U0154159

2011 不求人文化

2009 懶鬼子英日語

I'm 我識出版集團
I'm Publishing Group
www.17buy.com.tw

2006 意識文化

2005 易富文化

2004 我識地球村

2001 我識出版社

2011 不求人文化

2009 懶鬼子英日語

I'm 我識出版集團
I'm Publishing Group
www.17buy.com.tw

2006 意識文化

2005 易富文化

2004 我識地球村

2001 我識出版社

題解 in Topic Vocabulary at a Glance!

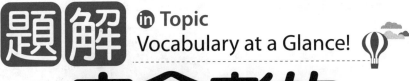

一定會考的 7,000單字

只要10天，掌握7,000單字和題型

1 ▸ 黃金10天完整模擬試題

7,000 單字權威林芯老師首創運用巨集資料數據庫，嚴選全國最擬真的模擬試題，以一天為一個單位，每天都能練習到四種不同的題型（包含詞彙題、綜合測驗、文意填填、閱讀測驗），就是要讓你在考前黃金 10 天，完全熟悉考題。

DAY 1

10天掌握 7,000 單字和題型

▸ Part 1｜詞 彙 題
▸ Part 2｜綜合測驗
▸ Part 3｜文意選填
▸ Part 4｜閱讀測驗

2 ▸ 完整翻譯及詳解

每題題目皆有林芯老師完整的中文翻譯以及詳細解說。除了了解題目意思以外，透過解說，讓你更融會貫通，解題更順手！不再一知半解地摸不著頭緒。

| Part 1 | 詞彙題｜Vocabulary Questions |

01 The director is in urgent need of a beautiful actress the play.
(A) aid
(B) act
(C) alarm
(D) bear

中譯｜導演急需一名漂亮的女演員來扮演這部戲中的主角。

解說｜本題考固定片語的用法。四個選項都是動詞，但是只有選項 (B) act 能夠與介系詞 as 連用，表示「扮演」，符合題意，所以正確選項為 (B)。

解答&技巧｜(B) 適用 TIP 1 適用 TIP 2

3 ▸ 獨家傳授解題技巧TIPS

每題題目下方皆附有解答以及適用技巧。林芯老師分析學測考題共有 16 個解題技巧，讓你解題不用再從第一個字看到最後一個字，透過老師獨家傳授的解題技巧，就是要讓你答題時比別人更快速、更準確。

02 The boss is _____ using airmail because it's expen
(A) against (B) aboriginal
(C) administrativ

中譯｜老闆反對使

解說｜依據題意
詞 using
詞。四個

應考攻略 Tips

TIP❶ 字彙量
累積一定的字彙量是應試的基本要求。常用 7,000 單字，其發音、字義、詞性轉換、詞型變化都是必須掌握的，此外，也要結合語境，正確判斷單字的意義。

TIP❷ 固定文法
所謂語法，就是遣詞造句的基本規則。句型與片語是文法規則的龐大重點，掌握必備的文法知識，在解題時才可以加以靈活運用。

TIP❸ 排除法
學測、指考、統測的選項通常為四選一，解題時可以先將一兩個明顯不符合題意或是錯誤的選項排除，再從剩下的選項中挑選正確答案。

TIP❹ 題意解析
有的題目所指的選項，其詞性、人稱、單複數、時態、語態等等一致，需要根據句意和題意，單字的意義，據而判斷出正確選項。

TIP❺ 注意代名詞
代名詞，可以分為人稱代名詞、所有格代名詞、反身代名詞、相互代名詞、不定代名詞、指示代名詞、疑問代名詞、不定代名詞。疑問是為了避免重複，代名詞的使用，通常而定之，正確理解代名詞的含義，才能正確理解文意內容。

TIP❻ 分別選項
閱讀選項時，可以按照詞性將選項分類，再根據題目列舉所謂詞的詞性，一一對應確認。如有明顯不符選項的選項，可以予直接刪去。

TIP❼ 代入法
克漏字與閱讀測驗通常是過考題文章內容的理解，確定文章主題後，將選項依次代入文中，以便找出最符合題意的選項。

TIP❽ 預覽題目
對於閱讀測驗題型，在閱讀文章之前，可以先看題目，以便掌握大略的文章內容，也可以先

應考攻略對照表

4 ▶ 完整網羅 7,000 單字

本書的目的就是要讓學生透過解題一網打盡 7,000 單字。老師細心地將每道題目中的 7,000 單字標示出來，並附上音標、詞性以及教育部公布的 7,000 單字級數。熟悉單字的同時，也能知道自己目前的程度在哪裡。老師也在每道題目裡另外補充進階的單字和片語，就是要讓你把握黃金 10 天，贏在起跑點上。

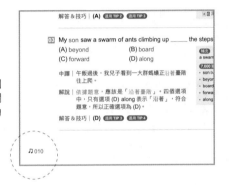

補充
act as ph 扮演

7,000 單字
- actress [ˈæktrɪs] n 1 女演員
- aid [ed] v 2 幫助
- act [ækt] v 1 扮演
- alarm [əˈlɑrm] v 2 警告
- bear [bɛr] v 2 承擔

● 詞性對照表：
n 名詞
v 動詞
a 形容詞
ad 副詞
ph 片語
prep 介係詞

● 教育部 7,000 單字級數對照表：
1 表示第一級
2 表示第二級
3 表示第三級
（以此類推）

5 ▶ 美籍老師 親錄 MP3

隨書附贈免費音檔，由美籍老師親自錄音，將每個單字及補充都詳細清晰地唸出，適合在零碎的時間用聲音記憶 7,000 單字。不只單字記熟，對於聽力也有幫助。

★本書附贈 CD 片內容音檔為 MP3 格式，收錄全書 7,000 單字及補充。

★音檔名稱即頁碼編號。

解答 & 技巧｜(A) 適用 TIP 2 適用 TIP 3

03 My son saw a swarm of ants climbing up _____ the steps
(A) beyond　　　　(B) board
(C) forward　　　 (D) along

補充
a swarm
- son l...
- beyon
- forwa
- board

7,000 單字

中譯｜午飯過後，我兒子看到一大群螞蟻正沿著臺階往上爬。

解說｜依據題意，應該是「沿著臺階」。四個選項中，只有選項 (D) along 表示「沿著」，符合題意，所以正確選項為 (D)。

解答 & 技巧｜(D) 適用 TIP 3 適用 TIP 4

♫ 010

6 ▶ 考前黃金 10 天 學習進度表

林芯老師特別規劃考前黃金 10 天學習進度表，要讓你在最關鍵的 10 天內放下單字書，專心練習考題。一天寫一回，只要 10 天就能完整網羅 7,000 單字！隨書附贈學習進度檢視表，讓你愈讀愈有信心！

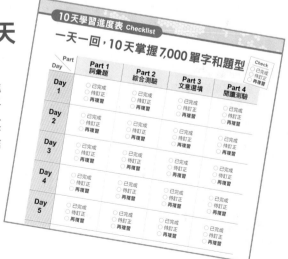

	Part 1 詞彙題	Part 2 綜合測驗	Part 3 文意選填	Part 4 閱讀測驗	Check
Day 1	○已完成 ○待訂正 ○再複習	○已完成 ○待訂正 ○再複習	○已完成 ○待訂正 ○再複習	○已完成 ○待訂正 ○再複習	
Day 2	○已完成 ○待訂正 ○再複習	○已完成 ○待訂正 ○再複習	○已完成 ○待訂正 ○再複習	○已完成 ○待訂正 ○再複習	
Day 3	○已完成 ○待訂正 ○再複習	○已完成 ○待訂正 ○再複習	○已完成 ○待訂正 ○再複習	○已完成 ○待訂正 ○再複習	
Day 4	○已完成 ○待訂正 ○再複習	○已完成 ○待訂正 ○再複習	○已完成 ○待訂正 ○再複習	○已完成 ○待訂正 ○再複習	
Day 5	○已完成 ○待訂正 ○再複習	○已完成 ○待訂正 ○再複習	○已完成 ○待訂正 ○再複習	○已完成 ○待訂正 ○再複習	

10 天學習進度表 Checklist

一天一回，10 天掌握 7,000 單字和題型

TIP❶ 字彙量

累積一定的字彙量是應試的基本要求。常用 7,000 單字，其發音、字義、詞性轉換、詞型變化都是必須熟記的，此外，也要結合語境，正確判斷單字或是文中的意義。

TIP❷ 固定文法

所謂語法，就是遣詞造句的基本規則。句型與片語是文法規則的兩大重點。掌握必備的文法知識，在解題時才可以加以靈活運用。

TIP❸ 排除法

學測、指考、統測的選項皆是四選一。解題時可以先將一兩個明顯不符合題意或是錯誤的選項排除，再從剩下的選項中挑選正確答案。

TIP❹ 題意辨析

有的題目所給的選項，其詞性、人稱、單複數、時態、語態等皆一致，需要根據句意判斷所缺單字的意義，進而選出正確選擇。

TIP❺ 推斷詞義

題目中或是所給文章中出現了生字時，若不影響答題，則可忽略；若影響題目理解，則需試著推斷詞意。除根據上下文推斷外，也可以根據構詞法加以推斷。至於衍生字，可以根據字首、字根、字尾推斷其含義；對於複合詞和混合詞，則可根據其構成部分而分別加以推斷。

TIP❻ 語感

對於個別較難的題目，如果無法只根據自己的英文知識加以判斷，則可借助語感。先閱讀題目，再將選項逐一代入細讀，感覺比較順的選項通常會是正確答案。平時也可以透過大量閱讀來培養語感。

TIP❼ 閱讀全文

對於克漏字題型，答題之前可以先快速閱讀全文，以掌握文章主旨，進而選出正確答案。快速閱讀時，文中的空缺若不影響理解內容，則可以暫時略過。

TIP❽ 注意連接詞

連接詞，通常是並列連接詞和從屬連接詞。按照詞義，可分為表示選擇或對等關係、表示解釋說明、表示總結、表示時間順序、表示因果關係、表示轉折關係、表示遞進等的連接詞。根據連接詞，可以判斷長句或是文章結構，加深理解。

TIP❾ 注意代名詞

代名詞，可以分為人稱代名詞、所有格代名詞、反身代名詞、相互代名詞、不定代名詞、疑問代名詞、關係代名詞等。代名詞的應用，通常是為了避免重複，其指代的內容要根據上下文而定。正確理解代名詞的含義，才能正確理解文章內容。

TIP❿ 分別選項

瀏覽選項時，可以按照詞性進行歸納分類，再根據題目判斷所缺單字的詞性，一一對應選擇，如有明顯不符題意的選項，則可直接刪去。

TIP⓫ 代入法

克漏字與閱讀測驗兩種題型通常是考對文章內容的理解，確定文章主題後，將選項依次代入文中，以便找出最符合題意的選項。

TIP⓬ 預覽題目

對於閱讀測驗題型，在閱讀文章之前，可以先看題目，以便掌握大略的文章內容。也可以先知道該從文章中找出什麼樣的答案，可以提高閱讀品質，以避免浪費過多時間在細讀文章上。

TIP⓭ 找關鍵字

預覽閱讀測驗的題目後，要試著從題目中找出關鍵字。疑問詞就是經常出現的關鍵字，例如：who、when、where、how 等，在閱讀文章時，看到與關鍵字有關的內容，可以先做記號，以便正確解題。

TIP⓮ 提取主旨

閱讀測驗的文章通常比較長，要在有限的時間內正確理解文章內容，必然要正確把握主旨。可以藉由段落主旨來彙整整篇文章的要旨，而段落主旨可以在每段的開頭或結尾找到。

TIP⓯ 比對選項

閱讀測驗中經常會出現判斷正誤的題目，解這類型的題目時可在文中找出相對應的出處，結合上下文，將各個選項一一加以比對，看是否與文章內容一致。

TIP⓰ 推論上下文

有的題目是要求從文中的某一段或是某一句中得出某個結論，在解這類題目時，一定要從文章的上下文尋找依據，特別要注意文章的語氣、脈絡等，才能正確從文中的敘述找出答案。

　　考前 10 天是最關鍵的黃金時期,各位同學都怎麼準備呢?是拿著單字書從 A-Z 開始胡亂背一通,還是乾脆放棄,當個佛系考生呢?雖然英文是一門需要長期累積的科目,但是只要有效率地規畫以及把握這黃金 10 天,還是有可能翻轉人生的!

　　為幫助考生克服在升學路上相當重要的 7,000 單字,於 2016 年出版《7,000 單字大數據》一書,並收到出版社的邀請,於 2018 年 9 月推出全新修訂版《題解一定會考的 7,000 單字》。但是到底要用什麼樣的方式記憶 7,000 單字才是最有效率的呢?其實很簡單!首先,放下你手上的單字書,拿起筆來,我們來練習考題!

　　考試最重要的就是要熟知哪類型的題目會考、哪些單字會出現在題目裡,並且以什麼樣的樣貌出現,絕非沒有頭緒地背單字。書中的考題都是運用巨集資料蒐集來的全國最擬真的模擬試題,絕對是最精華且最完整的。

　　考前 10 天透過重複且密集地練習題目,讓真正會考的 7,000 單字不斷地出現在句子裡、片語裡、文章裡,就像將這 7,000 單字慢慢輸入腦中,在腦中建構一個完整的 7,000 單字數據庫,唯有以這樣的方式,才有辦法將單字牢牢地記在你的長期記憶裡。

　　我長期在台灣教授英語課程,深知台灣學子準備考試的辛苦,所以希望能為台灣學子找到最輕鬆又最有效率的方式來準備這個繁瑣的考試!在此也非常感謝幫助我完成這本書的我的家人、朋友以及老師,同時也祝福每位考生都能順利拿到自己心目中的理想分數!

林芯
2018. 09

10天學習進度表 Checklist

一天一回，10天掌握 7,000 單字和題型

Part / Day	Part 1 詞彙題	Part 2 綜合測驗	Part 3 文意選填	Part 4 閱讀測驗
Day 1	○ 已完成 ○ 待訂正 ● 再複習	○ 已完成 ○ 待訂正 ● 再複習	○ 已完成 ○ 待訂正 ● 再複習	○ 已完成 ○ 待訂正 ○ 再複習
Day 2	○ 已完成 ○ 待訂正 ● 再複習	○ 已完成 ○ 待訂正 ● 再複習	○ 已完成 ○ 待訂正 ● 再複習	○ 已完成 ○ 待訂正 ● 再複習
Day 3	○ 已完成 ○ 待訂正 ● 再複習	○ 已完成 ○ 待訂正 ● 再複習	○ 已完成 ○ 待訂正 ● 再複習	○ 已完成 ○ 待訂正 ● 再複習
Day 4	○ 已完成 ○ 待訂正 ● 再複習	○ 已完成 ○ 待訂正 ● 再複習	○ 已完成 ○ 待訂正 ● 再複習	○ 已完成 ○ 待訂正 ○ 再複習
Day 5	○ 已完成 ○ 待訂正 ● 再複習	○ 已完成 ○ 待訂正 ● 再複習	○ 已完成 ○ 待訂正 ● 再複習	○ 已完成 ○ 待訂正 ● 再複習
Day 6	○ 已完成 ○ 待訂正 ● 再複習	○ 已完成 ○ 待訂正 ● 再複習	○ 已完成 ○ 待訂正 ● 再複習	○ 已完成 ○ 待訂正 ● 再複習
Day 7	○ 已完成 ○ 待訂正 ● 再複習	○ 已完成 ○ 待訂正 ● 再複習	○ 已完成 ○ 待訂正 ● 再複習	○ 已完成 ○ 待訂正 ● 再複習
Day 8	○ 已完成 ○ 待訂正 ● 再複習	○ 已完成 ○ 待訂正 ● 再複習	○ 已完成 ○ 待訂正 ● 再複習	○ 已完成 ○ 待訂正 ● 再複習
Day 9	○ 已完成 ○ 待訂正 ● 再複習	○ 已完成 ○ 待訂正 ● 再複習	○ 已完成 ○ 待訂正 ● 再複習	○ 已完成 ○ 待訂正 ● 再複習
Day 10	○ 已完成 ○ 待訂正 ● 再複習	○ 已完成 ○ 待訂正 ● 再複習	○ 已完成 ○ 待訂正 ● 再複習	○ 已完成 ○ 待訂正 ● 再複習

目錄 Contents

使用說明／002　　　應考攻略Tips／004　　　10 天學習進度表／006

Day 1

- **Part 1** 詞彙題 010
- **Part 2** 綜合測驗 016
- **Part 3** 文意選填 038
- **Part 4** 閱讀測驗 054

Day 2

- **Part 1** 詞彙題 072
- **Part 2** 綜合測驗 080
- **Part 3** 文意選填 100
- **Part 4** 閱讀測驗 116

Day 3

- **Part 1** 詞彙題 134
- **Part 2** 綜合測驗 142
- **Part 3** 文意選填 162
- **Part 4** 閱讀測驗 178

Day 4

- **Part 1** 詞彙題 196
- **Part 2** 綜合測驗 204
- **Part 3** 文意選填 224
- **Part 4** 閱讀測驗 240

Day 5

- **Part 1** 詞彙題 258
- **Part 2** 綜合測驗 266
- **Part 3** 文意選填 286
- **Part 4** 閱讀測驗 302

Day 6

- **Part 1** 詞彙題 320
- **Part 2** 綜合測驗 328
- **Part 3** 文意選填 348
- **Part 4** 閱讀測驗 354

Day 7

- **Part 1** 詞彙題 382
- **Part 2** 綜合測驗 390
- **Part 3** 文意選填 410
- **Part 4** 閱讀測驗 426

Day 8

- **Part 1** 詞彙題 444
- **Part 2** 綜合測驗 452
- **Part 3** 文意選填 472
- **Part 4** 閱讀測驗 488

Day 9

- **Part 1** 詞彙題 506
- **Part 2** 綜合測驗 514
- **Part 3** 文意選填 534
- **Part 4** 閱讀測驗 550

Day 10

- **Part 1** 詞彙題 568
- **Part 2** 綜合測驗 576
- **Part 3** 文意選填 596
- **Part 4** 閱讀測驗 612

學測必考片語補充／628

DAY 1

10 天掌握 7,000 單字和題型

Knowledge makes humble, ignorance makes proud.

知識使人謙虛，無知使人驕傲。

▶ **Part 1** ｜ 詞 彙 題

▶ **Part 2** ｜ 綜合測驗

▶ **Part 3** ｜ 文意選填

▶ **Part 4** ｜ 閱讀測驗

Part 1 詞彙題 | Vocabulary Questions

01 The director is in urgent need of a beautiful actress to _____ as the lead in the play.

(A) aid　　　　　　　(B) act

(C) alarm　　　　　(D) bear

補充
act as ph 扮演

7,000 單字
- actress [ˈæktrɪs] n 1 女演員
- aid [ed] v 2 幫助
- act [ækt] v 1 扮演
- alarm [əˈlɑrm] v 2 警告
- bear [bɛr] v 2 承擔

中譯｜導演急需一名漂亮的女演員來扮演這部戲中的主角。

解說｜本題考固定片語的用法。四個選項都是動詞，但是只有選項 (B) act 能夠與介系詞 as 連用，表示「扮演」，符合題意，所以正確選項為 (B)。

解答＆技巧｜**(B)** 適用 TIP 1　適用 TIP 2

---

02 The boss is _____ using airmail because it's expensive.

(A) against　　　　　(B) aboriginal

(C) administrative　　(D) affectionate

補充
be against ph 反對，違背

7,000 單字
- airmail [ˈɛrˌmel] n 1 航空郵件
- against [əˈgɛnst] prep 1 反對
- aboriginal [ˌæbəˈrɪdʒənl] a 6 土著的
- administrative [ədˈmɪnəˌstretɪv] a 6 管理的
- affectionate [əˈfɛkʃənɪt] a 6 深情的

中譯｜老闆反對使用航空郵件，因為很昂貴。

解說｜依據題意，空格後面的動詞 use 使用了動名詞 using，說明空格處的單字詞性應該為介系詞。四個選項中，只有選項 (A) against 是介系詞，其他三個選項都是形容詞，所以選 (A)。

解答＆技巧｜**(A)** 適用 TIP 2　適用 TIP 3

---

03 My son saw a swarm of ants climbing up _____ the steps after lunch.

(A) beyond　　　　　(B) board

(C) forward　　　　(D) along

補充
a swarm of ph 一大群

7,000 單字
- son [sʌn] n 1 兒子
- beyond [bɪˈjɑnd] prep 2 超越
- board [bord] v 2 登船
- forward [ˈfɔrwəd] ad 2 向前地
- along [əˈlɔŋ] prep 1 沿著

中譯｜午飯過後，我兒子看到一大群螞蟻正沿著臺階往上爬。

解說｜依據題意，應該是「沿著臺階」。四個選項中，只有選項 (D) along 表示「沿著」，符合題意，所以正確選項為 (D)。

解答＆技巧｜**(D)** 適用 TIP 3　適用 TIP 4

04 The barber smiled _____ the beggar and then began to give him a haircut.

(A) down

(B) below

(C) at

(D) by

補充
give sb. a haircut ph 幫某人理髮

7,000 單字
- barber [`barbɚ] n 1 理髮師
- down [daʊn] prep 1 向下
- below [bə`lo] prep 1 在下面
- at [æt] prep 1 朝
- by [baɪ] prep 1 透過

中譯｜理髮師對那個乞丐笑了笑，然後開始幫他理髮。

解說｜依據題意，空格處要選用合適的介系詞。動詞 smile 表示「微笑」，通常與介系詞 at 連用，表示「朝～微笑」，符合題意，所以選 (C)。

解答＆技巧｜**(C)** 適用 TIP 1 適用 TIP 2

---

05 I hear that the _____ in the zoo are fond of eating apples and bananas, so I buy some for them.

(A) apes

(B) garbage

(C) guavas

(D) jeeps

補充
be fond of ph 喜歡

7,000 單字
- banana [bə`nænə] n 1 香蕉
- ape [ep] n 1 猿
- garbage [`garbɪdʒ] n 2 垃圾
- guava [`gwavə] n 2 芭樂
- jeep [dʒip] n 2 吉普車

中譯｜聽説動物園裡的猿猴喜歡吃蘋果和香蕉，我就買了一些。

解說｜四個選項皆為名詞。依據題意，動詞 eat 在句中用來敘述主詞，因此能夠作主詞的只能是有生命的事物，選項 (A) apes 表示「猿猴」，是一種動物，所以正確選項為 (A)。

解答＆技巧｜**(A)** 適用 TIP 1 適用 TIP 4

---

06 A mosquito _____ my arm when I was bathing in the bathroom yesterday evening.

(A) jointed

(B) lent

(C) linked

(D) bit

補充
bathe in ph 在～中洗澡

7,000 單字
- arm [arm] n 1 手臂
- joint [dʒɔɪnt] v 2 連接
- lend [lɛnd] v 2 借出
- link [lɪŋk] v 2 連接
- bite [baɪt] v 1 咬

中譯｜昨天晚上我在浴室洗澡時，一隻蚊子叮了我的手臂。

解說｜四個選項皆為動詞。依據題意，應該是「蚊子叮了我的手臂」，選項 (D) bit 表示「咬」，所以正確選項為 (D)。

解答＆技巧｜**(D)** 適用 TIP 1 適用 TIP 4

DAY 1

Part 1
詞彙題
Day 1
完成 25%

Part 2
綜合測驗
Day 1
完成 50%

Part 3
文意選填
Day 1
完成 75%

Part 4
閱讀測驗
Day 1
完成 100%

07 It is said that this country has decided to _____ up the largest army in Africa.

(A) loaf　　　　(B) build
(C) mask　　　　(D) overpass

build up ph 建立

7,000 單字
- army [ˋɑrmɪ] n 1 軍隊
- loaf [lof] v 2 遊蕩
- build [bɪld] v 1 建造
- mask [mæsk] v 2 掩飾
- overpass [ˏovɚˋpæs] v 2 超越

中譯│據說，這個國家決定在非洲建立起一支規模最大的軍隊。

解說│本題考固定片語的用法。四個選項都是動詞，但只有選項 (B) build 能夠與副詞 up 連用，表示「建立」，符合題意，所以正確選項為 (B)。

解答&技巧│**(B)** 適用 TIP 1　適用 TIP 2

08 The desk is too _____ with so much dust and waste on it. You need to start cleaning it at once.

(A) dirty　　　　(B) absent
(C) peaceful　　　(D) playful

補充
at once ph 立刻，馬上

7,000 單字
- desk [dɛsk] n 1 書桌
- dirty [ˋdɝtɪ] a 1 髒的
- absent [ˋæbsn̩t] a 2 缺席的
- peaceful [ˋpisfəl] a 2 和平的
- playful [ˋplefəl] a 2 開玩笑的

中譯│書桌上有很多灰塵和垃圾，真是太髒了，你應該馬上開始清理。

解說│四個選項皆為形容詞。由後一句中的動詞 clean「打掃」可以判斷出，前一句中的形容詞應該用 dirty，表示「髒的」，所以正確選項為 (A)。

解答&技巧│**(A)** 適用 TIP 1　適用 TIP 4

09 The eagle is quite strong and capable of catching the small animals in the field with _____.

(A) pizza　　　　(B) pork
(C) ease　　　　(D) pot

補充
be capable of ph 有能力的
with ease ph 輕易地

7,000 單字
- eagle [ˋigl̩] n 1 鷹
- pizza [ˋpitsə] n 2 披薩
- pork [pork] n 2 豬肉
- ease [iz] n 1 輕鬆
- pot [pɑt] n 2 壺

中譯│那隻鷹很強壯，能夠輕易地抓到田野裡的小動物。

解說│本題考介系詞片語的用法。依據題意，四個選項都是名詞，但是只有選項 (C) ease 能夠與介系詞 with 連用，表示「輕易地」，所以正確選項為 (C)。

解答&技巧│**(C)** 適用 TIP 1　適用 TIP 2

10 She likes all the courses ＿＿＿＿ English because she hates to memorize English words.

(A) reply   (B) except

(C) salty   (D) screen

中譯｜她討厭背英文單字，所以在所有課程中，她唯獨不喜歡英語。

解說｜本題屬於因果關係題，根據後面的因「討厭背英文單字」可以判斷出，前面的果為「不喜歡英語」，所以要把英語「除去」，即選項 (B) except 符合題意。

解答＆技巧｜**(B)** 適用 TIP 1　適用 TIP 3

DAY
1

Part 1
詞
彙
題
Day 1
完成 25%

Part 2
綜
合
測
驗
Day 1
完成 50%

Part 3
文
意
選
填
Day 1
完成 75%

Part 4
閱
讀
測
驗
Day 1
完成 100%

補充
English word ph 英文單字

7,000 單字
• English [ˈɪŋglɪʃ] n 1 英語
• reply [rɪˈplaɪ] v 2 回覆
• except [ɪkˈsɛpt] prep 1 除了
• salty [ˈsɔltɪ] a 2 鹹的
• screen [skrin] n 2 螢幕

---

11 The conflicts between John and his teacher made it difficult for the teacher to judge his performance ＿＿＿＿.

【92年學測英文】

(A) objectively   (B) painfully

(C) excitedly   (D) intimately 熟悉地

中譯｜約翰和老師之間發生了衝突，這使得老師很難客觀地對約翰的表現作出評價。

解說｜四個選項皆為副詞。依據題意，應該是「很難客觀地評價」，選項 (A) objectively 表示「客觀地」，符合題意，所以正確選項為 (A)。

解答＆技巧｜**(A)** 適用 TIP 1　適用 TIP 4

補充
between A and B
ph 在 A 與 B 之間

7,000 單字
• judge [dʒʌdʒ] v 2 判斷
• objectively [əbˈdʒɛktɪvlɪ] ad 4 客觀地
• painfully [ˈpenfəlɪ] ad 2 痛苦地
• excitedly [ɪkˈsaɪtɪdlɪ] ad 2 興奮地
• intimately [ˈɪntəmɪtlɪ] ad 4 熟悉地

---

12 The boy worked very hard on the farm for ＿＿＿＿ that he would be dismissed by the boss.

(A) servant   (B) silent

(C) simply   (D) fear

中譯｜這個男孩努力在農場上工作，唯恐老闆把他開除了。

解說｜本題考介系詞片語的用法。四個選項中，只有名詞 fear 能夠與介系詞 for 連用，構成 for fear that，表示「害怕」，所以正確選項為 (D)。

解答＆技巧｜**(D)** 適用 TIP 1　適用 TIP 2

補充
work hard ph 辛勤工作
for fear that ph 唯恐

7,000 單字
• boy [bɔɪ] n 1 男孩
• servant [ˈsɝvənt] n 2 僕人
• silent [ˈsaɪlənt] a 2 沉默的
• simply [ˈsɪmplɪ] ad 2 簡單地
• fear [fɪr] n 1 害怕

13 The plane still _____ over this area slowly in spite of the heavy fog.

(A) flew   (B) slipped

(C) strung   (D) abounded

> 補充
> fly over ph 飛越
> heavy fog ph 濃霧

> 7,000 單字
> • fog [fɑg] n 1 霧
> • fly [flaɪ] v 1 飛
> • slip [slɪp] v 2 滑動
> • string [strɪŋ] v 2 紮
> • abound [əˋbaʊnd] v 6 富於

中譯｜儘管濃霧瀰漫，飛機還是緩慢地飛越了這個地區。

解說｜四個選項皆為動詞。根據固定用法，通常用 fly over 來表示「飛越」，符合題意，所以正確選項為 (A)。

解答＆技巧｜**(A)** 適用 TIP 1 適用 TIP 2

---

14 I will not make _____ of you because you are an excellent disabled dancer.

(A) abstraction   (B) bias

(C) fun   (D) abundance

> 補充
> make fun of ph 取笑

> 7,000 單字
> • dancer [ˋdænsɚ] n 1 舞蹈家
> • abstraction [æbˋstrækʃən] n 6 抽象
> • bias [ˋbaɪəs] n 6 偏見
> • fun [fʌn] n 1 樂趣
> • abundance [əˋbʌndəns] n 6 充裕

中譯｜我不會取笑你，因為你是一位非常優秀的身障舞蹈家。

解說｜四個選項皆為名詞。依據題意，四個選項中，只有選項 (C) fun 能夠與動詞 make 連用，構成 make fun of，表示「取笑」，符合題意，所以正確選項為 (C)。

解答＆技巧｜**(C)** 適用 TIP 2 適用 TIP 3

---

15 He _____ adding ham to the hamburger becaust it can make him fatter.

(A) certifies   (B) hates

(C) yearns   (D) wrestles

> 補充
> add to ph 添加

> 7,000 單字
> • ham [hæm] n 1 火腿
> • certify [ˋsɝtə͵faɪ] v 6 證明
> • hate [het] v 1 討厭
> • yearn [jɝn] v 6 渴望
> • wrestle [ˋrɛsl] v 6 摔角

中譯｜他不喜歡在漢堡裡面添加火腿，因為那樣會使他變得更胖。

解說｜四個選項皆為動詞。根據後一句中的 fatter 可以判斷出，主詞 he「討厭在漢堡裡面添加火腿」，即選項 (B) hates 符合題意。

解答＆技巧｜**(B)** 適用 TIP 1 適用 TIP 4

DAY
1

Part 1
詞
彙
題
Day 1
完成 25%

Part 2
綜
合
測
驗
Day 1
完成 50%

Part 3
文
意
選
填
Day 1
完成 75%

Part 4
閱
讀
測
驗
Day 1
完成 100%

16 The soldier got _____ in spite of carrying a submachine gun and a large bundle of bullets.

(A) witty   (B) vulgar

(C) hurt   (D) vogue

補充
get hurt ph 受傷
submachine gun ph 衝鋒槍

7,000 單字
• gun [gʌn] n 1 槍
• witty [ˋwɪtɪ] a 6 詼諧的
• vulgar [ˋvʌlgɚ] a 6 粗俗的
• hurt [hɝt] a 1 受傷的
• vogue [vog] a 6 時髦的

中譯 | 儘管帶了一把衝鋒槍和一大包子彈，那名戰士還是受傷了。

解說 | 依據題意，句中的 in spite of 意思是「儘管」，表示轉折，所以應該是「受傷了」，而動詞片語 get hurt 表示「受傷」，所以正確選項為 (C)。

解答＆技巧 | **(C)** 適用 TIP 1 適用 TIP 4

17 We believe the failure of the _____ innovation is temporary since we have the most advanced technology.

(A) technical   (B) vocational

(C) vocal   (D) variable

補充
technical innovation ph 技術創新

7,000 單字
• temporary [ˋtɛmpə͵rɛrɪ] a 5 暫時的
• technical [ˋtɛknɪkl] a 3 科技的
• vocational [voˋkeʃən] a 6 職業的
• vocal [ˋvokl] a 6 聲音的
• variable [ˋvɛrɪəbl] a 6 可變的

中譯 | 我們相信技術創新的失敗只是暫時性的，因為我們擁有最先進的技術。

解說 | 四個選項皆為形容詞。根據後一句中的名詞 technology 可以判斷出，應該是「技術創新」，即選項 (A) technical 符合題意。

解答＆技巧 | **(A)** 適用 TIP 1 適用 TIP 4

18 My girlfriend is in a bad _____ because the hairdresser has cut her hair too short.

(A) validity   (B) vanilla

(C) urgency   (D) temper

補充
be in a bad temper
ph 生氣，發脾氣

7,000 單字
• hair [her] n 1 頭髮
• validity [vəˋlɪdətɪ] n 6 有效性
• vanilla [vəˋnɪlə] n 6 香草
• urgency [ˋɝdʒənsɪ] n 6 緊急
• temper [ˋtɛmpɚ] n 3 脾氣

中譯 | 我女朋友很生氣，因為髮型師把她的頭髮剪得太短了。

解說 | 四個選項皆為名詞。依據題意，應該是「生氣」，而四個選項中，只有 temper 表示「脾氣」，可以構成固定片語 in a bad temper，表示「生氣」，所以正確選項為 (D)。

解答＆技巧 | **(D)** 適用 TIP 1 適用 TIP 2

19 He tried to add crystal sugar and blueberries to the ice cream in order to change _____ taste.

(A) its   (B) our

(C) her   (D) their

> 補充
> crystal sugar ph 冰糖
> ice cream ph 冰淇淋
>
> 7,000 單字
> • ice [aɪs] n 1 冰
> • its [ɪts] pron 1 它的
> • our [ˋaʊr] pron 1 我們的
> • her [hɝ] pron 1 她的
> • their [ðɛr] pron 1 他們的

中譯 | 他試著在冰淇淋裡面加入冰糖和藍莓來改變它的口味。

解說 | 四個選項皆為代名詞。依據題意，空格處所填的代名詞指的是 ice cream，表示物，通常要用代名詞 its 來指代，所以正確選項為 (A)。

解答＆技巧 | **(A)** 適用 TIP 4 適用 TIP 9

---

20 Those hunters _____ the tiger with several thick ropes after catching it with great effort.

(A) upheld   (B) upgraded

(C) tied   (D) unpacked

> 補充
> with great effort ph 費勁
>
> 7,000 單字
> • tiger [ˋtaɪgɚ] n 1 老虎
> • uphold [ʌpˋhold] v 6 支撐
> • upgrade [ˋʌpˋgred] v 6 升級
> • tie [taɪ] v 1 繫
> • unpack [ʌnˋpæk] v 6 卸下

中譯 | 那些獵人費了很大的勁捕到老虎後，用幾根粗繩子將牠捆了起來。

解說 | 四個選項皆為動詞。依據題意，應該是「用繩子捆起來」。四個選項中，只有選項 (C) tied 表示「繫，捆」，所以正確選項為 (C)。

解答＆技巧 | **(C)** 適用 TIP 3 適用 TIP 4

---

21 On receiving my letter of complaint, the hotel manager sent me a written _____.

【92年指考英文】

(A) consent   (B) scandal

(C) tornado   (D) apology

> 補充
> letter of complaint ph 投訴信
>
> 7,000 單字
> • my [maɪ] pron 1 我的
> • consent [kənˋsɛnt] n 5 同意
> • scandal [ˋskændḷ] n 6 醜聞
> • tornado [tɔrˋnedo] n 6 龍捲風
> • apology [əˋpɑlədʒɪ] n 4 道歉

中譯 | 一收到我的投訴信，飯店經理就發了一份書面道歉給我。

解說 | 四個選項皆為名詞。根據前一句中的 complaint「投訴」，可以判斷出，空格處應該填「道歉」，所以正確選項為 (D)。

解答＆技巧 | **(D)** 適用 TIP 1 適用 TIP 4

22 Herbs for the _____ of dysentery can be found easily by tribal people in Africa.

(A) transformation　　(B) interference

(C) prevention　　(D) substitution

補充
the prevention of ph 預防

7,000 單字
- tribal [ˈtraɪbl] a ④ 部落的
- transformation [ˌtrænsfɚˈmeʃən] n ⑥ 轉化
- interference [ˌɪntɚˈfɪrəns] n ⑤ 干擾
- prevention [prɪˈvɛnʃən] n ④ 預防
- substitution [ˌsʌbstəˈtjuʃən] n ⑥ 代替

中譯｜非洲部落的人能夠很容易找到預防痢疾的藥草。

解說｜四個選項皆為名詞。依據題意，herb「草藥」通常用於治療或預防疾病，而四個選項中，prevention 表示「預防」，所以正確選項為 (C)。

解答＆技巧｜**(C)**　適用 TIP 3　適用 TIP 4

---

23 His _____ for the government officials has caused great dissatisfaction to many people.

(A) destiny　　(B) contempt 表視

(C) transistor　　(D) isolation

補充
government official ph 政府官員

7,000 單字
- great [gret] a ① 重大的
- destiny [ˈdɛstənɪ] n ⑤ 命運
- contempt [kənˈtɛmpt] n ⑤ 輕視
- transistor [trænˈzɪstɚ] n ⑥ 電晶體
- isolation [ˌaɪslˈeʃən] n ④ 孤立

中譯｜他對政府官員的藐視已經引起了很多人的強烈不滿。

解說｜四個選項皆為名詞。依據題意，應該是「藐視引起不滿」，而四個選項中，只有選項 (B) contempt 表示「輕視，藐視」，符合題意，所以正確選項為 (B)。

解答＆技巧｜**(B)**　適用 TIP 3　適用 TIP 4

---

24 After a _____ day at work, David got hungry and sleepy and walked wearily back to his home.

(A) thrifty　　(B) theatrical

(C) supersonic　　(D) tiring

補充
back to ph 回到

7,000 單字
- sleepy [ˈslipɪ] a ② 想睡的
- thrifty [ˈθrɪftɪ] a ⑥ 節約的
- theatrical [θiˈætrɪkl] a ⑥ 戲劇性的
- supersonic [ˌsupɚˈsɑnɪk] a ⑥ 超音速的
- tiring [ˈtaɪrɪŋ] a ① 累人的

中譯｜工作勞累了一天，大衛又餓又睏，疲倦地走回了家。

解說｜四個選項皆為形容詞。由後一句中的 got hungry and sleepy 可以判斷出，前一句應該是「勞累了一天」，而選項 (D) tiring 表示「累人的」，所以正確選項為 (D)。

解答＆技巧｜**(D)**　適用 TIP 3　適用 TIP 4

Part 1
詞彙題
Day 1
完成 25%

Part 2
綜合測驗
Day 1
完成 50%

Part 3
文意選填
Day 1
完成 75%

Part 4
閱讀測驗
Day 1
完成 100%

Part 2 綜合測驗 | Comprehensive Questions

1 ▶

Most people are not aware of the hard work spent in collecting those __01__ animals that they pay to see in the zoo. When I was asked how I became an animal collector in the first __02__, my answer was always that I had been interested in animals. My parents told me that the first word I was able to say was not "mama" or "papa," but the word "zoo." When I grew __03__, we lived in the country, and I had a great number of pets, including owls and squirrels, and I spent most of my __04__ time exploring the countryside for live specimens to increase my collection of pets. Later on I went to the National Zoo in the hope of getting experience of the large animals, such as lions, bears and ostriches, which I couldn't keep at home. Though a collector's job is not easy and often full of disappointment, it will certainly __05__ to those who love animals.

01.
(A) deceptive
(B) fascinating
(C) grisly
(D) arrogant

02.
(A) half
(B) grade
(C) stage
(D) instance

03.
(A) older
(B) bigger
(C) smaller
(D) younger

04.
(A) full
(B) spare
(C) part
(D) exposure

05.
(A) due
(B) lead
(C) appeal
(D) turn

中譯｜很多人都不知道，要收集那些在動物園裡看到的迷人的動物是多麼的辛苦。被問及起初我是如何成為動物收集者時，我總是回答說，我一直都對動物非常感興趣。我的父母告訴我，我會說的第一個詞並不是「媽媽」或「爸爸」，而是「動物園」。長大後，我們住在鄉村，我有很多寵物，包括貓頭鷹和松鼠，我的空閒時間大多用在鄉間探索，以尋找活體樣本，增加我的寵物收藏。後來，為了能夠獲得一些飼養那些不能在家裡養的大型動物的經驗，如獅子、熊和駝鳥等，所以我去了國家動物園。收集工作並不輕鬆，也經常充滿了失望，然而，它確實是會吸引那些喜歡動物的人。

解說｜本篇短文是以「我」為主角來展開描述與動物有關的成長經歷，因此可以看作一篇敘事短文。第 1 題的四個選項都是形容詞，用來修飾後面的名詞 animals，透過詞義辨析可知，選項 (B) fascinating 意思是「迷人的」，符合題意，所以正確選擇為 (B)。第 2 題是考固定片語搭配，根據詞彙積累，in the first instance 表示「首先，起初」，最符合題意的選項是 (D)。第 3 題考單字比較級的用法，透過詞義辨析可知，要用 older 來表示「年長的」，即正確選項是 (A)。第 4 題根據上下文意思可知，要用固定搭配 spare time 來表示「空閒時間」，只有選項 (B) 符合題意。第 5 題要選擇可以跟介系詞 to 連用的動詞，透過將四個選項的動詞一一代入可知，選項 appeal to 表示「吸引」，最符合題意，所以選 (C)。

解答＆技巧｜ 01 **(B)**　02 **(D)**　03 **(A)**　04 **(B)**　05 **(C)**

適用 TIP 1　適用 TIP 2　適用 TIP 4　適用 TIP 7　適用 TIP 11

補充

be able to ph 能夠；mama n （兒語）媽媽；later on ph 後來；in the hope of ph 懷著～的希望；disappointment n 失望

7,000 單字

- people [ˋpip!] n 1 人
- aware [əˋwɛr] a 3 知道的
- zoo [zu] n 1 動物園
- collector [kəˋlɛktɚ] n 6 收藏家
- answer [ˋænsɚ] n 1 答案
- always [ˋɔlwez] ad 1 總是
- word [wɝd] n 1 詞語
- number [ˋnʌmbɚ] n 1 數量

- owl [aul] n 2 貓頭鷹
- squirrel [ˋskwɝəl] n 2 松鼠
- specimen [ˋspɛsəmən] n 5 樣本
- lion [ˋlaɪən] n 1 獅子
- bear [bɛr] n 1 熊
- spare [spɛr] a 4 空閒的
- exposure [ɪkˋspoʒɚ] n 4 暴露

DAY 1

Part 1
詞彙題
Day 1
完成 25%

Part 2
綜合測驗
Day 1
完成 50%

Part 3
文意選填
Day 1
完成 75%

Part 4
閱讀測驗
Day 1
完成 100%

2 ▶

Generally speaking, the British are widely ___01___ as quiet, shy and conservative. They are relaxed only with people they are familiar with. ___02___ strangers present, they often seem nervous, even embarrassed. You could examine the truth of this through taking a commuter train in the morning or evening. Businessmen and women who seem serious often sit in a corner reading their newspapers or dozing without talking to anybody to avoid being considered offensive.

It is ___03___ known that the British have a fancy for the discussion of the weather. Some people say that it is because the British weather ___04___ follows the forecast and always changes very quickly. Certainly, the British have little faith in the weathermen, who originally promise fine and sunny weather for the following day, but are often ___05___ wrong when a cloud brings rain to all districts! This is the reason why the British often take an umbrella even on a fine day.

01   (A) regarded   (B) replaced
           (C) proposed   (D) conducted

02   (A) Have   (B) For
           (C) With   (D) Since

03   (A) consequently   (B) generally
           (C) apparently   (D) deliberately

04   (A) always   (B) often
           (C) usually   (D) seldom

05   (A) supported   (B) witnessed
           (C) proved   (D) undergone

DAY
1

Part 1
詞
彙
題
Day 1
完成 25%

Part 2
綜
合
測
驗
Day 1
完成 50%

Part 3
文
意
選
填
Day 1
完成 75%

Part 4
閱
讀
測
驗
Day 1
完成 100%

中譯｜一般來說，英國人被廣泛認為是安靜、害羞且保守的人，他們只有和自己熟悉的人在一起才會放鬆。有陌生人在場時，他們通常看起來很緊張，甚至感到尷尬窘迫。你可以乘坐早晚通勤列車來檢驗這一情況的真實性。為了避免被認為自己無禮，那些看起來較嚴肅的商務人士通常都坐在角落看報紙或打盹，不與人交談。眾所周知，英國人喜歡討論天氣。一些人說這是因為英國的天氣很少跟預報的情況一致，且總是變化很快。確實，英國人不太信任天氣預報員，起初天氣預報員預報第二天天氣晴朗，但這通常證明是錯誤的，因為雲朵給所有地區帶來了降雨。因此，這就是為什麼英國人即使在晴朗的天氣裡也總是帶著雨傘。

解說｜本篇短文主要講述英國人的性格特點，以及他們喜歡談論天氣這一生活趣事，因此在答題前，可以閱讀全文，掌握短文大意。第 1 題考動詞的詞義辨析，根據上下文的意思可知，要選擇 regarded 與 as 連用，表示「認為」，所以正確選擇為 (A)。第 2 題選項的分詞構句做整個句子的伴隨副詞，通常要用介系詞 with 來引導，根據語感可以選出最符合題意的選項是 (C)。第 3 題要選出一個副詞來修飾後面的形容詞 known，透過將單字一一代入進行排除，可知 generally 符合題意，即正確選項是 (B)。第 4 題的四個選項都是副詞，根據上下文內容可知，要選擇表示否定的副詞 seldom，只有選項 (D) 符合題意。第 5 題考單字的用法。四個選項中只有動詞 proved 後面可以直接跟形容詞，表示「證明～」，所以選 (C)。

解答＆技巧｜ 01 **(A)** 02 **(C)** 03 **(B)** 04 **(D)** 05 **(C)**

適用 TIP 3　適用 TIP 4　適用 TIP 6　適用 TIP 7　適用 TIP 11

補充
generally speaking ph 一般來説；relaxed a 放鬆的；present a 在場的；
embarrassed a 尷尬的；weatherman n 天氣預報員

7,000 單字
- quiet [ˈkwaɪət] a 1 安靜的
- nervous [ˈnɝvəs] a 3 緊張的
- examine [ɪgˈzæmɪn] v 1 檢查
- truth [truθ] n 2 事實
- through [θru] prep 2 通過
- commuter [kəˈmjutɚ] n 5 通勤者
- newspaper [ˈnjuzˌpepɚ] n 1 報紙
- offensive [əˈfɛnsɪv] a 4 無禮的
- discussion [dɪˈskʌʃən] n 2 討論
- forecast [ˈforˌkæst] n 4 預報
- promise [ˈprɑmɪs] v 2 允諾
- umbrella [ʌmˈbrɛlə] n 2 傘
- propose [prəˈpoz] v 2 建議
- seldom [ˈsɛldəm] ad 3 很少
- witness [ˈwɪtnɪs] v 4 目擊

3 ▶ 92 年指考英文

The Internet has replaced books as a major source of information for Taiwanese primary school students, according to a recent survey. The survey was conducted last December, and it __01__ that 77 percent of the students considered the Internet to be the most convenient source of information. 14 percent of the respondents said they often turned to books for information instead of going online. Of all the students surveyed, 27 percent said they had never used the __02__.

The survey randomly selected 4,200 students in 26 primary schools in various parts of Taiwan to investigate their reading habits. A total of 4,017 questionnaires were properly __03__ by the respondents.

According to the survey, five percent of the school children indicated that they did not read any __04__ reading materials. Of those who read such materials, 25 percent liked to read comics, 20 percent fables and stories, 15 percent books on natural sciences, and 12.3 percent books on technology. The survey __05__ indicated that 45 percent of the school children read at least five books every month; another 45 percent of them read less than three per month.

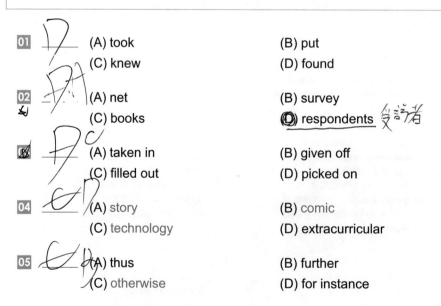

01 (A) took   (B) put
   (C) knew   (D) found

02 (A) net   (B) survey
   (C) books   (D) respondents 受訪者

03 (A) taken in   (B) given off
   (C) filled out   (D) picked on

04 (A) story   (B) comic
   (C) technology   (D) extracurricular

05 (A) thus   (B) further
   (C) otherwise   (D) for instance

DAY
1

Part 1
詞
彙
題
Day 1
完成 25%

Part 2
綜
合
測
驗
Day 1
完成 50%

Part 3
文
意
選
填
Day 1
完成 75%

Part 4
閱
讀
測
驗
Day 1
完成 100%

中譯｜ 根據最近的一項調查，網際網路已經取代書本，成為臺灣小學生的一種主要資訊來源。這項於去年十二月份進行的調查發現，百分之七十七的學生將網路當成是最方便的資訊來源。百分之十四的受訪者說，他們經常借助於書本而不是網路來尋求資訊。在所有接受調查的學生當中，百分之二十七的學生說他們從未使用過網路。

這項調查從臺灣不同地區的二十六所小學裡隨機挑選出四千兩百名學生來調查他們的閱讀習慣，共計有四千零十七份調查問卷由受訪者們恰當填寫。

根據調查，百分之五的學生表明他們沒有看過任何課外閱讀素材。在那些看過課外閱讀素材的學生當中，百分之二十五的學生喜歡看漫畫書，百分之二十的學生喜歡看寓言和故事書，百分之十五的學生喜歡看自然科學類的書籍，還有百分之十二點三的學生喜歡看科技方面的書籍。這項調查還進一步指出，百分之四十五的學生每個月至少閱讀五本書籍，而另外百分之四十五的學生則每個月少於三本。

解說｜ 首先可以閱讀全文來抓住本篇文章的主題「a recent survey」，即文章講述了在臺灣小學內部所進行的一項調查及其調查結果。第 1 題的空格之前的 it 作主詞，其後的 that 引導受詞子句，則第一題應選擇動詞，可以用代入法將四個選項一一代入題目，選出最符合題意的是 (D)。第 2 題之前有定冠詞 the，可知第 2 題應選擇名詞，再根據題意可判斷出，應選擇「網路」，即正確選項是 (A)。第 3 題是片語辨析，透過分析題意可知，要選擇「填寫」，即正確答案是 (C)。第 4 題是名詞辨析，可用排除法。後面的內容表示相反意義，而選項 (A)、(B)、(C) 都在後文中出現過，所以用排除法選 (D)。第 5 題要選出一個合適的副詞來修飾動詞 indicated，透過辨別詞義，只有選項 (B) further 符合題意，所以選 (B)。

解答 & 技巧｜ 01 (D)　02 (A)　03 (C)　04 (D)　05 (B)

適用 TIP 1　適用 TIP 3　適用 TIP 4　適用 TIP 7　適用 TIP 11

補充

Taiwanese ⓐ 臺灣的；respondent ⓝ 受訪者；randomly ⓪ 隨機地；reading habit ph 閱讀習慣；properly ⓪ 恰當地

7,000 單字

- book [bʊk] ⓝ 1 書
- source [sors] ⓝ 2 資源
- information [ˌɪnfɚ`meʃən] ⓝ 4 資訊
- conduct [kən`dʌkt] ⓥ 5 進行
- consider [kən`sɪdɚ] ⓥ 2 認為
- survey [sɚ`ve] ⓥ 3 研究
- select [sə`lɛkt] ⓥ 2 挑選
- questionnaire [ˌkwɛstʃən`ɛr] ⓝ 6 調查問卷

- material [mə`tɪrɪəl] ⓝ 2 材料
- fable [`febl] ⓝ 3 寓言
- science [`saɪəns] ⓝ 2 科學
- story [`storɪ] ⓝ 1 故事
- comic [`kɑmɪk] ⓝ 4 漫畫
- technology [tɛk`nɑlədʒɪ] ⓝ 3 技術，科技
- otherwise [`ʌðɚˌwaɪz] ⓪ 4 否則

4▶

The United States is famous for the major highway networks which are designed to help drivers __01__ from one place to another in the shortest time. Large highways often pass by scenic spots and small towns and generally connect with large urban centers; thus they __02__ become crowded with heavy traffic during rush hour, and these fast and direct ways may also become slow routes.

However, there is another possible route to take if you are not in a __03__ . Not far from the relatively new superhighways, there are usually older but less heavily traveled roads which will go __04__ the countryside. Some of these are good two-lane roads, while others are __05__ roads which curve through the country. Through these longer and slower routes, drivers would go to places where the air is cleaner and the scenery is more beautiful, and they may have a chance to pay a fresher visit to the world.

---

01 ___ (A) collect   (B) allow
        (C) add   (D) get

02 ___ (A) easily   (B) gladly
        (C) respectively   (D) profitably

03 ___ (A) time   (B) place
        (C) hurry   (D) driving

04 ___ (A) ahead   (B) through
        (C) abroad   (D) downhill

05 ___ (A) enjoyable   (B) splendid
        (C) amused   (D) uneven 不平的

中譯｜美國因主要高速公路網而出名，其設計是為了幫助司機們用最短的時間從一個地方到達另一個地方。大型高速公路經常經過風景名勝區和小城鎮，通常與大型市中心相連接，因此它們很容易在上下班尖峰時段變得交通擁擠，快速直達的通道也會變成一條非常慢速的路線。

然而，如果你不急的話，還有另一條可能採取的路線。在離相對來說比較新的超級高速公路的不遠處，經常有一些比較舊但是不太擁堵的道路，它們可以穿過鄉村。這些道路中有一些是良好的雙線道道路，其他則是路面不平的道路，彎彎曲曲地穿過鄉村。穿過這些較長且較緩慢的路線，司機們能前往空氣更清新，風景也更美麗的地方，並且他們也可以有機會對這個世界進行一次更加新鮮的拜訪。

解說｜本篇短文的主旨是講「美國高速公路」。第 1 題考四個動詞的詞義辨析。根據上下文的內容可知，只有動詞 get 與介系詞 to 搭配，表示「到達」符合題意，所以正確選擇為 (D)。第 2 題的四個選項都是副詞，用來修飾動詞 become。運用代入法將四個選項一一代入可知，要選擇副詞 easily，所以最符合題意的選項是 (A)。第 3 題考介系詞片語的固定搭配。運用排除法可知，in a hurry 表示「匆忙」，符合題意，即正確選項是 (C)。第 4 題考動詞 go 與介系詞的搭配用法，根據上下文內容可知，要用 go through 表示「穿過」，只有選項 (B) 符合題意。第 5 題的四個選項都是形容詞，來修飾名詞 roads。根據 roads 後面的形容詞子句可知，在鄉間彎曲的道路是不平坦的，而形容詞 uneven 表示「不平坦的」，所以選 (D)。

解答＆技巧｜ 01 (D)　 02 (A)　 03 (C)　 04 (B)　 05 (D)

適用 TIP 2　適用 TIP 3　適用 TIP 4　適用 TIP 11

補充

the United States ph 美國；heavy traffic ph 交通擁擠；rush hour ph 交通高峰期；relatively ad 相對地；superhighway n 超級高速公路

7,000 單字

- famous [ˈfeməs] a 2 著名的
- network [ˈnɛt,wɝk] n 3 網路
- highway [ˈhaɪ,we] n 2 高速公路
- design [dɪˈzaɪn] v 2 設計
- another [əˈnʌðɚ] a 1 另一個
- scenic [ˈsinɪk] a 6 風景優美的
- however [hauˈɛvɚ] conj 2 然而
- route [rut] n 4 路線

- less [lɛs] a 1 更少的
- traveled [ˈtrævld] a 2 旅客常到的
- countryside [ˈkʌntrɪ,saɪd] n 2 鄉村
- curve [kɝv] v 4 使彎曲
- collect [kəˈlɛkt] v 2 收集
- abroad [əˈbrɔd] ad 2 在國外
- splendid [ˈsplɛndɪd] a 4 傑出的

DAY 1

Part 1
詞彙題
Day 1
完成 25%

Part 2
綜合測驗
Day 1
完成 50%

Part 3
文意選填
Day 1
完成 75%

Part 4
閱讀測驗
Day 1
完成 100%

5 ▶

An old man died yesterday from being knocked down by a motorist because the driver had made no __01__ . When a policeman asked him to read the license plate of a car parked on the other __02__ of the road, the man said he couldn't read it correctly because it was foggy. However in fact, it was a sunny day. He said he had never needed glasses, though he had been involved in a __03__ accident the day before. Drivers' health problems often result in accidents like this. Last month, two motorists had died from traffic accidents. One died as a result of a blackout when driving __04__ the other man's car hit a tree. The second dead man had a brain disease, which would cause him to lose __05__ when he had a headache. In this case, it is not surprising that the accident prevention organizations are trying to persuade the government to introduce stricter controls over drivers.

01	(A) warning	(B) arrangement
	(C) brake	(D) guide

02	(A) side	(B) hand
	(C) part	(D) way

03	(A) definite	(B) perfect
	(C) exact	(D) similar

04	(A) when	(B) while
	(C) where	(D) till

05	(A) weight	(B) face
	(C) consciousness	(D) courage

中譯 │ 昨天，一位老人被一個駕車者撞倒後不治身亡，因為司機並沒有煞車。當一名員警要求他讀出停放在道路另一邊的車輛的車牌時，那名男子說他無法正確讀出，因為他覺得有霧。但實際上，那天是一個晴天。他說他從不需要戴眼鏡，儘管他前一天已經捲入一起類似的事故中。司機的健康問題通常會導致類似事故的發生。上個月，交通事故導致兩名駕車者死亡。其中一名死者是由於駕車時發生昏厥，而另一位死者是因為他的車撞到了樹。第二名死者患有腦部疾病，會在他頭痛時失去意識。在這種情況下，事故預防組織正試圖說服政府對駕駛員進行更為嚴格的管制，也就不足為奇了。

解說 │ 本篇短文講述了發生的幾起交通事故的原因和經過，答題時注意短文中出現的細節內容。第 1 題的四個選項都是名詞，透過閱讀全文可知，司機在撞人之前沒有煞車，要選用名詞 brake，所以正確選擇為 (C)。第 2 題考常識性的知識。道路的「另一邊」要表達為 the other side，最符合題意的選項是 (A)。第 3 題四個選項都是形容詞。根據上下文的內容可知，短文中提到的幾起交通事故的發生原因都是相似的，要用形容詞 similar，即正確選項是 (D)。第 4 題要選用符合題意的連接詞。句子前後說的是不同的情況，因此要選用表示轉折含義的連接詞 while，只有選項 (B) 符合題意。第 5 題考動詞 lose 的固定片語搭配用法。根據題意可知，lose consciousness 表示「失去意識」，符合短文內容所表達的含義，所以選 (C)。

解答&技巧 │ 01 **(C)**　02 **(A)**　03 **(D)**　04 **(B)**　05 **(C)**

適用 TIP 2　適用 TIP 4　適用 TIP 7　適用 TIP 8

補充

motorist n 駕車者；license plate ph 車牌；correctly ad 正確地；health n 健康；blackout n 昏厥

7,000 單字

- die [daɪ] v 1 死
- yesterday [ˋjɛstɚde] ad 1 昨天
- knock [nɑk] v 2 敲擊
- driver [ˋdraɪvɚ] n 1 駕駛員
- policeman [pəˋlismən] n 1 員警
- park [pɑrk] v 1 停放
- foggy [ˋfɑgɪ] a 2 有霧的
- sunny [ˋsʌnɪ] a 2 晴朗的

- glasses [ˋglæsɪz] n 1 眼鏡
- accident [ˋæksədənt] n 3 事故
- death [dɛθ] n 1 死亡
- persuade [pɚˋswed] v 3 說服
- brake [brek] n 3 煞車
- definite [ˋdɛfənɪt] a 4 確切的
- courage [ˋkɝɪdʒ] n 2 勇氣

DAY 1

Part 1
詞彙題
Day 1
完成 25%

Part 2
綜合測驗
Day 1
完成 50%

Part 3
文意選填
Day 1
完成 75%

Part 4
閱讀測驗
Day 1
完成 100%

Geography is in __01__ to the study of the relationship between people and the land. Geographers usually compare various places on the earth, but they will also consider the earth as a whole. Some geography books mainly __02__ on small areas like towns or cities, and some deal with states, regions, nations, or continents, but some geography books deal with the whole earth. Another way to divide the study of geography is to __03__ between physical geography and cultural geography. Physical geography focuses on the natural world, while cultural geography starts with human beings and studies how human beings and their environment __04__ each other. The main work of a geographer is to observe, record, and explain the differences between places, so if all places were alike, there would be no need for geographers any more. We know that no two places are __05__ the same; thus geography is a point of view, a special way of looking at places.

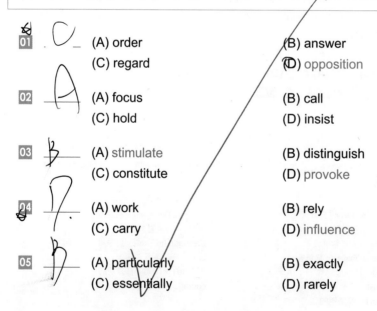

01 ___ (A) order   (B) answer
        (C) regard   (D) opposition

02 ___ (A) focus   (B) call
        (C) hold   (D) insist

03 ___ (A) stimulate   (B) distinguish
        (C) constitute (D) provoke

04 ___ (A) work   (B) rely
        (C) carry   (D) influence

05 ___ (A) particularly (B) exactly
        (C) essentially (D) rarely

DAY
1

Part 1
詞
彙
題
Day 1
完成 25%

Part 2
綜
合
測
驗
Day 1
完成 50%

Part 3
文
意
選
填
Day 1
完成 75%

Part 4
閱
讀
測
驗
Day 1
完成 100%

中譯｜ 地理學是關於研究人與大地之間的關係。地理學家通常對地球上各種不同的地方進行比較，但是他們也會視地球為一個整體。有些地理書籍主要關注小地方，像城鎮或是城市，有些涉及州、地區、國家或是大陸，但是有些地理書籍涉及到整個地球。另外一種劃分地理研究的方法是對自然地理學和人文地理學進行區分。自然地理學關注自然界，而人文地理學從人類入手，研究人類和他們居住的環境如何相互影響。地理學家的主要工作是觀察、記錄、解釋地方之間的差別，因此如果所有地方都相像，那麼就不再需要地理學家了。我們知道，沒有兩個地方是完全相同的，因此地理學是一種觀點，一種觀察地點的特殊方法。

解說｜ 本篇短文的主旨是「geography」，答題時要將地理學的相關知識考慮在內。第 1 題考介系詞片語的固定搭配用法。四個選項中，只有 regard 可以構成 in regard to 的固定搭配，表示「關於」，所以正確選擇為 (C)。第 2 題主要考能夠與介系詞 on 搭配的動詞的用法。根據上下文的內容可知，動詞 focus 與介系詞 on 搭配，表示「集中於」，符合題意，所以正確選項是 (A)。第 3 題的四個選項都是動詞，透過代入法將四個選項的單字一一代入，選出動詞 distinguish 最符合題意，即正確選項是 (B)。第 4 題四個選項都是動詞，只有 influence 符合題意與文法，所以正確選擇為 (D)。第 5 題的四個選項都是副詞，根據上下文的內容可知，要選擇 exactly 表示「完全地」，所以選 (B)。

解答＆技巧｜ 01 **(C)** 02 **(A)** 03 **(B)** 04 **(D)** 05 **(B)**
適用 TIP 2　適用 TIP 4　適用 TIP 7　適用 TIP 11

補充
geographer n 地理學家；physical geography ph 自然地理學；cultural geography ph 人文地理學；focus on ph 關注～；start with ph 以～開始

7,000 單字
- geography [ˋdʒɪˋɑgrəfɪ] n 2 地理
- relationship [rɪˋleʃənˋʃɪp] n 2 關係
- between [bɪˋtwin] prep 1 在兩者之間
- earth [ɝθ] n 1 地球
- state [stet] n 5 州
- physical [ˋfɪzɪkl] a 4 身體的
- cultural [ˋkʌltʃərəl] a 3 文化的
- environment [ɪnˋvaɪrənmənt] n 2 環境
- alike [əˋlaɪk] a 2 相似的
- thus [ðʌs] ad 1 因此
- view [vju] n 1 觀點
- opposition [ˌɑpəˋzɪʃən] n 6 反對
- stimulate [ˋstɪmjəˌlet] v 6 刺激
- provoke [prəˋvok] v 6 驅使
- influence [ˋɪnfluəns] v 2 影響

7 ▶ 92 年指考英文

Science makes possible use of new materials and new methods of producing objects. For example, some 20th-century chairs are made of steel and plastic. These materials, __01__ , were undreamed of in the 18th-century.

As new materials develop, one invention often __02__ another. Steel, for instance, was developed by engineers in the 19th-century. Because of its strength, steel soon became a useful building material. __03__ steel construction, buildings could then have a great many stories. But no one could be expected to walk up 8, 10, or 30 flights of __04__ . Therefore, to make tall buildings more accessible to their users, the elevator was invented. By providing much-needed space in a world __05__ people, tall buildings have solved many problems of cities and completely changed our way of life.

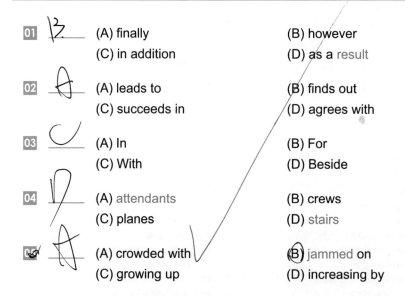

01 ___ (A) finally   (B) however
(C) in addition   (D) as a result

02 ___ (A) leads to   (B) finds out
(C) succeeds in   (D) agrees with

03 ___ (A) In   (B) For
(C) With   (D) Beside

04 ___ (A) attendants   (B) crews
(C) planes   (D) stairs

05 ___ (A) crowded with   (B) jammed on
(C) growing up   (D) increasing by

DAY
1

Part 1
詞
彙
題
Day 1
完成 25%

Part 2
綜
合
測
驗
Day 1
完成 50%

Part 3
文
意
選
填
Day 1
完成 75%

Part 4
閱
讀
測
驗
Day 1
完成 100%

中譯 科學讓使用新材料以及新方法來製造物品成為可能。例如，一些二十世紀的椅子就是由鋼鐵和塑膠製作而成的。然而，這些材料在十八世紀卻是做夢也想不到的。

隨著新型材料的發展，一項發明通常導致另一項發明的產生。例如，鋼是由十九世紀的工程師們發展而來的。由於它的強度，鋼很快成為一種有用的建築材料。隨著鋼結構的應用，建築物可以有很多樓層，但是沒有人會去爬八層、十層或者三十層的樓梯。因此，為了讓高樓大廈可以更加接近使用者，人們就發明了電梯。透過給這個人潮擁擠的世界提供亟需的空間，高樓大廈已經解決了城市中的很多難題，也徹底改變了我們的生活方式。

解說 本篇短文的主旨是「新型材料」，答題時要將建築學及一些與建築有關的發明考慮在內。第 1 題前後兩個句子所表達的含義相反，因此要用表示轉折的連接詞來引導，四個選項中只有 however 表示「然而」，所以正確選擇為 (B)。第 2 題考片語的用法。閱讀全文可知，此處要用 leads to 表示「導致」，即一項發明通常導致另一項發明的產生，因此最符合題意的選項是 (A)。第 3 題的句子是一個伴隨副詞子句，通常用 with 來引導，即正確選項是 (C)。第 4 題根據上下文內容可知，高層建築物有很多樓梯，即 stairs，只有選項 (D) 符合題意。第 5 題需要選用一個片語來充當 world 的後位修飾語，透過將四個選項一一代入可知，crowded with 表示「擁擠的」，符合題意，所以選 (A)。

解答＆技巧 | 01 **(B)**　02 **(A)**　03 **(C)**　04 **(D)**　05 **(A)**

適用 TIP 4　適用 TIP 7　適用 TIP 8　適用 TIP 11

> **補充**
> be made of ph 由～製成；undreamed a 夢想不到的；building material ph 建築材料；much-needed a 亟需的，很需要的；completely ad 完全地

> **7,000 單字**
> - method [ˈmɛθəd] n 2 方法
> - object [ˈɑbdʒɪkt] n 2 物體
> - example [ɪɡˈzæmpl] n 1 例子
> - chair [tʃɛr] n 1 椅子
> - plastic [ˈplæstɪk] n 3 塑膠
> - century [ˈsɛntʃʊrɪ] n 2 世紀
> - useful [ˈjusfəl] a 1 有用的
> - building [ˈbɪldɪŋ] n 1 建築物
>
> - construction [kənˈstrʌkʃən] n 4 建設
> - accessible [ækˈsɛsəbl] a 6 易接近的
> - elevator [ˈɛləˌvetɚ] n 2 電梯
> - result [rɪˈzʌlt] n 2 結果
> - attendant [əˈtɛndənt] n 6 侍者
> - stair [stɛr] n 1 樓梯
> - jam [dʒæm] v 2 使堵塞

It is said that a student once asked Albert Einstein, "What helped you the most with developing the __01__ of relativity?" Einstein replied with no hesitation, "Finding how to think about the problem."

Isaac Newton and several other scientists also have the same story. We have no idea whether these well-known conversations actually took __02__ or not, but we are willing to believe that they did and the answer was the same one as Einstein's, because this is the way making scientists work and science progress.

Scientists usually devote themselves __03__ the models of the structure that they are studying. Therefore, we possess many models of the structure of the universe and the atom, the models of the process by which the genetic pattern is __04__ from generation to generation, even the models of the economic system and so on. Some models are mathematical, but the most important requirement is that they see __05__ the relationships that determine why something works in such ways or how it is put together.

01. (A) volume   (B) theory
    (C) expectation   (D) compassion

02. (A) place   (B) back
    (C) for   (D) care

03. (A) for   (B) with
    (C) on   (D) to

04. (A) hindered   (B) suffered
    (C) passed   (D) hailed

05. (A) after   (B) through
    (C) free   (D) over

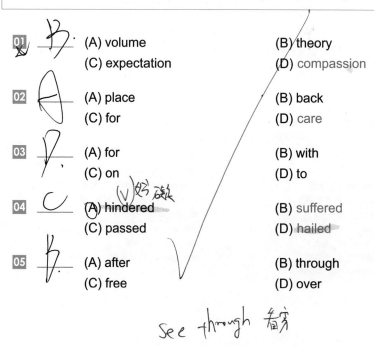

See through 看穿

中譯｜ 據説，曾經有一個學生問阿爾伯特‧愛因斯坦：「什麼是你發展相對論的重要推手？」愛因斯坦毫不猶豫地回答説：「發現如何思考問題。」
艾薩克‧牛頓以及其他幾位科學家都有相同的故事。我們不知道這些著名的談話是否真的發生過，但是我們願意相信真有其事，且答案與愛因斯坦的答案相同，因為這就是促使科學家們投入工作以及科學進步的方法。
科學家們經常致力於他們正在研究的結構模式。因此，我們能掌握到很多宇宙和原子的結構模式。基因形態代代相傳的過程模式，甚至是運用到經濟體系的模式等。有些模式為數學模式，然而，最重要的條件是，這些模式參透了決定事物運作方法和組合連結關係。

解説｜ 本篇短文講述了幾位科學家的事蹟，答題時可以考慮到這幾位科學家的學術研究成果。第 1 題考固定片語的搭配用法。依據題意可知，愛因斯坦發明的「相對論」可以表達為 theory of relativity，所以正確選擇為 (B)。第 2 題考與動詞 take 有關的固定片語用法。根據上下文內容可知，此處應該用表示「發生」的片語，即用 take place，所以最符合題意的選項是 (A)。第 3 題考介系詞的用法。根據積累的語法知識可知，動詞 devote 通常與介系詞 to 連用，表示「致力於」，即正確選項是 (D)。第 4 題考的是能夠與介系詞 from 連用的動詞。閱讀全文可知，此處應該用動詞 pass 表示「傳遞」，所以只有選項 (C) 符合題意。第 5 題考與動詞 see 連用的介系詞的用法。根據上下文內容可知，此處應該用介系詞 through，與動詞 see 連用表示「看穿」，所以選 (B)。

解答＆技巧｜ 01 **(B)**　02 **(A)**　03 **(D)**　04 **(C)**　05 **(B)**

適用 TIP 1　適用 TIP 2　適用 TIP 7

補充

relativity [n] 相對論；with no hesitation [ph] 毫不遲疑；have no idea [ph] 不知道；
the same... as [ph] 與～相同

7,000 單字

- student [ˋstjudn̩t] [n] ❶ 學生
- hesitation [͵hɛzəˋteʃən] [n] ❹ 猶豫
- several [ˋsɛvərəl] [a] ❶ 幾個的
- conversation [͵kɑnvɚˋseʃən] [n] ❷ 談話
- model [ˋmɑdl̩] [n] ❷ 模式
- structure [ˋstrʌktʃɚ] [n] ❸ 結構
- possess [pəˋzɛs] [v] ❹ 掌握
- universe [ˋjunə͵vɝs] [n] ❸ 宇宙

- pattern [ˋpætɚn] [n] ❷ 類型
- generation [͵dʒɛnəˋreʃən] [n] ❹ 一代
- mathematical [͵mæθəˋmætɪk] [a] ❸ 數學的
- compassion [kəmˋpæʃən] [n] ❺ 同情
- care [kɛr] [n] ❶ 關心
- suffer [ˋsʌfɚ] [v] ❸ 遭受
- hail [hel] [v] ❺ 招呼

DAY 1

Part 1
詞彙題
Day 1
完成 25%

Part 2
綜合測驗
Day 1
完成 50%

Part 3
文意選填
Day 1
完成 75%

Part 4
閱讀測驗
Day 1
完成 100%

9 ▶

When television began to develop at first, people who had become famous as radio announcers were hardly able to play an equal part. The biggest difficulty that they __01__ when they were trying to adjust themselves to the new medium was technical skill. For example, they had been used to __02__ on behalf of the listener when working in radio, which for others means that the announcer needs to be very good at talking. First of all, he should be able to create continuous visual images which could __03__ meanings to the sounds that the listener hears. However, the announcer sees everything with the viewer as to the television. Therefore, his duty is __04__ different. He has to make sure that the viewer does not miss any __05__ of interest, to help the viewer focus on particular things and understand the images on the television. In addition, he must also know the value of silence and how to use it when the pictures on the television speak for themselves.

01 ____ (A) experienced   (B) practiced
        (C) determined   (D) translated

02 ____ (A) seen   (B) saw
        (C) see   (D) seeing

03 ____ (A) appeal   (B) add
        (C) lead   (D) stick

04 ____ (A) naturally   (B) eventually
        (C) totally   (D) regularly

05 ____ (A) topic   (B) point
        (C) pattern   (D) information

中譯｜ 起初，電視開始發展時，那些早已成名的電台播音員幾乎無法與其平分秋色。他們在適應新媒體時所經歷的最大困難是技術技巧。例如，在電臺工作時，他們已經習慣代表聽眾來看事物，對於其他人來說，這種看意味著播音員需要非常善於言談。首先，他要能夠創造連續的視覺圖像，來增加聽眾聽到的聲音的含義。然而，至於電視機，播音員能夠看到觀眾看到的一切事物。因此，他的職責就完全不同。他必須確保觀眾不會錯過任何一個興趣點，幫助觀眾關注到特別的事物，理解電視上的圖像。此外，他也必須要知道沉默的效果，以及如何在電視上的圖片發威時保持沉默。

解說｜ 本篇短文的主旨是「電視」，答題時可以將電視的功用和特色考慮在內。第 1 題的四個選項都是動詞，根據上下文內容可知，此處應該選用動詞 experienced 表示「經歷」，所以正確選擇為 (A)。第 2 題考固定片語 be used to 的用法。根據所學的語法知識，be used to 中的 to 為介系詞，後面要用動名詞，即動詞 see 要用 seeing，所以最符合題意的選項是 (D)。第 3 題考能夠與介系詞 to 搭配使用的動詞。根據題意可知，應該選用動詞 add 表示「添加」，即正確選項是 (B)。第 4 題的四個選項都是副詞，用來修飾形容詞 different。根據上下文的內容可知，電臺播音員與電視播音員的職責是完全不同的，要選用副詞 totally，只有選項 (C) 符合題意。第 5 題涉及到固定片語的搭配。根據題意可知，point of interest 表示「興趣點」，符合題意，所以選 (B)。

解答＆技巧｜ 01 (A)　02 (D)　03 (B)　04 (C)　05 (B)

適用 TIP 1　適用 TIP 2　適用 TIP 4　適用 TIP 7

補充
announcer n 播音員；on behalf of ph 代表；be good at ph 擅長～；first of all ph 首先；themselves pron 他們自己

7,000 單字
- television [ˈtɛləˌvɪʒən] n 2 電視
- radio [ˈredɪo] n 1 廣播電台
- hardly [ˈhɑrdlɪ] ad 2 幾乎不
- difficulty [ˈdɪfəˌkʌltɪ] n 2 困難
- adjust [əˈdʒʌst] v 4 調整
- medium [ˈmidɪəm] n 3 媒介
- behalf [bɪˈhæf] n 5 代表
- mean [min] v 1 意味著
- continuous [kənˈtɪnjuəs] a 4 持續的
- visual [ˈvɪʒuəl] a 4 視覺的
- listener [ˈlɪsnɚ] n 2 聽眾
- image [ˈɪmɪdʒ] n 3 圖像
- translate [trænsˈlet] v 4 翻譯
- appeal [əˈpil] v 3 吸引
- stick [stɪk] v 2 堅持

Yesterday, 60,000 pounds __01__ of drugs being smuggled into Britain in boxes marked "Urgent Medical Supplies" were found at a London airport by the Customs officers. Five men were __02__ at the airport and underwent questioning, but they were unlikely to be the organizers. In fact, they said that they were unaware of what the goods in the boxes were and had actually acted in good __03__ in bringing them to Britain. This is the third time in this year that some people have attempted to smuggle illegal goods through Customs by disguising them to be medical supplies. Those illegal goods are frequently packed in special containers, with a warning to show that they may be damaged if not __04__ with care. The Customs officers said they were determined to put a stop to this practice and those people would have no way to get away with this any longer, because they had gained full cooperation of the international police who were also anxious to __05__ down the main source of supply.

01 (A) symbol (B) signature
(C) movement (D) worth

02 (A) arrested (B) harmed
(C) constructed (D) composed

03 (A) category (B) item
(C) faith (D) vibration

04 (A) designed (B) handled
(C) damaged (D) injured

05 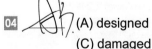 (A) fall (B) slow
(C) close (D) track

中譯｜昨天，倫敦一個機場的海關人員在標有「緊急醫療用品」的箱子裡發現了價值六萬英鎊的毒品，這些毒品正要被走私到英國。五名男子遭到逮捕並接受審問，但他們不大可能是組織者。事實上，他們說他們並不知道箱子裡裝了什麼貨物，他們實際上是出於好意才把貨物帶到英國。這是今年第三次有人試圖將違禁品偽裝成醫療用品透過海關來進行走私。那些違禁品時常包裝在特殊容器中，並帶有警示標誌，表明如果不小心處理，可能會損壞。海關人員說，他們決定制止這種行為，那些人再也無法僥倖逃脫，因為他們得到了也急於追捕主要供貨來源的國際刑警的全力配合。

解說｜本篇短文講述了發生在機場海關處的一起走私毒品的事件，並詳細介紹了其發生的過程和詳細情況。第 1 題的四個選項都是名詞，根據上下文的內容可知，此處應該選用名詞 worth 與介系詞 of 連用表示「價值」，所以正確選擇為 (D)。第 2 題的四個選項都是動詞。閱讀全文可知，應該是五名男子遭到逮捕，要用動詞 arrested，所以最符合題意的選項是 (A)。第 3 題涉及到動詞片語的固定搭配使用。根據平時所積累的語法知識可知，片語 act in good faith 表示「秉誠行事」，即正確選項是 (C)。第 4 題考動詞的使用。四個選擇都是動詞，但是根據上下文的內容可知，handle with care 表示「小心處理」，符合題意，所以只有選項 (B) 符合題意。第 5 題考與副詞 down 有關的動詞片語的用法。將四個選項一一代入可知，track down 表示「追捕」，符合題意，所以選 (D)。

解答＆技巧｜ 01 (D)　 02 (A)　 03 (C)　 04 (B)　 05 (D)
適用 TIP 1　適用 TIP 4　適用 TIP 7　適用 TIP 11

補充
Britain [n] 英國；unaware [a] 不知道的；illegal [a] 非法的；frequently [ad] 經常；
the international police [ph] 國際刑警

7,000 單字
- pound [paʊnd] [n] ② 英鎊
- smuggle [ˋsmʌgl̩] [v] ⑥ 走私
- box [bɑks] [n] ① 箱子
- urgent [ˋɝdʒənt] [a] ④ 緊急的
- airport [ˋɛr.port] [n] ① 機場
- customs [ˋkʌstəmz] [n] ⑤ 海關
- officer [ˋɔfəsɚ] [n] ① 官員
- question [ˋkwɛstʃən] [v] ① 質問

- organizer [ˋɔrgə.naɪzɚ] [n] ⑤ 組織者
- attempt [əˋtɛmpt] [v] ③ 試圖
- practice [ˋpræktɪs] [n] ① 實踐
- anxious [ˋæŋkʃəs] [a] ④ 急於～的
- signature [ˋsɪgnətʃɚ] [n] ④ 簽名
- arrest [əˋrɛst] [v] ② 逮捕
- vibration [vaɪˋbreʃən] [n] ⑥ 振動

DAY
1

Part 1
詞
彙
題
Day 1
完成 25%

Part 2
綜
合
測
驗
Day 1
完成 50%

Part 3
文
意
選
填
Day 1
完成 75%

Part 4
閱
讀
測
驗
Day 1
完成 100%

Part 3 文意選填 | Cloze Test

1▶

With the oil price __01__ up high in the global market, more attention has been drawn to the energy problem. There is no denying the fact that we are now facing another round of energy crisis. With the __02__ development of the industry and agriculture, the __03__ of energy has been dramatically increasing. Limited and non-renewable energy seems to be __04__ to meet the urgent needs of the economy. Recently scientists have been trying to discover and perfect other sources of energy: nuclear or atomic power, solar power, and synthetic fuels.

Nuclear power is supposed to offer some __05__, but fear of contamination just limits its use. The Three Mile Island accident in Pennsylvania in 1979, for example, had __06__ disastrous consequence for a long time, after nuclear waste material escaped into atmosphere. And power plant construction has greatly been __07__ since then.

Solar power, considered as another solution to the energy crisis, has been developing. Almost all energy __08__ from the sun. All other fuels might run out after a period of years, but the sun's power is limitless. Burning any fuel—oil, coal, or wood—probably causes pollution, but solar energy does not. However, solar energy has not been widely used in any country yet, since it seems to be __09__ and very expensive.

Furthermore, scientists are doing research to discover other sources of fuel. Strangely, some scientists have mixed alcohol with gasoline to __10__ fuel. This research is actually still in the developmental stage.

Nevertheless, there is still an immediate and viable solution to the problem—that is conservation, and it requires everyone's participation.

(A) rapid (B) unable (C) caused (D) assistance (E) climbing
(F) consumption (G) limited (H) conserve (I) derives (J) impractical

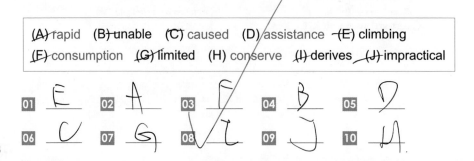

| 01 | E | 02 | A | 03 | F | 04 | B | 05 | D |
| 06 | C | 07 | G | 08 | I | 09 | J | 10 | H |

選項中譯｜迅速的；不能的；引起；幫助；攀升；消耗；限制；保存；源自；
不切實際的

中譯｜伴隨著國際市場上的石油價格上漲，人們更加關注能源問題。不可否認，我們正
面臨著新一輪的能源危機。隨著工業和農業的迅速發展，能源消耗量大幅增加。
有限而不可再生的能源似乎無法滿足經濟發展的迫切需求。近來，科學家們正試
著尋找及改善其他的能源：核能或是原子能、太陽能、合成燃料等。
核能是可以提供一些幫助的，不過，核能的利用卻因為害怕引起污染而受到限
制。例如，一九七九年賓夕法尼亞州的三哩島，因為核廢料擴散至空氣中，而
在之後造成長時間災難性的後果。而在那之後，發電廠的修建也受到了極大的限
制。
太陽能被認為是解決能源危機的另一種途徑，也在發展當中。幾乎所有的能源都
來自於太陽。其他的能源在若干年之後都可能面臨枯竭，而太陽能卻是永無止盡
的。石油、煤炭、木材等燃料的燃燒，都會造成污染，而太陽能卻不會。然而，
太陽能的利用似乎並不切合實際，費用也太過高昂，因此，在任何一個國家，太
陽能都尚未得到普及。
科學家們也在研究尋找其他的燃料。不可思議的是，有些科學家將酒精混入汽
油，以便節省燃料。事實上，這項研究仍然在實驗階段。
不論如何，還是有一種行之有效而又切實可行的方法來解決能源危機，那就是節
約利用，而這需要所有人的共同參與。

解譯｜閱讀全文可知，這篇文章的主題是應對能源危機的措施。
縱觀各選項，選項 (D)、(F) 是名詞，選項 (C)、(E)、(G)、(H)、(I) 是動詞，選
項 (A)、(B)、(J) 是形容詞。根據題意，第 3、5 題應選名詞，第 1、6、7、8、
10 題應選動詞，第 2、4、9 題應選形容詞。然後根據文章，依次作答。
第 1 題是選擇動詞，須與介系詞 up 進行搭配，有五個動詞可供選擇，即為選項
(C)、(E)、(G)、(H)、(I)。其中，只有選項 (E) climbing 可以，意為「攀升」，
即為正確答案。同樣，第 8 題所選的動詞需與介系詞 from 進行搭配，只有選項
(I) derives 可以，意為「源自於」。第 6 題是與名詞 consequence 進行搭配，
只有選項 (C) caused 可以，意為「引起～結果」。第 10 題是與名詞 fuel 進行
搭配，只剩下選項 (G) limited、(H) conserve 可供選擇，自然是選擇 (H)；而第
7 題則是選 (G)。
第 2 題是選擇形容詞，修飾名詞 development，有三個形容詞可供選擇，即為選
項 (A)、(B)、(J)。選項 (A) 意為「迅速的」，選項 (B) 意為「不能的」，選項 (J)
意為「不切實際的」，根據句意可知，應當是「工農業的迅速發展」，所以選
(A)。第 4 題，be unable to 可以視為固定搭配，意為「不能做某事」，所以選
(B)。第 9 題就只有選 (J)，句意為「太陽能的利用似乎並不切合實際」。
第 3 題是選擇名詞，用於 of 結構，意為「能源的～」。有兩個名詞可供選擇，

DAY
1

Part 1
詞
彙
題
Day 1
完成 25%

Part 2
綜
合
測
驗
Day 1
完成 50%

Part 3
文
意
選
填
Day 1
完成 75%

Part 4
閱
讀
測
驗
Day 1
完成 100%

即為選項 (D)、(F)，選項 (D) 意為「幫助」，選項 (F) 意為「消耗」，似乎都可以，暫且擱置。第 5 題也是選名詞，與動詞 offer 進行搭配，意為「提供～」，根據句意，應當是「提供幫助」，所以選 (D)，自然，第 3 題是選 (F)，意為「能源的消耗」。

解答＆技巧 | 01 (E)　02 (A)　03 (F)　04 (B)　05 (D)
　　　　　　06 (C)　07 (G)　08 (I)　09 (J)　10 (H)

適用 TIP 1　適用 TIP 2　適用 TIP 6　適用 TIP 7　適用 TIP 8
適用 TIP 9　適用 TIP 10　適用 TIP 11

補充

atomic power ph 原子能；solar power ph 太陽能；Three Mile Island ph 三哩島；
waste material ph 廢料；power plant ph 發電廠；energy crisis ph 能源危機

7,000 單字

- global [ˋglobl] a ③ 全球的
- draw [drɔ] v ① 拉
- round [raʊnd] n ① 一輪
- rapid [ˋræpɪd] a ② 快速的
- consumption [kənˋsʌmpʃən] n ⑥ 消耗
- atomic [əˋtɑmɪk] a ④ 原子的
- solar [ˋsolɚ] a ④ 太陽的
- synthetic [sɪnˋθɛtɪk] a ⑥ 合成的

- assistance [əˋsɪstəns] n ④ 幫助
- island [ˋaɪlənd] n ② 島
- cause [kɔz] v ① 引起
- alcohol [ˋælkəˌhɔl] n ④ 酒精
- gasoline [ˋgæsəˌlin] n ③ 汽油
- conserve [kənˋsɝv] v ⑤ 節約，保護，保存
- conservation [ˌkɑnsɚˋveʃən] n ⑥ 節約，保護，保存

MEMO

②▶

Everyone dreams. Those who claim that they never dream at all actually dream just as frequently as others, though they may not remember anything about what they have dreamt. Even those people, who are perfectly **01** _____ of dreaming night after night, seldom remember those dreams in great detail, merely retaining an untidy mixture of seemingly unrelated impressions. Dreams are not simply **02** _____ We generally dream with all our senses, so we are quite likely to experience sound, **03** _____ smell, and taste. It used to be believed that the soul of human had left the body when a person was sleeping. If the person were suddenly **04** _____ , the soul might not be able to return to the body in time; therefore, people had avoided waking a sleeping person.

Dreams are indeed reflections of people's inner spaces and a kind of **05** _____ between subconsciousness and consciousness. In many ancient civilizations, dreams have always been **06** _____ as a mystery. From ancient times to the present day, dream interpreting has always been quite **07** _____ . One of the best-known written documents in China is the book *Duke of Zhou Interprets Dreams*. It can be assumed that dreams have been believed to have a special **08** _____ even since then.

People have been making attempts to interpret dreams and to **09** _____ their significance. There are a great many books **10** _____ on the subject of dream interpretation, but unfortunately there are almost as many meanings for a particular dream as there are books.

DAY
1

Part 1
詞
彙
題
Day 1
完成 25%

Part 2
綜
合
測
驗
Day 1
完成 50%

Part 3
文
意
選
填
Day 1
完成 75%

Part 4
閱
讀
測
驗
Day 1
完成 100%

(A) regarded	(B) visual	(C) available	(D) aware	(E) significance
(F) connection	(G) touch	(H) explain	(I) awoken	(J) popular

01 _____	02 _____	03 _____	04 _____	05 _____
06 _____	07 _____	08 _____	09 _____	10 _____

選項中譯｜認為；可見的；可用的；意識到的；意義；聯繫；觸覺；解釋；叫醒；
　　　　　流行的

中譯｜每個人都會做夢。那些聲稱自己從不做夢的人，其實也和其他人一樣頻繁地做夢，不過，他們也許記不得自己做過什麼夢了。即便是那些確切地意識到自己在連夜做夢的人，也很少有人可以清楚地記得自己做過什麼夢，不過是些殘留下來的看似沒有什麼關聯的混亂印象。夢境不單只是視覺的。我們做夢時通常會調動所有的感官，所以我們很可能會聽到、觸摸到、聞到或是嗅到些什麼。過去有人認為，人在睡覺的時候，靈魂會離開身體。如果睡著的人突然被叫醒，靈魂就可能無法及時回歸到體內，所以過去人們會避免叫醒正在睡覺的人。

夢境，其實是人們內心世界的反映，也是意識和潛意識之間的一種聯繫。在很多的古文明中，夢境總是被認為十分神祕難解。從古至今，解夢都十分流行。中國最為著名的文字記載應該是《周公解夢》一書。可以推測，從那時候開始，人們就已經認為，夢境是有著某種特殊意義的了。

人們一直在試圖解夢，闡述其意義所在。已經有很多書在探討解夢之說。但不幸的是，對於某個具體的夢境，總有許多的解釋，正如有許多的解夢書一樣。

解譯｜閱讀全文可知，這篇文章的主題是解夢學的理論和相關發展。

縱觀各選項，選項 (E)、(F)、(G) 是名詞，選項 (A)、(H)、(I) 是動詞，選項 (B)、(C)、(D)、(J) 是形容詞。根據題意，第 3、5、8 題應選名詞，第 4、6、9 題應選動詞，第 1、2、7、10 題應選形容詞。然後根據文章，依次作答。

第 1 題是選擇形容詞，用於固定搭配 be... of，有四個形容詞可供選擇，即為選項 (B)、(C)、(D)、(J)。選項 (B) 意為「視覺的」，選項 (C) 意為「可用的」，選項 (D) 意為「意識到的」，選項 (J) 意為「流行的」，只有選項 (D) 可以，意為「意識到的，明白的」。第 2 題，根據句意可知，應當是「夢不只是～的」；第 7 題根據句意可知，應當是「解夢學是～的」；第 10 題根據句意可知，應當是「～的書」。分析句意可知，應當是第 2 題是選 (B)，意為「夢不只是視覺的」；第 7 題是選 (J)，意為「解夢學是流行的」；第 10 題是選 (C)，為「可用的書」。

第 3 題是選擇名詞，用於 sound, smell, and taste 的感官詞並列結構，有三個名詞可供選擇，即為選項 (E)、(F)、(G)，選項 (E) 意為「意義」，選項 (F) 意為「聯繫」，選項 (G) 意為「觸覺」，只有選項 (G) 符合要求。第 5 題也是選名詞，根據句意，應當是「意識和潛意識之間的一種～」；第 8 題根據句意，應當是「夢境是有著某種特殊的～」。分析句意可知，應當是第 5 題是選 (F)，意為「意識和潛意識之間的一種聯繫」；第 8 題是選 (E)，意為「夢境是有著某種特殊的意義」。

第 4 題是選擇動詞，須為被動語態，有三個動詞可供選擇，即為選項 (A)、(H)、

(I)。其中，選項 (A)、(I) 都是被動語態，根據句意，應當是「睡著的人突然被叫醒」，即選項 (I) 為正確答案。同樣，第 6 題所選的動詞，也應該用被動語態，只有選項 (A) 可以。而第 9 題則是只能選 (H)，意為「解釋其意義」。

解答&技巧 | **01** (D)　**02** (B)　**03** (G)　**04** (I)　**05** (F)
　　　　　　06 (A)　**07** (J)　**08** (E)　**09** (H)　**10** (C)

適用 TIP 1　適用 TIP 2　適用 TIP 6　適用 TIP 7　適用 TIP 8
適用 TIP 9　適用 TIP 10　適用 TIP 11

補充
in fact ph 事實上；night after night ph 連夜；in great detail ph 非常詳細地；in time ph 及時；make attempts to do sth. ph 嘗試做某事

7,000 單字
- anything [ˈɛnɪˌθɪŋ] pron 1 任何事物
- remember [rɪˈmɛmbɚ] v 1 記得
- mixture [ˈmɪkstʃɚ] n 3 混合
- touch [tʌtʃ] n 1 觸覺
- soul [sol] n 1 靈魂
- indeed [ɪnˈdid] ad 3 確實
- inner [ˈɪnɚ] a 3 內部的

- connection [kəˈnɛkʃən] n 3 連接，關係
- ancient [ˈenʃənt] a 2 古老的
- civilization [ˌsɪvləˈzeʃən] n 4 文明
- mystery [ˈmɪstərɪ] n 3 神祕
- significance [sɪgˈnɪfəkəns] n 4 意義
- explain [ɪkˈsplen] v 2 解釋
- interpretation [ɪnˌtɝprɪˈteʃən] n 5 解析，解釋

MEMO

DAY 1

Part 1
詞彙題
Day 1
完成 25%

Part 2
綜合測驗
Day 1
完成 50%

Part 3
文意選填
Day 1
完成 75%

Part 4
閱讀測驗
Day 1
完成 100%

3 ▶

Admittedly, he __01__ things might have been different, but who knows? These days he has more time to think. Of course, it's quite __02__ what comes to mind. Like the year he left home for the first time. It was a beautiful autumn morning. The woods were shades of gold and yellow, and the sun warmed his neck as he walked along. He then came to a point where the road __03__ in two, and he stood there, looking down those two roads for quite a long time, feeling it was a __04__ he couldn't take them both.

He remembers peering down one lane as far as he could see, to where it turned and __05__ in the mist, then setting off down the other. He thought that the one he had __06__ was a little less trodden path. But to tell the __07__., they might be trodden just about the same. The road was covered with __08__. He knew that he was the first one to come along that day because there were no footprints on the road, no blackened steps where the leaves had been trodden into the mud. He told himself that someday he would return to that __09__ in the road and take the other way, just to see where it would lead, but even then he knew he probably would not come back.

Still, when he thinks about that day and the road he chose, he cannot help __10__ what would have happened if he had gone the other way.

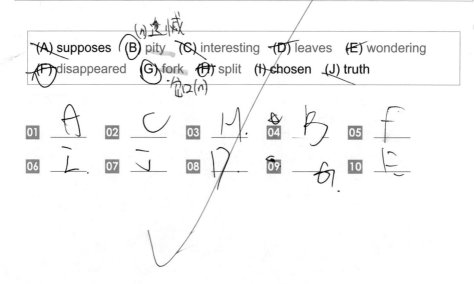

(A) supposes (B) pity (C) interesting (D) leaves (E) wondering
(F) disappeared (G) fork (H) split (I) chosen (J) truth

01	02	03	04	05
A	C	H	B	F

06	07	08	09	10
I	J	D	G	E

選項中譯｜ 推測；遺憾；有趣的；樹葉；想知道；消失；分岔口；分裂；選擇；事實

中譯｜ 他也知道，事情或許會有所不同，不過，誰知道呢？這幾天，他有更多的時間來思考。當然，他所想到的，是很有趣的事情。就像是那年，他第一次離開家的時候，是個美好的秋日清晨。樹林裡是深深淺淺的金色和黃色的色調，他在路上走著，太陽照得脖頸處暖洋洋的。後來，他走到了一處岔路口，面前有兩條路，他站在那裡，看了這兩條路很久，感覺很遺憾，他不能同時走這兩條路。

他記得，沿著一條路仔細地看過去，試圖看得更遠一些，視線所及，看到它轉了彎，消失在薄霧之中。然後，他走上了另一條路。他覺得自己選擇的這條路，走的人應該少一些。不過，說實話，這兩條路，走的人或許一樣多。他走的這條路，滿是落葉。他知道，自己應該是那一天最早走這條路的，因為，路上並沒有足跡，沒有那些落葉被踩踏後陷入泥濘中的深黑色足跡。他告訴自己，將來有一天，他要回到那個岔路口去，然後走另一條路，看看它是通往何處，不過，即便是在當時那個時候，他也知道，自己也許是不會再回去的了。

當他回想起那天的情形，回想起自己所選擇的路，他仍然忍不住要想，如果自己選擇的是另一條路，那麼，又會遇到什麼樣的情形呢？

解譯｜ 閱讀全文可知，這篇文章的主題是兩條路的選擇。

縱觀各選項，選項 (B)、(D)、(G)、(J) 是名詞，選項 (A)、(E)、(F)、(H)、(I) 是動詞，選項 (C) 是形容詞。根據題意，第 4、7、8、9 題應選名詞，第 1、3、5、6、10 題應選動詞，第 2 題應選形容詞。然後根據文章，依次作答。

第 1 題是選擇動詞，須為第三人稱單數形式，且引導受詞子句，有五個動詞可供選擇，即為選項 (A)、(E)、(F)、(H)、(I)。其中，只有選項 (A) 可以，即為正確答案。第 3 題，可以視為固定搭配，split in two / half 意為「一分為二」，所以選 (H)。第 5 題所選動詞須為過去式，只有選項 (F) 可以，句意為「消失在薄霧之中」。第 6 題所選動詞須為過去分詞，只有選項 (I) 可選擇。第 10 題則是選 (E)，構成固定搭配，意為「情不自禁地想知道」。

第 2 題是選擇形容詞，只有一個形容詞可供選擇，即為選項 (C)。

第 4 題是選擇名詞，有四個名詞可供選擇，即為選項 (B)、(D)、(G)、(J)，選項 (B) 意為「遺憾」，選項 (D) 意為「樹葉」，選項 (G) 意為「分岔口」，選項 (J) 意為「事實」，只有選項 (B) a pity，意為「遺憾、可惜」。第 7 題也是固定結構 to tell the truth，意為「說實話」，所以選 (J)。第 8 題，根據句意，應當是「道路鋪滿～」，只有選項 (D)、(G) 可供選擇，明顯應該選 (D)，意為「鋪滿樹葉」。自然，第 9 題是選 (G)，意為「岔路口」。

DAY
1

Part 1
詞
彙
題

Day 1
完成 25%

Part 2
綜
合
測
驗

Day 1
完成 50%

Part 3
文
意
選
填

Day 1
完成 75%

Part 4
閱
讀
測
驗

Day 1
完成 100%

解答&技巧 | **01** (A)　　**02** (C)　　**03** (H)　　**04** (B)　　**05** (F)
　　　　　　06 (I)　　**07** (J)　　**08** (D)　　**09** (G)　　**10** (E)

適用 TIP 1　　適用 TIP 2　　適用 TIP 6　　適用 TIP 7　　適用 TIP 8
適用 TIP 9　　適用 TIP 10　　適用 TIP 11

補充

of course ph 當然；come to mind ph 想到；split in two ph 一分為二；as far as ph 遠到；
to tell the truth ph 說實話

7,000 單字

- interesting [ˈɪntərɪstɪŋ] a 1 有趣的
- autumn [ˈɔtəm] n 1 秋天
- morning [ˈmɔrnɪŋ] n 1 早晨
- wood [wʊd] n 1 樹林
- shade [ʃed] n 3（色彩）濃淡，深淺
- gold [gold] n 1 金色
- neck [nɛk] n 1 脖子
- split [splɪt] v 4 分裂

- pity [ˈpɪtɪ] n 3 可惜，遺憾
- lane [len] n 2 鄉間小路
- disappear [ˌdɪsəˈpɪr] v 2 消失
- path [pæθ] n 2 小路
- leaf [lif] n 1 樹葉
- fork [fɔrk] n 1 岔口，分岔處
- wonder [ˈwʌndə] v 2 好奇，想知道

MEMO

④▶

Everyone might have __01__ from headaches, but so far medical researchers have not been __02__ what actually caused them. However, some new researches have indeed given us more information about common types of headaches and migraines.

Migraines should be the most __03__, which occur about eight to ten percent of all headaches, accompanied by a very sharp, throbbing pain. Most headaches, meanwhile, are tension headaches. They are unpleasant, of course, but not as painful as migraines. Usually tension headaches are experienced as variant aches on both sides of the head or in the back or the forehead. These headaches are usually __04__ by the tightening of the muscles of the head and the neck, which causes the blood __05__ to narrow, making it difficult for the brain to receive oxygen it needs.

Apparently migraines are inherited because several individuals in the same __06__ usually have them. It is believed that the brains of these individuals __07__ in unusual ways to small problems, like failing a test or eating unwisely. Sometimes there are warning __08__ before a migraine occurs, such as spots appearing before the eyes or a sick feeling in the stomach. If the person takes medicine or __09__ as soon as he or she begins to feel the headache coming on, it can be stopped. Caffeine and the medicine, called ergot, cause the blood vessels to narrow. Once the headache __10__ sleep and a cool towel on the head may help.

DAY
1

Part 1
詞
彙
題
Day 1
完成 25%

Part 2
綜
合
測
驗
Day 1
完成 50%

Part 3
文
意
選
填
Day 1
完成 75%

Part 4
閱
讀
測
驗
Day 1
完成 100%

(A) suffered (B) caused (C) family (D) signals (E) certain
(F) painful (G) occurs (H) vessels (I) caffeine (J) react

| 01 ____ | 02 ____ | 03 ____ | 04 ____ | 05 ____ |

| 06 ____ | 07 ____ | 08 ____ | 09 ____ | 10 ____ |

選項中譯｜遭受；引起；家庭；信號；確定的；痛苦的；發生；血管；咖啡因；反應

中譯｜也許每個人都有頭痛的經驗，不過，直到現在，醫學研究者仍然無法確信，究竟
是什麼引起了頭痛。不過，有些新的研究給予了我們更多關於常見頭痛和偏頭痛
的資訊。

偏頭痛應當是最痛苦的，有百分之八至百分之十的頭痛都是偏頭痛，發作時伴隨
著劇烈的抽痛。相比之下，大多數的頭痛，都是緊張性頭痛。當然，這些頭痛都
是令人不快的體驗，卻不像偏頭痛那樣令人痛苦。通常，緊張性頭痛發生在頭部
兩側、後方或是前額，伴隨著不同程度的疼痛，通常是由頭部、頸部的肌肉緊繃
引起的，會導致血管收縮，使得大腦難以獲得所需的氧氣。

偏頭痛似乎是遺傳的，同一家族中的不同個人通常都會患上偏頭痛。有人認為，
這些人的大腦會以不同的方式對某些小問題做出反應，例如考試不及格或是飲食
不當。有時候，偏頭痛在發作之前，會有警示性的信號，例如視線模糊或是反胃
想吐。如果在感覺偏頭痛有發作的跡象時，就服藥或是攝取咖啡因，是可以遏制
的。咖啡因和名為麥角鹼的藥物，可以引起血管收縮。一旦頭痛發作，睡眠和濕
毛巾冷敷頭部也許會有所幫助。

解譯｜閱讀全文可知，這篇文章的主題是頭痛和偏頭痛。

縱觀各選項，選項 (C)、(D)、(H)、(I) 是名詞，選項 (A)、(B)、(G)、(J) 是動詞，
選項 (E)、(F) 是形容詞。根據題意，第 5、6、8、9 題應選名詞，第 1、4、7、
10 題應選動詞，第 2、3 題應選形容詞。然後根據文章，依次作答。

第 1 題是選擇動詞，須與介系詞 from 進行搭配，有四個動詞可供選擇，即為
選項 (A)、(B)、(G)、(J)。其中，只有選項 (A) 可以，意為「遭受，經受」，即
為正確答案。同樣，第 4 題所選動詞須為被動語態，只有選項 (B) 可以，意為
「由～引起」。第 7 題所選動詞須為一般現在式，只有選項 (J) 可以，句意為「以
不同方式做出反應」。第 10 題所選動詞須為第三人稱單數形式，也只剩下選項
(G) 可供選擇，句意為「一旦頭痛發作」。

第 2 題是選擇形容詞，後接補語子句，有兩個形容詞可供選擇，即為選項 (E)、
(F)。選項 (E) 意為「確定的」，選項 (F) 意為「痛苦的」，只有選項 (E) 可以，
根據句意可知，應當是「醫學研究者仍然無法確信，究竟是什麼引起了頭痛」。
第 3 題，只有選項 (F) 可選，句意為「不像偏頭痛那樣令人痛苦」。

第 5 題是選擇名詞，與名詞 blood 連用，有四個名詞可供選擇，即為選項 (C)、
(D)、(H)、(I)，選項 (C) 意為「家庭」，選項 (D) 意為「信號」，選項 (H) 意為
「血管」，選項 (I) 意為「咖啡因」，只有選 (H)，構成固定搭配 blood vessel，
意為「血管」。第 6 題也是選名詞，根據前文中的 inherited「遺傳的」可知，
應當是「同一家族中的不同個人通常都會患上偏頭痛」，所以選 (C)。自然，
第 8 題所選名詞，與名詞 warning 連用，只有選項 (D)、(I) 可供選擇，應該是選
(D)，意為「警示信號」。第 9 題只有選 (I)，句意為「服藥或是攝取咖啡因」。

解答＆技巧｜ 01 **(A)** 02 **(E)** 03 **(F)** 04 **(B)** 05 **(H)**
06 **(C)** 07 **(J)** 08 **(D)** 09 **(I)** 10 **(G)**

適用 TIP 1　適用 TIP 2　適用 TIP 6　適用 TIP 7　適用 TIP 8
適用 TIP 9　適用 TIP 10　適用 TIP 11

DAY 1

Part 1
詞彙題
Day 1
完成 25%

補充

suffer from ph 遭受；migraine n 偏頭痛；blood vessel ph 血管；as soon as ph 一～就～；
ergot n 麥角鹼

7,000 單字

- certain [ˈsɝtən] a 1 確定的
- painful [ˈpenfəl] a 2 痛苦的
- side [saɪd] n 1 邊
- head [hɛd] n 1 頭
- forehead [ˈfɔrˌhɛd] n 3 額頭
- blood [blʌd] n 1 血
- vessel [ˈvɛsl̩] n 4 血管
- oxygen [ˈɑksədʒən] n 4 氧氣

- inherit [ɪnˈhɛrɪt] v 5 繼承，遺傳
- fail [fel] v 2 不及格
- test [tɛst] n 2 考試
- signal [ˈsɪɡn̩l] n 3 信號
- spot [spɑt] n 2 斑點
- sick [sɪk] a 1 噁心的，嘔吐的
- caffeine [ˈkæfiin] n 6 咖啡因

Part 2
綜合測驗
Day 1
完成 50%

Part 3
文意選填
Day 1
完成 75%

Part 4
閱讀測驗
Day 1
完成 100%

MEMO

5 ▶

The female __01__ force participation rate, i.e. FLFPR, has always been considered to reflect the economic status of women in a country or in a certain region. Besides, it is also an important __02__ reflecting the females' supply decisions.

Despite the experience of women in the labor market during the two World Wars, there is little evidence for a __03__ war-induced aberration. Female participation rates in 1951, compared with the rates in 1941, were just marginally higher, and still well under a quarter of the __04__ female labor force. Most were still young and __05__ and concentrated on the same narrow range of occupation. After the First World War, however, the growth in clerical occupation greatly __06__, and women made up the majority of the increase. In 1951 more than one out of every four employed women could be classed as clerical, and they __07__ fifty-seven percent of all clerical workers, a rise from fifty percent a decade before.

It is said that the wartime mobilization and the afterwar boom had given __08__ impetus to the growth of corporate capitalism. In the meanwhile, wartime labor __09__ and the introduction of capital intensive technology caused a revolution on the farm. Between 1941 and 1951, the number of occupied farms fell fifteen percent. And five years later, the number fell a further eight percent. Urbanization and the __10__ of the family production unit created the conditions for the revolution in women's labor market participation.

(A) labor (B) demand (C) single (D) temporary (E) index
(F) potential (G) decline (H) comprised (I) considerable
(J) expanded

---

01 _____ 02 _____ 03 _____ 04 _____ 05 _____

06 _____ 07 _____ 08 _____ 09 _____ 10 _____

選項中譯 | 勞動；需求；單身的；暫時的；指數；潛在的；衰落；組成；極大的；增加

中譯 | FLFPR，也就是女性勞動參與率，一直被認為能反映一個國家或是一個地區的女性經濟地位。此外，它也是反映女性勞動力供給決策的重要指標。

且不說兩次世界大戰期間女性在勞動市場的經歷，似乎沒有什麼證據可以顯示，女性勞動參與率存在著戰事所引起的暫時性偏差。與一九四一年相比，一九五一年的女性勞動參與率，只是略有上升，仍然低於女性勞動力潛在市場的四分之一。大多數都是年輕的單身女性，並且集中在有限的相似職業領域。然而，在第一次世界大戰之後，文書工作得到了極大的發展，女性勞動力為這樣的發展做出了絕大貢獻。一九五一年，多於四分之一的職業女性都是從事文書工作，她們佔據了文書工作者的百分之五十七，與十年前的百分之五十有所增長。

據說，戰時的動員和戰後的經濟增長，都極大地推動了企業資本主義的發展。同時，戰時勞動力需求和資本密集型技術，在農場引起了變革。一九四一年至一九五一年，農場的佔有率下降了十五個百分點。五年之後，這個數值又下降了八個百分點。都市化和個體家庭生產的衰落，為女性勞動參與的變革創造了條件。

解譯 | 閱讀全文可知，這篇文章的主題是女性勞動參與率。

縱觀各選項，選項 (A)、(B)、(E)、(G) 是名詞，選項 (H)、(J) 是動詞，選項 (C)、(D)、(F)、(I) 是形容詞。根據題意，第 1、2、9、10 題應選名詞，第 6、7 題應選動詞，第 3、4、5、8 題應選形容詞。然後根據文章，依次作答。

第 1 題是選擇名詞，與名詞 force 連用，且有形容詞 female 修飾，有四個名詞可供選擇，即為選項 (A)、(B)、(E)、(G)，選項 (A) 意為「勞動」，選項 (B) 意為「需求」、選項 (E) 意為「指數」，選項 (G) 意為「下降」，只有選 (A)，句意為「女性勞動參與率」。第 2 題也是選名詞，有形容詞 important 修飾，且後接現在分詞做修飾語，根據句意，應當是選 (E)，句意為「是反映女性勞動力供給決策的重要指標」。第 9 題所選名詞，有 wartime labor 作限定成分，應當是選 (B)，意為「戰時勞動力需求」。第 10 題只有選 (G)，句意為「個體家庭生產的衰落」。

第 3 題是選擇形容詞，與 war-induced 並列修飾名詞 aberration，有四個形容詞可供選擇，即為選項 (C)、(D)、(F)、(I)。選項 (C) 意為「單身的」，選項 (D) 意為「暫時的」，選項 (F) 意為「潛在的」，選項 (I) 意為「極大的」，根據句意可知，應當是「戰事所引起的暫時性偏差」，所以選 (D)。第 4 題，所選形容詞是修飾 female labor force，根據句意可知，應當是「女性勞動力潛在市場」，所以選 (F)。第 5 題，所選形容詞是與 young 並列作補語，根據句意可知，應當是「年輕的單身女性」，所以選 (C)。第 8 題就只有選 (I)，句意為「極大地推動了統合資本主義的發展」。

DAY
1

Part 1
詞
彙
題
Day 1
完成 25%

Part 2
綜
合
測
驗
Day 1
完成 50%

Part 3
文
意
選
填
Day 1
完成 75%

Part 4
閱
讀
測
驗
Day 1
完成 100%

第 6 題是選擇動詞，須為過去式，有兩個動詞可供選擇，即為選項 (H)、(J)，根據句意可知，應當是「文書工作得到了極大的發展」，只有選項 (J) 可以，即為正確答案。第 7 題所選的動詞，也是過去式，只能選 (H)，句意為「佔據了文書工作者的百分之五十七」。

解答＆技巧 | 01 (A)　02 (E)　03 (D)　04 (F)　05 (C)
　　　　　　06 (J)　07 (H)　08 (I)　09 (B)　10 (G)

適用 TIP 1　適用 TIP 2　適用 TIP 6　適用 TIP 7　適用 TIP 8
適用 TIP 9　適用 TIP 10　適用 TIP 11

補充

aberration n 偏差；marginally ad 稍微地；clerical a 文書的；
the First World War ph 第一次世界大戰；impetus n 促進；urbanization n 都市化

7,000 單字

- labor [ˈlebə] n 4 勞動
- reflect [rɪˈflɛkt] v 4 反映
- region [ˈridʒən] n 2 地區
- index [ˈɪndɛks] n 5 指數
- evidence [ˈɛvədəns] n 4 證據
- quarter [ˈkwɔrtə] n 2 四分之一
- single [ˈsɪŋgl] a 2 單身的
- war [wɔr] n 1 戰爭

- comprise [kəmˈpraɪz] v 6 組成
- before [bɪˈfor] ad 1 在～之前
- considerable [kənˈsɪdərəbl] a 3 相當大的
- corporate [ˈkɔrpərɪt] a 6 團體的，公司的
- capital [ˈkæpət] a 3 資本的
- intensive [ɪnˈtɛnsɪv] a 4 密集的
- production [prəˈdʌkʃən] n 4 生產

MEMO

MEMO

DAY
1

Part 1
詞
彙
題
Day 1
完成 **25**%

Part 2
綜
合
測
驗
Day 1
完成 **50**%

Part 3
文
意
選
填
Day 1
完成 **75**%

Part 4
閱
讀
測
驗
Day 1
完成 **100**%

The research on latent prints is conducted in a systematic and intelligent way. Investigators develop techniques to locate traces of fingerprints at a crime scene. The basic premise in searching for latent prints is to examine carefully those areas that would be most likely touched by people who have been on the spot. The natural manner in which a person would place his hands, in making an entrance or exit from a building or in handling a certain object, is the key to the discovery of latent prints.

Latent prints are likely to be found on any surface adjacent to or at the place where a forced entry has been made. The object with a smooth non-porous surface, if touched, is most likely to retain latent prints, while fingerprints on rough surfaces are usually of little value. Viewed under a reading glass, if the photographed fingermark does not disclose ridge detail, there may be a faint chance that you can find its value in identification. When fingermarks are found, it will be necessary, for the investigator, to compare them with the ones of people having legitimate access to the scene, so the traces might be eliminated as having evidentiary value if they prove to be from these persons.

Places to search for prints on an automobile are the rear view mirror, steering wheel hub, steering column, windshield, dashboard and the like. A fine brush or with an atomizer could be used for dusting off surfaces. The white powders used here are usually finely powdered white lead, talc or chalk, while the good black powder may be composed of lampblack, graphite, and powdered acacia. In developing latent prints, the common accepted method is to use the powder sparingly and brush lightly. However, powders should not be used if the fingermark is visible under oblique lighting. It can be photographed instead.

01 The word "intelligent" in the first paragraph is closest in meaning to _____.

(A) wise

(B) legal

(C) beautiful

(D) handsome

02 Which one of the following statements is true?

(A) Fingerprints on smooth non-porous surfaces are usually of great value.

(B) The research on latent prints is conducted in a casual way.

(C) Fingerprints on rough surfaces are usually of great value.

(D) Fingerprints at a crime scene are always neglected.

03 All the following substances may be the composition of the good black powder except _____.

(A) lampblack

(B) graphite

(C) powdered white lead

(D) powdered acacia

04 What is the main idea of the passage?

(A) Researches.

(B) Crime scenes.

(C) Photographs.

(D) Latent fingerprints.

DAY
1

Part 1
詞
彙
題
Day 1
完成 25%

Part 2
綜
合
測
驗
Day 1
完成 50%

Part 3
文
意
選
填
Day 1
完成 75%

Part 4
閱
讀
測
驗
Day 1
完成 100%

中譯｜有關潛伏指紋的研究，是以一種系統性、有智慧的方式來進行的。鑑識人員研發了相關技術，以找出犯罪現場的指紋跡證。尋找潛伏指紋的基本前提是仔細檢查那些極有可能被曾在場的人觸碰的地方。人們在進出建築物或是觸摸某個物體時，本能地放置手的方式，正是發現潛伏指紋的關鍵所在。

在強行進入發生的地方或附近，都可能找到潛伏指紋。光滑無孔的物體表面如果被觸及，就極有可能留下潛伏指紋；而粗糙表面上的指紋通常是沒有什麼價值的。透過放大鏡觀看，如果拍攝下來的指紋並無顯示具體的凹凸紋路，那麼，它通常是沒有什麼識別價值的。找到指紋後，鑑識人員有必要將它與有正當理由進出現場的人們的指紋進行對比，如此一來，如果可以證明指紋是這些人所有，就可以有足夠的證明理由，來排除這些跡證。

在汽車上，可以尋找指紋的地方，是後視鏡、方向盤底座、轉向機柱、擋風玻璃、儀錶板等。細毛刷，或是連同噴霧器一起，可以被用來為物體表面除塵。這裡所用的白色粉末通常是細緻的白色鉛粉、滑石粉或是粉筆末，而優質的黑色粉末也許是由燈黑、石墨和金合歡粉構成的。在進行指紋顯影時，普遍認可的方法是用少許粉末，輕輕拂掃。然而，如果指紋在低角度光源下可見，則不要用粉末，而是用攝影的方法來代替。

解譯｜在閱讀文章之前，先要預覽題目，然後再帶著問題針對性地閱讀文章。第 1 題是詞義辨析，第 2 題是判斷正誤，第 3 題是文意理解，第 4 題是概括主旨。理解了題目要求之後，閱讀全文，依次作答。

第 1 題是考形容詞 intelligent 的同義字。選項 (A) 意為「明智的，聰明的」，選項 (B) 意為「合法的」，選項 (C) 意為「漂亮的」，選項 (D) 意為「英俊的」。根據第 1 段首句內容可知，形容詞 intelligent 意為「明智的」，所以選 (A)。

第 2 題是判斷正誤，考的是細節，問的是，哪一項敘述是正確的。此題也可用排除法來解答。根據第 1 段首句內容可知，關於潛伏指紋的研究，是以一種系統性、有智慧的方式來進行的，而不是隨意進行，排除選項 (B)；根據第 1 段內容「Investigators develop techniques to locate traces of fingerprints at a crime scene」可知，犯罪現場的指紋並不是無人留意，排除選項 (D)；根據第 2 段內容「while fingerprints on rough surfaces are usually of little value」可知，粗糙表面上的指紋通常是沒有什麼價值的，排除選項 (C)。所以選 (A)。

第 3 題是文意理解，關鍵字是「composition of the good black powder」，即黑色粉末的構成，定位於第 3 段。根據第 3 句內容「while the good black powder may be composed of lampblack, graphite, and powdered acacia.」可知，排除選項 (A)、(B)、(D) 都是黑色粉末的構成成分；再根據第 3 句內容「The white powders used here are usually finely powdered white lead」可知，選項 (C) 是白色粉末的構成成分，所以選 (C)。

第 4 題是概括主旨。文中並沒有明顯的主旨句，需要根據各段內容加以概括。第 1 段是由潛伏指紋的研究而引出話題，第 2 段講述的是潛伏指紋的尋找發現，第 3 段講述的是潛伏指紋的採集。由此可知，短文內容是關於潛伏指紋的簡介，所以選 (D)。

解答＆技巧｜ **01 (A)** **02 (A)** **03 (C)** **04 (D)**

適用 TIP 1　適用 TIP 3　適用 TIP 7　適用 TIP 10　適用 TIP 11
適用 TIP 12　適用 TIP 13　適用 TIP 14　適用 TIP 15

補充

latent ⓐ 潛伏的，潛在的；adjacent ⓐ 接近的，毗連的；dashboard ⓝ 儀錶板；
acacia ⓝ 金合歡，刺槐；fingermark ⓝ 指痕，指印；oblique ⓐ 斜的

7,000 單字

- systematic [ˌsɪstə`mætɪk] ⓐ ④ 有系統的，有規劃的
- investigator [ɪn`vɛstəˌgetɚ] ⓝ ⑥ 鑑識人員，調查人員
- trace [tres] ⓝ ③ 痕跡
- entrance [`ɛntrəns] ⓝ ② 入口，進入
- discovery [dɪs`kʌvərɪ] ⓝ ③ 發現
- disclose [dɪs`kloz] ⓥ ⑥ 顯露
- compare [kəm`pɛr] ⓥ ② 比較
- legitimate [lɪ`dʒɪtəmɪt] ⓐ ⑥ 合理的，正當的

- eliminate [ɪ`lɪməˌnet] ⓥ ④ 消除，排除
- rear [rɪr] ⓐ ⑤ 後部的，後面的
- mirror [`mɪrɚ] ⓝ ② 鏡子
- wheel [hwil] ⓝ ② 輪子，方向盤
- column [`kɑləm] ⓝ ③ 柱
- windshield [`wɪndˌʃild] ⓝ ⑥ 擋風玻璃
- visible [`vɪzəb!] ⓐ ③ 可見的

Part 1
詞
彙
題
Day 1
完成 25%

Part 2
綜
合
測
驗
Day 1
完成 50%

Part 3
文
意
選
填
Day 1
完成 75%

Part 4
閱
讀
測
驗
Day 1
完成 100%

MEMO

♪ 057

Laughter should be a unifying force in a divided world. People may oppose each other on many different issues, nations may disagree about systems of government, and human relations may be plagued by ideological factions and political camps. However, we all share the ability to laugh. And laughter depends on the most complex and subtle of all human qualities— a sense of humor. Certain humor stereotypes have a universal appeal. The worldwide popularity of Charlie Chaplin's early films perfectly proves this. Any person at odds with others never fails to be amused.

A sense of humor may take various forms. Likewise, laughter may be anything from a refined smile to a wild roar, and the effect is always the same. Humor helps us to maintain a correct sense of values. It is just one of the qualities that political fanatics appear to lack. If we are aware of this, we may never make the mistake of taking ourselves too seriously. We should always be reminded that tragedy is not really far removed from comedy.

Humor should be one of the chief functions of satire and irony. Pains and sufferings are so grim, and we hover so often on the brink of disaster, failure, disease, etc. Cruel realities may plunge us into total despair. Under the circumstances, cartoons and satirical accounts of somber events could redress the balance, take the wind out of pompous and arrogant people's sails, and enable them to see that many of their actions are merely comic and absurd. We laugh because we are meant to laugh; but we are meant to weep, too. It is too powerful a weapon to be allowed to flourish. If happiness is one of the goals of life, then it is the sense of humor that provides the key.

01 We can learn from the first paragraph that the human quality laughter depends on is _____.

(A) a sense of satire

(B) a sense of humor

(C) a sense of responsibility

(D) a sense of history

02 Which one of the following statements is false?

(A) Any person at odds with others may share the ability to laugh.

(B) The popularity of Charlie Chaplin's early films shows that certain comic stereotypes have a universal appeal.

(C) Political fanatics all have a correct sense of values.

(D) Laughter may take various forms.

03 Which of the following statements about humor is not mentioned in the passage?

(A) Humor can help people to keep a correct sense of values.

(B) Humor can be regarded as one of the chief functions of satire and irony.

(C) Humor can lead us to find happiness.

(D) Humor may lead us to hover on the brink of pains and sufferings.

04 The word "redress" in the last paragraph is closest in meaning to _____.

(A) compensate

(B) reject

(C) advise

(D) invite

DAY
1

Part 1
詞
彙
題
Day 1
完成 25%

Part 2
綜
合
測
驗
Day 1
完成 50%

Part 3
文
意
選
填
Day 1
完成 75%

Part 4
閱
讀
測
驗
Day 1
完成 100%

中譯｜在充滿分歧的世界中，笑應當是有著消融分歧的力量的。人們也許會因為諸多不同的事件而觀點對立，國家也許會因為政治體系而產生分歧，人際關係也許會因為意識形態派系和政治陣營而受阻。然而，我們都有著笑的本能。笑則是依賴於幽默感——人們共有最複雜最微妙的本質。某些幽默模式有著普遍的吸引力。卓別林早期的電影在全世界普及正說明了這一點。與他人格格不入的人也會被逗笑。

幽默感有各式各樣的表現形式，同樣，笑可以是微笑，也可以是狂笑，如此種種，效果皆同。幽默感幫助我們保持正確的價值觀，這正是政治狂熱者所缺乏的特質。如果我們可以意識到這一點，也許就不會犯過於看重自己的錯誤。我們應當時刻記得，其實，悲劇之於喜劇，距離並不遙遠。

幽默應當是諷刺和反語的主要功能之一。苦難折磨是如此令人沮喪，我們也總是掙扎在災難、失敗、疾病等邊緣。殘酷的現實也許會令我們完全絕望，在這種處境中，漫畫和對某些政治事物的諷刺挖苦可以使人得以重獲平衡，使自負而傲慢的人們變得洩氣，使他們意識到，自己的諸多行為也不過是可笑而荒謬的。我們笑，是因為我們想笑；然而，我們也會想哭。這是效能強大的武器，決不能放任它隨意發展。如果幸福是我們的生活目標，那麼，幽默感就是開啟幸福的鑰匙。

解譯｜在閱讀文章之前，先要預覽題目，然後再帶著問題有針對性地閱讀文章。第 1、3 題是文意理解，第 2 題是判斷正誤，第 4 題是詞義辨析。理解了題目要求之後，閱讀全文，依次作答。

第 1 題是文意理解，問的是，笑所依賴的人類本質。根據第 1 段第 4 句內容「And laughter depends on the most complex and subtle of all human qualities—a sense of humor.」可知，笑是依賴於幽默感——人們共有最複雜最微妙的本質，與選項 (B) 相符，而其他選項在文中並沒有提及，因此排除，所以選 (B)。

第 2 題是判斷正誤，考的是細節，問哪一項是錯誤的。根據第 2 段內容「Humor helps us to maintain a correct sense of values. It is just one of the qualities that political fanatics appear to lack.」可知，政治狂熱者缺乏幽默感，也無法保持正確的價值觀，與選項 (C) 的敘述明顯不符，所以選 (C)。

第 3 題同樣是文意理解，關於幽默的敘述，哪一項在文中並沒有提及。其關鍵字是 humor，即幽默。根據第 2 段內容「Humor helps us to maintain a correct sense of values.」判斷，幽默感幫助我們保持正確的價值觀，與選項 (A) 相符；根據第 3 段首句內容「Humor should be one of the chief functions of satire and irony.」可知，幽默是諷刺和反語的主要功用之一，與選項 (B) 相符。再根據第 3 段最後一句內容「If happiness is one of the goals of life, then it is the sense of humor that provides the key.」可知，幽默感就是開啟幸福的鑰匙，與選項 (C) 相符。這三個選項都可以排除，只有選項 (D) 在文中找不到相關敘述，所以選 (D)。

第 4 題是考動詞 redress 的同義字。選項 (A) 意為「補償」，選項 (B) 意為「拒絕」，選項 (C) 意為「建議」，選項 (D) 意為「邀請」。根據第 3 段內容可知，動詞 redress 意為「補償」，所以選 (A)。

解答&技巧 | 01 (B)　02 (C)　03 (D)　04 (A)

適用 TIP 1　適用 TIP 3　適用 TIP 7　適用 TIP 10　適用 TIP 11
適用 TIP 12　適用 TIP 13　適用 TIP 15

補充
ideological ⓐ 意識形態的；worldwide ⓐ 遍及全世界的；satire ⓝ 諷刺，譏諷；satirical ⓐ 諷刺的；redress the balance ⓟ 使恢復平衡，均衡

7,000 單字

- laughter [ˋlæftɚ] ⓝ ③ 笑，笑聲
- disagree [͵dɪsəˋgri] ⓥ ② 不同意，有分歧
- faction [ˋfækʃən] ⓝ ⑥ 派系，派別
- camp [kæmp] ⓝ ① 陣營
- subtle [ˋsʌtl] ⓐ ⑥ 細微的，難以察覺的
- humor [ˋhjumɚ] ⓝ ② 幽默
- stereotype [ˋstɛrɪə͵taɪp] ⓝ ⑤ 老一套，模式化
- odds [ɑds] ⓝ ⑤ 可能性，機會

- amuse [əˋmjuz] ⓥ ④ 逗笑
- fanatic [fəˋnætɪk] ⓝ ③ 狂熱者
- comedy [ˋkɑmədɪ] ⓝ ④ 喜劇
- irony [ˋaɪrənɪ] ⓝ ⑥ 反語，諷刺
- failure [ˋfeljɚ] ⓝ ② 失敗
- plunge [plʌndʒ] ⓥ ⑤ 陷入
- arrogant [ˋærəgənt] ⓐ ⑥ 傲慢的

MEMO

DAY
1

Part 1
詞
彙
題
Day 1
完成 25%

Part 2
綜
合
測
驗
Day 1
完成 50%

Part 3
文
意
選
填
Day 1
完成 75%

Part 4
閱
讀
測
驗
Day 1
完成 100%

The newspaper must provide the readers with unalloyed, unslanted, and objectively selected facts. With regard to the complex news recently, the newspaper must provide more facts and supply more interpretation on these facts. It should be the most important assignment that journalism has been confronted with—to make clear to the readers the everyday events, to make international news as understandable as community news, to recognize that there is no longer such a thing as "local" news because any event in the international area may have a local effect on manpower draft, on economic strain, etc.

There is a widespread view in journalism that when you embark on interpretation, you are entering the swirling tides of opinion as choppy as dangerous waters. However, this is nonsense.

The opponents of interpretation insist that the writer and the editor shall confine himself to the "facts." This insistence raises two questions: What are the facts? Are there enough bare facts?

As to the first question, we should find out how a so-called "factual" story comes about. Hypothetically, the reporter collects fifty facts; out of these fifty, his space allotment is necessarily restricted. Then he selects ten, which he considers the most important. This is the first judgment. Next, he or his editor decides which of these ten facts shall constitute the headline news. This is the second judgment. Lastly, it is up to the chief editor to determine whether the article shall be presented on the front page with a large impact. This is the third judgment.

Thus, in the presentation of a so-called "factual" or "objective" story, there should be at least three judgments involved. And these three judgments have something in common with those judgments involved in interpretation, in which reporters and editors, with their general background and news neutralism, finally come to a conclusion as to the significance of the news.

01 The word "interpretation" in the first paragraph is closest in meaning to _____.

(A) explanation
(B) entrance
(C) emergency
(D) experience

02 Which of the following statements about the assignment of journalism is not mentioned in the passage?

(A) To inform readers of the daily news.
(B) To make international news easy to understand.
(C) To choose as many facts as possible.
(D) To realize that international news may have a local effect.

03 Which one of the following statements about the so-called factual story is true?

(A) There is no space allotment when the reporter collects facts.
(B) The reporter should select the most important facts within his space allotment.
(C) The first judgment is to decide which fact can constitute the lead of the piece.
(D) The second judgement is to decide where the article should be presented.

04 What is the main idea of the passage?

(A) Interpretation of news.
(B) Choice of facts.
(C) Subjective and objective opinions.
(D) Editors' work.

DAY 1

Part 1
詞彙題
Day 1
完成 25%

Part 2
綜合測驗
Day 1
完成 50%

Part 3
文意選填
Day 1
完成 75%

Part 4
閱讀測驗
Day 1
完成 100%

中譯｜報紙必須為讀者提供純粹的、無偏見的、客觀挑選的事實報導。對於近來複雜的新聞，報紙必須提供更多的事實，也必須提供這些事實的闡述。這應當是新聞界所面臨的最重要的任務——為讀者說明日常所發生的事，並且使國際新聞如同社區新聞一般易於理解，也要意識到當地新聞已經不復存在，因為，國際範圍內的任何事件都可能會對當地的人力流通、經濟壓力等產生影響。

新聞界有一種廣為流傳的觀點，認為開始闡述事實之時，也就是涉入了觀念思潮的漩渦中——如同有波浪起伏的危險水域。然而，這其實是妄言。

反對闡述事實的人則堅持認為，作者和編輯應當受限於事實。這樣的主張提出了兩個問題：什麼是事實？有沒有足夠的基本事實？

對於第一個問題，我們應當去尋找所謂的事實究竟是如何產生的。假定，記者收集了五十個事實，而在這五十個事實當中，他的報紙版面配置是必定要受到限制的。然後，這個記者選出他認為最重要的十個事實。這就是第一次判斷。接下來，這個記者或是他的編輯要決定，這十個事實中有哪一個可以作為頭條新聞。這就是第二次判斷。最後要取決於主編，即這篇文稿是否要放在有重要影響力的第一頁。這就是第三次判斷。

這樣來看，在所謂的事實或是客觀的故事敘述中，應當包括至少三次的判斷。這三次判斷，與事實闡述中所包含的判斷有些共同之處，記者和編輯都要運用自己的知識背景概況和新聞中立主義，來最終得出結論，判定新聞的意義。

解譯｜在閱讀文章之前，先要預覽題目，然後再帶著問題有針對性地閱讀文章。第 1 題是詞義辨析，第 2 題是文意理解，第 3 題是判斷正誤，第 4 題是概括主旨。理解了題目要求之後，閱讀全文，依次作答。

第 1 題是考名詞 interpretation 的同義字。選項 (A) 意為「解釋」，選項 (B) 意為「進入」，選項 (C) 意為「緊急事件」，選項 (D) 意為「經驗」。根據第 1 段內容可知，名詞 interpretation 意為「闡述」，所以選 (A)。

第 2 題是文意理解，關於新聞界的任務，哪一項敘述在文中沒有提及。根據第 1 段最後一句內容可知，選項 (A) 告知讀者日常新聞，選項 (B) 使國際新聞易於理解，選項 (D) 意識到國際新聞也許會對當地產生影響，這些都是新聞界所面臨的最重要的任務。而選項 (C) 選擇盡可能多的事實，在文中找不到相關敘述，所以選 (C)。

第 3 題是判斷正誤，考的是細節，問的是，關於所謂的事實的敘述，哪一項是正確的。很明顯，其關鍵字是 so-called factual story，因此，定位於第 4 段。根據第 4 段第 2 句內容「his space allotment is necessarily restricted」可知，記者的報紙版面配置是受到限制的，所以，選項 (A) 敘述錯誤，排除；根據第 4 段倒數第 4 行內容可知，決定頭條新聞，這是第二次判斷，選項 (C) 敘述錯誤，排除；再根據第 4 段倒數第 3 行內容可知，文稿的位置是第三次判斷，選項 (D) 敘述錯誤，也可以排除。而根據第 4 段第 3 句內容「Then he selects ten, which he considers most important.」可知，記者要選出他認為最重要的事實，與選項 (B) 相符。所以選 (B)。

第 4 題是概括主旨。文中並沒有明顯的主旨句，需要根據各段內容加以概括。第 1 段是由新聞界的任務而引出話題，第 2 段講述的是新聞闡述的錯誤觀點，第 3、4、5 段講述的是所謂的新聞事實的決斷過程。由此可知，短文內容是簡述新聞的闡述，所以選 (A)。

解答＆技巧｜ 01 (A)　 02 (C)　 03 (B)　 04 (A)

適用 TIP 1　適用 TIP 3　適用 TIP 7　適用 TIP 10　適用 TIP 11
適用 TIP 12　適用 TIP 13　適用 TIP 14　適用 TIP 15

補充
unalloyed ⓐ 純粹的，不混雜的；unslanted ⓐ 無偏見的，不歪曲的；manpower ⓝ 人力；choppy ⓐ 波浪起伏的；neutralism ⓝ 中立

7,000 單字
- journalism [ˋdʒɝnḷɪzm] ⓝ 5 新聞學，新聞界
- understandable [ˌʌndɚˋstændəbḷ] ⓐ 5 可以理解的
- draft [dræft] ⓝ 4 選派
- strain [stren] ⓝ 5 壓力
- embark [ɪmˋbɑrk] ⓥ 6 開始，從事
- nonsense [ˋnɑnsɛns] ⓝ 4 胡說，廢話
- insist [ɪnˋsɪst] ⓥ 2 堅持，堅決主張
- editor [ˋɛdɪtɚ] ⓝ 3 編輯，編者
- confine [kənˋfaɪn] ⓥ 4 限制
- insistence [ɪnˋsɪstəns] ⓝ 6 堅持，主張
- reporter [rɪˋportɚ] ⓝ 2 記者
- constitute [ˋkɑnstəˌtjut] ⓥ 4 組成，構成
- objective [əbˋdʒɛktɪv] ⓐ 4 客觀的
- general [ˋdʒɛnərəl] ⓐ 1 整體的，總的
- conclusion [kənˋkluʒən] ⓝ 3 結論

MEMO

DAY 1

Part 1 詞彙題 Day 1 完成 25%
Part 2 綜合測驗 Day 1 完成 50%
Part 3 文意選填 Day 1 完成 75%
Part 4 閱讀測驗 Day 1 完成 100%

Despite the marvelous progress made in every field of study, the methods of testing a student's knowledge and ability still remain as primitive as they have ever been. It is indeed odd that after all these years, educators still fail to find anything more efficient and reliable than examinations. Examinations may be a good means of testing memory or the knack of working effectively under extreme pressure, but they can tell nothing about a student's true ability and aptitude.

As anxiety-makers, examinations, the mark of success or failure in our society, should be second to none. A student's whole future may be simply decided in one fateful day. Nobody can work best if he is in mortal terror, or after a sleepless night. However, this is precisely what the examination system expects students to do. The moment a student attends school, he enters a world of vicious competition, where success and failure are clearly defined and measured.

A good education should actually train students to think for themselves. The examination system in reality does anything but that. That is a pity. What has to be learned is rigidly laid down by the syllabus, and students are simply forced to memorize it. Examinations restrict students' reading and induce cramming, rather than enable students to read widely and seek more knowledge. Besides, examinations lower the standards of teaching since they deprive the teacher of all freedoms.

In addition, the results of examinations depend so much on a subjective assessment by the anonymous examiners. Examiners always have to mark stacks of hastily scrawled scripts in a limited amount of time. They may get tired and hungry and therefore make mistakes. However, their word carries weight. After a judge's decision is made, people still have the right of appeal. But after an examiner's word is put on the paper, students have no right to do anything but accept it.

01 We can learn from the second paragraph that the fate of students is directly decided by _____.

(A) education

(B) teachers

(C) examinations

(D) schools

02 According to the passage, what is the most important function of a good education?

(A) To encourage students to read widely.

(B) To encourage students to learn as much knowledge as possible.

(C) To train students to think on their own.

(D) To encourage students to fight for a bright future.

03 We can learn from the passage that the author's attitude toward examinations is _____.

(A) critical

(B) indifferent

(C) detest

(D) approval

04 What is the main idea of the passage?

(A) Examinations are a means to test students' knowledge and ability.

(B) Examinations actually have a pernicious influence on education.

(C) Examinations are anxiety-makers.

(D) Examinations are a burden on teachers and students.

DAY
1

Part 1
詞
彙
題
Day 1
完成 25%

Part 2
綜
合
測
驗
Day 1
完成 50%

Part 3
文
意
選
填
Day 1
完成 75%

Part 4
閱
讀
測
驗
Day 1
完成 100%

中譯│儘管各個學科領域都已經有了極大的進展，然而，考查學生知識和能力的方法，
卻還是一如既往。事實上，這麼多年過去之後，教育學家們仍然沒有找到比考試
更有效、更可靠的方法，這是很反常的。考試也許是考驗記憶力的好方法，或是
在極度壓力下有效工作的訣竅，然而，它卻無法測知學生的真正能力和天賦。

考試在我們的社會中，是成功或是失敗的評定標識，成為造成焦慮的始作俑者，
無出其右。學生的未來，有可能在決定性的一日之間，就被輕易判定。在極度的
恐慌下，或是在一夜無眠之後，沒有人還能表現得很好。然而，這正是考試系統
所期望學生們做到的事情。學生入學讀書的時候，也就進入了激烈的競爭世界，
在這裡，成功和失敗都是清楚地規定和衡量的。

事實上，好的教育應當訓練學生獨立思考。而現實中的考試系統，做了很多，卻
是唯獨沒有做到這一點，令人遺憾。學生們所要學習的內容，都是教學大綱所嚴
格設定的，他們也只是簡單地被迫記憶而已。考試是限制學生的閱讀，引發填鴨
式教學，而不是讓學生廣泛閱讀，獲取更多的知識。此外，考試也剝奪了教師的
所有自由，因此降低了教學水準。

除此之外，考試結果過度依賴於匿名閱卷人員的主觀評定。閱卷人員總是要在有
限的時間之內批閱大量匆忙作答的試卷。他們也許會感覺疲倦和饑餓，也會因此
出錯。但是，他們的評語卻有舉足輕重的分量。法官做出判決之後，人們還可以
有上訴權。閱卷人員在考卷上做出評語之後，學生們除了接受之外別無選擇。

解譯│在閱讀文章之前，先要預覽題目，然後再帶著問題有針對性地閱讀文章。第 1、
2 題是文意理解，第 3 題是細節推斷，第 4 題是概括主旨。理解了題目要求之
後，閱讀全文，依次作答。

第 1 題是文意理解，關鍵字為 the fate of students，即為學生的命運，定位於第
2 段。根據第 2 段首句和第 2 句內容可知，考試是成功或是失敗的評定標識，學
生的未來，也許是在決定性的一日之間，就被輕易判定，由此推斷，學生的命運
是直接由考試所決定的，所以選 (C)。

第 2 題同樣是文意理解，問的是，好的教育最重要的功用。根據第 3 段首句內
容「A good education should actually train students to think for themselves.」
判斷，好的教育應當訓練學生獨立思考，與選項 (C) 相符。選項 (A) 鼓勵學生廣
泛閱讀、選項 (B) 鼓勵學生盡可能地多學知識、選項 (D) 鼓勵學生為美好的未來
而奮鬥，都在文中沒有提及，可以排除。所以選 (C)。

第 3 題是細節推斷，問的是，作者對於考試持何種看法。在第 1 段中，作者明
確指出，考試無法衡量學生的能力和水準。第 2 段則是點明，考試殘酷地決定學
生的命運。第 3 段則是指出，考試對於學生和老師的負面影響。第 4 段則是說，
閱卷制度的不合理性。這一切都說明，對於考試，作者是持批評態度的。所以選
(A)。

第 4 題是概括主旨。文中並沒有明顯的主旨句，需要根據各段內容加以概括。第
1 段是由教育現狀而引出話題；第 2 段講述的是考試輕易決定學生的成敗，引發
極度焦慮；第 3 段講述的是考試限制了教育的發展，對學生和老師都有極大的負

面影響；第 4 段講述的是考試結果受閱卷人員影響，並且不容學生置疑反抗。由此可知，短文內容是簡述考試對於教育的負面影響，所以選 (B)。

解答&技巧 | 01 **(C)** 02 **(C)** 03 **(A)** 04 **(B)**

適用 TIP 3　適用 TIP 7　適用 TIP 11　適用 TIP 12　適用 TIP 13
適用 TIP 14　適用 TIP 15　適用 TIP 16

補充

educator ⓝ 教育家；knack ⓝ 技巧，訣竅；fateful ⓐ 決定性的，重大的；
sleepless ⓐ 失眠的，不眠的；precisely ⓐⓓ 正好，恰恰；rigidly ⓐⓓ 嚴格地，不易改變地

7,000 單字

- marvelous [ˈmɑrvələs] ⓐ ③ 驚人的
- primitive [ˈprɪmətɪv] ⓐ ④ 舊式的，原始的
- odd [ɑd] ⓐ ⑤ 奇怪的
- reliable [rɪˈlaɪəbl] ⓐ ③ 可靠的，可信賴的
- examination [ɪgˌzæməˈneʃən] ⓝ ① 考試
- aptitude [ˈæptəˌtjud] ⓝ ⑥ 天資，天賦
- mortal [ˈmɔrtl] ⓐ ⑤ 極度的，極大的
- vicious [ˈvɪʃəs] ⓐ ⑥ 劇烈的

- memorize [ˈmɛməˌraɪz] ⓥ ③ 記憶
- induce [ɪnˈdjus] ⓥ ⑤ 引起，產生
- deprive [dɪˈpraɪv] ⓥ ⑥ 剝奪
- subjective [səbˈdʒɛktɪv] ⓐ ⑥ 主觀的
- anonymous [əˈnɑnəməs] ⓐ ⑥ 匿名的，不具名的
- examiner [ɪgˈzæmɪnə] ⓝ ④ 考試委員，檢查者
- script [skrɪpt] ⓝ ⑥ 筆試答案卷

MEMO

DAY 1

Part 1 詞彙題
Day 1
完成 25%

Part 2 綜合測驗
Day 1
完成 50%

Part 3 文意選填
Day 1
完成 75%

Part 4 閱讀測驗
Day 1
完成 100%

DAY 2

All things are difficult before they are easy.
凡事必先難後易。

▶ Part 1 ｜詞 彙 題
▶ Part 2 ｜綜合測驗
▶ Part 3 ｜文意選填
▶ Part 4 ｜閱讀測驗

Part 1 詞彙題｜Vocabulary Questions

---

01 Five men were killed in the tragic car accident last week due to the _____ of the petrol.

(A) span　　　　　　(B) sociology

(C) solitude　　　　(D) leak

中譯｜汽油洩漏導致五個人在上周發生的悲慘車禍中喪生。

解說｜四個選項皆為名詞。依據題意，應該是「汽油洩漏」，四個選項中，只有選項 (D) leak 表示「洩漏」，所以正確選項為 (D)。

解答&技巧｜**(D)** 適用 TIP 1　適用 TIP 4

> **補充**
> car accident ph 車禍，交通事故
>
> **7,000 單字**
> • tragic [ˈtrædʒɪk] a 4 悲劇的
> • span [spæn] n 6 跨度
> • sociology [ˌsoʃɪˈɑlədʒɪ] n 6 社會學
> • solitude [ˈsɑləˌtjud] n 6 孤獨
> • leak [lik] n 3 洩漏

---

02 Since she is very _____ of her weight, she often exercises in her leisure time.

(A) sneaky　　　　(B) conscious

(C) skeptical　　　(D) shrewd

中譯｜她非常在意自己的體重，所以經常在閒暇時間運動。

解說｜本題是因果關係句。由後一句的果「經常運動」，可以推斷出，前一句的因「在意體重」，所以應該選 (B) conscious。

解答&技巧｜**(B)** 適用 TIP 1　適用 TIP 4

> **補充**
> be conscious of ph 意識到，在意
>
> **7,000 單字**
> • leisure [ˈliʒɚ] a 4 空閒的
> • sneaky [ˈsnikɪ] a 6 鬼鬼祟祟的
> • conscious [ˈkɑnʃəs] a 3 意識到的
> • skeptical [ˈskɛptɪkl] a 6 懷疑的
> • shrewd [ʃrud] a 6 精明的

---

03 The young man _____ his opponent with all his effort in order to marry the lady.

(A) shoplifted　　　(B) seduced

(C) retrieved　　　(D) defeated

中譯｜為了跟那位女士結婚，這個年輕人盡全力打敗了他的對手。

解說｜四個選項皆為動詞。依據題意，應該是「打敗對手」。將四個選項一一代入可知，選項 (D) defeated 表示「打敗」，符合題意。

解答&技巧｜**(D)** 適用 TIP 3　適用 TIP 4

> **補充**
> marry sb. ph 和某人結婚
>
> **7,000 單字**
> • lady [ˈledɪ] n 1 女士
> • shoplift [ˈʃɑpˌlɪft] v 6 從商店中偷東西
> • seduce [sɪˈdjus] v 6 引誘
> • retrieve [rɪˈtriv] v 6 找回
> • defeat [dɪˈfit] v 4 打敗

04 He decided to ＿＿＿＿ his wedding until his parents and sister came back from America.

(A) relay   (B) relish

(C) postpone   (D) simplify

補充
come back from ph 從～回來

7,000 單字
- America [əˋmɛrɪkə] n 3 美國
- relay [rɪˋle] v 6 轉達
- relish [ˋrɛlɪʃ] v 6 品味
- postpone [postˋpon] v 3 延期
- simplify [ˋsɪmpləˌfaɪ] v 6 簡化

中譯｜他決定延後婚禮，直到他父母和妹妹從美國回來。

解說｜四個選項皆為動詞。由連接詞 until 可以推斷出，空格處的動詞應該用「延後」，選項 (C) postpone 表示「延後」，符合題意，所以正確選項為 (C)。

解答＆技巧｜**(C)** 適用 TIP 4　適用 TIP 8

---

05 Living in a highly competitive society, arming yourself with as much knowledge as possible is ＿＿＿＿ for you.

(A) tolerant   (B) renowned

(C) favorable   (D) regardless

補充
arm with ph 武裝，裝備

7,000 單字
- you [ju] pron 1 你
- tolerant [ˋtɑlərənt] a 4 寬容的
- renowned [rɪˋnaʊnd] a 6 著名的
- favorable [ˋfevərəbl] a 4 有利的
- regardless [rɪˋgɑrdlɪs] a 6 不管

中譯｜生活在一個競爭相當激烈的社會裡，用盡可能多的知識來武裝自己是非常有利的。

解說｜四個選項皆為形容詞。根據前一句的副詞子句可以推斷出，空格處應該是「有利的」，所以選項 (C) favorable 表示「有利的」，符合題意。

解答＆技巧｜**(C)** 適用 TIP 3　適用 TIP 4

---

06 Sometimes it's better not to put your graduation date on the resume in case it subjects you to age ＿＿＿＿.

(A) possession   (B) rehearsal

(C) discrimination   (D) rebellion

補充
in case ph 以防
subject to ph 使遭受

7,000 單字
- resume [ˋrɛzjuˋme] n 5 簡歷
- possession [pəˋzɛʃən] n 4 擁有
- rehearsal [rɪˋhɝsl] n 6 排演
- discrimination [dɪˌskrɪməˋneʃən] n 6 歧視
- rebellion [rɪˋbɛljən] n 6 叛亂

中譯｜有時不要將畢業日期寫進簡歷中，以防使你受到年齡歧視。

解說｜四個選項皆為名詞。選項 (C) discrimination 可以與名詞 age 搭配，表示「年齡歧視」，而其他三個選項都不可以進行搭配，所以正確選項為 (C)。

解答＆技巧｜**(C)** 適用 TIP 3　適用 TIP 4

DAY 2

Part 1
詞彙題
Day 2
完成 25%

Part 2
綜合測驗
Day 2
完成 50%

Part 3
文意選填
Day 2
完成 75%

Part 4
閱讀測驗
Day 2
完成 100%

07 I think his remark on the investment plan is on the _____, so you should not treat it as rubbish.

(A) realism   (B) mark

(C) ravage   (D) query

中譯｜我認為他對於投資計畫的評論很中肯，所以你不應該認為那毫無價值。

解說｜本題考介系詞片語的用法。四個選項中，只有選項 (B) mark 能夠與介系詞 on 搭配，構成 on the mark 表示「中肯」，符合題意，所以正確選項為 (B)。

解答＆技巧｜**(B)** 〔適用 TIP 1〕 〔適用 TIP 2〕

> 補充
> investment plan ph 投資計畫
> on the mark ph 中肯的，切題的
>
> 7,000 單字
> • rubbish [ˈrʌbɪʃ] n 5 垃圾
> • realism [ˈrɪəlɪzəm] n 6 現實主義
> • mark [mɑrk] n 2 標誌
> • ravage [ˈrævɪdʒ] n 6 蹂躪
> • query [ˈkwɪrɪ] n 6 疑問

---

08 The couple broke up with each other, which announced the irretrievable _____ of their marriage.

(A) radiator   (B) breakdown

(C) prosecution   (D) propeller

中譯｜那對夫婦分手了，這宣告了他們婚姻破裂且無法挽回。

解說｜四個選項皆為名詞。依據題意，應該是「分手宣告了婚姻破裂」。選項 (B) breakdown 表示「破裂」，符合題意，所以正確選項為 (B)。

解答＆技巧｜**(B)** 〔適用 TIP 1〕 〔適用 TIP 4〕

> 補充
> break up with ph 跟～分手
>
> 7,000 單字
> • irretrievable [ˌɪrɪˈtrivəbl] a 6 不能彌補的
> • radiator [ˈredɪˌetə] n 6 散熱器
> • breakdown [ˈbrekˌdaun] n 6 故障
> • prosecution [ˌprɑsɪˈkjuʃən] n 6 起訴
> • propeller [prəˈpɛlə] n 6 螺旋槳

---

09 With the whole county in the dark, the workers had to work around the clock to _____ the power lines.

(A) repair   (B) prosecute

(C) purify   (D) oblige

中譯｜整個縣都陷入了黑暗中，因此工人們不得不晝夜不停地修理輸電線。

解說｜依據題意，由「黑暗」可以推斷出輸電線壞掉，需要「修理」，而選項 (A) repair 表示「修理」，符合題意，所以正確選項為 (A)。

解答＆技巧｜**(A)** 〔適用 TIP 1〕 〔適用 TIP 4〕

> 補充
> around the clock ph 晝夜不停地
>
> 7,000 單字
> • county [ˈkaʊntɪ] n 2 縣
> • repair [rɪˈpɛr] v 3 修理
> • prosecute [ˈprɑsɪˌkjut] v 6 起訴
> • purify [ˈpjʊrəˌfaɪ] v 6 淨化
> • oblige [əˈblaɪdʒ] v 6 迫使

10 Julie wants to buy a _____ computer so that she can carry it around when she travels.

【93年學測英文】

(A) memorable   (B) portable

(C) predictable   (D) readable

中譯｜朱莉想買一台可攜式電腦，以便在旅行時隨身攜帶。

解說｜四個選項皆為形容詞。由後一句中的 carry it around，可以推斷出是小型的可攜式電腦，所以選項 (B) portable 表示「手提的，便攜的」，符合題意。

解答＆技巧｜**(B)** 適用 TIP 1 適用 TIP 4

補充
portable computer ph 可攜式電腦
carry sth. around ph 隨身攜帶

7,000 單字
- that [ðæt] conj 1 以至於
- memorable [ˋmɛmərəbl] a 4 難忘的
- portable [ˋportəbl] a 4 手提的
- predictable [prɪˋdɪktəbl] a 4 可預言的
- readable [ˋridəbl] a 1 可讀的

---

11 It is unfortunate that Peter's poor pension got him into economic _____ after his retirement.

(A) nurture   (B) nuisance

(C) crisis   (D) oppression

中譯｜很不幸地，彼得退休後，他那少得可憐的退休金使他陷入了經濟危機。

解說｜四個選項皆為名詞。依據題意，應該是「經濟危機」，因為題目中提到了退休金。選項 (C) crisis 表示「危機」，符合題意。

解答＆技巧｜**(C)** 適用 TIP 1 適用 TIP 4

補充
get into ph 陷入

7,000 單字
- pension [ˋpɛnʃən] n 6 退休金
- nurture [ˋnɝtʃɚ] n 6 養育
- nuisance [ˋnjusns] n 6 討厭的人（事、物）
- crisis [ˋkraɪsɪs] n 2 危機
- oppression [əˋprɛʃən] n 6 鎮壓

---

12 Jack has no time for ice skating which he takes to, _____ alone growing flowers in the garden.

(A) originate   (B) persevere

(C) phase   (D) let

中譯｜傑克沒時間去從事他喜歡的滑冰運動，更不必說在花園裡種花了。

解說｜本題考固定片語的用法。四個選項中，只有選項 (D) let 能夠與 alone 搭配，構成 let alone，表示「更不必說」，符合題意，所以正確選項為 (D)。

解答＆技巧｜**(D)** 適用 TIP 1 適用 TIP 2

補充
ice skating ph 滑冰
take to ph 喜歡

7,000 單字
- skating [ˋsketɪŋ] n 3 滑冰
- originate [əˋrɪdʒə.net] v 6 發源
- persevere [.pɝsəˋvɪr] v 6 堅持
- phase [fez] v 6 逐步執行
- let [lɛt] v 1 允許

DAY 2

Part 1 詞彙題
Day 2 完成 25%

Part 2 綜合測驗
Day 2 完成 50%

Part 3 文意選填
Day 2 完成 75%

Part 4 閱讀測驗
Day 2 完成 100%

13 Why do we have to put up with his _____? We should bravely struggle against him.

(A) piety   (B) poacher

(C) threat   (D) originality

中譯｜我們為什麼要忍受他的威脅？我們應該勇敢地進行反抗。

解說｜四個選項皆為名詞。由後一句中的 struggle「反抗」，可以推斷出前一句應該是「忍受威脅」，所以選項 (C) threat 符合題意。

解答＆技巧｜**(C)** 適用 TIP 1   適用 TIP 4

補充
put up with ph 忍受
struggle against ph 與～作鬥爭

7,000 單字
- why [hwaɪ] ad 1 為什麼
- piety [`paɪətɪ] n 6 虔誠
- poacher [`potʃə] n 6 偷獵者
- threat [θrɛt] n 3 威脅
- originality [ə,rɪdʒə`nælətɪ] n 6 創造性，獨創性

---

14 Trust me, a more _____ argument can help you win the debate competition without a hitch.

(A) nutrient   (B) peculiar

(C) nutritious   (D) persuasive

中譯｜相信我，一個更有說服力的論點會幫助你順利贏得辯論賽。

解說｜四個選項皆為形容詞。依據題意，要想「贏得辯論賽」，論據應該是「有說服力的」，選項 (D) persuasive 表示「有說服力的」，符合題意。

解答＆技巧｜**(D)** 適用 TIP 1   適用 TIP 4

補充
without a hitch ph 順利地

7,000 單字
- hitch [hɪtʃ] n 6 故障
- nutrient [`njutrɪənt] a 6 營養的
- peculiar [pɪ`kjuljə] a 4 特殊的
- nutritious [nju`trɪʃəs] a 6 滋養的
- persuasive [pə`swesɪv] a 4 有說服力的

---

15 Inspired by his teammates, John finally beat his opponent and won the _____ in the match.

(A) championship   (B) navigation

(C) momentum   (D) lounge

中譯｜在隊友們的鼓舞下，約翰最終打敗了對手，在比賽中贏得了冠軍。

解說｜本題考固定片語的用法。依據題意，要表示「贏得冠軍」可以說 win the championship，是一個固定搭配，所以選項 (A) 是正確答案。

解答＆技巧｜**(A)** 適用 TIP 1   適用 TIP 2

補充
win the championship
ph 贏得冠軍

7,000 單字
- teammate [`tim,met] n 2 隊友
- championship [`tʃæmpɪən,ʃɪp] n 4 冠軍稱號
- navigation [,nævə`geʃən] n 6 航行
- momentum [mo`mɛntəm] n 6 勢頭
- lounge [laʊndʒ] n 6 休息室

16 As is known to the whole world, the Statue of Liberty has become the most important _____ of America.

(A) skylight   (B) lunatic

(C) landmark   (D) malaria

補充
the whole world ph 全世界

7,000 單字
- statue [ˋstætʃu] n ③ 雕像
- skylight [ˋskaɪ͵laɪt] n ③ 天窗
- lunatic [ˋlunə͵tɪk] n ⑥ 瘋子
- landmark [ˋlænd͵mɑrk] n ④ 地標
- malaria [məˋlɛrɪə] n ⑥ 瘧疾

中譯│自由女神像聞名於世，已經成為了美國最重要的地標。

解說│四個選項皆為名詞。將四個選項的單字一一代入可知，應該是「地標」，要用 landmark 來表示，所以選項 (C) 是正確答案。

解答＆技巧│**(C)** 〔適用 TIP 4〕〔適用 適用 TIP 11〕

---

17 Mary usually buys things on _____, so that later she finds most of the things she bought are useless.

(A) accident   (B) compliment

(C) justification   (D) impulse

補充
on impulse ph 一時衝動

7,000 單字
- useless [ˋjuslɪs] a ① 無用的
- accident [ˋæksədənt] n ③ 事故
- compliment [ˋkɑmpləmənt] n ⑤ 恭維
- justification [͵dʒʌstəfəˋkeʃən] n ⑤ 辯護
- impulse [ˋɪmpʌls] n ⑤ 衝動

中譯│瑪麗經常憑藉一時衝動而買東西，以致於後來她發現所買的大部分東西都是無用的。

解說│本題考介系詞片語的用法。將四個選項一一代入，只有選項 (D) impulse 能夠與介系詞 on 搭配，構成 on impulse，表示「一時衝動」，符合題意，所以正確選項為 (D)。

解答＆技巧│**(D)** 〔適用 TIP 1〕〔適用 TIP 2〕

---

18 The children are so naive that they may not _____ between their imagination and the real world.

(A) irritate   (B) undertake

(C) manipulate   (D) differentiate

補充
real world ph 現實世界

7,000 單字
- real [ˋrɪəl] a ① 真實的
- irritate [ˋɪrə͵tet] v ⑥ 刺激
- undertake [͵ʌndɚˋtek] v ⑥ 承擔
- manipulate [məˋnɪpjə͵let] v ⑥ 操縱
- differentiate [͵dɪfəˋrenʃɪ͵et] v ⑥ 區分

中譯│孩子們太天真了，他們無法將想像與真實世界進行區分。

解說│本題考動詞之間的辨析。依據題意，應該是「區分」。選項 (D) differentiate 表示「區分」，且能夠與 between 連用，表示「在～中進行區分」，所以選項 (D) 是正確答案。

解答＆技巧│**(D)** 〔適用 TIP 1〕〔適用 TIP 4〕

DAY
2

Part 1
詞
彙
題
Day 2
完成 25%

Part 2
綜
合
測
驗
Day 2
完成 50%

Part 3
文
意
選
填
Day 2
完成 75%

Part 4
閱
讀
測
驗
Day 2
完成 100%

19 The little boy is so _____ that he always asks his parents and teachers a lot of strange questions.

(A) accurate   (B) inquisitive

(C) manageable   (D) joyous

中譯｜這個小男孩非常好問,總是向他的父母和老師問很多奇怪的問題。

解說｜四個選項皆為形容詞。由後一句中的動詞 ask,可以推斷出前一句的形容詞應該是「好問的」,所以選項 (B) inquisitive 是正確答案。

解答 & 技巧｜**(B)** 〔適用 TIP 1〕 〔適用 TIP 4〕

> **補充**
> a lot of ph 許多
>
> **7,000 單字**
> • lot [lɑt] n 1 大量
> • accurate [ˈækjərɪt] a 3 精確的
> • inquisitive [ɪnˈkwɪzətɪv] a 3 好問的
> • manageable [ˈmænɪdʒəbl] a 3 易管理的
> • joyous [ˈdʒɔɪəs] a 6 令人高興的

---

20 We can see from his strong sense of dedication to work that he is a(an) _____ man.

(A) forthcoming   (B) invaluable

(C) ingenious   (D) ambitious

中譯｜我們可以從他強烈的事業心看出,他是一個有雄心壯志的人。

解說｜四個選項皆為形容詞。依據題意,由 strong sense of dedication 可以推斷出,他是一個「有雄心壯志的人」,選項 (D) ambitious 符合題意。

解答 & 技巧｜**(D)** 〔適用 TIP 1〕 〔適用 TIP 4〕

> **補充**
> sense of ph ～的感覺
>
> **7,000 單字**
> • dedication [ˌdɛdəˈkeʃən] n 6 奉獻
> • forthcoming [ˌforθˈkʌmɪŋ] a 6 即將來臨的
> • invaluable [ɪnˈvæljəbl] a 6 無價的
> • ingenious [ɪnˈdʒinjəs] a 6 有獨創性的
> • ambitious [æmˈbɪʃəs] a 4 野心勃勃的

---

21 Just observe how others interact with tourists and do _____, and then you can become an experienced tour guide.

(A) edgewise   (B) likewise

(C) incidental   (D) clockwise

中譯｜觀察其他人如何與遊客們進行互動,然後照著做,你就會變成一名經驗豐富的導遊。

解說｜依據題意,要選擇副詞來修飾動詞 do,選項 (C) 是形容詞,排除。將選項 (A)、(B) 和 (C) 代入可知,選項 (B) likewise 表示「同樣地,照樣地」,符合題意,所以正確選項為 (B)。

解答 & 技巧｜**(B)** 〔適用 TIP 3〕 〔適用 TIP 11〕

> **補充**
> interact with ph 與～互動、交流
> tour guide ph 導遊
>
> **7,000 單字**
> • tour [tʊr] n 2 旅遊
> • edgewise [ˈɛdʒˌwaɪz] ad 5 沿邊
> • likewise [ˈlaɪkˌwaɪz] ad 6 同樣地
> • incidental [ˌɪnsəˈdɛntl] a 6 附帶的
> • clockwise [ˈklɑkˌwaɪz] ad 5 順時針方向地

22 John had failed to pay his phone bills for months, so his telephone was
_____ last week.

【93年學測英文】

(A) interrupted (B) disconnected
(C) excluded (D) discriminated

DAY
2

Part 1
詞
彙
題
Day 2
完成 25%

Part 2
綜
合
測
驗
Day 2
完成 50%

Part 3
文
意
選
填
Day 2
完成 75%

Part 4
閱
讀
測
驗
Day 2
完成 100%

補充
phone bill ph 電話帳單
for months ph 好幾個月

7,000 單字
• his [hɪz] pron ❶ 他的
• interrupt [ˌɪntəˈrʌpt] v ❸ 打斷
• disconnect [ˌdɪskəˈnɛkt]
  v ❹ 切斷（水、電、瓦斯、電
  話等的）供應
• exclude [ɪkˈsklud] v ❺ 排除
• discriminate [dɪˈskrɪməˌnet]
  v ❺ 歧視

中譯｜約翰已經好幾個月沒有繳電話費了，所以他上
星期被停話了。

解說｜本題是因果關係句。由前一句的因「沒有繳電
話費」，可以推斷出後一句的果「被停話」，
所以選項 (B) disconnected 符合題意。

解答＆技巧｜**(B)** 適用 TIP 1 適用 TIP 4

23 Lily usually _____ the used bottles instead of throwing them into the trash
bins.

(A) hunches (B) recycles
(C) disguises (D) hospitalizes

補充
trash bin ph 垃圾箱

7,000 單字
• trash [træʃ] n ❸ 垃圾
• hunch [hʌntʃ] v ❻ 聳起，拱起
• recycle [riˈsaɪkl] v ❹ 回收再利用
• disguise [dɪsˈɡaɪz] v ❹ 掩飾
• hospitalize [ˈhɑspɪtḷˌaɪz]
  v ❻ 使住院

中譯｜莉莉通常會回收那些用過的瓶子，而不是將它
們扔進垃圾箱裡。

解說｜本題中的連接詞片語 instead of 表示相反關
係。依據題意，「沒有扔進垃圾箱」的相反
結果應該是「回收再利用」，所以選項 (B)
recycles 是正確答案。

解答＆技巧｜**(B)** 適用 TIP 1 適用 TIP 4

24 The bonus system of this company has attracted many applicants for its
_____ positions.

(A) hospitable (B) evident
(C) honorary (D) vacant

補充
bonus system ph 獎金制度

7,000 單字
• bonus [ˈbonəs] n ❺ 獎金
• hospitable [ˈhɑspɪtəbl]
  a ❻ 友好熱情的
• evident [ˈɛvədənt] a ❹ 明顯的
• honorary [ˈɑnəˌrɛrɪ] a ❻ 榮譽的
• vacant [ˈvekənt] a ❸ 空缺的

中譯｜這家公司的獎金制度已經吸引了很多人前來應
徵空缺職位。

解說｜四個選項皆為形容詞。依據題意，應該是「應
徵空缺職位」，而 vacant position 是固定搭
配，表示「空缺職位」，所以正確選項是(D)。

解答＆技巧｜**(D)** 適用 TIP 2 適用 TIP 4

Part 2　綜合測驗 | Comprehensive Questions

1 ▶ 93 年指考英文

Children's encounters with poetry should include three types of response—enjoyment, exploration, and deepening understanding. These do not occur always as __01__ steps but may happen simultaneously. Certainly, children must start with enjoyment __02__ their interest in poetry dies. But if from the beginning they find delight in the poems they hear or read, they are ready and eager to __03__ further—more books and more poems of different sorts. Even the youngest children can learn to see implications __04__ the obvious. To read for hidden meanings is to identify with the poet, and to ask the poet's questions. This is reading for deeper understanding, __05__ a thoughtful look at what lies beneath the surface. Enjoyment, exploration, and deeper understanding must all be part of children's experience with poetry if we are to help them love it.

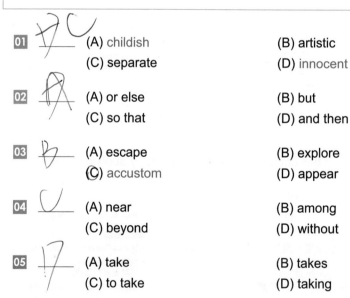

01   (A) childish   (B) artistic
      (C) separate   (D) innocent

02   (A) or else   (B) but
      (C) so that   (D) and then

03   (A) escape   (B) explore
      (C) accustom   (D) appear

04   (A) near   (B) among
      (C) beyond   (D) without

05   (A) take   (B) takes
      (C) to take   (D) taking

中譯｜兒童在接觸到詩時，應該有三種類型的反應——享受、探索和深層理解。這些反應並不總是單獨發生，也有可能同時發生。當然，兒童的第一反應一定是享受，否則他們對於詩的興趣將會消失殆盡。但是，如果他們一開始就對聽到的或是所讀的詩產生喜愛之情，他們就會準備好，並且急於對更多不同類型的書籍和詩進行更進一步的探索。即便是最小的孩子也可以學著理解表面意義之外的深層含義。讀出隱藏的含義就是與詩人產生共鳴，問出詩人的提問。這種閱讀是為了獲得深層理解，對置於表面下的事物進行深思的觀察。如果我們想要幫助兒童喜愛詩，他們就要歷經享受、探索和深層理解的所有階段。

解說｜本篇短文的主旨是「兒童與詩」，詳細介紹了兒童閱讀詩的過程及方式。第 1 題句子中的連接詞 but 表示轉折，but 之後的內容是同時發生，則 but 之前的選項應該選擇單獨發生，即用 separate，所以正確選擇為 (C)。第 2 題考連接詞的用法。根據上下文的內容可知，要選用 or else 表示「否則，要不然」，來說明選項之後的情況表示假設，所以最符合題意的選項是 (A)。第 3 題的四個選項都是動詞，閱讀全文可知，對書本和知識應該是「探索」，要用 explore，即正確選項是 (B)。第 4 題是關於介系詞的選取。根據題意可知，此處應該用 beyond 表示「超過，超越」，只有選項 (C) 符合題意。第 5 題考語法知識，即動詞用在副詞子句中時，要用動名詞，因此要用 taking，所以選 (D)。

解答&技巧｜ 01 **(C)** 02 **(A)** 03 **(B)** 04 **(C)** 05 **(D)**
適用 TIP 2　適用 TIP 4　適用 TIP 7　適用 TIP 8

補充
simultaneously [ad] 同時地；understanding [n] 理解；certainly [ad] 當然；reading [n] 閱讀；to do sth. [ph] 打算做某事

7,000 單字
- encounter [ɪnˋkaʊntə] [n] 4 遇到
- poetry [ˋpoɪtrɪ] [n] 1 詩
- type [taɪp] [n] 2 類型
- response [rɪˋspɑns] [n] 3 反應
- step [stɛp] [n] 1 步驟
- happen [ˋhæpən] [v] 1 發生
- delight [dɪˋlaɪt] [n] 4 高興
- poem [ˋpoɪm] [n] 2 詩
- read [rid] [v] 1 讀
- sort [sɔrt] [n] 2 種類
- poet [ˋpoɪt] [n] 2 詩人
- thoughtful [ˋθɔtfəl] [a] 4 深思的
- childish [ˋtʃaɪldɪʃ] [a] 2 幼稚的
- innocent [ˋɪnəsn̩t] [a] 3 天真的
- accustom [əˋkʌstəm] [v] 5 使習慣於

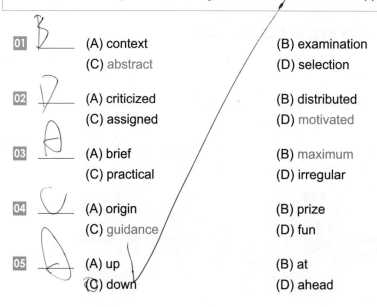

Many teachers think that the students have the responsibilities for learning. If the students are given a reading assignment, even if they will not discuss it in class or take an ___01___ , they should get familiar with the information in the reading. The ideal student should be ___02___ to learn for the sake of learning instead of only taking an interest in getting high grades. Sometimes homework is returned to the student with ___03___ written comments but with no grade. Even so, the student is responsible for finishing it carefully.

If research is assigned, the professor would expect the student to complete it actively with very little ___04___ . Professors usually have much other work to do besides teaching and limited time they could spend on the student outside of class; therefore, it is the student's responsibility to look things ___05___ in books, magazines, and articles in the library to get information they need. If the student has problems with classroom work, he should consult the professor during office hours or make an appointment.

01 ___ (A) context   (B) examination
        (C) abstract   (D) selection

02 ___ (A) criticized   (B) distributed
        (C) assigned   (D) motivated

03 ___ (A) brief   (B) maximum
        (C) practical   (D) irregular

04 ___ (A) origin   (B) prize
        (C) guidance   (D) fun

05 ___ (A) up   (B) at
        (C) down   (D) ahead

DAY 2

Part 1
詞彙題
Day 2
完成 25%

Part 2
綜合測驗
Day 2
完成 50%

Part 3
文意選填
Day 2
完成 75%

Part 4
閱讀測驗
Day 2
完成 100%

中譯｜ 許多老師都認為學生有學習的責任。如果老師要求學生閱讀某物，即使他們不在課堂上進行討論，也不進行考試，他們也應該熟悉閱讀資料。理想的學生應該受到激發，為了學問進行學習，而不是僅僅對考取高分感興趣。有時，老師將家庭作業返還給學生，上面有簡短的書面批註而沒有分數，即便如此，學生也有責任認真完成作業。

如果被分配了研究任務，教授會希望學生在不太需要指導的情況下積極主動地完成它。除了教學外，教授通常還有很多其他的工作要做，課外花費在學生身上的時間很有限，因此，學生就有責任在圖書館裡查閱書籍、雜誌和文章，來獲取他所需要的資訊。如果學生對於課堂作業有困難，他應該在辦公時間諮詢教授，或是進行預約。

解說｜ 本篇短文的主旨是「學習」，教導學生了解正確以及有效的學習目的和學習方法。第 1 題考動詞片語的固定用法。依據題意可知，「考試」應該表達為 take an examination，所以正確選擇為 (B)。第 2 題的四個選項都是形容詞，根據上下文的內容可知，要選用 motivated 表示「有積極性的」，即要積極主動地學習，所以最符合題意的選項是 (D)。第 3 題的四個選項都是形容詞，根據前後文的意思可知，written comments 應該是「簡明的」，即 brief，所以正確選項是 (A)。第 4 題要選用一個名詞，而依據題意可知，教授提供給學生的應該是「指導」，即 guidance，只有選項 (C) 符合題意。第 5 題考與動詞 look 有關的片語的用法。依據題意可知，「查閱」要用 look up，所以選 (A)。

解答＆技巧｜ 01 (B)　02 (D)　03 (A)　04 (C)　05 (A)

適用 TIP 1　適用 TIP 2　適用 TIP 4　適用 TIP 7

補充

high grades ph 高分；carefully ad 認真地；actively ad 積極地；limited a 有限的；classroom n 教室

7,000 單字

- teacher [ˈtitʃɚ] n 1 老師
- have [hæv] v 1 有
- discuss [dɪˈskʌs] v 2 討論
- class [klæs] n 1 班級
- ideal [aɪˈdiəl] a 3 理想的
- interest [ˈɪntərɪst] n 1 興趣
- homework [ˈhom.wɝk] n 1 家庭作業
- assign [əˈsaɪn] v 4 指派

- professor [prəˈfɛsɚ] n 4 教授
- article [ˈɑrtɪkl] n 2 文章
- library [ˈlaɪ.brɛri] n 2 圖書館
- abstract [ˈæbstrækt] n 4 摘要
- motivate [ˈmotə.vet] v 4 激發
- maximum [ˈmæksəməm] a 4 最多的
- guidance [ˈgaɪdn̩s] n 3 指導

3▶

A plane was out of control and was moving unsteadily __01__ the airport. Although the passengers had __02__ the seat belts, they were still thrown forward. After a while, a flight attendant came. She calmly informed the passengers that the pilot had fainted and asked which passenger knew how to control the machine. Then a man got up and walked into the pilot's cabin.

After moving the pilot aside, the man sat in the pilot's seat and listened carefully to the urgent __03__ sent by radio from the airport. Now, the plane was dangerously __04__ to the ground, but it soon began to climb. The man had to circle over the airport several times in order to get to know how to control the plane. According to the instructions, the man had to guide the plane toward the airfield and prepare to land. When the plane touched the ground, it shook __05__ and then moved rapidly along the runway. After a long run, the plane finally stopped safely.

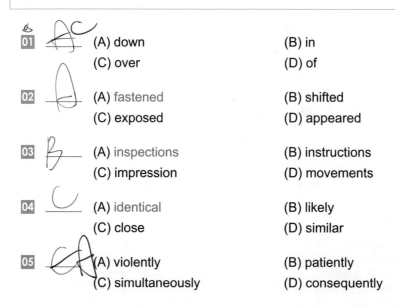

01   (A) down   (B) in
      (C) over   (D) of

02   (A) fastened   (B) shifted
      (C) exposed   (D) appeared

03   (A) inspections   (B) instructions
      (C) impression   (D) movements

04   (A) identical   (B) likely
      (C) close   (D) similar

05   (A) violently   (B) patiently
      (C) simultaneously   (D) consequently

中譯 | 一架飛機失去了控制，正搖搖擺擺地在飛機場上方飛行。儘管乘客們已經扣緊了安全帶，他們的身體仍然向前衝去。不久，一位空服員過來了。她非常冷靜地通知大家，飛行員已經昏迷了，並且詢問有哪位乘客知道如何控制機器。然後，一名男子起身走進了駕駛艙。

把飛行員移到旁邊後，那名男子坐到駕駛座上，認真聽取機場透過無線電傳來的緊急指令。現在，飛機非常危險地接近地面，但是不久又開始上升。那名男子不得不在飛機場上空盤旋幾次，以便知道如何操控飛機。依照指令，那名男子操縱飛機開往飛機場，並且準備著陸。當接觸到地面時，飛機劇烈搖晃，然後沿著跑道快速移動。經過長時間的滑行，飛機終於安全停了下來。

解說 | 本篇短文主要講述了飛機失控，以及最終如何平安降落的事件。第 1 題要選用合適的介系詞。依據題意，「在飛機場上方」要用介系詞 over，所以正確選擇為 (C)。第 2 題的四個選項都是動詞，而根據平時所積累的有關乘坐飛機的知識可知，乘客應該是繫上安全帶，要選用動詞 fasten，所以最符合題意的選項是 (A)。第 3 題的四個選項都是名詞。依據題意可知，機場透過無線電發送的是緊急指令，即 instructions，所以正確選項是 (B)。第 4 題要選用合適的形容詞。根據上下文的內容可知，當飛機不斷下降時，就會接近地面，即用 close 表示「接近的」，只有選項 (C) 符合題意。第 5 題考副詞的用法。飛機接觸地面時，會劇烈搖晃，副詞 violently 最符合題意，所以選 (A)。

解答&技巧 | 01 **(C)** 02 **(A)** 03 **(B)** 04 **(C)** 05 **(A)**

適用 TIP 1 適用 TIP 2 適用 TIP 4 適用 TIP 7

補充
unsteadily ad 不平穩地；airfield n （小型）機場；runway n 跑道；finally ad 最終；safely ad 安全地

7,000 單字
- plane [plen] n 1 飛機
- control [kən`trol] n 1 控制
- passenger [`pæsṇdʒɚ] n 2 乘客
- forward [`fɔrwəd] ad 2 向前
- inform [ɪn`fɔrm] v 3 通知
- pilot [`paɪlət] n 3 飛行員
- faint [fent] v 3 昏倒
- machine [mə`ʃin] n 1 機器

- cabin [`kæbɪn] n 3 客艙
- climb [klaɪm] v 1 爬
- instruction [ɪn`strʌkʃən] n 3 指令
- land [lænd] n 1 陸地
- fasten [`fæsṇ] v 3 使固定
- inspection [ɪn`spɛkʃən] n 4 檢查
- identical [aɪ`dɛntɪkḷ] a 4 同一的

DAY 2
Part 1
詞彙題
Day 2
完成 25%
Part 2
綜合測驗
Day 2
完成 50%
Part 3
文意選填
Day 2
完成 75%
Part 4
閱讀測驗
Day 2
完成 100%

4 ▶ 94 年學測英文

Experts say that creativity by definition means going against the tradition and breaking the rules. To be creative, you must dare __01__ , and courageously express your own outlook and __02__ what makes you unique. But does our society encourage children to break the rules? I'm afraid the answer is no. The famous film director Ang Lee recalls his father's disappointment with him when he was young. __03__ a small child, he would pick up a broom and pretend to be playing guitar for the entertainment of family guests. Then, when he was studying film in college, he would exhaust himself just for a performance tour. His father, __04__ always hoped that he would get a PhD and become a professor, __05__ with a scoff, "What is all this nonsense?!" But it later turned out that it was exactly his courage to "rebel" and to express his own ideas that mark his films with distinct creativity.

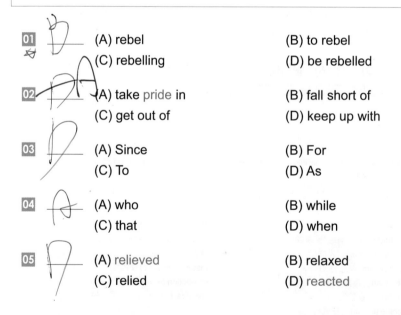

01	(A) rebel	(B) to rebel
	(C) rebelling	(D) be rebelled
02	(A) take pride in	(B) fall short of
	(C) get out of	(D) keep up with
03	(A) Since	(B) For
	(C) To	(D) As
04	(A) who	(B) while
	(C) that	(D) when
05	(A) relieved	(B) relaxed
	(C) relied	(D) reacted

DAY
2

Part 1
詞
彙
題
Day 2
完成 25%

Part 2
綜
合
測
驗
Day 2
完成 50%

Part 3
文
意
選
填
Day 2
完成 75%

Part 4
閱
讀
測
驗
Day 2
完成 100%

中譯｜專家們說，從定義上來講，創造性意味著反對傳統、打破規則。想要富有創造性，你必須敢於反抗，勇敢地表達出自己的觀點，並且對那些使自己成為獨一無二的事物引以為傲。但是我們的社會鼓勵孩子們打破規則嗎？恐怕不是這樣。著名電影導演李安回想起，小時候他的父親對他感到很失望。作為一個孩童，他會拾起一把掃帚，假裝是在彈吉他為客人們助興。然後，上大學主修電影時，他會僅僅為了一次巡迴演出而把自己累得精疲力竭。他的父親，那個總是希望他能夠拿到博士學位，成為一名教授的人，卻嘲笑著反應道：「都在胡搞些什麼？！」然而後來，事實證明，正是他敢於反抗以及表達自己的勇氣才使得他的電影具有獨特的創造性。

解說｜本篇短文的主旨是「創造性」，並列舉了一些人物的事例來表現這一主旨。第 1 題考動詞 dare 的用法。根據所學的語法知識可知，動詞 dare 後面一般接不定詞來表示敢於做某事，即用 to rebel 的形式，所以正確選擇為 (B)。第 2 題考動詞片語的用法。依據題意可知，此處應該選用 take pride in 表示「因～而自豪」，所以最符合題意的選項是 (A)。第 3 題是一個伴隨副詞子句，通常用 as 來引導，在此處表示「作為」，所以正確選項是 (D)。第 4 題涉及到指示代名詞的用法。此處的選項指代之前的名詞 father，是一個人，要用指示代名詞 who，只有選項 (A) 符合題意。第 5 題考動詞的用法。將四個選項的動詞一一代入可知，只有動詞 reacted 表示「反應」，符合題意，所以選 (D)。

解答＆技巧｜ 01 (B)　 02 (A)　 03 (D)　 04 (A)　 05 (D)
適用 TIP 1　 適用 TIP 2　 適用 TIP 9　 適用 TIP 11

補充
courageously [ad] 勇敢地；a performance tour [ph] 巡迴演出；PhD [ph] 博士學位；scoff [n] 嘲笑；exactly [ad] 正好地

7,000 單字
- expert [ˈɛkspɝt] [n] 2 專家
- creativity [ˌkrieˈtɪvətɪ] [n] 4 創造性
- definition [ˌdɛfəˈnɪʃən] [n] 3 定義
- tradition [trəˈdɪʃən] [n] 2 傳統
- outlook [ˈaʊtˌlʊk] [n] 6 觀點
- unique [juˈnik] [a] 4 獨一無二的
- child [tʃaɪld] [n] 1 兒童
- broom [brum] [n] 3 掃帚
- guitar [ɡɪˈtɑr] [n] 2 吉他
- guest [ɡɛst] [n] 1 客人
- exhaust [ɪɡˈzɔst] [v] 4 排出
- rebel [rɪˈbɛl] [v] 4 反抗
- pride [praɪd] [n] 2 驕傲
- relieve [rɪˈliv] [v] 4 解除
- react [rɪˈækt] [v] 3 反應

5 ▶

Among all studies, the study of words and word origins is the most interesting one. According to the study, each language may __01__ from several earlier languages, and the words of a language can even date back to two or three different languages. Therefore, the words contained in one language may also gradually change __02__ other languages and receive new meanings.

__03__ the word "etiquette" for example. It was originally a French word and meant a label or a sign. Later on, it passed into Spanish but kept its __04__ meaning. For this reason, today in Spanish the word "etiquette" means the small tags that a store gives to a suit or a dress. However, in French, the word "etiquette" changes into another different meaning, that is, the custom written on small cards to guide the visitors how to dress themselves and prepare during an important ceremony, __05__ at the royal court. Therefore, the word "etiquette" now indicates the correct manners that people should follow.

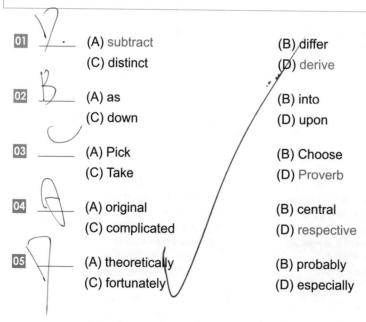

01 _____ (A) subtract (B) differ
　　　　　　(C) distinct (D) derive

02 _____ (A) as (B) into
　　　　　　(C) down (D) upon

03 _____ (A) Pick (B) Choose
　　　　　　(C) Take (D) Proverb

04 _____ (A) original (B) central
　　　　　　(C) complicated (D) respective

05 _____ (A) theoretically (B) probably
　　　　　　(C) fortunately (D) especially

中譯｜在所有的研究中，有關字彙和字源的研究最為有趣。研究顯示，每一種語言都可能起源於幾種早期的語言，其字彙甚至可能追溯到兩種或三種不同的語言。因此，一種語言裡所包含的字彙也有可能會轉變成其他的語言，獲得新的含義。

以單字「etiquette」為例。它最初是一個法語單字，意思是標籤或者符號。後來，它逐漸變成西班牙語，但是保留了最初的含義。因此，如今在西班牙語中，單字「etiquette」的意思是商店給一套衣服或一件洋裝所貼的小標籤。然而，在法語中，單字「etiquette」變成了另外一種不同的含義，那就是寫在小卡上的慣例習俗，用於指導訪客如何在重要儀式上（特別是在宮廷場合上內）正確著裝以及準備。因此，如今單字「etiquette」表示人們應該遵守的正確禮儀。

解說｜本篇短文講述了字彙的起源以及轉變，並列舉實例來詳細介紹字彙的轉變過程。第 1 題考與介系詞 from 連用的動詞的用法。根據上下文的內容可知，此處應該選用 derive 表示「起源」，所以正確選擇為 (D)。第 2 題考動詞 change 後面所接介系詞的用法。根據所學的語法知識可知，動詞 change 後面通常接介系詞 into，表示「轉變成」，所以最符合題意的選項是 (B)。第 3 題涉及到固定搭配的使用。「以～為例」是一個固定搭配，即 take... for example，要用動詞 take 來引導，即正確選項是 (C)。第 4 題的四個選項都是形容詞，根據上下文的內容可知，應該選用 original 表示「原來的」，只有選項 (A) 符合題意。第 5 題要選用合適的副詞。根據上下文的內容可知，royal court 是之前所說情況的一種特例，要用副詞 especially 來引導，所以選 (D)。

解答&技巧｜ 01 (D)　02 (B)　03 (C)　04 (A)　05 (D)

適用 TIP 1　適用 TIP 2　適用 TIP 4　適用 TIP 7

補充
earlier ⓐ 早期的；gradually ⓐ 逐漸地；etiquette ⓝ 禮儀；originally ⓐ 最初；Spanish ⓝ 西班牙語

7,000 單字
• origin [ˋɔrədʒɪn] ⓝ ③ 起源
• language [ˋlæŋgwɪdʒ] ⓝ ② 語言
• date [det] ⓥ ① 始於，源自
• receive [rɪˋsiv] ⓥ ① 接到，收到
• meaning [ˋminɪŋ] ⓝ ② 意義
• tag [tæg] ⓝ ③ 標籤
• give [gɪv] ⓥ ① 給予
• dress [drɛs] ⓝ ② 洋裝

• prepare [prɪˋpɛr] ⓥ ① 準備
• indicate [ˋɪndə͵ket] ⓥ ② 指出
• follow [ˋfɑlo] ⓥ ① 遵循
• subtract [səbˋtrækt] ⓥ ② 減去
• derive [dɪˋraɪv] ⓥ ⑥ 源於
• proverb [ˋprɑvɜb] ⓝ ④ 諺語
• respective [rɪˋspɛktɪv] ⓐ ⑥ 各自的

DAY 2

Part 1
詞彙題
Day 2
完成 25%

Part 2
綜合測驗
Day 2
完成 50%

Part 3
文意選填
Day 2
完成 75%

Part 4
閱讀測驗
Day 2
完成 100%

6 ▶ 92 年指考英文

If you plan to begin a new job, you should think about the basic strengths and weaknesses that you __01__ . Success or failure you get in your work would depend on your ability to use your strengths and weaknesses to a great __02__ , and your attitude would be of the utmost importance.

There are two kinds of people in this world. The first kind of people begins a new job, but he believes that he isn't going to like it or his weaknesses must __03__ his success. However, the other kind of people is sure that he is as capable as anyone else in doing the work, and he is willing to make a brave __04__ with all his potential strengths; thus he would have a chance to do the work well. It is true that strengths are the prerequisite skills for a particular job. If a person lacks these skills, weaknesses would be the only things left to him, and he would come to __05__ in the end.

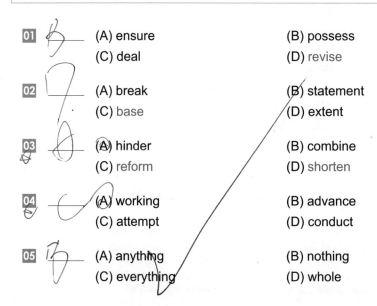

01 _____ (A) ensure   (B) possess
        (C) deal   (D) revise

02 _____ (A) break   (B) statement
        (C) base   (D) extent

03 _____ (A) hinder   (B) combine
        (C) reform   (D) shorten

04 _____ (A) working   (B) advance
        (C) attempt   (D) conduct

05 _____ (A) anything   (B) nothing
        (C) everything   (D) whole

中譯｜如果你打算開始一份新的工作，你應該思考一下你所具備的基本優勢與不足。你在工作中獲得成功還是遭遇失敗，很大程度上取決於你善用優點或缺點的能力，而你的態度將極其重要。

世界上有兩種人。第一種人開始一份新的工作，但是他相信自己不會喜歡這份工作，或者他的缺點必定會阻礙他獲得成功。然而，另一種人確信他和其他人一樣有能力來做這份工作，並且他願意用他所有潛在的優點勇敢地進行嘗試，這樣他就會有機會把工作做好。確實，強項是做某項特殊工作的首要技能，如果一個人缺少了這些技能，他就只剩下缺點，最終將一事無成。

解說｜本篇短文講述了決定工作成敗的因素，即個人所具備的優點和缺點會導致工作的成敗。第 1 題考動詞的用法。依據題意，優點和缺點是一個人所具備的能力，要用動詞 possess 來表示，所以正確選擇為 (B)。第 2 題考固定片語的搭配。「在很大程度上」可以表達為 to a great extend，所以最符合題意的選項是 (D)。第 3 題的四個選項都是動詞。根據上下文的內容可知，缺點會阻礙成功，要用動詞 hinder 表示「阻礙」，即正確選項是 (A)。第 4 題考固定片語的用法。根據所學的知識，「嘗試」可以表達為 make an attempt，所以只有選項 (C) 符合題意。第 5 題涉及到跟動詞 come 相關的片語的用法。依據題意可知，缺點會導致一個人最終一事無成，即 come to nothing，所以選 (B)。

解答&技巧｜ 01 **(B)** 02 **(D)** 03 **(A)** 04 **(C)** 05 **(B)**

適用 TIP 1　適用 TIP 2　適用 TIP 4　適用 TIP 7

補充
think about ph 考慮；weakness n 弱點；be of the utmost importance ph 極其重要的；
be going to do sth. ph 將要做某事；prerequisite a 必備的，先決條件的

7,000 單字

- plan [plæn] n 1 計畫
- job [dʒab] n 1 工作
- strength [strɛŋθ] n 3 長處
- utmost [ˈʌt.most] a 6 極度的
- importance [ɪmˈpɔrtns] n 2 重要性
- kind [kaɪnd] n 1 種類
- world [wɝld] n 1 世界
- success [səkˈsɛs] n 2 成功

- capable [ˈkepəbl] a 3 有能力的
- anyone [ˈɛnɪ.wʌn] pron 2 任何人
- potential [pəˈtɛnʃəl] a 5 潛在的
- revise [rɪˈvaɪz] v 4 修正
- base [bes] n 1 基礎
- reform [rɪˈfɔrm] v 4 改革
- shorten [ˈʃɔrtn̩] v 3 縮短

DAY 2

Part 1
詞
彙
題
Day 2
完成 25%

Part 2
綜
合
測
驗
Day 2
完成 50%

Part 3
文
意
選
填
Day 2
完成 75%

Part 4
閱
讀
測
驗
Day 2
完成 100%

7 ▶ 94 年學測英文

European politicians are trying to get the UK Government to make cigarette companies print photos on the packets. These photos will show __01__ smoking damages your health. The shocking pictures include images of smoke-damaged lungs and teeth, with reminders in large print that smokers die younger. The picture __02__ have been used in Canada for the last four years. It has been very successful and has led to a 44% __03__ in smokers wanting to kick the habit. At the moment EU tobacco manufacturers only have to put written health warnings on cigarette packets __04__ the dangers of smoking. The aim of the campaign is to remind people of the damage the deadly weed does to their body. It is believed that this would be to the best interest of all people, __05__ teens who might be tempted to start smoking. These dreadful photos may change the impression among teenagers that smoking is cool and sexy.

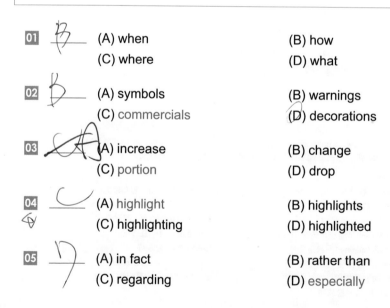

| 01 | (A) when | (B) how |
| | (C) where | (D) what |

| 02 | (A) symbols | (B) warnings |
| | (C) commercials | (D) decorations |

| 03 | (A) increase | (B) change |
| | (C) portion | (D) drop |

| 04 | (A) highlight | (B) highlights |
| | (C) highlighting | (D) highlighted |

| 05 | (A) in fact | (B) rather than |
| | (C) regarding | (D) especially |

中譯｜歐洲政治家們正試圖使英國政府讓菸草公司在包裝上印製圖片。這些圖片將會展示香菸如何損害健康。這些令人震驚的圖片包括因吸菸而損害的肺和牙齒，以及大字體印刷的標識語「吸菸者更易過早死亡」。過去四年間，這種圖片警示已經在加拿大獲得使用，結果很成功，並且使戒菸人數增長了百分之四十四。現在，歐盟菸草製造商不得不在香菸包裝上印製書面的健康警語來強調吸菸的危害。這項活動的宗旨在於提醒人們注意那些致命的菸草對他們的身體所造成的危害，相信這將會符合所有人的利益，尤其是那些可能因受到誘惑而開始吸菸的青少年。這些可怕的圖片也許會改變吸菸留給青少年的冷酷、性感的印象。

解說｜本篇短文主要講述了吸菸與健康危害，以及在香菸包裝上印刷健康警示的重要性。第 1 題主要考連接詞的用法。依據題意，香菸損害健康的方式要用 how 來引導，所以正確選擇是 (B)。第 2 題的四個選項都是名詞。根據上下文的內容可知，這些圖片起了警示的作用，要用 warning 來表示，所以最符合題意的選項是 (B)。第 3 題考名詞的用法。依據題意，圖片警示獲得了成功，因此戒菸人數應該是上升，要用 increase，即正確選項是 (A)。第 4 題考常用的語法知識，即動詞在句中作副詞時，要用動名詞，只有選項 (C) 符合題意。第 5 題選項後面的情況是前面所述情況的一種特例，一般用副詞 especially 來引導，所以選 (D)。

解答＆技巧｜ 01 (B) 02 (B) 03 (A) 04 (C) 05 (D)
適用 TIP 2　適用 TIP 4　適用 TIP 8

補充
UK ph 英國；shocking a 使人震驚的；smoker n 吸菸者；EU ph 歐盟；warning n 警示

7,000 單字
- politician [ˌpɑləˈtɪʃən] n 3 政治家
- photo [ˈfoto] n 2 照片
- packet [ˈpækɪt] n 5 小包
- reminder [rɪˈmaɪndə] n 5 提醒物
- print [prɪnt] n 1 印刷
- kick [kɪk] v 1 戒掉（惡習）
- tobacco [təˈbæko] n 3 菸草
- manufacturer [ˌmænjəˈfæktʃərə] n 4 製造商
- campaign [kæmˈpen] n 4 活動
- dreadful [ˈdrɛdfəl] a 5 可怕的
- cool [kul] a 1 冷靜的
- commercial [kəˈmɝʃəl] n 3 商業的
- portion [ˈporʃən] n 3 部分
- highlight [ˈhaɪˌlaɪt] v 6 強調
- especially [əˈspɛʃəlɪ] ad 2 尤其

What happened in the USA? How did the critics think of the new play? Which country won the World Cup football game? Many events take __01__ in the world every day. Once they happen, reporters will be on the __02__ to gather the newest news, and newspapers will offer the details to the readers.

One basic __03__ of newspapers is to get most of the news as quickly as possible from its source and then to tell it to people who want to know it. Lots of inventions, such as radio, telegraph and television, and also the development of magazines and other means of communication have brought competition for newspapers. But this competition spurred the newspapers on. Today, more and more newspapers are printed and read because they have made __04__ use of the newer and faster means of communication to improve the speed and efficiency of their operations. Nowadays, competition also leads newspapers to __05__ to many other fields, and the newspapers begin to educate and influence readers about politics and other important matters.

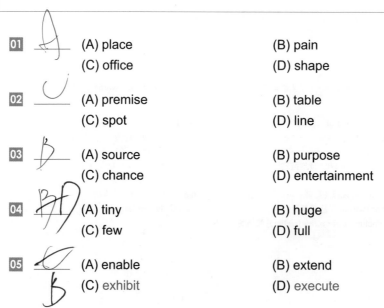

01	(A) place	(B) pain
	(C) office	(D) shape
02	(A) premise	(B) table
	(C) spot	(D) line
03	(A) source	(B) purpose
	(C) chance	(D) entertainment
04	(A) tiny	(B) huge
	(C) few	(D) full
05	(A) enable	(B) extend
	(C) exhibit	(D) execute

中譯｜美國發生了什麼事？評論家們認為那齣新劇怎麼樣？哪個國家贏得了世界盃足球賽？每天世界上都會發生很多事情，它們一旦發生，記者們就會到現場收集最新的資訊，而報紙也會為讀者提供詳細情況。

　　報紙的一個基本目的是為了盡快從來源地收集到大多數資訊，然後將其告訴給那些想要了解情況的人。很多發明，像無線電廣播、電報和電視，還有雜誌的發展以及其他的交流方式都給報紙帶來了競爭。但是這些競爭推動了報紙的發展。如今，愈來愈多的報紙被印出和被閱讀，是因為他們充分利用了更新、更快捷的交流方式來提高操作的速率以及效率。現在，競爭也引領報紙朝其他許多領域擴展，報紙開始教育並影響讀者關注政治以及其他重要的事件。

解說｜本篇短文主要講述了報紙的發明及發展過程。第 1 題考與動詞 take 相關的片語的用法。根據上下文的內容可知，應該是事件發生，應該選用 take place，而其他選項都不符合題意，所以正確選擇為 (A)。第 2 題主要考介系詞片語的用法。將四個選項一一代入可知，on the spot 表示「在場」，符合題意，所以正確選項是 (C)。第 3 題中，to 後面的句子表示目的，所以前面所說的應該是報紙的目的，應該選擇 purpose，即正確選項是 (B)。第 4 題考固定片語的用法。根據所學的知識，make full use of 表示「充分利用」，符合題意，所以正確選項是 (D)。第 5 題的四個選項都是動詞。根據上下文的內容可知，競爭導致報紙在很多領域得以擴展，應該選擇 extend 表示「擴展」，所以選 (B)。

解答＆技巧｜ 01 (A)　 02 (C)　 03 (B)　 04 (D)　 05 (B)

適用 TIP 2　適用 TIP 4　適用 TIP 7　適用 TIP 11

補充
USA ph 美國；the World Cup ph 世界盃；reader n 讀者；quickly ad 快速地；
more and more... ph 愈來愈多的～

7,000 單字

- critic [ˋkrɪtɪk] n 4 評論家
- play [ple] n 1 戲劇
- cup [kʌp] n 1 獎盃
- football [ˋfʊtˌbɔl] n 2 足球（美式英語為 soccer）
- game [gem] n 1 比賽
- basic [ˋbesɪk] a 1 基本的
- news [njuz] n 1 新聞
- telegraph [ˋtɛləˌgræf] n 4 電報

- communication [kəˌmjunəˋkeʃən] n 4 交流
- competition [ˌkɑmpəˋtɪʃən] n 4 競爭
- efficiency [ɪˋfɪʃənsɪ] n 4 效率
- operation [ˌɑpəˋreʃən] n 4 操作
- politics [ˋpɑlətɪks] n 3 政治
- exhibit [ɪgˋzɪbɪt] v 4 展示
- execute [ˋɛksɪˌkjut] v 5 實行

DAY
2

Part 1
詞
彙
題
Day 2
完成 25%

Part 2
綜
合
測
驗
Day 2
完成 50%

Part 3
文
意
選
填
Day 2
完成 75%

Part 4
閱
讀
測
驗
Day 2
完成 100%

9 ▶ 92 年指考英文

Nowadays, reading is not relaxing any longer for many people because they must read letters, reports, trade publications and interoffice communications to keep up their work, let __01__ newspapers and magazines which contain numerous words. Whether you want to get a job or get __02__ in one, your ability to read and comprehend quickly can determine the success you can achieve. However, an unfortunate fact that we have to face is that most of us are poor readers, for most of us have developed poor reading habits at an early age and never got __03__ them.

According to the study, words play an important role in the human languages. Taken __04__ , words have little meaning, but if they are put together into phrases, sentences and paragraphs, their meanings would become full and complete. Unfortunately, most of the __05__ readers often read one word at a time or reread words or passages. This is a bad habit in reading, and the readers may fail to comprehend the whole information quickly and correctly.

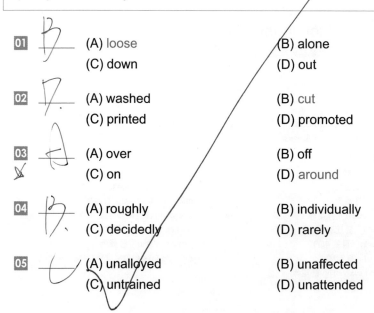

01 ____ (A) loose   (B) alone
    (C) down   (D) out

02 ____ (A) washed   (B) cut
    (C) printed   (D) promoted

03 ____ (A) over   (B) off
    (C) on   (D) around

04 ____ (A) roughly   (B) individually
    (C) decidedly   (D) rarely

05 ____ (A) unalloyed   (B) unaffected
    (C) untrained   (D) unattended

中譯｜ 現今，對於大多數人來說，閱讀已經變得不再那麼輕鬆了，因為他們必須閱讀信函、報告、商業出版品和各部門之間的通信來維持他們的工作，更不必說閱讀報紙以及雜誌那些包含很多文字的讀物了。不管你想得到一份工作，還是想在工作中獲得晉升，你所具備的快速閱讀理解能力能夠決定你所取得的成功。然而，我們不得不面對的一個不幸的事實是，我們大多數人的閱讀能力都比較差，因為大部分的人早年就養成了很差的閱讀習慣，也一直沒有克服這些習慣。

研究顯示，字彙在人類語言中發揮了重要作用。如果單一放置，字彙的意義不大，但是如果將它們組成片語、句子和段落，他們的意義就會變得很完整。不幸的是，大多數未經訓練的讀者通常一次只讀一個單字，或是重讀單字或段落，這是不好的閱讀習慣，讀者也許會無法快速、正確地理解整體資訊。

解說｜ 本篇短文講述了閱讀的方法和技巧，以及養成良好閱讀習慣的重要性。第 1 題考固定片語的用法。let 通常與 alone 搭配使用，表示「更不必說」，符合題意，所以正確選項為 (B)。第 2 題考動詞 get 的用法。get 後面通常接動詞的過去分詞，表示被動。此處涉及工作，應該是 get promoted 表示「得到晉升」，所以最符合題意的選項是 (D)。第 3 題考與動詞 get 相關的片語的用法。一些不好的閱讀習慣需要克服，即用 get over 表示「克服」，所以正確選項是 (A)。第 4 題的四個選項都是副詞。句中 but 之後的情況表示將單字放在一起，所以前面的情況應該表示相反，即單字單獨放置，要用 individually，只有選項 (B) 符合題意。第 5 題要選擇合適的形容詞。將四個選項一一代入可知，只有 untrained 表示「未經訓練的」符合題意，所以選 (C)。

解答＆技巧｜ 01 **(B)** 02 **(D)** 03 **(A)** 04 **(B)** 05 **(C)**

適用 TIP 1　適用 TIP 2　適用 TIP 7　適用 TIP 11

補充

unfortunate Ⓐ 不幸的；trade publication Ⓟ 商業出版品；interoffice Ⓐ 辦公室之間的；keep up Ⓟ 保持；unfortunately Ⓐ 不幸地

7,000 單字

- nowadays [ˈnaʊəˌdez] Ⓐ 4 現今
- letter [ˈlɛtɚ] Ⓝ 1 信
- report [rɪˈport] Ⓝ 1 報告
- magazine [ˌmægəˈzin] Ⓝ 2 雜誌
- numerous [ˈnjumərəs] Ⓐ 4 很多的
- comprehend [ˌkɑmprɪˈhɛnd] Ⓥ 5 理解
- achieve [əˈtʃiv] Ⓥ 3 完成
- phrase [frez] Ⓝ 2 片語

- sentence [ˈsɛntəns] Ⓝ 1 句子
- paragraph [ˈpærəˌgræf] Ⓝ 4 段落
- complete [kəmˈplit] Ⓥ 2 完成
- whole [hol] Ⓐ 1 整個的
- loose [lus] Ⓐ 3 鬆開的
- cut [kʌt] Ⓥ 1 切
- around [əˈraʊnd] Ⓐ 1 在附近

DAY 2

Part 1
詞彙題
Day 2
完成 25%

Part 2
綜合測驗
Day 2
完成 50%

Part 3
文意選填
Day 2
完成 75%

Part 4
閱讀測驗
Day 2
完成 100%

10 ▶ 94 年指考英文

After a long day working in the office, Alexander hailed a taxi to take him home. Squeezing his body into the taxi, he noticed the shiny interior and the smell of brand new leather. After informing the driver of his __01__ , Alexander resorted to his reading of Dan Brown's intelligent thriller, *The Da Vinci Code*. Five minutes into the journey, he was on page 120: "... his Mona Lisa is neither male nor female..." Suddenly, Alexander __02__ and noticed that the driver had detoured from the familiar route. To redirect the driver, Alexander tapped him on the shoulder. Out of the blue, the driver screamed, lost control of the car, and almost hit a bus. The cab went up on the footpath and __03__ stopped centimeters away from a shop window. For a second, everything went quiet in the cab. Then the driver said, "Look, mate! Don't ever do that again. You scared the living daylights out of me!" Alexander apologized and said, "I didn't __04__ that a little tap would scare you so much." The driver replied, "Sorry, sir. It's not really your __05__ . Today is my first day as a cab driver. I've been driving a funeral van for the last 25 years."

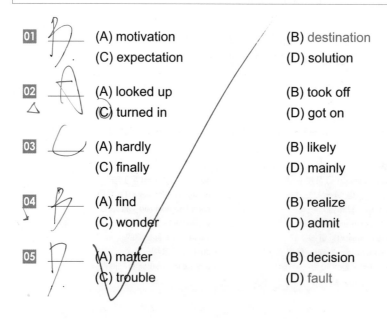

01   (A) motivation   (B) destination
       (C) expectation   (D) solution

02   (A) looked up   (B) took off
       (C) turned in   (D) got on

03   (A) hardly   (B) likely
       (C) finally   (D) mainly

04   (A) find   (B) realize
       (C) wonder   (D) admit

05   (A) matter   (B) decision
       (C) trouble   (D) fault

中譯 一整天的辦公室工作之後，亞歷山大招了一輛計程車搭回家。身體擠進計程車內後，他注意到車子內部閃閃發亮，也聞到了全新的皮革的味道。告知司機自己的目的地後，亞歷山大開始閱讀丹‧布朗的推理驚悚小說《達芬奇密碼》。行進五分鐘後，他讀到了一百二十頁：「～他的蒙娜麗莎既不是男人也不是女人～」突然，亞歷山大抬起頭來，注意到司機從一條熟路繞道行駛。為了讓司機改變方向，亞歷山大在他的肩膀上輕輕地拍了拍。意外地，司機大聲尖叫起來，車子失控了，幾乎要撞上一輛公車。計程車行駛到人行道上，終於在離一家商店櫥窗的幾公分處停了下來。片刻間，車子內一片寂靜。於是司機說道：「聽著，老兄！再也不要那樣做了！你把我嚇得魂都沒了！」亞歷山大道歉說：「我沒意識到輕輕拍你就能把你嚇成這樣。」司機回答說：「抱歉，先生，這真不是你的錯。今天是我第一天開計程車，過去二十五年裡我一直都開殯葬車。」

解說 本篇短文講述了主角亞歷山大下班後乘坐計程車時發生的故事。第 1 題的四個選項都是名詞。依據題意，亞歷山大應該是將自己的目的地告訴給司機，因此要選 destination，即正確選擇為 (B)。第 2 題考動詞片語的用法。根據上下文的內容可知，亞歷山大先是在看書，然後才抬起頭來發現了情況，因此要選擇 looked up 表示「抬起頭來」，最符合題意的選項是 (A)。第 3 題的四個選項都是副詞。將四個選項一一代入可知，只有 finally 符合題意，即正確選項是 (C)。第 4 題要選擇合適的動詞。根據上下文的內容可知，應該是沒有意識到，即用動詞 realize 表示「意識到」，所以只有選項 (B) 符合題意。第 5 題的四個選項都是名詞。根據前後句意思可知，應該選擇 fault 表示「錯誤」，所以選 (D)。

解答&技巧 01 (B) 02 (A) 03 (C) 04 (B) 05 (D)

適用 TIP 1　適用 TIP 4　適用 TIP 7　適用 TIP 11

DAY 2

Part 1
詞彙題
Day 2
完成 25%

Part 2
綜合測驗
Day 2
完成 50%

Part 3
文意選填
Day 2
完成 75%

Part 4
閱讀測驗
Day 2
完成 100%

補充
redirect ⓥ 使改變方向；out of the blue ㏗ 突然地；footpath ⓝ 人行道，小徑；daylights ⓝ 知覺，神智；really ⓐⓓ 實際上

7,000 單字
- office [ˈɔfɪs] ⓝ 1 辦公室
- interior [ɪnˈtɪrɪə] ⓝ 5 內部
- brand [brænd] ⓝ 2 烙印
- leather [ˈlɛðə] ⓝ 3 皮革
- resort [rɪˈzɔrt] ⓥ 5 憑藉
- intelligent [ɪnˈtɛlədʒənt] ⓐ 4 智能的
- thriller [ˈθrɪlə] ⓝ 5 驚險小說（或電影、戲劇）
- shoulder [ˈʃoldə] ⓝ 1 肩膀
- cab [kæb] ⓝ 1 計程車
- mate [met] ⓝ 2 老兄
- apologize [əˈpɑləˌdʒaɪz] ⓥ 4 道歉
- funeral [ˈfjunərəl] ⓝ 4 葬禮
- van [væn] ⓝ 3 廂型車
- destination [ˌdɛstəˈneʃən] ⓝ 5 目的地
- fault [fɔlt] ⓝ 2 錯誤

Part 3 文意選填 | Cloze Test

1▶

Currently, the ___01___ of traffic in most cities all over the world continues to expand. Therefore, many problems have been caused, such as serious air pollution, ___02___ delays, and the greater risk of accidents. Undoubtedly, something must be done, but it often seems to be quite difficult to ___03___ people into changing their habits and leaving their cars at home.

A possible method of solving this problem is to make it much more ___04___ for people to drive their own cars by increasing charges for parking and imposing heavier ___05___ for anyone who breaks the traffic law. In addition, with a special electronic card fixed to the windscreen of the car, drivers could be required to ___06___ for choosing particular routes at different times of the day. The system, known as road pricing, has already been adopted in a great many cities.

Another way of dealing with the problem is to provide cheap parking on the outskirts of the city, and keep ___07___ control over the number of vehicles allowed into the center. Drivers and their ___08___ then could choose a special bus service for the final stage of their journey.

To provide good public transport is, of course, the most important thing. However, in order to get people to give up the comfort of their own cars, public transport must be made reliable, ___09___ and comfortable. Besides, ___10___ should be kept at a relatively acceptable level.

(A) persuade   (B) fares   (C) volume   (D) passengers   (E) pay
(F) lengthy   (G) gines   (H) expensive   (I) strict   (J) convenient

| 01 ____ | 02 ____ | 03 ____ | 04 ____ | 05 ____ |
| 06 ____ | 07 ____ | 08 ____ | 09 ____ | 10 ____ |

選項中譯｜勸說；票價；數量；乘客；支付；很長的；罰款；昂貴的；嚴格的；方便的

中譯｜現今，世界上的大多數城市中，交通量都在持續增長，因此引起了很多問題，例如嚴重的空氣污染、長時間的滯留、更高的事故發生率。無疑，必須對此採取措施，不過，勸說人們改變自己的習慣而把自己的車子留在家裡，似乎是相當困難的。

解決這個問題的可能途徑之一，是收取更高的停車費，並且對那些違反交通規則的人處以更高的罰金，從而使人們開自家車的花費變得更高。此外，也可以把一種特製的電子卡片固定在車子的擋風玻璃上，以便在一天中的不同時段，對選取某些特殊路線的司機收取費用。這樣的體系，被稱為道路收費制度，已經在很多城市實施。

解決這個問題的另一種方式，是在城市郊區提供廉價的停車區位，並且對進入市中心的車輛數目加以嚴格控制。至於通往市區的最後一段路程，司機和乘客們可以選擇特定的公車服務。

當然，提供良好的公共運輸系統是最重要的。不過，為了讓人們放棄自家車的舒適，必須確保公共運輸系統是可靠、便利而舒適的。此外，票價也應該控制在相對易於接受的範圍之內。

解譯｜閱讀全文可知，這篇文章的主題是交通管制問題。

縱觀各選項，選項 (B)、(C)、(D)、(G) 是名詞，選項 (A)、(E) 是動詞，選項 (F)、(H)、(I)、(J) 是形容詞。根據題意，第 1、5、8、10 題應選名詞，第 3、6 題應選動詞，第 2、4、7、9 題應選形容詞。然後根據文章，依次作答。

第 1 題是選擇名詞，用於 of 結構，意為「交通的～」。有四個名詞可供選擇，即為選項 (B)、(C)、(D)、(G)，選項 (B) 意為「票價」，選項 (C) 意為「數量」，選項 (D) 意為「乘客」，選項 (G) 意為「罰款」，根據句意，應當是「交通量持續增長」，所以選 (C)。第 5 題也是選名詞，與動詞 impose 進行搭配，且有形容詞比較級 heavier 修飾，可以視為固定用法，意為「處以更高的罰金」，所以選 (G)。第 8 題所選名詞須為表示人的名詞複數形式，是與 drivers 並列作主詞，所以選 (D)。而第 10 題則是選 (B)，意為「票價也應該控制在相對易於接受的範圍之內」。

第 2 題是選擇形容詞，修飾名詞 delays，有四個形容詞可供選擇，即為選項 (F)、(H)、(I)、(J)。選項 (F) 意為「很長的」，選項 (H) 意為「昂貴的」，選項 (I) 意為「嚴格的」，選項 (J) 意為「方便的」，根據句意可知，應當是「長時間的滯留」，所以選 (F)。第 4 題所選形容詞，有比較級成分 more 修飾，須為多音節形容詞，選項 (H)、(J) 可供選擇，根據句意，應當是「使人們開自家車的花費變得更高」，所以選 (H)。第 7 題，修飾名詞 control，所以選 (I)，意為「實行嚴格控制」。第 9 題就只有選 (J)，句意為「確保公共運輸系統是可靠、便利而舒適的」。

DAY
2

Part 1
詞
彙
題
Day 2
完成 25%

Part 2
綜
合
測
驗
Day 2
完成 50%

Part 3
文
意
選
填
Day 2
完成 75%

Part 4
閱
讀
測
驗
Day 2
完成 100%

第 3 題是選擇動詞，有兩個動詞可供選擇，即為選項 (A)、(E)。persuade sb. into doing sth. 可以視為固定搭配，意為「勸説某人做某事」，所以選 (A)。第 6 題則是選 (E)，句意為「在不同時段，對選取某些特殊路線的司機收取費用」。

解答 & 技巧 | 01 (C)　02 (F)　03 (A)　04 (H)　05 (G)
　　　　　　06 (E)　07 (I)　08 (D)　09 (J)　10 (B)

適用 TIP 1　適用 TIP 2　適用 TIP 6　適用 TIP 7　適用 TIP 8
適用 TIP 9　適用 TIP 10　適用 TIP 11

補充

air pollution ph 空氣污染；persuade sb. into doing sth. ph 勸説某人做某事；
impose heavy fines for ph 對～處以高額罰金；traffic law ph 交通規則；
keep strict control over ph 對～加以嚴格控制

7,000 單字

- volume [ˈvɑljəm] n 3 數量，大量
- traffic [ˈtræfɪk] n 2 交通
- lengthy [ˈlɛŋθɪ] a 6 漫長的，冗長的
- delay [dɪˈle] n 2 延遲
- charge [tʃɑrdʒ] n 2 費用
- fine [faɪn] n 1 罰款
- break [brek] v 1 違背
- pay [pe] v 1 支付

- adopt [əˈdɑpt] v 3 採取
- cheap [tʃip] a 2 便宜的
- outskirts [ˈaut͵skɝts] n 5 郊區，市郊
- strict [strɪkt] a 2 嚴格的
- vehicle [ˈviɪkl] n 3 交通工具
- convenient [kənˈvinjənt] a 2 方便的
- fare [fɛr] n 3 票價

MEMO

❷►

Most population growth, until recently, has actually occurred in relatively __01__ urban environments. In other words, even though we witness rapid population growth, that would not mean all the cities will be filled with people. Otherwise the urban areas would __02__ to become more crowded.

Historically, we find that people always moved to ports or __03__ where there were many natural resources. Later, with transportation becoming relatively cheaper, other geographical locations gradually became __04__ of economic activity. One __05__ that determines where people would move, even when transportation became cheaper, should be income. Generally, people working in cities earn higher incomes than those working in __06__ areas. Hence population has tended to increase in some major urban centers, until the 1970s.

Recently population has shifted out of the Northeast in America to the South and to the West, simply for the more __07__ climate. If people could not benefit from living in large cities, there would likely be a population distribution into the entire land area. Probably, if this were the case, there would be less concern over population __08__. Indeed, if you start a cross-country drive or plane trip, you can easily understand how sparsely populated those __09__ areas really are. However, it is not to say that we should not do anything about population growth. Anyway, the shortage of people in certain areas merely __10__ that overpopulation is really only a problem in overcrowded urban environments.

DAY
2

Part 1
詞
彙
題
Day 2
完成 25%

Part 2
綜
合
測
驗
Day 2
完成 50%

Part 3
文
意
選
填
Day 2
完成 75%

Part 4
閱
讀
測
驗
Day 2
完成 100%

(A) dense　(B) rural　(C) demonstrates　(D) tend　(E) pleasant
(F) locations　(G) explosion　(H) underdeveloped　(I) factor　(J) centers

01 ___	02 ___	03 ___	04 ___	05 ___
06 ___	07 ___	08 ___	09 ___	10 ___

選項中譯｜稠密的；農村的；表明；傾向於；宜人的；地點；激增；不發達的；
因素；中心

中譯｜直到最近，大多數的人口增長，事實上都是在人口較為密集的城市環境中。換言之，即便是人口迅速增長，也並不意味著，所有的城市都會人滿為患。要不然，城市地區就會變得更為擁擠了。

我們可以發現，歷史上，人們通常會遷往港口或是那些擁有很多自然資源的地方。後來，交通運輸變得較為廉價之後，其他地方也逐漸成為了經濟活動的中心。決定人們遷往何處的一個因素，是收入水準，即便是在交通運輸變得較為廉價之後，也是如此。通常而言，與那些在鄉村地區工作的人相比，在城市中工作的人，收入水準要高一些。因此，直到二十世紀七〇年代，一些主要的城市中心，人口數量都是在增長的。

近來，美國的人口從東北部遷往南部和西部，只是為了相對宜人的氣候條件。如果人們在大城市中的生活無法得益，就可能遷往所有的領土範圍中的任何一處地方。也許，如果這成為事實的話，也就不必如此憂慮人口激增的問題了。事實上，如果你開車或是乘飛機遊遍全國的話，就可以很容易地發現，在那些不發達地區，人口分布是多麼地稀疏。不過，這也不是說，對於人口增長，我們就該毫無所為。不論如何，某些地方的人口短缺只不過是說明，人口過剩只是發生在過度擁擠的城市中。

解譯｜閱讀全文可知，這篇文章的主題是城市中的人口增長。

縱觀各選項，選項 (F)、(G)、(I)、(J) 是名詞，選項 (C)、(D) 是動詞，選項 (A)、(B)、(E)、(H) 是形容詞。根據題意，第 3、4、5、8 題應選名詞，第 2、10 題應選動詞，第 1、6、7、9 題應選形容詞。然後根據文章，依次作答。

第 1 題是選擇形容詞，與形容詞 urban 並列修飾名詞 environment，有四個形容詞可供選擇，即為選項 (A)、(B)、(E)、(H)。選項 (A) 意為「稠密的」，選項 (B) 意為「農村的」，選項 (E) 意為「宜人的」，選項 (H) 意為「不發達的」，根據句意可知，應當是「人口較為密集的城市環境」，所以選 (A)。第 6 題，可以視為固定搭配，rural areas 意為「農村地區」，所以選 (B)。第 7 題，修飾名詞 climate，且有比較級成分 more 修飾，須為多音節形容詞，所以選 (E)，意為「相對宜人的氣候條件」。第 9 題就只有選 (H)，句意為「不發達地區」。

第 2 題是選擇動詞，須與介系詞進行搭配，有兩個動詞可供選擇，即為選項 (C)、(D)。tend to do sth. 可以視為固定搭配，意為「傾向於做某事」，所以選 (D)。第 10 題則是選 (C)，意為「某些地方的人口短缺只不過是說明～」。

第 3 題是選擇名詞，與複數名詞 ports 並列，且後接 where 引導的關係子句。有四個名詞可供選擇，即為選項 (F)、(G)、(I)、(J)，選項 (F) 意為「地點」，選項 (G) 意為「激增」，選項 (I) 意為「因素」，選項 (J) 意為「中心」，根據句意，應當是選複數形式的地點名詞，所以選 (F)。第 4 題所選名詞，是用於 of 結構，

意為「經濟活動的～」，根據句意，應當是「經濟活動中心」，所以選 (J)。第 5 題則是選 (I)，意為「決定人們遷往何處的一個因素」。自然，第 8 題是選 (G)，可以視為固定用法，population explosion 意為「人口激增」。

解答＆技巧｜ 01 (A)　02 (D)　03 (F)　04 (J)　05 (I)
06 (B)　07 (E)　08 (G)　09 (H)　10 (C)

適用 TIP 1　適用 TIP 2　適用 TIP 6　適用 TIP 7　適用 TIP 8
適用 TIP 9　適用 TIP 10　適用 TIP 11

補充
population growth ph 人口增長；tend to ph 傾向於，趨於；historically ad 在歷史上；
natural resources ph 自然資源；benefit from ph 從～中得益；overpopulation n 人口過剩

7,000 單字

- dense [dɛns] a 4 密集的
- fill [fɪl] v 1 充滿
- tend [tɛnd] v 3 傾向於
- move [muv] v 1 搬遷
- port [port] n 2 港口
- location [loˋkeʃən] n 4 位置，地方
- natural [ˋnætʃərəl] a 2 自然的
- geographical [dʒɪəˋgræfɪkl] a 5 地理的

- earn [ɝn] v 2 賺
- rural [ˋrʊrəl] a 4 農村的
- pleasant [ˋplɛzənt] a 2 宜人的，合意的
- distribution [ˌdɪstrəˋbjuʃən] n 4 分散，分配
- explosion [ɪkˋsploʒən] n 4 激增
- trip [trɪp] n 1 旅行
- demonstrate [ˋdɛmənˌstret] v 4 證明，顯示

Part 1
詞
彙
題
Day 2
完成 25%

Part 2
綜
合
測
驗
Day 2
完成 50%

Part 3
文
意
選
填
Day 2
完成 75%

Part 4
閱
讀
測
驗
Day 2
完成 100%

MEMO

3▸

Memorial Day was originally established to __01__ the Civil War dead. Shortly after the __02__ and bloody Civil War between the North and South, the women of Columbus, Mississippi decorated the graves of both Confederate and Union soldiers, thus honoring the war dead who were their enemies along with their defenders. Northerners were greatly touched and considered it as a __03__ of national unity. In 1868, Decoration Day—now called Memorial Day—became a __04__ holiday.

Memorial Day now officially honors all American servicemen who give their lives for their country. Unofficially the holiday has been extended beyond its military connection and become a day of general __05__ to the dead. On Memorial Day, __06__ are always crowded with people who come to place flowers on the graves of their loved ones.

In most states, Memorial Day is __07__ on the last Monday in May or on May 30. However, there are some __08__ to this custom. Some southern states observe __09__ army. This holiday falls on April 26 in Florida and Georgia, on the last Monday in April in Alabama and Mississippi, and on May 10 in North and South Carolina.

The military fashion of Memorial Day is evident in the parades and customs, which solemnly mark the occasion. __10__ exercises are also held at Gettysburg National Military Park in Pennsylvania and at the National Cemetery in Arlington, Virginia.

(A) Military   (B) cemeteries   (C) legal   (D) Confederate   (E) honor
(F) bitter   (G) tribute   (H) exceptions   (I) celebrated   (J) symbol

| 01 ____ | 02 ____ | 03 ____ | 04 ____ | 05 ____ |
| 06 ____ | 07 ____ | 08 ____ | 09 ____ | 10 ____ |

DAY
2

Part 1
詞
彙
題
Day 2
完成 25%

Part 2
綜
合
測
驗
Day 2
完成 50%

Part 3
文
意
選
填
Day 2
完成 75%

Part 4
閱
讀
測
驗
Day 2
完成 100%

選項中譯｜軍事的；墓地；法定的；南方邦聯的；致敬；慘痛的；致哀；例外；慶祝；象徵

中譯｜設立陣亡將士紀念日，最初是為了紀念在南北戰爭中犧牲的將士。南北方慘痛而血腥的內戰過後不久，密西西比州哥倫布的婦女們，裝點了南方邦聯將士和北方各州將士的墓地，以此紀念那些守衛者和他們的敵人。北方人十分感動，認為這是國家統一的象徵。一八六八年，陣亡將士紀念日，起初稱為 Decoration Day，如今稱為 Memorial Day，成為法定假日。

如今，官方的陣亡將士紀念日，是紀念那些為國家獻出生命的所有軍人。而在非正式的意義上，這個節日已經不再局限於軍事意義，而是成為了向逝者憑弔致哀的日子。在陣亡將士紀念日這一天，墓園通常會擠滿前來為深愛的逝者獻花的人們。

在多數的州中，陣亡將士紀念日是在五月的最後一個禮拜一或是在五月三十日。然而，這項習俗也有例外情況。南方的一些州是紀念南方邦聯的軍隊。在佛羅里達州和喬治亞州，這個節日是在四月二十六日；在阿拉巴馬州和密西西比州，則是在四月的最後一個禮拜一；而在北卡羅萊納州和南卡羅萊納州，則是在五月十日。

陣亡將士紀念日的軍事風格表現在遊行和習俗中，鄭重地突顯了這個節日。在賓夕法尼亞州的蓋茨堡國家軍事公園和維吉尼亞州的阿靈頓國家公墓，還會舉行軍事演習。

解譯｜閱讀全文可知，這篇文章的主題是美國的陣亡將士紀念日。

縱觀各選項，選項 (B)、(G)、(H)、(J) 是名詞，選項 (E)、(I) 是動詞，選項 (A)、(C)、(D)、(F) 是形容詞。根據題意，第 3、5、6、8 題應選名詞，第 1、7 題應選動詞，第 2、4、9、10 題應選形容詞。然後根據文章，依次作答。

第 1 題是選擇動詞，有兩個動詞可供選擇，即為選項 (E)、(I)，根據句意可知，應當是「紀念在南北戰爭中犧牲的將士」，所以選 (E)。第 7 題則是選 (I)，為被動語態。

第 2 題是選擇形容詞，與形容詞 bloody 並列，修飾名詞 Civil War，有四個形容詞可供選擇，即為選項 (A)、(C)、(D)、(F)。選項 (A) 意為「軍事的」，選項 (C) 意為「法定的」，選項 (D) 意為「南方邦聯的」，選項 (F) 意為「慘痛的」，根據句意可知，應當是「慘痛而血腥的內戰」，所以選 (F)。第 4 題所選形容詞，可以視為固定搭配，legal holiday 意為「法定假日」，所以選 (C)。第 9 題所選形容詞，也可以視為固定用法，Confederate army 意為「美國南方邦聯軍隊」，所以選 (D)。第 10 題則是選 (A)，也是固定搭配，military exercises 意為「軍事演習」。

第 3 題是選擇名詞，用於 of 結構，意為「國家統一的～」。有四個名詞可供選擇，即為選項 (B)、(G)、(H)、(J)，選項 (B) 意為「墓地」，選項 (G) 意為「致

107

哀」，選項 (H) 意為「例外」，選項 (J) 意為「象徵」，根據句意，應當是「國家統一的象徵」，所以選 (J)。第 5 題所選名詞，根據句意，應當是「向逝者憑弔致哀的日子」，所以選 (G)。第 6 題所選名詞，根據句意，應當是「墓園通常會擠滿前來為深愛的逝者獻花的人們」，所以選 (B)。第 8 題則是選 (H)，與介系詞 to 連用，意為「～的例外」。

解答＆技巧 | **01** (E)　　**02** (F)　　**03** (J)　　**04** (C)　　**05** (G)
　　　　　 06 (B)　　**07** (I)　　**08** (H)　　**09** (D)　　**10** (A)

適用 TIP 1　適用 TIP 2　適用 TIP 6　適用 TIP 7　適用 TIP 8
適用 TIP 9　適用 TIP 10　適用 TIP 11

補充

Memorial Day ph 美國陣亡將士紀念日；Civil War ph 美國南北戰爭；legal holiday ph 法定假日；military exercises ph 軍事演習；Gettysburg National Military Park ph 美國蓋茨堡國家軍事公園；National Cemetery ph 美國國家公墓

7,000 單字

- memorial [mə`morɪəl] n 4 紀念
- establish [ə`stæblɪʃ] v 4 建立
- honor [`ɑnɚ] v 3 尊敬
- civil [`sɪvl] a 3 國內的
- bitter [`bɪtɚ] a 2 慘痛的
- bloody [`blʌdɪ] a 2 血腥的
- grave [grev] n 4 墳墓
- dead [dɛd] a 1 死去的

- enemy [`ɛnəmɪ] n 2 敵人
- symbol [`sɪmbl] n 2 象徵
- unity [`junətɪ] n 3 統一
- decoration [ˌdɛkə`reʃən] n 4 勳章
- tribute [`trɪbjut] n 5 敬意
- cemetery [`sɛməˌtɛrɪ] n 6 墓地
- military [`mɪləˌtɛrɪ] a 2 軍事的

MEMO

❹▸ 93 年學測英文

Although stories about aliens have never been officially confirmed, their existence has been widely speculated upon.

Many people believe that __01__ from outer space have visited us for centuries. Some say that life on Earth __02__ "out there" and was seeded here. Others say that aliens have __03__ what happens on Earth, and are responsible for quite a few legends, and that the ancient Greek and Roman gods, __04__ the fairies and dwarfs in many classic tales, were in fact "space people" living here. Still __05__ say that aliens were responsible for the growth of highly evolved civilizations which have __06__ perished, including the Incan and Mayan civilizations and the legendary Atlantis.

A lot of ancient civilizations, __07__ the Egyptians, Hindus, Greeks, and Mayans, have left writings and __08__ which indicate contacts with superior beings "from the stars." Many believe that the aliens are here to help us, while others hold that the aliens intend us __09__. Still others think that most aliens visit Earth to study us like our scientists study primitive natives and animals, and have no interest in helping us __10__.

It is difficult to comment conclusively on these theories in general, apart from saying that any and all of them might be possible. Maybe time will tell.

(A) as well as   (B) beings   (C) drawings   (D) in any way
(E) kept an eye on   (F) like   (G) others   (H) originated   (I) since
(J) harm

| 01 _____ | 02 _____ | 03 _____ | 04 _____ | 05 _____ |
| 06 _____ | 07 _____ | 08 _____ | 09 _____ | 10 _____ |

DAY 2

Part 1
詞
彙
題
Day 2
完成 25%

Part 2
綜
合
測
驗
Day 2
完成 50%

Part 3
文
意
選
填
Day 2
完成 75%

Part 4
閱
讀
測
驗
Day 2
完成 100%

選項中譯｜和；生物；圖畫；不論如何；留意；像；其他人；起源於；此後；傷害

中譯｜關於外星人的故事從未獲得官方證實，但是，對於外星人的存在，卻有著種種推測。

很多人相信，幾世紀以來，來自太空的生物都來訪問過我們。有人說，地球上的生命就是起源於太空中的，後來才在地球上扎根繁衍。也有人說，外星人一直都在關注著地球上發生的事情，他們與很多的傳說有關，而且，古希臘、古羅馬的眾神，和很多經典故事中的仙女、小矮人，事實上都是生活在地球上的外星人。還有人說，外星人與那些先進的隨後消失的文明的發展有關，包括印加文明、馬雅文明和傳奇的亞特蘭提斯。

很多的古文明，例如古埃及文明、古印度文明、古希臘文明、馬雅文明，都留下了相關的文字和圖畫，表明了和來自太空的高等生物的接觸。很多人相信，外星人是來到這裡幫助我們的，不過，也有人認為，外星人是想要傷害我們。也有人認為，多數外星人來到地球，是為了研究我們，就像我們的科學家研究原始人和動物一樣，並沒有要幫助我們的意願。

只能說，這些理論假說中的某一些或是全部都是有可能的，卻很難對這些理論假說總結性地加以評論。也許，時間會證明一切。

解譯｜閱讀全文可知，這篇文章的主題是關於外星人的推測。

縱觀各選項，選項 (A) 是連接詞片語，選項 (E) 是動詞片語，選項 (D) 是副詞片語，選項 (B)、(C)、(G)、(J) 是名詞，選項 (H) 是動詞，選項 (F) 是連接詞，選項 (I) 是副詞。根據題意，第 1、5、8、9 題應選名詞，第 2、3 題應選動詞，第 6、10 題應選副詞，第 4、7 題應選連接詞。然後根據文章，依次作答。

第 1 題是選擇名詞，為複數形式。有四個名詞可供選擇，即為選項 (B)、(C)、(G)、(J)，選項 (B) 意為「生物」，選項 (C) 意為「圖畫」，選項 (G) 意為「其他人」，選項 (J) 意為「傷害」，根據句意，應當是「來自太空的生物」，所以選 (B)。第 5 題所選名詞，根據句意，應當是「還有人說〜」，所以選 (G)。第 8 題則是選 (C)，句意為「留下了相關的文字和圖畫」。第 9 題選 (J)，句意為「外星人想要傷害我們」。

第 2 題是選擇動詞，須為過去式，有兩個動詞可供選擇，即為選項 (E)、(H)，根據句意，應當是「起源於太空」，所以選 (H)。第 3 題則是選 (E)，可以視為固定搭配，**keep an eye on** 意為「留心，關注」，句意為「關注著地球上發生的事情」。

第 4 題是選擇連接詞，有兩個連接詞可供選擇，即為選項 (A)、(F)。選項 (A) 意為「和」，選項 (F) 意為「像」，根據句意，應當是「古希臘、古羅馬的眾神，和很多經典故事中的仙女、小矮人」，所以選 (A)。第 7 題則是選 (F)，意為「例如古埃及文明、古印度文明、古希臘文明、馬雅文明」。

第 6 題是選擇副詞，有兩個副詞可供選擇，即為選項 (D)、(I)。選項 (D) 意為「不論如何」，選項 (I) 意為「此後」，根據句意，應當是「隨後消失的文明」，所以選 (I)。第 10 題則是選 (D)，意為「並沒有要幫助我們的意願。」

解答＆技巧 | 01 (B)　02 (H)　03 (E)　04 (A)　05 (G)

06 (I)　07 (F)　08 (C)　09 (J)　10 (D)

適用 TIP 1　適用 TIP 2　適用 TIP 6　適用 TIP 7　適用 TIP 8

適用 TIP 9　適用 TIP 10　適用 TIP 11

補充

Greek ⓐ / ⓝ 希臘的，希臘人；Roman ⓐ 羅馬的；Incan ⓐ 印加文化的；

Mayan ⓐ / ⓝ 馬雅的，馬雅人；Atlantis ⓝ 亞特蘭提斯；Egyptian ⓝ 埃及人；Hindu ⓝ 印度人

7,000 單字

- alien [ˈelɪən] ⓝ 5 外星人
- confirm [kənˈfɝm] ⓥ 2 確信
- existence [ɪgˈzɪstəns] ⓝ 3 存在
- speculate [ˈspɛkjəˌlet] ⓥ 6 推測
- legend [ˈlɛdʒənd] ⓝ 4 傳說
- fairy [ˈfɛrɪ] ⓝ 3 仙子，精靈
- dwarf [dwɔrf] ⓝ 5 小矮人
- classic [ˈklæsɪk] ⓐ 2 經典的

- tale [tel] ⓝ 1 故事
- perish [ˈpɛrɪʃ] ⓥ 5 毀滅
- legendary [ˈlɛdʒəndˌɛrɪ] ⓐ 6 傳奇的
- contact [ˈkɑntækt] ⓝ 2 接觸
- harm [hɑrm] ⓝ 3 傷害
- comment [ˈkɑmɛnt] ⓥ 4 評論
- maybe [ˈmebɪ] ⓐⓓ 1 也許

Part 1
詞
彙
題
Day 2
完成 25%

Part 2
綜
合
測
驗
Day 2
完成 50%

Part 3
文
意
選
填
Day 2
完成 75%

Part 4
閱
讀
測
驗
Day 2
完成 100%

MEMO

5 ▶

The foregoing picture of the potential __01__ of the microelectronic revolution is hardly possible to inspire great expectations of the employees. After all this picture is too bleak.

The new technology indeed opens up a __02__ of exciting possibilities. Like the last industrial revolution, in the long __03__ the new revolution may open up as many new jobs as it destroys. But the peasants of the nineteenth-century Britain, the harness makers of twentieth-century North America, and the women of early industrial Canada were __04__ to leave the land and move into the mills and urban squalor. Besides, it is also __05__ comfort to the office workers, bank teller and production-line workers who are made redundant by electronic technology. They will be mostly __06__ to lose more jobs to the chip.

To women, the challenge of the chip is __07__. The first one is employment. The potentially most-affected __08__ are those traditionally considered women's work. Given that women are expected to make up seventy percent of all new entrants to the labor force, the employment __09__ are indeed bleak, unless women can break through traditional occupational ghettos. The second challenge is the quality of work, decent wage levels, access to job ladders, work safety, agreeable work environment, regular employment, and the absence of the stresses. However, whether these challenges can be removed or not still __10__ to be seen.

(A) remains   (B) run   (C) host   (D) twofold   (E) prospects
(F) implications   (G) likely   (H) occupations   (I) scant   (J) forced

01 _____   02 _____   03 _____   04 _____   05 _____

06 _____   07 _____   08 _____   09 _____   10 _____

選項中譯｜留待；時期；許多；雙重的；前景；可能的影響；可能的；職業；不足的；被迫

中譯｜之前的關於微電子變革潛在影響的陳述，對於員工來說，幾乎是沒有什麼樂觀前景的。畢竟，這樣的陳述過於黯淡。

新技術的確提供了很多令人振奮的可能性。正如上一次的工業革命一般，從長遠來看，新變革也許會推垮很多工作崗位，卻也會提供同樣多的新工作崗位。但是，十九世紀的英國農民們，二十世紀的北美馬具製造者們，以及加拿大工業革命早期的女性，都是被迫離開自己的家園，遷往工廠和城區污濁地。此外，電子技術使得辦公室職員、銀行出納員、生產線工人們成為冗員而被裁撤，對於他們而言，新技術也不會是什麼慰藉。微晶片很可能奪去更多的工作崗位。

對於女性而言，微晶片帶來的挑戰是雙重性的。第一是職業。最可能受到影響的職業，都是那些歷來由女性擔任的職業。考慮到女性佔據勞動市場中新工作者的百分之七十，女性如果不能打破傳統職業分布常規，職業前景就的確是十分黯淡了。第二重挑戰在於工作品質、可觀的薪資水準、工作等級的便利性、工作安全、宜人的工作環境、常規職業以及壓力的缺乏。然而，這些挑戰能否得到解決，尚未可知。

解譯｜閱讀全文可知，這篇文章的主題是微電子變革的影響。

縱觀各選項，選項 (B)、(C)、(E)、(F)、(H) 是名詞，選項 (A)、(J) 是動詞，選項 (D)、(G)、(I) 是形容詞。根據題意，第 1、2、3、8、9 題應選名詞，第 4、10 題應選動詞，第 5、6、7 題應選形容詞。然後根據文章，依次作答。

第 1 題是選擇名詞，用於 of 結構，有五個名詞可供選擇，即為選項 (B)、(C)、(E)、(F)、(H)，選項 (B) 意為「時期」，選項 (C) 意為「很多」，選項 (E) 意為「前景」，選項 (F) 意為「可能的影響」，選項 (H) 意為「職業」，根據句意，應當是「微電子變革的潛在影響」，所以選 (F)。第 2 題所選名詞，可以視為固定搭配 a host of 意為「很多，大量」，所以選 (C)。第 3 題所選名詞，也可以視為固定搭配，in the long run 意為「從長遠來看」，所以選 (B)。第 8 題所選名詞，根據句意，應當是「最可能受到影響的職業」，所以選 (H)。第 9 題則是選 (E)，意為「職業前景的確是十分黯淡」。

第 4 題是選擇動詞，須為被動語態，有兩個動詞可供選擇，即為選項 (A)、(J)。只有選項 (J) 符合要求，句意為「被迫離開家園」，即為正確答案。第 10 題則是選 (A)，可以視為固定搭配，remain to be seen 意為「尚未可知，有待觀察」。

第 5 題是選擇形容詞，修飾名詞 comfort，有三個形容詞可供選擇，即為選項 (D)、(G)、(I)。選項 (D) 意為「雙重的」，選項 (G) 意為「可能的」，選項 (I) 意為「不足的」，根據句意可知，應當是「也不是什麼慰藉」，所以選 (I)。第 6 題所選形容詞，可以視為固定搭配，be likely to do sth. 意為「有可能做某事」，所以選 (G)。第 7 題則是選 (D)，句意為「微晶片帶來的挑戰是雙重性的」。

DAY 2

Part 1
詞彙題
Day 2
完成 25%

Part 2
綜合測驗
Day 2
完成 50%

Part 3
文意選填
Day 2
完成 75%

Part 4
閱讀測驗
Day 2
完成 100%

解答&技巧 | **01** (F)　**02** (C)　**03** (B)　**04** (J)　**05** (I)
　　　　　06 (G)　**07** (D)　**08** (H)　**09** (E)　**10** (A)

適用 TIP 1　適用 TIP 2　適用 TIP 6　適用 TIP 7　適用 TIP 8
適用 TIP 9　適用 TIP 10　適用 TIP 11

補充

foregoing ⓐ 在前的，上述的；microelectronic ⓐ 微電子的；a host of ⓟ許多，眾多；
squalor ⓝ 污穢，卑微；entrant ⓝ 新成員；ghetto ⓝ 某些階層、集體的聚居區

7,000 單字

- implications [ˌɪmplɪˈkeʃənz]
  ⓝ ⑥ 可能的影響，可能的後果
- inspire [ɪnˈspaɪr] ⓥ ④ 啟示，啟迪
- bleak [blik] ⓐ ⑥ 黯淡的，無望的
- destroy [dɪˈstrɔɪ] ⓥ ③ 破壞
- peasant [ˈpɛznt] ⓝ ⑤ 農民
- harness [ˈhɑrnɪs] ⓝ ⑤ 馬具
- mill [mɪl] ⓝ ③ 工廠，磨坊
- bank [bæŋk] ⓝ ① 銀行

- teller [ˈtɛlɚ] ⓝ ⑤ 出納員
- redundant [rɪˈdʌndənt] ⓐ ⑥ 被解雇的，失業的
- chip [tʃɪp] ⓝ ③ 微晶片
- prospect [ˈprɑspɛkt] ⓝ ⑤ 前景
- decent [ˈdisn̩t] ⓐ ⑥ 可觀的，體面的
- ladder [ˈlædɚ] ⓝ ③ 梯子，階梯
- regular [ˈrɛgjəlɚ] ⓐ ② 常規的

MEMO --

MEMO

DAY
2

Part 1
詞
彙
題
Day 2
完成 25%

Part 2
綜
合
測
驗
Day 2
完成 50%

Part 3
文
意
選
填
Day 2
完成 75%

Part 4
閱
讀
測
驗
Day 2
完成 100%

The ship Titanic sank on its maiden voyage in 1912 after striking an iceberg, and carried more than 1,500 passengers to death. After resting on the ocean floor for nearly a century, Titanic seemed to come alive again.

The story of Titanic had been commonly found in print, on film, in poetry and in song. However, what had been legendary finally became real. Viewing videotapes and photographs of the sunken leviathan, millions of people around the world could sense the ruined splendor of the lost age. Views of the railings, where doomed passengers and crew members stood, evoked images of the moonless night, 74 years ago, when the ship slipped beneath the waves.

The two-minute videotape and nine photographs, all in color and shot 12,500ft under the North Atlantic, were a tiny sample of 60 hours of video and 60,000 stills garnered during the twelve-day exploration of the undersea craft. The videotape and photographs were released at a Washington press conference conducted by Marine Geologist Robert Ballard, 44 years old, who led the teams from the Woods Hole Oceanographic Institution that found and revisited Titanic.

Besides the highlights of what has already become the most celebrated feat of underwater exploration, some startling new information was as well revealed. The deep-diving craft failed to find the 300ft gash that, according to the legend, was torn in the Titanic's hull when the ship plowed into the iceberg. It is, therefore, supposed that the collision had buckled the ship's plates instead, allowing water to pour in. There is some evidence that the ship broke apart not when it hit bottom, but as it sank: the stern, which settled on the bottom almost 1,800ft from the bow, had swiveled 180° on its way down.

01 The word "lengendary" in the first paragraph is closest in meaning to _____.

(A) imaginary

(B) fabled

(C) mortal

(D) virtual

02 Which one of the following statements about Titanic is true?

(A) Titanic sank on its maiden voyage in 1912.

(B) Titanic carried one thousand passengers to death after striking the iceberg.

(C) The story of Titanic can hardly be found nowadays.

(D) The sunken Titanic has been resting on the ocean floor for fifty years.

03 Which of the following statements is not mentioned in the passage?

(A) The 300ft gash of Titanic's hull was actually found.

(B) Videotapes of Titanic evoked sad memories of viewers.

(C) Marine Geologist Robert Ballard found and revisited Titanic.

(D) Videotape and photographs about Titanic were released at a press conference.

04 What is the main idea of the passage?

(A) Press conference of Titanic.

(B) Discovery of the sunken ship.

(C) Exploration of Titanic.

(D) The story of Titanic.

DAY
2

Part 1
詞
彙
題
Day 2
完成 25%

Part 2
綜
合
測
驗
Day 2
完成 50%

Part 3
文
意
選
填
Day 2
完成 75%

Part 4
閱
讀
測
驗
Day 2
完成 100%

中譯｜一九一二年，鐵達尼號郵輪在首次航行中撞上冰山而沉沒，致使一千五百多名乘客喪生。在海底沉沒了將近一個世紀之後，鐵達尼號似乎是再度引起了關注。

鐵達尼號的故事在出版物中、在影片中、在詩中、在歌曲中都是普遍可見的。然而，這些傳奇最終成為了現實。觀看著這艘沉沒的龐然大物的錄影和照片，世界上有數百萬的人們可以感受到那個逝去的時代中湮滅的輝煌。欄杆的場景，那些已逝的乘客和船員曾經站立的地方，喚起人們的回憶，想像著那個無月之夜，這艘郵輪淹沒在浪濤之下。

在北大西洋海面下一萬兩千五百英尺深處，為期十二天的海底輪船探險中，拍攝了六十小時的影片和六萬張定格畫面，人們所看到的這兩分鐘長的彩色錄影和九張彩色照片，就是其中的一小部分樣品。錄影和照片是在華盛頓的記者招待會上發佈的，這次招待會是由四十四歲的海洋地質學家羅伯特‧巴拉德舉辦的，也就是他，領導著伍茲霍爾海洋研究所的團隊，找到並且再度探訪了鐵達尼號。

除了這些最為著名的海底探險亮點之外，記者會也揭示了一些令人吃驚的新資訊。傳說中，鐵達尼號撞上冰山時，船體裂開了三百英尺的切口，但是，深潛海底的探險船並沒有找到這個切口。因此，有人推測，撞擊冰山，只是使得鐵達尼號的船體彎曲變形，海水進而倒灌。鐵達尼號船尾距離船頭幾乎有一千八百英尺遠，並且在沉沒過程中發生了一百八十度旋轉，這就表明，鐵達尼號並不是在撞擊冰山底部時發生斷裂，而是在沉沒時才發生的。

解譯｜在閱讀文章之前，先要預覽題目，然後再帶著問題有針對性地閱讀文章。第 1 題是詞義辨析，第 2 題是判斷正誤，第 3 題是文意理解，第 4 題是概括主旨。理解了題目要求之後，閱讀全文，依次作答。

第 1 題是考形容詞 legendary 的同義字。選項 (A) 意為「想像的」，選項 (B) 意為「傳奇的」，選項 (C) 意為「極度的」，選項 (D) 意為「實質上的」。根據第 1 段內容可知，形容詞意為「傳奇的」，所以選 (B)。

第 2 題是判斷正誤，考的是細節，關於鐵達尼號的敘述，哪一項是正確的。很明顯，其關鍵字是 Titanic。根據第 1 段首句內容「The ship Titanic sank on its maiden voyage in 1912 after striking an iceberg」可知，選項 (A) 是正確的。同樣，此題也可以用排除法來解答。根據第 1 段內容可知，鐵達尼號致使一千五百多名乘客喪生，而不是一千名乘客，排除選項 (B)；根據第 2 段內容可知，鐵達尼號的故事是普遍可見的，並不罕見，排除選項 (C)；並且，鐵達尼號在海底已經沉沒了一個世紀，而不是五十年，排除選項 (D)。所以選 (A)。

第 3 題是文意理解，問的是哪一項敘述在文中沒有提及。可以用排除法來解答。根據第 2 段最後一句內容判斷，鐵達尼號的影像引起了觀眾的悲傷回憶，與選項 (B) 相符；選項 (C) 與第 3 段最後一句內容相符，而選項 (D) 是與第 3 段倒數第 2 行內容相符。只有選項 (A)，無法在文中找到相關敘述，所以選 (A)。

第 4 題是概括主旨。文中並沒有明顯的主旨句，需要根據各段內容加以概括。第 1 段講述的是鐵達尼號的簡介，第 2 段講述的是有關鐵達尼號的錄影和照片，第 3 段講述的是鐵達尼號的探險成果發佈，第 4 段講述的是有關鐵達尼號沉沒真相的最新資訊。由此可知，短文內容是簡述鐵達尼號的探險，所以選 (C)。

解答&技巧 | **01** (B)　**02** (A)　**03** (A)　**04** (C)

適用 TIP 1　適用 TIP 3　適用 TIP 7　適用 TIP 10　適用 TIP 11

適用 TIP 12　適用 TIP 13　適用 TIP 14　適用 TIP 15

補充

leviathan n 龐然大物；evoke v 引起，喚起；moonless a 無月的；railing n 欄杆，扶手；
undersea a 海面下的；oceanographic a 海洋學的

7,000 單字

- maiden [ˈmedn̩] a 5 首次的，初次的
- voyage [ˈvɔɪɪdʒ] n 4 航行
- splendor [ˈsplɛndə] n 5 華麗，輝煌
- beneath [bɪˈniθ] prep 3 在～下
- wave [wev] n 2 浪濤
- videotape [ˈvɪdɪoˈtep] n 5 錄影，錄影帶
- exploration [ˌɛkspləˈreʃən] n 6 探查，探險
- craft [kræft] n 4 船舶

- press [prɛs] n 2 新聞界，報界
- institution [ˌɪnstəˈtjuʃən] n 6 機構
- plow [plaʊ] v 5 破浪航行
- buckle [ˈbʌkl̩] v 6 變形，弄彎
- allow [əˈlaʊ] v 1 允許
- pour [por] v 3 灌，注
- stern [stɜn] n 5 船尾

Part 1
詞
彙
題
Day 2
完成 25%

Part 2
綜
合
測
驗
Day 2
完成 50%

Part 3
文
意
選
填
Day 2
完成 75%

Part 4
閱
讀
測
驗
Day 2
完成 100%

MEMO

The great majority of men may successfully resist all attempts to make them change their style of clothes. However, this does not apply to women. The conclusions to be drawn are obvious. Men are too sensible to let themselves be bullied by fashion designers, while the constantly changing fashions of women's clothes reflect fickleness and instability of women.

Each year a few so-called top designers in Paris or London lay down the law, and women around the whole world rush to obey. The decrees of the designers are somehow unpredictable and dictatorial. Being mercilessly exploited and black-mailed by the designers and the big stores year after year, women should have only themselves to blame. They always shudder at the thought of appearing in public in fashionable clothes. Clothes, which have been worn only a few times, may simply be forgotten because of the dictates of fashion. Women are always standing in front of a wardrobe packed full of clothes, and complaining sadly that they have nothing to wear.

Changing fashions are nothing more than the deliberate creation of waste. Many women squander vast sums of money annually to replace clothes that have hardly been worn because they will put up with little discomfort in the matter of fashion. Being unwilling to discard clothing in this way, some women may waste hours of their time altering the dresses they have. Hem-lines are taken up or let down; waist-lines are taken in or let out; neck-lines are lowered or raised, and so on.

There is no denying that the fashion industry seldom contributes anything really important to society. Fashion designers are seldom concerned with vital things like warmth, comfort and durability. What they are interested in is merely outward appearance.

01 The word "fashion" in the first paragraph is closest in meaning to _____.

(A) vogue
(B) design
(C) decoration
(D) necessity

02 Why are women mercilessly exploited by fashion designers and big stores?

(A) They always spend much money on clothing.
(B) They want to look beautiful.
(C) They love new clothes.
(D) They are too vain.

03 What are fashion designers interested in?

(A) Durability.
(B) Outward appearance.
(C) Comfort.
(D) Warmth.

04 What is the main idea of the passage?

(A) New fashions in clothes are quite popular among women.
(B) Women are commercially exploited by new fashions in clothing.
(C) Women don't have a basic quality of reliability.
(D) Top designers have the exclusive right to create new fashion.

DAY
2

Part 1
詞
彙
題
Day 2
完成 25%

Part 2
綜
合
測
驗
Day 2
完成 50%

Part 3
文
意
選
填
Day 2
完成 75%

Part 4
閱
讀
測
驗
Day 2
完成 100%

中譯 | 對於那些企圖讓他們改變衣著風格的種種方式，大多數的男性也許可以成功地抵制。然而，這並不適用於女性。結論是顯而易見的。男性過於理智，並不會被時尚設計師脅迫；而女裝不斷變化著的時尚則反映出女性的善變和不穩定性。

每年，巴黎和倫敦的所謂的優秀設計師會設定規則，全世界的女性都會爭相遵從。設計師的決定可以說是難以預計的、專斷的。女性年復一年地被設計師和大型店鋪利用、訛詐，也只能歸責於自身。一想到穿著時尚的衣著出現在公共場合，她們總是興奮地發抖。因為時尚所限，只穿過少數幾次的衣服，也許就會被遺忘。女性總是站在滿是衣服的衣櫥前，哀傷地抱怨說，她們沒有可穿的衣服。不斷變化著的時尚，其實是蓄意的浪費。很多女性每年都花費大筆的錢，來更換那些幾乎不曾穿過的衣服，因為，在時尚問題上，她們可以忍受些許的不適。有些女性不願就此丟棄那些衣服，也許就會花費數小時的時間來改造。褶邊翻上去或是放下來，腰線收縮或是放寬，領口開低或是拉高，如此種種。

不可否認，時尚產業對社會並沒有什麼真正的貢獻。時尚設計師極少關注諸如溫暖、舒適和耐用之類的重要事宜。他們感興趣的，也只是外在形象而已。

解譯 | 在閱讀文章之前，先要預覽題目，然後再帶著問題有針對性地閱讀文章。第 1 題是詞義辨析，第 2、3 題是文意理解，第 4 題是概括主旨。理解了題目要求之後，閱讀全文，依次作答。

第 1 題是考名詞 fashion 的同義字。選項 (A) 意為「時尚」，選項 (B) 意為「設計」，選項 (C) 意為「裝飾」，選項 (D) 意為「必需品」。根據第 1 段內容可知，名詞 fashion 意為「時尚」，所以選 (A)。

第 2 題是文意理解，問的是為什麼女性會被時尚設計師和大型店鋪利用，可以定位於第 2 段。可以推知，女性被商家利用，是因為她們自身愛慕虛榮，即為選項 (D)。而選項 (A) 是說女性總是花錢買衣服，選項 (B) 是說女性喜歡漂亮，選項 (C) 喜歡新衣服，都是女性愛慕虛榮的細節表現，所以選 (D)。

第 3 題同樣是文意理解，考的是細節，問的是時尚設計師們關注的是什麼，可以定位於第 4 段。在文中有直接的敘述，是最後一句內容「What they are interested in is merely outward appearance」可知，他們關注的只是外在形象，所以選 (B)。同樣，此題也可以用排除法來解答。根據第 2 句內容「Fashion designers are seldom concerned with vital things like warmth, comfort and durability.」可知，設計師甚少關注溫暖、舒適、耐用，排除選項 (A)、(C)、(D)，所以選 (B)。

第 4 題是概括主旨。文中並沒有明顯的主旨句，需要根據各段內容加以概括。第 1 段是由男性和女性對於衣著的不同態度而引出話題，第 2 段講述的是女性愛慕虛榮而被設計師和服飾店利用，第 3 段講述的是追求時尚其實是浪費，第 4 段講述的是時尚產業於社會無益。由此可知，短文內容是說，為求商業效益，女性在衣著時尚方面被利用，所以選 (B)。

解答＆技巧 | **01 (A)**　**02 (D)**　**03 (B)**　**04 (B)**

適用 TIP 1　適用 TIP 3　適用 TIP 7　適用 TIP 10　適用 TIP 11
適用 TIP 12　適用 TIP 13　適用 TIP 14　適用 TIP 15

補充

decree ⓝ 命令，法令，政令；unpredictable ⓐ 不可預知的；dictatorial ⓐ 獨斷的，獨裁的；squander ⓥ 浪費，揮霍；durability ⓝ 耐用，耐久

7,000 單字

- resist [rɪ`zɪst] ⓥ ③ 抵抗，抵制
- obey [ə`be] ⓥ ② 遵從，順從
- exploit [ɪk`splɔɪt] ⓥ ⑥ 利用，剝削
- blame [blem] ⓥ ③ 責怪
- shudder [`ʃʌdɚ] ⓥ ⑤ 顫慄
- wardrobe [`wɔrd.rob] ⓝ ⑥ 衣櫥
- deliberate [dɪ`lɪbərɪt] ⓐ ⑥ 蓄意的，故意的
- creation [krɪ`eʃən] ⓝ ④ 產生，創造

- replace [rɪ`ples] ⓥ ③ 代替
- waist [west] ⓝ ② 腰
- lower [`loɚ] ⓥ ② 降低
- contribute [kən`trɪbjut] ⓥ ④ 貢獻
- vital [`vaɪtl] ⓐ ④ 極重要的
- comfort [`kʌmfɚt] ⓝ ③ 舒適
- appearance [ə`pɪrəns] ⓝ ② 外表，外觀

Part 1
詞
彙
題
Day 2
完成 25%

Part 2
綜
合
測
驗
Day 2
完成 50%

Part 3
文
意
選
填
Day 2
完成 75%

Part 4
閱
讀
測
驗
Day 2
完成 100%

MEMO

♪ 123

A sense of humor is just one of the many things shared by Alfred and Anthony Melillo, 64-year-old twin brothers from East Haven who made history in February 2002. On Christmas Eve, 1992, Anthony had a heart transplant from a 21-year-old donor. Two days before Valentine's Day in 2002, Alfred received a 19-year-old heart, marking the first time on record that twin adults each received heart transplants.

"I'm 15 minutes older than him, but now I'm younger because of my heart, and I'm not going to respect him," Alfred said with a grin, pointing to his brother while talking to a roomful of reporters, who laughed frequently at their jokes.

While the twins knew that genetics might have played a role in their condition, they recognized that their eating habits might have also contributed to their heart problems. "We'd put half a pound of butter on a steak. I overdid it on all the food that tasted good, so I guess I deserved what I got for not dieting properly."

The discussion moved to Anthony's recovery. In the five years since his heart transplant, he had been on an exercise program where he regularly rode a bicycle for five miles, swam each day, and walked a couple of miles. He was still on medication, but not nearly as much as Alfred, who was just in the early stage of his recovery.

"Right now I feel pretty young, and I'm doing very well," Anthony said. "I feel like a new person." Alfred said his goal, of course, was to feel even better than his brother. But, he added, "I love my brother very much. We're very close, and I'm sure we'll do just fine."

01 This article is mainly about _____.

(A) the danger of heart transplant surgery
(B) becoming young by getting a new heart
(C) the effect of genetics on the heart
(D) the twin brothers who received heart transplants

02 What did Alfred and Anthony have in common?

(A) Lifespan.
(B) Career goals.
(C) A sense of humor.
(D) Love for bicycling.

03 What did Alfred and Anthony think caused their heart problems?

(A) Exercise.
(B) Diet.
(C) Surgery.
(D) Medicines.

04 Why did Alfred say, "I'm 15 minutes older than him, but now I'm younger because of my heart"?

(A) His heart transplant surgery was more successful than Anthony's.
(B) His recovery from the heart surgery was faster than Anthony's.
(C) His exercise program was better than Anthony's.
(D) His new heart was younger than Anthony's.

中譯｜阿爾弗雷德・梅利洛和安東尼・梅利洛，這一對來自美國東港的六十四歲雙胞胎兄弟，於二〇〇二年創造了歷史。幽默感只是這兩對兄弟的共有特性之一。一九九二年聖誕前夕，安東尼接受了心臟移植手術，捐獻者是一位二十一歲的年輕人。二〇〇二年情人節的前兩天，阿爾弗雷德也接受了心臟移植手術，捐獻者是一位十九歲的年輕人。成年雙胞胎都接受心臟移植手術，這還是有史以來的第一次。

「我比他早出生十五分鐘，不過，因為心臟的緣故，現在我比他年輕一些了，但是我不會尊重他的。」當著一屋子的記者，阿爾弗雷德露齒而笑，指著他的兄弟安東尼這樣說。兩兄弟的幽默笑話常常逗得記者們發笑。

雙胞胎兄弟知道，他們的病症也許與遺傳學理論有關，他們也承認，心臟問題可能也是和自己的飲食習慣有關。「我們喜歡在牛排上塗半磅的奶油。我更是在所有美味的食物上都塗過多的奶油，所以，我想，以這樣不恰當的飲食習慣來說，目前的狀況也是我應得的。」

話題轉向了安東尼的恢復情況。他接受心臟移植手術後的五年時間裡，一直在參加一項運動計畫，定期騎自行車五英里，每天游泳，散步走幾英里。他還在接受藥物治療，只是很有限的治療，不像是阿爾弗雷德，他才剛剛開始恢復。

「現在，我感覺自己很年輕，一切也都很好，」安東尼說，「我感覺，自己像是重生了一樣。」阿爾弗雷德說，他的目標，自然是要恢復得比他兄弟還好。不過，他又說，「我很愛我弟弟。我們關係很好，我相信，我們都會好好地活下去。」

解譯｜在閱讀文章之前，先要預覽題目，然後再帶著問題有針對性地閱讀文章。第 1 題是概括主旨，第 2、3、4 題是文意理解。理解了題目要求之後，閱讀全文，依次作答。主旨題可以留在最後解答。

第 2 題是文意理解，問的是，阿爾弗雷德和安東尼有什麼共同之處。在文中可以找到明確的敘述，定位於第 1 段首句「A sense of humor is just one of the many things shared by Alfred and Anthony Melillo」，與選項 (C) 相符。其他三個選項，在文中找不到相關敘述，也可以排除。所以選 (C)。

第 3 題也是文意理解，問的是，阿爾弗雷德和安東尼認為，是什麼引起了他們的心臟病。根據第 3 段首句內容「they recognized that their eating habits might have also contributed to their heart problems.」可知，他們承認，心臟問題可能和飲食習慣有關，與選項 (B) 相符。其他三個選項，在文中找不到相關敘述。所以選 (B)。

第 4 題同樣是文意理解，問的是，阿爾弗雷德為什麼會說「I'm 15 minutes older than him, but now I'm younger because of my heart」。這句話是出現在文中第 2 段的首句位置，答案應該可以定位於第 1 段。根據第 1 段第 2、3 句內容可知，安東尼接受的心臟移植手術，捐獻者是一位二十一歲的年輕人。而阿爾弗雷德接受的心臟移植手術，捐獻者是一位十九歲的年輕人。選項 (B) 意為「他接受移植的心臟比安東尼的心臟要年輕一些」，與此相符，所以選 (D)。

DAY
2

Part 1
詞
彙
題
Day 2
完成 25%

Part 2
綜
合
測
驗
Day 2
完成 50%

Part 3
文
意
選
填
Day 2
完成 75%

Part 4
閱
讀
測
驗
Day 2
完成 100%

第 1 題是概括主旨。文中並沒有明顯的主旨句，需要根據各段內容加以概括。第 1 段是由阿爾弗雷德和安東尼的心臟移植手術而展開敘述，第 2 段講述的是兩兄弟的幽默，第 3 段講述的是他們的發病原因，第 4 段講述的是他們的恢復狀況，第 5 段講述的是他們的感想。由此可知，短文內容是簡述接受心臟移植手術的雙胞胎兄弟，與選項 (D) 相符，所以選 (D)。

解答＆技巧 | 01 (D)　02 (C)　03 (B)　04 (D)

適用 TIP 1　適用 TIP 2　適用 TIP 3　適用 TIP 7　適用 TIP 10
適用 TIP 11　適用 TIP 12　適用 TIP 13　適用 TIP 14　適用 TIP 15

補充
make history ph 載入史冊，創造歷史；point to ph 指向；eating habits ph 飲食習慣；
contribute to ph 引起；be on medication ph 進行藥物治療

7,000 單字

- twin [twɪn] n 3 雙胞胎
- brother [ˋbrʌðɚ] n 1 兄弟
- transplant [ˋtræns͵plænt] n 6 移植
- donor [ˋdonɚ] n 6 捐獻者
- grin [ɡrɪn] n 3 露齒而笑
- laugh [læf] v 1 發笑
- genetics [dʒəˋnɛtɪks] n 6 遺傳學
- butter [ˋbʌtɚ] n 1 奶油

- steak [stek] n 2 牛排
- overdo [͵ovɚˋdu] v 5 過分，過火
- recovery [rɪˋkʌvərɪ] n 4 恢復，痊癒
- bicycle [ˋbaɪsɪkl] n 1 自行車
- couple [ˋkʌpl] n 2 對，雙
- medication [͵mɛdɪˋkeʃən] n 6 藥物治療
- stage [stedʒ] n 2 階段

MEMO

Joy and sadness are experienced by people around the world. It turns out that the expression of many emotions may be universal. Smiling is apparently a universal sign of friendliness and approval. Baring the teeth in a hostile way, according to Charles Darwin in the 19th century, might be a universal sign of anger. Darwin, the originator of the theory of evolution, believed that the universal recognition of facial expressions would have survival value. Facial expressions, for example, could signal the approach of enemies or friends in the absence of language.

Most investigators concur that the emotions could be manifested by facial expressions. Psychological researchers generally discover that facial expressions reflect emotional states. In fact, various emotional states give rise to certain patterns of electrical activity in the facial muscles and in the brain. But the facial-feedback hypothesis argues that the causal relationship between emotions and facial expressions can also work in the opposite direction. According to this hypothesis, signals from the facial muscles, i.e. feedback, are sent back to emotion centers of the brain, so a person's facial expression can influence his emotional state.

The free expression by outward signs of emotions may intensify it. On the other hand, the repression, as far as possible, of all outward signs softens our emotions. Smiling may lead to feelings of good will, for example, and frowning to anger.

Psychological researches have announced some interesting findings concerning the facial-feedback hypothesis. Causing participants in experiments to smile, for example, leads them to give more positive feelings and to regard cartoons as being more humorous. When they are caused to frown, they regard cartoons as being more aggressive.

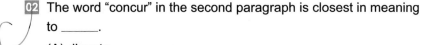

01 Why does the author mention "Baring the teeth in a hostile way" in the first paragraph?

(A) To give an example of facial expressions whose meaning are widely understood.

(B) To introduce Darwin's theory of evolution.

(C) To show facial expressions are quite important.

(D) To show the discovery of investigators.

02 The word "concur" in the second paragraph is closest in meaning to _____.

(A) dispute

(B) disagree

(C) agree

(D) discuss

03 Which one of the following statements is true?

(A) Facial expressions of many emotions prove to be universal.

(B) Emotions cannot be demonstrated by facial expressions.

(C) Facial expressions seldom reflect emotional states.

(D) Facial expressions have no survival value actually.

04 What is the main idea of the passage?

(A) Darwin's theory of evolution.

(B) Joy and sadness.

(C) The facial-feedback hypothesis.

(D) The relationship between facial expressions and emotions.

DAY
2

Part 1
詞
彙
題
Day 2
完成 25%

Part 2
綜
合
測
驗
Day 2
完成 50%

Part 3
文
意
選
填
Day 2
完成 75%

Part 4
閱
讀
測
驗
Day 2
完成 100%

中譯│全世界的人們都會有快樂和悲傷的體驗。事實證明，許多情緒的表達都是普遍共通的。微笑似乎是友好和認同的共同標誌。十九世紀的查爾斯‧達爾文認為，表示敵意地露出牙齒，也許是憤怒的共同標誌。進化論的創始人達爾文認為，面部表情的普遍認知將會具有生存價值。例如，在缺少語言的情況下，面部表情能發出訊號，幫你判斷前來的是敵是友。

大多數的調查研究者一致同意，情緒可以借由面部表情清晰地表露出來。心理學研究學者通常會發現，面部表情可以反映情緒狀況。事實上，不同的情緒狀況會引起面部肌肉和大腦的某種電波活動。然而，面部表情回饋假說則是認為，情緒和面部表情之間的因果關係，也會以相反的方式而發生。這項假說認為，來自面部肌肉的信號，即為回饋資訊，將被傳遞回大腦的情緒中心，因此，人的面部表情可以影響他的情緒狀況。

外在的情緒的自由表達也許會助長這種情緒。另一方面，盡可能地壓抑外在的情緒則會弱化這種情緒。例如，微笑也許會引起善意的情緒，而皺眉則會引起憤怒。

心理學研究學者公佈了有關面部表情回饋假說的一些有趣的發現。例如，在實驗中，讓參與者微笑，會使他們表現出更多的積極情緒，認為漫畫更為幽默；如果讓參與者皺眉，他們則會認為漫畫更有攻擊性。

解譯│在閱讀文章之前，先要預覽題目，然後再帶著問題有針對性地閱讀文章。第 1 題是細節推斷，第 2 題是詞義辨析，第 3 題是判斷正誤，第 4 題是概括主旨。理解了題目要求之後，閱讀全文，依次作答。

第 1 題是細節推斷，問的是，文中列舉這樣一個例子，意圖何在，關鍵字是 Baring the teeth in a hostile way，即表示敵意地露出牙齒，定位於第 1 段。根據第 1 段內容判斷，引述這個例子，目的與上一句的微笑例子相同，都是為了證明前文所提到的，許多情緒的表達都是普遍共通的，所以選 (A)。

第 2 題是考動詞 concur 的同義字。選項 (A) 意為「爭論」，選項 (B) 意為「反對」，選項 (C) 意為「同意」，選項 (D) 意為「討論」。根據第 2 段內容可知，動詞 concur 意為「同意」，所以選 (C)。

第 3 題是判斷正誤，考的是細節，問的是，哪一項敘述是正確的。根據第 1 段 第 2 句 內 容「It turns out that the expression of many emotions may be universal.」可知，事實證明，許多情緒的表達都是普遍共通的，與選項 (A) 相符。同樣，此題也可以用排除法來解答。根據第 2 段首句內容「the emotions could be manifested by facial expressions.」可知，選項 (B) 敘述錯誤，排除；根據第 2 段第 2 句內容「facial expressions reflect emotional states」，排除選項 (C)；根據第 1 段倒數第 2 行內容「the universal recognition of facial expressions would have survival value」，排除選項 (D)。所以選 (A)。

第 4 題是概括主旨。文中並沒有明顯的主旨句，需要根據各段內容加以概括。第 1 段是由快樂和悲傷而引出話題，第 2 段講述的是情緒可以由面部表情表現，第 3 段講述的是情緒和面部表情的相互影響，第 4 段講述的是面部表情回饋假說的一些有趣的發現。由此可知，短文內容是簡述情緒和面部表情的關係，所以選 (D)。

解答＆技巧 ┃ **01 (A)** ❘ **02 (C)** ❘ **03 (A)** ❘ **04 (D)**

適用 TIP 1　適用 TIP 3　適用 TIP 7　適用 TIP 10　適用 TIP 11
適用 TIP 12　適用 TIP 13　適用 TIP 14　適用 TIP 15　適用 TIP 16

DAY
2

Part 1
詞
彙
題
Day 2
完成 25%

Part 2
綜
合
測
驗
Day 2
完成 50%

Part 3
文
意
選
填
Day 2
完成 75%

Part 4
閱
讀
測
驗
Day 2
完成 100%

補充

sadness ⓝ 悲傷；originator ⓝ 創始者，發起人；concur ⓥ 同意；hypothesis ⓝ 假設，假說；
repression ⓝ 壓抑，抑制

7,000 單字

- universal [ˌjunəˈvɝsl] ⓐ ④ 普遍的，通用的
- approval [əˈpruvl] ⓝ ④ 贊成，認可
- hostile [ˈhɑstɪl] ⓐ ⑤ 有敵意的，不友好的
- anger [ˈæŋgɚ] ⓝ ① 憤怒
- evolution [ˌɛvəˈluʃən] ⓝ ⑥ 進化
- recognition [ˌrɛkəgˈnɪʃən] ⓝ ④ 認識，承認
- absence [ˈæbsn̩s] ⓝ ② 缺乏，缺少
- manifest [ˈmænəˌfɛst] ⓥ ⑤ 證明，顯示

- electrical [ɪˈlɛktrɪkl̩] ⓐ ③ 電的
- send [sɛnd] ⓥ ① 發送
- participant [parˈtɪsəpənt] ⓝ ⑤ 參與者
- smile [smaɪl] ⓝ ① 微笑
- cartoon [karˈtun] ⓝ ② 漫畫
- frown [fraʊn] ⓥ ④ 皺眉
- aggressive [əˈgrɛsɪv] ⓐ ④ 尋釁的，攻擊性的

MEMO --

DAY 3

Always make a total effort, even when the odds are against you.
— *Arnold Palmer*

永遠盡全力，即便成功的機會不高。
——阿諾德‧帕爾默

▶ **Part 1**｜詞 彙 題

▶ **Part 2**｜綜合測驗

▶ **Part 3**｜文意選填

▶ **Part 4**｜閱讀測驗

Part 1 | 詞彙題 | Vocabulary Questions

01 Advertisements will bring more _____ for the new products produced by our company.

(A) inference
(B) fragment
(C) fracture
(D) publicity

中譯｜廣告將會為我們公司生產的產品帶來更多的宣傳。

解說｜四個選項皆為名詞。依據題意，應該是「廣告帶來宣傳」。選項 (D) publicity 表示「宣傳」，符合題意，所以正確選項為 (D)。

解答＆技巧｜**(D)** 適用 TIP 1　適用 TIP 4

02 Elderly people and people with disabilities have _____ to buy train tickets compared with young people.

(A) regularity
(B) freak
(C) priority
(D) friction

中譯｜與年輕人相比，老年人和身心障礙者享有購買火車票的優先權。

解說｜四個選項皆為名詞。依據題意，應該是「享有優先權」，選項 (C) priority 可以與動詞 have 搭配，構成 have priority to do sth.，表示「優先做某事」，所以正確選項是 (C)。

解答＆技巧｜**(C)** 適用 TIP 1　適用 TIP 2

03 It has been raining for half a year, so there is an _____ supply of fresh water in this area.

(A) valiant
(B) ultimate
(C) abundant
(D) epidemic

中譯｜這個地區連續下雨長達半年之久，所以有著充足的淡水。

解說｜本題考句子之間的因果關係。由前一句的因「下雨長達半年之久」，可以推斷出後一句的果「有充足的淡水」，即選項 (C) 是正確答案。

解答＆技巧｜**(C)** 適用 TIP 1　適用 TIP 4

04 Our chemistry teacher has asked for a one-month marriage leave, so we need another teacher to _____ for him.

(A) verge   (B) navigate

(C) rehearse   (D) substitute

中譯｜我們的化學老師請了一個月的婚假，所以我們需要另外一位老師來替代他。

解說｜四個選項皆為動詞。依據題意，應該是「替代」，選項 (D) substitute 表示「替代，替換」，符合題意，所以正確選項是 (D)。

解答＆技巧｜**(D)** 適用 TIP 1   適用 TIP 4

補充
marriage leave ph 婚假

7,000 單字
- chemistry [ˋkɛmɪstrɪ] n 4 化學
- verge [vɝdʒ] v 6 瀕臨
- navigate [ˋnævəˏget] v 5 駕駛
- rehearse [rɪˋhɝs] v 6 排練
- substitute [ˋsʌbstəˏtjut] v 5 代替

---

05 Routine _____ work, such as regular checking and repairing, can keep these facilities in good condition.

(A) veterinarian   (B) eloquence

(C) maintenance   (D) alliance

中譯｜定期檢查和修理屬於日常維修工作，能夠使這些設備保持完好無損。

解說｜四個選項皆為名詞。依據題意，定期檢查和修理應該屬於日常維修工作，選項 (C) maintenance 表示「維修，維護」，符合題意。

解答＆技巧｜**(C)** 適用 TIP 1   適用 TIP 4

補充
be in good condition ph 完好無損

7,000 單字
- such [sʌtʃ] a 1 這樣的
- veterinarian [ˏvɛtərəˋnɛrɪən] n 6 獸醫
- eloquence [ˋɛləkwəns] n 6 口才
- maintenance [ˋmentənəns] n 5 維護
- alliance [əˋlaɪəns] n 6 聯盟

---

06 Once people pass the tests for professional _____, they may have more opportunities to find a well-paid job.

(A) virtues   (B) veterans

(C) certificates   (D) perseverances

中譯｜一旦人們通過了專業證書考試，他們就更有機會找到一份高薪的工作。

解說｜本題考名詞片語的用法。四個選項皆為名詞，將其一一代入可知，選項 (C) certificates 表示「證書」，與 professional 連用表示「專業資格證書」，符合題意。

解答＆技巧｜**(C)** 適用 TIP 2   適用 TIP 11

補充
professional certificate ph 專業證書

7,000 單字
- well-paid [ˋwɛlˋped] a 1 薪資優厚的
- virtue [ˋvɝtʃu] n 4 美德
- veteran [ˋvɛtərən] n 6 老兵
- certificate [səˋtɪfəkɪt] n 5 證書
- perseverance [ˏpɝsəˋvɪrəns] n 6 堅持不懈

DAY 3

Part 1
詞彙題
Day 3
完成 25%

Part 2
綜合測驗
Day 3
完成 50%

Part 3
文意選填
Day 3
完成 75%

Part 4
閱讀測驗
Day 3
完成 100%

07 Although Tom has not met his elementary school classmate for ten years, he can still _____ her clearly.

(A) nominate　　　　(B) visualize

(C) prolong　　　　(D) victimize

補充

elementary school ph 小學

7,000 單字
- classmate [ˋklæs͵met] n 6 同班同學
- nominate [ˋnɑmə͵net] v 5 提名
- visualize [ˋvɪʒʊə͵laɪz] v 6 想像
- prolong [prəˋlɔŋ] v 5 延長
- victimize [ˋvɪktɪ͵maɪz] v 6 使受害

中譯｜儘管湯姆和他的小學同學已經十年沒見面了，但他仍然能夠清楚地想像出她的樣子。

解說｜四個選項皆為動詞。依據題意，在沒見面的情況下，應該是「想像」她的樣子，選項 (B) visualize 表示「使形象化，想像」，符合題意，是正確選項。

解答＆技巧｜**(B)**　適用 TIP 1　適用 TIP 4

---

08 The vendor said that selling fried chicken at the night market is the most _____ business and he has earned much money from it.

(A) plentiful　　　　(B) victorious

(C) profitable　　　　(D) productive

補充

fried chicken ph 炸雞
night market ph 夜市

7,000 單字
- chicken [ˋtʃɪkɪn] n 1 雞肉
- plentiful [ˋplɛntɪfəl] a 4 豐富的
- victorious [vɪkˋtorɪəs] a 6 勝利的
- profitable [ˋprɑfɪtəbl] a 4 有利可圖的
- productive [prəˋdʌktɪv] a 4 生產的

中譯｜那個小販說，在夜市裡賣炸雞是最賺錢的生意，他已經靠它賺了很多錢。

解說｜四個選項皆為形容詞。由 earned much money 可以推斷出「賣炸雞是最賺錢的生意」，選項 (C) profitable 表示「有利可圖的」，符合題意。

解答＆技巧｜**(C)**　適用 TIP 1　適用 TIP 4

---

09 With an excellent _____ of French, she is assigned to translate these business contracts.

(A) writing　　　　(B) vineyard

(C) command　　　　(D) vitality

補充

business contract ph 商業合約

7,000 單字
- French [frɛntʃ] n 6 法語
- writing [ˋraɪtɪŋ] n 1 書寫
- vineyard [ˋvɪnjəd] n 6 葡萄園
- command [kəˋmænd] n 3 掌握
- vitality [vaɪˋtælətɪ] n 6 活力

中譯｜她的法語學得很出色，所以被指派翻譯這些商業合約。

解說｜四個選項皆為名詞。依據題意，應該是「法語學得很出色」，四個選項中，command 表示「掌握，運用能力」，所以選項 (C) 符合題意。

解答＆技巧｜**(C)**　適用 TIP 1　適用 TIP 4

10 All the students are required to attend the two-day _____ program so that they can have a complete understanding of the university they are admitted to.

【93年指考英文】

(A) orientation　　(B) accomplishment
(C) enthusiasm　　(D) independence

補充
orientation program ph 新生訓練
be admitted to
ph 獲准進入，允許加入

7,000 單字
• admit [əd`mɪt] v ③ 准許進入
• orientation [ˌorɪɛn`teʃən] n ④（新生）情況介紹、訓練
• accomplishment [ə`kɑmplɪʃmənt] n ④ 成就
• enthusiasm [ɪn`θjuzɪ͵æzəm] n ④ 熱心
• independence [ˌɪndɪ`pɛndəns] n ② 獨立性

中譯｜所有學生都應該參加為期兩天的新生訓練，以便他們對於自己錄取的大學有一個徹底的了解。

解說｜四個選項皆為名詞。依據題意，要想「了解大學」，學生就要參加「新生訓練」，而 orientation program 是一個固定搭配，表示「新生訓練」，所以選項 (A) 符合題意。

解答&技巧｜ **(A)** 適用 TIP 2　適用 TIP 4

11 She gets a poor salary every month, so she cannot afford the _____ deluxe toiletries.

(A) luxury　　(B) license
(C) sphere　　(D) spiral

補充
get a salary ph 領薪水

7,000 單字
• salary [`sælərɪ] n ③ 薪水
• luxury [`lʌkʃərɪ] n ④ 奢侈
• license [`laɪsṇs] n ④ 執照
• sphere [sfɪr] n ⑥ 球體
• spiral [`spaɪrəl] n ⑥ 螺旋

中譯｜她每個月領取微薄的薪水，所以買不起那些奢侈的高級盥洗用品。

解說｜四個選項皆為名詞。依據題意，「微薄的薪水」應該與「奢侈的高級盥洗用品」形成對比，構成因果關係，所以選項 (A) luxury 符合題意。

解答&技巧｜ **(A)** 適用 TIP 1　適用 TIP 4

12 He is so experienced in buying and selling stocks that he is bound to make a _____.

(A) sponsor　　(B) decision
(C) stability　　(D) fortune

補充
be bound to ph 必定

7,000 單字
• bound [baʊnd] a ⑥ 必然的
• sponsor [`spɑnsɚ] n ⑥ 贊助商
• decision [dɪ`sɪʒən] n ② 決定
• stability [stə`bɪlətɪ] n ⑥ 穩定性
• fortune [`fɔrtʃən] n ③ 財富

中譯｜他在買賣股票方面經驗很豐富，所以他肯定會發財。

解說｜本題考動詞片語的用法。將四個選項的名詞一一代入空格，選項 (D) fortune 與動詞 make 構成片語 make a fortune，表示「發財」，符合題意，所以選項 (D) 是正確答案。

解答&技巧｜ **(D)** 適用 TIP 2　適用 TIP 11

13 The young man _____ his post as chief editor because of a better job in another company.

(A) retreated   (B) revived

(C) strangled   (D) resigned

補充
chief editor ph 總編輯

7,000 單字
- chief [tʃif] a 1 主要的
- retreat [rɪ'trit] v 4 撤退
- revive [rɪ'vaɪv] v 5 使復興
- strangle ['stræŋgl] v 6 勒死
- resign [rɪ'zaɪn] v 4 辭職

中譯｜這個年輕人之所以辭去總編輯的職位，是因為他在另一家公司找到了更好的工作。

解說｜本題是因果關係句。由後一句的因「在另一家公司找到了更好的工作」，可以推斷出前一句的果「辭去總編輯的職位」，所以選項 (D) resigned 符合題意。

解答&技巧｜**(D)** 適用 TIP 1　適用 TIP 4

---

14 The little boy's quick recovery from the brain surgery has _____ all the doctors and nurses.

(A) suffocated   (B) amazed

(C) terminated   (D) recurred

補充
brain surgery ph 腦部手術

7,000 單字
- nurse [nɝs] n 1 護士
- suffocate ['sʌfə.ket] v 6 使窒息
- amaze [ə'mez] v 3 使吃驚
- terminate ['tɝmə.net] v 6 終止
- recur [rɪ'kɝ] v 6 復發

中譯｜這個小男孩進行了腦部手術，但很快就恢復了健康，這使所有醫生和護士都感到吃驚。

解說｜四個選項皆為動詞。依據題意，應該是快速恢復健康使醫生和護士感到吃驚，選項 (B) amazed 表示「使吃驚」，符合題意。

解答&技巧｜**(B)** 適用 TIP 3　適用 TIP 4

---

15 It is a common _____ to take a bottle of champagne as a gift when you are invited to a dinner.

(A) recipient   (B) courtesy

(C) acceptance   (D) raft

補充
a bottle of ph 一瓶

7,000 單字
- champagne [ʃæm'pen] n 6 香檳
- recipient [rɪ'sɪpɪənt] n 6 領受者
- courtesy ['kɝtəsɪ] n 4 禮貌
- acceptance [ək'sɛptəns] n 4 接受
- raft [ræft] n 6 救生艇

中譯｜你被邀請參加晚宴時，帶一瓶香檳是一個很普遍的禮節。

解說｜四個選項皆為名詞。依據題意，參加晚宴時帶酒是一個禮節，用於表示禮貌，選項 (B) courtesy 表示「禮節」，符合題意，是正確答案。

解答&技巧｜**(B)** 適用 TIP 1　適用 TIP 4

16 Constantly _____ your anti-virus software can prevent your computer from being attacked by new viruses.

(A) presiding

(B) overlooking

(C) esteeming

(D) updating

補充
anti-virus software ph 防毒軟體

7,000 單字
- virus [ˈvaɪrəs] n 4 病毒
- preside [prɪˈzaɪd] v 6 主持
- overlook [ˌovɚˈlʊk] v 4 忽略
- esteem [ɪsˈtim] v 5 尊敬
- update [ʌpˈdet] v 5 更新

中譯 | 不斷更新防毒軟體能夠防止新的病毒攻擊你的電腦。

解說 | 四個選項皆為動詞，將其一一代入可知，應該是「不斷更新防毒軟體」。選項 (D) updating 表示「更新」，符合題意。

解答&技巧 | **(D)** 適用 TIP 4 適用 TIP 11

17 He has invented many new machines and is honored as the most creative and _____ engineer.

(A) pathetic

(B) outright

(C) innovative

(D) presidential

補充
be honored as ph 被譽為

7,000 單字
- engineer [ˌɛndʒəˈnɪr] n 3 工程師
- pathetic [pəˈθɛtɪk] a 6 可憐的
- outright [ˈaʊtˌraɪt] a 6 完全的
- innovative [ˈɪnoˌvetɪv] a 6 革新的
- presidential [ˌprɛzədɛnʃəl] a 6 總統的

中譯 | 他發明了很多新機器，被譽為是最富有創造力和革新精神的工程師。

解說 | 四個選項皆為形容詞。由題目中的「發明了很多新機器」可以推斷出，他是「富有革新精神的」，選項 (C) innovative 能夠表達這一含義，是正確選項。

解答&技巧 | **(C)** 適用 TIP 1 適用 TIP 4

18 This new worker is so _____ that she always breaks bottles when she puts them on the shelves.

(A) religious

(B) visual

(C) clumsy

(D) intimate

補充
break sth. ph 打碎東西

7,000 單字
- shelf [ʃɛlf] n 2 架子
- religious [rɪˈlɪdʒəs] a 3 宗教的
- visual [ˈvɪʒuəl] a 4 視覺的
- clumsy [ˈklʌmzɪ] a 4 笨拙的
- intimate [ˈɪntəmɪt] a 4 親密的

中譯 | 這名新來的工人笨手笨腳的，她總是在將瓶子放到架子上時打碎瓶子。

解說 | 四個選項皆為形容詞。由題目中的「總是打碎瓶子」可以推斷出，這個工人「笨手笨腳」，而選項 (C) clumsy 表示「笨拙的」，符合題意。

解答&技巧 | **(C)** 適用 TIP 1 適用 TIP 4

Part 1
詞彙題
Day 3
完成 25%

Part 2
綜合測驗
Day 3
完成 50%

Part 3
文意選填
Day 3
完成 75%

Part 4
閱讀測驗
Day 3
完成 100%

19 This entrepreneur has made substantial donations to _____ in order to help those poor children.

(A) charity   (B) bulletin

(C) outrage   (D) nominee

> 補充
> make donations to charity
> ph 向慈善團體捐贈

> 7,000 單字
> • entrepreneur [ˌɑntrəprəˋnɜ]
>   n 4 企業家
> • charity [ˋtʃærətɪ] n 4 慈善團體
> • bulletin [ˋbulətɪn] n 4 公告
> • outrage [ˋaut͵redʒ] n 6 憤怒
> • nominee [ˌnɑməˋni] n 6 被提名者

中譯│這名企業家已經做了大量的善捐給慈善團體來幫助那些可憐的孩子。

解說│四個選項皆為名詞，將其一一代入可知，應該是「慈善團體」，選項 (A) charity 表示「慈善團體」，符合題意。

解答&技巧│**(A)** 適用 TIP 1 適用 TIP 4

---

20 This reporter was given _____ of having an interview with the famous enterpriser, which made others quite envious.

(A) mischief   (B) privilege

(C) involvement   (D) nomination

> 補充
> have an interview with ph 採訪

> 7,000 單字
> • enterpriser [ˋɛntɚ͵praɪzɚ]
>   n 5 企業家
> • mischief [ˋmɪstʃɪf] n 4 惡作劇
> • privilege [ˋprɪvlɪdʒ] n 4 特權
> • involvement [ɪnˋvɑlvmənt]
>   n 4 牽連
> • nomination [ˌnɑməˋneʃən]
>   n 6 提名

中譯│這名記者被給予特權採訪那位著名的企業家，這使其他人非常羨慕。

解說│四個選項皆為名詞。依據題意，應該是有特權進行採訪，所以才讓其他人羨慕，選項 (B) privilege 表示「特權」，是正確答案。

解答&技巧│**(B)** 適用 TIP 1 適用 TIP 4

---

21 The tourists enjoyed wholeheartedly the _____ scenery along the coastal highway between Hualien and Ilan. 【93年指考英文】

(A) airtight   (B) breathtaking

(C) sentimental   (D) eccentric

> 補充
> coastal highway ph 海岸公路

> 7,000 單字
> • wholeheartedly [ˌholˋhɑrtɪdlɪ]
>   ad 1 全神貫注地
> • airtight [ˋɛr͵taɪt] a 5 緊密的
> • breathtaking [ˋbrɛθ͵tekɪŋ]
>   a 5 驚人的
> • sentimental [ˌsɛntəˋmɛntl]
>   a 6 傷感的
> • eccentric [ɪkˋsɛntrɪk] a 6 古怪的

中譯│遊客們沿著花蓮與宜蘭之間的濱海公路全神貫注地欣賞著令人驚歎的美景。

解說│四個選項皆為形容詞，將其一一代入可知，應該是「令人驚歎的美景」，選項 (B) breathtaking 表示「驚人的」，符合題意。

解答&技巧│**(B)** 適用 TIP 1 適用 TIP 4

22 To these sportsmen, winning the match is the primary task, and the others are all _____.

(A) notorious   (B) secondary

(C) notable   (D) mournful

中譯｜對於這些運動員來說，贏得比賽是首要任務，其他的都是次要的。

解說｜四個選項皆為形容詞。依據題意，the match 與 the others 形成對比，所以形容詞 primary 應該與空格處的形容詞形成對比，選項 (B) secondary 表示「次要的」，符合題意。

解答＆技巧｜**(B)** 〔適用 TIP 1〕〔適用 TIP 4〕

> 〔補充〕
> primary task ph 首要任務
> 〔7,000 單字〕
> - sportsman [ˈsportsmən] n 4 運動員
> - notorious [noˈtorɪəs] a 6 聲名狼藉的
> - secondary [ˈsɛkənˌdɛrɪ] a 3 次要的
> - notable [ˈnotəbl] a 5 顯著的
> - mournful [ˈmornfəl] a 6 悲哀的

---

23 After we passed through a long and narrow _____ by train, we saw a beautiful village.

(A) mouthpiece   (B) temple

(C) tunnel   (D) channel

中譯｜我們坐火車穿過一條狹長的隧道後，就看到了一座漂亮的村莊。

解說｜四個選項皆為名詞。依據題意，應該是「火車通過了隧道」，選項 (C) tunnel 表示「隧道」，符合題意，其他三個選項都不符合題意。

解答＆技巧｜**(C)** 〔適用 TIP 3〕〔適用 TIP 4〕

> 〔補充〕
> pass through ph 穿過
> 〔7,000 單字〕
> - we [wi] pron 1 我們
> - mouthpiece [ˈmauθˌpis] n 6 代言人
> - temple [ˈtɛmpl] n 2 寺廟
> - tunnel [ˈtʌnl] n 2 隧道
> - channel [ˈtʃænl] n 3 海峽

---

24 Water pollution has caused serious environmental damage, so we should take measures to _____ it.

(A) haste   (B) retain

(C) refresh   (D) remedy

中譯｜水污染引起了嚴重的環境破壞，所以我們應該採取措施來補救。

解說｜四個選項皆為動詞。依據題意，應該是「採取措施來補救」，選項 (D) remedy 表示「補救」，符合題意，其他三個選項都不符合題意。

解答＆技巧｜**(D)** 〔適用 TIP 1〕〔適用 TIP 4〕

> 〔補充〕
> environmental damage ph 環境破壞
> 〔7,000 單字〕
> - should [ʃud] aux 1 應該
> - haste [hest] v 4 趕快
> - retain [rɪˈten] v 4 保持
> - refresh [rɪˈfrɛʃ] v 4 更新
> - remedy [ˈrɛmədɪ] v 4 補救

DAY 3

Part 1 詞彙題
Day 3 完成 25%

Part 2 綜合測驗
Day 3 完成 50%

Part 3 文意選填
Day 3 完成 75%

Part 4 閱讀測驗
Day 3 完成 100%

Part 2 綜合測驗 | Comprehensive Questions

Many students find that __01__ university courses is very confusing and frustrating because the course generally lasts for one or two hours, and the teacher usually illustrates the talk with slides, writes up some important information on the blackboard, distributes reading materials or gives assignments to the students. Some students often __02__ write on notebooks in classes, but when they leaves the classes, they may find that they cannot understand what they have written and even catch the __03__ points.

Most universities would provide courses which teach the skills that the students need to help them be effective. For example, most students have difficulty in __04__ the language skills required in college study; thus they must take measures to tackle the problem. One way to __05__ the difficulties is to attend the language skills classes which most colleges provide during the academic year, and the other is to find a study partner with whom you could exchange ideas and share progress.

01 _____ (A) extending   (B) performing
         (C) attending   (D) attributing

02 _____ (A) continuously   (B) normally
         (C) logically   (D) repeatedly

03 _____ (A) entry   (B) delivery
         (C) main   (D) neutral

04 _____ (A) preventing   (B) acquiring
         (C) withstanding   (D) sustaining

05 _____ (A) acknowledge   (B) argue
         (C) predict   (D) overcome

DAY
3

Part 1
詞彙題
Day 3
完成 25%

Part 2
綜合測驗
Day 3
完成 50%

Part 3
文意選填
Day 3
完成 75%

Part 4
閱讀測驗
Day 3
完成 100%

中譯｜許多學生發現參加大學課程非常令人困惑，也令人沮喪，因為課程通常會持續一至兩個小時，老師經常用幻燈片來舉例說明所說的內容，在黑板上詳細記載一些重要資訊，分發閱讀材料或是出作業給學生們。課堂上，一些學生經常不停地在筆記本上寫東西，但是下課時，他們會發現他們不理解自己都寫了些什麼，甚至無法抓住要點。

許多大學會為學生提供課程，教授他們所需的技能來幫助他們變得有效率。例如，大多數學生在獲取大學課程所需的語言技能時都會遇到困難，這樣他們就必須採取措施來處理困難。一種克服困難的方法是參加大學在學年裡所提供的語言技能課程，而另一種方法是尋找一位學習夥伴，你可以和他一起交流想法、分享學習進度。

解說｜本篇短文的主旨是「大學課程」，主要講述了有效學習大學課程的方法。第 1 題要選擇合適的動詞，而四個選項之所以都用現在分詞，是因為在句中作主詞。根據所學知識，表示「參加課程」時，要用動詞 attend，所以正確選擇為 (C)。第 2 題的四個選項都是副詞。將四個選項一一代入可知，continuously 表示「連續不斷地」符合題意，所以最佳選項是 (A)。第 3 題主要考名詞片語的固定搭配。根據所學的知識，「要點」為 main point，即正確選項是 (C)。第 4 題將四個選項一一代入可知，acquiring 表示「習得，獲得」，在文中符合題意，所以只有選項 (B) 符合題意。第 5 題要選擇合適的動詞。依據題意，「克服困難」為 overcome the difficulties，要用動詞 overcome，所以選 (D)。

解答 & 技巧｜ 01 **(C)** 02 **(A)** 03 **(C)** 04 **(B)** 05 **(D)**

適用 TIP 1　適用 TIP 2　適用 TIP 4　適用 TIP 11

補充

confusing ⓐ 困惑的；frustrating ⓐ 沮喪的；reading materials ⓟʰ 閱讀材料；give an assignment ⓟʰ 出作業；language skills ⓟʰ 語言能力

7,000 單字

- university [ˌjunəˋvɝsətɪ] ⓝ 4 大學
- course [kors] ⓝ 1 課程
- illustrate [ˋɪləstret] ⓥ 4 舉例說明
- blackboard [ˋblækˌbord] ⓝ 2 黑板
- notebook [ˋnotˌbʊk] ⓝ 2 筆記本
- catch [kætʃ] ⓥ 1 理解
- point [pɔɪnt] ⓝ 1 要點
- effective [ɪˋfɛktɪv] ⓐ 2 有效的

- tackle [ˋtækl] ⓥ 5 處理
- difficulty [ˋdɪfəˌkʌltɪ] ⓝ 2 困難
- exchange [ɪksˋtʃendʒ] ⓝ 3 交換
- extend [ɪkˋstɛnd] ⓥ 4 延長
- delivery [dɪˋlɪvərɪ] ⓝ 3 遞送
- neutral [ˋnjutrəl] ⓐ 6 中立的
- predict [prɪˋdɪkt] ⓥ 4 預言

Whether children, adults, or even elders, people all use language as a 01 to broaden their knowledge and the world around. New born babies are not able to use this valuable tool. But 02 language develops and humans evolve, the possibilities for people's future attainments and cultural growth have increased.

Many linguists 03 our ability to produce and use language to evolution. They claim that we possess an innate language ability provided by our highly evolved brain, but the lower organisms do not. People who are in 04 of this innateness theory say that our organization for language is inborn as a function of the brain, though the language itself has developed gradually.

Nowadays, more and more schools have discovered that it is best to teach the students foreign languages when they are in the lower grades, because young children can often learn several languages easily, while adults have to spend more time in 05 another language, especially when the rules of their first language have become quite fixed.

01 _____ (A) group   (B) constitution
         (C) formation   (D) means

02 _____ (A) with   (B) as
         (C) when   (D) after

03 _____ (A) attribute   (B) confirm
         (C) convince   (D) inform

04 _____ (A) honor   (B) ignorance
         (C) support   (D) advance

05 _____ (A) learn   (B) learning
         (C) learned   (D) to learn

中譯｜不管是小孩、大人，或甚至是老人，人們都把語言當做一種工具來擴展知識以及周圍的世界。新生兒不會使用這種重要的工具。但是隨著語言的發展以及人類的進化，人們成就未來以及取得文化發展的可能性已經有所增加。

許多語言學家將我們創作以及使用語言的能力歸因於進化。他們聲稱我們擁有高度進化的大腦提供我們先天語言能力，但是低等生物卻沒有這種能力。支持這種天賦論的人們說，儘管語言本身已經在逐步發展，但是我們的語言組織天生就是大腦的一種功能。

如今，愈來愈多的學校發現，最好在低年級就教授學生們外語，因為幼兒通常可以輕易地學好幾種語言，而成年人卻必須花費更多的時間來學習另外一種語言，特別是當他們的母語規則變得十分牢固。

解說｜本篇短文的主旨是「語言」，答題時可以將語言的特點和用法考慮在內。第 1 題的四個選項都是名詞。依據題意可知，語言應該是擴展知識的一種工具，即 means，所以正確選擇為 (D)。第 2 題所在的句子是一個伴隨副詞子句，根據所學的語法知識，應該用 as 來表示「隨著」，所以最符合題意的選項是 (B)。第 3 題考動詞片語的固定搭配。根據上下文的內容可知，題意應該是將創作以及使用語言的能力歸因於進化，要用動詞 attribute 與介系詞 to 搭配，所以正確選項是 (A)。第 4 題根據上下文的內容可知，選項前後所說的情況是一致的，所以提到的科學家是支持這一理論的，要用 in support of 表示「支持」，只有選項 (C) 符合題意。第 5 題考動詞 spend 的用法。spend 後面接介系詞 in 時，其後的動詞要用動名詞，即 learning，所以選 (B)。

解答＆技巧｜ 01 (D)　 02 (B)　 03 (A)　 04 (C)　 05 (B)

　　適用 TIP 1　適用 TIP 2　適用 TIP 4　適用 TIP 7

補充
newborn ⓐ 新生的；linguist ⓝ 語言學家；innate ⓐ 先天的；innateness ⓝ 天賦；inborn ⓐ 天生的

7,000 單字
- adult [ə`dʌlt] ⓝ ❶ 成年人
- even [`ivən] ⓐⓓ ❶ 甚至
- knowledge [`nɑlɪdʒ] ⓝ ❷ 知識
- tool [tul] ⓝ ❶ 工具
- produce [prə`djus] ⓥ ❷ 生產
- claim [klem] ⓥ ❷ 聲稱
- organism [`ɔrgən,ɪzm] ⓝ ❻ 生物體
- organization [,ɔrgənə`zeʃən] ⓝ ❷ 組織

- discover [dɪs`kʌvə] ⓥ ❶ 發現
- grade [gred] ⓝ ❷ 等級
- quite [kwaɪt] ⓐⓓ ❶ 相當
- formation [fɔr`meʃən] ⓝ ❹ 形成
- convince [kən`vɪns] ⓥ ❹ 說服
- ignorance [`ɪgnərəns] ⓝ ❸ 無知
- advance [əd`væns] ⓝ ❷ 發展

DAY 3

Part 1
詞彙題
Day 3
完成 25%

Part 2
綜合測驗
Day 3
完成 50%

Part 3
文意選填
Day 3
完成 75%

Part 4
閱讀測驗
Day 3
完成 100%

3 ▶ 94 年指考英文

Today, with a couple of clicks, you can go anywhere in the world without leaving your computer. So it should come as little __01__ that the Internet has headlined the top 25 innovations of the past quarter century, according to a panel of technology leaders assembling to promote inventiveness. In creating the list, the group __02__ twenty-five non-medically related technological innovations that have become widely used since 1980. These innovations are readily recognizable by most Americans, have had a direct impact on our everyday lives, and may also dramatically affect our lives __03__. The top innovation, the Web, was created by British software consultant Tim Berners-Lee. __04__ by a multitude of information systems requiring complicated access, Berners-Lee fashioned a universal one that made information readily __05__. He created HTML (hypertext markup language) and its rule of usage (HTTP, hypertext transfer protocol). In 1991 he unveiled the World Wide Web. Today, this No. 1 invention has become so commonplace that it is almost taken for granted.

01 _____ (A) agreement (B) surprise
(C) belief (D) concern

02 _____ (A) gives in (B) takes over
(C) singles out (D) turns down

03 _____ (A) for a moment (B) at that time
(C) from then on (D) in the future

04 _____ (A) Having frustrated (B) Frustrated
(C) To be frustrated (D) Been frustrated

05 _____ (A) available (B) consistent
(C) important (D) unforgettable

中譯｜如今，只要點擊幾下，你無需離開電腦就能夠暢遊世界。聚集商討如何推進創造力發展的一組科技領導人說，網路已名列過去二十五年裡排名前二十五項創新發明之首，這一點都不令人驚奇。在列清單時，小組人員就挑選出了從一九八〇年開始就被廣泛運用的二十五項非醫學相關的技術創新。這些創新很快地被大多數美國人認可，對我們的日常生活造成了直接影響，也可能大幅地影響我們未來的生活。名列第一的發明是由英國的軟體顧問提姆‧伯納－李所開發的全球資訊網。因為許多資訊系統進入取得的方式都很繁雜，伯納－李曾為此感到沮喪。他設計了一套通用系統，使獲取資訊變得十分便捷。他創立了 HTML（超文字標示語言）以及其使用規則 HTTP（超文字傳輸協定）。一九九一年，他公開了全球資訊網。如今，這項名列第一的發明已經變得普遍到人們覺得理所當然。

解說｜本篇短文主要介紹了網路技術的發明以及應用。第 1 題的四個選項都是名詞。將四個選項一一代入可知，只有 surprise 符合題意，所以正確選擇為 (B)。第 2 題主要考動詞片語的用法。依據題意可知，應該選擇 singles out 表示「挑選」，所以最符合題意的選項是 (C)。第 3 題句中的 may 表示「可能，也許」，說明未來的情況，所以時間副詞要選擇 in the future 表示「將來」，即正確選項是 (D)。第 4 題句中的介系詞 by 表示原因，而 frustrated 與主詞 Berners-Lee 之間是主動關係，所以只有選項 (B) 符合題意。第 5 題的四個選項都是形容詞，將其一一代入可知，information 應該是「可以使用」，要用 available 來表示，所以選 (A)。

解答＆技巧｜ 01 **(B)** 02 **(C)** 03 **(D)** 04 **(B)** 05 **(A)**

適用 TIP 1　適用 TIP 2　適用 TIP 7　適用 TIP 11

> **補充**
>
> inventiveness n 有創造力；British a 英國的；hypertext n 超文字；markup language ph 標示語言；protocol n 協議

> **7,000 單字**
>
> - today [tə`de] ad 1 現今
> - click [klɪk] n 3 點擊
> - computer [kəm`pjutɚ] n 2 電腦
> - panel [`pænl] n 4 專門小組
> - assemble [ə`sɛmbl] v 4 聚集
> - innovation [ˌɪnə`veʃən] n 6 創新
> - affect [ə`fɛkt] v 3 影響
> - software [`sɔftˌwɛr] n 4 軟體
>
> - consultant [kən`sʌltənt] n 4 顧問
> - access [`æksɛs] n 4 進入
> - usage [`jusɪdʒ] n 4 使用
> - commonplace [`kɑmənˌples] a 5 平凡的
> - almost [`ɔlˌmost] ad 1 幾乎
> - belief [bɪ`lif] n 2 信賴
> - concern [kən`sɜn] n 3 關心

DAY 3

Part 1
詞彙題
Day 3
完成 25%

Part 2
綜合測驗
Day 3
完成 50%

Part 3
文意選填
Day 3
完成 75%

Part 4
閱讀測驗
Day 3
完成 100%

A great change has come to the shopping habits in the United States of the last century. Early in the 1900s, nearly every American town and city had a Main Street which was always in the heart. There, shoppers could walk into the stores to look at all __01__ of merchandise, including clothing, furniture, hardware and groceries. In addition, some other shops, such as drugstores, restaurants and hairdressing shops, would also __02__ services.

But in the 1950s, things began to change. With more and more automobiles __03__ into Main Street, fewer parking spaces were available to shoppers. Under the __04__ the merchants began to take an interest in the open spaces outside the city because open space was much-needed for the car-driving customers. Therefore, shopping centers which were far away from crowded city centers and with plenty of free parking __05__ were built and attracted thousands of customers. Later on, many shopping centers gradually developed into small cities themselves.

01 _____ (A) sorts   (B) genders
          (C) unions   (D) conditions

02 _____ (A) design   (B) abandon
          (C) offer   (D) waive

03 _____ (A) dipping   (B) crowding
          (C) merging   (D) blundering

04 _____ (A) guns   (B) influences
          (C) hammers   (D) circumstances

05 _____ (A) spaces   (B) orbits
          (C) stickers   (D) terraces

DAY
3

Part 1
詞彙題
Day 3
完成 25%

Part 2
綜合測驗
Day 3
完成 50%

Part 3
文意選填
Day 3
完成 75%

Part 4
閱讀測驗
Day 3
完成 100%

中譯｜上個世紀，美國人的購物習慣發生了很大變化。二十世紀初期，幾乎美國的每一個城鎮和都市的中心都有一個大街。在那裡，購物者可以走進商店，瀏覽包括服裝、傢具、五金器具和雜貨在內的各種各樣的商品。此外，一些其他的商店，如藥妝店、餐廳和美髮店也會提供服務。

但是在二十世紀五〇年代，這種情況發生了變化。隨著愈來愈多的汽車湧入大街，可供購物者使用的停車位變得更少，在這種情況下，商人們開始對城外的空地感興趣，因為駕車的顧客急需空地。因此，遠離擁擠的市中心且帶有免費停車位的購物中心得以建造，並且吸引了成千上萬的顧客。後來，許多購物中心自己逐漸發展成為小型城市。

解說｜本篇短文的主旨是「美國人的購物習慣」，答題時可以將美國社會的發展過程以及文化特點考慮在內。第 1 題考介系詞片語的固定用法。依據題意可知，「所有種類」可以表達為 all sorts of，所以正確選擇為 (A)。第 2 題的四個選項都是動詞，將其一一代入可知，「提供服務」可以表達為 offer services，最符合題意的選項是 (C)。第 3 題主要考與介系詞 into 搭配的動詞的用法。根據上下文的內容可知，crowding into 表示「湧入，擠入」，最符合題意，所以正確選項是 (B)。第 4 題考固定片語作副詞的用法。「在這種情況下」可以表達為 under the circumstances，在句中作副詞，所以只有選項 (D) 符合題意。第 5 題考名詞片語的用法。「停車位」為 a parking space，文章裡為複數，要用 spaces 表示，所以選 (A)。

解答＆技巧｜01 (A)　02 (C)　03 (B)　04 (D)　05 (A)
適用 TIP 1　適用 TIP 2　適用 TIP 7　適用 TIP 11

補充
shopping habits ph 購物習慣；American a 美國的；hairdressing n 美髮；Main Street ph 主街；crowded a 擁擠的

7,000 單字
- change [tʃendʒ] n 2 變化
- nearly [ˋnɪrlɪ] ad 2 幾乎
- street [strit] n 1 街道
- hardware [ˋhɑrd͵wɛr] n 4 五金器具
- restaurant [ˋrɛstərənt] n 2 餐廳
- available [əˋveləbl] a 3 可利用的
- merchant [ˋmɝtʃənt] n 3 商人
- customer [ˋkʌstəmə] n 2 顧客
- center [ˋsɛntə] n 1 中心
- plenty [ˋplɛntɪ] n 3 大量
- union [ˋjunjən] n 4 聯合
- abandon [əˋbændən] v 4 遺棄
- merge [mɝdʒ] v 6 合併
- orbit [ˋɔrbɪt] n 4 軌道
- terrace [ˋtɛrəs] n 5 梯田

As far as we know, music has many forms, and most countries have music __01__ of their own. But when jazz was born, America had no prominent music style yet. People didn't know when jazz was invented or by whom, only knowing that it was heard __02__ the first time in the early 1900s. Classical music follows formal European traditions, but jazz is spontaneous and free in form which bubbles with energy and expresses the moods, interests, and emotions of the people.

It is said that African slaves in America were the jazz pioneers. At the beginning they were brought to Southern States as slaves, and those plantation owners always __03__ them to work long hours. When the slaves died, their friends and relatives would form processions to carry the body to the cemetery, __04__ by a band. On the way to the cemetery the band would play slow and solemn music, but on the return __05__ the melody of the music turned to be happy and joyful, which made everyone want to dance. And it was the early form of jazz.

01 _____ (A) discoveries   (B) resources
         (C) styles   (D) originals

02 _____ (A) for   (B) to
         (C) with   (D) up

03 _____ (A) demonstrated   (B) composed
         (C) hosted   (D) forced

04 _____ (A) whistled   (B) accompanied
         (C) presented   (D) showed

05 _____ (A) commission   (B) mechanism
         (C) load   (D) journey

中譯 | 據我們所知，音樂有多種形式，並且大多數國家都有其各自的音樂風格。但是當爵士樂產生時，美國卻還沒有比較顯著的音樂風格。人們不知道爵士樂是在什麼時候由誰發明的，只知道首次聽到爵士樂是在二十世紀初期。古典音樂遵循刻板的歐洲傳統，但是爵士樂是一種自發的自由形式，它充滿了活力，表達人們的情緒、興趣以及情感。

據說，美國黑奴是爵士樂的創始人。起初，他們被當做奴隸帶到美國南方諸州，那些莊園園主經常迫使他們長時間地工作。黑奴死後，他們的朋友和親屬會組成隊伍，將遺體帶到基地，還有一個樂隊相伴。在去基地的途中，樂隊會演奏緩慢而莊嚴的音樂，但是在回程中，音樂的旋律變得歡快愉悦，使得每個人都想跳舞。這就是爵士樂的早期形式。

解說 | 本篇短文主要介紹了爵士樂的特色以及發展過程。第 1 題的四個選項都是名詞，將其一一代入可知，只有 style 與 music 搭配構成 music style 表示「音樂風格」，符合題意，所以正確選擇為 (C)。第 2 題主要考介系詞片語的固定用法。依據題意，「第一次」可以表達為 for the first time，要用介系詞 for 來引導，所以最符合題意的選項是 (A)。第 3 題將四個動詞選項一一代入可知，只有 forced 表示「強迫」符合題意，所以正確選項是 (D)。第 4 題所在的句子在文中作伴隨副詞，依據題意，accompanied 表示被動，且與介系詞 by 搭配表示「由～陪同」，只有選項 (B) 符合題意。第 5 題主要考名詞片語的用法。根據所學的知識，「回程」可以表達為 return journey，名詞 journey 符合題意，所以選 (D)。

解答＆技巧 | 01 (C)　02 (A)　03 (D)　04 (B)　05 (D)

適用 TIP 1　適用 TIP 2　適用 TIP 4　適用 TIP 11

補充
America n. 美國；African a. 非裔的；at the beginning ph. 起初；Southern States ph. 南方諸州；
on the way to ph. 去～的路上

7,000 單字

- music [ˈmjuzɪk] n. 1 音樂
- style [staɪl] n. 3 風格
- jazz [dʒæz] n. 2 爵士樂
- invent [ɪnˈvɛnt] v. 2 發明
- formal [ˈfɔrml] a. 2 正式的
- spontaneous [spanˈtenɪəs] a. 6 自發的
- bubble [ˈbʌbl] v. 3 沸騰
- energy [ˈɛnədʒɪ] n. 2 活力

- slave [slev] n. 3 奴隸
- procession [prəˈsɛʃən] n. 5 隊伍
- solemn [ˈsɑləm] a. 5 莊嚴的
- original [əˈrɪdʒənl] n. 3 原型
- whistle [ˈhwɪsl] v. 3 吹口哨
- commission [kəˈmɪʃən] n. 5 委員會
- mechanism [ˈmɛkəˌnɪzəm] n. 6 機制

DAY 3

Part 1
詞彙題
Day 3
完成 25%

Part 2
綜合測驗
Day 3
完成 50%

Part 3
文意選填
Day 3
完成 75%

Part 4
閱讀測驗
Day 3
完成 100%

There are two kinds of words in every language. Taken together, they will __01__ the whole vocabulary. Those words that we learn from the members of our family or familiar associates and are generally used in daily __02__ are called "popular words." They concern the common things of life. Even if we could not read or write, we should know them correctly. They belong to the people of the whole world and are not the exclusive share of certain individuals.

On the other hand, there are also some other words that we __03__ seldom used in daily conversations. These words are called "learned words." They are learned not from our families or other people, but from books we read or lectures we attend. Nearly every __04__ person knows their meanings, but they will not use these words at home or in the marketplace. The biggest difference between these two kinds of words __05__ in the right understanding of linguistic process and the usage occasion.

01 _____ (A) compose　　　　　(B) hire
　　　　　 (C) adopt　　　　　　 (D) apply

02 _____ (A) wages　　　　　　(B) inspections
　　　　　 (C) telegraphs　　　　 (D) conversations

03 _____ (A) formally　　　　　(B) comparatively
　　　　　 (C) principally　　　　 (D) primarily

04 _____ (A) legal　　　　　　 (B) national
　　　　　 (C) educated　　　　　(D) qualified

05 _____ (A) takes　　　　　　 (B) lies
　　　　　 (C) adepts　　　　　　(D) gets

DAY
3

Part 1
詞
彙
題
Day 3
完成 25%

Part 2
綜
合
測
驗
Day 3
完成 50%

Part 3
文
意
選
填
Day 3
完成 75%

Part 4
閱
讀
測
驗
Day 3
完成 100%

中譯｜每一種語言中都有兩種單詞。把它們放在一起，就構成了完整的詞彙。那些我們從家人或是熟悉的同伴那裡學到的詞彙叫做「流行語」。它們通常用於日常會話，涉及到生活中的普通事物，即使我們不會讀寫，我們也應該正確地了解它們。它們屬於全世界的人類，而不屬於某個個體獨有。

另一方面，還有其他一些詞，我們相對地在平常的會話中很少使用。這些詞被稱為「書面詞」。這些詞不是透過我們的家人或是其他人學到，而是從我們所讀的書本或參加的課程中學到的。幾乎每一個受過教育的人都知道它們的含義，但是他們不會在家裡或是市場使用這些詞。這兩種詞彙之間最大的區別在於正確理解語言過程以及使用場合。

解說｜本篇短文的主旨是「詞彙的構成」，講述了詞彙的組成類別以及使用方法。第1題依據題意，要用動詞 compose 來表示「構成」，所以正確選擇為 (A)。第 2 題的四個選項都是名詞，將其一一代入可知，daily conversations 表示「日常會話」，最符合題意，所以最佳選項是 (D)。第 3 題要選擇合適的副詞。將四個選項的副詞一一代入可知，只有 comparatively 表示「相對來說」符合題意，即正確選項是 (B)。第 4 題依據題意可知，了解單字含義的人肯定是受過教育的人，要用 educated 表示「受教育的」來修飾 person，所以只有選項 (C) 符合題意。第 5 題主要考動詞片語的用法。根據上下文的內容可知，lie in 表示「在於」，最符合題意，所以選 (B)。

解答＆技巧｜ 01 (A)　02 (D)　03 (B)　04 (C)　05 (B)

適用 TIP 1　適用 TIP 2　適用 TIP 4　適用 TIP 11

補充

even if [ph] 即便；on the other hand [ph] 另一方面；daily conversation [ph] 日常談話；marketplace [n] 市場；linguistic [a] 語言學的

7,000 單字

- together [tə`gɛðɚ] [ad] ① 一起
- vocabulary [və`kæbjəˌlɛrɪ] [n] ② 詞彙
- member [`mɛmbɚ] [n] ② 成員
- family [`fæməlɪ] [n] ① 家庭
- associate [ə`soʃɪˌet] [n] ④ 夥伴
- write [raɪt] [v] ① 寫
- individual [ˌɪndə`vɪdʒʊəl] [n] ③ 個人
- lecture [`lɛktʃɚ] [n] ④ 演講

- attend [ə`tɛnd] [v] ② 參加
- occasion [ə`keʒən] [n] ③ 場合
- compose [kəm`poz] [v] ④ 組成
- hire [haɪr] [v] ② 雇用
- apply [ə`plaɪ] [v] ② 申請
- wage [wedʒ] [n] ③ 薪資
- legal [`ligl] [a] ② 合法的

7 ▶ 95 年學測英文

Dear Son,

I am very happy to hear that you are doing well in school. However, I am very concerned with the way you __01__ money. I understand that college students like to __02__ parties, movies, and lots of activities, but you also have to learn how to do without certain things. After all, you must live within a limited budget.

__03__ the extra money you want for this month, I am sorry that I have decided not to send it to you because I think it is time for you to learn how to live without my help. If I give you a hand every time you have problems with money now, what will you do when you no longer have me to support you? Besides, I remember telling you I used to have two part-time jobs when I was in college just to __04__. So, if you need money now, you should try either finding a job or cutting down on your __05__.

I understand it is not easy to live on your own. But learning to budget your money is the first lesson you must learn to be independent. Good luck, son. And remember: never spend more than you earn.

Love,

Mom

01 _____ (A) manage   (B) restrict
           (C) charge   (D) deposit

02 _____ (A) indulge in   (B) dwell in
           (C) attend to   (D) apply to

03 _____ (A) Regarded   (B) To regard
           (C) Being regarded   (D) Regarding

04 _____ (A) catch up   (B) get my way
           (C) keep in touch   (D) make ends meet

05 _____ (A) spirits   (B) expenses
           (C) savings   (D) estimates

中譯｜親愛的兒子：

聽說你在學校表現良好，我很高興。但是，我非常關心你的理財方法。我理解大學生喜歡沉溺於聚會、看電影以及許多活動，但是你也得學習如何在沒有這些活動的情況下生活。畢竟，你的生活預算非常有限。

關於這個月你額外要求的錢，抱歉我已經決定不寄給你，因為我想是時候讓你學著在沒有我的幫助下生活。如果現在每一次你遇到資金困難，我都對你施以援手，那麼我不再支援你時，你該怎麼辦呢？此外，我記得告訴過你，我上大學時經常做兩份兼職工作來平衡收支。因此，如果你現在需要錢，你可以嘗試著找一份工作或者削減你的開支。

我明白獨立生活並不容易，但是學習預算開支是你學會獨立的第一門必修課。祝你好運，兒子。要記得：絕對不要花得比賺得多。

愛你的媽媽

解說｜這是媽媽寫給兒子的一封信，就兒子理財方面的事宜提出建議。第 1 題的四個選項都是動詞。根據上下文的內容可知，「理財」可以表達為 manage money，要用動詞 manage，所以正確選擇為 (A)。第 2 題考動詞片語的用法。將四個片語一一代入文中可知，indulge in 表示「沉溺於」，符合題意，而其他選項皆不符合題意，所以最佳選項是 (A)。第 3 題選項所在的句子在文中作伴隨副詞，且表主動，所以動詞 regard 要用現在分詞 regarding 表示「關於」，即正確選項是 (D)。第 4 題也是考動詞片語的用法。將四個選項一一代入可知，make ends meet 表示「平衡收支」，符合題意，所以選項 (D) 符合題意。第 5 題要選擇合適的名詞。依據題意，expense 表示「花費」，符合題意，所以選 (B)。

解答&技巧｜ 01 (A)　02 (A)　03 (D)　04 (D)　05 (B)

適用 TIP 1　適用 TIP 2　適用 TIP 7　適用 TIP 11

補充

concerned a 擔心的；without one's help ph 沒有某人的幫助；part-time a 兼職的；
on one's own ph 依靠某人自己；learn to do sth. ph 學會做某事

7,000 單字

- hear [hɪr] v 1 聽
- school [skul] n 1 學校
- money [ˋmʌnɪ] n 1 錢
- college [ˋkɑlɪdʒ] n 3 大學
- movie [ˋmuvɪ] n 1 電影
- budget [ˋbʌdʒɪt] n 3 預算
- month [mʌnθ] n 1 月
- support [səˋport] v 2 支持

- either [ˋiðɚ] conj 1 或者
- lesson [ˋlɛsn̩] n 1 課
- manage [ˋmænɪdʒ] v 3 管理
- deposit [dɪˋpɑzɪt] v 5 存（錢）
- indulge [ɪnˋdʌldʒ] v 5 沉溺
- expense [ɪkˋspɛns] n 3 花費
- estimate [ˋɛstəˏmet] n 4 估計

Nowadays, cars have become the most popular sort of transportation and have completely __01__ horses as a means of everyday transportation in America. According to statistics, most of the Americans are able to buy cars, and they use cars nearly in each __02__ of the everyday life. The average price of the car has increased with the development of the economy. American car manufacturers have been always trying to improve their products and work __03__ , and as a result, the yearly income of the American family has increased faster than the price of cars. Therefore, an American family only needs to pay a small part of their total __04__ for a new car. In addition, most of the cars are __05__ superior to the models manufactured from previous years; thus the influence of the automobile on America is as important as that of the economy, and Americans also spend more money on their cars than other things.

01 _____ (A) denied   (B) ridiculed
         (C) classified   (D) replaced

02 _____ (A) personnel   (B) field
         (C) percentage   (D) family

03 _____ (A) influence   (B) expectation
         (C) efficiency   (D) excursion

04 _____ (A) earnings   (B) propositions
         (C) predictions   (D) deviances

05 _____ (A) suddenly   (B) proportionally
         (C) technically   (D) regularly

中譯｜如今在美國，汽車已經成為最流行的運輸方式，也完全代替馬匹作為一種日常的交通工具。據統計，大多數美國人都能夠購買汽車，幾乎用於日常生活的每個領域。隨著經濟的發展，汽車的平均價格有所提升。美國的汽車製造商一直試圖提升他們產品和工作效率，使美國家庭的年收入要比汽車價格增得更快。因此，一個美國家庭只需要花費總收入的一小部分就可以購買汽車。此外，大多數汽車在技術上要比早些年生產的汽車更好，所以汽車對美國造成的影響與經濟造成的影響同等重要，相比於其他事物，美國人也花費更多的錢在汽車上。

解說｜本篇短文的主旨是「美國的汽車」，答題時可以將美國的經濟情況和工業發展考慮在內。第 1 題的四個選項都是動詞。依據題意，汽車取代馬作為一種交通工具，要用 replace 表示「取代」，所以正確選擇為 (D)。第 2 題要選擇合適的名詞。依據題意，「領域」可以用 field 來表達，所以最符合題意的選項是 (B)。第 3 題主要考名詞片語的用法。依據題意，「工作效率」可以表達為 work efficiency，即正確選項是 (C)。第 4 題的四個選項都是名詞。根據上下文的內容可知，「總收入」可以表達為 total earnings，所以只有選項 (A) 符合題意。第 5 題要選擇合適的副詞。將四個選項的副詞一一代入可知，只有 technically 表示「技術上」符合題意，所以選 (C)。

解答＆技巧｜ 01 **(D)** 　 02 **(B)** 　 03 **(C)** 　 04 **(A)** 　 05 **(C)**

適用 TIP 1 　 適用 TIP 2 　 適用 TIP 4 　 適用 TIP 11

補充

everyday ⓐ 日常的；as a means of ⓟⓗ 作為～的工具；with the development of ⓟⓗ 隨著～的發展；as... as ⓟⓗ 和～一樣；spend money on... ⓟⓗ 把錢花在～上

7,000 單字

- car [kɑr] ⓝ ① 汽車
- transportation [ˌtrænspɚˈteʃən] ⓝ ④ 運輸
- statistics [stəˈtɪstɪks] ⓝ ⑤ 統計
- able [ˈebl] ⓐ ① 有能力的
- life [laɪf] ⓝ ① 生活
- average [ˈævərɪdʒ] ⓐ ③ 平均的
- economy [ɪˈkɑnəmɪ] ⓝ ④ 經濟
- improve [ɪmˈpruv] ⓥ ② 改善

- product [ˈprɑdəkt] ⓝ ③ 產品
- income [ˈɪnˌkʌm] ⓝ ② 收入
- manufacture [ˌmænjəˈfæktʃɚ] ⓥ ④ 製造
- automobile [ˈɔtəməˌbil] ⓝ ③ 汽車
- personnel [ˌpɜsṇˈɛl] ⓝ ⑤ 人事部門
- earnings [ˈɜnɪŋz] ⓝ ③ 收入
- prediction [prɪˈdɪkʃən] ⓝ ⑥ 預報

DAY 3

Part 1
詞彙題
Day 3
完成 25%

Part 2
綜合測驗
Day 3
完成 50%

Part 3
文意選填
Day 3
完成 75%

Part 4
閱讀測驗
Day 3
完成 100%

9 ▶ 92 年指考英文

People usually regard marriage as a formal contract which should be noted, but the form of this contract could be different in different societies. For example, in Western societies, a man and a woman should go to an official recognized by the state for **01** in order that they could be given the status of legal marriage. However, in some African societies, marriage is **02** by formally exchanging goods instead of official registration. In general, the bridegroom has **03** to make a payment of goods to the bride's kin, but sometimes it is the bridegroom's kin that make a payment to the bride.

Nuer is a people living in Southern Sudan, and in this people, bride **04**, which is the payment made to the bride's kin is in the form of cattles. After the amount of bride wealth is **05** upon, and the formal payment is made, the marriage between the bridegroom and his bride should become legal, and their offspring of them will also become acceptable.

01 _____ (A) communication (B) registration
(C) connection (D) contemplation

02 _____ (A) programmed (B) identified
(C) cultivated (D) legalized

03 _____ (A) responsibility (B) divorce
(C) payment (D) cost

04 _____ (A) shape (B) size
(C) wealth (D) type

05 _____ (A) called (B) agreed
(C) known (D) named

中譯｜人們通常認為婚姻是一種正式契約，應該被記載下來，但是這種契約形式在每個社會都有所不同。例如，在西方社會，一個男人和一個女人應該去一位國家認可的官員那裡進行登記，以便得到合法婚姻的身份。但是，在非洲社會，婚姻是透過正式交換物品而變得合法，並不是透過官方登記。通常，新郎有責任給予新娘親屬物品，但有時新郎的親屬也會為新娘支付。

努爾族是一個生活在南蘇丹的民族，在這個民族裡，新娘聘禮，也就是給新娘親屬的報酬，是以牛為形式的。新娘聘禮的數量經過商定以及正式付款後，新郎和新娘之間的婚姻就變得合法，他們的後代子孫也會為人接受。

解說｜本篇短文列舉實例介紹了婚姻的不同習俗。第 1 題的四個選項都是名詞。依據題意，男人和女人應該是去登記結婚，要用 registration 表示「登記」，所以正確選擇為 (B)。第 2 題要選擇合適的動詞。根據上下文的內容可知，正式交換物品後，婚姻就合法了，所以要用 legalized 表示「合法」，最符合題意的選項是 (D)。第 3 題考動詞片語的用法。根據所學的知識，有責任做某事可以表達為 have responsibility to do sth.，要用名詞 responsibility，所以正確選項是 (A)。第 4 題依據題意可知，選項指代的事物是 cattle，是一種聘禮，可以用 wealth 來表達，所以只有選項 (C) 符合題意。第 5 題考動詞片語的搭配。依據題意，「就某事達成一致意見」可以表達為 agree upon，而其他選項皆不符合題意，所以選 (B)。

解答＆技巧｜ 01 **(B)** 02 **(D)** 03 **(A)** 04 **(C)** 05 **(B)**
適用 TIP 1 　適用 TIP 2 　適用 TIP 9 　適用 TIP 11

補充
African ⓐ 非洲的；formally ⓐⓓ 正式地；Nuer ⓝ 努爾人；Sudan ⓝ 蘇丹；in the form of ⓟⓗ 以～形式

7,000 單字
- form [fɔrm] ⓝ ② 形式
- contract [ˋkɑntrækt] ⓝ ③ 契約
- official [əˋfɪʃəl] ⓐ ② 正式的
- status [ˋstetəs] ⓝ ④ 身份
- marriage [ˋmærɪdʒ] ⓝ ② 婚姻
- registration [ˌrɛdʒɪˋstreʃən] ⓝ ④ 登記
- bridegroom [ˋbraɪd͵grʊm] ⓝ ④ 新郎
- bride [braɪd] ⓝ ③ 新娘
- cattle [ˋkætl̩] ⓝ ③ 牛
- amount [əˋmaʊnt] ⓝ ② 數量
- offspring [ˋɔf͵sprɪŋ] ⓝ ⑥ 後代
- acceptable [əkˋsɛptəbl̩] ⓐ ③ 可接受的
- contemplation [ˌkɑntɛmˋpleʃən] ⓝ ⑥ 沉思
- cultivate [ˋkʌltə͵vet] ⓥ ⑥ 培養
- wealth [wɛlθ] ⓝ ③ 財富

DAY
3

Part 1
詞
彙
題
Day 3
完成 25%

Part 2
綜
合
測
驗
Day 3
完成 50%

Part 3
文
意
選
填
Day 3
完成 75%

Part 4
閱
讀
測
驗
Day 3
完成 100%

10 ▶ 95 年學測英文

Fans of professional baseball and football argue continually over which is America's favorite sport. Though the figures on attendance for each vary with every new season, certain __01__ remain the same. To begin with, football is a quicker, more physical sport, and football fans enjoy the emotional involvement they feel while watching. Baseball, on the other hand, seems more mental, like chess, and __02__ those fans that prefer a quieter, more complicated game. __03__, professional football teams usually play no more than fourteen games a year. Baseball teams, however, play __04__ every day for six months. Finally, football fans seem to love the half-time activities, the marching bands, and the pretty cheerleaders. __05__, baseball fans are more content to concentrate on the game's finer details and spend the breaks between innings filling out their own private scorecards.

01 _____ (A) agreements   (B) arguments
          (C) accomplishments   (D) arrangements

02 _____ (A) attracted   (B) is attracted
          (C) attract   (D) attracts

03 _____ (A) In addition   (B) As a result
          (C) In contrast   (D) To some extent

04 _____ (A) hardly   (B) almost
          (C) somehow   (D) rarely

05 _____ (A) Even so   (B) For that reason
          (C) On the contrary   (D) By the same token

中譯｜職業棒球和美式足球的球迷們不斷爭論著何者才是美國最受喜愛的運動。儘管每個新賽季兩個球賽的出席人數都有所變化，但是爭論點還是沒變。首先，美式足球是一種節奏較快、動作較激烈的運動，球迷們享受那種在看球賽時所感受到的情感投入，另一方面，棒球和下西洋棋一樣，似乎更像是腦力運動，吸引了比較喜歡安靜、較複雜比賽的球迷。此外，職業美式足球隊一年通常比賽不超過十四場。然而，棒球隊幾乎可以在長達六個月的賽季內每天出賽。最後，美式足球迷似乎很喜歡觀看中場休息時的活動、遊行樂隊，還有漂亮的啦啦隊。反之，棒球迷更滿足於專注看比賽中的細節，並在每局結束的休息時間填寫他們自己的計分卡。

解說｜本篇短文的主旨是「棒球和美式足球」，答題時可以將這兩種運動的比賽規則考慮在內。第 1 題的四個選項都是名詞。依據題意，兩種運動之間一直存在著爭議，可以用 arguments 來表示「爭議」，所以正確選擇為 (B)。第 2 題考語法知識的運用。依據題意，動詞 attract 與主詞 baseball 之間是主動關係，要用主動形式。而 attract 在句中與 seems 表並列關係，也要用第三人稱單數形式，所以要用 attracts，正確選項是 (D)。第 3 題選項之後的情況是前面情況的補充，可以用 in addition 來引導，最符合題意的選項是 (A)。第 4 題將四個選項一一代入可知，只有副詞 almost 符合題意，所以最佳選項是 (B)。第 5 題選項前後說的是不同運動的球迷，要用表示對比關係的片語 on the contrary，所以選 (C)。

解答&技巧｜ 01 (B)　02 (D)　03 (A)　04 (B)　05 (C)

適用 TIP 1　適用 TIP 2　適用 TIP 4　適用 TIP 11

補充

continually [ad] 持續地；complicated [a] 複雜的；half-time [n] 半場；cheerleader [n] 啦啦隊隊員；scorecard [n] 記分卡

7,000 單字

- fan [fæn] [n] ③ 愛好者
- professional [prəˋfɛʃən] [a] ④ 專業的
- baseball [ˋbes͵bɔl] [n] ① 棒球
- argue [ˋɑrgju] [v] ② 爭論
- favorite [ˋfevərɪt] [a] ② 最喜愛的
- remain [rɪˋmen] [v] ③ 保持
- begin [bɪˋgɪn] [v] ① 開始
- emotional [ɪˋmoʃən] [a] ④ 情緒的

- chess [tʃɛs] [n] ② 西洋棋
- prefer [prɪˋfɝ] [v] ② 更喜歡
- pretty [ˋprɪtɪ] [a] ① 漂亮的
- concentrate [ˋkɑnsɛn͵tret] [v] ④ 集中
- attract [əˋtrækt] [v] ③ 吸引
- somehow [ˋsʌm͵haʊ] [ad] ③ 以某種方式
- contrary [ˋkɑntrɛrɪ] [n] ④ 相反

DAY 3

Part 1 詞彙題
Day 3 完成 25%

Part 2 綜合測驗
Day 3 完成 50%

Part 3 文意選填
Day 3 完成 75%

Part 4 閱讀測驗
Day 3 完成 100%

Part 3 文意選填 | Cloze Test

1▸

A paradox is actually an apparent __01__ that is nevertheless somehow true. It might be either a situation or a statement. Aesop's __02__ of *The Traveler* just illustrates a paradoxical situation.

As a __03__ of speech, paradox is simply a statement. Alexander Pope once wrote a literary critic that his time would "damn with faint praise." Clearly, he was using a literal paradox. Anyway, how can a man be damned by praising? But Pope's paradox will not be strange when we __04__ that damn is being used figuratively, and that Pope means that a praise, which is much too reserved, may damage an author with the public almost as much as adverse __05__ .

When we understand all the conditions and circumstances __06__ in a paradox, we may find that what at first seemed impossibilities is actually entirely __07__ and not strange at all. The paradox of the cold hands and hot porridge is not __08__ to anyone who knows that a stream of air directed upon an object of different temperature will tend to bring that object closer to its own temperature. In a paradoxical statement the contradiction usually __09__ from one of the words being used figuratively or in more than one sense.

The value of paradox is its typical value. Its seeming __10__ startles the reader into attention, and, by the fact of its apparent absurdity, underscores the truth of what is being said.

(A) criticism   (B) contradiction   (C) impossibility   (D) figure   (E) strange
(F) realize   (G) fable   (H) stems   (I) plausible   (J) involved

---

01 _____   02 _____   03 _____   04 _____   05 _____

06 _____   07 _____   08 _____   09 _____   10 _____

選項中譯｜批評；矛盾；不可能性；修辭手法；奇怪的；意識到；寓言；源自；
似乎可信的；包括在內的

中譯｜似是而非的雋語其實是看似矛盾、卻又言之有理的敘述手法，可以是某種狀況，
也可以是某種陳述。《旅行者》這則伊索寓言，所闡述的就是似是而非的狀況。
作為一種修辭手法，似是而非的雋語只是一種敘述。亞歷山大·蒲柏曾寫過一段
文學評論，說他的一生將會是寓褒於貶。明顯地，他是用了字面上看似矛盾的
雋語。不論如何，一個人怎麼會因為褒揚而受到貶抑呢？不過，damn（嚴厲批
評）是使用了修辭意義，蒲柏的意思是說，關於含蓄的褒揚，也許會像非難一
樣，損傷作者的名譽，如果我們可以意識到這一點，蒲柏似是而非的雋語也就不
足為奇了。
如果我們能夠理解似是而非的雋語中包含的所有條件和情形，我們也許會發現，
那些起初看來是不可能的事實，事實上完全是可信的，根本不足為奇。氣流流經
不同溫度的物體時，會使得這個物體的溫度接近於自身的溫度，如果明白這一
點，關於涼手和熱粥的那則雋語，也就不足為奇了。在似是而非的敘述中，矛盾
之處通常在於，某個單字使用了修辭意義，或是某個單字有多義性。
似是而非的雋語，其價值在於它本身的獨特意義。看起來不可能的事實，可以引
起讀者的注意，而且，看似荒謬的事實，也可以用來強調真正想要陳述的事實。

解譯｜閱讀全文可知，這篇文章的主題是似是而非的雋語。
縱觀各選項，選項 (A)、(B)、(C)、(D)、(G) 是名詞，選項 (F)、(H) 是動詞，選
項 (E)、(I)、(J) 是形容詞。根據題意，第 1、2、3、5、10 題應選名詞，第 4、
9 題應選動詞，第 6、7、8 題應選形容詞。然後根據文章，依次作答。
第 1 題是選擇名詞，須為可數名詞單數，有五個名詞可供選擇，即為選項 (A)、
(B)、(C)、(D)、(G)，選項 (A) 意為「批評」，選項 (B) 意為「矛盾」，選項 (C)
意為「不可能性」，選項 (D) 意為「修辭手法」，選項 (G) 意為「寓言」，根據
句意，應當是「似是而非的雋語是看似矛盾、卻又言之有理的陳述」，所以選
(B)。第 2 題所選名詞，Aesop's fable 意為伊索寓言，所以選 (G)。第 3 題所選
名詞，可以視為固定搭配，figure of speech 意為「修辭手法」，所以選 (D)。第
5 題所選名詞，也可以視為固定表達，adverse criticism 意為「非難」，所以選
(A)。第 10 題則是選 (C)，意為「看起來不可能的事實」。
第 4 題是選擇動詞，主詞為第二人稱複數，有兩個動詞可供選擇，即為選項
(F)、(H)。只有選項 (F) 符合要求，句意為「如果我們可以意識到這一點」。第
9 題則是選 (H)，可以視為固定搭配，stem from 意為「源自於」。
第 6 題是選擇形容詞，用來後位修飾 conditions and circumstances，有三個形
容詞可供選擇，即為選項 (E)、(I)、(J)。選項 (E) 意為「奇怪的」，選項 (I) 意
為「可信的」，選項 (J) 意為「包含在內的」，根據句意可知，應當是「似是而
非的雋語中包含的所有條件和情形」，所以選 (J)。第 7 題所選形容詞，根據句

DAY
3

Part 1
詞
彙
題
Day 3
完成 25%

Part 2
綜
合
測
驗
Day 3
完成 50%

Part 3
文
意
選
填
Day 3
完成 75%

Part 4
閱
讀
測
驗
Day 3
完成 100%

意可知，應當是「那些起初看來是不可能的事實，事實上完全是可信的」，所以選 (I)。第 8 題則是選 (E)，意為「關於涼手和熱粥的那則雋語，也就不足為奇了。」。

解答&技巧 | 01 (B)　02 (G)　03 (D)　04 (F)　05 (A)
　　　　　　06 (J)　07 (I)　08 (E)　09 (H)　10 (C)

適用 TIP 1　適用 TIP 2　適用 TIP 6　適用 TIP 7　適用 TIP 8
適用 TIP 9　適用 TIP 10　適用 TIP 11

補充
Alexander Pope n 亞歷山大・蒲柏；plausible a 似乎可信的，貌似有理的；
paradoxical a 似是而非的，自相矛盾的；absurdity n 悖理，荒謬；underscore v 強調

7,000 單字

- paradox [ˋpærəˏdɑks] n 5 似是而非的人或事
- contradiction [ˏkɑntrəˋdɪkʃən] n 6 矛盾
- fable [ˋfebl] n 3 寓言
- traveler [ˋtrævlɚ] n 3 旅行者
- figure [ˋfɪgjɚ] n 2 修辭
- literary [ˋlɪtəˏrɛrɪ] a 4 文學的
- damn [dæm] v 4 嚴厲批評
- praise [prez] n 2 讚揚

- literal [ˋlɪtərəl] a 6 字面意義的
- damage [ˋdæmɪdʒ] v 2 毀滅
- involve [ɪnˋvɑlv] v 4 包括
- stream [strim] n 2 流，流動
- air [ɛr] n 1 空氣
- stem [stɛm] v 4 來自，起源於
- attention [əˋtɛnʃən] n 2 注意

MEMO

----

❷▸

It doesn't __01__ which room a family chooses to gather in. It might be a corner of the kitchen, or a paneled den. That's all right. What really matters is whether they choose to be together. As is __02__ to all, it is the support, strength, bonds and traditions of the family that give us what all of us need in life. A good home is undoubtedly of great significance. Home, to some __03__, should be the stage on which the drama of life is played. It's the place where children learn to __04__ right from wrong, where ancient ideals like courage, honesty, respect for oneself and others, etc. are passed down from one __05__ to the next.

Nowadays, we are concerned about the erosion of these values that should be taught at home. We have seen the rising problems of society, such as broken homes, crimes, drugs, and __06__ delinquency, and been greatly shocked by the trauma they inflict on families, especially on children. Overburdened schools surely can no longer __07__ these problems confronting our society. If there is a way to save this situation, it should be the home. Just turn to the home, the place where we can regain the values that will probably __08__ these ills.

For many years, experts have always been dedicated to helping people create __09__ environments for their homes. But we should know it takes more than fine-quality furnishing to make a good home. It actually takes the love, respect and understanding of those who __10__ it together.

(A) comfortable (B) extent (C) juvenile (D) matter (E) share
(F) distinguish (G) solve (H) known (I) cure (J) generation

01 _____ 02 _____ 03 _____ 04 _____ 05 _____

06 _____ 07 _____ 08 _____ 09 _____ 10 _____

DAY 3

Part 1 詞彙題 Day 3 完成 25%

Part 2 綜合測驗 Day 3 完成 50%

Part 3 文意選填 Day 3 完成 75%

Part 4 閱讀測驗 Day 3 完成 100%

165

選項中譯 | 舒適的；範圍；少年的；關係重大；共同擁有；區別；解決；知道；治癒；
一代

中譯 | 家庭成員選擇在哪個房間聚集，並不重要。也許是在廚房的一個角落，也許是在
一個有鑲板的小房間，都是可以的。真正重要的是，他們是否會選擇聚集在一
起。眾所周知，來自家庭的支持、力量、親情、傳統，是我們所有人在生活中都
需要的。好的家庭無疑是十分重要的。在某種程度上，家庭是生活這齣戲劇的演
出場地。它是孩子們學習明辨是非的地方，也是諸如勇氣、誠信、自重與尊重他
人等古老的理念，代代傳承的地方。

如今，我們都十分擔心這些在家中學習的價值觀正遭到侵蝕。我們能看到愈來愈
多的社會問題，例如家庭破碎、犯罪、毒品、少年犯罪等，這些問題會讓家庭甚
至是孩子們遭受嚴重創傷，為此我們都感到極為震驚。學校已經不堪重負，自然
無法解決我們的社會所面臨的這些問題。如果說，有什麼辦法來改變這種局面，
那就是家庭。重視家庭吧，我們在家庭中重建價值觀，才可能解決這些問題。

很多年來，專家們都在致力於幫助人們創造舒適的家庭環境。但是，我們應該明
白，好的家庭所需要的，並不只是高級的傢俱裝飾，事實上，好的家庭需要每個
家庭成員的愛心、尊重和理解。

解譯 | 閱讀全文可知，這篇文章的主題是家庭環境。

縱觀各選項，選項 (B)、(J) 是名詞，選項 (D)、(E)、(F)、(G)、(H)、(I) 是動詞，
選項 (A)、(C) 是形容詞。根據題意，第 3、5 題應選名詞，第 1、2、4、7、8、
10 題應選動詞，第 6、9 題應選形容詞。然後根據文章，依次作答。

第 1 題是選擇動詞，有六個動詞可供選擇，即為選項 (D)、(E)、(F)、(G)、(H)、
(I)。it doesn't matter... 可以視為固定搭配，意為「～並不重要」，所以選 (D)。
第 2 題所選動詞，也是固定搭配，as is known to all 意為「眾所周知」，所以選
(H)。第 4 題所選動詞，可以視為固定表達，distinguish right from wrong 意為
「明辨是非」，所以選 (F)。第 7 題所選動詞，是與名詞 problem 進行搭配，意
為「解決問題」，所以選 (G)。第 8 題所選動詞，則是與名詞 ill 進行搭配，所以
選 (I)，意為「消除弊病，解決困難」。第 10 題則是選 (E)。

第 3 題是選擇名詞，有兩個名詞可供選擇，即為選項 (B)、(J)，選項 (B) 意為
「範圍」，選項 (J) 意為「一代」。to some extent 可以視為固定搭配，意為「在
某種程度上」，所以選 (B)。第 5 題所選名詞，也可以視為固定搭配，from one
generation to the next 意為「代代相傳」，所以選 (J)。

第 6 題是選擇形容詞，修飾名詞 delinquency，有兩個形容詞可供選擇，即為選
項 (A)、C)。juvenile delinquency 可以視為固定表達，意為「少年犯罪」，所以
選 (C)。第 9 題所選形容詞，修飾名詞 environments，即為選項 (A)，意為「舒
適的環境」。

解答 & 技巧｜ 01 **(D)** 02 **(H)** 03 **(B)** 04 **(F)** 05 **(J)**
06 **(C)** 07 **(G)** 08 **(I)** 09 **(A)** 10 **(E)**

適用 TIP 1　適用 TIP 2　適用 TIP 6　適用 TIP 7　適用 TIP 8
適用 TIP 9　適用 TIP 10　適用 TIP 11

補充

den n 小房間；distinguish right from wrong ph 明辨是非；delinquency n 罪行；
erosion n 侵蝕；inflict v 使遭受

7,000 單字

- matter [`mætɚ] v ① 要緊，關係重大
- gather [`gæðɚ] v ② 集合，聚集
- corner [`kɔrnɚ] n ② 角落
- kitchen [`kɪtʃɪn] n ① 廚房
- panel [`pænl] v ④ 用鑲板鑲嵌
- bond [bɑnd] n ④ 聯繫，關聯
- extent [ɪk`stɛnt] n ④ 程度
- drama [`drɑmə] n ② 戲劇

- distinguish [dɪ`stɪŋgwɪʃ] v ④ 分辨
- honesty [`ɑnɪstɪ] n ③ 誠信
- crime [kraɪm] n ② 犯罪
- juvenile [`dʒuvənl] a ⑤ 少年的
- trauma [`trɔmə] n ⑥ 創傷，痛苦
- cure [kjʊr] v ② 治癒
- comfortable [`kʌmfɚtəbl] a ② 舒適的

Part 1
詞
彙
題
Day 3
完成 25%

Part 2
綜
合
測
驗
Day 3
完成 50%

Part 3
文
意
選
填
Day 3
完成 75%

Part 4
閱
讀
測
驗
Day 3
完成 100%

MEMO

Passover, a tribute to freedom, has been regarded as one of the most important Jewish holidays. It __01__ the liberation of the Hebrews from slavery in ancient Egypt.

Almost four thousand years ago, according to the Book of *Exodus*, the Hebrews in Egypt were miserably kept in __02__. They were forced to be workers to build great Egyptian monuments. Moses once asked Pharaoh, the ruler of Egypt, to permit the Hebrews to make a __03__ pilgrimage, but Pharaoh refused. For this, God punished Egypt with a series of horrible __04__. And the last and the worst plague was the death of every first born. The Hebrews luckily escaped this punishment by __05__ their doorposts with the blood of a lamb. The Angel of Death just "passed over" these households marked with blood. Thus the holiday was called Passover.

After this plague, Pharaoh finally agreed to __06__ the Hebrews. But he changed his mind then and sent his soldiers after them. Another __07__ allowed the Hebrews to escape from the Egyptian pursuers. When preparing to flee from Egypt, the Hebrews ate matzos (flat, unleavened slabs of bread) because there was no time to wait for the __08__ to rise.

Today, Jews all over the world __09__ Passover and eat matzos in memory of the hardship and their ancestors' sufferings. Orthodox and __10__ Jews outside Israel observe the holiday for eight days, while Reform Jews and Israeli Jews for seven days.

(A) conservative   (B) plagues   (C) commemorates   (D) miracle
(E) observe   (F) bondage   (G) release   (H) religious   (I) dough
(J) sprinkling

01 _____   02 _____   03 _____   04 _____   05 _____

06 _____   07 _____   08 _____   09 _____   10 _____

選項中譯｜保守派的；災難；紀念；奇蹟；慶祝；奴役；釋放；宗教的；生麵團；灑

中譯｜逾越節，是向自由獻禮的節日，被認為是最重要的猶太節日之一，是為了紀念古埃及時的希伯來人擺脫奴役命運。

《出埃及記》一書中說，大約在四千年前，埃及的希伯來人遭受著悲慘的奴役。他們被迫成為工人，修建巨型的埃及紀念碑。摩西曾經請求法老，也就是埃及的統治者，允許猶太人進行宗教朝聖，法老卻拒絕了。為此，上帝用一連串的災難來懲罰埃及。最後一次災難也是最嚴重的，每個長子都面臨著死亡的命運。因為希伯來人把羊血灑在門柱上，所以幸運地躲過了這次懲罰。死亡天使越過了這些灑上羊血的人家，所以，這個節日就被稱為逾越節。

這次瘟疫結束後，法老終於同意釋放希伯來人。不過，他隨後又改變了主意，命令士兵前去追趕。奇蹟再度幫希伯來人躲過了埃及人的追捕。準備逃離埃及的時候，因為沒有時間等生麵團發酵，希伯來人就吃了 matzos（未經發酵的扁平厚麵包）。

如今，世界各地的猶太人都慶祝逾越節，並且食用未發酵的麵包，紀念前人所經歷的苦難和遭遇。在以色列境外的正統派猶太教徒和保守派猶太教徒，過逾越節時會慶祝八天，而改革派猶太教徒和以色列的猶太人則是慶祝七天。

解譯｜閱讀全文可知，這篇文章的主題是逾越節的由來與習俗。

縱觀各選項，選項 (B)、(D)、(F)、(I) 是名詞，選項 (C)、(E)、(G)、(J) 是動詞，選項 (A)、(H) 是形容詞。根據題意，第 2、4、7、8 題應選名詞，第 1、5、6、9 題應選動詞，第 3、10 題應選形容詞。然後根據文章，依次作答。

第 1 題是選擇動詞，須為第三人稱單數形式，有四個動詞可供選擇，即為選項 (C)、(E)、(G)、(J)。只有選項 (C) 符合要求，句意為「紀念古埃及時的希伯來人擺脫奴役命運」。第 5 題所選動詞，須為動名詞，所以選 (J)，句意為「希伯來人把羊血灑在門柱上，才幸運地躲過了這次懲罰」。第 6 題所選動詞，是與名詞 Hebrews 進行搭配，所以選 (G)，意為「釋放希伯來人」。第 9 題則是選 (E)，意為「慶祝逾越節」。

第 2 題是選擇名詞，有四個名詞可供選擇，即為選項 (B)、(D)、(F)、(I)，選項 (B) 意為「災難」，選項 (D) 意為「奇蹟」，選項 (F) 意為「奴役」，選項 (I) 意為「生麵團」，keep sb. in bondage 可以視為固定搭配，意為「使某人被奴役」，所以選 (F)。第 4 題所選名詞，根據句意，應當是「上帝用一連串的瘟疫來懲罰埃及」，所以選 (B)。第 7 題所選名詞，根據句意，應當是「奇蹟再度幫希伯來人躲過了埃及人的追捕」，所以選 (D)。第 8 題則是選 (I)，意為「沒有時間等生麵團發酵」。

第 3 題是選擇形容詞，修飾名詞 pilgrimage，有兩個形容詞可供選擇，即為選項 (A)、(H)。選項 (A) 意為「保守的」，選項 (H) 意為「宗教的」，根據句意可知，應當是「宗教朝聖」，所以選 (H)。第 10 題則是選 (A)，句意為「保守派猶太教徒」。

DAY 3

Part 1 詞彙題 Day 3 完成 25%

Part 2 綜合測驗 Day 3 完成 50%

Part 3 文意選填 Day 3 完成 75%

Part 4 閱讀測驗 Day 3 完成 100%

解答＆技巧 | **01** (C)　**02** (F)　**03** (H)　**04** (B)　**05** (J)
06 (G)　**07** (D)　**08** (I)　**09** (E)　**10** (A)

適用 TIP 1　適用 TIP 2　適用 TIP 6　適用 TIP 7　適用 TIP 8
適用 TIP 9　適用 TIP 10　適用 TIP 11

補充

Passover n 逾越節；Hebrew n 希伯來人，猶太人；*Exodus* n 《出埃及記》；Pharaoh n 法老；
pilgrimage n 朝聖；The Angel of Death ph 死亡天使，死神；matzo n 未發酵的麵包；
Orthodox a 正統派的

7,000 單字

- holiday [ˋhɑlə‚de] n 1 節日
- commemorate [kəˋmɛmə‚ret] v 6 紀念
- liberation [‚lɪbəˋreʃən] n 6 解放
- slavery [ˋslevərɪ] n 6 奴隸制度，奴隸身份
- bondage [ˋbɑndɪdʒ] n 6 奴役，束縛
- monument [ˋmɑnjəmənt] n 4 紀念碑
- religious [rɪˋlɪdʒəs] a 3 宗教的
- plague [pleg] n 5 災難

- sprinkle [ˋsprɪŋkl] v 3 灑
- lamb [læm] n 1 羔羊
- angel [ˋendʒl] n 3 天使
- household [ˋhaʊs‚hold] n 4 家庭
- dough [do] n 5 生麵團
- hardship [ˋhɑrdʃɪp] n 4 苦難
- ancestor [ˋænsɛstə] n 4 祖先

MEMO

DAY
3

Part 1
詞
彙
題
Day 3
完成 25%

Part 2
綜
合
測
驗
Day 3
完成 50%

Part 3
文
意
選
填
Day 3
完成 75%

Part 4
閱
讀
測
驗
Day 3
完成 100%

4▶

The meal schedule may __01__ on weekends and holidays. In many families, Sunday brunch is traditional. Brunch, just as the name __02__, is a combination of breakfast and lunch. It is usually served between eleven o'clock and noon, including typical breakfast food plus cheese, fruit, cake, perhaps cold fish as well. Brunch should be __03__ enough to sustain people until dinnertime.

If they go to church on Sunday morning, families may have their __04__ weekday breakfast after services, and then eat the biggest meal of the day at about two o'clock. The main meal is simply called dinner, no matter when it is served. After dinner in mid-afternoon, a smaller evening meal, i.e. __05__, is served around seven o'clock. And on Saturday evenings, many people eat very late dinners, especially those who choose to __06__ out. Crowds always begin to __07__ into restaurants at about seven o'clock, and some people may dine continental style as late as nine or ten o'clock.

On Sundays and holidays, weather __08__, families often eat outdoors. Picnics in parks, backyard barbecues (charcoal-broiled steaks or hamburgers), neighborhood roasts, clambakes (New England-style picnics where clams, lobsters, and potatoes are steamed on a bed of hot stones under a layer of wet seaweed) are all popular.

By tradition, Sunday is a day of __09__. Many women also take a rest from kitchen. Families often go out for a casual Sunday dinner. Those with young children may enjoy a quick and __10__ meal at a drive-through restaurant, where food is brought to and eaten in a car.

(A) vary　(B) supper　(C) inexpensive　(D) substantial　(E) permitting
(F) implies　(G) usual　(H) rest　(I) pour　(J) dine

---

01 ＿＿＿　02 ＿＿＿　03 ＿＿＿　04 ＿＿＿　05 ＿＿＿

06 ＿＿＿　07 ＿＿＿　08 ＿＿＿　09 ＿＿＿　10 ＿＿＿

選項中譯｜改變；晚餐；廉價的；可觀的；允許；暗示；平常的；休息；湧入；進餐

中譯｜在週末和假日，用餐安排可能會有所變動。有很多的家庭，在周日吃早午餐已經成為慣例。早午餐，顧名思義，就是早餐和午餐的結合，通常是在十一點和中午之間的時間段用餐，吃的是典型的早餐食物和乳酪、水果、蛋糕，也許還有涼拌魚肉。早午餐份量應夠多，才能支撐人們捱到晚餐時間。

如果禮拜天早上要去教堂，做完禮拜之後，這些家庭也許會像平常的工作日一樣吃早餐，然後在下午兩點左右吃當天的正餐。不論是在什麼時候吃，主餐都會稱為 dinner（正餐）。下午三點左右吃過正餐之後，在七點左右還要吃較為簡單些的晚餐，稱為 supper。周六晚上，很多人的正餐都吃得很晚，特別是那些出去吃飯的人。大約在七點左右，人們開始湧進餐館，有些保持歐洲大陸用餐習慣的人則是在九點或是十點才會吃飯。

在周日和假日，如果天氣允許的話，一家人通常會去戶外吃飯。在公園野餐，後院燒烤（木炭烤肉排或是漢堡），社區烤肉，海邊海味野餐會（新英格蘭風格的野餐，蛤蜊、龍蝦、馬鈴薯等放在熱石頭上，墊著濕的海藻蒸）都很流行。

根據傳統，周日是休息時間。很多女性也不再下廚，而是選擇休息。家人們通常出去吃休閒的週末大餐。那些帶著小孩子的家庭，可能會去免下車餐館吃飯，把食物帶到車上享用，既快速又便宜。

解譯｜閱讀全文可知，這篇文章的主題是用餐安排。

縱觀各選項，選項 (B)、(H) 是名詞，選項 (A)、(E)、(F)、(I)、(J) 是動詞，選項 (C)、(D)、(G) 是形容詞。根據題意，第 5、9 題應選名詞，第 1、2、6、7、8 題應選動詞，第 3、4、10 題應選形容詞。然後根據文章，依次作答。

第 1 題是選擇動詞，須為動詞原形，有五個動詞可供選擇，即為選項 (A)、(E)、(F)、(I)、(J)，根據句意可知，應當是「在週末和假日，用餐安排可能會有所變動」，所以選 (A)。第 2 題所選動詞，根據句意可知，應當是「顧名思義」，所以選 (F)。第 6 題所選動詞，可以視為固定搭配，意為「在外吃飯」，所以選 (J)。第 7 題所選動詞，也可以視為固定搭配，pour into 意為「湧入」，所以選 (I)。第 8 題則是選 (E)，是獨立分詞，可以視為常用表達，weather permitting 意為「如果天氣允許的話」。

第 3 題是選擇形容詞，有三個形容詞可供選擇，即為選項 (C)、(D)、(G)。選項 (C) 意為「便宜的」，選項 (D) 意為「可觀的」，選項 (G) 意為「平常的」，根據句意可知，應當是「早午餐應當足夠豐富，才能支撐人們捱到晚餐時間」，所以選 (D)。第 4 題所選形容詞，根據句意可知，應當是「像工作日一樣吃早餐」，所以選 (G)。第 10 題則是選 (C)，句意為「去免下車餐館吃飯，可以把食物帶到車上享用，快速又便宜」。

第 5 題是選擇名詞，有兩個名詞可供選擇，即為選項 (B)、(H)，選項 (B) 意為「晚餐」，選項 (H) 意為「休息」，根據句意，應當是「七點左右還要吃較為簡單些的晚餐，稱為 supper，所以選 (B)。第 9 題則是選 (H)，意為「周日是休息時間」。

解答&技巧｜ 01 (A)　02 (F)　03 (D)　04 (G)　05 (B)
　　　　　 06 (J)　07 (I)　08 (E)　09 (H)　10 (C)

適用 TIP 1　適用 TIP 2　適用 TIP 6　適用 TIP 7　適用 TIP 8
適用 TIP 9　適用 TIP 10　適用 TIP 11

補充

dinnertime ⓝ 晚餐時間；main meal ⓟⓗ 主餐；clambake ⓝ 海邊海味野餐會；
seaweed ⓝ 海草，海藻；drive-through ⓐ 免下車服務的

7,000 單字

- meal [mil] ⓝ② 餐，飯食
- weekend [`wik`ɛnd] ⓝ① 週末
- brunch [brʌntʃ] ⓝ② 早午餐
- imply [ɪm`plaɪ] ⓥ④ 暗示
- lunch [lʌntʃ] ⓝ① 午餐
- noon [nun] ⓝ① 正午
- typical [`tɪpɪkl] ⓐ③ 典型的，有代表性的
- plus [plʌs] ⓟⓡⓔⓟ② 加

- substantial [səb`stænʃəl] ⓐ⑤ 可觀的，大量的
- service [`sɝvɪs] ⓝ① 禮拜，祈禱儀式
- supper [`sʌpɚ] ⓝ① 晚餐
- continental [ˌkɑntə`nɛnt] ⓐ⑤ 歐洲大陸情調的
- picnic [`pɪknɪk] ⓝ② 野餐
- hamburger [`hæmbɝɡɚ] ⓝ② 漢堡
- lobster [`lɑbstɚ] ⓝ③ 龍蝦

MEMO

DAY **3**

Part 1 詞彙題　Day 3 完成 25%
Part 2 綜合測驗　Day 3 完成 50%
Part 3 文意選填　Day 3 完成 75%
Part 4 閱讀測驗　Day 3 完成 100%

♫173

Blue whales are known as the largest __01__ . The tongue of a blue whale can __02__ as much as a small elephant. Blue whales can weigh 150 tons or so. Huge as they are, blue whales are actually graceful. They can swim fast and make quick turns.

__03__ of teeth, the blue whale has blubber looking like a large comb. The blue whale eats small shrimplike krill. The blue whale opens its mouth to let in water and krill. Then it closes its mouth and __04__ the water out, the baleen keeps the krill __05__ . There are a lot of krill in Antarctica, making the ocean orange. A hungry blue whale can eat 8,000 pounds of krill every day.

Female whales are called cows, and the babies are called calves. Blue whales usually give __06__ to their babies in warm waters. Blue whale calves grow much faster than other animals. During the first seven months, they can gain about 200 pounds every day.

In spring, when the calf is a few months old, the mother and the baby begin __07__ , hoping to find more food. Antarctica is their __08__ . The baby lives on its mother's milk. The travel might __09__ the baby and mother many weeks.

When autumn comes, the young whale should be old enough and large enough to take __10__ of itself. Then it will make the return trip to warm waters alone.

(A) inside   (B) animals   (C) take   (D) Instead   (E) forces
(F) migrating   (G) destination   (H) weigh   (I) care   (J) birth

01 _____   02 _____   03 _____   04 _____   05 _____

06 _____   07 _____   08 _____   09 _____   10 _____

選項中譯｜在裡面；動物；花費；代替；迫使；遷移；目的地；重；照顧；出生

中譯｜眾所周知，藍鯨是體型最大的動物。一隻藍鯨的舌頭重量，和一頭小象的重量相當。藍鯨可以重達一百五十噸左右。體形雖然龐大，藍鯨們卻很優雅。他們游得很快，也能快速地掉頭轉彎。

藍鯨沒有牙齒，但他們有鯨脂，看起來像是一把大梳子。藍鯨所吃的是蝦米似的小磷蝦。藍鯨張開嘴巴，讓水和磷蝦進入口中，然後閉上嘴巴，將水排出，鯨鬚會把磷蝦留在藍鯨體內。南極洲的海洋中，有很多的磷蝦，使得海水看起來都是橘色的。一隻饑餓的藍鯨每天可以吃八千磅的磷蝦。

雌鯨稱為 cow，小鯨則稱為 calf。藍鯨在溫暖的水域裡生下小藍鯨。小藍鯨的成長速度，比其他動物都快。在最初的七個月裡，他們每天大約會增重兩百磅。

在春天，當小鯨有幾個月大時，母鯨和小鯨開始遷移，希望找到更多的食物。南極洲是牠們的目的地。小鯨是以母鯨的奶水為生。母鯨和小鯨們的旅行，也許會歷時數周。

到了秋天，小鯨的年齡也已經足夠大，體型也足夠大，可以自己照顧自己。這時候，牠會獨自返回暖水域。

解譯｜閱讀全文可知，這篇文章的主題是藍鯨。

縱觀各選項，選項 (B)、(G)、(I)、(J) 是名詞，選項 (C)、(E)、(F)、(H) 是動詞，選項 (A)、(D) 是副詞。根據題意，第 1、6、8、10 題應選名詞，第 2、4、7、9 題應選動詞，第 3、5 題應選副詞。然後根據文章，依次作答。

第 1 題是選擇名詞，有四個名詞可供選擇，即為選項 (B)、(G)、(I)、(J)，選項 (B) 意為「動物」，選項 (G) 意為「目的地」，選項 (I) 意為「照顧」，選項 (J) 意為「出生」，根據句意，應當是「藍鯨是體型最大的動物」，所以選 (B)。第 6 題所選名詞，可以視為固定搭配，give birth to 意為「生產」，所以選 (J)。第 8 題所選名詞，根據句意，應當是「南極洲是牠們的目的地」，所以選 (G)。第 10 題則是選 (I)，也可以視為固定搭配，take care of 意為「照顧」。

第 2 題是選擇動詞，有四個動詞可供選擇，即為選項 (C)、(E)、(F)、(H)，根據句意，應當是「藍鯨的舌頭重量」，所以選 (H)。第 4 題所選動詞，根據句意，應當是「將水排出」，所以選 (E)。第 7 題所選動詞，是用於固定搭配，begin doing sth. 意為「開始做某事」，所以選 (F)。第 9 題則是選 (C)，意為「母鯨和小鯨的旅行，也許會歷時數周」。

第 3 題是選擇副詞，有兩個副詞可供選擇，即為選項 (A)、(D)。選項 (A) 意為「在裡面」，選項 (D) 意為「代替」，根據句意可知，應當是「把磷蝦留在藍鯨體內」，所以選 (D)。第 5 題則是選 (A)。

DAY
3

Part 1
詞
彙
題
Day 3
完成 25%

Part 2
綜
合
測
驗
Day 3
完成 50%

Part 3
文
意
選
填
Day 3
完成 75%

Part 4
閱
讀
測
驗
Day 3
完成 100%

解答＆技巧 | **01** (B)　**02** (H)　**03** (D)　**04** (E)　**05** (A)
　　　　　　06 (J)　**07** (F)　**08** (G)　**09** (C)　**10** (I)

適用 TIP 1　適用 TIP 2　適用 TIP 6　適用 TIP 7　適用 TIP 8
適用 TIP 9　適用 TIP 10　適用 TIP 11

補充

blubber n 鯨脂；krill n 磷蝦；baleen n 鯨鬚；enough... to ph 足夠～做某事；take care of ph 照顧

7,000 單字

- whale [hwel] n 2 鯨魚
- animal [ˈænəml] n 1 動物
- tongue [tʌŋ] n 2 舌頭
- elephant [ˈɛləfənt] n 1 大象
- graceful [ˈgresfəl] a 4 優雅的
- comb [kom] n 2 梳子
- Antarctica [ænˈtɑrktɪkə] n 6 南極洲
- orange [ˈɔrɪndʒ] a 1 橙色的

- cow [kaʊ] n 1 母獸
- baby [ˈbebɪ] n 1 幼獸
- calf [kæf] n 5 幼獸
- birth [bɝθ] n 1 出生
- spring [sprɪŋ] n 1 春天
- migrate [ˈmaɪˌgret] v 6 遷徙
- take [tek] v 1 花費

MEMO

MEMO

DAY
3

Part 1
詞
彙
題
Day 3
完成 25%

Part 2
綜
合
測
驗
Day 3
完成 50%

Part 3
文
意
選
填
Day 3
完成 75%

Part 4
閱
讀
測
驗
Day 3
完成 100%

Part 4 閱讀測驗 | Reading Questions

Historians, who seek to identify the circumstances that encouraged the emergence of feminist movements, have thoroughly investigated the mid-nineteenth-century economic and social conditions affecting the status of women in America. However, they have analyzed less fully the development of specifically feminist ideas and activities during the same period. Furthermore, the ideological origins of feminism have been obscured. Feminist activists who have been described as "solitary" and "individual theorists" were in fact related to a movement, i.e. utopian socialism, which was already popularizing feminist ideas after the first women's rights conference.

The Saint-Simonians should be the earliest and most popular of the utopian socialists. The specifically feminist part of Saint-Simonianism has, however, been less studied than the group's contribution to early socialism. That is regrettable. By 1832, feminism had been the central concern of Saint-Simonianism and entirely absorbed its adherents' energy. Some historians have misunderstood Saint-Simonianism. However, many feminist ideas can be traced to Saint-Simonianism.

Saint-Simon's followers, many of whom were women, based on their feminism interpretation of this system to reorganize the world by replacing brute force with the rule of spiritual powers. The new world order would be ruled together by a male, representing reflection, and a female, representing sentiment. The Saint-Simonians did not reject the belief that there were innate differences between men and women. However, they foresaw an equally important social and political role for both sexes in their Utopia.

Only a few Saint-Simonians opposed a definition of sexual equality based on gender distinction. The minority believed that individuals of both sexes were born similar in capacity and character, and they ascribed male-female differences to socialization and education.

01 What does the word "which"in the last line of the first paragraph refer to?

(A) Feminist activists.

(B) Utopian socialism.

(C) The first women's rights conference.

(D) Feminist ideas.

02 What's the meaning of the word "Saint-Simonians" in the second paragraph?

(A) A kind of movements.

(B) A kind of organizations.

(C) A kind of beliefs.

(D) The group of people who follow and support Saint-Simonianism.

03 The word "oppose" in the last paragraph is closest in meaning to _____.

(A) attack

(B) contradict

(C) observe

(D) demand

04 What is the main idea of the passage?

(A) Socialism.

(B) Utopia.

(C) Feminism.

(D) The status of women.

DAY
3

Part 1
詞
彙
題
Day 3
完成 25%

Part 2
綜
合
測
驗
Day 3
完成 50%

Part 3
文
意
選
填
Day 3
完成 75%

Part 4
閱
讀
測
驗
Day 3
完成 100%

中譯｜歷史學家試圖探索促成女性主義運動出現的情形，也深入地研究了十九世紀中期影響美國女性地位的經濟條件和社會條件。然而，對於同一時期，明確的女性主義觀點的發展狀況，他們並沒有進行全面分析。而且，女性主義的意識起源也很模糊。事實上，那些被形容為是孤獨的以及個人主義者的女性主義者，都會和某一項社會運動聯繫在一起，即烏托邦社會主義。烏托邦社會主義自從第一屆女性會議召開之後，就已經使女性主義理念普及化。

聖西門主義者應當是最早也最流行的烏托邦社會主義者。然而，相較於聖西門主義本身對於早期社會主義的貢獻，此流派中女性主義的部分研究也較為有限，令人遺憾。直至一八三二年，女性主義已經成為聖西門主義所關注的核心問題，並且完全吸引了擁護者的精力。有些歷史學家對聖西門主義有些誤解。然而，很多的女性主義理念都源自於聖西門主義。

基於她們對聖西門主義系統的女性主義詮釋，以女性為主要追隨者的聖西門主義者認為以新的方式建構這個世界，應該要以精神力量的規則來取代暴力。新的世界秩序應當是由男性和女性共同控制，男性代表著思考，而女性則是代表著情感。聖西門主義者並不否認男女生來就有著區別的理念。然而，在他們的烏托邦中，他們預見了一種對於男性和女性都同等重要的社會和政治角色。

只有少數的聖西門主義者將概念建立在性別平等上，反對性別差異的觀念。這些少數人認為，在能力和性格方面，男性和女性都是生來相似的，並且認為男女差異是由社會化和教育所引起的。

解譯｜在閱讀文章之前，先要預覽題目，然後再帶著問題有針對性地閱讀文章。第 1 題是文意理解，第 2 題是詞義推斷，第 3 題是詞義辨析，第 4 題是概括主旨。理解了題目要求之後，閱讀全文，依次作答。

第 1 題是文意理解，問的是關係代名詞 which 所指代的內容。通常來說，在關係子句中，which 所指代的內容，可以是之前所說的某個無生命物體的名詞，也可以是子句前的這個句子。根據第 1 段最後一句內容判斷，which 在此處應該是指代名詞，即先行詞 utopian socialism。所以選 (B)。

第 2 題是詞義推斷，單字 Saint-Simonian 較為少見，僅僅根據固有的詞彙量，也許無法得知詞義。而形近字 Saint-Simon 和 Saint-Simonianism，均在後文中出現，由此可以加以推斷。根據構詞法，字尾 -nism 是表示某種主義或是理論，而字尾 -ian 則是表示某一類人。再結合語境，可以推斷，Saint-Simon 最為簡單，應該是個人名，而 Saint-Simonianism 則是 Saint-Simon 的理念，至於 Saint-Simonian，就應該是擁護 Saint-Simonianism 的人。所以選 (D)。

第 3 題是考動詞 oppose 的同義字。選項 (A) 意為「攻擊」，選項 (B) 意為「反駁」，選項 (C) 意為「觀察」，選項 (D) 意為「要求」。根據第 4 段內容可知，意為「反對」，所以選 (B)。

第 4 題是概括主旨。文中並沒有明顯的主旨句，需要根據各段內容加以概括。第 1 段是女性主義起源，第 2 段講述的是聖西門主義與女性主義的關係，第 3 段講述的是聖西門主義者的女性主義理念，第 4 段講述的是少數聖西門主義者的觀念。由此可知，短文內容是簡述女性主義，所以選 (C)。

解答＆技巧 | **01 (B)**　**02 (D)**　**03 (B)**　**04 (C)**

適用 TIP 1　適用 TIP 2　適用 TIP 3　適用 TIP 5　適用 TIP 7　適用 TIP 10
適用 TIP 11　適用 TIP 12　適用 TIP 13　適用 TIP 14　適用 TIP 15

DAY
3

Part 1
詞
彙
題
Day 3
完成 25%

Part 2
綜
合
測
驗
Day 3
完成 50%

Part 3
文
意
選
填
Day 3
完成 75%

Part 4
閱
讀
測
驗
Day 3
完成 100%

補充

emergence [n] 出現；feminist [n] 男女平等主義者，女性主義者；ideological [a] 意識形態的；
feminism [n] 女性主義；utopian [a] 烏托邦的，理想國的

7,000 單字

- historian [hɪsˋtorɪən] [n] ❸ 歷史學家
- analyze [ˋænḷˌaɪz] [v] ❹ 分析
- obscure [əbˋskjur] [v] ❻ 使不分明，遮掩
- activist [ˋæktəvɪst] [n] ❻ 積極分子
- solitary [ˋsɑləˌtɛrɪ] [a] ❺ 孤獨的
- socialism [ˋsoʃəlˌɪzəm] [n] ❻ 社會主義
- socialist [ˋsoʃəlɪst] [n] ❻ 社會主義者
- contribution [ˌkɑntrəˋbjuʃən] [n] ❹ 貢獻

- misunderstand [ˋmɪsʌndɚˋstænd] [v] ❹ 誤解
- system [ˋsɪstəm] [n] ❶ 系統
- brute [brut] [a] ❻ 粗暴的，無理性的
- reflection [rɪˋflɛkʃən] [n] ❹ 沉思，思考
- sentiment [ˋsɛntəmənt] [n] ❺ 情感
- distinction [dɪˋstɪŋkʃən] [n] ❺ 區別
- character [ˋkærɪktɚ] [n] ❷ 性格

MEMO

In some countries where racial prejudice is acute, violence has been taken for granted as a means of mopping up differences. The white man imposes his rule by brute force, while the black man protests by setting fire to cities and by looting and pillaging. Important people on both sides, who would in other respects appear to be reasonable men, calmly argue in favor of violence—as if it were a legitimate solution. But when it comes to the crunch, no actual progress has been made at all. This realization is really frightening and despairing.

The recorded history of the human race, the tedious documentation of violence, has actually taught us nothing. We haven't fully understood that violence never solves a problem but makes it more acute. The sheer horror, the bloodshed and the suffering, as a matter of fact, means nothing.

The truly reasonable men, who know where the solutions lie, find it harder and harder to get an ear. They are mostly despised, mistrusted and even persecuted because they advocate such apparently outrageous things as law enforcement. If we could make full use of half the energy that goes into violent acts, if our efforts were directed at cleaning up the slums and ghettos and at improving living-standards and providing education and employment, we would have found an appropriate solution to this problem. Our strength is somehow sapped because it has to eliminate the mess left by violence in its wake. In a well-directed effort, it would not be impossible to fulfill the ideals of a stable social program. The benefits derived from constructive solutions are everywhere obvious around us. Genuine and lasting solutions should always be possible.

01 Which of the following statements about truly reasonable men is the most appropriate?

(A) They have difficulty in advocating law enforcement.

(B) They are always looked down upon.

(C) They are even persecuted.

(D) They can't get a hearing.

02 The word "outrageous" in the third paragraph is closest in meaning to _____.

(A) unusual

(B) shocking

(C) offensive

(D) immoral

03 According the author, which is the best way to solve racial prejudice?

(A) Technology.

(B) Law enforcement.

(C) Education.

(D) Knowledge.

04 What is the main idea of the passage?

(A) Racial prejudice.

(B) Conflicts between the white men and the black men.

(C) Violence as a legitimate solution.

(D) Violence can do nothing to diminish racial prejudice.

DAY
3

Part 1
詞
彙
題
Day 3
完成 25%

Part 2
綜
合
測
驗
Day 3
完成 50%

Part 3
文
意
選
填
Day 3
完成 75%

Part 4
閱
讀
測
驗
Day 3
完成 100%

中譯｜在一些種族歧視十分嚴重的國家，暴力被視為是消除異己理所當然的一種手段。白人用暴力來強加管制，而黑人則是在城市中放火、搶劫掠奪，以示抗議。雙方的重要人物，在其他方面，似乎都是明理之人，卻都支持使用暴力——似乎這是正當的解決辦法。然而，暴力在關鍵時刻，並沒有達成什麼實質性的進展。這樣的認知的確令人恐慌、絕望。

人類種族的歷史，也就是一連串暴力的冗長記載，都沒有讓我們從中學到教訓。我們並沒有完全理解，暴力永遠都無法解決問題，只會激化問題。事實上，極度的恐慌、流血犧牲和苦難，都沒有意義。

真正明理的人們，知道如何尋求解決之道，卻愈來愈難得到認同。他們提倡法令施行這種顯然是非比尋常的做法，因此大多受人鄙視，不被信任，甚至是受到迫害。如果我們可以把來施行暴力行徑精力的一半好好充分利用，來努力整頓貧民窟、改善生活水準、提供教育和就業機會，我們也許會找到解決這個問題的正確方法。我們的精力不得不用來消除暴力引起的混亂狀況，因此逐漸削弱。如果在目標明確的狀況下努力，實現穩定的社會規劃也並非是全無可能。有建設性的解決辦法所帶來的益處，在我們身邊隨處都是顯而易見的。真誠而持久的解決辦法總是可能存在的。

解譯｜在閱讀文章之前，先要預覽題目，然後再帶著問題有針對性地閱讀文章。第 1、3 題是文意理解，第 2 題是詞義辨析，第 4 題是概括主旨。理解了題目要求之後，閱讀全文，依次作答。

第 1 題是文意理解，考的是細節，問的是關於真正明理的人們的敘述，哪一項是最為恰當的。很明顯，其關鍵字是 truly reasonable men，因此，定位於第 3 段。根據第 1、2 句內容可知，他們愈來愈難得到認同，他們提倡法令施行這種顯然是非比尋常的做法，因此，大多受人鄙視，不被信任，甚至是受到迫害。選項 (B)、(C)、(D) 都只是其中的一個細節表現，可以排除。只有選項 (A) 最為全面，所以選 (A)。

第 2 題是考形容詞 outrageous 的同義字。形容詞 outrageous 意為「駭人的；蠻橫無禮的；不道德的；不尋常的；不依慣例的」，而選項 (A) 意為「不尋常的」，選項 (B) 意為「驚人的」，選項 (C) 意為「無禮的」，選項 (D) 意為「不道德的」，都可以表示一定程度上的相似意義。根據第 3 段內容可知，形容詞 outrageous 意為「不尋常的」，所以選 (A)。

第 3 題同樣是文意理解，問的是消除種族偏見的最佳方式。根據第 2 段內容可知，法制才是最佳方式，而選項 (A)、(C)、(D) 在文中並未提及，也可以排除。所以選 (B)。

第 4 題是概括主旨。文中並沒有明顯的主旨句，需要根據各段內容加以概括。第 1 段是在某些國家，大肆使用暴力來解決種族問題；第 2 段講述的是人類歷史證明，暴力並不能夠解決種族問題；第 3 段講述的是法制才是真正持久的解決方法。由此可知，短文內容是說暴力無法解決種族問題，所以選 (D)。

解答 & 技巧 | **01 (A)** **02 (A)** **03 (B)** **04 (D)**

適用 TIP 1　適用 TIP 2　適用 TIP 3　適用 TIP 7　適用 TIP 10
適用 TIP 11　適用 TIP 12　適用 TIP 13　適用 TIP 14　適用 TIP 15

補充

loot ⓥ 搶奪；pillage ⓥ 掠奪；bloodshed ⓝ 流血，殺害；mistrust ⓥ 不信任；persecute ⓥ 迫害；ghetto ⓝ 貧民區

7,000 單字

- racial [ˈreʃəl] ⓐ③ 種族的
- prejudice [ˈprɛdʒədɪs] ⓝ⑥ 偏見
- acute [əˈkjut] ⓐ⑥ 嚴重的
- mop [mɑp] ⓥ③ 擦
- solution [səˈluʃən] ⓝ② 解決辦法
- actual [ˈæktʃuəl] ⓐ③ 實際的
- realization [ˌrɪələˈzeʃən] ⓝ⑥ 認知，認識
- tedious [ˈtidɪəs] ⓐ⑥ 煩人的，厭倦的
- sheer [ʃɪr] ⓐ⑥ 完全的，十足的

- despise [dɪˈspaɪz] ⓥ⑤ 鄙視
- violent [ˈvaɪələnt] ⓐ③ 暴力的，強烈的
- mess [mɛs] ⓝ③ 混亂狀態
- wake [wek] ⓝ② （事過之後的）痕跡，狀況
- fulfill [fʊlˈfɪl] ⓥ④ 完成，實現
- constructive [kənˈstrʌktɪv] ⓐ④ 建設性的，有助益的

MEMO

♩ 185

DAY 3 — Part 1 詞彙題 Day 3 完成 25% / Part 2 綜合測驗 Day 3 完成 50% / Part 3 文意選填 Day 3 完成 75% / Part 4 閱讀測驗 Day 3 完成 100%

People considering robotic surgery for prostate cancer shouldn't trust the rosy ads, which simply promotes the expensive technology over the low-tech surgery. According to a new survey, complains about sexual problems and urinary leakage were equally common after the two procedures.

The new study, published in the *Journal of Clinical Oncology*, is based on the responses from more than 600 prostate cancer patients on Medicare, the government's health insurance for the elderly. Overall, there is no significant difference between the two patient groups, though urinary problems seemed to be slightly more common after the robotic procedure.

Robotic prostatectomy has caught on rapidly in the U.S., in spite of the fact that there is no good evidence to show it's better than traditional prostate removal. It is, however, much more expensive, adding some $2,000 in hospital costs per procedure.

The robots, which cost a couple million dollars each, indeed have some advantages. For example, they reduce blood loss, which helps surgeons see better when operating. However, there is no denying that it doesn't treat cancer any better than the old surgery. Still, it doesn't have any proven benefit in terms of side effects. Patients who consider surgery should, therefore, look for experienced surgeons, rather than simply focus on technology.

One study has found that every year more than 120,000 American men diagnosed with prostate cancer are ideal candidates for observation, or watchful waiting. But the majority of them end up having surgery, radiation or other treatments instead.

01 The word "significant" in the second paragraph is closest in meaning to _____.

(A) preferable

(B) strange

(C) important

(D) necessary

02 Which one of the following statements is true?

(A) Both kinds of operations may resultin sexual problems and urinary leakage.

(B) All the ads about robotic prostatectomy are untruthful.

(C) Robotic surgery is cheaper than low-tech surgery.

(D) Robotic surgery is better than the traditional one.

03 According to the passage, patients who are considering surgery should focus their attention on _____.

(A) surgeons

(B) robots

(C) rosy ads

(D) other cancer patients

04 What is the author's attitude towards robotic prostatectomy?

(A) Indifferent.

(B) Objective.

(C) Subjective.

(D) Ambiguous.

DAY
3

Part 1
詞
彙
題
Day 3
完成 25%

Part 2
綜
合
測
驗
Day 3
完成 50%

Part 3
文
意
選
填
Day 3
完成 75%

Part 4
閱
讀
測
驗
Day 3
完成 100%

中譯｜考慮接受機器人手術治療攝護腺癌的人們，不應該相信那些一味推廣昂貴的新科技手術、而貶低舊技術手術的華而不實的廣告。一項新的調查發現，有很多人在抱怨採用新舊兩種技術治療，同樣都會導致性功能問題和小便失禁。

這項新研究發表於《臨床腫瘤學雜誌》上，是基於超過六百位攝護腺癌症病患的反應，這些攝護腺癌症病患都有接受政府提供給老年人的 Medicare 醫療健康保險。總體來說，接受機器人手術的病人，泌尿問題似乎是稍微普遍一些，不過，兩組病人並沒有什麼顯著的區別。

並沒有什麼有力的證據證明，機器人攝護腺切除手術比傳統手術更好，但機器人攝護腺切除手術卻在美國迅速流行。不過，它的費用也高得多，相較於傳統手術，每次手術費用大約會高出兩千美元。

一台價值幾百萬美元的機器人的確是有一些優勢。例如，它們減少了失血量，動手術時可以幫助醫生看得更清晰。但是，不可否認它並不比傳統手術更能治療癌症，而且在緩解副作用方面，也沒有什麼確切的益處。因此想要接受手術的病人，應該去尋求有經驗的手術醫生，而不是單單把焦點放在新科技。

有研究發現，每年有超過十二萬被診斷患有攝護腺癌症的美國人，適合接受觀察，或是謹慎地等待治療。然而，他們其中大多數人最後還是接受了手術、放射療法或是其他治療方法。

解譯｜在閱讀文章之前，先要預覽題目，然後再帶著問題有針對性地閱讀文章。第 1 題是詞義辨析，第 2 題是判斷正誤，第 3、4 題是文意理解。理解了題目要求之後，閱讀全文，依次作答。

第 1 題是考形容詞 significant 的同義字。選項 (A) 意為「更好的」，選項 (B) 意為「奇怪的」，選項 (C) 意為「重大的」，選項 (D) 意為「必要的」。根據第 2 段內容可知，意為「重大的，顯著的」，所以選 (C)。

第 2 題是判斷正誤，考的是細節，問的是關於機器人手術和傳統手術的敘述，哪一項是正確的。根據第 2 段最後一句內容可知，這兩種手術之後，都存在泌尿問題，與選項 (A) 相符。同樣，此題也可以用排除法來解答。根據第 3 段內容可知，機器人手術費用較高，卻也不見得比傳統手術效果更好，排除選項 (C)、(D)；而選項 (B) 在文中並未提及，也可以排除。所以選 (A)。

第 3 題是文意理解，問的是考慮接受手術的病人，應當考慮什麼。根據第 5 段最後一句內容「Patients who consider surgery should, therefore, look for experienced surgeons, rather than simply focus on technology.」可知，病人應該把焦點放在有經驗的手術醫生，所以選 (A)。

第 4 題同樣是文意理解，問的是作者對於機器人手術的態度。縱觀全文，作者先是由調查結果引出了機器人手術的話題，再根據文獻記載對這項手術提出質疑，接著告誡病人們，應該把焦點放在醫生而不僅僅是技術，由此可知，作者對此的態度是十分客觀的，所以選 (B)。

解答＆技巧 | **01 (C)** **02 (A)** **03 (A)** **04 (B)**

適用 TIP 1　適用 TIP 2　適用 TIP 3　適用 TIP 7　適用 TIP 10
適用 TIP 11　適用 TIP 12　適用 TIP 13　適用 TIP 15　適用 TIP 16

DAY
3

Part 1
詞
彙
題
Day 3
完成 25%

Part 2
綜
合
測
驗
Day 3
完成 50%

Part 3
文
意
選
填
Day 3
完成 75%

Part 4
閱
讀
測
驗
Day 3
完成 100%

補充

complain about ph 抱怨；health insurance ph 健康保險；be based on ph 基於；
catch on ph 流行，受歡迎；tens of thousands ph 成千上萬，數以萬計

7,000 單字

- surgery [ˈsɝdʒərɪ] n 4 手術
- complaint [kəmˈplent] n 3 抱怨
- journal [ˈdʒɝnḷ] n 3 期刊
- clinical [ˈklɪnɪkḷ] a 6 臨床的
- spite [spaɪt] n 3 不顧
- removal [rɪˈmuvḷ] n 6 移除

- surgeon [ˈsɝdʒən] n 4 外科醫師
- operate [ˈɑpəˌret] v 2 動手術
- diagnose [ˈdaɪəgnoz] v 6 診斷
- candidate [ˈkændədet] n 4 候選人
- observation [ˌɑbzɚˈveʃən] n 4 觀察

MEMO

Generally speaking, there is no way of repairing a severed spinal cord. But the research team took nasal stem cells and implanted them into the damaged area. Surprisingly, these cells formed a bridge, along which the nerve fibers re-grew and re-connected.

The research involved rats. These rats were unable to climb a metal ladder, after one of their front paws had been paralyzed to mimic a spinal cord injury. After an injection of stem cells, the rats were able to move nearly as well as uninjured animals. According to the research, paralyzed rats could walk again after a combination of electrical-chemical stimulation and rehabilitation training. Some newspaper reports were prompted talking of "new hope" for paralyzed patients.

The research is actually conducted in this way: the team injected chemicals into the paralyzed rats, aiming at stimulating neurons that control lower body movement. Shortly after the injection, the spinal cords of the rats were stimulated with electrodes.

Then the rats were placed in a harness on a treadmill, which gave them the impression of having a working spinal column. Next, they were encouraged to move towards the end of a platform where a chocolate reward was waiting for them. Over time the animals learned to walk and even run again.

What does this mean for paralyzed patients?

Some scientists are optimistic that patient trials would begin in a year or two. Others give a mixed response to the findings. Overall, the research should be groundbreaking. However, questions would still remain before its usefulness in humans could be finally determined.

That term "neuroplasticity" is crucial. It means the ability of the brain and spinal cord to adapt and recover from moderate injury. And researchers have been trying to exploit for many years. Some people still have the question whether the improvements in the paralyzed rats might in part be due to spontaneous recovery—neuroplasticity—rather than the combination of interventions.

01 The word "implanted" in the first paragraph is closest in meaning to _____.

(A) transported

(B) grew

(C) inserted

(D) delivered

02 Which of the following statements is true?

(A) After the nasal stem cells were implanted, the damaged fibers still remained the same.

(B) Generally a severed spinal cord is impossible to be repaired.

(C) Both front paws of the rats involved in the research had been paralyzed.

(D) With the injection of stem cells, the paralyzed rats still could not move.

03 Which of the following statements about the research of paralyzed rats is not mentioned in the passage?

(A) Some newspaper reports were optimistic about the research of paralyzed rats.

(B) Some scientists believe that patient trials may begin soon.

(C) The research of paralyzed rats is groundbreaking, anyway.

(D) The usefulness of the research in humans has already been determined.

04 What is the author's attitude towards the research of paralyzed rats?

(A) Objective.

(B) Doubtful.

(C) Critical.

(D) Ambiguous.

DAY
3

Part 1
詞
彙
題
Day 3
完成 25%

Part 2
綜
合
測
驗
Day 3
完成 50%

Part 3
文
意
選
填
Day 3
完成 75%

Part 4
閱
讀
測
驗
Day 3
完成 100%

中譯 | 通常來說，斷裂的脊髓是無法修復的。但研究小組卻取來鼻部幹細胞，然後植入受損區。意外的是，這些幹細胞組成一座橋，神經纖維沿著這座橋再生，並且重新連接。

這項研究是以老鼠為實驗對象。這些老鼠的一隻前爪癱瘓，無法爬金屬梯，以此來模擬骨髓受傷。經過幹細胞注射後，牠們幾乎能夠像未受傷的動物一樣活動。在實驗中，老鼠經過電化學刺激和恢復訓練組合療法後，就能夠再次行走。有新聞報導說，癱瘓病人有了新希望。

這項研究其實是在癱瘓的老鼠體內注入藥物，目的是要刺激那些控制肢體運動的神經元。注射後不久，老鼠的脊髓接受了電極刺激。老鼠被套上背帶，放在一台跑步機上，讓牠們覺得自己的脊柱可以正常工作，接下來在平臺的另一端放有一塊巧克力獎品，以此鼓勵牠們走過去。經過一段時間，牠們就學會了走路，甚至能夠再次奔跑。

這對於癱瘓病人有什麼意義？

有些科學家很樂觀地預計，一兩年之內就會在病人身上嘗試此療法。對這項研究結果，其他科學家卻是反應各異。總括來說，這項研究是有開拓性的，但是在確定這樣的方法在人類身上的可用性之前，許多問題也仍然存在。

神經可塑性這個詞是關鍵所在。它是指大腦和脊髓適應中度損傷並且恢復的能力——這也是研究者們多年以來一直在努力探索的。也有人懷疑，癱瘓老鼠的功能性改善，也許有一部分原因是牠自身的恢復能力——神經的可塑性——而不是多種人工干預相結合的治療。

解譯 | 在閱讀文章之前，先要預覽題目，然後再帶著問題有針對性地閱讀文章。第 1 題是詞義辨析，第 2 題是判斷正誤，第 3、4 題是文意理解。理解了題目要求之後，閱讀全文，依次作答。

第 1 題是考動詞 implant 的同義字。選項 (A) 意為「運輸」，選項 (B) 意為「生長」，選項 (C) 意為「移植」，選項 (D) 意為「傳送」。根據第 1 段內容可知，動詞 implant 意為「移植」，所以選 (C)。

第 2 題是判斷正誤，考的是細節，問的是哪一項敘述是正確的。根據第 1 段首句內容「Generally speaking, there is no way of repairing a severed spinal cord.」可知，切斷了的脊髓通常是無法修復的，與選項 (B) 相符。同樣，此題也可以用排除法來解答。根據第 1 段最後一句內容可知，幹細胞植入後，神經纖維再生並且重新連接，選項 (A) 敘述錯誤，排除；根據第 2 段第 2 句可知，研究中的老鼠，只是一隻前爪癱瘓，選項 (C) 錯誤；根據第 2 段第 3 句內容可知，經過幹細胞注射後，老鼠能夠像未受傷的動物一樣活動，選項(D)錯誤。所以選(B)。

第 3 題是文意理解，問的是關於癱瘓老鼠的研究，哪一項敘述在文中沒有提及。第 2 段最後一句內容與選項 (A) 相符，第 4 段首句內容與選項 (B) 相符，第 4 段第 3 句內容選項 (C) 相符。只有選項 (D)，在文中找不到相關敘述，所以選 (D)。

第 4 題同樣是文意理解，問的是對於癱瘓老鼠的研究，作者持何種態度。縱觀全文，作者先是由幹細胞實驗引出話題，再介紹癱瘓老鼠實驗，接著闡述了各方對於這項研究的觀點。由此可知，作者對此是持客觀態度的。所以選 (A)。

解答&技巧 | 01 (C)　02 (B)　03 (D)　04 (A)

適用 TIP 1　適用 TIP 2　適用 TIP 3　適用 TIP 7　適用 TIP 10

適用 TIP 11　適用 TIP 12　適用 TIP 13　適用 TIP 15　適用 TIP 16

補充

spinal cord ph 脊髓；stem cell ph 幹細胞；nerve fiber ph 神經纖維；neuron n 神經元，神經細胞；
recover from ph 恢復

7,000 單字

- cord [kɔrd] n 4 索狀組織
- bridge [brɪdʒ] n 1 橋
- nerve [nɜv] n 3 神經
- metal [ˋmɛtl] a 2 金屬的
- paw [pɔ] n 3 爪子
- paralyze [ˋpærə͵laɪz] v 6 使麻痺，使癱瘓
- mimic [ˋmɪmɪk] v 6 模擬
- injection [ɪnˋdʒɛkʃən] n 6 注射，注入

- stimulation [͵stɪmjəˋleʃən] n 6 刺激
- inject [ɪnˋdʒɛkt] v 6 注射，注入
- platform [ˋplæt͵fɔrm] n 2 平臺
- optimistic [͵ɑptəˋmɪstɪk] a 3 樂觀的
- trial [ˋtraɪəl] n 2 試用
- crucial [ˋkruʃəl] a 6 關鍵的
- moderate [ˋmɑdərɪt] a 4 適度的

MEMO

DAY 3

Part 1
詞
彙
題
Day 3
完成 25%

Part 2
綜
合
測
驗
Day 3
完成 50%

Part 3
文
意
選
填
Day 3
完成 75%

Part 4
閱
讀
測
驗
Day 3
完成 100%

DAY 4

The greater the struggle, the more glorious the triumph.
— Nick Vujicic

挑戰愈艱鉅，勝利愈輝煌。
──尼克・胡哲

▶ **Part 1** | 詞 彙 題

▶ **Part 2** | 綜合測驗

▶ **Part 3** | 文意選填

▶ **Part 4** | 閱讀測驗

Part 1 詞彙題 | Vocabulary Questions

---

01 The tourists are _____ by the scenic beauty of Bali and unwilling to leave.

(A) notified   (B) complicated

(C) fascinated   (D) suspended

中譯｜遊客們被巴里島的美麗風景迷住了，不願意離開。

解說｜四個選項皆為動詞。依據題意，應該是「被巴里島的美麗風景迷住了」，選項 (C) fascinated 表示「使著迷」，符合題意，其他三個選項都不符合題意。

解答＆技巧｜**(C)** 適用 TIP 1　適用 TIP 4

> **補充**
> scenic beauty ph 美麗的風景
>
> **7,000 單字**
> - unwilling [ʌn`wɪlɪŋ] a 2 不情願的
> - notify [`notə͵faɪ] v 5 通知
> - complicate [`kɑmplə͵ket] v 4 使複雜化
> - fascinate [`fæsn͵et] v 5 使著迷
> - suspend [sə`spɛnd] v 5 暫停

---

02 Mary described her journey to London in _____ detail, which made us quite yearning.

(A) militant   (B) vivid

(C) missionary   (D) courageous

中譯｜瑪麗以生動的細節描述了她的倫敦之旅，這令我們非常嚮往。

解說｜四個選項皆為形容詞。依據題意，應該是「以生動的細節描述了她的倫敦之旅」，選項 (B) vivid 表示「生動的」，符合題意，其他三個選項都不符合題意。

解答＆技巧｜**(B)** 適用 TIP 1　適用 TIP 4

> **補充**
> in detail ph 詳細地
>
> **7,000 單字**
> - yearning [`jɜnɪŋ] a 6 嚮往的
> - militant [`mɪlətənt] a 6 好戰的
> - vivid [`vɪvɪd] a 3 生動的
> - missionary [`mɪʃən͵ɛrɪ] a 6 傳教的
> - courageous [kə`redʒəs] a 4 有膽量的

---

03 With no war and conflict in the world, all people can live in peace and _____ with one another.

(A) monopoly   (B) harmony

(C) morality   (D) texture

中譯｜如果世界上沒有了戰爭與衝突，所有人就能夠和平共存、和睦相處。

解說｜四個選項皆為名詞。依據題意，應該是「和平共存、和睦相處」，選項 (B) harmony 表示「和睦」，符合題意，其他三個選項都不符合題意。

解答＆技巧｜**(B)** 適用 TIP 1　適用 TIP 4

> **補充**
> live in peace ph 和平共處
>
> **7,000 單字**
> - one [wʌn] num 1 一
> - monopoly [mə`nɑplɪ] n 6 壟斷
> - harmony [`hɑrmənɪ] n 4 和諧
> - morality [mə`rælətɪ] n 6 道德
> - texture [`tɛkstʃə] n 6 質地

04 These two tribes fought against each other in order to _____ their own independence.

(A) volunteer　　　　(B) scatter
(C) preserve　　　　(D) motivate

中譯｜這兩個部落之間互相爭鬥，以維護他們各自的獨立。

解說｜四個選項皆為動詞。依據題意，應該是「互相爭鬥以維護他們各自的獨立」，選項 (C) preserve 表示「維護」，符合題意，其他三個選項都不符合題意。

解答＆技巧｜**(C)** 適用 TIP 1　適用 TIP 4

補充
fight against ph 反抗，對抗
7,000 單字
• tribe [traɪb] n 3 部落
• volunteer [ˌvɑlənˈtɪr] v 4 自願
• scatter [ˈskætɚ] v 3 使散開
• preserve [prɪˈzɝv] v 4 維護
• motivate [ˈmotəˌvet] v 4 激發

05 The photographer kept on moving around, trying to shoot the target object from different _____.

(A) mottos　　　　(B) naturalists
(C) angles　　　　(D) inputs

中譯｜攝影師不停地走來走去，試圖從不同角度來拍攝目標物。

解說｜四個選項皆為名詞。依據題意，應該是「從不同角度來拍攝目標物」，選項 (C) angles 表示「角度」，符合題意，其他三個選項都不符合題意。

解答＆技巧｜**(C)** 適用 TIP 1　適用 TIP 4

補充
target object ph 目標物體
7,000 單字
• photographer [fəˈtɑgrəfɚ] n 2 攝影師
• motto [ˈmato] n 6 座右銘
• naturalist [ˈnætʃərəlɪst] n 6 自然主義者
• angle [ˈæŋgl] n 3 角度
• input [ˈɪnˌpʊt] n 4 輸入

06 Please show your _____ for purchasing this refrigerator if you claim a refund.

(A) navel　　　　(B) receipt
(C) metropolitan　　(D) metaphor

中譯｜如果你要求退還購買這台冰箱的錢，請出示你的收據。

解說｜四個選項皆為名詞。依據題意，應該是「出示收據」，選項 (B) receipt 表示「收據」，符合題意，其他三個選項都不符合題意。

解答＆技巧｜**(B)** 適用 TIP 1　適用 TIP 4

補充
claim a refund ph 要求退款
7,000 單字
• refrigerator [rɪˈfrɪdʒəˌretɚ] n 2 冰箱
• navel [ˈnevl] n 6 肚臍
• receipt [rɪˈsit] n 3 收據
• metropolitan [ˌmɛtrəˈpɑlətn] n 6 大都市人
• metaphor [ˈmɛtəfɚ] n 6 隱喻

DAY 4

Part 1 詞彙題
Day 4 完成 25%

Part 2 綜合測驗
Day 4 完成 50%

Part 3 文意選填
Day 4 完成 75%

Part 4 閱讀測驗
Day 4 完成 100%

07 Having stayed in Japan for six years, Linda is _____ in Japanese besides English.

(A) promising   (B) ethical

(C) fluent   (D) feasible

補充
be fluent in ph （語文）流利的

7,000 單字
- in [ɪn] prep **1** 在～裡
- promising [`prɑmɪsɪŋ] a **4** 有希望的
- ethical [`ɛθɪk!] a **6** 道德的
- fluent [`ɛfluənt] a **4** 流利的
- feasible [`fizəb!] a **6** 可行的

中譯 | 琳達在日本待了六年，除了英語，她還會說流利的日語。

解說 | 四個選項皆為形容詞。依據題意，應該是「會說流利的日語」，選項 (C) fluent 表示「流利的」，符合題意，是正確選項。

解答＆技巧 | **(C)** 適用 TIP 1 適用 TIP 4

---

08 Although he is a chef, Roberto _____ cooks his own meals. 【94年學測英文】

(A) rarely   (B) bitterly

(C) naturally   (D) skillfully

補充
cook a meal ph 做飯

7,000 單字
- chef [ʃɛf] n **5** 廚師
- rarely [`rɛrlɪ] ad **2** 很少
- bitterly [`bɪtəlɪ] ad **2** 悲痛地
- naturally [`nætʃərəlɪ] ad **2** 自然地
- skillfully [`skɪlfəlɪ] ad **2** 巧妙地

中譯 | 雖然羅伯托是一名廚師，但他很少給自己做飯。

解說 | 四個選項皆為副詞。依據題意，although 表示轉折，所以應該是「很少給自己做飯」，選項 (A) rarely 意思是「很少」，表示否定，符合題意，其他三個選項都不符合題意。

解答＆技巧 | **(A)** 適用 TIP 1 適用 TIP 4

---

09 The police made a thorough _____ of the fire and finally knew about the cause of it.

(A) faculty   (B) extension

(C) federation   (D) investigation

補充
make an investigation
ph 進行調查

7,000 單字
- thorough [`θɝo] a **4** 徹底的
- faculty [`fæk!tɪ] n **6** 科
- extension [ɪk`stɛnʃən] n **5** 延長
- federation [ˌfɛdə`reʃən] n **6** 聯邦
- investigation [ɪnˌvɛstə`geʃən] n **4** 調查

中譯 | 員警對火災進行了徹底調查，最終了解了失火的原因。

解說 | 四個選項皆為名詞。依據題意，應該是「對火災進行了徹底調查」，選項 (D) investigation 表示「調查」，符合題意，其他三個選項都不符合題意。

解答＆技巧 | **(D)** 適用 TIP 1 適用 TIP 4

10 He stayed up late last night to finish the capital project, so he is drinking a lot of coffee to keep _____ now.

(A) fireproof　　　　(B) formidable

(C) awake　　　　　(D) frail

補充
capital project ph 資金計畫

7,000 單字
- late [let] ad ① 遲地
- fireproof [`faɪr͵pruf] a ⑥ 防火的
- formidable [`fɔrmɪdəbl] a ⑥ 令人敬畏的
- awake [ə`wek] a ② 清醒的
- frail [frel] a ⑥ 脆弱的

中譯｜昨天晚上他熬夜做完了資金計畫，所以現在他正在大量喝咖啡來保持清醒。

解說｜四個選項皆為形容詞。依據題意，應該是「喝咖啡來保持清醒」，選項 (C) awake 表示「清醒的」，與 keep 連用表示「保持清醒」，符合題意。

解答＆技巧｜**(C)** 適用 TIP 2　適用 TIP 4

---

11 Today the general manager has to attend seven meetings, so it is really a _____ schedule for him.

(A) explicit　　　　(B) dual

(C) tight　　　　　(D) documentary

補充
general manager ph 總經理

7,000 單字
- seven [`sɛvn̩] num ① 七
- explicit [ɪk`splɪsɪt] a ⑥ 明確的
- dual [`djuəl] a ⑥ 雙重的
- tight [taɪt] a ③ 緊湊的
- documentary [͵dɑkjə`mɛntərɪ] a ⑥ 記錄的

中譯｜今天總經理要參加七個會議，所以這對他來說，真的是一個緊湊的日程。

解說｜四個選項皆為形容詞。依據題意，應該是「緊湊的日程」，選項 (C) tight 表示「緊湊的」，符合題意，是正確選項。

解答＆技巧｜**(C)** 適用 TIP 1　適用 TIP 4

---

12 He finished drinking all the beer within the shortest time, so he finally won the drinking _____.

(A) drill　　　　　(B) doctrine

(C) diversity　　　　(D) contest

補充
the shortest time ph 最短時間

7,000 單字
- beer [bɪr] n ② 啤酒
- drill [drɪl] n ④ 訓練
- doctrine [`dɑktrɪn] n ⑥ 教義
- diversity [daɪ`vɝsətɪ] n ⑥ 多樣性
- contest [`kɑntɛst] n ④ 比賽

中譯｜他在最短的時間內喝完了所有啤酒，所以他最終贏得了喝酒比賽。

解說｜四個選項皆為名詞。依據題意，應該是「贏得了喝酒比賽」，選項 (D) contest 表示「比賽」，符合題意，是正確選項。

解答＆技巧｜**(D)** 適用 TIP 1　適用 TIP 4

DAY
4

Part 1
詞
彙
題
Day 4
完成 25%

Part 2
綜
合
測
驗
Day 4
完成 50%

Part 3
文
意
選
填
Day 4
完成 75%

Part 4
閱
讀
測
驗
Day 4
完成 100%

13 Learning to do household _____ helps the children cultivate patience and develop a sense of responsibility.

(A) missions　　　(B) chores

(C) diversions　　(D) distractions

補充

household chores ph 家務

7,000 單字
- patience [ˈpeʃəns] n 3 耐心
- mission [ˈmɪʃən] n 3 使命
- chore [tʃor] n 4 雜務
- diversion [daɪˈvɝʒən] n 6 轉移
- distraction [dɪˈstrækʃən] n 6 消遣

中譯｜學習做家務有助於培養孩子的耐心和責任感。

解說｜四個選項皆為名詞。依據題意，應該是「學習做家務」，選項 (B) chores 表示「雜務」，而 house chores 表示「家務」，符合題意，其他三個選項都不符合題意。

解答＆技巧｜**(B)**　適用 TIP 2　適用 TIP 4

---

14 The tsunami had resulted in the death of thousands of people, which was the most serious natural _____ in this area.

(A) diplomacy　　(B) directory

(C) descendant　(D) disaster

補充

thousands of ph 成千上萬的

7,000 單字
- tsunami [tsuˈnɑmɪ] n 6 海嘯
- diplomacy [dɪˈploməsɪ] n 6 外交
- directory [dəˈrɛktərɪ] n 6 目錄
- descendant [dɪˈsɛndənt] n 6 後裔
- disaster [dɪˈzæstɚ] n 4 災難

中譯｜海嘯導致了上千人死亡，是這個地區發生過最嚴重的一次自然災害。

解說｜四個選項皆為名詞。依據題意，應該是「最嚴重的一次自然災害」，選項 (D) disaster 表示「災害」，符合題意，是正確選項。

解答＆技巧｜**(D)**　適用 TIP 1　適用 TIP 4

---

15 The factory was closed down last month because of its _____ accounting.

(A) dental　　　(B) delinquent

(C) false　　　 (D) cordial

補充

close down ph 關閉，查封
false accounting ph 偽造帳目

7,000 單字
- factory [ˈfæktərɪ] n 1 工廠
- dental [ˈdɛntl] a 6 牙齒的
- delinquent [dɪˈlɪŋkwənt] a 6 有過失的
- false [fɔls] a 1 偽造的
- cordial [ˈkɔrdʒəl] a 6 熱忱的

中譯｜這家工廠偽造帳目，於上個月被查封了。

解說｜四個選項皆為形容詞。依據題意，應該是「工廠偽造帳目而被查封」，選項 (C) false 表示「偽造的」，符合題意，其他三個選項都不符合題意。

解答＆技巧｜**(C)**　適用 TIP 1　適用 TIP 4

16 I don't know for sure what I am going to do this weekend, but _____ I plan to visit an old friend of mine in southern Taiwan. 【94年指考英文】

(A) tentatively   (B) inevitably

(C) unknowingly   (D) numerously

中譯 | 我還不確定這個週末要做什麼，但我暫時打算去拜訪一位住在南台灣的朋友。

解說 | 四個選項皆為副詞。依據題意，應該是「暫時打算去拜訪一位朋友」，選項 (A) tentatively 表示「暫時地」，符合題意，是正確選項。

解答＆技巧 | **(A)** 適用 TIP 1　適用 TIP 4

補充
for sure ph 確實

7,000 單字
- sure [ʃʊr] ad 1 確切地
- tentatively [ˋtɛntətɪvlɪ] ad 5 暫時地
- inevitably [ɪnˋɛvətəblɪ] ad 6 不可避免地
- unknowingly [ʌnˋnoɪŋlɪ] ad 5 不知不覺地
- numerously [ˋnjumərəslɪ] ad 4 無數地

---

17 Because of _____ differences, students in this university speak different dialects.

(A) compatible   (B) comparative

(C) communicative   (D) regional

中譯 | 由於地區差異，這所大學的學生說不同的方言。

解說 | 本題為因果關係句。依據題意，應該是「地區差異導致這所大學的學生說不同的方言」，選項 (D) regional 表示「地區的」，符合題意，其他三個選項都不符合題意。

解答＆技巧 | **(D)** 適用 TIP 3　適用 TIP 4

補充
regional difference ph 地區差異

7,000 單字
- dialect [ˋdaɪəlɛkt] n 5 方言
- compatible [kəmˋpætəbl] a 6 相容的
- comparative [kəmˋpærətɪv] a 6 比較的
- communicative [kəˋmjunəˏketɪv] a 6 健談的
- regional [ˋridʒənl] a 3 地區的

---

18 The security guard saw a man steal the bike on a CCTV _____.

(A) coincidence   (B) monitor

(C) closure   (D) bureaucracy

中譯 | 保全人員在閉路監視器上看到了一名男子在偷自行車。

解說 | 四個選項皆為名詞。依據題意，應該是「在閉路監視器上看到有人在偷自行車」，選項 (B) monitor 表示「監視器」，符合題意，其他三個選項都不符合題意。

解答＆技巧 | **(B)** 適用 TIP 1　適用 TIP 4

補充
security guard ph 保全人員，警衛

7,000 單字
- bike [baɪk] n 1 自行車
- coincidence [koˋɪnsɪdəns] n 6 巧合
- monitor [ˋmɑnətə] n 4 監視器
- closure [ˋkloʒə] n 6 關閉
- bureaucracy [bjuˋrɑkrəsɪ] n 6 官僚主義

DAY
4

Part 1
詞
彙
題
Day 4
完成 25%

Part 2
綜
合
測
驗
Day 4
完成 50%

Part 3
文
意
選
填
Day 4
完成 75%

Part 4
閱
讀
測
驗
Day 4
完成 100%

19 If you can pass through a three-month check, I will _____ you for a promotion as marketing manager.

(A) vibrate (B) wade

(C) recommend (D) contemplate

補充
marketing manager ph 行銷經理
7,000 單字
· three [θri] num 1 三
· vibrate [ˈvaɪbret] v 5 振動
· wade [wed] v 5 跋涉
· recommend [ˌrɛkəˈmɛnd]
  v 5 推薦
· contemplate [ˈkɑntɛmˌplet]
  v 5 沉思

中譯｜如果你能通過為期三個月的考核，我就推薦你升職當行銷經理。

解說｜本題為條件副詞子句。依據題意，應該是「推薦你升職當行銷經理」，選項 (C) recommend 表示「推薦」，符合題意，其他三個選項都不符合題意。

解答＆技巧｜**(C)** 適用 TIP 1 適用 TIP 4

---

20 The dark brown trousers have _____ to light brown under the impact of direct sunlight.

(A) cycled (B) faded

(C) loosened (D) creaked

補充
dark brown ph 深棕色
7,000 單字
· trousers [ˈtrauzɚz] n 1 褲子
· cycle [ˈsaɪk!] v 4 循環
· fade [fed] v 3 褪色
· loosen [ˈlusn̩] v 3 鬆開
· creak [krik] v 5 使咯吱咯吱響

中譯｜在陽光直接照射的影響下，褲子由深棕色褪色成了淺棕色。

解說｜四個選項皆為動詞。依據題意，應該是「褲子由深棕色褪色成了淺棕色」，選項 (B) faded 表示「褪色」，符合題意，是正確選項。

解答＆技巧｜**(B)** 適用 TIP 1 適用 TIP 4

---

21 My neighbor comes to my home nearly every day, and her _____ visit makes me feel tired.

(A) desirable (B) descriptive

(C) frequent (D) destructive

補充
every day ph 每天
7,000 單字
· tired [taɪrd] a 1 疲倦的
· desirable [dɪˈzaɪrəb!]
  a 3 令人滿意的
· descriptive [dɪˈskrɪptɪv]
  a 5 描寫的
· frequent [ˈfrikwənt] a 3 頻繁的
· destructive [dɪˈstrʌktɪv]
  a 5 破壞的

中譯｜我的鄰居幾乎每天都來我家，她頻繁的拜訪我使我感到很厭煩。

解說｜本題是由 and 連接的並列句。依據題意，應該是「頻繁的拜訪」，選項 (C) frequent 表示「頻繁的」，符合題意，其他三個選項都不符合題意。

解答＆技巧｜**(C)** 適用 TIP 3 適用 TIP 4

22 The driver _____ the traffic regulations and was subjected to severe criticism and punishment.

(A) dispensed   (B) violated

(C) elevated   (D) invaded

中譯｜那名司機違反了交通規則，受到了嚴厲的批評與處罰。

解說｜四個選項皆為動詞。依據題意，應該是「司機違反了交通規則」，選項 (B) violated 表示「違反」，符合題意，是正確選項。

解答＆技巧｜ **(B)** 　適用 TIP 1 　適用 TIP 4

補充
traffic regulations ph 交通規則

7,000 單字
- regulation [ˌrɛgjə`leʃən] n 4 規則
- dispense [dɪ`spɛns] v 5 分配
- violate [`vaɪəˌlet] v 4 違反
- elevate [`ɛləˌvet] v 5 提升
- invade [ɪn`ved] v 4 侵略

---

23 Few boys can perform ballet as well as girls do; however, jack is an _____.

(A) endeavor   (B) exaggeration

(C) exception   (D) evergreen

中譯｜很少有男孩跳芭蕾舞能跳得跟女孩一樣好，然而，傑克是個例外。

解說｜本題中的 however 表示轉折，依據題意，應該是「傑克是個例外」，選項 (C) exception 表示「例外」，符合題意，其他三個選項都不符合題意。

解答＆技巧｜ **(C)** 　適用 TIP 1 　適用 TIP 4

補充
as well as ph 和～一樣

7,000 單字
- ballet [`bæle] n 4 芭蕾舞
- endeavor [ɪn`dɛvə] n 5 努力
- exaggeration [ɪgˌzædʒə`reʃən] n 5 誇張
- exception [ɪk`sɛpʃən] n 4 例外
- evergreen [`ɛvəˌgrin] n 5 常綠樹

---

24 If you want the sponge to dry quickly, you should _____ the water out of it.

(A) exclaim   (B) squeeze

(C) freeze   (D) flip

中譯｜如果你想讓海綿快點乾，就把它裡面的水擠出來。

解說｜本題是一個條件句，依據題意，應該是「把海綿裡的水擠出來」，選項 (B) squeeze 表示「擠出」，符合題意，是正確選項。

解答＆技巧｜ **(B)** 　適用 TIP 1 　適用 TIP 4

補充
out of ph 自～離開

7,000 單字
- sponge [spʌndʒ] n 5 海綿
- exclaim [ɪks`klem] v 5 呼喊
- squeeze [skwiz] v 3 擠出
- freeze [friz] v 3 冰凍
- flip [flɪp] v 5 輕彈

DAY
4

Part 1
詞
彙
題
Day 4
完成 25%

Part 2
綜
合
測
驗
Day 4
完成 50%

Part 3
文
意
選
填
Day 4
完成 75%

Part 4
閱
讀
測
驗
Day 4
完成 100%

Part 2 綜合測驗 | Comprehensive Questions

 ▶

Many people have a wrong idea that when they get old, their families will place them in __01__ homes. Thus they have to live with strangers for the rest of their lives, and their grown children may visit them __02__ , and they will also have no visitors. But this has been proved to be imaginary. In fact, most of the family members would like to provide care to the __03__ people, and they believe that they are the best people for the job. They think that they can take care of the elderly people better than anyone else, and they are willing to do the job themselves.

Many __04__ say that they have an obligation to help the old people and helping others would make them feel more useful. They also hope that they could deserve care when they become old and dependent. By this __05__ , providing care for the elderly people and being taken care of could be a mutually satisfying experience for everyone in the world.

01 _____ (A) nursing   (B) motor
                   (C) mobile   (D) initiative

02 _____ (A) independently   (B) mutually
                   (C) occasionally   (D) similarly

03 _____ (A) night   (B) elderly
                   (C) white   (D) village

04 _____ (A) characters   (B) policemen
                   (C) workmen   (D) caregivers

05 _____ (A) time   (B) token
                   (C) means   (D) way

中譯｜ 許多人都錯誤地認為，當他們年老時，他們的家人會把他們安置到養老院裡。這樣他們就不得不跟陌生人一起度過餘生，他們的成年子女也許只會偶爾來看望他們，平常也沒有人會來拜訪。但是這種想法證明只是一種假想。事實上，大多數家庭成員都願意為老人提供關懷與照料，他們相信他們是做這項工作的最佳人選。他們認為他們能夠比其他人更好地照顧老人，並且很願意自己來做這項工作。

許多看護者說，他們有義務幫助老人，並且幫助別人會使他們感到更有用處。他們也希望當他們變得年老、需要依賴他人時，可以值得別人關心。由此看來，對於世界上的所有人來說，關心老年人與被照顧會是一種相互令人滿意的體驗。

解說｜ 本篇短文的主題是「養老」，講述了老人和年輕人對待養老的不同的態度。第 1 題依據題意，要選擇跟老人相關的地方，而 nursing home 意思是「養老院」，符合題意，所以正確選擇為 (A)。第 2 題要選擇合適的副詞來修飾動詞 visit，將四個選項一一代入，副詞 occasionally 意思是「偶爾」，符合題意，所以最佳選項是 (C)。第 3 題要選擇可以用於修飾人的形容詞，而依據題意要選擇「老年人」，可以用 elderly people 來表達，即正確選項是 (B)。第 4 題四個選項都是名詞，但是跟照顧老人相關的是 caregivers，意思是「看護人」，只有選項 (D) 符合題意。第 5 題考跟介系詞 by 相關的介系詞片語的用法。依據題意，by this token 意思是「由此看來」，符合題意，所以選 (B)。

解答&技巧｜ **01 (A) 02 (C) 03 (B) 04 (D) 05 (B)**

適用 TIP 1   適用 TIP 2   適用 TIP 4   適用 TIP 7

補充

grown ⓐ 成年的；family member ph 家庭成員；mutually ad 共同地；satisfying ⓐ 令人滿意的；everyone pron 人人

7,000 單字

- wrong [rɔŋ] ⓐ 1 錯誤的
- idea [aɪˋdiə] n 1 想法
- place [ples] v 1 放置
- prove [pruv] v 1 證明
- imaginary [ɪˋmædʒəˏnɛrɪ] ⓐ 4 虛構的
- provide [prəˋvaɪd] v 2 提供
- better [ˋbɛtə] ad 1 更好地
- obligation [ˏɑbləˋgeʃən] n 6 義務

- deserve [dɪˋzɝv] v 4 應得
- become [bɪˋkʌm] v 1 變成
- dependent [dɪˋpɛndənt] ⓐ 4 依靠的
- mobile [ˋmobɪl] ⓐ 3 非固定的
- initiative [ɪˋnɪʃətɪv] ⓐ 6 主動的
- village [ˋvɪlɪdʒ] n 2 村莊
- token [ˋtokən] n 5 記號

DAY 4

Part 1
詞彙題
Day 4
完成 25%

Part 2
綜合測驗
Day 4
完成 50%

Part 3
文意選填
Day 4
完成 75%

Part 4
閱讀測驗
Day 4
完成 100%

Nowadays, most countries in the world have built canals near the __01__ and made them parallel to the coast. The size of a canal mainly depends on the kind of boats which go through it. Generally a canal must be wide enough to __02__ two large boats to pass each other easily, and deep enough to leave about two feet of water beneath the keel of the large boat.

Some famous canals, such as the Suez and the Panama, could save the ships much time of shipment by __03__ their voyage by a thousand miles. With canals, a large quantity of goods could be shipped more cheaply by boat than by any other means of transport, and the risks could also be __04__. Of all the canals, some permit boats to reach cities that are not located on the coast, and some others could drain lands with too much water, helping to irrigate fields that lack water and __05__ water power for factories and mills.

01 _____ (A) ocean   (B) valley
          (C) land   (D) forest

02 _____ (A) leak   (B) survey
          (C) permit   (D) observe

03 _____ (A) escaping   (B) shortening
          (C) drying   (D) affording

04 _____ (A) revealed   (B) exposed
          (C) opened   (D) reduced

05 _____ (A) develop   (B) furnish
          (C) uncover   (D) discover

中譯｜當今，世界上的大多數國家都在沿海處修建了運河，並且使運河與海岸平行。運河的大小主要取決於穿過運河的船隻種類。通常來說，一個運河的寬度必須要能夠允許兩隻大船輕易地交錯通過，深度也要足夠讓大船船底下方留出兩呎水深。一些著名的運河，如蘇伊士運河和巴拿馬運河，可以透過將航程縮短一千英哩，為船隻節省很多運送時間。有了運河，大量貨物能夠用船隻進行運輸，比用其他任何運輸方式都更為廉價，風險也會降低。在所有的運河中，一些運河允許船隻到達那些並不位於沿海地區的城市，而其他的一些運河則可以將水太多的陸地排乾，來幫助灌溉那些缺水的田地，以及為工廠、製造廠等提供水力發電。

解說｜本篇短文的主旨是「運河」，介紹了運河的修建、特點以及好處。第 1 題是常識性的問題。運河一般修建在沿海處，便於海洋運輸，所以第一個空格要選擇 ocean，正確選擇為 (A)。第 2 題考能夠與介系詞 to 連用的動詞。將四個選項一一代入可知，只有 permit 表示「允許」符合題意，所以最佳選項是 (C)。第 3 題要選擇合適的動詞。依據題意，要想節省時間，就要縮短航程，只有 shortening 表示「縮短」符合題意，即正確選項是 (B)。第 4 題的四個選項都是動詞。根據上下文的內容可知，運河可以降低運輸的風險，而 reduced 表示「降低」，所以只有選項 (D) 符合題意。第 5 題將四個選項的動詞一一代入空格，只有 furnish 表示「提供，供應」符合題意，所以選 (B)。

解答＆技巧｜ 01 (A)　 02 (C)　 03 (B)　 04 (D)　 05 (B)

適用 TIP 1　適用 TIP 2　適用 TIP 7　適用 TIP 11

補充
Suez n 蘇伊士；Panama n 巴拿馬；on the coast ph 在沿海地區；cheaply ad 廉價地；
irrigate v 灌溉

7,000 單字

- canal [kə`næl] n 5 運河
- parallel [`pærə‚lɛl] a 5 平行的
- coast [kost] n 1 海岸
- boat [bot] n 1 船
- large [lardʒ] a 1 大的
- water [`wɔtɚ] n 1 水
- ship [ʃɪp] n 1 船
- mile [maɪl] n 1 英哩

- transport [`træns‚pɔrt] n 3 運輸
- drain [dren] v 3 排出，排捍
- field [fild] n 2 田地
- valley [`vælɪ] n 2 山谷
- observe [əb`zɝv] v 3 觀察
- shorten [`ʃɔrtn] v 3 縮短
- furnish [`fɝnɪʃ] v 4 提供

DAY
4

Part 1
詞
彙
題
Day 4
完成 25%

Part 2
綜
合
測
驗
Day 4
完成 50%

Part 3
文
意
選
填
Day 4
完成 75%

Part 4
閱
讀
測
驗
Day 4
完成 100%

More than forty universities have been built in Britain. Among all of them, eight universities are completely new, and ten other ones are created by __01__ old colleges of technology into universities. Meanwhile, the number of students at the universities has doubled, from 70,000 to more than 200,000. Nearly all the universities are private, and each one has its own governing councils, __02__ local businessmen, local politicians and academics. In addition, nearly all the funds used for the universities __03__ from state grants.

At the universities, all the students need to pay fees and living costs, but they may receive help from the local authority. Many students will choose to take full-time or part-time jobs in the summer __04__ , but they do not normally do that during the academic year. Though the Department of Education will take responsibility for the payment covering the whole expenditure of the universities, it does not have direct control because it must take the __05__ of the University Grants Committee.

01 _____ (A) making   (B) consisting
(C) taking   (D) converting

02 _____ (A) inclusive   (B) including
(C) conclusive   (D) concluding

03 _____ (A) derive   (B) define
(C) involve   (D) elaborate

04 _____ (A) profit   (B) experiment
(C) vacation   (D) travel

05 _____ (A) pleasure   (B) advice
(C) shelter   (D) grade

DAY
4

Part 1
詞
彙
題
Day 4
完成 25%

Part 2
綜
合
測
驗
Day 4
完成 50%

Part 3
文
意
選
填
Day 4
完成 75%

Part 4
閱
讀
測
驗
Day 4
完成 100%

中譯｜英國已經建立了超過四十所大學。其中，八所大學是完全新建的，而其他十所是由舊的技術學院轉變而來的。與此同時，大學生的數量也已經翻倍，從七萬人增加到二十多萬人。幾乎所有的大學都是私立的，每一所都有它自己的學生自治會，包括地方商人和從政者，以及大學教師。此外，幾乎所有用於大學的基金都來自國家撥款。

在大學裡，所有學生都需要支付學費和生活費，但是他們可以獲得地方當局的幫助。許多學生選擇在暑假期間做全職或兼職工作，但是他們通常不會在學年裡這樣做。儘管教育部門會負責支付大學的全部開支，但是沒有直接支配，因為它必須聽從大學教育資助委員會的意見。

解說｜本篇短文的主旨是「英國的大學」，詳細介紹了英國大學的建立和學生的上學問題。第 1 題要選擇合適的動詞。依據題意，另外十所學校應該是由舊的學院轉變而來的，而 converting 表示「轉化，改變」，所以正確選項為 (D)。第 2 題空格後面的句子作整個句子的伴隨副詞，且與主句是包含關係，including 意思是「包括」，所以最符合題意的選項是 (B)。第 3 題根據上下文的內容可知，要選擇「來自於」，可以用 derive form 來表達，所以正確選項是 (A)。第 4 題主要考名詞片語的用法。依據題意，「暑假」可以表達為 summer vacation，只有選項 (C) 符合題意。第 5 題的四個選項都是名詞，但是依據上下文，take the advice 表示「採納建議」，符合題意，所以選 (B)。

解答＆技巧｜ 01 **(D)**　 02 **(B)**　 03 **(A)**　 04 **(C)**　 05 **(B)**

適用 TIP 1　適用 TIP 2　適用 TIP 4　適用 TIP 7

補充
governing council ph 學生自治會；living costs ph 生活費；full-time a 全職的；
normally ad 正常地；University Grants Committee ph 大學教育資助委員會

7,000 單字

- among [ə`mʌŋ] prep 1 在～之中
- create [krɪ`et] v 2 創造
- meanwhile [`min‚hwaɪl] ad 3 同時
- private [`praɪvɪt] a 2 私人的
- council [`kaʊnsl] n 4 委員會
- fund [fʌnd] n 3 基金
- grant [grænt] n 5 獎學金，助學金
- authority [ə`θɔrətɪ] n 4 權威

- academic [‚ækə`dɛmɪk] a 4 學院的
- department [dɪ`pɑrtmənt] n 2 部門
- education [‚ɛdʒu`keʃən] n 2 教育
- convert [kən`vɝt] v 5 轉變
- inclusive [ɪn`klusɪv] a 6 包括的
- elaborate [ɪ`læbə‚ret] v 5 精心製作
- profit [`prɑfɪt] n 3 利潤

4 ▶ 95 年指考英文

Young visitors to museums often complain about having museum feet, the tired feeling one gets after spending too much time in a museum. A case of museum feet makes one feel like saying: "This is __01__ . I could have done the painting myself. When can we sit down? What time is it?"

Studies of museum behavior show that the average visitor spends about four seconds looking at one object. For young visitors, the time span can be __02__ shorter. Children are more interested in smells, sounds, and the "feel" of a place than looking at a work of art. If they stay in a museum too long, a feeling of boredom and monotony will build up, leading __03__ to impatience and fatigue.

To __04__ museum feet, try not to have children look at too many things in one visit. It is reported that young visitors get more out of a visit if they focus on __05__ nine objects. One and a half hours is the ideal time to keep their eyes and minds sharp, and their feet happy!

| 01 | _____ | (A) boring | (B) difficult |
| | | (C) cool | (D) exciting |

| 02 | _____ | (A) almost | (B) also |
| | | (C) even | (D) meanwhile |

| 03 | _____ | (A) efficiently | (B) eventually |
| | | (C) fortunately | (D) permanently |

| 04 | _____ | (A) affect | (B) approach |
| | | (C) assure | (D) avoid |

| 05 | _____ | (A) no better than | (B) no less than |
| | | (C) no more than | (D) no sooner than |

中譯 │ 參觀博物館的年輕人時常會抱怨走到腳痠而有博物館症候群（museum feet），這種疲憊感是因為在博物館裡耗了太多時間而產生的。有這種症狀的人會想說：「這真的好無聊喔，這種畫我自己也能畫。我們什麼時候可以能坐下來？現在幾點了？」

博物館行為的研究顯示，每位參觀者平均花約四秒鐘觀賞一件作品。對於年紀較輕的參觀者，所花的時間可能更短。對孩子們來說，味道、聲音以及一個地方的「感覺」比較容易提起他們的興趣，而不是去觀看一件藝術作品。如果他們在博物館待太久，就會愈來愈覺得無聊與單調，最後導致不耐煩與疲憊。

為了避免得到這種博物館症候群，試著不要讓孩子一次參觀太多物品。根據報導，年紀較輕的參觀者如果一次參觀不超過九件物品，可以學到更多的東西。而若要他們保持眼睛敏銳和頭腦的清晰，腳步還要輕鬆的話，一個半鐘頭是最理想的時間。

解說 │ 本篇短文介紹了在參觀博物館時經常發生的一種現象「博物館症候群」（museum feet）。第 1 題根據上下文的內容可知，有 museum feet 這種症狀的人會對所參觀的事物感到無趣，而 boring 意思是「無聊的」，符合題意，所以正確選項為 (A)。第 2 題要選擇合適的副詞來修飾形容詞比較級 shorter。依據題意，even 可以修飾比較級，所以最符合題意的選項是 (C)。第 3 題將四個選項的副詞一一代入可知，eventually 表示「最終」符合題意，即正確選項是 (B)。第 4 題根據上下文的內容可知，後面講的是避免產生 museum feet 的方法，所以要選用動詞 avoid，只有選項 (D) 符合題意。第 5 題依據題意可知，看的物品愈少，收穫就會愈多，no more than 符合題意，所以選 (C)。

解答&技巧 │ 01 **(A)**　02 **(C)**　03 **(B)**　04 **(D)**　05 **(C)**

適用 TIP 1　適用 TIP 2　適用 TIP 7　適用 TIP 11

補充

tired ⓐ 疲倦的；spend too much time ⓟʰ 花費過多時間；interested ⓐ 感興趣的；impatience ⓝ 不耐煩；one and a half hours ⓟʰ 一個半小時

7,000 單字

- museum [mjuˈzɪəm] ⓝ ② 博物館
- complain [kəmˈplen] ⓥ ② 抱怨
- case [kes] ⓝ ① 情況
- sit [sɪt] ⓥ ① 坐
- second [ˈsɛkənd] ⓝ ① 秒
- smell [smɛl] ⓝ ① 氣味
- art [ɑrt] ⓝ ① 藝術
- long [lɔŋ] ⓐᵈ ① 長期地

- monotony [məˈnɑtənɪ] ⓝ ⑥ 單調
- fatigue [fəˈtig] ⓝ ⑤ 疲勞
- focus [ˈfokəs] ⓥ ② 集中
- mind [maɪnd] ⓝ ① 頭腦
- sharp [ʃɑrp] ⓐ ① 敏銳的
- also [ˈɔlso] ⓐᵈ ① 也
- approach [əˈprotʃ] ⓥ ③ 接近

DAY 4

Part 1
詞
彙
題
Day 4
完成 25%

Part 2
綜
合
測
驗
Day 4
完成 50%

Part 3
文
意
選
填
Day 4
完成 75%

Part 4
閱
讀
測
驗
Day 4
完成 100%

Children can model themselves largely on their parents, and they will do so mainly __01__ identification. Once they believe that they have the same qualities and feelings as their parents, they will identify with them. What the parents do and say as well as the things they do to the children will __02__ influence the children's behavior. Therefore, the parents must __03__ behave like the type of person they want their children to become.

The parents' actions will also affect the self-image of the children. If the children see many positive qualities in their parents, they will likely learn to behave in a positive way and vice versa. Although the children can modify their self-images themselves, they may also be __04__ by peer groups.

According to the study, some events may have a permanent effect on the children's behavior. For example, if the children know they are loved, they can accept the divorce or death of their parents. But if they feel unloved, they will regard such events __05__ rejection or punishment.

01 _____ (A) through   (B) with
(C) onto   (D) upon

02 _____ (A) inexplicably   (B) inexpressibly
(C) inevitably   (D) luckily

03 _____ (A) subjectively   (B) consistently
(C) inextricably   (D) inexpediently

04 _____ (A) classified   (B) discovered
(C) invented   (D) influenced

05 _____ (A) as   (B) to
(C) for   (D) in

DAY
4

Part 1
詞
彙
題
Day 4
完成 25%

Part 2
綜
合
測
驗
Day 4
完成 50%

Part 3
文
意
選
填
Day 4
完成 75%

Part 4
閱
讀
測
驗
Day 4
完成 100%

中譯｜兒童在很大程度上能夠模仿他們的父母，他們主要透過認同來進行模仿。一旦他們相信自己有著和父母一樣的特質和感覺，就會對父母產生認同。父母做的事、說的話，以及對孩子們所做的事情，都會不可避免地影響到孩子們的行為。因此，父母想要孩子成為什麼樣的人，他們本身的表現就必須與那樣的人一致。

父母的行為也會影響到孩子的自我形象。如果孩子從父母身上看到了正面的特質，他們很可能會積極地學著那樣做，反之亦然。儘管孩子能夠自己修改形象，但是他們也會受到同儕團體的影響。

據調查，某些事情能夠對孩子的行為造成永久性的影響。例如，如果孩子們知道有人愛自己，他們就能夠接受父母離婚或是死亡。但是如果他們沒有感受到愛，他們就會認為這些事情是對他們的拒絕或者懲罰。

解說｜本篇短文的主旨是「兒童行為模仿」，說明了父母的行為對孩子的行為所產生的影響。第 1 題要選合適的介系詞。依據題意，identification（認同）是兒童進行模仿的方法，可以用 through 來表示「通過」，所以正確選擇為 (A)。第 2 題四個選項都是副詞，將其一一代入空格，inevitably 意思是「不可避免地」符合題意，所以最佳選項是 (C)。第 3 題要選擇合適的副詞來修飾動詞 behave。依據題意，consistently 意思是「一貫地，一致地」符合題意，所以正確選項是 (B)。第 4 題要選擇合適的動詞。依據題意，兒童會受到同儕的影響，應該選用 influenced，只有選項 (D) 符合題意。第 5 題考語法知識的應用。動詞 regard 通常與介系詞 as 連用，表示「把～認作」，所以選 (A)。

解答＆技巧｜ 01 (A)　02 (C)　03 (B)　04 (D)　05 (A)

適用 TIP 1　適用 TIP 2　適用 TIP 4　適用 TIP 11

補充
self-image n 個人形象；vice versa ph 反之亦然；peer group ph 同儕團體；
have an effect on ph 對～產生影響；unloved a 不被喜愛的

7,000 單字
- identification [aɪ͵dɛntəfəˋkeʃən] n 4 認同
- believe [bɪˋliv] v 1 相信
- quality [ˋkwɑlətɪ] n 2 品質
- feeling [ˋfilɪŋ] n 1 感覺
- behavior [bɪˋhevjɚ] n 4 行為
- action [ˋækʃən] n 1 行動
- behave [bɪˋhev] v 3 表現
- positive [ˋpɑzətɪv] a 2 積極的

- modify [ˋmɑdə͵faɪ] v 5 修改
- peer [pɪr] n 4 同儕
- permanent [ˋpɝmənənt] a 4 永久的
- effect [ɪˋfɛkt] n 2 效果
- love [lʌv] v 1 愛
- rejection [rɪˋdʒɛkʃən] n 4 反對
- classify [ˋklæsə͵faɪ] v 4 分類

It is the meteors and rays from the sun and other stars that make space a dangerous place. But atmosphere should be our __01__ blanket on earth. Light is essential and helpful for making the food we eat, and heat could make our environments tolerable and allow some ultraviolet rays to __02__ the atmosphere. According to the study, various kinds of cosmic rays could come through the air from outer space, but large quantities of radiation from the sun have been screened __03__ . The scientists say that as soon as human leave the atmosphere, they will be __04__ to the radiation. However, specially-made spacesuits for the astronauts or the walls of the spacecraft could prevent a lot of radiation damage. Radiation can cause the greatest danger to explorers in space, but people living on the earth receive radiation from the sun, cosmic rays and radioactive minerals all the time, and the amount of radiation can __05__ according to the different places that people live.

01 _____ (A) protective   (B) clay
               (C) impervious   (D) drainage

02 _____ (A) shift   (B) convert
               (C) modify   (D) penetrate

03 _____ (A) onto   (B) off
               (C) down   (D) upward

04 _____ (A) modified   (B) caught
               (C) exposed   (D) accepted

05 _____ (A) enlarge   (B) enforce
               (C) remain   (D) vary

DAY
4

Part 1
詞
彙
題
Day 4
完成 25%

Part 2
綜
合
測
驗
Day 4
完成 50%

Part 3
文
意
選
填
Day 4
完成 75%

Part 4
閱
讀
測
驗
Day 4
完成 100%

中譯｜流星以及來自太陽和其他恆星的輻射線使太空成為一個危險的地方。但是大氣層是我們在地球上的保護層。光對於製造我們所吃的食物是必要且有益的，熱能幫助我們有一個可耐環境，允許一些紫外線穿透大氣層。研究指出，各種不同種類的宇宙射線能夠從外太空穿過空氣，但是大量來自太陽的輻射卻被遮擋。科學家們說，只要人們離開了大氣層，他們就會暴露在輻射之中。但是，為太空人特製的太空衣或是太空船的艙壁能夠阻止許多輻射的危害。輻射會對太空中的探險家造成最嚴重的傷害，但是生活在地球上的人們一直都受到來自太陽、宇宙射線以及放射性礦物質的輻射，並且輻射量會根據所居住的地點不同而變化。

解說｜本篇短文的主旨是「宇宙射線」，答題時可以將一些太空知識考慮在內。第 1 題考名詞片語的固定用法。依據題意，「保護層」可以表達為 protective blanket，所以正確選擇為 (A)。第 2 題考我們對於自然知識的了解。據我們所知，一些紫外線可以穿透大氣層，而 penetrate 意思是「穿透」，所以最符合題意的選項是 (D)。第 3 題考語法知識的運用。動詞 screen 通常與副詞 off 連用，表示「擋開，遮罩」，所以正確選項是 (B)。第 4 題考動詞片語的用法。依據題意，be exposed to 表示「暴露於」，符合上下文的意思，所以只有選項 (C) 符合題意。第 5 題的四個選項都是動詞，依據題意，動詞 vary 意思是「變化」，符合題意，所以選 (D)。

解答＆技巧｜ 01 (A) 02 (D) 03 (B) 04 (C) 05 (D)

適用 TIP 1　適用 TIP 2　適用 TIP 7　適用 TIP 11

補充
meteor n 流星；ultraviolet a 紫外線的；explorer n 探險家；cosmic a 宇宙的；
radioactive a 放射性的

7,000 單字

- ray [re] n 3 射線
- sun [sʌn] n 1 太陽
- space [spes] n 1 太空
- dangerous [ˋdendʒərəs] a 2 危險的
- essential [ɪˋsɛnʃəl] a 4 必要的
- helpful [ˋhɛlpfəl] a 2 有幫助的
- atmosphere [ˋætməs͵fɪr] n 4 大氣
- outer [ˋautɚ] a 3 外部的

- quantity [ˋkwɑntətɪ] n 2 數量
- radiation [͵redɪˋeʃən] n 6 輻射
- astronaut [ˋæstrə͵nɔt] n 5 太空人
- spacecraft [ˋspes͵kræft] n 5 太空船
- prevent [prɪˋvɛnt] v 3 阻止
- penetrate [ˋpɛnə͵tret] v 5 穿透
- enforce [ɪnˋfors] v 4 實施

7 ▶ 96 年學測英文

All dogs deserve to look and feel their best. After a spa treatment at Happy Puppy, dogs come home __01__ pampered and relaxed. At Happy Puppy, your dog can enjoy a half day of care and then be taken to the salon at naptime. Here all the dogs are given a bath using professional shampoo and conditioners in a massaging tub. Their relaxing bath will be __02__ a full fluff dry and brush-out. When you arrive for pick-up, your dog will be well-exercised and beautiful.

You can also bring your dog to Happy Puppy and wash it yourself. We supply everything, __03__ waist-high tubs, shampoo, and towels. This service is available seven days a week during normal operating hours.

__04__ Happy Puppy is a relatively new service, we benefit from more than 20 years of experience in breeding and caring for dogs. We are completely __05__ to helping dogs enjoy a full and active life. Our well-trained staff will provide the best possible service for you and your dog.

| 01 | _____ | (A) will feel | (B) to feel |
| | | (C) have felt | (D) feeling |

| 02 | _____ | (A) counted on | (B) followed by |
| | | (C) turned into | (D) started with |

| 03 | _____ | (A) concerning | (B) showing |
| | | (C) including | (D) relating |

| 04 | _____ | (A) Although | (B) Because |
| | | (C) Once | (D) Until |

| 05 | _____ | (A) devoted | (B) determined |
| | | (C) delighted | (D) directed |

中譯｜所有的狗狗都應該擁有最美麗的外表與最舒服的心情。在《快樂狗狗》享受過水療按摩後，狗狗都可以帶著感到倍受寵愛又輕鬆的心情回家。在《快樂狗狗》裡，您的狗狗可以享受半天的照料，然後會在小睡的時間被帶到美容沙龍裡。在這裡，所有的狗狗都可以在按摩浴缸裡沐浴，享受專業洗髮精和潤髮乳。在放鬆的沐浴之後，會接著將狗狗的毛吹到乾爽並膨膨鬆鬆的，再好好地梳理。您來接狗狗的時候，牠們不但已經充分運動過了，而且也非常漂亮。

您也可以把狗狗帶來《快樂狗狗》，親自為牠洗澡。我們提供所有設備，包括高度及腰的澡盆、洗髮精和毛巾。一週七天正常營業時間裡都有這項服務。

雖然《快樂狗狗》算是比較新的服務，但是二十多年的培育以及照料狗狗的經驗使我們受益匪淺。我們完全致力於幫助狗狗享受豐富、活躍的生活。我們受過良好訓練的員工將竭盡所能，提供您和狗狗最好的服務。

解說｜本篇短文實際上相當於一則宣傳廣告，向人們介紹「快樂狗狗」能夠為狗狗們提供的服務。第1題空格處所填的動詞在句中修飾狗狗，要用現在分詞，即 feeling，所以正確選擇為 (D)。第2題的四個選項都是動詞片語，將其一一代入可知，followed by 意思是「然後，跟隨」，最符合短文的意思，所以最符合題意的選項是 (B)。第3題空格後面的內容是前面內容的具體說明，屬於包含關係，要用 including 來引導，所以正確選項是 (C)。第4題中兩個子句之間是轉折關係，後面沒有用連接詞 but，則空格處可以用 Although 表示「儘管」，所以只有選項 (A) 符合題意。第5題的四個選項中，能夠與介系詞 to 連用，且後面的動詞用動名詞的只有 devote，所以選 (A)。

解答&技巧｜ 01 **(D)**　02 **(B)**　03 **(C)**　04 **(A)**　05 **(A)**

適用 TIP 1　適用 TIP 2　適用 TIP 8　適用 TIP 11

補充

spa n 礦泉；pampered a 嬌寵的；salon n 院，廳；naptime n 小睡時間；fluff n 絨毛

7,000 單字

- dog [dɔg] n 1 狗
- puppy [ˈpʌpɪ] n 2 小狗
- shampoo [ʃæmˈpu] n 3 洗髮精
- wash [wɑʃ] v 1 洗
- tub [tʌb] n 3 浴盆
- towel [ˈtauəl] n 2 毛巾
- normal [ˈnɔrml] a 3 正常的
- hour [aur] n 1 小時

- benefit [ˈbɛnəfɪt] v 3 受惠
- experience [ɪkˈspɪrɪəns] n 2 經驗
- breed [brid] v 4 飼養
- active [ˈæktɪv] a 2 積極的
- staff [stæf] n 3 職員
- count [kaunt] v 1 計算
- devote [dɪˈvot] v 4 致力於

DAY 4

Part 1
詞彙題
Day 4
完成 25%

Part 2
綜合測驗
Day 4
完成 50%

Part 3
文意選填
Day 4
完成 75%

Part 4
閱讀測驗
Day 4
完成 100%

One day someone sent a police officer some fresh mushrooms. He was so happy that he wanted to __01__ the mushrooms with other officers. Thus when it was breakfast time the next day, all the officers found some mushrooms on their plates.

Before they began to eat, one officer suggested the dog should __02__ the mushrooms first in case they were __03__. The dog seemed to like the mushrooms very much, and then all the officers began to enjoy their mushrooms.

However, an hour later, the gardener rushed into the room and said that the dog died. Every officer was very __04__, and they immediately drove their cars to the nearest hospital. In the hospital, the doctors helped them get rid of the __05__ mushrooms with pumps, and later they returned to the police station. They were eager to know in which way the dog died, so they called the gardener. Surprisingly, the gardener said, "It was killed by a car."

01 _____ (A) comply   (B) share
(C) encounter   (D) reckon

02 _____ (A) tried   (B) to try
(C) trying   (D) try

03 _____ (A) poisonous   (B) disappointed
(C) careless   (D) unforgettable

04 _____ (A) shy   (B) cheerful
(C) astonished   (D) returned

05 _____ (A) hurried   (B) residual
(C) frightened   (D) sweet

中譯｜有一天，有人寄送了一些新鮮的蘑菇給一位警察。他很高興，想與其他的同仁一起分享，於是第二天吃早餐的時候，所有警察的盤子裡都有一些蘑菇。

開始吃之前，一位同仁建議說，應該讓狗先試吃一下蘑菇，以防蘑菇有毒。狗看起來很喜歡吃蘑菇，然後所有人就開始享用他們的蘑菇。

然而，一個小時後，園丁衝進房間說狗死了。每一位警察都非常震驚，他們立即駕車前往最近的醫院。在醫院裡，醫生用幫浦幫他們除去殘餘的蘑菇，稍後他們返回警察局。他們急於知道狗是怎麼死的，因此他們叫來了園丁。令人意外的是，園丁說：「牠是被車撞死的。」

解說｜本篇短文講述了一則搞笑的故事。第 1 題的四個選項都是動詞，但是能夠與介系詞 with 連用且符合題意的動詞只有 share，意思是「分享」，所以正確選項為 (B)。第 2 題考動詞 suggest 的語法知識的應用。根據所學的語法知識，動詞 suggest 後面的子句中要用原形動詞，因此要用 try，正確選項是 (D)。第 3 題的四個選項都是形容詞，將其一一代入，只有 poisonous 表示「有毒的」，符合上下文的意思，即正確選項是 (A)。第 4 題依據題意可以判斷出，聽到消息後的反應應該是「震驚的」，可以用 astonished 來表達，故選項 (C)。第 5 題根據上下文的內容可知，在人體內的應該是殘餘的蘑菇，可以用 residual 表示「殘餘的」，所以選 (B)。

解答&技巧｜ 01 **(B)** 02 **(D)** 03 **(A)** 04 **(C)** 05 **(B)**

適用 TIP 1 　適用 TIP 2 　適用 TIP 7 　適用 TIP 11

補充

the next day ph 次日；in case ph 如果；rush into ph 衝進；police station ph 警察局；surprisingly ad 令人驚訝地

7,000 單字

- police [pə`lis] n 1 員警
- fresh [frɛʃ] a 1 新鮮的
- mushroom [`mʌʃrum] n 3 蘑菇
- breakfast [`brɛkfəst] n 1 早餐
- suggest [sə`dʒɛst] v 3 建議
- gardener [`gɑrdənə] n 2 園丁
- hospital [`hɑspɪtl] n 2 醫院
- rid [rɪd] v 3 擺脫

- pump [pʌmp] n 2 幫浦
- return [rɪ`tɜn] v 1 返回
- station [`steʃən] n 1 站
- eager [`igə] a 3 急切的
- reckon [`rɛkən] v 5 估算
- poisonous [`pɔɪznəs] a 4 有毒的
- cheerful [`tʃɪrfəl] a 3 快樂的

DAY 4

Part 1
詞彙題
Day 4
完成 25%

Part 2
綜合測驗
Day 4
完成 50%

Part 3
文意選填
Day 4
完成 75%

Part 4
閱讀測驗
Day 4
完成 100%

People living in this city had __01__ from the sound of bells for two weeks, because four students from a college of higher education were standing in the bell tower of the church and rang the bells nonstop in order to protest __02__ heavy trucks running day and night through the narrow High Street. Most of the people said that the sound of bells made it __03__ for them to sleep at night and seriously influenced their work and life.

One of the protesters, a biology student, said, "If those heavy trucks must run through the narrow street, they could build a new road that goes round the town. Our city isn't large, and the narrow streets are not __04__ for heavy traffic."

The other three students said that what they did was to make the government officials realize the seriousness of this thing, and it was __05__ time that they solved this problem. They would keep doing this until the government officials could pay attention to it.

01 _____ (A) suffered   (B) tested
(C) determined   (D) pleased

02 _____ (A) on   (B) up
(C) against   (D) to

03 _____ (A) terrible   (B) difficult
(C) hopeful   (D) serious

04 _____ (A) applied   (B) passed
(C) entered   (D) prepared

05 _____ (A) low   (B) wrong
(C) high   (D) right

DAY 4

Part 1
詞彙題
Day 4
完成 25%

Part 2
綜合測驗
Day 4
完成 50%

Part 3
文意選填
Day 4
完成 75%

Part 4
閱讀測驗
Day 4
完成 100%

中譯｜居住在這個城市的人們遭受鐘聲之苦已經長達兩個星期，因為來自一所高等教育學院的四名學生正站在教堂的鐘樓上，不停地敲鐘，以反對重型卡車日夜穿過狹窄的大街。大多數人說，鐘聲使他們在夜晚難以入睡，嚴重影響了他們的工作和生活。

其中一位反對者是一名生物系的學生，他說：「如果那些重型卡車必須穿過狹窄的街道，他們可以繞城修建一條新道路。我們的城市並不大，那些狹窄的街道不是為重型卡車準備的。」

其他三名學生說，他們所做的事情是為了讓政府官員意識到此事的重要性，並且是時候解決這個難題了。他們會持續這個行動，直到能夠引起政府官員的注意。

解說｜本篇短文講述了幾名大學生透過敲鐘來表達抗議的一起事件。第 1 題根據上下文的內容可知，人們對鐘聲是厭惡的，無法容忍的，可以用 suffer from 來表示「遭受，忍受」，所以正確選項為 (A)。第 2 題要選擇能夠與動詞 protest 連用的介系詞。依據題意，學生們的這種行為是為了進行反抗，則用介系詞 against 可以表示反抗，所以最符合題意的選項是 (C)。第 3 題依據題意應該是「難以入睡」，要選擇 difficult 表示「困難的」，正確選項是 (B)。第 4 題要選擇能夠與介系詞 for 連用的動詞。依據題意，prepared 表示「準備」與上下文意思相符，所以選項 (D) 符合題意。第 5 題考語法知識的應用。表示「是時候～」可以說 it's high time...，所以選 (C)。

解答＆技巧｜ 01 **(A)**　02 **(C)**　03 **(B)**　04 **(D)**　05 **(C)**

適用 TIP 1　適用 TIP 2　適用 TIP 7　適用 TIP 11

補充

college of higher education ph 高等教育學院；nonstop ad 不停地；seriously ad 嚴重地；protester n 反對者；seriousness n 嚴重

7,000 單字

- city [ˋsɪtɪ] n 1 城市
- sound [saʊnd] n 1 聲音
- bell [bɛl] n 1 鈴聲
- tower [ˋtaʊɚ] n 2 塔
- protest [prəˋtɛst] v 4 抗議
- biology [baɪˋɑlədʒɪ] n 4 生物
- heavy [ˋhɛvɪ] a 1 沉重的
- truck [trʌk] n 2 卡車

- narrow [ˋnæro] a 2 狹窄的
- town [taʊn] n 1 城鎮
- realize [ˋrɪəˌlaɪz] v 2 意識到
- until [ənˋtɪl] conj 1 直到
- terrible [ˋtɛrəbl] a 2 可怕的
- hopeful [ˋhopfəl] a 4 有希望的
- enter [ˋɛntɚ] v 1 進入

Many people know that exercise is a good way to keep __01__ and lose weight, but they know little about how to exercise properly; thus they may run __02__ trouble when they exercise.

According to a recent study, when specific muscles are exercised, not only the fat in the neighboring area but also fat from all over the body is burned up. Muscles which are not exercised are easy to __03__ their strength, and to regain it needs 48 to 72 hours. Therefore, if you want to keep a normal level of __04__ strength, you'd better exercise every other day.

To lose weight you should always prepare to sweat when exercising because sweating helps reduce body temperature in order to prevent overheating. As we know, walking is the best and easiest exercise, which can help the __05__ of blood throughout the whole body and also have a direct effect on your feeling of health. So it is good for you to walk at least 20 minutes every day.

01 _____ (A) healthy   (B) silence
           (C) house   (D) still

02 _____ (A) out   (B) short
           (C) pope   (D) into

03 _____ (A) reply   (B) lose
           (C) raise   (D) destroy

04 _____ (A) yielding   (B) ionic
           (C) physical   (D) mechanical

05 _____ (A) working   (B) circulation
           (C) exercise   (D) growth

中譯│ 很多人都知道，運動是保持健康和減肥的一種好方法，但是他們很少了解如何正確地運動，因此在運動時就可能會遇到困難。

最近的一項研究指出，當特定的肌肉得到鍛鍊時，除了附近部位的脂肪，全身的脂肪也都會燃燒。沒有得到鍛鍊的肌肉很容易失去肌力，並且重新獲得肌力需要四十八到七十二個小時。因此，如果你想要保持正常水準的體力，你最好每隔一天運動一次。

為了減肥，你應該隨時準備好在運動時出汗，因為出汗會幫助降低體溫，以防體溫過高。正如我們所知，走路是最好也是最容易的運動方式，能夠幫助全身的血液循環，也會直接讓你感受到對健康的影響。因此每天至少走路二十分鐘對你很有益處。

解說│ 本篇短文的主旨是「運動」，介紹了運動的好處及方法。第 1 題考與動詞 keep 相關的片語的用法。依據題意，運動可以「保持健康」，可以表達為 keep healthy，所以正確選項為 (A)。第 2 題考與動詞 run 相關的片語的用法。根據上下文的內容，不了解運動方法會導致在運動中遇到困難，而 run into 表示「遇到」符合題意，所以最佳選項是 (D)。第 3 題根據常識性的知識可知，肌肉不得到鍛鍊就會失去力量，而動詞 lose 表示「失去」符合題意，所以正確選項是 (B)。第 4 題考名詞片語的用法。依據題意，「體力」可以表達為 physical strength，只有選項 (C) 符合題意。第 5 題要選擇合適的名詞。依據題意，「血液循環」可以表達為 the circulation of blood，所以選 (B)。

解答＆技巧│ 01 **(A)**　02 **(D)**　03 **(B)**　04 **(C)**　05 **(B)**

適用 TIP 1　適用 TIP 2　適用 TIP 7　適用 TIP 11

補充

neighboring a 鄰近的；regain v 重新獲得；keep a normal level of ph 保持～的正常水準；every other day ph 每隔一天；body temperature ph 體溫

7,000 單字

- exercise [ˈɛksɚˌsaɪz] n 2 運動
- lose [luz] v 2 失去
- weight [wet] n 1 體重
- run [rʌn] v 1 奔跑
- muscle [ˈmʌsl̩] n 3 肌肉
- fat [fæt] n 1 脂肪
- burn [bɝn] v 2 燃燒
- level [ˈlɛvl̩] n 1 水準

- sweat [swɛt] v 3 出汗
- reduce [rɪˈdjus] v 3 降低
- silence [ˈsaɪləns] n 2 沉默
- raise [rez] v 1 提高
- yield [jild] v 5 屈服
- mechanical [məˈkænɪkl̩] a 4 機械的
- circulation [ˌsɝkjəˈleʃən] n 4 循環

DAY 4

Part 1
詞
彙
題
Day 4
完成 25%

Part 2
綜
合
測
驗
Day 4
完成 50%

Part 3
文
意
選
填
Day 4
完成 75%

Part 4
閱
讀
測
驗
Day 4
完成 100%

Part 3 文意選填 | Cloze Test

1▸

Most mammals usually look like their parents when they are born. They have the same shape as their parents, but not the same __01__ . The baby mammals should __02__ on their mothers for a living. The mother mammals will produce milk for their young. As the babies __03__ up, they gradually change in size. Some other changes also take __04__ in their body during the period. When they become adults, these mammals will also be parents of babies.

Babies of some mammals, such as opossums and kangaroos, when they are born, are too small or weak to live independently. So they cannot leave their mother. These babies will stay in special __05__ that the mothers have until they are __06__ enough to live out by themselves.

If you keep a cat or any other kind of animals as a __07__ at home, you can observe the mother feeding her young after it gives birth to babies.

If you know actually an animal __08__ to the mammals, then you may know some basic information about the animal at once, even if you don't know much about it before. You know that when it was born, it must have __09__ on the milk of the mother. Besides, you can also know that the animal should be a lung-breather, quite __10__ a gill-breather.

(A) pet　(B) depend　(C) unlike　(D) pouches　(E) lived
(F) size　(G) grow　(H) strong　(I) belongs　(J) place

01 ＿＿＿　02 ＿＿＿　03 ＿＿＿　04 ＿＿＿　05 ＿＿＿

06 ＿＿＿　07 ＿＿＿　08 ＿＿＿　09 ＿＿＿　10 ＿＿＿

選項中譯｜寵物；依靠；不像；育兒袋；生活；大小；成長；強壯的；屬於；地方

中譯｜ 大多數的哺乳動物，剛出生時，都與自己的父母很相似。牠們有著和父母相同的外形，只是大小不同。哺乳動物的寶寶必須依靠母親生存，雌性哺乳動物將分泌奶水，來餵養寶寶。寶寶在成長的過程中，體型會逐漸發生變化。在這期間，也會發生一些別的變化。成年後，這些哺乳動物將會產下自己的寶寶。

一些哺乳動物——例如負鼠、袋鼠——的寶寶，出生時，或是太小，或是太過虛弱，並不能夠獨自生活。所以，牠們不能離開母體。這些寶寶會停留在母體特殊的育兒袋中，直到牠們變得足夠強壯，能夠獨自生存。

如果你家裡養了貓，或是有其他任何一種動物作寵物，當牠生育寶寶後，你可以觀察牠如何餵養寶寶。

如果你知道某種動物屬於哺乳動物，即便之前並不了解這種動物，也可以立即知道關於這種動物的基本資訊。你可以知道，牠出生的時候，必定是以母親的乳汁為生的。此外，你也可以知道，這種動物應該是用肺呼吸的，而不是用腮呼吸的。

解譯｜ 閱讀全文可知，這篇文章的主題是哺乳動物。

縱觀各選項，選項 (A)、(D)、(F)、(J) 是名詞，選項 (B)、(E)、(G)、(I) 是動詞，選項 (C) 是介系詞，選項 (H) 是形容詞。根據題意，第 1、4、5、7 題應選名詞，第 2、3、8、9 題應選動詞，第 6 題應選形容詞，第 10 題應選介系詞。然後根據文章，依次作答。

第 1 題是選擇名詞，有四個名詞可供選擇，即為選項 (A)、(D)、(F)、(J)，選項 (A) 意為「寵物」，選項 (D) 意為「育兒袋」，選項 (F) 意為「大小」，選項 (J) 意為「地方」，根據句意，應當是「牠們有著和父母相同的外形，只是大小不同」，所以選 (F)。第 4 題所選名詞，可以視為固定搭配，take place 意為「發生」，所以選 (J)。第 5 題所選名詞，根據句意，應當是「寶寶會停留在母體的特殊的育兒袋中」，所以選 (D)。第 7 題則是選 (A)，也可以視為固定搭配，keep... as a pet 意為「養～作為寵物」。

第 2 題是選擇動詞，須與介系詞 on 進行搭配，有四個動詞可供選擇，即為選項 (B)、(E)、(G)、(I)。只有選項 (B) 符合要求，depend on 意為「依靠」。第 3 題所選動詞，是與介系詞 up 進行搭配，grow up 意為「長大」，所以選 (G)。第 8 題所選動詞，是與介系詞 to 進行搭配，belong to 意為「屬於」，所以選 (I)。第 9 題則是選 (E)，也可以視為固定搭配，live on 意為「以～為生」。

第 6 題是選擇形容詞，只有一個形容詞可供選擇，即為選項 (H)，句意為「直到牠們變得足夠強壯，能夠獨自生存」。

第 10 題是選擇介系詞，只有一個介系詞可供選擇，即為選項 (C)。

解答&技巧 ┃ 01 (F)　　02 (B)　　03 (G)　　04 (J)　　05 (D)
06 (H)　　07 (A)　　08 (I)　　09 (E)　　10 (C)

適用 TIP 1　適用 TIP 2　適用 TIP 6　適用 TIP 7　適用 TIP 8
適用 TIP 9　適用 TIP 10　適用 TIP 11

補充

opossum ⓝ 負鼠；independently ⓐⓓ 獨立地；pouch ⓝ 育兒袋；unlike prep 不相似，不同；
gill ⓝ 鰓

7,000 單字

- mammal [ˋmæml] ⓝ 5 哺乳動物
- parent [ˋpɛrənt] ⓝ 1 雙親之一
- depend [dɪˋpɛnd] ⓥ 2 依靠
- kangaroo [͵kæŋgəˋru] ⓝ 3 袋鼠
- weak [wik] ⓐ 1 虛弱的
- leave [liv] ⓥ 1 離開
- special [ˋspɛʃəl] ⓐ 1 特別的

- strong [strɔŋ] ⓐ 1 強壯的
- cat [kæt] ⓝ 1 貓
- pet [pɛt] ⓝ 1 寵物
- home [hom] ⓝ 1 家
- know [no] ⓥ 1 知道
- belong [bəˋlɔŋ] ⓥ 1 屬於
- lung [lʌŋ] ⓝ 3 肺

MEMO

❷▶

DAY
4

Part 1
詞
彙
題
Day 4
完成 25%

Part 2
綜
合
測
驗
Day 4
完成 50%

Part 3
文
意
選
填
Day 4
完成 75%

Part 4
閱
讀
測
驗
Day 4
完成 100%

Early Tudor England, to a __01__ extent, was self-sufficient. Practically all the __02__ of life—food, clothing, fuel and housing—were produced from native resources by native effort. And it was to satisfy these __03__ needs that the great mass of the population labored at the daily tasks. Production was, for the most part, organized in __04__ small units. In the country, the farm, the hamlet and the village lived on what they could grow or make for themselves, and on the sale of any __05__ in the local market town, while in the towns craftsmen __06__ themselves to their one-man business, making the boots and shoes, the caps and the cloaks, the implement and harness of townsmen and countrymen alike. Once a week, town folks and country dwellers would meet to make __07__ at a market, which came near to realizing the medieval idea of direct contact between producer and consumer. This was the traditional economy, which was hardly __08__ for some centuries, and which set the pattern of work and the standard of life of perhaps nine out of every ten English men and women. The work was long and hard, and the __09__ of life achieved was almost unimaginably low. Most Englishmen lied by a diet which was often meager and always monotonous, wore __10__ and ill-fitting clothes which harbored dirt undermine, and lived in holes whose squalor would affront the modern slum dwellers.

(A) applied   (B) altered   (C) coarse   (D) large   (E) innumerable
(F) necessities   (G) standard   (H) exchange   (I) surplus   (J) primary

01 _____   02 _____   03 _____   04 _____   05 _____

06 _____   07 _____   08 _____   09 _____   10 _____

227

選項中譯｜應用；改變；粗糙的；很大的；無以計數的；必需品；水準；交換；剩餘；
　　　　基本的

中譯｜在都鐸王朝早期，英國在很大程度上是自給自足的。事實上，所有的生活必需品
　　　——食物、衣物、燃料、住宅——都是本國勞動力利用本土資源生產製造的，而
　　　且正是為了滿足這些基本需求，每天都有大批人在勞動。這些生產製造大多是在
　　　無以計數的小作坊中進行的。在鄉下，農場、部落、村莊，居民們賴以為生的，
　　　是自己所種植的作物、生產製造的產品，或是在當地集鎮出售多餘的產品。而在
　　　市鎮中，手工藝者們從事個體經營，製造市民和鄉下人都需要的靴子、鞋子、
　　　帽子、斗篷、農具、馬具。每週一次，市鎮和鄉村居民會在某個集市上進行交
　　　易，這有些近似於中世紀所說的生產者和消費者之間的直接交流。這就是傳統經
　　　濟，在幾個世紀中幾乎都沒有什麼改變，也確立了生產模式和九成英國人的生活
　　　水準。長時間的艱苦勞作，所換來的卻是無法想像的低劣生活水準。大多數的英
　　　國人，吃的是單調乏味卻又少得可憐的食物，穿的是做工粗糙、遍佈灰塵而日益
　　　黯淡的不合身的衣服，住的是連現在的貧民窟居民都會感到難堪的骯髒淒慘的洞
　　　穴。

解譯｜閱讀全文可知，這篇文章的主題是都鐸王朝早期英國居民的生計。
　　　縱觀各選項，選項 (F)、(G)、(H)、(I) 是名詞，選項 (A)、(B) 是動詞，選項 (C)、
　　　(D)、(E)、(J) 是形容詞。根據題意，第 2、5、7、9 題應選名詞，第 6、8 題應
　　　選動詞，第 1、3、4、10 題應選形容詞。然後根據文章，依次作答。
　　　第 1 題是選擇形容詞，有四個形容詞可供選擇，即為選項 (C)、(D)、(E)、(J)。
　　　選項 (C) 意為「粗糙的」，選項 (D) 意為「很大的」，選項 (E) 意為「無以計數
　　　的」，選項 (J) 意為「基本的」，to a large extent 可以視為固定搭配，意為「在
　　　很大程度上」，所以選 (D)。第 3 題所選形容詞，根據句意，應當是「滿足這些
　　　基本需求」，所以選 (J)。第 4 題所選形容詞，根據句意，應當是「無以計數的
　　　小作坊」，所以選 (E)。第 10 題則是選 (C)，句意為「做工粗糙的衣服」。
　　　第 2 題是選擇名詞，用於 of 結構，有四個名詞可供選擇，即為選項 (F)、(G)、
　　　(H)、(I)，選項 (F) 意為「必需品」，選項 (G) 意為「水準」，選項 (H) 意為「交
　　　換」，選項 (I) 意為「剩餘」，all the necessities of life 可以視為固定搭配，意
　　　為「所有的生活必需品」，所以選 (F)。第 5 題所選名詞，根據句意，應當是「出
　　　售多餘的產品」，所以選 (I)。第 7 題所選名詞，也可以視為固定搭配，make
　　　exchange 意為「進行交換」，所以選 (H)。第 9 題則是選 (G)，standard of life
　　　意為「生活水準」。
　　　第 6 題是選擇動詞，有兩個動詞可供選擇，即為選項 (A)、(B)，可以視為固定搭
　　　配，apply oneself to 意為「專注於，集中精力做某事」，所以選 (A)。第 8 題則
　　　是選 (B)，意為「在幾個世紀中幾乎都沒有什麼改變」。

解答&技巧 | 01 **(D)**　02 **(F)**　03 **(J)**　04 **(E)**　05 **(I)**
06 **(A)**　07 **(H)**　08 **(B)**　09 **(G)**　10 **(C)**

適用 TIP 1　適用 TIP 2　適用 TIP 6　適用 TIP 7　適用 TIP 8
適用 TIP 9　適用 TIP 10　適用 TIP 11

DAY
4

Part 1
詞
彙
題
Day 4
完成 25%

Part 2
綜
合
測
驗
Day 4
完成 50%

Part 3
文
意
選
填
Day 4
完成 75%

Part 4
閱
讀
測
驗
Day 4
完成 100%

補充

Tudor a 都鐸王朝的；to a large extent ph 在很大程度上；native resources ph 本土資源；
for the most part ph 多半，在很大程度上；affront v 冒犯，侮辱

7,000 單字

- sufficient [sə`fɪʃənt] a 3 足夠的
- necessity [nə`sɛsətɪ] n 3 必需品
- native [`netɪv] a 3 本地的
- primary [`praɪ͵mɛrɪ] a 3 基本的
- mass [mæs] n 2 大量
- surplus [`sɝpləs] n 6 盈餘，剩餘
- boot [but] n 3 靴子
- implement [`ɪmpləmənt] n 6 工具

- medieval [͵midɪ`ivəl] a 6 中世紀的
- direct [də`rɛkt] a 1 直接的
- monotonous [mə`nɑtənəs] a 6 單調乏味的，厭倦的
- coarse [kors] a 4 粗糙的
- undermine [͵ʌndɚ`maɪn] v 6 漸漸削弱
- hole [hol] n 1 洞穴
- slum [slʌm] n 6 貧民窟

MEMO

♫229

3 ▶ 95 年學測英文

Good health is not something you are able to buy, nor can you get it back with a quick __01__ to a doctor. Keeping yourself healthy has to be your own __02__. If you mistreat your body by keeping bad habits, __03__ symptoms of illness, and ignoring common health rules, even the best medicine can be of little use.

Nowadays health specialists __04__ the idea of wellness for everybody. Wellness means __05__ the best possible health within the limits of your body. One person may need fewer calories than another. Some people might prefer a lot of __06__ exercise to more challenging exercise. While one person enjoys playing seventy-two holes of golf a week, another would rather play competitive games of tennis.

Understanding the needs of your body is the __07__. Everyone runs the risk of accidents, and no one can be sure of avoiding __08__ diseases. Nevertheless, poor diet, stress, a bad working environment, and carelessness can __09__ good health. By changing your habits or the conditions surrounding you, you can __10__ the risk or reduce the damage of diseases.

(A) ruin (B) visit (C) neglecting (D) lower (E) easier
(F) responsibility (G) chronic (H) key (I) promote (J) achieving

01 _____   02 _____   03 _____   04 _____   05 _____

06 _____   07 _____   08 _____   09 _____   10 _____

選項中譯｜ 損害；拜訪；忽視；降低；更簡單的；責任；慢性的；關鍵；提倡；達到

中譯｜ 健康並不是你可以買來的，也不是快速地看過醫生之後就可以重新得到的。保持健康必須是自己的責任。如果你因養成了不好的習慣，忽視疾病的症狀，並無視常規的健康法則，對自己的身體不好，那麼，即便是最好的藥也不會有什麼作用。

如今，健康專家提倡針對大眾的健康概念。健康，意味著在個人身體極限範圍之內，達到可能的最佳健康狀況。一個人所需要的熱量也許比另一個人所需要的少一些。有些人也許會願意進行大量簡單些的運動，而不是進行挑戰性的運動。一個人也許喜歡每週打七十二洞的高爾夫球，另一個人也許願意進行競爭性更強的網球運動。

明白自己的身體所需，才是關鍵。每個人都可能遇到意外事故，也沒有人可以確信自己不會感染慢性疾病。然而，不健康的飲食、壓力、糟糕的工作環境、粗心，都會損害健康狀況。改變自己的習慣，或是改變周遭的環境，可以降低患病機率，或是減少對身體健康狀況的損害。

解譯｜ 閱讀全文可知，這篇文章的主題是健康問題。

縱觀各選項，選項 (B)、(F)、(H) 是名詞，選項 (A)、(C)、(D)、(I)、(J) 是動詞，選項 (E)、(G) 是形容詞。根據題意，第 1、2、7 題應選名詞，第 3、4、5、9、10 題應選動詞，第 6、8 題應選形容詞。然後根據文章，依次作答。

第 1 題是選擇名詞，有三個名詞可供選擇，即為選項 (B)、(F)、(H)。選項 (B) 表示「拜訪」，選項 (F) 表示「責任」，選項 (H) 表示「關鍵」，根據句意可知，應當是「去看醫生」，所以選 (B)，意為「拜訪」，其實是由動詞片語 visit a doctor 演化而來。同樣，第 2 題也是選擇名詞，根據文意，應當是「保持健康必須是自己的責任」，所以選 (F)，意為「責任」。那麼，就只剩下一個名詞可供選擇，即為選項 (H)，正好留給需要選擇名詞的第 7 題。根據文意，應當是「明白自己的身體所需，才是關鍵」。

第 3、4、5、9、10 題是選擇動詞，有五個動詞可供選擇，即為選項 (A)、(C)、(D)、(I)、(J)。其中，第 9、10 題可視為固定搭配，ruin health 意為「損害健康」，lower the risk 意為「降低風險」，由此可判斷選擇 (A)、(D)。第 3、4、5 題是根據文意和單字字義選擇，不作贅述。

第 6 題是選擇形容詞，有兩個形容詞可供選擇，即為選項 (E)、(G)。同樣是根據文意和單字字義選擇，亦不再贅述。

Part 1
詞彙題
Day 4
完成 25%

Part 2
綜合測驗
Day 4
完成 50%

Part 3
文意選填
Day 4
完成 75%

Part 4
閱讀測驗
Day 4
完成 100%

解答＆技巧 | 01 **(B)**　02 **(F)**　03 **(C)**　04 **(I)**　05 **(J)**
06 **(E)**　07 **(H)**　08 **(G)**　09 **(A)**　10 **(D)**

適用 TIP 1　適用 TIP 2　適用 TIP 6　適用 TIP 7　適用 TIP 10　適用 TIP 11

補充

get back ph 恢復，取回；keep healthy ph 保持健康；be of little use ph 不起作用；
prefer... to... ph 寧願選擇～而不選擇～；run the risk of ph 冒～風險

7,000 單字

- health [hɛlθ] n 1 健康
- doctor [ˈdɑktɚ] n 1 醫生
- neglect [nɪɡˈlɛkt] v 4 忽視
- symptom [ˈsɪmptəm] n 6 症狀
- specialist [ˈspɛʃəlɪst] n 5 專家
- within [wɪˈðɪn] prep 2 在～之內
- golf [ɡɑlf] n 2 高爾夫
- tennis [ˈtɛnɪs] n 2 網球

- nevertheless [ˌnɛvɚðəˈlɛs] conj 4 然而
- surround [səˈraʊnd] v 3 圍繞
- ruin [ˈrʊɪn] v 4 損害
- visit [ˈvɪzɪt] v 1 拜訪
- responsibility [rɪˌspɑnsəˈbɪlətɪ] n 3 責任
- chronic [ˈkrɑnɪk] a 6 慢性的
- promote [prəˈmot] v 3 提倡

MEMO

④ ▶

In January, 1848, James Marshall ___01___ gold on Johann Sutter's property when looking for a location to build a sawmill. He and Sutter agreed immediately that it must be kept ___02___ from others. However, workers who were building the sawmill soon ___03___ the news. By May, the gold ___04___ had started.

By 1849, a large number of people had come from the United States and from Mexico, Australia, Hawaii, China and Europe. Among these people who set out to find gold, only a few were experienced ___05___. Some of them even had never mined before. The ___06___ of gold seekers and pioneers chose the overland route to reach California, crossing the vast plains, the Rocky Mountains, and possibly deserts, while trying their best to ___07___ being attacked by Native Americans. These gold seekers were merely chasing the dream of striking it rich, looking for adventure, seeking a career change, or running from their problems and responsibilities.

Many people gained nothing there and became ___08___ then. Some of them set up businesses later to supply the miners with provisions, laundry, liquor, gambling, and other goods and services. All of these supplies were high-priced, so, even if a miner did strike gold, it would have been spent quickly. Most miners had to work hard to make enough money to ___09___ food and necessary supplies.

Admittedly, a great deal of gold was mined in California. However, only a few people made rich strikes. Despite this fact, a great many miners still ___10___ to come here to chase the dream.

DAY
4

Part 1
詞
彙
題
Day 4
完成 25%

Part 2
綜
合
測
驗
Day 4
完成 50%

Part 3
文
意
選
填
Day 4
完成 75%

Part 4
閱
讀
測
驗
Day 4
完成 100%

(A) discovered   (B) majority   (C) spread   (D) continued   (E) disappointed
(F) secret   (G) miners   (H) rush   (I) avoid   (J) purchase

---

01 _____   02 _____   03 _____   04 _____   05 _____

06 _____   07 _____   08 _____   09 _____   10 _____

選項中譯｜發現；大多數；傳播；繼續；失望的；祕密；礦工；繁忙的活動；避免；
購買

中譯｜一八四八年一月，詹姆士‧馬歇爾在尋找興建鋸木廠的地點時，在喬安‧薩特的
領地上發現了黃金。隨即，他和薩特都同意將此事保密，不告訴別人。那些修建
鋸木廠的工人卻很快傳出了這個消息。到五月時，淘金熱已經開始。

到一八四九年，來自美國、墨西哥、澳大利亞、夏威夷、中國和歐洲的大批淘金
客湧入。在這些前來淘金的人流中，只有小部分人曾經做過礦工，有些人之前甚
至都沒有挖礦經驗。大多數的淘金客和拓荒者們，選擇走陸路去加州，這期間他
們要穿過廣闊的平原、洛磯山脈，也有可能還要途經沙漠，也要盡最大努力來躲
避印第安人的突襲。這些淘金客只是前來追尋夢想，有人希望發財，有人尋求冒
險，有人尋求職業轉變，也有人則是想擺脫麻煩或是逃避責任。

很多人並沒有在那裡得到什麼，隨即變得失望。之後，有些人創建了自己的事
業，為礦工提供食物、洗衣服務、酒類、賭場，以及其他的商品和服務。這些商
品和服務都十分昂貴，所以即便礦工淘到了金子，也必定會很快消費掉。為了購
買足夠的食物和必需品，大部分礦工都不得不賣力地工作。

的確是有大量的黃金在加州被開採出來。然而，發財的也只是一小部分人。雖然
事實是如此，依然有很多人繼續前來追尋夢想。

解譯｜閱讀全文可知，這篇文章的主題是淘金熱。

縱觀各選項，選項 (B)、(G)、(H) 是名詞，選項 (A)、(C)、(D)、(I)、(J) 是動詞，
選項 (E)、(F) 是形容詞。根據題意，第 4、5、6 題應選名詞，第 1、3、7、9、
10 題應選動詞，第 2、8 題應選形容詞。然後根據文章，依次作答。

第 1 題是選擇動詞，有五個動詞可供選擇，即為選項 (A)、(C)、(D)、(I)、(J)，
根據句意可知，應當是「發現黃金」，所以選 (A)。第 3 題所選動詞，是與名詞
news 進行搭配，所以選 (C)，意為「傳播消息」。第 7 題所選動詞，可以視為
固定搭配，avoid doing sth. 意為「避免做某事」，所以選 (I)。第 9 題所選動詞，
根據句意可知，應當是「購買足夠的食物和必需品」，所以選 (J)。第 10 題則是
選 (D)，continue to do sth. 意為「繼續做某事」。

第 2 題是選擇形容詞，有兩個形容詞可供選擇，即為選項 (E)、(F)。選項 (E)
意為「失望的」，選項 (F) 意為「祕密的」，可以視為固定搭配，keep sth.
secret from 意為「不讓某人知道」，所以選 (F)。第 8 題則是選 (E)，become
disappointed 意為「變得失望」。

第 4 題是選擇名詞，有三個名詞可供選擇，即為選項 (B)、(G)、(H)，選項 (B)
意為「大多數」，選項 (G) 意為「礦工」，選項 (H) 意為「繁忙的活動」，可以
視為固定表達，the gold rush 意為「淘金熱」，所以選 (H)。第 5 題所選名詞，
根據句意可知，應當是「只有小部分人曾經做過礦工」，所以選 (G)。第 6 題則
是選 (B)，the majority of 意為「大多數的」。

解答&技巧 | **01** (A) **02** (F) **03** (C) **04** (H) **05** (G)
06 (B) **07** (I) **08** (E) **09** (J) **10** (D)

適用 TIP 1 適用 TIP 2 適用 TIP 6 適用 TIP 7 適用 TIP 8
適用 TIP 9 適用 TIP 10 適用 TIP 11

DAY
4

Part 1
詞
彙
題
Day 4
完成 25%

Part 2
綜
合
測
驗
Day 4
完成 50%

Part 3
文
意
選
填
Day 4
完成 75%

Part 4
閱
讀
測
驗
Day 4
完成 100%

補充

sawmill n 鋸木廠；Mexico n 墨西哥；Hawaii n 夏威夷；the Rocky Mountains ph 洛磯山脈；
provision n 供應

7,000 單字

- agree [ə`gri] v **1** 同意
- spread [sprɛd] v **2** 傳播
- miner [`maɪnɚ] n **3** 礦工
- mine [maɪn] v **2** 開礦
- pioneer [ˌpaɪə`nɪr] n **4** 拓荒者
- cross [krɔs] v **2** 穿過
- vast [væst] a **4** 巨大的
- avoid [ə`vɔɪd] v **2** 避免

- attack [ə`tæk] v **2** 攻擊
- adventure [əd`vɛntʃɚ] n **3** 冒險
- career [kə`rɪr] n **4** 事業
- laundry [`lɔndrɪ] n **3** 洗衣店
- goods [gʊdz] n **4** 貨物
- purchase [`pɝtʃəs] v **5** 購買
- continue [kən`tɪnju] v **1** 繼續

MEMO --

♫ 235

The brain of human beings is quite __01__ from the brain of animals. God gives each person a brain, a mind to think. Our mind helps us to __02__, feel and choose. We are able to know and learn anything. Our mind helps us to be creative. An animal, being not creative, will never be able to make a spaceship or a rocket __03__.

The two large __04__ of the brain are known as the cerebrum. Each hemisphere could be __05__ divided into lobes. We store different kinds of __06__ in different parts of our brains. Among these parts, there is one area that saves only pictures of things we see. Another area remembers how those things are __07__. As for the area that stores smells and sounds, it is very close to the area that stores feelings. That's why we sometimes feel __08__ when we smell homemade bread, or feel sad when we hear a love song.

Our brain also gives orders for our lungs to __09__, for our organs to function, and for our muscles to move. Playing such an important __10__, our brain weighs only about three pounds. Scientists say that people use only a small part of the brain throughout their lives.

(A) forever   (B) different   (C) arranged   (D) role   (E) understand
(F) further   (G) breathe   (H) happy   (I) hemispheres   (J) information

---

01 _____   02 _____   03 _____   04 _____   05 _____

06 _____   07 _____   08 _____   09 _____   10 _____

DAY
4

Part 1
詞
彙
題
Day 4
完成 25%

Part 2
綜
合
測
驗
Day 4
完成 50%

Part 3
文
意
選
填
Day 4
完成 75%

Part 4
閱
讀
測
驗
Day 4
完成 100%

選項中譯｜永遠；不同的；安排；角色；理解；進一步；呼吸；高興的；半球；資訊

中譯｜人的頭腦與動物的頭腦有所不同。上帝賜予每個人頭腦，來幫助思考。頭腦幫助我們理解、感覺和選擇，我們可以了解和學習任何東西。頭腦幫助我們具有創造力。動物是沒有創造力的，牠們永遠也不會製造出太空船或是火箭。

頭腦中的兩個大半球，被稱為大腦。每個半球都可以進一步分為腦葉。我們在大腦裡的不同區位儲存著不同的資訊。在這些區位中，有一個區位只負責儲存我們所看到的事物的圖像。另一個區位則是負責記憶這些事物是如何排列的。儲存氣味和聲音的區位，與儲存感覺的區位相鄰近。這就可以解釋，為什麼有時當你聞到家裡做的麵包時會感到高興，或聽一首愛情歌曲時會感到悲傷。

大腦也會下達命令，讓肺呼吸，讓器官運轉，讓肌肉運動。大腦有如此多的功能，卻僅有三磅重。科學家們說，在一生中，人們也只是利用了大腦的一小部分。

解譯｜閱讀全文可知，這篇文章的主題是我們的大腦。

縱觀各選項，選項 (A)、(F) 是副詞，選項 (B)、(H) 是形容詞，選項 (C)、(E)、(G) 是動詞，選項 (D)、(I)、(J) 是名詞。根據題意，第 1、8 題應選形容詞，第 2、7、9 題應選動詞，第 3、5 題是副詞，第 4、6、10 題應選名詞。然後根據文章，依次作答。

第 1 題是選擇形容詞，有兩個形容詞可供選擇，即為選項 (B)、(H)。選項 (B) 意為「不同的」，選項 (H) 意為「高興的」，be different from 可以視為固定搭配，意為「與～不同」，所以選 (B)。第 8 題則是選 (H)，feel happy 意為「感到高興」。

第 2 題是選擇動詞，有三個動詞可供選擇，即為選項 (C)、(E)、(G)，根據句意，應當是「頭腦幫助我們理解、感覺和選擇」，所以選 (E)。第 7 題所選動詞，根據句意，應當是「這些事物是如何排列的」，所以選 (C)。第 9 題則是選 (G)，意為「大腦下達命令，讓肺呼吸」。

第 3 題是選擇副詞，有兩個副詞可供選擇，即為選項 (A)、(F)。選項 (A) 意為「永遠」，選項 (F) 意為「進一步」，根據句意，應當是「動物永遠也不會製造出太空船或是火箭」，所以選 (A)。第 5 題則是選 (F)，be further divided into 意為「進一步分為」。

第 4 題是選擇名詞，有三個名詞可供選擇，即為選項 (D)、(I)、(J)，選項 (D) 意為「角色」，選項 (I) 意為「半球」，選項 (J) 意為「資訊」，根據句意，應當是「頭腦中的兩個大半球，被稱為大腦」，所以選 (I)。第 6 題所選名詞，根據句意，應當是「在大腦裡的不同區位儲存著不同的資訊」，所以選 (J)。第 10 題則是選 (D)，play an important role 意為「起重要作用」。

解答＆技巧 | **01** (B)　**02** (E)　**03** (A)　**04** (I)　**05** (F)
　　　　　　06 (J)　**07** (C)　**08** (H)　**09** (G)　**10** (D)

適用 TIP 1　適用 TIP 2　適用 TIP 6　適用 TIP 7　適用 TIP 8
適用 TIP 9　適用 TIP 10　適用 TIP 11

補充

be different from ph 與～不同；help sb. to do sth. ph 幫助某人做某事；cerebrum n 大腦；
lobe n 肺葉，腦葉；homemade a 自製的，自家做的

7,000 單字

- brain [bren] n 2 大腦
- understand [ˌʌndɚˋstænd] v 1 理解
- choose [tʃuz] v 2 選擇
- creative [krɪˋetɪv] a 3 創造性的
- spaceship [ˋspes͵ʃɪp] n 5 太空船
- forever [fɚˋɛvɚ] ad 3 永遠
- hemisphere [ˋhɛməs͵fɪr] n 6 半球
- area [ˋɛrɪə] n 1 地區

- picture [ˋpɪktʃɚ] n 1 圖片
- arrange [əˋrendʒ] v 2 安排
- sometimes [ˋsʌm͵taɪmz] ad 1 有時候
- happy [ˋhæpɪ] a 1 高興的
- bread [brɛd] n 1 麵包
- song [sɔŋ] n 1 歌曲
- breathe [brið] v 3 呼吸

MEMO

MEMO

DAY 4

Part 1
詞彙題
Day 4
完成 **25%**

Part 2
綜合測驗
Day 4
完成 **50%**

Part 3
文意選填
Day 4
完成 **75%**

Part 4
閱讀測驗
Day 4
完成 **100%**

閱讀測驗 | Reading Questions

Salt levels in bread have fallen by about one third during the past decade, with some falling by up to 40%. There is wide variation in the amount of salt found in loaves. Most are within half a gram of the current guideline of 1.1g of salt per 100g of bread—about two thick slices.

Eating too much salt might lead to high blood pressure, which in turn increases the risk of developing heart disease. Recommended dietary salt levels vary with age. Adults should have no more than 6g of salt in their diet per day, while the tolerable daily intake of salt for toddlers are meant to be no more than 2g. It is the high levels of salt hidden in everyday food, such as bread, that puts up the blood pressure of both adults and children.

CASH (Campaign for Action on Salt and Health) makes recommendations to consumers that they should pay close attention to nutrition labels, if possible, to find out how much salt bread contains. Fresh breads, however, from in-store bakeries or high-street supermarkets, mostly have no nutritional labeling. Thus people cannot tell how much salt they contain. Besides, bakery bread always has higher levels than the packaged products. It is quite outrageous that bread still contains so much salt. The Department of Health should make sure that all bread is clearly labeled and that all manufacturers try to reduce the salt in bread according to the salt target.

The available wrapped sliced bread mostly meets the salt targets. Some manufacturers indeed work towards targets for salt reduction, and provide color-coded food labels to help customers. But more measures are still needed in order to reduce the salt content in bread.

01 The word "current" in the first paragraph is the closest in meaning to _____.

(A) outdated

(B) future

(C) past

(D) present

02 Which one of the following statements is true?

(A) Salt levels in bread have greatly increased during the past decade.

(B) Recommended dietary salt levels are actually different with age.

(C) Fresh breads from in-store bakeries are usually with the lowest salt levels.

(D) Fresh breads are always clealy labelled.

03 Which of the following statements is not mentioned in the passage?

(A) Women should have more salt in their daily diet than men.

(B) CASH recommends that consumers should find out how much salt bread contains.

(C) The amount of salt in loaves usually vary with brands.

(D) Salt levels of bakery bread are always higher than that of the packaged bread.

04 What is the main idea of the passage?

(A) Various brands of bread.

(B) Recommendations of CASH.

(C) Salt levels in bread.

(D) Dietary salt levels.

DAY
4

Part 1
詞
彙
題
Day 4
完成 25%

Part 2
綜
合
測
驗
Day 4
完成 50%

Part 3
文
意
選
填
Day 4
完成 75%

Part 4
閱
讀
測
驗
Day 4
完成 100%

中譯 | 在過去的十年中，麵包的含鹽量下降了大約三分之一，有些甚至是下降了百分之四十。不同品牌的麵包，含鹽量也是各不相同。大多數都與當前的指標——每一百克，即兩厚片麵包中含一點一克鹽——上下相差不到半克。

吃太多鹽會導致高血壓，進而增加心臟病的發病率。對不同年齡層的人，建議的食鹽量也不同。每天的食鹽攝入量，成人不該超過六克，兒童則是不該超過兩克。成人和兒童血壓升高的原因，正是日常所吃的食物——例如麵包——中含鹽量過多。

CASH（低鹽與健康運動）建議消費者，如果可以，應該特別留意營養標籤上的含鹽量說明。然而，商場裡及沿街的麵包坊裡的新鮮麵包，大多是沒有營養標籤的，人們也就無法確認其中究竟含有多少鹽。此外，相較於包裝的麵包，麵包坊的麵包含鹽量通常會更高。麵包中仍含有這麼多鹽，是十分嚇人的。衛生部應當確保所有麵包都清楚地標示了營養成分，所有生產商也都盡力按照含鹽量指標來降低麵包中的含鹽量。

大多數的包裝切片麵包已經符合含鹽量指標。有些生產商的確是在盡力按照指標要求來降低含鹽量，也提供了彩色營養標籤，幫助顧客做出選擇。然而，要降低麵包中的含鹽量，我們還需要採取更多的措施。

解譯 | 在閱讀文章之前，先要預覽題目，然後再帶著問題有針對性地閱讀文章。第 1 題詞義辨析，第 2 題是判斷正誤，第 3 題是文意理解，第 4 題是概括主旨。理解了題目要求之後，閱讀全文，依次作答。

第 1 題是考 current 的同義字。current 可以作形容詞，意為「現行的；當前的；通用的」；也可以作名詞，意為「流；傾向」。選項 (A) 意為「過時的」，選項 (B) 意為「未來的」，選項 (C) 意為「過去的」，選項 (D) 意為「現在的」。根據第 1 段內容可知，current 在文中是作形容詞，意為「現行的」，所以選 (D)。

第 2 題是判斷正誤，考的是細節，問的是哪一項敘述是正確的。根據第 2 段第 2 句內容「Recommended dietary salt levels vary with age.」可知，對不同年齡層的人，建議的食鹽量也不同，與選項 (B) 相符。同樣，此題也可以用排除法來解答。根據第 1 段首句內容可知，在過去的十年中，麵包的含鹽量是在下降，而不是增長，排除選項 (A)；根據第 3 段第 2 句及第 3 句內容可知，商場中的麵包通常是沒有標籤的，含鹽量也是不確定的，排除選項 (C)、(D)。所以選 (B)。

第 3 題是文意理解，問的是哪一項敘述在文中沒有提及。第 3 段首句內容與選項 (B) 相符，第 1 段第 2 句內容與選項 (C) 相符，第 3 段第 4 句內容選項 (D) 相符。只有選項 (A)，在文中找不到相關敘述。所以選 (A)。

第 4 題是概括主旨。文中並沒有明顯的主旨句，需要根據各段內容加以概括。第 1 段是由麵包含鹽量的降低而引出話題，第 2 段講述的是食鹽攝取量不應該過多，第 3 段講述的是低鹽與健康運動的建議，第 4 段是簡略加以總結。由此可知，短文內容是簡述麵包中的含鹽量問題，所以選 (C)。

解答＆技巧 | 01 **(D)** 02 **(B)** 03 **(A)** 04 **(C)**

適用 TIP 1 適用 TIP 2 適用 TIP 3 適用 TIP 7 適用 TIP 10
適用 TIP 11 適用 TIP 12 適用 TIP 13 適用 TIP 14 適用 TIP 15

補充

up to ph 多達；Campaign for Action on Salt and Health ph 低鹽與健康運動；
if possible ph 如果可以；pay close attention to ph 密切注意，特別留意；
the Department of Health ph 衛生部，衛生局

7,000 單字

- salt [sɔlt] n 1 鹽
- third [θɝd] n 1 三分之一
- variation [ˌvɛrɪ`eʃən] n 6 變化，變動
- gram [græm] n 3 克
- guideline [`ɡaɪdˌlaɪn] n 5 指標，準則
- slice [slaɪs] n 3 薄片
- pressure [`prɛʃɚ] n 3 壓力
- tolerable [`tɑlərəbl] a 4 可承受的

- recommendation [ˌrɛkəmɛn`deʃən] n 6 推薦
- nutrition [nju`trɪʃən] n 6 營養
- supermarket [`supɚˌmɑrkɪt] n 2 超市
- bakery [`bekərɪ] n 2 麵包店
- outrageous [aut`redʒəs] a 6 不尋常的
- target [`tɑrɡɪt] n 2 目標
- reduction [rɪ`dʌkʃən] n 4 減少

MEMO

DAY 4

Part 1
詞彙題
Day 4
完成 25%

Part 2
綜合測驗
Day 4
完成 50%

Part 3
文意選填
Day 4
完成 75%

Part 4
閱讀測驗
Day 4
完成 100%

Dr. Thompson was pleased. Just three months after moving to the small Midwestern town, he had been invited to address an evening meeting of the Chamber of Commerce. Here was the perfect opportunity to show his knowledge of modern medicine and to get his practice off to a flourishing start. With this in mind, the doctor prepared carefully.

On the night of his speech, Dr. Thompson was delighted to see that the meeting hall was full. After being introduced, he strode confidently to the lectern and announced his topic: "Recent Advances in Medicine." He began with a detailed discussion of Creutzfeldt-Jakob Disease, a rare brain disorder that had recently been covered in the *New England Journal of Medicine*. Next he outlined the progress that had been made in studying immune system disorders.

Just about this time, halfway through his speech, Dr. Thompson began to notice certain restlessness in his audience. People were murmuring and shuffling their feet. Someone in the fourth row seemed to be glancing at a newspaper. Nevertheless, Dr. Thompson plowed on. He had saved the best for last. He quoted extensively from an article in the *Lancet* about genetic research, feeling sure his audience would be impressed by his familiarity with this prestigious British medical journal.

Then the speech was over. Dr. Thompson had expected to be surrounded by enthusiastic people, congratulating him and asking questions. Instead he found himself standing alone. Finally the president of the Chamber of Commerce came up to him. "Something tells me," said Dr. Thompson, "that my speech was not very successful. I can't understand it. I worked so hard to make it interesting." "Oh, it was a fine speech," replied the president. "But maybe it would have gone over better with a different audience. Creutzfeldt-Jakob Disease is not exactly a factor in these people's everyday experience. You know, here we are in January. If you'd talked about ways to avoid getting the flu, you'd have had them on the edge of their seats!"

01 What is the main message of the passage?

(A) A good speaker has to be fully prepared regardless of the audience.

(B) A good speaker should display his learning to the audience in an enthusiastic way.

(C) The more a speaker wants to please the audience, the more likely he will succeed.

(D) The key to a successful speech is to make it meaningful and relevant to the audience.

02 What was the reaction of the audience to Dr. Thompson's speech?

(A) They were bored because the medical topics were not their daily concerns.

(B) They did not understand him, so they could only discuss among themselves.

(C) They were impressed by his familiarity with advanced research in medicine.

(D) They congratulated him on the success of the speech and asked him questions.

03 Which topic was NOT mentioned in the doctor's speech?

(A) Genetic research.

(B) Flu.

(C) Immune system disorder.

(D) Creutzfeldt-Jakob disease.

04 What does "had them on the edge of their seats" mean in the last sentence of the passage?

(A) Had them stand up.

(B) Took them by surprise.

(C) Caught their full attention.

(D) Aroused their suspicion.

中譯 ｜ 湯普森醫生很高興。他搬到這個中西部小鎮上居住才三個月,就受到邀請在商會的晚間會議致辭。這是個絕佳的機會來展示他的現代醫學知識,也可以為他的診所打響知名度。抱著這樣的想法,這位醫生認真地做好準備。

在他演講的那天晚上,看到會議室坐滿了聽眾,湯普森醫生很高興。主持人介紹過他的身份之後,他信心滿懷地闊步走上講臺,宣佈了他的演講題目,「醫學的最新發展狀況」。他的演講是以庫賈氏病的詳細解說開始的,庫賈氏病是一種少見的大腦功能障礙,最近在《新英格蘭醫學期刊》上有過報導。接下來,他概括性簡述了有關免疫系統功能障礙的研究進展。

就在演講進行到一半的這時候,湯普森醫生開始注意到聽眾們的坐立不安。人們都在低聲說話,還晃動著腳。第四排的某些人似乎是在瀏覽報紙。然而,湯普森醫生依然努力地繼續演講。他把最精彩的內容放在了最後來講。他延伸性地引述了《刺胳針》上的一篇關於基因研究的文章,確信以他對這份頗有盛名的英國醫學期刊的熟稔,必定會給聽眾們留下深刻的印象。

然後,演講就結束了。湯普森醫生期待熱情洋溢的聽眾們上前來簇擁著他,祝賀他,或是向他詢問問題。然而,他卻只是孤零零地站在那裡。最後,商會主席走到他面前。湯普森醫生說,「看來,我的演講並不是很成功。我無法理解。我是如此地努力,想要讓這次演講有趣一些。」「哦,演講是很好,」這位主席說,「不過,如果換一批聽眾,也許會更受歡迎一些。以這些人的日常經歷來說,他們並不熟悉庫賈氏病。你要知道,現在是一月份,如果你講的是如何避免感染流感,就能緊緊抓住聽眾們的注意力。」

解譯 ｜ 在閱讀文章之前,先要預覽題目,然後再帶著問題有針對性地閱讀文章。第 1 題是概括主旨,第 2、3、4 題是文意理解。理解了題目要求之後,閱讀全文,依次作答。主旨題可以留在最後解答。

第 2 題是文意理解,問的是湯普森醫生的聽眾作何反應。關鍵字是「the reaction of the audience」,定位於第 3 段。文中列舉了聽眾們種種不耐煩的表現,對湯普森醫生的演講並不感興趣,原因在第 4 段結尾處有所表現,因為,演講的話題並不是他們所關注的。選項 (A) 意為「他們感到厭煩,因為醫學話題不是他們所關注的內容」,與此相符。同樣,此題也可以用排除法來解答。選項 (B) 意為「他們不理解他,所以他們只能自己討論」,在文中並沒有相關敘述;選項 (C) 意為「他對醫學領域最新研究進展的熟悉,令他們印象深刻」,選項 (D) 意為「他們祝賀他的演講取得成功,並且向他詢問問題」,與第 3 段內容不符,也可以排除。所以選 (A)。

第 3 題也是文意理解,問的是在這位醫生的演講中,哪一項話題並沒有涉及到。選項 (A) 意為「基因研究」,選項 (B) 意為「流感」,選項 (C) 意為「免疫系統功能紊亂」,選項 (D) 意為「庫賈氏病」。根據第 2 段內容可知,選項 (A)、(C)、(D) 都在演講中有所涉及,只有選項 (B),在文中找不到相關敘述。所以選 (B)。

第 4 題同樣是文意理解，問的是短文的最後一句中所說的「had them on the edge of their seats」，是什麼意思。這是較為口語化的表達，意為「吸引某人的注意力」，與選項 (C) 相符，所以選 (C)。

第 5 題是概括主旨。文中並沒有明顯的主旨句，需要根據各段內容加以概括。第 1 段講述的是湯普森醫生受邀致辭，第 2 段講述的是他的演講進程，第 3 段講述的是聽眾們的反應，第 4 段講述的是演講結束後商會主席的安慰解說。由此推斷，短文內容想要說明的是，成功的演講，應當是有趣味性的，也要與聽眾密切相關，與選項 (D) 敘述相符，所以選 (D)。

解答＆技巧 | **01 (D)** **02 (A)** **03 (B)** **04 (C)**

適用 TIP 1　適用 TIP 2　適用 TIP 3　適用 TIP 7　適用 TIP 10
適用 TIP 11　適用 TIP 12　適用 TIP 13　適用 TIP 14　適用 TIP 15

補充
Chamber of Commerce ph 商會；meeting hall ph 會議室，會議廳；
Creutzfeldt-Jakob Disease ph 庫賈氏病；immune system ph 免疫系統
the New England Journal of Medicine ph 《新英格蘭醫學期刊》

7,000 單字

- address [əˋdrɛs] v 1 致辭
- chamber [ˋtʃembɚ] n 4 議院，議會
- commerce [ˋkɑmɝs] n 4 商務
- hall [hɔl] n 2 廳堂
- stride [straɪd] v 5 大步走
- disorder [dɪsˋɔrdɚ] n 4 紊亂
- outline [ˋaʊt͵laɪn] v 3 概述
- notice [ˋnotɪs] v 1 注意

- audience [ˋɔdɪəns] n 3 聽眾
- glance [glæns] v 3 瞥，看
- quote [kwot] v 3 引用
- genetic [dʒəˋnɛtɪk] a 6 基因的
- familiarity [fə͵mɪlɪˋærətɪ] n 6 通曉，熟悉
- enthusiastic [ɪn͵θjuzɪˋæstɪk] a 5 熱情的
- congratulate [kənˋgrætʃə͵let] v 4 祝賀

MEMO

When preparing lunch for children, you should be particularly careful, since children are among the most vulnerable to severe consequences of food poisoning.

Before preparation, remember to wash your hands with warm water and soap for 20 seconds. The countertop, the sink, the cutting board, along with some other cooking utensils, should be washed carefully as well. For the sake of convenience, you can choose to use a spray-on bleach product. In a word, everything that comes into contact with raw meat, poultry, fish or eggs should be thoroughly cleaned immediately after use.

A standard rule of food safety is to keep cold food cold and hot food hot. Insulated lunch boxes prove to be much safer. The best box (hard-sided or soft) should have an insulated lining and a pocket in which to place a thin freezer pack, so as to help keep the contents cold before they are consumed.

What to put in those boxes? Food like peanut butter and sliced cheese that can tolerate room temperatures without spoiling are OK, especially if insulation is lacking. Pantry-safe food that can be packed in easy-to-open containers can be considered as well. Tuna, for example, should be a good choice, since it can be eaten out of a flip-top can, with or without bread.

Boxed milk or juice sold unrefrigerated can be another safe bet. Various sandwiches—with lunch meats, tuna or egg salad—can be made the night before. Lettuce and tomatoes can be packed separately so that they can be put on the sandwich before eating. Dried fruits and whole fruits like apples, bananas, oranges and grapes can round out the meal, since they can be kept safely at room temperature. But all fresh fruits, even those that will be peeled, must be washed before they are put in the lunch box.

01 Which one of the following statements is true?

(A) Insulated lunch boxes are actually not a good choice for children.

(B) In order to ensure food safety, we should keep cold food cold and hot food hot.

(C) Children are unlikely to suffer from the consequence of food poisoning.

(D) Spray-on bleach products could not be used to clean cooking utensils.

02 Which of the following statements is not mentioned in the passage?

(A) Peanut butter and sliced cheese can stand the room temperature without spoiling.

(B) Boxed milk or juice can be prepared for children's lunch.

(C) Various sandwiches should be avoided in children's lunch food for the sake of safety.

(D) Fresh fruits should be washed before being put into the lunch box.

03 The word "bet" in the last paragraph is closest in meaning to _____.

(A) situation

(B) gamble

(C) race

(D) competition

04 What is the main idea of the passage?

(A) Food poisoning.

(B) Food safety.

(C) Preparation of lunch for children.

(D) Boxed lunch.

DAY 4

Part 1
詞彙題
Day 4
完成 25%

Part 2
綜合測驗
Day 4
完成 50%

Part 3
文意選填
Day 4
完成 75%

Part 4
閱讀測驗
Day 4
完成 100%

中譯│兒童最容易受到食物中毒的嚴重危害，所以為孩子們做午餐時應該要格外注意。準備食物前，要用溫水和肥皂洗手二十秒。廚房流理台、水槽、砧板，以及其他的廚具，也要仔細清洗。為求方便，可以用消毒噴劑。總之，接觸過生肉、家禽、魚或蛋類的所有器具，使用完後，都要立即徹底清洗。

保證食品安全的準則之一，就是讓冷的食物保持冷藏，而讓熱的食物保溫。使用保溫飯盒更安全一些。最好的飯盒（硬盒或是軟盒），要有保溫內襯和裝有輕薄冷凍包的口袋，確保食物在食用前保持冷藏。

飯盒裡應該裝什麼食物呢？花生醬和切片乳酪之類的食物就可以，它們能夠在室溫下，尤其是在沒有保溫包裝的情況下保存。適宜裝在易開容器中的食品，也可以考慮。例如，鮪魚就是很好的選擇，可以裝在翻蓋易開罐，可以配麵包食用，也可以不配。

室溫出售的盒裝牛奶或果汁，也是很安全的。不同種類的三明治——搭配午餐肉、鮪魚或雞蛋沙拉的三明治——可以在前一天晚上準備。生菜和番茄可以單獨裝起來，食用之前，加在三明治上即可。附上水果乾，以及蘋果、香蕉、柳丁和葡萄之類的整顆水果，因為可以在室溫下保存，這樣就是完整的一餐。不過，所有的新鮮水果，即使是剝皮後才吃的水果，放入飯盒之前，也必須清洗。

解譯│在閱讀文章之前，先要預覽題目，然後再帶著問題有針對性地閱讀文章。第 1 題是判斷正誤，第 2 題是文意理解，第 3 題是詞義辨析，第 4 題是概括主旨。理解了題目要求之後，閱讀全文，依次作答。

第 1 題是判斷正誤，考的是細節，問的是哪一項敘述是正確的。根據第 3 段首句內容「A standard rule of food safety is to keep cold food cold and hot food hot.」可知，為保食物安全，應該讓冷的食物保持冷藏，而讓熱的食物保溫，與選項 (B) 相符。同樣，此題也可以用排除法來解答。根據第 3 段 2 句內容可知，保溫飯盒更安全一些，是很好的選擇，排除選項 (A)；根據第 1 段內容可知，兒童最容易受到食物中毒的嚴重危害，而不是不可能受到危害，排除選項 (C)；根據第 2 段第 3 句內容可知，可以用消毒噴劑清洗廚具，排除選項 (D)。所以選 (B)。

第 2 題是文意理解，問的是哪一項敘述在文中沒有提及。第 4 段第 2 句內容與選項 (A) 相符，第 5 段首句內容與選項 (B) 相符，第 5 段最後一句內容與選項 (D) 相符。只有選項 (C)，在文中找不到相關敘述。所以選 (C)。

第 3 題是考 bet 的同義字。bet 可以作動詞，意為「賭博」；也可以作名詞，意為「賭博；賭注；意見；預言；選擇」。根據最後一段內容可知，bet 在文中是作名詞，意為「選擇」。選項 (A) 意為「選擇」，選項 (B) 意為「賭博」，選項 (C) 意為「比賽」，選項 (D) 意為「競爭」。所以選 (A)。

第 4 題是概括主旨。文中並沒有明顯的主旨句，需要根據各段內容加以概括。第 1 段是引出話題，第 2 段講述的是準備食物前的事宜，第 3 段講述的是保證食物安全的準則，第 4 段講述的是飯盒裡應該放的食物，第 5 段講述的是午餐的輔助搭配。由此可知，短文內容是簡述兒童的午餐製備，所以選 (C)。

解答＆技巧 │ **01 (B)** **02 (C)** **03 (A)** **04 (C)**

適用 **TIP 1** 適用 **TIP 2** 適用 **TIP 3** 適用 **TIP 7** 適用 **TIP 10**

適用 **TIP 11** 適用 **TIP 12** 適用 **TIP 13** 適用 **TIP 14** 適用 **TIP 15**

DAY
4

補充

food poisoning ph 食物中毒；cutting board ph 砧板；cooking utensils ph 廚具；
for the sake of convenience ph 為求方便；peanut butter ph 花生醬

7,000 單字

- vulnerable [ˋvʌlnərəb!] a 6 易受傷害的
- severe [səˋvɪr] a 4 嚴重的
- consequence [ˋkɑnsə͵kwɛns] n 4 結果
- soap [sop] n 1 肥皂
- utensil [juˋtɛns!] n 6 用具
- convenience [kənˋvinjəns] n 4 方便
- bleach [blitʃ] n 5 漂白劑
- raw [rɔ] a 3 生的

- poultry [ˋpoltrɪ] n 5 家禽
- pocket [ˋpɑkɪt] n 1 口袋
- peanut [ˋpi͵nʌt] n 2 花生
- tolerate [ˋtɑlə͵ret] v 4 承受
- spoil [spɔɪl] v 3 損壞
- sandwich [ˋsændwɪtʃ] n 2 三明治
- salad [ˋsæləd] n 2 沙拉

Part 1
詞
彙
題

Day 4
完成 25%

Part 2
綜
合
測
驗

Day 4
完成 50%

Part 3
文
意
選
填

Day 4
完成 75%

Part 4
閱
讀
測
驗

Day 4
完成 100%

MEMO --

Pop stars enjoy a style of living, which is similar to the prerogative of the royalty. Whenever and wherever they are, the excited crowds always try to get close to their idols or at least catch a brief glimpse. The stars are always being surrounded by a permanent entourage of managers, press agents and bodyguards. Photographs of them regularly appear in the press, and all their comings and goings are reported. Just like the royalty, pop stars are news. They are not only private individuals, but public property.

However, pop stars are confronted with great inconvenience as well. It may be unpleasant, or even dangerous, for them to make unscheduled appearances in public, since they must be constantly shielded from the adoring crowds.

The financial rewards pop stars receive for this sacrifice cannot be calculated. Actually, their rates of pay are astronomical. Society rewards top entertainers lavishly, and famous stars always enjoy fame, wealth and adulation on an unprecedented scale. Nobody could begrudge them their rewards. Pop stars earn vast sums in foreign currency, and the taxman should only be grateful for their massive annual contributions to the exchequer.

People engaged in humdrum jobs may complain about the successes and rewards of pop stars. Actually, there is nothing to be said against it. But these people who make envious remarks should know that the most famous stars only represent the tip of the iceberg. For every famous star, there are hundreds of others struggling to earn a living. Everyone who attempts to become a star should inevitably take enormous risks, and be aware that only a handful of competitors ever get to the very top. Moreover, years of concentrated efforts may be rewarded with complete failure.

01 What does the first sentence in the first paragraph mean?

(A) Pop stars' lifestyles are just the same as that of the royalty.

(B) Pop stars enjoy the treatment that only belonged to the royalty in the past.

(C) Pop stars are as rich as the royalty.

(D) Pop stars' life is as luxurious as that of the royalty.

02 The word "confronted" in the second paragraph is closest in meaning to _____.

(A) faced

(B) suffered

(C) pushed

(D) led

03 What is the author's attitude toward pop stars' high income?

(A) Critical.

(B) Approval.

(C) Indifferent.

(D) Disapproval.

04 What is the main idea of the passage?

(A) Pop stars and the royalty.

(B) Pop stars' high income.

(C) Pop stars' lifestyle.

(D) Pop stars' inconvenience.

DAY
4

Part 1
詞
彙
題
Day 4
完成 25%

Part 2
綜
合
測
驗
Day 4
完成 50%

Part 3
文
意
選
填
Day 4
完成 75%

Part 4
閱
讀
測
驗
Day 4
完成 100%

中譯｜明星們的生活方式，與王室的特權相似。不論他們身在何時何地，激動的人群總是試圖接近他們的偶像，或至少只是短暫的一瞥。明星們總是被固定的隨行人員——經紀人、宣傳人員和保鑣——包圍著。他們的照片定期出現在報章雜誌裡，他們的一舉一動也隨時都會被報導，正如王室一般，明星們就是新聞。他們不只是個人，也是公眾人物。

然而，明星們也面臨著極大的不便之處。如果是未經計畫地出現在公眾場合，情形有可能會不太愉快，甚至是危險的，因為他們必須持續地與那些崇拜人群隔離開來。

因為有這樣的犧牲，明星們所獲得的經濟收入難以計算。事實上，他們的報酬高昂得無法估計。社會對於優秀演藝人員總是慷慨相酬，明星們也總是享有前所未有的名望、財富和吹捧。沒有人可以忌妒他們的報酬。明星們賺取巨額的外幣，稅務員也應當感謝他們每年為財政部所做出的貢獻。

那些工作較為單調的人們也許會抱怨明星們的成功和報酬。事實上，這也無可厚非。不過，這些做忌妒之語的人們也要知道，最著名的明星只代表冰山一角。對於每一個明星而言，都有數以百計的同行在為生存而掙扎。每一個試圖成為明星的人，都不可避免地要承擔極大的風險，也要明白，只有少數人可以成為頂尖人物。而且，多年的辛苦努力也許會以徹底失敗而告終。

解譯｜在閱讀文章之前，先要預覽題目，然後再帶著問題有針對性地閱讀文章。第 1、3 題是文意理解，第 2 題是詞義辨析，第 4 題是概括主旨。理解了題目要求之後，閱讀全文，依次作答。

第 1 題是文意理解，問的是第 1 段首句的意義。原句為「Pop stars enjoy a style of living, which is similar to the prerogative of the royalty.」主要子句是闡述明星們的生活方式，關係子句是對先行詞 style of living 作進一步的解說，意為與王室的特權相似。全句意義整合之後，即為明星們的生活方式，與王室的特權相似，與選項 (D) 最為相符，所以選 (D)。

第 2 題是考動詞 confront 的同義字。選項 (A) 意為「面臨」，選項 (B) 意為「遭受」，選項 (C) 意為「推動」，選項 (D) 意為「引領」。根據第 2 段內容可知，confront 意為「面臨」，所以選 (A)。

第 3 題同樣是文意理解，問的是對於明星們的高收入，作者持何種態度。可以定位於第 2、3 段。作者先是表明了明星們有高收入的原因，再指出社會和稅務方面對明星收入的態度，接著直接表明，「Nobody could begrudge them their rewards.」。由此可知，作者對此是持支持態度的。所以選 (B)。

第 4 題是概括主旨。文中並沒有明顯的主旨句，需要根據各段內容加以概括。第 1 段是由明星們的生活方式而引出話題，第 2 段講述的是明星們的不便之處，第 3 段講述的是明星們的高收入，第 4 段講述的是明星們風光背後的艱辛。由此可知，短文內容是簡述明星們的生活方式，所以選 (C)。

解答＆技巧 | **01 (D)** **02 (A)** **03 (B)** **04 (C)**

適用 TIP 1　適用 TIP 2　適用 TIP 7　適用 TIP 10　適用 TIP 11
適用 TIP 12　適用 TIP 13　適用 TIP 14　適用 TIP 15　適用 TIP 16

補充

prerogative ⓝ 特權；entourage ⓝ 隨行人員；inconvenience ⓝ 不便；unpleasant ⓐ 不愉快的；
astronomical ⓐ 天文數字的

7,000 單字

- pop [pɑp] ⓝ 3 流行
- royalty [ˋrɔɪəltɪ] ⓝ 6 王室成員
- idol [ˋaɪdl̩] ⓝ 4 偶像
- brief [brif] ⓐ 2 短暫的
- glimpse [glɪmps] ⓝ 4 一瞥，一看
- bodyguard [ˋbɑdɪ͵gɑrd] ⓝ 5 保鏢
- shield [ʃild] ⓥ 5 保護
- financial [faɪˋnænʃəl] ⓐ 4 財務的

- sacrifice [ˋsækrə͵faɪs] ⓝ 4 犧牲
- calculate [ˋkælkjə͵let] ⓥ 4 計算
- fame [fem] ⓝ 4 名望
- currency [ˋkɝənsɪ] ⓝ 5 貨幣
- remark [rɪˋmɑrk] ⓝ 4 評論
- struggle [ˋstrʌgl̩] ⓥ 2 奮鬥
- enormous [ɪˋnɔrməs] ⓐ 4 極大的

DAY 4

Part 1 詞彙題　Day 4 完成 25%

Part 2 綜合測驗　Day 4 完成 50%

Part 3 文意選填　Day 4 完成 75%

Part 4 閱讀測驗　Day 4 完成 100%

MEMO

DAY 5

Success is a journey, not a destination.
The doing is often more important than the outcome.
— *Arthur Ashe*

成功是一個旅程，不是終點，所做的事比結果還重要。
——亞瑟‧艾許

▶ **Part 1** │ 詞 彙 題

▶ **Part 2** │ 綜合測驗

▶ **Part 3** │ 文意選填

▶ **Part 4** │ 閱讀測驗

01 Many people are fond of wearing cotton _____ in summer because it breathes.

(A) fabric   (B) coverage
(C) aircraft   (D) airline

補充
cotton fabric ph 棉布

7,000 單字
• cotton [ˋkɑtn] n 2 棉花
• fabric [ˋfæbrɪk] n 5 布料
• coverage [ˋkʌvərɪdʒ] n 6 覆蓋
• aircraft [ˋɛr͵kræft] n 2 飛機
• airline [ˋɛr͵laɪn] n 2 航空公司

中譯｜很多人喜歡在夏天穿棉布衣服，因為它透氣。

解說｜四個選項皆為名詞。依據題意，應該是「在夏天穿棉布衣服」，選項 (A) fabric 表示「布料」，符合題意，其他三個選項都不符合題意。

解答&技巧｜**(A)** 適用 TIP 3　適用 TIP 4

---

02 The passengers _____ escaped death when a bomb exploded in the subway station, killing sixty people. 【95年學測英文】

(A) traditionally   (B) valuably
(C) loosely   (D) narrowly

補充
escape death ph 死裡逃生
subway station ph 地鐵車站

7,000 單字
• subway [ˋsʌb͵we] n 2 地鐵
• traditionally [trəˋdɪʃənlɪ] ad 2 傳統地
• valuably [ˋvæljuəblɪ] ad 3 有價值地
• loosely [ˋluslɪ] ad 3 寬鬆地
• narrowly [ˋnæ:rolɪ] ad 2 勉強地

中譯｜一顆炸彈在地鐵車站爆炸，六十個人被炸死，而乘客們勉強死裡逃生。

解說｜四個選項皆為副詞。依據題意，應該是「乘客們勉強死裡逃生」，選項 (D) narrowly 表示「勉強地」，符合題意，其他三個選項都不符合題意。

解答&技巧｜**(D)** 適用 TIP 1　適用 TIP 4

---

03 After you wash the crystal glassware, you can _____ them with newspaper and make them shine.

(A) recall   (B) clarify
(C) borrow   (D) polish

補充
crystal glassware ph 水晶玻璃器皿

7,000 單字
• crystal [ˋkrɪstl] n 5 水晶
• recall [rɪˋkɔl] v 4 回想起
• clarify [ˋklærə͵faɪ] v 4 澄清
• borrow [ˋbɑro] v 2 借
• polish [ˋpɑlɪʃ] v 4 擦亮

中譯｜清洗過那些水晶玻璃器皿後，你可以用報紙擦亮它們，讓它們閃閃發光。

解說｜四個選項皆為動詞。依據題意，應該是「用報紙擦拭水晶玻璃器皿」，選項 (D) polish 表示「擦亮」，符合題意，是正確選項。

解答&技巧｜**(D)** 適用 TIP 3　適用 TIP 4

04 The disabled man overcame all _____ to win the first prize in the drawing contest and deserved the praise from people.

(A) privacies   (B) ambitions

(C) bookcases   (D) obstacles

中譯｜那名身障者克服所有障礙，在畫畫比賽中贏得了第一名，理應得到人們的稱讚。

解說｜四個選項皆為名詞。依據題意，應該是「身障者克服所有障礙」，選項 (D) obstacles 表示「障礙」，符合題意，其他三個選項都不符合題意。

解答＆技巧｜**(D)** 　適用 TIP 3 　適用 TIP 4

補充
first prize ph 第一名

7,000 單字
- disabled [dɪsˋeblɖ] a 6 身心障礙的
- privacy [ˋpraɪvəsɪ] n 4 隱私
- ambition [æmˋbɪʃən] n 3 野心
- bookcase [ˋbʊk͵kes] n 2 書櫃
- obstacle [ˋɑbstəkl̩] n 4 障礙

---

05 People who are over the age of eighteen are emotionally _____ and should behave responsibly.

(A) bony   (B) mature

(C) familiar   (D) childlike

中譯｜年滿十八歲的人情感已成熟，應該負責任地行事。

解說｜四個選項皆為形容詞。依據題意，應該是「情感已成熟」，選項 (B) mature 表示「成熟的」，符合題意，是正確選項。

解答＆技巧｜**(B)** 　適用 TIP 1 　適用 TIP 4

補充
the age of ph ～的年齡

7,000 單字
- eighteen [ˋeˋtin] num 1 十八
- bony [ˋbonɪ] a 2 骨瘦如柴的
- mature [məˋtjʊr] a 3 成熟的
- familiar [fəˋmɪljə] a 3 熟悉的
- childlike [ˋtʃaɪld͵laɪk] a 2 天真爛漫的

---

06 Generally speaking, the air fare for the international flight is much more expensive than the _____ one.

(A) classic   (B) crazy

(C) distant   (D) domestic

中譯｜一般來說，國際航班的機票價格要比國內航班的機票價格貴很多。

解說｜四個選項皆為形容詞。依據題意，應該是「國際航班的機票價格比國內航班的機票價格貴」，選項 (D) domestic 表示「國內的」，符合題意。

解答＆技巧｜**(D)** 　適用 TIP 3 　適用 TIP 4

補充
air fare ph 機票價格

7,000 單字
- is [ɪz] v 1 是
- classic [ˋklæsɪk] a 2 經典的
- crazy [ˋkrezɪ] a 2 瘋狂的
- distant [ˋdɪstənt] a 2 遙遠的
- domestic [dəˋmɛstɪk] a 3 國內的

DAY
5

Part 1
詞
彙
題
Day 5
完成 25%

Part 2
綜
合
測
驗
Day 5
完成 50%

Part 3
文
意
選
填
Day 5
完成 75%

Part 4
閱
讀
測
驗
Day 5
完成 100%

07 Mark always _____ about his new smart phone before his colleagues, which was aversive to them.

(A) boasted   (B) dropped

(C) gossiped   (D) confessed

> 補充
> smart phone ph 智慧型手機
>
> 7,000 單字
> • aversive [ə`vɜsɪv] a 4 反感的
> • boast [bost] v 4 吹噓
> • drop [drɑp] v 2 滴下
> • gossip [`gɑsəp] v 3 傳播流言蜚語
> • confess [kən`fɛs] v 4 承認

中譯 | 馬克總是在同事面前吹噓他新買的智慧型手機，這令他們感到很反感。

解說 | 本題是由 which 引導的非限定關係子句。依據題意，應該是「在同事面前吹噓新買的智慧型手機」，選項 (A) boasted 表示「吹噓」，符合題意。

解答&技巧 | **(A)** 適用 TIP 1 適用 TIP 4

---

08 The millionaire was so _____ that he never gave the poor a penny, let alone making donations to the refugees.

(A) stingy   (B) eastern

(C) elder   (D) exact

> 補充
> let alone ph 更不必說
>
> 7,000 單字
> • millionaire [ˌmɪljən`ɛr]
>   n 3 百萬富翁
> • stingy [`stɪndʒɪ] a 4 吝嗇的
> • eastern [`istən] a 2 東方的
> • elder [`ɛldə] a 2 年長的
> • exact [ɪg`zækt] a 2 準確的

中譯 | 這個富翁非常吝嗇，他從來不給窮人一分錢，更不必說捐錢給難民了。

解說 | 四個選項皆為形容詞。依據題意，應該是「富翁非常吝嗇」，選項 (A) stingy 表示「吝嗇的」，符合題意，是正確答案。

解答&技巧 | **(A)** 適用 TIP 1 適用 TIP 4

---

09 The salesman says that this suitcase is strong and _____ and I can use it for a long time.

(A) giant   (B) durable

(C) hateful   (D) magnetic

> 補充
> for a long time ph 很長時間
>
> 7,000 單字
> • suitcase [`sut.kes] n 5 手提箱
> • giant [`dʒaɪənt] a 2 巨大的
> • durable [`djurəbl] a 4 耐用的
> • hateful [`hetfəl] a 2 可憎的
> • magnetic [mæg`nɛtɪk]
>   a 4 有磁性的

中譯 | 推銷員說這種手提箱結實耐用，我可以用很久。

解說 | 四個選項皆為形容詞。依據題意，應該是「手提箱結實耐用」，選項 (B) durable 表示「耐用的」，符合題意，其他三個選項都不符合題意。

解答&技巧 | **(B)** 適用 TIP 1 適用 TIP 4

DAY
5

Part 1
詞
彙
題
Day 5
完成 25%

Part 2
綜
合
測
驗
Day 5
完成 50%

Part 3
文
意
選
填
Day 5
完成 75%

Part 4
閱
讀
測
驗
Day 5
完成 100%

10 No matter how difficult the work may be, Jason always _____ in finishing it before he goes home.

(A) hunts

(B) persists

(C) unfolds

(D) unifies

補充
go home ph 回家

7,000 單字
• how [haʊ] ad 1 如何
• hunt [hʌnt] v 2 打獵
• persist [pəˋsɪst] v 5 堅持
• unfold [ʌnˋfold] v 6 打開
• unify [ˋjunəˏfaɪ] v 6 統一

中譯｜無論遇到多麼困難的工作，傑森總是堅持在回家之前完成它。

解說｜本題是一個讓步副詞子句。依據題意，應該是「堅持在回家之前完成工作」，選項 (B) persists 表示「堅持」，符合題意，其他三個選項都不符合題意。

解答&技巧｜ **(B)** 適用 TIP 3 適用 TIP 4

---

11 According to the law, if a young child commits a crime, his parents should be held _____ for his criminal act.

(A) eligible

(B) dispensable

(C) credible

(D) accountable

補充
commit a crime ph 犯罪

7,000 單字
• commit [kəˋmɪt] v 4 犯罪
• eligible [ˋɛlɪdʒəbl] a 6 合格的
• dispensable [dɪˋspɛnsəbl]
  a 5 可有可無的
• credible [ˋkrɛdəbl] a 6 可信的
• accountable [əˋkaʊntəbl]
  a 6 有責任的

中譯｜法律規定，如果幼兒犯罪，將由其父母來承擔責任。

解說｜四個選項皆為形容詞。依據題意，應該是「父母承擔責任」，選項 (D) accountable 表示「有責任的」，符合題意，是正確選項。

解答&技巧｜ **(D)** 適用 TIP 1 適用 TIP 4

---

12 Although this baby is one month _____, he is still healthy under the special care of the babysitter.

(A) preventive

(B) premature

(C) unanimous

(D) progressive

補充
special care ph 特別照料

7,000 單字
• babysitter [ˋbebɪsɪtə] n 2 保姆
• preventive [prɪˋvɛntɪv]
  a 6 預防的
• premature [ˏpriməˋtjʊr]
  a 6 早產的
• unanimous [juˋnænəməs]
  a 6 意見一致的
• progressive [prəˋgrɛsɪv]
  a 6 進步的

中譯｜儘管這個嬰兒早產了一個月，但是在保姆的特別照料下，他仍然很健康。

解說｜四個選項皆為形容詞。依據題意，應該是「嬰兒早產了一個月」，選項 (B) premature 表示「早產的」，符合題意，其他三個選項都不符合題意。

解答&技巧｜ **(B)** 適用 TIP 1 適用 TIP 4

13 Do not just sit and wait _____ for a good chance to come to you. You have to take the initiative and create chances for yourself.　　　【95年指考英文】

(A) consciously
(B) passively
(C) reasonably
(D) subjectively

中譯｜不要只是被動地坐著等待好時機來找你，你要採取主動，為自己創造機會。

解說｜本題可看做一個祈使句。依據題意，應該是「被動地坐著等待好時機」，選項 (B) passively 表示「被動地」，符合題意。

解答＆技巧｜**(B)** 〔適用 TIP 3〕 〔適用 TIP 4〕

〔補充〕
take the initiative ph 採取主動

〔7,000 單字〕
- do [du] aux 1 助動詞
- consciously [ˈkɑnʃəslɪ] ad 3 自覺地
- passively [ˈpæsɪvlɪ] ad 4 被動地
- reasonably [ˈriznəblɪ] ad 3 合理地
- subjectively [səbˈdʒɛktɪvlɪ] ad 6 主觀地

---

14 You should buy used cars with _____ because some used car dealers may be dishonest.

(A) dignity
(B) upbringing
(C) caution
(D) vaccine

中譯｜你在購買二手車時要謹慎，因為有些二手車商可能不誠實。

解說｜四個選項皆為名詞。依據題意，應該是「購買二手車時要謹慎」，選項 (C) caution 表示「謹慎」，而 with caution 表示「謹慎地」，符合題意。

解答＆技巧｜**(C)** 〔適用 TIP 1〕 〔適用 TIP 4〕

〔補充〕
used car ph 二手車

〔7,000 單字〕
- dealer [ˈdilɚ] n 4 業者
- dignity [ˈdɪgnətɪ] n 4 尊嚴
- upbringing [ˈʌpˌbrɪŋɪŋ] n 6 養育
- caution [ˈkɔʃən] n 5 謹慎
- vaccine [ˈvæksin] n 6 疫苗

---

15 Her career _____ most of her time, so she has no extra time to knit a sweater for her husband.

(A) animates
(B) occupies
(C) asserts
(D) activates

中譯｜她的事業佔用了她大多數的時間，所以她沒有多餘的時間為丈夫織毛衣。

解說｜四個選項皆為動詞。依據題意，應該是「事業佔用了她大多數的時間」，選項 (B) occupies 表示「佔用」，符合題意，是正確選項。

解答＆技巧｜**(B)** 〔適用 TIP 1〕 〔適用 TIP 4〕

〔補充〕
extra time ph 額外時間

〔7,000 單字〕
- sweater [ˈswɛtɚ] n 2 毛衣
- animate [ˈænəˌmet] v 6 使有生氣
- occupy [ˈɑkjəˌpaɪ] v 4 佔據
- assert [əˈsɝt] v 6 維護
- activate [ˈæktəˌvet] v 5 啟動

16 This criminal has made a _____ how he and his accomplices stole the jewelry.

(A) assumption
(B) asylum
(C) confession
(D) boycott

補充
make a confession ph 招供

7,000 單字
- accomplices [əˋkɑmplɪs] n 6 幫兇
- assumption [əˋsʌmpʃən] n 6 假定
- asylum [əˋsaɪləm] n 6 庇護
- confession [kənˋfɛʃən] n 5 坦白
- boycott [ˋbɔɪˏkɑt] n 6 聯合抵制

中譯｜這個犯人已經招認了他如何與同夥一起偷竊珠寶。

解說｜四個選項皆為名詞。依據題意，應該是「犯人招認如何與同夥一起偷竊珠寶」，選項 (C) confession 表示「坦白」，而片語 make a confession 表示「招供」，符合題意。

解答＆技巧｜**(C)** 適用 TIP 2 適用 TIP 4

---

17 I have got the teaching _____ and am certified to teach high school here.

(A) qualification
(B) bombard
(C) biochemistry
(D) byte

補充
high school ph 中學

7,000 單字
- here [hɪr] ad 1 這裡
- qualification [ˏkwɑləfəˋkeʃən] n 6 資格
- bombard [bɑmˋbɑrd] n 6 射石砲
- biochemistry [ˏbaɪoˋkɛmɪstrɪ] n 6 生物化學
- byte [baɪt] n 6 位元組

中譯｜我已經獲得了教師資格，有資格在這裡教高中。

解說｜四個選項皆為名詞。依據題意，應該是「獲得了教師資格」，選項 (A) qualification 表示「資格」，符合題意，其他三個選項都不符合題意。

解答＆技巧｜**(A)** 適用 TIP 1 適用 TIP 4

---

18 What I want to say is that this college student _____ to work in the restaurant instead of being forced.

(A) capsules
(B) captions
(C) defines
(D) volunteers

補充
college student ph 大學生

7,000 單字
- force [fors] v 1 強迫
- capsule [ˋkæpsl] v 6 濃縮
- caption [ˋkæpʃən] v 6 加標題
- define [dɪˋfaɪn] v 3 闡釋
- volunteer [ˏvɑlənˋtɪr] v 4 自願做

中譯｜我想說的是，這名大學生是自願在這家餐廳工作，而不是被強迫的。

解說｜本題是一個名詞子句。由 not forced 可以推斷出，應該是「自願在這家餐廳工作」，選項 (D) volunteers 表示「自願做」，符合題意。

解答＆技巧｜**(D)** 適用 TIP 1 適用 TIP 4

DAY 5

Part 1 詞彙題 Day 5 完成 25%
Part 2 綜合測驗 Day 5 完成 50%
Part 3 文意選填 Day 5 完成 75%
Part 4 閱讀測驗 Day 5 完成 100%

♫ 263

19 The plane will take off in twenty minutes, so we should hurry up to go _____.

(A) aboard   (B) diameter

(C) disclosure   (D) emigration

補充
take off ph 起飛

7,000 單字
- twenty [ˈtwɛntɪ] num 1 二十
- aboard [əˈbord] ad 3 在飛機上
- diameter [daɪˈæmətɚ] n 6 直徑
- disclosure [dɪsˈkloʒɚ] n 6 披露
- emigration [ˌɛməˈɡreʃən] n 6 移民

中譯｜飛機還有二十分鐘就要起飛了，我們要抓緊時間登機。

解說｜依據題意，應該是「抓緊時間登機」，選項 (A) aboard 表示「在飛機上」，而 go aboard 表示「登機」，符合題意。

解答&技巧｜**(A)** 適用 TIP 2 適用 TIP 10

---

20 The policemen thought it was not an _____ death because there was a knife in the abdomen of the dead man.

(A) emphatic   (B) equivalent

(C) accidental   (D) versatile

補充
accidental death ph 意外死亡

7,000 單字
- abdomen [ˈæbdəmən] n 4 腹部
- emphatic [ɪmˈfætɪk] a 6 著重的
- equivalent [ɪˈkwɪvələnt] a 6 等價的
- accidental [ˌæksəˈdɛnt] a 4 意外的
- versatile [ˈvɝsətl] a 6 多功能的

中譯｜員警認為這不是意外死亡，因為死者的腹部插著一把刀。

解說｜四個選項皆為形容詞。依據題意，應該是「不是意外死亡」，選項 (C) accidental 表示「意外的」，符合題意，是正確選項。

解答&技巧｜**(C)** 適用 TIP 1 適用 TIP 4

---

21 The accountant was _____ of embezzling public funds and arrested by the police.

(A) repaid   (B) accused

(C) reproduced   (D) resided

補充
public funds ph 公款

7,000 單字
- accountant [əˈkauntənt] n 4 會計（師）
- repay [rɪˈpe] v 5 回報
- accuse [əˈkjuz] v 4 控告
- reproduce [ˌriprəˈdjus] v 5 複製
- reside [rɪˈzaɪd] v 5 居住

中譯｜這名會計被指控挪用公款，遭到了警方的逮捕。

解說｜四個選項皆為動詞。依據題意，應該是「會計被指控挪用公款」，選項 (B) accused 表示「指控」，而片語 be accused of 表示「被指控～」，符合題意。

解答&技巧｜**(B)** 適用 TIP 2 適用 TIP 4

DAY
5

Part 1
詞
彙
題
Day 5
完成 25%

Part 2
綜
合
測
驗
Day 5
完成 50%

Part 3
文
意
選
填
Day 5
完成 75%

Part 4
閱
讀
測
驗
Day 5
完成 100%

22 The teacher asked him to _____ himself with the usage of the adjectives within a week and then have a test.

(A) retort   (B) acquaint

(C) reverse   (D) scramble

補充
acquaint oneself with
ph 熟悉，了解

7,000 單字
- adjective [ˈædʒɪktɪv] n 4 形容詞
- retort [rɪˈtɔrt] v 6 反駁
- acquaint [əˈkwent] v 4 使熟悉
- reverse [rɪˈvɝs] v 5 顛倒
- scramble [ˈskræmbl] v 5 搶奪

中譯｜老師要求他在一周之內了解形容詞的用法，然後進行測驗。

解說｜四個選項皆為動詞。依據題意，應該是「了解形容詞的用法」，選項 (B) acquaint 表示「了解」，而 acquaint oneself with 表示「熟悉，了解」，符合題意。

解答＆技巧｜ **(B)** 適用 TIP 2　適用 TIP 4

---

23 He has studied English for about eight years, so I think his knowledge of English is _____ for this job.

(A) adequate   (B) shabby

(C) structural   (D) vertical

補充
be adequate for ph 對～是足夠的

7,000 單字
- eight [et] num 1 八
- adequate [ˈædəkwɪt] a 4 充足的
- shabby [ˈʃæbɪ] a 5 破舊的
- structural [ˈstrʌktʃərəl] a 5 結構上的
- vertical [ˈvɝtɪk!] a 5 垂直的

中譯｜他已經學了八年英語，所以我認為他所掌握的英語知識對於這項工作來說是足夠的。

解說｜四個選項皆為形容詞。依據題意，應該是「掌握的英語知識是足夠的」，選項 (A) adequate 表示「足夠的」，符合題意，是正確選項。

解答＆技巧｜ **(A)** 適用 TIP 1　適用 TIP 4

---

24 Ruth is a very _____ person. She cannot take any criticism and always finds excuses to justify herself. 【96年學測英文】

(A) shameful   (B) wholesome

(C) defensive   (D) outgoing

補充
justify oneself ph 為自己辯解

7,000 單字
- excuse [ɪkˈskjuz] n 2 理由
- shameful [ˈʃemfəl] a 4 可恥的
- wholesome [ˈholsəm] a 5 健全的
- defensive [dɪˈfɛnsɪv] a 4 防禦的
- outgoing [ˈaʊtˌɡoɪŋ] a 5 外出的

中譯｜露絲是一個防禦性很強的人，她無法接受任何批評，總是找理由來為自己辯解。

解說｜四個選項皆為動詞。依據題意，應該是「露絲是一個防禦性很強的人」，選項 (C) defensive 表示「防禦的，戒備的」，符合題意。

解答＆技巧｜ **(C)** 適用 TIP 3　適用 TIP 4

Part 2 綜合測驗 │ Comprehensive Questions

 ► 96 年學測英文

Whenever I set foot on the soil of Rwanda, a country in east-central Africa, I feel as if I have entered paradise: green hills, red earth, sparkling rivers and mountain lakes. Herds of goats and cows __01__ enormous horns graze the lush green fields. Although located close to the equator, Rwanda's thousand hills, __02__ from 1,500 m to 2,500 m in height, ensure that the temperature is pleasant all year around. And being a tiny country, everything in Rwanda is __03__ in a few hours, and the interesting spots can be explored comfortably in a couple of weeks. But __04__, Rwanda is a symbol of the triumph of the human spirit over evil. Though it was once known to the world for the 1994 tribal conflict that resulted in about one million deaths, Rwanda has __05__ the mass killing. Now it is healing and prospering and greets visitors with open arms.

01 _____ (A) into (B) with
(C) for (D) from

02 _____ (A) differing (B) wandering
(C) ranging (D) climbing

03 _____ (A) off the record (B) beyond doubt
(C) in touch (D) within reach

04 _____ (A) worst of all (B) for that matter
(C) above all (D) at most

05 _____ (A) survived (B) transformed
(C) recovered (D) endangered

中譯 每當我來到盧安達——位於非洲中部與東部的一個國家——我就會覺得自己仿佛已經進入了天堂——青山、紅土、閃閃發光的河流以及山間湖泊。有著巨大的角的山羊和牛成群地在肥沃的綠地上吃草。雖然地處赤道附近，但是盧安達有成千上萬海拔高度在一千五百到兩千五百公尺的範圍內的山丘，使得全年氣溫適宜。作為一個小國家，所有地方都在幾個小時內就能到達的距離，也可以在幾周內舒舒服服地探索有趣的景點。但最重要的是，盧安達是人文精神戰勝邪惡的勝利象徵。盧安達於一九九四年發生的部落衝突導致了大約一百萬人死亡，儘管它曾因此而聞名於世，但是它在大屠殺中倖存了下來。如今，它正在恢復繁榮景象，熱情地迎接遊客。

解說 本篇短文介紹了盧安達這個國家的概況，答題時可以將一些歷史知識考慮在內。第 1 題要選擇合適的介系詞。依據題意，enormous horns 是 goats and cows 本身的所有物，要用 with 表示「帶有」，所以正確選擇為 (B)。第 2 題空格處的動詞在句中修飾山丘，而動詞 range 能夠與介系詞 from 連用，表示「從～到～範圍」，符合題意，所以最佳選項是 (C)。第 3 題考介系詞片語的用法。根據上下文的內容可知，盧安達是一個小國家，所到之處僅需幾個小時，而 be within reach 意思是「可到達的距離」，符合題意，所以正確選項是 (D)。第 4 題考介系詞片語的用法。將四個選項的片語一一代入，只有 above all 符合題意，所以最佳選項是 (C)。第 5 題考動詞的辨析。依據題意，應該是在大屠殺中倖存下來，要用 survive 表示「倖存」，所以選 (A)。

解答＆技巧 | 01 (B)　02 (C)　03 (D)　04 (C)　05 (A)

適用 TIP 1　適用 TIP 2　適用 TIP 7　適用 TIP 11

補充

Rwanda [n] 盧安達；Africa [n] 非洲；sparkling [a] 閃亮的；all year around [ph] 一年到頭；comfortably [ad] 舒適地

7,000 單字

- whenever [hwɛnˋɛvɚ] [ad] 2 不論何時
- foot [fʊt] [n] 1 腳
- paradise [ˋpærəˌdaɪs] [n] 3 天堂
- hill [hɪl] [n] 1 小山
- herd [hɝd] [n] 4 獸群
- goat [got] [n] 2 山羊
- lush [lʌʃ] [a] 6 蒼翠繁茂的
- locate [loˋket] [v] 2 定位

- height [haɪt] [n] 2 高度
- triumph [ˋtraɪəmf] [n] 4 勝利
- tribal [traɪbl] [a] 4 部落的
- wander [ˋwɑndɚ] [v] 3 漫步
- above [əˋbʌv] [prep] 1 在～之上
- survive [səˋvaɪv] [v] 2 倖存
- endanger [ɪnˋdendʒɚ] [v] 4 危及

DAY 5

Part 1
詞彙題
Day 5
完成 25%

Part 2
綜合測驗
Day 5
完成 50%

Part 3
文意選填
Day 5
完成 75%

Part 4
閱讀測驗
Day 5
完成 100%

▶

I suppose that most parents must have read bedtime stories to their children and they may have realized it is so difficult to find a good children's book. If the authors write something very difficult in the stories, the children can't __01__ their meanings easily and correctly.

The best children's books should not be too difficult or too simple, but could __02__ the children who hear the stories and the adults who read them. However, it is unfortunate that there are few books like this in the market now, so it should be a big problem to find the __03__ bedtime stories for the children.

It is true that many books which are regarded as works of children's literature are actually __04__ for adults. If the parents want to choose the right books for their children, just leave the children in the bookshops or libraries, and they will be quite willing to choose the books written in a(an) __05__ way or full of stories and jokes which are good for them to hear and learn.

01	_____	(A) refuse	(B) follow
		(C) mention	(D) refer
02	_____	(A) acknowledge	(B) accustom
		(C) satisfy	(D) capture
03	_____	(A) right	(B) short
		(C) hopeful	(D) frozen
04	_____	(A) seized	(B) understood
		(C) decomposed	(D) written
05	_____	(A) dull	(B) imaginative
		(C) dizzy	(D) savage

中譯 | 我想很多父母一定為自己的孩子讀過床邊故事，他們或許已經意識到，要找到一本好的兒童讀物非常困難。如果作者在故事裡寫了一些很難的東西，孩子們就不能容易且正確地理解它們的含義。

最好的兒童讀本不應該太難，也不應該太簡單，既要能夠使聽故事的孩子們滿意，也要使讀故事的大人滿意。然而不幸的是，如今這類書本在市場上很少銷售，因此為孩子們找到合適的床邊故事是一個大難題。

確實，很多被認為是兒童文學的作品實際上是為成年人而寫的。如果父母想要為孩子選擇恰當的書籍，就把孩子留在書店或是圖書館裡，他們會非常樂意選擇那些富有想像力的書籍，或是有益於他們聆聽或學習的故事書或笑話集。

解說 | 本篇短文的主旨是「兒童讀物」，介紹了如何為孩子尋求最好的睡前讀物。第 1 題要選擇合適的動詞。根據上下文的內容，「理解含義」可以表達為 follow one's meaning，用動詞 follow 來表示「理解」，所以正確選項為 (B)。第 2 題考動詞的辨析。將四個選項的動詞一一代入，只有 satisfy 符合題意，所以最佳選項是 (C)。第 3 題的四個選項都是形容詞。依據題意，應該是找到合適的床邊故事，而「合適的」可以用 right 來表達，所以正確選項是 (A)。第 4 題考動詞的辨析。根據上下文的內容，此句是被動句，主詞是 books，動詞用 written 符合題意，所以正確選擇為 (D)。第 5 題依據題意，兒童喜歡看富有想像力的書籍，可以用 imaginative 表示「富有想像力的」，所以選 (B)。

解答＆技巧 | 01 (B)　02 (C)　03 (A)　04 (D)　05 (B)

適用 TIP 1　適用 TIP 4　適用 TIP 7　適用 TIP 11

補充
bedtime n 就寢時間；easily ad 容易地；be regarded as ph 被視為～；actually ad 實際上；bookshop n 書店

7,000 單字
- suppose [sə`poz] v 3 猜想
- find [faɪnd] v 1 找到
- author [`ɔθɚ] n 3 作者
- something [`sʌmθɪŋ] pron 1 某事
- simple [`sɪmpl] a 1 簡單的
- few [fju] a 1 很少的
- market [`mɑrkɪt] n 1 市場
- true [tru] a 1 真實的
- right [raɪt] a 1 正確的
- willing [`wɪlɪŋ] a 2 樂意的
- joke [dʒok] n 1 笑話
- learn [lɚn] v 1 學習
- capture [`kæptʃɚ] v 3 俘獲
- dizzy [`dɪzɪ] a 2 頭暈目眩的
- savage [`sævɪdʒ] a 5 野蠻的

DAY 5

Part 1
詞彙題
Day 5
完成 25%

Part 2
綜合測驗
Day 5
完成 50%

Part 3
文意選填
Day 5
完成 75%

Part 4
閱讀測驗
Day 5
完成 100%

Nowadays, more and more students choose to study in hot majors, such as foreign languages, international business and law, etc. As a result, fewer and fewer students will choose scientific majors, __01__ math, physics and biology, or art majors, like history, Chinese and philosophy. Though many students have __02__ up their interests and chosen the hot majors, the number of the "hot" majors is limited, so not every student can study in them.

To be __03__, if one has no interest in his work or study, he could not do well in it. One of my friends comes from the countryside, and her parents are both farmers. Though she likes history, she chose English as her major because she wants to __04__ a happier and better life in the future. But later on, she found that she was not interested in English at all, and all the subjects __05__ to English were tiresome to her, so she felt very upset. By this token, choosing the major according to the interests should be the best way to succeed.

01 _____ (A) such   (B) so
            (C) which   (D) like

02 _____ (A) dried   (B) given
            (C) set   (D) cleaned

03 _____ (A) hateful   (B) distorted
            (C) honest   (D) inflated

04 _____ (A) live   (B) spend
            (C) cost   (D) save

05 _____ (A) studied   (B) arranged
            (C) settled   (D) related

中譯｜如今，愈來愈多的學生選擇主修熱門科系，如外語、國際貿易、法律等。結果，愈來愈少的學生會選擇像數學、物理、生物這樣的科學專業，以及歷史、中文、哲學之類的藝術專業。儘管很多學生都放棄了他們的興趣，選擇熱門科系，但是熱門科系的人數有限，因此並非每一位學生都能夠學習。

老實說，如果一個人對他的工作或是學習不感興趣，他就不會做好。我的一個朋友來自農村，她的父母都是農夫。儘管她喜歡歷史，但她卻選擇主修英語，因為她希望以後過更幸福、更好的生活。但是後來，她發現她對英語一點都不感興趣，所有跟英語有關的課程對她而言都很無聊，因此她感到很沮喪。由此看來，根據興趣來選擇主修科系應該是成功的最好方法。

解說｜本篇短文介紹了大學生在選擇主修科系時的傾向性和盲目性。第 1 題空格後面的內容是前面內容的舉例，要用表示「像」的介系詞 like，所以正確選擇為 (D)。第 2 題考能夠跟介系詞 up 連用的動詞。依據題意，很多學生為了選擇熱門科系而放棄了自己的興趣，而 give up 表示「放棄」，所以最符合題意的選項是 (B)。第 3 題考固定片語的用法。將四個選項一一代入空格，只有 honest 能夠與 to be 搭配構成 to be honest 表示「老實說」，所以正確選項是 (C)。第 4 題考動詞片語的固定用法。依據題意，「過生活」可以表達為 live a life，要用動詞 live 來引導，只有選項 (A) 符合題意。第 5 題考能夠與介系詞 to 連用的動詞。根據上下文的內容，應該是所有跟英語相關的課程，可以用 related 來表示「有關係的」，所以選 (D)。

解答＆技巧｜ 01 (D) 02 (B) 03 (C) 04 (A) 05 (D)
適用 TIP 1　適用 TIP 2　適用 TIP 7　適用 TIP 11

補充
art majors ph 藝術類主修科目；hot majors ph 熱門主修科目；have no interest in ph 對～不感興趣；do well in ph 擅長；not at all ph 一點也不

7,000 單字
- hot [hɑt] a 1 熱門的
- major [ˈmedʒɚ] n 3 主修科目，專業
- foreign [ˈfɔrɪn] a 1 外國的
- international [ˌɪntɚˈnæʃən] a 2 國際的
- law [lɔ] n 1 法律
- scientific [ˌsaɪənˈtɪfɪk] a 3 科學的
- physics [ˈfɪzɪks] n 4 物理學
- history [ˈhɪstərɪ] n 1 歷史
- philosophy [fəˈlɑsəfɪ] n 4 哲學
- study [ˈstʌdɪ] v 1 學習
- friend [frɛnd] n 1 朋友
- future [ˈfjutʃɚ] n 2 未來
- tiresome [ˈtaɪrsəm] a 4 令人厭煩的，無聊的
- dry [draɪ] v 1 乾燥
- distorted [dɪsˈtɔrtɪd] a 6 歪曲的

4 ▶ 96 年指考英文

Recent studies show that levels of happiness for most people change throughout their lives. In a British study between 1991 and 2003, people were asked how satisfied they are __01__ their lives. The resulting statistics graph shows a smile-shaped curve. Most of the people __02__ happy and become progressively less happy as they grow older. For many of them, the most miserable period in their life is their 40s. __03__ , their levels of happiness climb. Furthermore, it seems that men are slightly happier on average than women in their teens, but women bounce back and overtake men __04__ in life. The low point seems to last longer for women—throughout their 30s and 40s, only climbing __05__ women reach 50. Men, on the other hand, have the lowest point in their 40s, going up again when they reach 50.

01 _____   (A) for   (B) with
                 (C) at   (D) of

02 _____   (A) end up   (B) pass by
                 (C) start off   (D) go on

03 _____   (A) After that   (B) By that time
                 (C) Not for long   (D) Before now

04 _____   (A) sooner   (B) later
                 (C) earlier   (D) slower

05 _____   (A) once   (B) unless
                 (C) before   (D) since

中譯｜最近的研究顯示，大多數人的幸福程度在一生中都會發生變化。在一九九一年至二〇〇三年的一項英國研究中，人們被問及自己對生活的滿意程度。結果統計圖顯示出一個笑臉形狀的曲線圖表。大多數人開始時很幸福，隨著年齡增長，他們逐漸變得不那麼幸福。對他們大多數人來說，四十幾歲是他們一生中最悲慘的時期。之後，他們的幸福程度有所攀升。此外，在青少年時期，男人似乎平均要比女人更幸福，但是在後來的生活中，女人會反彈回升並超過男人。女人幸福的最低點似乎持續時間更長──貫穿三十到四十幾歲，一旦她們到五十歲，才有所回升。而另一方面，男人幸福的最低點是在四十幾歲的時候，五十歲時又會上升。

解說｜本篇短文介紹了處於不同年齡階段的人們其幸福程度所發生的變化。第 1 題考語法知識的應用。動詞 satisfy 通常與介系詞 with 連用構成 be satisfied with 表示「對～滿意」，所以正確選項為 (B)。第 2 題考動詞片語的用法。依據題意，應該是大多數人剛開始很幸福，可以用 start off 表示「開始」，所以最符合題意的選項是 (C)。第 3 題考介系詞片語的用法。依據題意，空格前後的內容表示遞進關係，後面的內容發生在前面內容之後，要用 After that 來連接，即正確選項是 (A)。第 4 題中，根據上下文的內容可知，青少年時期男人比較幸福，但是女人在後來的生活中更幸福，要用 later 來表示「後來」，只有選項 (B) 符合題意。第 5 題要選擇合適的連接詞。將四個選項一一代入空格，只有 once 符合題意，所以選 (A)。

解答＆技巧｜ 01 **(B)** 02 **(C)** 03 **(A)** 04 **(B)** 05 **(A)**

適用 TIP 1　適用 TIP 2　適用 TIP 8　適用 TIP 11

補充

happiness n 幸福；satisfied a 感到滿意的；progressively ad 日益地；slightly ad 稍微；on average ph 平均

7,000 單字

- recent [ˈrisn̩t] a 2 最近的
- show [ʃo] v 1 顯示
- most [most] a 1 大部分的
- throughout [θruˈaʊt] prep 2 貫穿
- graph [ɡræf] n 6 圖表
- miserable [ˈmɪzərəbl] a 4 悲慘的
- period [ˈpɪrɪəd] n 2 時期
- furthermore [ˈfɝðəˌmor] ad 4 此外

- teens [tinz] n 2 十幾歲（十三至十九歲）
- bounce [baʊns] v 4 彈跳
- overtake [ˌovəˈtek] v 4 追過
- last [læst] v 1 持續
- only [ˈonlɪ] ad 1 僅僅
- end [ɛnd] v 1 結束
- unless [ʌnˈlɛs] conj 3 除非

DAY
5

Part 1
詞
彙
題
Day 5
完成 25%

Part 2
綜
合
測
驗
Day 5
完成 50%

Part 3
文
意
選
填
Day 5
完成 75%

Part 4
閱
讀
測
驗
Day 5
完成 100%

Nowadays, the rocket engine has become an impressive __01__ of the new space age. During the past decades, the rocket engine has been powerful enough to launch astronauts and land them on the moon __02__ the earth's gravitational pull. Therefore, the moon has become the target for space exploration.

The rocket was invented in China over 800 years ago. At that time, it was only a relatively simple __03__ . With the development of technology, the __04__ burned in the rocket engine has changed into gas, and the roar of the rocket engine is steady, like that of a waterfall or a thunderstorm. When the hot and rapid expanding gas escapes from the opening that faces backward, the gas is radiated with great force, and then it pushes the rocket in the __05__ direction. What the rocket engine operates follows the laws of nature: "For every action, there is an equal and opposite reaction," which was discovered by Sir Isaac Newton.

01 _____ (A) portrait   (B) picture
        (C) exhibition   (D) symbol

02 _____ (A) beyond   (B) with
        (C) on   (D) in

03 _____ (A) head   (B) body
        (C) device   (D) furniture

04 _____ (A) coal   (B) fuel
        (C) water   (D) oil

05 _____ (A) same   (B) before
        (C) opposite   (D) after

中譯｜如今，火箭發動機已經成為新太空時代一個令人印象深刻的標誌。在過去數十年間，火箭發動機已經足夠強大，能夠超越地球的萬有引力，將太空人送往太空，並讓他們登陸月球。因此，月球現在已經成為太空探索的目標。

中國在八百多年前發明了火箭。在那時，火箭只是一種相對簡單的裝置。隨著科技的發展，用於火箭發動機燃燒的燃料已經變成了氣體，它的轟鳴聲很平穩，像瀑布或是雷雨的聲音。當又熱又快速的膨脹氣體通過面向後方的通道逸出時，氣體在強大的推動力作用下噴射出，然後推動火箭朝相反方向運行。火箭發動機的操作遵循「每一個作用力都有一個大小相等、方向相反的反作用力」的自然定律，而這個定律是由艾薩克·牛頓爵士發現的。

解說｜本篇短文介紹了火箭的發明和操作原理。第 1 題的四個選項都是名詞，將其一一代入空格，只有 symbol 符合題意，所以正確選擇為 (D)。第 2 題考介系詞的用法。根據常識，火箭只有超越了地球引力才能夠進入太空，要用 beyond 表示「超越」，所以最符合題意的選項是 (A)。第 3 題要選擇合適的名詞。根據上下文的內容可知，火箭是一種裝置，可以用 device 來表示「裝置」，即正確選項是 (C)。第 4 題根據對火箭知識的了解，在火箭中燃燒的是燃料，可以用 fuel 表示「燃料」，只有選項 (B) 符合題意。第 5 題根據所學知識，火箭在發射過程中，受到力的作用會朝相反方向運行，即 opposite direction，所以選 (C)。

解答＆技巧｜ `01` **(D)**　`02` **(A)**　`03` **(C)**　`04` **(B)**　`05` **(C)**

[適用 TIP 1]　[適用 TIP 2]　[適用 TIP 7]　[適用 TIP 11]

補充

rocket engine ph 火箭引擎；gravitational a 重力的；China n 中國；thunderstorm n 雷雨；law of nature ph 自然法則

7,000 單字

- rocket [ˋrɑkɪt] n 3 火箭
- engine [ˋɛndʒən] n 3 發動機，引擎
- impressive [ɪmˋprɛsɪv] a 3 令人印象深刻的
- age [edʒ] n 1 時代
- decade [ˋdɛked] n 3 十年
- powerful [ˋpaʊəfəl] a 2 強有力的
- pull [pʊl] n 1 拉力
- moon [mun] n 1 月亮

- ago [əˋgo] ad 1 以前
- roar [ror] n 3 咆哮
- waterfall [ˋwɔtəˌfɔl] n 2 瀑布
- backward [ˋbækwəd] ad 2 向後
- radiate [ˋrediˌet] v 6 輻射
- portrait [ˋportret] n 3 肖像
- furniture [ˋfɝnɪtʃə] n 3 傢具

DAY 5

Part 1
詞
彙
題
Day 5
完成 25%

Part 2
綜
合
測
驗
Day 5
完成 50%

Part 3
文
意
選
填
Day 5
完成 75%

Part 4
閱
讀
測
驗
Day 5
完成 100%

According to the survey, some kind of specialized training is needed for most worthwhile careers. Therefore, the choice of an occupation should be made before one chooses a ___01___ in universities. However, most people don't actually make their career plans until they begin to work or they have decided to change their job, for the ___02___ of economic and industrial changes or the desire to improve their position. Therefore, the idea of "one perfect job" does not ___03___ in fact. Under the circumstances, young people had better enter into a flexible training program which will teach them to fit for a ___04___ of work rather than for a single job.

In reality, many young people have made their career plans without the help from a competent vocational counselor or psychologist. They choose their lifework at ___05___ or even drift from job to job because they know little about the occupational world or their own abilities, which leads them to work unhappily or with no satisfaction.

01 _____ (A) partner   (B) curriculum
          (C) friend   (D) companion

02 _____ (A) result   (B) process
          (C) preface   (D) reason

03 _____ (A) exist   (B) bloom
          (C) wither   (D) decay

04 _____ (A) lot   (B) plenty
          (C) field   (D) little

05 _____ (A) leisure   (B) random
          (C) times   (D) heart

DAY
5

Part 1
詞
彙
題
Day 5
完成 25%

Part 2
綜
合
測
驗
Day 5
完成 50%

Part 3
文
意
選
填
Day 5
完成 75%

Part 4
閱
讀
測
驗
Day 5
完成 100%

中譯 │ 據調查，很多值得從事的職業都需要某種專門訓練。因此，在選擇職業之前，應該先選擇大學的課程。然而，因為經濟和產業變動，或是因為他們想要提升自己的職位，很多人實際上直到開始工作或是準備換工作時，才開始做職涯規劃。因此，「一份完美的工作」的理念實際上並不存在。在這種情況下，年輕人最好參加靈活的培訓計畫，這將會教導他們勝任一個工作領域，而不僅僅是一份單一的工作。

實際上，很多年輕人在做職涯規劃時，身邊並沒有稱職的職涯顧問或是心理學家幫助。他們隨意選擇工作，甚至頻繁地換工作，因為他們很少了解職業領域或是自己的能力，這導致工作得不開心或是不滿意。

解說 │ 本篇短文的主旨是「職涯規劃」，講述了職涯規劃的重要性以及年輕人應該如何做好職涯規劃。第 1 題要選擇合適的名詞。根據上下文的內容可知，在大學裡選擇的應該是課程，可以用 curriculum 來表達，所以正確選項為 (B)。第 2 題考介系詞片語的用法。四個選項中，只有 reason 能夠與介系詞 for 連用構成 for the reason of 表示「因為」，所以最符合題意的選項是 (D)。第 3 題的四個選項都是動詞，將其一一代入，只有動詞 exist 符合題意，即正確選項是 (A)。第 4 題根據上下文的內容可知，與一份單一的工作相對的是一個工作領域，可以用 field 來表示「領域」，所以只有選項 (C) 符合題意。第 5 題考能夠與介系詞 at 搭配使用的片語的用法。依據題意，at random 表示「隨意」符合題意，所以選 (B)。

解答＆技巧 │ **01 (B)** **02 (D)** **03 (A)** **04 (C)** **05 (B)**

適用 TIP 1 　 適用 TIP 2 　 適用 TIP 7 　 適用 TIP 11

補充

specialized ⓐ 專門的；career plans ph 職涯規劃；teach sb. to do sth. ph 教某人做某事；occupational ⓐ 職業的；unhappily ad 不高興地

7,000 單字

- need [nid] ⓥ 1 需要
- worthwhile [ˋwɝθˋhwaɪl] ⓐ 5 值得做的
- decide [dɪˋsaɪd] ⓥ 1 決定
- industrial [ɪnˋdʌstrɪəl] ⓐ 3 工業的
- desire [dɪˋzaɪr] ⓝ 2 要求
- position [pəˋzɪʃən] ⓝ 1 職位
- perfect [ˋpɝfɪkt] ⓐ 2 完美的
- circumstance [ˋsɝkəm.stæns] ⓝ 4 情況

- flexible [ˋflɛksəbl] ⓐ 4 靈活的
- counselor [ˋkaʊnslɚ] ⓝ 5 顧問
- psychologist [saɪˋkɑlədʒɪst] ⓝ 4 心理學家
- curriculum [kəˋrɪkjələm] ⓝ 5 課程
- wither [ˋwɪðɚ] ⓥ 5 枯萎
- decay [dɪˋke] ⓥ 5 衰退
- random [ˋrændəm] ⓐ 6 隨機的

Many people choose an occupation for its real or imagined prestige, which has proved to be a mistake. It is true that too many students or their parents have a __01__ for choosing the professional fields, but disregard the small proportion of job openings in the professions and also the extremely high educational and personal __02__ . Therefore, the imagined or real prestige of a profession is not really helpful in choosing it as a life work. In addition, people working on these occupations are not always well paid. Knowing that there are plenty of jobs in the machine building and the handicraft industry, the majority of young people should take these fields into serious __03__ .

Generally speaking, before making an occupational choice, one should think over what he really wants to get or what life he wants to live in the future. Different people __04__ for jobs for different purposes, such as social prestige, intellectual satisfaction, security and money, etc. Therefore, different occupational __05__ will get people different demands and rewards.

01 _____ (A) choice (B) taste
    (C) preference (D) eyesight

02 _____ (A) properties (B) requirements
    (C) equations (D) consumptions

03 _____ (A) accommodation (B) identification
    (C) entertainment (D) consideration

04 _____ (A) seek (B) appeal
    (C) stick (D) turn

05 _____ (A) health (B) negligence
    (C) choice (D) disease

DAY
5

Part 1
詞
彙
題
Day 5
完成 25%

Part 2
綜合測驗
Day 5
完成 50%

Part 3
文意選填
Day 5
完成 75%

Part 4
閱讀測驗
Day 5
完成 100%

中譯｜ 很多人為了真實存在或是想像中的聲譽名望而選擇職業，但這已經證明是一個錯誤。確實，太多學生以及他們的父母偏向選擇專業領域，卻忽視了這些領域僅有很小比例的職缺，也忽視了極高的學歷與個人條件的要求。因此，想像中或是真實的專業名望並不會真正有助於選擇它作為一項畢生的事業。此外，從事這些職業的人並不總是有很高的報酬。了解到機械製造業和手工業有很多工作，大多數年輕人應該認真考慮一下這些領域。

一般來講，選擇職業前，一個人應該仔細考慮一下他真正想得到什麼，或是以後他想過什麼樣的生活。不同人會為了不同的目的而尋找工作，如社會榮譽、知識滿意度、安全感、金錢等。因此，選擇不同的職業將會給人們帶來不同的需求以及回報。

解說｜ 本篇短文講述了大學生應當如何選擇職業。第 1 題要選擇合適的名詞。將四個選項的名詞一一代入，只有 have a preference for 表示「偏向」符合題意，所以正確選項為 (C)。第 2 題的四個選項都是名詞。根據上下文的內容可知，應該是學歷和個人條件的要求，可以用 requirements 來表示「要求」，所以最符合題意的選項是 (B)。第 3 題考詞彙知識的應用。依據題意，take... into consideration 表示「將～考慮在內」，consideration 符合題意，即正確選項是 (D)。第 4 題考能夠與介系詞 for 搭配使用的動詞。依據題意，seek for 表示「尋找」符合上下文的意思，所以只有選項 (A) 符合題意。第 5 題根據本篇短文的主旨，主要講的是職業選擇，而 choice 表示「選擇」，所以選 (C)。

解答&技巧｜ 01 **(C)** 02 **(B)** 03 **(D)** 04 **(A)** 05 **(C)**

適用 TIP 1 適用 TIP 2 適用 TIP 7 適用 TIP 11

補充

professional field ph 專業領域；extremely ad 極度地；well paid ph 待遇優厚的；
think over ph 考慮；in the future ph 將來

7,000 單字

- occupation [ˌɑkjəˈpeʃən] n 4 職業
- prestige [presˈtiʒ] n 6 聲望
- many [ˈmɛnɪ] a 1 很多的
- proportion [prəˈporʃən] n 5 比例
- handicraft [ˈhændɪˌkræft] n 5 手工藝
- majority [məˈdʒɔrətɪ] n 3 多數
- social [ˈsoʃəl] a 2 社會的
- intellectual [ˌɪntlˈɛktʃʊəl] a 4 智力的

- security [sɪˈkjurətɪ] n 3 安全
- will [wɪl] aux 1 將要
- demand [dɪˈmænd] n 4 需求
- eyesight [ˈaɪˌsaɪt] n 6 視力
- property [ˈprɑpɚtɪ] n 3 性質
- equation [ɪˈkweʃən] n 6 相等
- consideration [kənˌsɪdəˈreʃən] n 3 考慮

8 ▶ 96 年指考英文

Average global temperature has increased by almost 1° F over the past century. Scientists expect it to increase an __01__ 2° to 6° F over the next one hundred years. This may not sound like much, but it could change the Earth's climate as __02__ before.

Climate change may affect people's health both directly and indirectly. For instance, heat stress and other heat-related health problems are caused directly by very warm temperatures. __03__ , human health can also be affected by ecological disturbances, changes in food and water supplies, as well as coastal flooding. How people and nature __04__ climate change will determine how seriously it affects human health. Generally, poor people and poor countries are __05__ probable to have the money and resources they need to cope with health problems due to climate change.

| 01 | _____ | (A) extreme | (B) additional |
| | | (C) immediate | (D) original |

| 02 | _____ | (A) ever | (B) never |
| | | (C) always | (D) yet |

| 03 | _____ | (A) Suddenly | (B) Previously |
| | | (C) Exclusively | (D) Indirectly |

| 04 | _____ | (A) result from | (B) count on |
| | | (C) adapt to | (D) stand for |

| 05 | _____ | (A) less | (B) very |
| | | (C) most | (D) further |

中譯 | 上個世紀，全球平均溫度上升了華氏一度。科學家們預計，接下來的一百年裡全球平均溫度將會再上升華氏二到六度。這聽起來也許並不多，但是它會前所未有地改變地球的氣候。

氣候變化會直接和間接地影響人們的健康。例如，過於溫暖的氣候會直接導致熱應力和其他與熱相關的健康問題。而人類健康也會間接受到生態失調、食品供應和水供應的改變以及海岸洪災的影響。人類和自然適應氣候變化的程度將會決定氣候變化影響人類健康的程度。一般來說，窮人和貧窮的國家比較不可能擁有處理氣候變化引起的健康問題所需的金錢和資源。

解說 | 本篇短文講述了全球氣溫升高將會對人類和自然造成的影響。第 1 題將四個選項一一代入空格可知，additional 表示「額外的」符合題意，所以正確選擇為 (B)。第 2 題根據上下文的內容可知，這種氣溫變化對氣候造成的影響是前所未有的，可以用 as never before 來表達，所以最符合題意的選項是 (B)。第 3 題根據上下文的內容，前面已經說了直接影響，則空格後面的應該是間接的影響，可以用 indirectly 表示「間接地」，即正確選項是 (D)。第 4 題依據題意，應該是人類和自然適應氣候變化，要用 adapt to 表示「適應」，所以只有選項 (C) 符合題意。第 5 題根據上下文的內容可知，窮人和貧窮的國家擁有所需的金錢和資源的可能性更少，要用 less 來修飾 probable，所以選 (A)。

解答＆技巧 | `01` **(B)**　`02` **(B)**　`03` **(D)**　`04` **(C)**　`05` **(A)**

`適用 TIP 1`　`適用 TIP 2`　`適用 TIP 7`　`適用 TIP 11`

DAY 5

Part 1
詞彙題
Day 5
完成 25%

Part 2
綜合測驗
Day 5
完成 50%

Part 3
文意選填
Day 5
完成 75%

Part 4
閱讀測驗
Day 5
完成 100%

補充
climate change ph 氣候變化；directly ad 直接地；indirectly ad 間接地；coastal a 沿海；
health problem ph 健康問題

7,000 單字

- increase [ɪn`kris] v 2 增加
- past [pæst] a 1 過去的
- climate [`klaɪmɪt] n 2 氣候
- stress [strɛs] n 2 壓力
- warm [wɔrm] a 1 溫暖的
- human [`hjumən] n 1 人類
- disturbance [dɪs`tɝbəns] n 6 干擾
- food [fud] n 1 食物

- nature [`netʃə] n 1 自然
- poor [pʊr] a 1 貧窮的
- probable [`prɑbəbl] a 3 很可能的
- cope [kop] v 4 處理
- extreme [ɪk`strim] a 3 極端的
- ever [`ɛvə] ad 1 曾經
- adapt [ə`dæpt] v 4 適應

Clothing has __01__ our values and lifestyles more vividly than any other human activities in daily life. According to the survey, the dress of a person has been regarded as a sign language to __02__ some complex information and is also as a basis to form an immediate impression. In addition, compared with women, men possess less clothing consciousness.

The clothing culture has gradually changed as men's clothes have more variety and color. At present, white-collar workers especially __03__ dress as a symbol of capacity. They believe that proper clothes could greatly impress and influence others in the work __04__ , so they extremely concern about the impressions that their clothing makes on their superiors. Although blue-collar workers are less concerned about the clothing they wear, they have recognized that any difference for the pattern of the dress could draw ridicule from other __05__ workers. No matter how the pattern of the dress has changed, the importance of dress has still not diminished.

01 _____ (A) considered   (B) guessed
(C) calculated   (D) reflected

02 _____ (A) draw   (B) communicate
(C) write   (D) shift

03 _____ (A) view   (B) defeat
(C) conquer   (D) reject

04 _____ (A) function   (B) leader
(C) situation   (D) preparation

05 _____ (A) machine   (B) municipal
(C) excavation   (D) fellow

中譯│相比於其他任何的人類活動，衣著在日常生活中更加強烈地反映出我們的價值觀以及生活方式。據調查，一個人的衣著被認為是一種符號語言，用於交流一些複雜的資訊，也作為即時印象的基礎。此外，與女人相比，男人更不具備服裝意識。

隨著男人的服裝具有更多的種類和顏色，服裝文化已經逐漸發生了變化。目前，白領階級尤其將衣著看作是一種能力的象徵。他們相信合適的服裝能夠在工作場合中給人留下很好的印象，也會很大程度地造成影響，因此他們極其關注自己的服裝給上司所留下的印象。儘管藍領階級較少關注他們所穿的服裝，但是他們已經察覺到，服裝款式的任何變化都能夠引起其他同事的嘲笑。不管服裝的款式如何變化，服裝的重要性仍然沒有減弱。

解說│本篇短文的主旨是「衣著」，講述了服裝對人們的工作和生活所造成的影響。第 1 題的四個選項都是動詞，將其一一代入空格，只有 reflected 表示「反映」符合題意，所以正確選擇為 (D)。第 2 題根據上下文的內容，language 是用於交流的，可以用 communicate 表示「交流」，所以最符合題意的選項是 (B)。第 3 題主要考能夠與介系詞 as 搭配使用的動詞。四個選項中，只有 view 能夠與 as 連用，表示「將～看做～」，符合題意，即正確選項是 (A)。第 4 題考名詞片語的用法。依據題意，「工作場合」可以表達為 work situation，所以選項 (C) 符合題意。第 5 題將四個選項一一代入空格可知，fellow workers 表示「同事」，符合題意，所以選 (D)。

解答＆技巧│ **01 (D)** **02 (B)** **03 (A)** **04 (C)** **05 (D)**

適用 TIP 1　適用 TIP 2　適用 TIP 7　適用 TIP 11

補充
lifestyle n 生活方式；vividly ad 清晰地；consciousness n 意識；white-collar a 白領階級的；blue-collar a 藍領階級的

7,000 單字
- clothing [ˈkloðɪŋ] n 2 服裝
- value [ˈvælju] n 2 價值
- other [ˈʌðɚ] a 1 其他的
- person [ˈpɝsn̩] n 1 人
- basis [ˈbesɪs] n 2 基礎
- immediate [ɪˈmidɪɪt] a 3 立即的
- culture [ˈkʌltʃɚ] n 2 文化
- worker [ˈwɝkɚ] n 1 工人

- capacity [kəˈpæsətɪ] n 4 能力
- impress [ɪmˈprɛs] v 3 給人留下印象
- superior [səˈpɪrɪɚ] n 3 上級
- ridicule [ˈrɪdɪkjul] n 6 嘲笑
- diminish [dəˈmɪnɪʃ] v 6 減少
- shift [ʃɪft] v 4 轉變
- municipal [mjuˈnɪsəpl̩] n 6 市政的

DAY
5

Part 1
詞
彙
題
Day 5
完成 25%

Part 2
綜
合
測
驗
Day 5
完成 50%

Part 3
文
意
選
填
Day 5
完成 75%

Part 4
閱
讀
測
驗
Day 5
完成 100%

In one hot summer evening, when I finished all the office work, I decided to ___01___ a movie. I was so happy at the ___02___ of air-conditioning in the theater and delicious popcorn.

Sitting in the theater I felt quite cool and comfortable. But when the movie began, I had to look through the ___03___ between the two tall heads in front of me and keep changing the angle from time to time because the girl often leaned ___04___ to talk to the boy, or the boy leaned over to kiss the girl. Then I became so impatient and angry.

I thought the movie would be an English one and good for my English, but later I found out that it was an Italian movie which was so boring. An hour later I decided to give up on the movie and ___05___ on my popcorn. I bought so much popcorn, and it really tasted good. After a while I heard no sound of the movie but only the sound of the popcorn crunching between my teeth.

01 _____   (A) look   (B) browse
            (C) scan   (D) see

02 _____   (A) thought   (B) foot
            (C) peak   (D) discretion

03 _____   (A) blank   (B) break
            (C) opening   (D) crack

04 _____   (A) form   (B) over
            (C) up   (D) onto

05 _____   (A) rely   (B) hang
            (C) insist   (D) concentrate

DAY
5

Part 1
詞
彙
題
Day 5
完成 25%

Part 2
綜
合
測
驗
Day 5
完成 50%

Part 3
文
意
選
填
Day 5
完成 75%

Part 4
閱
讀
測
驗
Day 5
完成 100%

中譯｜ 在一個炎熱的夏夜，下班後我決定去看電影。一想到電影院裡的空調以及美味的爆米花，我就很高興。

坐在電影院裡，我感到很涼爽，也很愜意。但是當電影開始時，我不得不從擋在前面的兩顆頭之間的縫隙看過去，並且時不時地得變換角度，因為那個女孩經常彎下身子與那個男孩談話，或是那個男孩傾身去吻那個女孩。於是我變得非常不耐煩，很生氣。

我本以為這會是一部英文電影，會對我的英文有所幫助，但是後來我發現那是一部無聊的義大利文電影。一個小時後，我決定放棄看電影，專心吃爆米花。我買了很多爆米花，它們真得很美味。不久，我就聽不到電影的聲音了，只聽到爆米花在我的牙齒間咬碎的聲音。

解說｜ 本篇短文講述了主角「我」下班後看電影的事情。第 1 題依據題意，「看電影」要表達為 see a movie，要用動詞 see，所以正確選擇為 (D)。第 2 題考介系詞片語的用法。根據上下文的內容，應該是「一想到」，可以用 at the thought of 來表達，所以最符合題意的選項是 (A)。第 3 題的四個選項都是名詞，依據題意，應該是「縫隙」，可以用 crack 來表達，即正確選項是 (D)。第 4 題要選擇合適的副詞。根據所學的知識，lean over 表示「傾斜，彎下」，符合題意，所以最佳選項是 (B)。第 5 題考能夠與介系詞 on 搭配的動詞的用法。依據題意，concentrate on 表示「專心於」符合題意，所以選 (D)。

解答＆技巧｜ **01 (D)** **02 (A)** **03 (D)** **04 (B)** **05 (D)**

適用 TIP 1 適用 TIP 2 適用 TIP 7 適用 TIP 11

補充

in front of ph 在～面前；from time to time ph 不時地；English a 英語的；Italian a 義大利語的；
boring a 無聊的

7,000 單字

- evening [ˈivnɪŋ] n 1 晚上
- finish [ˈfɪnɪʃ] v 1 完成
- work [wɝk] n 1 工作
- air-conditioning [ˈɛrkənˈdɪʃənɪŋ] n 3 空調
- delicious [dɪˈlɪʃəs] a 2 美味的
- popcorn [ˈpɑpˌkɔrn] n 1 爆米花
- theater [ˈθɪətɚ] n 2 劇院
- tall [tɔl] a 1 高的

- kiss [kɪs] v 1 吻
- angry [ˈæŋgrɪ] a 1 生氣的
- good [gʊd] a 1 好的
- crunch [krʌntʃ] v 5 咬碎
- browse [braʊz] v 5 瀏覽
- peak [pik] n 3 最高點
- crack [kræk] n 4 裂縫

Water may come in the form of solid, __01__, or gas. It usually changes with __02__. At room temperature, water is liquid. When temperature falls below zero degree centigrade, water is solid, i.e. ice. __03__, water will become steam.

Two types of thermometers are used to __04__ the temperature of water. One is the Fahrenheit thermometer, named after the inventor Daniel Gabriel Fahrenheit. The __05__ thermometer is the centigrade thermometer. The temperature scale is also known as Celsius, named after Anders Celsius, a Swedish scientist. According to the centigrade thermometer, the freezing __06__ of water is 0°C, and the boiling point is 100°C.

When water freezes, it expands and takes up more __07__. The __08__ of ice is lower than that of water. So ice will __09__ in the water. Animals living in the ponds or streams can escape to the bottom, in order to __10__ cold winter. A glacier is a huge amount of ice that moves down a slope or land area, i.e. a huge mountain of ice on land. Lumps of ice may break away from land and move out into the oceans. These floating mountains of ice are called icebergs. The word "berg" means "mountain."

(A) liquid   (B) point   (C) Heated   (D) temperature   (E) survive
(F) density   (G) float   (H) space   (I) other   (J) measure

01 _____   02 _____   03 _____   04 _____   05 _____

06 _____   07 _____   08 _____   09 _____   10 _____

DAY
5

Part 1
詞
彙
題
Day 5
完成 25%

Part 2
綜
合
測
驗
Day 5
完成 50%

Part 3
文
意
選
填
Day 5
完成 75%

Part 4
閱
讀
測
驗
Day 5
完成 100%

選項中譯 | 液體；點；被加熱；溫度；倖存；密度；漂浮；空間；另外的；測量

中譯 | 水的形態可以是固態、液態或氣態，通常會隨著溫度的變化而改變。在室溫下，水是液態的。當溫度低於攝氏零度時，水就變成了固態——冰。受熱時，水將變成蒸汽。

測量水溫會用到兩種溫度計。一種是華氏溫度計，以其創始人丹尼爾·加布里埃爾·華倫海特的名字而命名。另一種溫度計是攝氏溫度計。這種溫標也稱為攝氏度，以一名瑞典科學家安德斯·攝爾修斯的名字而命名。依照攝氏溫度計，水的冰點是 0°C，沸點是 100°C。

當水結冰時，會發生膨脹而佔據更多的空間。冰的密度比水輕，因此冰可以浮在水面上。冬天期間，生活在溪流和池塘裡的動物，會躲到溪流或池塘底部，以便度過寒冬。冰河是指從斜坡或陸地上滑下來的大量冰塊，也就是陸地上的大冰山。冰塊也許會脫離陸地滑進海洋，那些飄移的冰山稱為 iceberg。單字 berg 意為「山」。

解譯 | 閱讀全文可知，這篇文章的主題是水的不同形態。

縱觀各選項，選項 (A)、(B)、(D)、(F)、(H) 是名詞，選項 (C)、(E)、(G)、(J) 是動詞，選項 (I) 是代名詞。根據題意，第 1、2、6、7、8 題應選名詞，第 3、4、9、10 題應選動詞，第 5 題應選代名詞。然後根據文章，依次作答。

第 1 題是選擇名詞，用於與 solid、gas 的並列結構，有五個名詞可供選擇，即為選項 (A)、(B)、(D)、(F)、(H)，選項 (A) 意為「液體」，選項 (B) 意為「溫度中的度」，選項 (D) 意為「溫度」，選項 (F) 意為「密度」，選項 (H) 意為「空間」，所以選 (A)。第 2 題所選名詞，根據句意，應當是「水的形態隨著溫度的變化而改變」，所以選 (D)。第 6 題所選名詞，可以視為固定表達，freezing point 意為「冰點」，所以選 (B)。第 7 題所選名詞，也可以視為固定表達，take up... space 意為「佔據～空間」，所以選 (H)。第 8 題則是選 (F)，the density of 意為「～的密度」。

第 3 題是選擇動詞，有四個動詞可供選擇，即為選項 (C)、(E)、(G)、(J)，根據句意，應當是「受熱時，水將變成蒸汽」，是用被動形式作伴隨副詞，表示條件，所以選 (C)。第 4 題所選動詞，根據句意，應當是「測量水溫會用到兩種溫度計」，所以選 (J)。第 9 題所選動詞，根據句意，應當是「冰可以浮在水面上」，所以選 (G)。第 10 題則是選 (E)，survive cold winter 意為「度過寒冬」。

第 5 題是選擇代名詞，只有一個代名詞可供選擇，即為選項 (I)，one... the other 意為「一個～另一個～」。

解答＆技巧 | **01** (A)　**02** (D)　**03** (C)　**04** (J)　**05** (I)
　　　　　 06 (B)　**07** (H)　**08** (F)　**09** (G)　**10** (E)

適用 TIP 1　適用 TIP 2　適用 TIP 6　適用 TIP 7　適用 TIP 8
適用 TIP 9　適用 TIP 10　適用 TIP 11

補充

degree centigrade ph 攝氏溫度；**Fahrenheit** a 華氏的；**Celsius** a 攝氏的；**Swedish** a 瑞典的；
berg n 山

7,000 單字

- solid [ˈsɑlɪd] n 3 固體
- liquid [ˈlɪkwɪd] n 2 液體
- gas [gæs] n 1 氣體
- temperature [ˈtɛmprətʃɚ] n 3 溫度
- steam [stim] n 2 蒸汽
- thermometer [θɚˈmɑmətɚ] n 6 溫度計
- measure [ˈmɛʒɚ] v 2 計量
- inventor [ɪnˈvɛntɚ] n 3 發明家

- centigrade [ˈsɛntəˌgred] a 5 攝氏的
- scale [skel] n 3 標度，刻度
- float [flot] v 3 漂浮
- escape [əˈskep] v 3 躲避
- pond [pɑnd] n 1 池塘
- slope [slop] n 3 斜坡
- iceberg [ˈaɪsˌbɝg] n 4 冰山

MEMO

②►

DAY
5

Part 1
詞
彙
題
Day 5
完成 25%

Part 2
綜
合
測
驗
Day 5
完成 50%

Part 3
文
意
選
填
Day 5
完成 75%

Part 4
閱
讀
測
驗
Day 5
完成 100%

In North America, the grasslands are called the Great Plains, __01__ from Canada to Texas in the center of the continent. In South America, to the north and south of the Amazon rainforest are llanos. In Africa, savannas wind around the outside of the rainforests near the __02__ . In South Africa, the treeless grassland is called the veld. In Europe and Asia, the grasslands are called steppes, stretching across the center of the two __03__ . And in Australia, the grasslands __04__ the central desert.

Grasslands can be __05__ into three different types: prairies, steppes, and savannas.

The word prairie comes from the French word for meadow. Steppes have less rain and shorter grass, __06__ to prairies. Grass on the steppes usually grows in little bunches, rather than spreads out evenly like a lawn. Both steppes and prairies have hot summer and cold winter. On the western side of the Great Plains, near the rain __07__ of the Rocky Mountains, are steppes, not prairies.

Savannas are the grasslands in the __08__ , between the Tropics of Cancer and Capricorn, around the equator. Savannas seldom have changes in temperature all the year around, but there is a great change in __09__ . Savannas have a wet season and a __10__ season. Plants have to manage to survive without rain for months during the dry season, and, when the wet season comes, live through heavy rains. Most savannas are in Africa, some in South America and Australia as well.

(A) stretching (B) divided (C) tropics (D) circle (E) equator
(F) dry (G) continents (H) rainfall (I) shadow (J) compared

---

01 _____ **02** _____ **03** _____ **04** _____ **05** _____

06 _____ **07** _____ **08** _____ **09** _____ **10** _____

選項中譯 | 延伸；劃分；熱帶地區；環繞；赤道；乾的；大陸；降雨量；陰影；被比較

中譯 | 在北美洲，草原被稱為大平原，從加拿大延伸到大陸中部的德州。在南美洲，林木稀疏的大草原 llano 分布在亞馬遜熱帶雨林的北部和南部。在非洲，熱帶草原位於赤道附近的熱帶雨林邊緣。在南非，不長樹木的草原稱為疏林草原 veld。在歐洲和亞洲，草原被稱為乾草原 steppe，分布在這兩個大陸中部。在澳洲，草原環繞在中部沙漠的周邊。

草原可以分為三種不同類別：大草原 prairie、無林大草原 steppe 和熱帶亞熱帶大草原 savanna。

大草原 prairie 一詞源於法國的「草地 meadow」一詞。相較於大草原，無林大草原雨水較少，草也矮一些。無林大草原的草通常是一簇簇地生長，而不是像草坪一樣成片分布。無林大草原和大草原，都有炎熱的夏天和寒冷的冬天。在大平原的西部、洛磯山脈的雨影區附近，是無林大草原，而不是大草原。

熱帶亞熱帶大草原是在赤道附近、南北回歸線之間的熱帶地區。一年四季溫度都沒有什麼變化，降雨量卻有很大的差異。熱帶亞熱帶大草原有乾季和雨季。在乾季，連續數月都沒有降水，植物不得不設法生存；而當雨季到來，植物也必須經受得住大雨襲擊。熱帶亞熱帶大草原大多數是在非洲，南美洲和澳洲也有一些。

解譯 | 閱讀全文可知，這篇文章的主題是草原的不同類別。

縱觀各選項，選項 (C)、(E)、(G)、(H)、(I) 是名詞，選項 (A)、(B)、(D)、(J) 是動詞，選項 (F) 是形容詞。根據題意，第 2、3、7、8、9 題應選名詞，第 1、4、5、6 題應選動詞，第 10 題應選形容詞。然後根據文章，依次作答。

第 1 題是選擇動詞，有四個動詞可供選擇，即為選項 (A)、(B)、(D)、(J)。只有選項 (A) 符合要求，stretch from... to 意為「從～延伸到」。第 4 題所選動詞，根據句意，應當是「草原環繞在中部沙漠的周邊」，所以選 (D)。第 5 題所選動詞，可以視為固定搭配，be divided into 意為「被分為」，所以選 (B)。第 6 題則是選 (J)，也可以視為固定搭配，compared to 意為「相較於」。

第 2 題是選擇名詞，有五個名詞可供選擇，即為選項 (C)、(E)、(G)、(H)、(I)，選項 (C) 意為「熱帶地區」，選項 (E) 意為「赤道」，選項 (G) 意為「大陸」，選項 (H) 意為「降雨量」，選項 (I) 意為「陰影」，根據句意，應當是「熱帶草原位於赤道附近的熱帶雨林邊緣」，所以選 (E)。第 3 題所選名詞，根據句意，應當是「分布在這兩個大陸中部」，所以選 (G)。第 7 題所選名詞，可以視為固定表達，rain shadow 意為「雨影區」，所以選 (I)。第 8 題所選名詞，可以視為固定表達，in the tropics 意為「在熱帶地區」，所以選 (C)。第 9 題則是選 (H)，意為「降雨量有很大的差異」。

第 10 題是選擇形容詞，只有一個形容詞可供選擇，即為選項 (F)，dry season 意為「乾季」。

解答&技巧 | `01` **(A)** `02` **(E)** `03` **(G)** `04` **(D)** `05` **(B)**
`06` **(J)** `07` **(I)** `08` **(C)** `09` **(H)** `10` **(F)**

適用 TIP 1　適用 TIP 2　適用 TIP 6　適用 TIP 7　適用 TIP 8
適用 TIP 9　適用 TIP 10　適用 TIP 11

DAY
5

Part 1
詞
彙
題
Day 5
完成 25%

Part 2
綜
合
測
驗
Day 5
完成 50%

Part 3
文
意
選
填
Day 5
完成 75%

Part 4
閱
讀
測
驗
Day 5
完成 100%

補充

rainforest n 雨林；savanna n 熱帶亞熱帶大草原；equator n 赤道；veld n 南非的疏林草原；
steppe n 樹木稀少的草原

7,000 單字

- plain [plen] n 2 平原
- stretch [strɛtʃ] v 2 延伸
- continent [ˋkɑntənənt] n 3 大陸
- circle [ˋsɝkl] v 2 環繞
- central [ˋsɛntrəl] a 2 中央的
- prairie [ˋprɛrɪ] n 5 北美洲的大草原
- meadow [ˋmɛdo] n 3 草地
- bunch [bʌntʃ] n 3 簇

- lawn [lɔn] n 3 草坪（人為照顧的）
- summer [ˋsʌmɚ] n 1 夏天
- western [ˋwɛstɚn] a 2 西方的
- shadow [ˋʃædo] n 3 陰影
- tropics [ˋtrɑpɪks] n 6 熱帶
- rainfall [ˋrɛn͵fɔl] n 4 降雨量
- without [wɪˋðaʊt] prep 2 無，沒有

MEMO

Scientists call the smallest bits of matter atoms and ___01___ . They cannot be seen even with the ___02___ . Millions of molecules ___03___ the tiniest speck of dust.

All the matter is made of tiny atoms and molecules. The smallest piece of sugar, as well as the smallest drop of water, has millions of molecules. We can change the size and shape of a certain substance by heating, cooling, or ___04___ it. All these changes are ___05___ changes, which do not change one substance into another. Clay is still clay even if it is molded, and sugar is still sugar even if it is added to cereal.

Not all changes are physical changes. Sometimes when certain changes take place, a new substance will come into ___06___ . The new substance does not look like the ___07___ one. Neither does it act as the previous substance. This kind of change is a ___08___ change. A growing plant shows a chemical change. The nutrients and water from the soil and air is changed to cells of the plant. Chemical changes may take place when two kinds of substances are ___09___ . When baking a cake, a chemical change occurs. The different kinds of mixed substances induce changes as the cake is being ___10___ . The old substances join together in a certain way to compose a new substance.

(A) molecules   (B) being   (C) baked   (D) microscopes   (E) smashing
(F) physical   (G) mixed   (H) compose   (I) chemical   (J) previous

---

01 _____   02 _____   03 _____   04 _____   05 _____

06 _____   07 _____   08 _____   09 _____   10 _____

選項中譯│分子；存在；烘烤；顯微鏡；粉碎；物理的；混合；組成；化學的；之前的

中譯│科學家把最小量的物質稱為原子和分子。即使在顯微鏡下，也看不到原子和分子。塵埃的最小顆粒就是由數百萬的分子構成的。

所有的物質都是由微小的原子和分子構成的。最小的一顆糖、最小的一滴水，都是由數百萬的分子構成的。我們可以加熱、冷卻、粉碎某種物質，來改變它的大小和形狀。所有的這些變化都是物理變化，不會將一種物質變為另一種物質。黏土即便是被做成模型，也還是黏土。糖即便是被加入麥片中，也還是糖。

並非所有的變化都是物理變化。有時候，某些變化發生，就會產生新的物質。這種新的物質與舊的物質不同，所產生的作用也不同。這種變化就是化學變化。一株正在生長的植物所顯示的就是化學變化。土壤和空氣提供的營養和水分變成了植物的細胞。當兩種物質混合在一起時，就有可能會發生化學變化。烤蛋糕的時候，化學變化就會發生。在烤蛋糕時，各種不同的東西混合在一起，引起變化。舊的物質以某種方式結合在一起，產生新的物質。

解譯│閱讀全文可知，這篇文章的主題是物理變化和化學變化。

縱觀各選項，選項 (A)、(B)、(D) 是名詞，選項 (C)、(E)、(G)、(H) 是動詞，選項 (F)、(I)、(J) 是形容詞。根據題意，第 1、2、6 題應選名詞，第 3、4、9、10 題應選動詞，第 5、7、8 題應選形容詞。然後根據文章，依次作答。

第 1 題是選擇名詞，用於與 atoms 的並列結構，有三個名詞可供選擇，即為選項 (A)、(B)、(D)，選項 (A) 意為「原子」，選項 (B) 意為「存在」，選項 (D) 意為「顯微鏡」，根據句意，應當 (A)。第 2 題所選名詞，根據句意，應當是「即使在顯微鏡下，也看不到原子和分子」，所以選 (D)。第 6 題則是選 (B)，come into being 可以視為固定搭配，意為「開始存在」。

第 3 題是選擇動詞，有四個動詞可供選擇，即為選項 (C)、(E)、(G)、(H)，根據句意，應當是「塵埃的最小顆粒就是由數百萬的分子構成的」，所以選 (H)。第 4 題所選動詞，應為動名詞，所以選 (E)。第 9 題所選動詞，須為被動語態，根據句意可知，應當是「兩種物質混合在一起」，所以選 (G)。第 10 題則是選 (C)，bake a cake 意為「烤蛋糕」。

第 5 題是選擇形容詞，有三個形容詞可供選擇，即為選項 (F)、(I)、(J)。選項 (F) 意為「物理的」，選項 (I) 意為「化學的」，選項 (J) 意為「之前的」，根據句意可知，應當是「這些變化都是物理變化，不會將一種物質變為另一種物質」，所以選 (F)。第 7 題所選形容詞，根據句意可知，應當是「新的物質與舊的物質不同」，所以選 (J)。第 8 題則是選 (I)，句意為「這種變化是化學變化」。

DAY
5

Part 1
詞
彙
題
Day 5
完成 25%

Part 2
綜
合
測
驗
Day 5
完成 50%

Part 3
文
意
選
填
Day 5
完成 75%

Part 4
閱
讀
測
驗
Day 5
完成 100%

解答＆技巧 | **01** (A)　**02** (D)　**03** (H)　**04** (E)　**05** (F)
　　　　　06 (B)　**07** (J)　**08** (I)　**09** (G)　**10** (C)

適用 TIP 1　適用 TIP 2　適用 TIP 6　適用 TIP 7　適用 TIP 8
適用 TIP 9　適用 TIP 10　適用 TIP 11

補充

speck [n] 顆粒；be made of [ph] 由〜組成；as well as [ph] 和，同；millions of [ph] 數百萬的；physical changes [ph] 物理變化；chemical changes [ph] 化學變化

7,000 單字

- atom [ˋætəm] [n] **4** 原子
- molecule [ˋmɑləˏkjul] [n] **5** 分子
- microscope [ˋmaɪkrəˏskop] [n] **4** 顯微鏡
- dust [dʌst] [n] **3** 灰塵
- tiny [ˋtaɪnɪ] [a] **1** 極小的
- sugar [ˋʃʊgɚ] [n] **1** 糖
- substance [ˋsʌbstəns] [n] **3** 物質
- smash [smæʃ] [v] **5** 粉碎

- clay [kle] [n] **2** 黏土
- add [æd] [v] **1** 加
- cereal [ˋsɪrɪəl] [n] **2** 穀類食物，麥片
- previous [ˋpriviəs] [a] **3** 在前的
- chemical [ˋkɛmɪkl̩] [a] **2** 化學的
- soil [sɔɪl] [n] **1** 土壤
- bake [bek] [v] **2** 烘烤

MEMO

④ ▶

DAY
5

Part 1
詞
彙
題
Day 5
完成 25%

Part 2
綜
合
測
驗
Day 5
完成 50%

Part 3
文
意
選
填
Day 5
完成 75%

Part 4
閱
讀
測
驗
Day 5
完成 100%

According to the tradition laid down by ancient customs, people usually stay up late on New Year's Eve, waiting for the __01__ of the New Year. When the clock __02__ twelve at midnight, people blow horns, set off __03__ and say "Happy New Year" to each other. And __04__ can be seen in different cities on New Year's Day.

In a little town in England, people gather around a fire on New Year's Eve. The band plays songs. It is their custom to stay up until the fire goes out. They __05__ the New Year in this way, though no one knows actually when and how it started.

In Japan, people eat fish on New Year's Day, __06__ it will bring them good health.

In Belgium, farmers say "Happy New Year" to all animals on the morning of New Year's Day.

In Vienna, Austria, people __07__ a pig on the morning of New Year's Day. They believe they will have good __08__ in the new year if they catch the pig.

In Scotland, people think that the first boy to come to a house on New Year's Eve will bring good luck. If a girl is the first to come, she may bring bad luck.

The Chinese Spring Festival is according to the __09__ calendar, different from New Year's Day, which __10__ on the first day in January. The festival is usually at the end of January or the beginning of February. The elders of the family will put money in a little red envelope and give it to children as a Spring Festival gift, hoping to bring good luck.

(A) firecrackers (B) arrival (C) luck (D) welcome (E) falls
(F) strikes (G) hoping (H) lunar (I) chase (J) parades

---

01 _____   02 _____   03 _____   04 _____   05 _____

06 _____   07 _____   08 _____   09 _____   10 _____

選項中譯｜鞭炮；到來；運氣；歡迎；發生在；敲；希望；農曆的；追趕；遊行

中譯｜依照古老的習俗，人們在除夕夜要熬夜，等待新年的到來。當午夜凌晨，十二點的鐘聲響起，人們會吹響號角，燃放鞭炮，相互問候「新年快樂」。在元旦當天，很多城市都會舉行遊行。

在英格蘭的一個小鎮上，除夕夜時，人們聚集在火堆旁。樂隊演奏歌曲。依照習俗，人們要熬夜，直到火堆熄滅。他們以這樣的方式來迎接新年，卻沒有人知道，這樣的習俗是起源於什麼時候，又是如何開始的。

在日本，元旦當天，人們要吃魚，這樣做是希望可以為自己帶來健康。

在比利時，新年的早晨，農民要對所有的動物說「新年快樂」。

在奧地利維也納，新年的早晨，人們要追趕一頭豬，他們認為如果能夠抓到這頭豬，在新的一年中就會有好運氣。

在蘇格蘭，人們認為，除夕夜第一個進入屋子的男孩，會帶來好運氣。如果第一個進來的是女孩，則會帶來壞運氣。

中國的春節則是依照農曆，與元旦不同，並不是在一月的第一天，而是在一月底或是二月初。家族中的長輩要把壓歲錢放在小紅包裡，作為春節禮物送給孩子們，希望能帶來好運。

解譯｜閱讀全文可知，這篇文章的主題是新年慶祝與習俗。

縱觀各選項，選項 (A)、(B)、(C)、(J) 是名詞，選項 (D)、(E)、(F)、(G)、(I) 是動詞，選項 (H) 是形容詞。根據題意，第 1、3、4、8 題應選名詞，第 2、5、6、7、10 題應選動詞，第 9 題應選形容詞。然後根據文章，依次作答。

第 1 題是選擇名詞，用於 of 結構，有四個名詞可供選擇，即為選項 (A)、(B)、(C)、(J)，選項 (A) 意為「鞭炮」，選項 (B) 意為「到來」，選項 (C) 意為「運氣」，選項 (J) 意為「遊行」，根據句意，應當是「等待新年的到來」，所以選 (B)。第 3 題所選名詞，可以視為固定搭配，set off firecrackers 意為「放鞭炮」，所以選 (A)。第 4 題所選名詞，根據句意，應當是「很多城市都會舉行遊行」，所以選 (J)。第 8 題則是選 (C)，good luck 意為「好運」。

第 2 題是選擇動詞，有五個動詞可供選擇，即為選項 (D)、(E)、(F)、(G)、(I)。只有選項 (F) 符合要求，意為「鐘敲響報時」。第 5 題所選動詞，根據句意，應當是「以這樣的方式來迎接新年」，所以選 (D)。第 6 題所選動詞，是用現在分詞表示伴隨狀況，所以選 (G)。第 7 題所選動詞，根據句意，應當是「追趕」，所以選 (I)。第 10 題則是選 (E)，fall on 意為「發生在某一天」。

第 9 題是選擇形容詞，只有一個形容詞可供選擇，即為選項 (H)，lunar calendar 意為「農曆」。

解答＆技巧 | **01** (B)　**02** (F)　**03** (A)　**04** (J)　**05** (D)
　　　　　　06 (G)　**07** (I)　**08** (C)　**09** (H)　**10** (E)

適用 TIP 1　適用 TIP 2　適用 TIP 6　適用 TIP 7　適用 TIP 8
適用 TIP 9　適用 TIP 10　適用 TIP 11

補充

lay down ph 明確規定；New Year's Day ph 元旦；Happy New Year ph 新年快樂；
good luck ph 好運；bad luck ph 霉運

7,000 單字

- tradition [trə`dɪʃən] n 4 傳統
- arrival [ə`raɪvl] n 3 到來
- clock [klɑk] n 1 時鐘
- strike [straɪk] v 2 時鐘敲響
- blow [blo] v 1 吹
- horn [hɔrn] n 3 號角
- parade [pə`red] n 3 遊行
- fire [faɪr] n 1 火

- band [bænd] n 1 樂隊
- welcome [`wɛlkəm] v 1 歡迎
- chase [tʃes] v 1 追趕
- pig [pɪg] n 1 豬
- luck [lʌk] n 2 運氣
- envelope [`ɛnvə.lop] n 2 信封
- January [`dʒænju.ɛrɪ] n 1 一月

DAY 5

Part 1 詞彙題 Day 5 完成 25%
Part 2 綜合測驗 Day 5 完成 50%
Part 3 文意選填 Day 5 完成 75%
Part 4 閱讀測驗 Day 5 完成 100%

MEMO

♪297

5 ▶

When World War I finally came to an end in 1918, in order to avoid such terrible __01__ and bloodshed, an international association was established by the leading nations involved in the war. The association is known as the League of Nations, __02__ to find peace between countries. The League began to fall apart in the 1930s after several member states challenged its authority. With the __03__ of the Second World War in 1939, the League of Nations ceased to exist. But there were moves to establish a new organization to __04__ it.

In 1941, American President Franklin D. Roosevelt, and British Prime __05__ Winston Churchill, signed the *Atlantic Charter*. The charter pledged to respect fellowmen's legal rights, to maintain peace, and to promote disarmament as well as economic __06__ .

In 1944, representatives from the United States, the USSR, China, and Great Britain attended a series of meetings in the U.S. They __07__ up the idea of establishing an international peacekeeping organization. The first conference of the United Nations (UN) was held in San Francisco in 1945, and the UN charter was __08__ in October in the same year.

Peace and security are the most important aim of the UN. The UN also has many other __09__ , known as agencies, dealing with worldwide problems. Some of these agencies provide aid for people in need, such as refugees. Others are concerned with health matters, living and working conditions, human __10__ , etc.

(A) signed   (B) outbreak   (C) Minister   (D) rights   (E) slaughter
(F) prosperity   (G) aiming   (H) branches   (I) brought   (J) replace

---

01 _____   02 _____   03 _____   04 _____   05 _____

06 _____   07 _____   08 _____   09 _____   10 _____

選項中譯｜簽署；爆發；部長；權利；殺戮；繁榮；力求；分支；提出；代替

DAY
5

Part 1
詞
彙
題
Day 5
完成 25%

Part 2
綜
合
測
驗
Day 5
完成 50%

Part 3
文
意
選
填
Day 5
完成 75%

Part 4
閱
讀
測
驗
Day 5
完成 100%

中譯｜一九一八年，第一次世界大戰終於結束，為了避免如此殘酷的殺戮和流血犧牲，主要的參戰國成立了一個國際性組織。這個組織就是國際聯盟，旨在維持國與國之間的和平。二十世紀三〇年代，繼幾個成員國挑戰國際聯盟的權威之後，國際聯盟開始瓦解。一九三九年，隨著第二次世界大戰爆發，國際聯盟不復存在，卻建立了新的組織來代替它。

一九四一年，美國總統富蘭克林·羅斯福和英國首相溫斯頓·邱吉爾簽署《大西洋憲章》。憲章保證，尊重人民的合法權利，維護和平，推動裁軍和經濟繁榮。

一九四四年，美國、蘇聯、中國和英國的代表們，在美國參加了一系列會議。他們提出了成立國際維和組織的理念。一九四五年，聯合國首次會議在舊金山召開，同年十月，簽署聯合國憲章。

和平和安全是聯合國的最重要的目標。聯合國也有許多其他的分支，稱為理事處，負責處理世界性問題。有些機構是為有需要的人們——例如難民——提供幫助。其他機構則是關注健康事宜、生活和工作環境、人權等問題。

解譯｜閱讀全文可知，這篇文章的主題是國際維和組織的發展。

縱觀各選項，選項 (B)、(C)、(D)、(E)、(F)、(H) 是名詞，選項 (A)、(G)、(I)、(J) 是動詞。根據題意，第 1、3、5、6、9、10 題應選名詞，第 2、4、7、8 題應選動詞。然後根據文章，依次作答。

第 1 題是選擇名詞，用於與 bloodshed 的並列結構，有六個名詞可供選擇，即為選項 (B)、(C)、(D)、(E)、(F)、(H)，選項 (B) 意為「爆發」，選項 (C) 意為「部長」，選項 (D) 意為「權利」，選項 (E) 意為「殺戮」，選項 (F) 意為「繁榮」，選項 (H) 意為「分支」，所以選 (E)。第 3 題所選名詞，根據句意，應當是「隨著第二次世界大戰的爆發」，所以選 (B)。第 5 題所選名詞，可以視為固定表達，prime minister 意為「首相，總理」，所以選 (C)。第 6 題所選名詞，economic prosperity 意為「經濟繁榮」，所以選 (F)。第 9 題所選名詞，根據句意，應當是「聯合國也有許多其他的分支」，所以選 (H)。第 10 題則是選 (D)，human right 意為「人權」。

第 2 題是選擇動詞，須為現在分詞，作目的副詞，有四個動詞可供選擇，即為選項 (A)、(G)、(I)、(J)。只有選項 (G) 符合要求，可以視為固定搭配，aim to do sth. 意為「力圖做某事」。第 4 題所選動詞，根據句意，應當是「建立了新的組織來代替它」，所以選 (J)。第 7 題所選動詞，可以視為固定搭配，bring up the idea of 意為「提出～觀點」，所以選 (I)。第 8 題則是選 (A)，意為「簽署聯合國憲章」。

解答&技巧 | 01 (E)　02 (G)　03 (B)　04 (J)　05 (C)
06 (F)　07 (I)　08 (A)　09 (H)　10 (D)

適用 TIP 1　適用 TIP 2　適用 TIP 6　適用 TIP 7　適用 TIP 8
適用 TIP 9　適用 TIP 10　適用 TIP 11

補充

League of Nations ph 國際聯盟；charter n 憲章；USSR ph 蘇聯；San Francisco ph 舊金山；
the United Nations ph 聯合國

7,000 單字

- slaughter [ˈslɔtɚ] n 5 屠殺
- league [lig] n 5 聯盟
- aim [em] v 2 旨在
- peace [pis] n 2 和平
- outbreak [ˈaʊtˌbrek] n 6 爆發
- cease [sis] v 4 停止
- exist [ɪgˈzɪst] v 2 存在
- prime [praɪm] a 4 最主要的

- minister [ˈmɪnɪstɚ] n 4 部長，大臣
- pledge [plɛdʒ] v 5 保證
- prosperity [prɑsˈpɛrətɪ] n 4 繁榮
- series [ˈsiriz] n 5 系列
- conference [ˈkɑnfərəns] n 4 會議
- agency [ˈedʒənsɪ] n 4 機構，理事處
- refugee [ˌrɛfjʊˈdʒi] n 4 難民

MEMO

MEMO

DAY
5

Part 1
詞
彙
題
Day 5
完成 25%

Part 2
綜
合
測
驗
Day 5
完成 50%

Part 3
文
意
選
填
Day 5
完成 75%

Part 4
閱
讀
測
驗
Day 5
完成 100%

Part 4 閱讀測驗 | Reading Questions

Recently, there are a lot of ridiculous sayings about the "great classless society." It is said that the existing monarchies have lost all political authority; inherited wealth has become less because of the taxation. As a system of government, monarchy has totally lost public trust. On the contrary, many countries under the rule of law or people have gained complete victory. But these views may not be true.

It may not be the case that all men will be equal if the society provides everybody with the same educational opportunities. Actually, when God gives special gifts and ability to a person, the principle of equality may not be taken into consideration. The popularity of education has created a new class system instead of the old one.

Genuine ability, animal cunning, and the knack of seizing opportunities, all of these can bring material rewards. When people get rich, they may try to ensure their children to get the best opportunities and have a good start in life. In the western society, private schools have more advantages than state schools, which is obviously good for the rich and bad for the poor. But the private schools would not be banned because, in a democratic nation, it is people's right and freedom to choose what kind of education they want for their children. In this case, the new elite education will have the chance to retain its life, which means an able child from a rich family can succeed ahead of his poorer peers. Money is also an effective weapon to achieve political purposes. Without strong economic support, it may be difficult to become a leader of a democratic country.

01 The word "knack" in the third paragraph is closest in meaning to _____.

(A) skill

(B) information

(C) equipment

(D) procedure

02 According to the third paragraph, who are likely to obtain more rapid success?

(A) Children from a rich family.

(B) Children from a poor family.

(C) Children of many gifts.

(D) Children with good education opportunities.

03 According to the author, what is the meaning of class divisions?

(A) Capitalism and socialism.

(B) Genius and stupidity.

(C) Different opportunities for the rich and the poor.

(D) Oppressor and the oppressed.

04 We can learn from the passage that _____.

(A) God will bring us a classless society.

(B) Equality of opportunity has not eliminated the class system.

(C) There is no classless society on the earth.

(D) All of people have the same equality of education.

DAY
5

Part 1
詞
彙
題
Day 5
完成 25%

Part 2
綜
合
測
驗
Day 5
完成 50%

Part 3
文
意
選
填
Day 5
完成 75%

Part 4
閱
讀
測
驗
Day 5
完成 100%

中譯｜最近，關於「偉大的無階級社會」有很多荒謬的說法。據說，現存的君主制已經喪失了所有的政治權威。由於稅收，人們所繼承的遺產變得更少。作為一個政府體系，君主制已經完全喪失了公眾的信任。相反地，很多由律法和人們進行統治的社會卻是獲得了極大的勝利。但是，這些觀點也許並非正確。

如果社會為所有人提供同樣的受教育機會，所有人也未必就都是平等的。事實上，上帝給予某個人特殊天賦和能力時，就不會將平等原則考慮在內。教育的普及創建了新的階級制度來替代舊的制度。

真才實學、動物般的狡猾、抓住機遇的能力，這些，都能夠獲得物質回報。人們變得富有時，也許會盡力確保孩子們獲得最好的機會，有個好的人生開端。在西方社會，相較於公立學校，私立學校具備更多的優勢，這對富人有利，卻對窮人有害。但是，私立學校並不會受到禁止，因為在民主國家，人們享有權利和自由來選擇讓孩子接受何種教育。在這樣的情形下，新的精英教育將有機會得以存在，這就意味著，與貧困家庭的同儕相比，來自富裕家庭的、有能力的孩子，將會領先一步獲得成功。金錢也是一種用來達成政治目的的有效手段。如果沒有強大的經濟支持，也許就難以成為民主國家的領導者。

解譯｜在閱讀文章之前，先要預覽題目，然後再帶著問題有針對性地閱讀文章。第 1 題是詞義辨析，第 2、3、4 題是文意理解。理解了題目要求之後，閱讀全文，依次作答。

第 1 題是考名詞 knack 的同義字。選項 (A) 意為「技巧」，選項 (B) 意為「資訊」，選項 (C) 意為「設備」，選項 (D) 意為「程序」。根據第 3 段內容可知，名詞 knack 在文中意為「技巧」，所以選 (A)。

第 2 題是文意理解，考的是細節，問的是根據第 3 段，誰有可能迅速獲得成功。第 3 段主要是說，因為貧富差距，孩子們的受教育機會並不均等，人生際遇也不相同。根據第 3 段倒數第 4 行內容「an able child from a rich family can succeed ahead of his poorer peers」可知，與貧困家庭的同儕相比，來自富裕家庭的孩子，將會領先一步獲得成功，與選項 (A) 相符。同樣，此題也可以用排除法來解答。選項 (B) 明顯錯誤，可以排除；選項 (C)、(D) 固然是成功的因素之一，卻不是這篇短文的意義所在，也可以排除。所以選 (A)。

第 3 題也是文意理解，問的是在作者看來，所謂的階級劃分意義何在。縱觀全文，作者先是引出階級社會的話題，再指明教育導致新階級制度的產生，接著闡述貧富差距對受教育機會的影響。由此可知，所謂的階級劃分，即為貧富階層的不同機遇，與選項 (C) 相符。選項 (A) 意為「資本主義和社會主義」，選項 (B) 意為「天才和蠢材」，選項 (D) 意為「壓迫者和被壓迫者」，在文中找不到相關敘述。所以選 (C)。

第 4 題同樣是文意理解，問的是根據這篇短文，可以得出什麼結論。根據第 3 題的分析，短文主旨可以概括為，隨著教育的發展，階級劃分從政治制度層面轉為機會際遇層面，貧富差距正是引起機會際遇差別的主要因素，選項 (B) 意為「機會均等並沒有消除階級體系」，與此相符。選項 (A) 意為「上帝將會帶來無階級

社會」，選項 (C) 意為「無階級社會根本不會存在」，選項 (D) 意為「所有人都享有均等的受教育機會」，在文中並沒有相關敘述。所以選 (B)。

解答＆技巧 | **01 (A)** **02 (A)** **03 (C)** **04 (B)**

適用 TIP 1　適用 TIP 2　適用 TIP 3　適用 TIP 7　適用 TIP 10　適用 TIP 11
適用 TIP 12　適用 TIP 13　適用 TIP 14　適用 TIP 15　適用 TIP 16

補充

inherited a 繼承的；monarchy n 君主制；taxation n 稅收制度；knack n 技巧；
obviously ad 顯然地

7,000 單字

- ridiculous [rɪ`dɪkjələs] a 5 荒謬的
- political [pə`lɪtɪkl̩] a 3 政治的
- government [`gʌvɚnmənt] n 2 政府
- principle [`prɪnsəpl̩] n 2 原則
- equality [i`kwɑlətɪ] n 4 平等
- genuine [`dʒɛnjuɪn] a 4 真誠的
- cunning [`kʌnɪŋ] a 4 狡猾的
- seize [siz] v 3 抓住

- ban [bæn] v 5 禁止
- democratic [ˌdɛmə`krætɪk] a 3 民主的
- nation [`neʃən] n 1 國家
- elite [i`lit] n 6 精英
- ahead [ə`hɛd] prep 1 領先於
- weapon [`wɛpən] n 2 行動，手段
- leader [`lidɚ] n 1 領導人

MEMO

DAY
5

Part 1
詞
彙
題
Day 5
完成 25%

Part 2
綜
合
測
驗
Day 5
完成 50%

Part 3
文
意
選
填
Day 5
完成 75%

Part 4
閱
讀
測
驗
Day 5
完成 100%

One thousand years ago in the Southwest of North America, the Hopi and Zuni Indians were building houses with adobe—sun baked brick plastered with mud. These buildings looked remarkably like modern apartment houses. Some were four stories high and could hold about a thousand people, along with store rooms for grain and other goods. These buildings were mostly put up against cliffs, in order to make construction easier and serve as a defense against enemies. They were really villages in themselves, as soon after Spanish explorers discovered them and called them "pueblos," which means "town" in Spanish.

The people of the Pueblos planted corn, beans and squash. They made wonderful pottery and wove marvelous baskets, some of which are so amazing that they could hold water. The Southwest of North America has always been a dry place, where water is scarce. The Hopi and Zuni brought water from streams to their fields and gardens through irrigation ditches. Water was so important that it occupied a major position in their religion. They created elaborate ceremonies and religious rituals to bring rain.

The lifestyle of those less settled Indian groups was simpler and more strongly influenced by the nature. One example is the Shoshone and Ute, they loafed about arid mountainous regions and ate seeds and small animals such as small rabbits and snakes. Another example is the ancestors of today's Inuit; they lived on the frozen seas in igloos built of blocks of packed snow and hunted seals, walruses, and the great whales. In summer, they fished for salmon and hunted the caribou.

The Plains Indians, which includes the Cheyenne, Pawnee, and Sioux tribes, lived on the grasslands between the Rocky Mountains and the Mississippi River. They hunted bison, also known as "buffalo." They ate its meat as their main source of food and made their clothing and covering of their tents and Tipis with its hide.

01 What is the main idea of the passage?

(A) The buildings of early American Indians.

(B) The movement of American Indians.

(C) The religion of American Indians.

(D) The lifestyle of American Indian tribes in early North America.

02 We can learn from the passage that the houses of the Hopi and Zuni were _____.

(A) very big

(B) highly developed

(C) easy to defend

(D) quickly built

03 According to the passage, which of the following statements about the Indians of North America is true?

(A) All American Indians' living places are like modern apartment houses.

(B) The Cheyenne, Pawnee, and Sioux tribes like loafing about the dry and mountainous lands.

(C) Food was so important that it occupied a major position in their religion.

(D) The Plains Indians' chief food is buffalo's meat.

04 The word "hide" in the last paragraph is closest in meaning to _____.

(A) place

(B) skin

(C) fur

(D) feather

DAY
5

Part 1
詞
彙
題
Day 5
完成 25%

Part 2
綜
合
測
驗
Day 5
完成 50%

Part 3
文
意
選
填
Day 5
完成 75%

Part 4
閱
讀
測
驗
Day 5
完成 100%

中譯 | 一千年以前，在北美洲的西南部，霍皮人和祖尼人兩支印第安部落，用泥磚——也就是曬乾的燒結磚塗上灰泥——來建造房屋。他們建造的房屋頗像現代的公寓，有些房子是四層樓高，能容納一千人，普有貯藏糧食和其他物品的儲藏室。這些房子通常緊靠懸崖而建，是為了易於修建，也為了防禦敵人。這些建築群實際上就是一個個村莊。不久，西班牙探險者發現了這些建築群，稱之為「pueblos」，在西班牙語中意為「城鎮」。

pueblos 的居民種植玉米、豆類和南瓜類植物。他們能製造出精美的陶器，編織極好的籃子，有些籃子甚至能用來盛水，令人感到十分驚訝。北美西南部是個乾旱的地方，極度缺水。霍皮人和祖尼人用灌溉水渠將水從小溪引到自家的田地和菜園裡。對於他們來說，水非常重要，也在他們的宗教信仰裡佔據了主要地位，為此，他們創立了精細的宗教儀式來求雨。

那些居無定所的印第安人，生活方式相對簡單一些，受大自然的影響也更大一些。像肖松尼族印第安人和猶特人，流浪在乾旱多山的地區，靠吃植物種子和小型動物（兔子、蛇）為生。另一個例子就是現在的因紐特人的祖先，他們居住在冰冷海邊的圓頂小屋裡，這些小屋是用堅硬的雪塊砌成的。他們以捕獵海豹、海象和鯨魚為生。夏天的時候，他們還捕獵鮭魚和馴鹿。

「平原印第安人」包括夏安族人、波尼族人以及蘇族人，他們居住在洛磯山脈和密西西比河之間的大草原上，捕獵北美野牛。野牛肉是他們的主要食物來源，牛皮則用於製作衣物和帳篷。

解譯 | 在閱讀文章之前，先預覽題目，然後再帶著問題有針對性地閱讀文章。第 1 題是概括主旨，第 2 題是細節推斷，第 3 題是判斷正誤，第 4 題是詞義推斷。理解了題目要求之後，閱讀全文，依次作答。主旨題可以留在最後解答。

第 2 題是考細節，關鍵字是 the houses of the Hopi and Zuni，即為霍皮人和祖尼人的房子。透過細讀第 1 段可知，早在一千年前，霍皮人和祖尼人建造的房屋就已經和現代的公寓相仿，可以推斷出，他們的房屋建造技術很發達。選項 (A)、(D) 在文章中都沒有提到；第 1 段中說，房屋臨懸崖而建，是為了方便建房，也是為了防禦敵人，並沒有提到防禦是否容易，所以選項 (C) 與文意不符；均可排除，所以選 (B)。

第 3 題是判斷正誤，關鍵字是 the Indians of North America，即為北美印第安人。根據文章第 1 段內容可知，霍皮人和祖尼人的房屋像現代化的公寓，第三段講到，也有一些住處不太固定的印第安人，過著流浪的生活，或是住在寒冷的雪屋裡，選項 (A) 以全蓋偏，可以排除。根據第三段可知，是肖松尼族印第安人和猶特人，流浪在乾旱多山的地區，而不是夏安族人、波尼族人以及蘇族人，選項 (B) 張冠李戴，也可以排除。根據第二段可知，水在北美印第安人的宗教信仰裡佔據很重要的地位，而不是食物，排除選項 (C)。選項 (D) 說，「平原印第安人」的主要食物來源是野牛肉，與最後一段內容相符，所以選 (D)。

第 4 題是考單字 hide 的同義字。hide 通常是用作動詞，意為「躲藏；隱蔽」，卻也可以用作名詞，意為「獸皮」。最後一段中說，「平原印第安人」吃掉野牛

的肉，將野牛的皮做成衣服和帳篷，顯然根據語意，可以判斷出 hide 在文中是作為名詞，表示「野牛的皮」。四個選項中的單字，只有選項 (B) 與原文意思最接近，所以選 (B)。

第 1 題是概括主旨。閱讀全文，歸納 4 段內容可知，作者主要是描述了北美地區不同印第安部落的不同的生活方式。選項 (A) 只是印第安人生活方式的一個方面，選項 (B)、(C) 在文中都沒有提到，均可排除，所以選 (D)。

解答&技巧 | **01 (D) 02 (B) 03 (D) 04 (B)**

適用 TIP 1 適用 TIP 3 適用 TIP 5 適用 TIP 7 適用 TIP 11

適用 TIP 12 適用 TIP 14 適用 TIP 15

補充

look like ph 看起來像；put up against... ph 依～而建；soon after ph 不久；
so that ph 如此～以至於～；such as ph 例如

7,000 單字

- apartment [əˋpɑrtmənt] n 2 公寓
- grain [gren] n 3 穀物
- cliff [klɪf] n 4 懸崖
- defense [dɪˋfɛns] n 4 防禦
- wonderful [ˋwʌndɚfəl] a 2 極好的
- pottery [ˋpɑtərɪ] n 3 陶器
- scarce [skɛrs] a 3 稀少的
- ditch [dɪtʃ] n 3 溝

- religion [rɪˋlɪdʒən] n 3 宗教
- ceremony [ˋsɛrəˏmonɪ] n 5 儀式
- ritual [ˋrɪtʃʊəl] n 6 程序，儀節
- mountainous [ˋmaʊntənəs] a 4 山地的，多山的
- seal [sil] n 3 海豹
- salmon [ˋsæmən] n 5 鮭魚
- buffalo [ˋbʌfˏlo] n 3 野牛

MEMO

DAY 5

Part 1
詞
彙
題
Day 5
完成 25%

Part 2
綜
合
測
驗
Day 5
完成 50%

Part 3
文
意
選
填
Day 5
完成 75%

Part 4
閱
讀
測
驗
Day 5
完成 100%

As is known to all, William Shakespeare is the only one industry in Stratford-upon-Avon. There are two entirely different branches. One is the Royal Shakespeare Company (RSC), which offers excellent plays at the Shakespeare Memorial Theater on the Avon; the other is the townsfolk, who mainly live on the tourists who come to visit Anne Hathaway's Cottage, Shakespeare's birthplace and the other sights.

The rich residents of Stratford don't think that the theater increases their income. They don't like the RSC's actors actually, but what is extremely ironic is, Shakespeare, the person they live off at the present time, was an actor, too.

The separation between the tourists is not absolute. The sightseers usually visit Warwick Castle and Blenheim Palace. They almost never see the plays, and some of them even don't know there is a theater in Stratford. Yet the playgoers not only see the plays, but they also go sightseeing. The sightseers visit every place they want to go in one day and leave the town when it's dark. The playgoers spend the night in the town; some of them even stay for four or five nights and naturally bring much money to the local hotels and restaurants. So according to the RSC, it is the playgoers that increase the town's income. But the townsfolk don't agree with the RSC, and local council refuses to offer subsidy to it.

The townsfolk don't think that the Royal Shakespeare Company needs a subsidy because the theater has enough audience. It has broken attendance records for three years in a row, and the number of audience is still growing. But they do not know that the cost of the theater is increasing, while the ticket prices remain the same. If the theater increases prices, the loyal customers may not come to Stratford any more. The purpose they come there is to watch the plays, rather than to see the sights.

01 Which of the following statements is true according to the first two paragraphs?

(A) The actors of the RSC copy Shakespeare on stage.

(B) The two branches in Stratford-upon-Avon are on bad terms.

(C) The townsfolk can't earn money from tourism.

(D) The townsfolk don't think the RSC makes contribution to the town's income.

02 We cam learn from the third paragraph that _____.

(A) the sightseers don't like visiting the Castle and the Palace separately

(B) the sightseers spend less money than the playgoers

(C) the playgoers do less shopping than the sightseers

(D) the playgoers only go to the theater in town

03 The townsfolk think that the RSC shouldn't be offered subsidy because _____.

(A) they can increase the ticket prices to cover the spending

(B) the company is badly managed

(C) the actors are not welcomed

(D) the number of the audience is rising

04 We can infer from the passage that the author _____.

(A) agrees with both sides

(B) indifferent to both sides

(C) feels pity for the RSC

(D) supports the townsfolk's opinion

DAY 5

Part 1
詞彙題
Day 5 完成 25%

Part 2
綜合測驗
Day 5 完成 50%

Part 3
文意選填
Day 5 完成 75%

Part 4
閱讀測驗
Day 5 完成 100%

中譯｜眾所周知，威廉·莎士比亞是英國史特拉福鎮的唯一產業，它有兩個完全不同的分支。一是皇家莎士比亞劇團，在莎士比亞紀念劇院上演多部優秀戲劇；另一支則是史特拉福鎮居民，主要是以招待遊客為生，這些遊客是來參觀安妮·海瑟薇的小屋、莎士比亞出生地以及其他景點。

富裕的史特拉福鎮居民並不認為，劇院增加了他們的收入。實際上，他們並不喜歡劇院的演員，然而頗諷刺的是，他們如今是憑靠莎士比亞為生，而莎士比亞本人也是個戲劇演員。

遊客之間的分歧也不是絕對的。觀光者通常會參觀華威城堡和布倫海姆宮，他們幾乎從不去看戲劇，有些人甚至不知道史特拉福鎮還有劇院。不過，戲劇迷們並不只是去看戲劇，他們也去觀光。觀光者們會在一天的時間內看完他們想看的景點，然後在天黑前離開；戲迷們則是在鎮裡過夜，有些戲迷甚至會停留四五個晚上，這自然會給當地的旅店和餐館帶來很大的利潤。因此劇院認為，是戲迷們令鎮裡增加了收入。居民們卻不認同這一觀點，當地政府也拒絕給劇院提供經濟補貼。

居民們認為，劇院不需要補貼，因為劇院有足夠多的觀眾，已經打破了連續三年以來的就座率記錄，觀眾人數也還在增加。但是居民們並不知道，劇院的花費在增長，票價卻沒有改變。如果劇院提高票價，忠實觀眾也許就不會再到史特拉福來，他們來此是為了看戲，而不是為了參觀景點。

解譯｜在閱讀文章之前，先要預覽題目，然後再帶著問題有針對性地閱讀文章。第 1 題是判斷正誤，第 2、3、4 題是文意理解。理解了題目要求之後，閱讀全文，依次作答。

第 1 題是判斷正誤，考的是細節，問的是根據前兩段，哪一項敘述是正確的。根據第 2 段首句內容「The rich residents of Stratford don't think that the theater increases their income.」可知，史特拉福鎮居民並不認為，劇院令他們增加了收入。選項 (D) 意為「鎮上的居民認為，莎士比亞劇團並沒有增加鎮裡的收入」，與此相符。同樣，此題也可以用排除法來解答。選項 (A) 意為「莎士比亞劇團的演員在舞臺上模仿莎士比亞」，選項 (B) 意為「史特拉福鎮的這兩個分支，關係並不和睦」，在文中都找不到相關敘述，可以排除；再根據第 1 段倒數第 2 行內容可知，鎮上的居民是以旅遊業為生，而選項 (C) 意為「從旅遊業中，鎮上的居民並沒有賺取錢」，明顯錯誤，排除。所以選 (D)。

第 2 題是文意理解，問的是根據第 3 段，可以得出什麼結論。根據第 3 段內容可知，相較於觀光者，戲迷們看戲、參觀景點，為鎮裡創造了更多的收入，與選項 (B) 相符。其他三個選項，在文中都找不到相關敘述。所以選 (B)。

第 3 題也是文意理解，問的是鎮上的居民認為，當地政府不應該給莎士比亞劇院提供經濟補貼的原因。在文中有直接的敘述，根據第 4 段首句內容可知，居民們認為劇院不需要補貼，是因為劇院有足夠多的觀眾，與選項 (D) 相符。所以選 (D)。

第 4 題同樣是文意理解，問的是作者持何種態度。選項 (A) 意為「對於雙方的觀點，作者都是贊成的」，選項 (B) 意為「對於雙方的觀點，作者是漠不關心的」，選項 (C) 意為「作者為莎士比亞劇團感到遺憾」，選項 (D) 意為「作者支持鎮上居民的觀點」。根據第 4 段內容可知，劇院的花費在增長，票價卻沒有改變，當地政府卻不給劇院提供經濟補貼。由此可知，作者是對此感到遺憾，所以選 (C)。

解答＆技巧 ┃ **01** (D)　**02** (B)　**03** (D)　**04** (C)

適用 TIP 1　適用 TIP 2　適用 TIP 3　適用 TIP 7　適用 TIP 10
適用 TIP 11　適用 TIP 12　適用 TIP 13　適用 TIP 15　適用 TIP 16

補充

as is known to all ph 眾所周知；live on ph 靠～生活；at the present time ph 目前；
agree with ph 同意；not... any more ph 不再

7,000 單字

- branch [bræntʃ] n 2 分支
- excellent [ˈɛkslənt] a 2 傑出的
- cottage [ˈkɑtɪdʒ] n 4 小屋
- resident [ˈrɛzədənt] n 5 居民
- ironic [aɪˈrɑnɪk] a 6 諷刺的
- absolute [ˈæbsəˌlut] a 4 絕對的
- castle [ˈkæsl] n 2 城堡
- palace [ˈpælɪs] n 3 宮殿

- sightseeing [ˈsaɪtˌsiɪŋ] n 4 觀光，遊覽
- attendance [əˈtɛndəns] n 5 到場，參加
- ticket [ˈtɪkɪt] n 1 票
- loyal [ˈlɔɪəl] a 4 忠誠的
- copy [ˈkɑpɪ] v 2 複製
- indifferent [ɪnˈdɪfərənt] a 5 漠不關心的
- opinion [əˈpɪnjən] n 2 看法

MEMO

DAY 5

Part 1
詞彙題
Day 5
完成 25%

Part 2
綜合測驗
Day 5
完成 50%

Part 3
文意選填
Day 5
完成 75%

Part 4
閱讀測驗
Day 5
完成 100%

Sleep should be absolutely necessary for a healthy and happy life. What should you do if you are too busy to have enough sleep? In this case, sleep quality should be more important. Here are some ways to improve your sleep quality.

1. Avoid Caffeine before You Sleep

If you drink a cup of coffee at sleeping time, it will be difficult for you to fall asleep. Caffeine not only exists in coffee, but also in chocolate, tea and soda. So you should avoid these things before going to bed.

2. Don't Drink Too Much Water after 6:00 P.M.

If you drink too much water after 6 o'clock p.m., it will seriously affect the quality of sleep. You may wake up many times to go to the bathroom during the night.

3. Keep a Stable Sleeping Time

Researches show that people who go to sleep and get up at regular times have a better sleep quality. You can sleep for eight hours or six hours a day. It's all up to you. But you should remember to go to sleep and get out of bed at a fixed time each day.

4. Reading Easy Books before Sleeping

Many people like watching TV before going to sleep. And many times they have been so absorbed in the plot and forget the time. They will stay up later than the regular bedtime. Thus sleep patterns will be disturbed. So before you go to bed, you can read some easy paper books. Reading can make you feel relaxed and quickly fall asleep.

5. Create Comfortable Sleeping Environment

Adjust the temperature in your bedroom to suit your preferences. You can install appropriate curtains to keep off the sun. Keep your pets outside the bedroom if you want to get some sleep.

01 What is the main idea of the passage?

(A) How to build a comfortable sleeping environment.

(B) Things you should do and shouldn't do before bedtime.

(C) Coffee is bad for human body.

(D) How to improve your sleep quality.

02 According to the passage, why should you not drink too much water after 6 p.m.?

(A) Drinking too much water after 6 p.m. is harmful to humans' health.

(B) If you drink too much water, you cannot get up early in the morning.

(C) Drinking too much water after 6 p.m. will cause you to wake up and go to the bathroom many times and affect your sleep quality.

(D) After drinking a lot of water, you will not want to sleep.

03 Which one of the following statements is true?

(A) When it's weekend, you should get up late to get more sleep.

(B) If you cannot sleep, you should read some detective novels.

(C) Whether it's a weekend or a workday, you should not change your sleeping time.

(D) Reading some difficulty paper books or e-books when you cannot sleep.

04 Which is not the proper way to create a comfortable sleeping environment?

(A) Adjust the temperature in your bedroom to suit your needs.

(B) Install proper curtains to block out the light.

(C) Keep your pets in your bedroom.

(D) Do not watch TV in your bedroom.

DAY
5

Part 1
詞
彙
題
Day 5
完成 25%

Part 2
綜
合
測
驗
Day 5
完成 50%

Part 3
文
意
選
填
Day 5
完成 75%

Part 4
閱
讀
測
驗
Day 5
完成 100%

中譯｜健康而幸福的生活中，睡眠是十分必要的。如果因為太忙而無法獲得充足的睡眠，該怎麼辦？在這種情況下，睡眠品質就更為重要。以下是一些改善睡眠品質的方法。

1. 睡覺前避免攝取咖啡因

如果在睡覺前喝咖啡，會難以入眠。咖啡因不只是存在於咖啡中，巧克力、茶和汽水中也都含有咖啡因。所以，睡覺前應當避免攝取這些。

2. 下午六點後不要喝太多水

下午六點以後，如果喝太多的水，會嚴重影響睡眠品質。在半夜時你可能會因為要去洗手間而醒來多次。

3. 保持穩定的睡眠時間

研究顯示，按照固定的時間入睡、起床的人，睡眠品質更好。每天睡八個小時或是六個小時，都是取決於自己。不過，你應該記得，每天都要在固定的時間入睡、起床。

4. 睡前看些輕鬆易讀的書

很多人喜歡在睡覺前看電視。很多時候，他們被電視情節深深吸引而忘記了時間，就會比平常晚睡。這樣睡眠模式就會被打亂。因此，入睡前可以看一些輕鬆易讀的紙本書。閱讀會讓你感到放鬆，快速入睡。

5. 創造舒適的睡眠環境

將臥室的溫度調到你覺得最舒適的狀態。安裝合適的窗簾，以遮擋陽光。想要好好睡一覺的時候，也不要讓寵物留在臥室裡。

解譯｜在閱讀文章之前，先要預覽題目，然後再帶著問題有針對性地閱讀文章。第 1 題是概括主旨，第 2、4 題是文意理解，第 3 題是判斷正誤。理解了題目要求之後，閱讀全文，依次作答。

第 1 題是概括主旨。文中有明確的主旨句，根據第 1 段最後一句內容「Here are some ways to improve your sleep quality.」可知，文章主旨為，改善睡眠品質的方法，與選項 (D) 相符。所以選 (D)。

第 2 題是文意理解，問的是為什麼下午六點後不要喝太多水。可以定位於第 5 段。文中說，六點以後如果喝太多的水，會嚴重影響睡眠品質。在半夜時你可能會因為要去洗手間而醒來多次，與選項 (C) 相符。所以選 (C)。

第 3 題是判斷正誤，考的是細節，問的是哪一項敘述是正確的。根據第 3 條建議可知，每天都要在固定的時間入睡、起床，與選項 (C) 相符。同樣，此題也可以用排除法來解答。選項 (A) 明顯不符合第 3 條建議，排除；根據第 4 條建議，睡前要看些輕鬆易讀的書，排除選項 (B)、(D)。所以選 (C)。

第 4 題同樣是文意理解，問的是創造舒適的睡眠環境。可以定位於最後一段。文中說，要將臥室的溫度調到你覺得舒適的狀態，安裝合適的窗簾，不要讓寵物留在臥室裡。選項 (C) 明顯是與第 3 項建議不符。所以選 (C)。

解答&技巧 | **01 (D)**　**02 (C)**　**03 (C)**　**04 (C)**

適用 TIP 1　適用 TIP 2　適用 TIP 3　適用 TIP 7　適用 TIP 10

適用 TIP 11　適用 TIP 12　適用 TIP 13　適用 TIP 14　適用 TIP 15

DAY 5

Part 1
詞
彙
題
Day 5
完成 25%

Part 2
綜
合
測
驗
Day 5
完成 50%

Part 3
文
意
選
填
Day 5
完成 75%

Part 4
閱
讀
測
驗
Day 5
完成 100%

補充

lead a... life ph 過～的生活；too... to... ph 太～而不能～；in this case ph 在這種情況下；
get out of bed ph 起床；stay up ph 熬夜

7,000 單字

- caffeine [ˈkæfim] n 6 咖啡因
- coffee [ˈkɔfɪ] n 1 咖啡
- chocolate [ˈtʃɑkəlɪt] n 2 巧克力
- soda [ˈsodə] n 1 蘇打
- bathroom [ˈbæθˌrum] n 1 洗手間
- stable [ˈstebl] a 3 穩定的
- bed [bɛd] n 1 床
- plot [plɑt] n 4 情節

- forget [fɚˈgɛt] v 1 忘記
- disturb [dɪsˈtɝb] v 4 擾亂
- paper [ˈpepɚ] n 1 紙
- curtain [ˈkɝtn] n 2 窗簾
- bedroom [ˈbɛdˌrum] n 2 臥室
- detective [dɪˈtɛktɪv] a 4 偵探的
- proper [ˈprɑpɚ] a 3 適當的

MEMO

DAY 6

When a man has put a limit on what he will do,
he has put a limit on what he can do.
— *Charles M. Schwab*

當一個人為自己將做的事設限，他也為自己能做的事設限。
──查爾斯‧施瓦布

▶ **Part 1**｜詞 彙 題

▶ **Part 2**｜綜合測驗

▶ **Part 3**｜文意選填

▶ **Part 4**｜閱讀測驗

Part 1 詞彙題 | Vocabulary Questions

01 If you become our company's sole _____, then you are entitled to sell our products in this area.

(A) yarn
(B) wreath
(C) yacht
(D) agent

中譯｜如果你成為我們公司的獨家代理商，那麼你就有權在這個地區銷售我們的產品。

解說｜四個選項皆為名詞。依據題意，應該是「公司的獨家代理商」，選項 (D) agent 表示「代理商」，而 sole agent 表示「獨家代理商」，符合題意，是正確選項。

解答&技巧｜**(D)** 適用 TIP 2　適用 TIP 4

02 She likes rainy days, so it is _____ for her to wander in the rain with an umbrella.

(A) worthy
(B) agreeable
(C) accessory
(D) amiable

中譯｜她喜歡下雨天，所以打著傘在雨中漫步對她來說是令人愉快的。

解說｜四個選項皆為形容詞。依據題意，應該是「在雨中漫步是令人愉快的」，選項 (B) agreeable 表示「令人愉快的」，符合題意。

解答&技巧｜**(B)** 適用 TIP 1　適用 TIP 4

03 Several bank robberies have happened recently, so the bank is _____ to the danger.

(A) analytical
(B) antibiotic
(C) applicable
(D) alert

中譯｜最近發生了多起銀行盜竊案，所以銀行對這種危險有警覺。

解說｜四個選項皆為形容詞。依據題意，應該是「對這種危險有警覺」，選項 (D) alert 表示「警覺的」，符合題意，其他三個選項都不符合題意。

解答&技巧｜**(D)** 適用 TIP 1　適用 TIP 4

04 Although this man is forty years old, he looks still full of _____ vigor.

(A) youthful   (B) approximate

(C) authentic   (D) biological

中譯｜儘管這個人四十歲了，但他看起來仍然充滿了年輕活力。

解說｜四個選項皆為形容詞。依據題意，應該是「充滿了年輕活力」，選項 (A) youthful 表示「年輕的」，而 youthful vigor 表示「年輕活力」，符合題意。

解答＆技巧｜**(A)** 適用 TIP 2　適用 TIP 4

補充
years old ph ～歲

7,000 單字
- vigor [ˋvɪgɚ] n 5 活力
- youthful [ˋjuθfəl] a 4 年輕的
- approximate [əˋprɑksəmɪt] a 6 大概的
- authentic [ɔˋθɛntɪk] a 6 真正的
- biological [͵baɪəˋlɑdʒɪkl] a 6 生物的

---

05 Tomorrow will be the couple's wedding _____, which shows that they have been married for one year.

(A) binoculars   (B) blunder

(C) anniversary   (D) bout

中譯｜明天是這對夫婦的結婚周年紀念日，這說明他們已經結婚一年了。

解說｜四個選項皆為名詞。依據題意，應該是「結婚周年紀念日」，選項 (C) anniversary 表示「周年紀念日」，符合題意，其他三個選項都不符合題意。

解答＆技巧｜**(C)** 適用 TIP 1　適用 TIP 4

補充
wedding anniversary ph 結婚周年紀念日

7,000 單字
- tomorrow [təˋmɔro] n 1 明天
- binoculars [bɪˋnɑkjələs] n 6 雙筒望遠鏡
- blunder [ˋblʌndɚ] n 6 大錯
- anniversary [͵ænəˋvɝsərɪ] n 4 周年紀念日
- bout [baʊt] n 6 回合

---

06 My little niece always throws the glasses to the ground, which _____ me a lot.

(A) caresses   (B) caters

(C) annoys   (D) civilizes

中譯｜我的小姪女總是把杯子摔到地上，這讓我感到很厭煩。

解說｜四個選項皆為動詞。依據題意，應該是「讓我感到很厭煩」，選項 (C) annoys 表示「使煩惱」，符合題意，是正確選項。

解答＆技巧｜**(C)** 適用 TIP 3　適用 TIP 4

補充
throw sth. to the ground ph 朝地面摔某物

7,000 單字
- niece [nis] n 2 姪女
- caress [kəˋrɛs] v 6 愛撫
- cater [ˋketɚ] v 6 投合
- annoy [əˋnɔɪ] v 4 惹惱，令人不快（厭煩）
- civilize [ˋsɪvə͵laɪz] v 6 使文明

DAY
6

Part 1
詞
彙
題
Day 6
完成 25%

Part 2
綜
合
測
驗
Day 6
完成 50%

Part 3
文
意
選
填
Day 6
完成 75%

Part 4
閱
讀
測
驗
Day 6
完成 100%

07 Employees who travel on business also enjoy travel _____ except fixed salary.

(A) chuckle   (B) allowance

(C) clarity   (D) clearance

> **補充**
> on business ph 出差
>
> **7,000 單字**
> • fixed [fɪkst] a 4 固定的
> • chuckle [ˋtʃʌkl̩] n 6 輕笑
> • allowance [əˋlaʊəns] n 4 津貼
> • clarity [ˋklærətɪ] n 6 清楚
> • clearance [ˋklɪrəns] n 6 清除

中譯 | 除了固定薪資外，出差的員工還享有出差津貼。

解說 | 四個選項皆為名詞。依據題意，應該是「享有出差津貼」，選項 (B) allowance 表示「津貼」，而 travel allowance 表示「出差津貼」，符合題意。

解答&技巧 | **(B)** 適用 TIP 2   適用 TIP 4

---

08 He learns to take photographs only on weekends, so he is a(an) _____ photographer.

(A) coherent   (B) amateur

(C) colloquial   (D) competent

> **補充**
> on weekends ph 每逢週末
>
> **7,000 單字**
> • photograph [ˋfotəˏgræf] n 2 照片
> • coherent [koˋhɪrənt] a 6 連貫的
> • amateur [ˋæməˏtʃʊr] a 4 業餘的
> • colloquial [kəˋlokwɪəl] a 6 口語的
> • competent [ˋkɑmpətənt] a 6 勝任的

中譯 | 他只在週末學習攝影，所以他是一名業餘攝影師。

解說 | 四個選項皆為形容詞。依據題意，應該是「業餘攝影師」，選項 (B) amateur 表示「業餘的」，符合題意，是正確答案。

解答&技巧 | **(B)** 適用 TIP 1   適用 TIP 4

---

09 An honest person is faithful to his promise. Once he makes a _____, he will not go back on his own word.

【96年指考英文】

(A) prescription   (B) commitment

(C) frustration   (D) transcript

> **補充**
> be faithful to ph 對～忠誠
> make a commitment ph 承諾
>
> **7,000 單字**
> • an [æn] art 1 一
> • prescription [prɪˋskrɪpʃən] n 6 處方
> • commitment [kəˋmɪtmənt] n 6 承諾
> • frustration [ˏfrʌsˋtreʃən] n 4 挫折
> • transcript [ˋtrænˏskrɪpt] n 6 成績單

中譯 | 一個誠實的人會忠於自己的諾言。一旦他許下承諾，就不會食言。

解說 | 四個選項皆為名詞。依據題意，應該是「許下承諾」，選項 (B) commitment 表示「承諾」，符合題意，其他三個選項都不符合題意。

解答&技巧 | **(B)** 適用 TIP 3   適用 TIP 4

10 After sending many _____ letters, he was finally hired by a foreign insurance company.

(A) complement   (B) complexion
(C) application   (D) deficiency

中譯｜在寄出很多求職信之後，他終於被一家外商保險公司錄用了。

解說｜四個選項皆為名詞。依據題意，應該是「寄出很多求職信」，選項 (C) application 表示「申請」，而 application letter 表示「求職信」，符合題意。

解答＆技巧｜**(C)** 適用 TIP 2　適用 TIP 4

補充
foreign company ph 外商公司

7,000 單字
- insurance [ɪnˈʃʊrəns] n 4 保險
- complement [ˈkɑmpləmənt] n 6 補足
- complexion [kəmˈplɛkʃən] n 6 膚色
- application [ˌæpləˈkeʃən] n 4 申請
- deficiency [dɪˈfɪʃənsɪ] n 6 缺陷

11 You could imitate foreigners' pronunciation and _____ when you are a beginner in English.

(A) defect   (B) density
(C) intonation   (D) ebb

中譯｜初學英語時，你可以模仿外國人的發音和語調。

解說｜四個選項皆為名詞。依據題意，應該是「模仿外國人的發音和語調」，選項 (C) intonation 表示「語調」，符合題意，其他三個選項都不符合題意。

解答＆技巧｜**(C)** 適用 TIP 1　適用 TIP 4

補充
beginner in English ph 英語初學者

7,000 單字
- pronunciation [prəˌnʌnsɪˈeʃən] n 4 發音
- defect [dɪˈfɛkt] n 6 缺點
- density [ˈdɛnsətɪ] n 6 密度
- intonation [ˌɪntoˈneʃən] n 4 語調
- ebb [ɛb] n 6 衰退

12 This book has been translated into several languages for _____ next month, and by then the readers could buy it in the bookstore.

(A) ecstasy   (B) ecology
(C) emigrant   (D) publication

中譯｜這本書已經被翻譯成好幾種語言，準備下個月出版，到時候讀者就可以到書店購買了。

解說｜四個選項皆為名詞。依據題意，應該是「準備下個月出版」，選項 (D) publication 表示「出版」，符合題意，其他三個選項都不符合題意。

解答＆技巧｜**(D)** 適用 TIP 1　適用 TIP 4

補充
by then ph 到那時候

7,000 單字
- this [ðɪs] pron 1 這個
- ecstasy [ˈɛkstəsɪ] n 6 狂喜
- ecology [ɪˈkɑlədʒɪ] n 6 生態（學）
- emigrant [ˈɛməgrənt] n 6 移民
- publication [ˌpʌblɪˈkeʃən] n 4 出版

DAY 6

Part 1 詞彙題　Day 6 完成 25%
Part 2 綜合測驗　Day 6 完成 50%
Part 3 文意選填　Day 6 完成 75%
Part 4 閱讀測驗　Day 6 完成 100%

13 In consideration of your extensive experience in marketing, we have decided to _____ you as the new sales manager.

(A) emigrate
(B) enrich
(C) appoint
(D) erode

補充
sales manager ph 業務經理
7,000 單字
• extensive [ɪkˋstɛnsɪv] a 5 廣泛的
• emigrate [ˋɛmə͵gret] v 6 移民
• enrich [ɪnˋrɪtʃ] v 6 使富足
• appoint [əˋpɔɪnt] v 4 任命
• erode [ɪˋrod] v 6 腐蝕

中譯｜考慮到你在行銷方面的豐富經驗，我們已經決定任命你為新的業務經理。

解說｜四個選項皆為動詞。依據題意，應該是「決定任命你為新的業務經理」，選項 (C) appoint 表示「任命」，符合題意，其他三個選項都不符合題意。

解答＆技巧｜**(C)** 適用 TIP 1　適用 TIP 4

---

14 We have been aware of the truth of the kidnapping, so you should feel _____ for telling lies.

(A) exotic
(B) exquisite
(C) fabulous
(D) ashamed

補充
feel ashamed for
ph 為～感到羞愧
7,000 單字
• kidnapping [ˋkɪdnæpɪŋ] n 6 綁架
• exotic [ɛgˋzatɪk] a 6 異國的
• exquisite [ˋɛkskwɪzɪt] a 6 精緻的
• fabulous [ˋfæbjələs] a 6 絕佳的
• ashamed [əˋʃemd] a 4 慚愧的

中譯｜我們已經了解了這起綁架案的真相，所以你應該為你說的這些謊話感到羞愧。

解說｜四個選項皆為形容詞。依據題意，應該是「為謊話感到羞愧」，選項 (D) ashamed 表示「羞愧的」，符合題意，是正確選項。

解答＆技巧｜**(D)** 適用 TIP 1　適用 TIP 4

---

15 I am totally unaware of the knowledge of computer programming, so I am just a _____.

(A) layman
(B) famine
(C) fertility
(D) grocer

補充
be unaware of ph 不知道
7,000 單字
• programming [ˋprogræmɪŋ]
　n 3 程式設計
• layman [ˋlemən] n 6 外行人
• famine [ˋfæmɪn] n 6 饑荒
• fertility [fɝˋtɪlətɪ] n 6 肥沃
• grocer [ˋgrosɚ] n 6 食品雜貨商

中譯｜我完全不懂電腦程式設計方面的知識，所以我只是一個外行人。

解說｜四個選項皆為名詞。依據題意，應該是「是一個外行人」，選項 (A) layman 表示「外行人」，符合題意，其他三個選項都不符合題意。

解答＆技巧｜**(A)** 適用 TIP 1　適用 TIP 4

16 I will forgive you if you can give me _____ that things like this will never happen again.

(A) guerrilla   (B) habitat

(C) assurance   (D) hacker

補充
like this ph 像這樣

7,000 單字
• forgive [fəˋgɪv] v 2 原諒
• guerrilla [gəˋrɪlə] n 6 游擊隊員
• habitat [ˋhæbə‚tæt] n 6 棲息地
• assurance [əˋʃʊrəns] n 4 保證
• hacker [ˋhækə] n 6 電腦駭客

中譯｜如果你能向我保證，這類事情永遠不會再發生，我就原諒你。

解說｜四個選項皆為名詞。依據題意，應該是「向我保證」，選項 (C) assurance 表示「保證」，符合題意，是正確選項。

解答＆技巧｜**(C)** 適用 TIP 1　適用 TIP 4

---

17 You should put the mutton in the _____ to keep it fresh on such hot summer days.

(A) hereafter   (B) freezer

(C) hospitality   (D) humanitarian

補充
keep fresh ph 保鮮

7,000 單字
• mutton [ˋmʌtn] n 5 老羊肉
• hereafter [hɪrˋæftə] n 6 今後
• freezer [ˋfrizə] n 2 冷凍庫
• hospitality [‚hɑspɪˋtælətɪ] n 6 好客
• humanitarian [hju‚mænəˋtɛrɪən] n 6 人道主義者

中譯｜在這樣炎熱的夏天，你應該把羊肉放進冷凍庫裡保鮮。

解說｜四個選項皆為名詞。依據題意，應該是「把羊肉放進冷凍庫裡保鮮」，選項 (B) freezer 表示「冷凍庫」，符合題意，其他三個選項都不符合題意。

解答＆技巧｜**(B)** 適用 TIP 3　適用 TIP 4

---

18 David likes to see science fiction films, so these science fiction video disks have much _____ for him.

(A) hygiene   (B) hypocrisy

(C) attraction   (D) illusion

補充
video disk ph 影碟

7,000 單字
• fiction [ˋfɪkʃən] n 4 虛構
• hygiene [ˋhaɪdʒin] n 6 衛生
• hypocrisy [hɪˋpɑkrəsɪ] n 6 虛偽
• attraction [əˋtrækʃən] n 4 吸引力
• illusion [ɪˋljuʒən] n 6 幻覺

中譯｜大衛喜歡看科幻電影，所以這些科幻影碟對他來說具有很大的吸引力。

解說｜四個選項皆為名詞。依據題意，應該是「對他來說具有很大的吸引力」，選項 (C) attraction 表示「吸引力」，符合題意，其他三個選項都不符合題意。

解答＆技巧｜**(C)** 適用 TIP 3　適用 TIP 4

DAY 6

Part 1
詞彙題
Day 6
完成 25%

Part 2
綜合測驗
Day 6
完成 50%

Part 3
文意選填
Day 6
完成 75%

Part 4
閱讀測驗
Day 6
完成 100%

19 Ann enjoyed going to the flower market. She believed that the ＿＿＿＿ of flowers refreshed her mind.

【97年學測英文】

(A) installment　　　　(B) dominance

(C) appliance　　　　(D) fragrance

補充
flower market ph 花市

7,000 單字
- the [ðə] art 1 這
- installment [ɪnˋstɔlmənt] n 4 安裝
- dominance [ˋdɑmənəns] n 6 優勢
- appliance [əˋplaɪəns] n 4 器具
- fragrance [ˋfregrəns] n 4 香味

中譯｜安喜歡去花卉市場，她認為花香能夠使她重新提起精神。

解說｜四個選項皆為名詞。依據題意，應該是「花香能夠使她重新提起精神」，選項 (D) fragrance 表示「香味」，符合題意，其他三個選項都不符合題意。

解答＆技巧｜**(D)**　適用 TIP 1　適用 TIP 4

---

20 When the reporter asked questions about extramarital affairs, the artist kept in ＿＿＿＿ silence.

(A) integrated　　　　(B) legislative

(C) awkward　　　　(D) mellow

補充
extramarital affair ph 婚外情

7,000 單字
- extramarital [ˌɛkstrəˋmærɪt] a 6 婚外的
- integrated [ˋɪntəˌgretɪd] a 6 整合的
- legislative [ˋlɛdʒɪsˌletɪv] a 6 立法的
- awkward [ˋɔkwəd] a 4 尷尬的
- mellow [ˋmɛlo] a 6 （聲音）圓潤的

中譯｜當記者問到有關婚外情的問題時，那位藝人尷尬地保持了沉默。

解說｜本題是一個時間副詞子句。依據題意，應該是「藝人尷尬地保持了沉默」，選項 (C) awkward 表示「尷尬的」，符合題意，是正確選項。

解答＆技巧｜**(C)**　適用 TIP 3　適用 TIP 4

---

21 For the convenience of chemotherapy, the girl shaved all her hair off and became ＿＿＿＿.

(A) bald　　　　(B) mischievous

(C) miraculous　　　　(D) mute

補充
for the convenience of ph 為了～的方便

7,000 單字
- chemotherapy [ˌkɛmoˋθɛrəpɪ] n 6 化學療法
- bald [bɔld] a 4 禿頭的
- mischievous [ˋmɪstʃɪvəs] a 6 淘氣的
- miraculous [mɪˋrækjələs] a 6 不可思議的
- mute [mjut] a 6 啞的

中譯｜為了方便化療，這個女孩剃光了所有頭髮，變成了光頭。

解說｜四個選項皆為形容詞。依據題意，應該是「變成了光頭」，選項 (A) bald 表示「禿頭的」，符合題意，其他三個選項都不符合題意。

解答＆技巧｜**(A)**　適用 TIP 3　適用 TIP 4

22 We will go _____ if we are not able to recover the economic losses by next month.

(A) narrative   (B) naval

(C) bankrupt   (D) operational

中譯｜如果到下個月我們還無法彌補經濟損失，我們將面臨破產。

解說｜四個選項皆為形容詞。依據題意，應該是「面臨破產」，選項 (C) bankrupt 表示「破產的」，而 go bankrupt 表示「破產」，符合題意。

解答＆技巧｜**(C)**　適用 TIP 2　適用 TIP 4

補充
go bankrupt ph 破產

7,000 單字
- by [baɪ] prep **1** 不遲於
- narrative [ˈnærətɪv] a **6** 敘述的
- naval [ˈnevl̩] a **6** 海軍的
- bankrupt [ˈbæŋkrʌpt] a **4** 破產的
- operational [ˌɑpəˈreʃən] a **6** 操作的

---

23 The little boy's got sand in his eyes, so he is _____ rapidly.

(A) oppressing   (B) outfitting

(C) blinking   (D) overlapping

中譯｜小男孩的眼睛裡進了沙子，所以他一直在快速地眨眼睛。

解說｜四個選項皆為動詞。依據題意，應該是「快速地眨眼睛」，選項 (C) blinking 表示「眨眼睛」，符合題意，其他三個選項都不符合題意。

解答＆技巧｜**(C)**　適用 TIP 1　適用 TIP 4

補充
in the eye ph 在眼裡

7,000 單字
- rapidly [ˈræpɪdlɪ] ad **2** 快速地
- oppress [əˈprɛs] v **6** 壓迫
- outfit [ˈaʊt.fɪt] v **6** 配備
- blink [blɪŋk] v **4** 眨眼
- overlap [ˌovɚˈlæp] v **6** 重疊

---

24 You can boil the corn in the pot and also _____ it on the grill.

(A) broil   (B) ponder

(C) populate   (D) precede

中譯｜你可以把玉米放到鍋裡煮，也可以把它放到烤架上燒烤。

解說｜四個選項皆為動詞。依據題意，應該是「放到烤架上燒烤」，選項 (A) broil 表示「燒烤」，符合題意，是正確選項。

解答＆技巧｜**(A)**　適用 TIP 1　適用 TIP 4

補充
and also ph 而且

7,000 單字
- grill [grɪl] n **6** 烤架
- broil [brɔɪl] v **4** 烤
- ponder [ˈpɑndɚ] v **6** 考慮
- populate [ˈpɑpjə.let] v **6** 居住於
- precede [prɪˈsid] v **6** 領先

DAY 6

Part 1
詞彙題
Day 6
完成 25%

Part 2
綜合測驗
Day 6
完成 50%

Part 3
文意選填
Day 6
完成 75%

Part 4
閱讀測驗
Day 6
完成 100%

Part 2 綜合測驗 | Comprehensive Questions

 97 年學測英文

What is so special about green tea? The Chinese and Indians **01** it for at least 4,000 years to treat everything from headache to depression. Researchers at Purdue University recently concluded that a compound in green tea **02** the growth of cancer cells. Green tea is also helpful **03** infection and damaged immune function. The secret power of green tea is its richness in a powerful antioxidant.

Green tea and black tea come from the same plant. Their **04** is in the processing. Green tea is dried but not fermented, and this shorter processing gives it a lighter flavor than black tea. It also helps retain the tea's beneficial chemicals. That is **05** green tea is so good for health. The only reported negative effect of drinking green tea is a possible allergic reaction and insomnia due to the caffeine it contains.

01 _____ (A) would use   (B) are using
(C) had used   (D) have been using

02 _____ (A) looks after   (B) slows down
(C) takes over   (D) turns out

03 _____ (A) for   (B) from
(C) at   (D) inside

04 _____ (A) weight   (B) purpose
(C) difference   (D) structure

05 _____ (A) whether   (B) whenever
(C) what   (D) why

中譯｜綠茶有什麼特殊之處呢？中國人和印度人在四千多年間一直使用綠茶來治療各種疾病，包括頭痛和抑鬱症在內。美國普渡大學的研究人員近期指出，綠茶裡含有的一種化合物能夠減緩癌細胞的生長。綠茶也有助於治療傳染病和受損的免疫功能。綠茶的祕密威力在於它富含很強的抗氧化劑。

綠茶和紅茶出產於同一種植物。它們的不同之處在於加工。綠茶經過乾燥處理，但沒有被發酵，加工時間較短，口味要比紅茶更為清淡，也有利於保留茶中的有益化學物質。這就是綠茶有益於健康的原因。唯一報導過的有關飲用綠茶的負面效果，是綠茶中含有的咖啡因可能會引起過敏反應和失眠。

解說｜本篇短文主要介紹了綠茶的功用以及加工。第 1 題考時態的用法。根據上下文的內容，空格後面有時間副詞 for at least 4,000 years，表示持續到現在的時間，所以動詞 use 要用現在完成進行式，即 have been using，所以正確選擇為 (D)。第 2 題要選擇合適的動詞片語。依據題意，綠茶對身體有益，應該是能夠減緩癌細胞的生長，而「減緩」可以表達為 slows down，所以最符合題意的選項是 (B)。第 3 題考固定片語的用法。「有益於」可以表達為 be helpful for，要用介系詞 for，即正確選項是 (A)。第 4 題空格後面的內容說的是紅茶和綠茶的不同之處，所以空格處應該用 difference 表示「不同」，只有選項 (C) 符合題意。第 5 題根據所學的知識，「就是～的原因」可以表達為 that is why，要用 why 來引導，所以選 (D)。

解答＆技巧｜ 01 (D) 02 (B) 03 (A) 04 (C) 05 (D)

適用 TIP 1　適用 TIP 2　適用 TIP 4　適用 TIP 11

補充

Chinese n 中國人；Indian n 印度人；Purdue University ph 美國普渡大學；richness n 富裕；antioxidant n 抗氧化劑

7,000 單字

- tea [ti] n 1 茶
- year [jɪr] n 1 年
- treat [trit] v 2 治療
- conclude [kən`klud] v 3 推斷
- cancer [`kænsɚ] n 2 癌症
- infection [ɪn`fɛkʃən] n 4 感染
- immune [ɪ`mjun] a 6 免疫的
- secret [`sikrɪt] n 2 祕密

- plant [plænt] n 1 植物
- flavor [`flevɚ] n 3 味道
- beneficial [ˌbɛnə`fɪʃəl] a 5 有益的
- negative [`nɛɡətɪv] a 2 負的
- allergic [ə`lɝdʒɪk] a 5 對～過敏的
- slow [slo] v 1 放慢
- difference [`dɪfərəns] n 2 不同

DAY 6

Part 1
詞彙題
Day 6
完成 25%

Part 2
綜合測驗
Day 6
完成 50%

Part 3
文意選填
Day 6
完成 75%

Part 4
閱讀測驗
Day 6
完成 100%

According to the survey, nearly every country has suffered from inflation, which is an __01__ condition that prices for consumer goods increase, but the value of money decreases.

There are several reasons for inflation. The major and most important reason is the excessive government spending. To be __02__, if the government intends to finance a war or carry out some social __03__, it would spend more money than it has received through taxes and other revenues, which could create a deficit. And in order to offset this deficit, the Treasury Department could __04__ more paper money to expand the money supply, which is used to meet the debts of government and will cause the value of the dollar to decrease.

Another reason for inflation may occur when the money supply increases faster than the supply of goods. If people have more money, they will spend more money on those popular goods like televisions and computers, which can result in a shortage. And then the industry will produce more goods __05__ higher prices to satisfy demand.

01 _____ (A) social   (B) economic
         (C) environmental   (D) familiar

02 _____ (A) automatic   (B) excessive
         (C) percussive   (D) specific

03 _____ (A) programs   (B) statistics
         (C) welfare   (D) capital

04 _____ (A) invent   (B) control
         (C) issue   (D) employ

05 _____ (A) of   (B) at
         (C) with   (D) in

DAY
6

Part 1
詞
彙
題
Day 6
完成 25%

Part 2
綜
合
測
驗
Day 6
完成 50%

Part 3
文
意
選
填
Day 6
完成 75%

Part 4
閱
讀
測
驗
Day 6
完成 100%

中譯｜據調查，幾乎每一個國家都經歷過通貨膨脹。通貨膨脹是一種日用消費品的價格提高，但是貨幣價值卻有所降低的經濟狀況。

通貨膨脹有幾種原因，最主要也是最重要的原因是由於政府過度支出。具體來說，如果政府打算提供經費在戰爭或是開展某些社會事業上，就會花費更多的錢，超過了透過稅收或是其他收益獲得的錢，導致財政赤字。為了補償這種赤字，財政部門會發行更多的紙幣來擴大貨幣供給，用於滿足政府債務，也會導致美元貶值。

當貨幣供給的增長速率超過貨物供需時，也會導致通貨膨脹。如果人們擁有更多的錢，他們將會花費更多的錢來購買那些人氣商品，例如電視機和電腦，這會導致商品短缺。然後產業就會生產更多價位更高的商品以滿足需求。

解說｜本篇短文的主旨是「通貨膨脹」，答題時可以將有關通貨膨脹和經濟發展的知識考慮在內。第 1 題依據題意可知，通貨膨脹是一種經濟狀況，要用 economic 表示「經濟的」，所以正確選擇為 (B)。第 2 題空格後面的內容是前面內容的具體說明，而四個選項中，只有 specific 能夠與 to be 搭配構成 to be specific 表示「具體地說」，所以最符合題意的選項是 (D)。第 3 題考名詞片語的用法。依據題意，「社會事業」可以表達為 social programs，此處應選擇 programs，即正確選項是 (A)。第 4 題的四個選項都是動詞。根據上下文的內容可知，發行貨幣要用動詞 issue 來表示「發行」，只有選項 (C) 符合題意。第 5 題考介系詞片語的用法。根據所學的知識，「以某種價格」可以表達為 at... price，要用介系詞 at，所以選 (B)。

解答 & 技巧｜ 01 **(B)** 02 **(D)** 03 **(A)** 04 **(C)** 05 **(B)**

適用 TIP 1　適用 TIP 2　適用 TIP 7　適用 TIP 11

補充

spending n 花費；carry out ph 實行；Treasury Department ph 財政部；offset v 補償；result in ph 導致

7,000 單字

- every [ˈɛvrɪ] a 1 每一的
- inflation [ɪnˈfleʃən] n 4 通貨膨脹
- condition [kənˈdɪʃən] n 3 狀況
- consumer [kənˈsjumɚ] n 4 消費者
- decrease [ˈdikris] n 4 減少
- excessive [ɪkˈsɛsɪv] a 6 過多的
- intend [ɪnˈtɛnd] v 4 打算
- finance [faɪˈnæns] v 4 供給經費

- expand [ɪkˈspænd] v 4 擴大
- debt [dɛt] n 2 債務
- supply [səˈplaɪ] n 2 供給
- shortage [ˈʃɔrtɪdʒ] n 5 短缺
- environmental [ɪnˌvaɪrənˈmɛntl] a 3 環境的
- specific [spɪˈsɪfɪk] a 3 特殊的
- welfare [ˈwɛlˌfɛr] n 4 福利

When you buy fewer goods but with the same amount of money, inflation is the problem because __01__ the period of inflation, there is usually a rise in the price of goods and service. Thus your money could buy less.

Generally speaking, people who live on a fixed income suffer from the inflation most. For example, retired workers and elderly people could face serious problems in __02__ their incomes to meet their needs during the inflation because retirement income or any __03__ income usually does not rise as fast as the prices, and then most of the retired people must cut their spending to __04__ up with the rising prices.

On the other hand, though people who are working have higher incomes, they may also suffer from the inflation, for the cost of living goes up, too. Even if they earn the same amount of money, they are not able to buy the same amount of goods and services. Therefore, they must earn more money to keep up their __05__ of living.

01 _____ (A) on   (B) during
          (C) with   (D) upon

02 _____ (A) consuming   (B) demanding
          (C) increasing   (D) spending

03 _____ (A) fixed   (B) maintained
          (C) described   (D) displayed

04 _____ (A) prolong   (B) count
          (C) stretch   (D) keep

05 _____ (A) ratio   (B) standard
          (C) percentage   (D) proportion

中譯｜當你用同樣的錢卻買到了更少的商品時，通貨膨脹就是問題所在，因為在通貨膨脹時期，商品和服務的價格通常會上漲，於是你的錢就會買到更少的東西。

通常來說，靠固定薪資生活的人是通貨膨脹的最大受害者。例如，在通貨膨脹期間，退休員工和老年人要想增加收入來滿足他們的需求，可能會有困難，因為退休金或是其他任何的固定收入通常沒有物價增加的快，那麼大多數的退休人員就必須縮減開支來跟上物價的上漲。

另一方面，儘管正在工作的人有著更高的收入，但是他們也會受通貨膨脹之苦，因為生活費也會增加。即使他們賺到了同樣的錢，卻不能夠買到同樣的商品和服務。因此，他們必須賺更多的錢來維持他們的生活水準。

解說｜本篇短文講述了導致通貨膨脹的原因以及通貨膨脹對人們的生活造成的影響。第 1 題要選擇合適的介系詞。依據題意，「在～期間」可以表達為 during the period of，要用介系詞 during，所以正確選擇為 (B)。第 2 題根據上下文的內容可知，要想滿足需求，就需要增加收入，應該用動詞 increase 表示「增加」，所以最符合題意的選項是 (C)。第 3 題依據題意可知，本段講述的是固定薪資與通貨膨脹之間的關係，所以此處應該用 fixed 表示「固定的」，即正確選項是 (A)。第 4 題的四個選項都是動詞。根據所學的知識，keep up 意思是「保持」，符合題意，所以最佳選項是 (D)。第 5 題考名詞片語的用法。依據題意，「生活標準」應該表達為 standard of living，所以本題選 (B)。

解答＆技巧｜ 01 **(B)**　02 **(C)**　03 **(A)**　04 **(D)**　05 **(B)**

適用 TIP 1　適用 TIP 2　適用 TIP 4　適用 TIP 11

補充

fixed ⓐ 固定的；retired ⓐ 退休的；retirement ⓝ 退休；suffer from ⓟⓗ 遭受；living ⓝ 生計

7,000 單字

- buy [baɪ] ⓥ 1 買
- rise [raɪz] ⓝ 1 上升
- price [praɪs] ⓝ 1 價格
- face [fes] ⓥ 1 面對
- serious [ˈsɪrɪəs] ⓐ 2 嚴重的
- fast [fæst] ⓐⓓ 1 快速地
- though [ðo] ⓒⓞⓝⓙ 1 儘管
- cost [kɔst] ⓝ 1 花費
- too [tu] ⓐⓓ 1 也
- keep [kip] ⓥ 1 保持
- during [ˈdjurɪŋ] prep 1 在～期間
- maintain [menˈten] ⓥ 2 維持
- display [dɪˈsple] ⓥ 2 顯示
- ratio [ˈreʃo] ⓝ 5 比率
- percentage [pəˈsɛntɪdʒ] ⓝ 4 百分比

DAY 6

Part 1
詞彙題
Day 6
完成 25%

Part 2
綜合測驗
Day 6
完成 50%

Part 3
文意選填
Day 6
完成 75%

Part 4
閱讀測驗
Day 6
完成 100%

Although many blind people are __01__ using Braille, thousands of other blind people still find it difficult to learn the system. Therefore, they are __02__ off from the world of books and newspapers and have to rely on their families or friends to read to them.

However, a new machine has been designed to provide __03__ to the sightless, which is a major breakthrough in history. It is said that a camera in the machine could scan any page in a book, interpret the print into sounds, and then deliver them __04__ to the listener. By pressing the appropriate buttons on the keyboard, a blind person can read any book or document.

At present, this machine is very expensive, but the scientists are trying to invent a smaller but improved version that has a lower price. Thus more blind people could __05__ to buy one. Moreover, many manufacturers also have great interest in this machine, and they believe it will sell well in the future market.

01 _____   (A) heavenly   (B) skillfully
              (C) culturally   (D) commercially

02 _____   (A) dwell   (B) press
              (C) urge   (D) shut

03 _____   (A) aid   (B) execution
              (C) process   (D) expression

04 _____   (A) visually   (B) mentally
              (C) orally   (D) physically

05 _____   (A) stride   (B) afford
              (C) haul   (D) trail

中譯｜ 儘管很多盲人很熟練地使用布萊葉點字法，但是仍然有其他成千上萬的盲人覺得這種系統很難學習。因此，他們與書本和報紙的聯繫被切斷了，不得不依靠家人或朋友來為他們閱讀。

然而，有一種新機器已經設計出來了，專為盲人提供幫助，是歷史上的一個突破。據說，機器裡的一個攝影機能夠對一本書裡的任何一頁進行掃描，把印刷的內容轉成聲音，然後以口語方式傳達給聽者。透過按壓鍵盤上對應的按鈕，盲人就能夠閱讀任何書籍或是文件。

目前，這種機器非常昂貴，不過科學家們正試圖發明一種更小、更先進，而價格更低的版本，這樣更多的盲人就能夠買得起一台機器。此外，很多製造商也對這種機器非常感興趣，他們相信它在未來的市場中會賣得很好。

解說｜ 本篇短文介紹了一種專為盲人設計發明的閱讀機器。第 1 題要選擇合適的副詞來修飾動詞 using。將四個選項一一代入空格，只有 skillfully 符合題意，所以正確選擇為 (B)。第 2 題要選擇能夠與副詞 off 搭配使用的被動式動詞。選項中只有 shut 為被動式且能夠與 off 連用構成 shut off 表示「使隔絕」，所以最符合題意的選項是 (D)。第 3 題依據題意可知，新機器的發明是為了幫助盲人，所以為盲人提供的是幫助，名詞 aid 表示「幫助」，即正確選項是 (A)。第 4 題根據上下文的內容可知，這種機器是可以口頭發音的，而 orally 表示「口頭地」，所以選項 (C) 符合題意。第 5 題的四個選項都是動詞。依據題意，應該是買得起一台機器，可以用 afford to 來表達，所以選 (B)。

解答＆技巧｜ 01 (B)　02 (D)　03 (A)　04 (C)　05 (B)

適用 TIP 1　適用 TIP 2　適用 TIP 5　適用 TIP 7　適用 TIP 11

補充

Braille ⓝ 布萊葉盲人點字法；sightless ⓐ 失明的；improved ⓐ 改善的；blind people ⓟⓗ 盲人；sell well ⓟⓗ 暢銷

7,000 單字

- blind [blaɪnd] ⓐ ② 失明的
- thousand [ˈθaʊznd] ⓝ ① 一千
- still [stɪl] ⓐⓓ ① 仍然
- rely [rɪˋlaɪ] ⓥ ③ 依靠
- breakthrough [ˈbrek͵θru] ⓝ ⑥ 突破
- scan [skæn] ⓥ ⑤ 掃描
- interpret [ɪnˋtɝprɪt] ⓥ ④ 翻譯
- appropriate [əˋproprɪət] ⓐ ④ 合適的

- button [ˋbʌtn̩] ⓝ ② 按鈕
- keyboard [ˈki͵bord] ⓝ ③ 鍵盤
- document [ˈdɑkjəmənt] ⓝ ⑤ 文件
- dwell [dwɛl] ⓥ ⑤ 居住
- urge [ɝdʒ] ⓥ ④ 督促
- haul [hɔl] ⓥ ⑤ 拖拉
- trail [trel] ⓥ ③ 追蹤

DAY
6

Part 1
詞彙題
Day 6
完成 25%

Part 2
綜合測驗
Day 6
完成 50%

Part 3
文意選填
Day 6
完成 75%

Part 4
閱讀測驗
Day 6
完成 100%

5 ▶ 97 年學測英文

A wise woman traveling in the mountains found a precious stone. The next day she met another traveler who was hungry. The wise woman generously opened her bag to __01__ her food with the traveler. When the hungry traveler saw the precious stone, he asked her to give it to him. The woman did __02__ without hesitation. The traveler left, rejoicing. If he sold the stone, he thought, he __03__ enough money for the rest of his life. But in a few days he came back to find the woman. When he found her, he said, "I know how valuable this stone is, but I'm giving it back to you, __04__ that you can give me something even more precious. You gave me the stone without asking for anything __05__. Please teach me what you have in your heart that makes you so generous."

01 _____
(A) give
(B) bring
(C) share
(D) earn

02 _____
(A) so
(B) such
(C) as
(D) thus

03 _____
(A) had
(B) had had
(C) would have
(D) would have had

04 _____
(A) hope
(B) hoping
(C) hoped
(D) to hope

05 _____
(A) on leave
(B) by surprise
(C) off record
(D) in return

中譯｜一個聰明的女人在山上旅行時發現了一塊寶石。第二天，她遇到了另一個旅行者，那個旅行者很餓。那個聰明的女人慷慨地打開自己的袋子，與旅行者分享自己的食物。饑餓的旅行者看到了那塊寶石，要求她把寶石給他。女人毫不猶豫地這樣做了。旅行者高興地離開了。他想著，如果把寶石賣了，他將會有足夠的錢來度過餘生。但是幾天後，他回來尋找那個女人。他找到她後，就說：「我知道這塊寶石有多麼珍貴，但是我把它還給你，希望你能給我一些更珍貴的東西。你把寶石給了我，卻沒有要求任何回報，請教教我你內心所懷為何，能使你如此慷慨大度。」

解說｜本題講述了一則有關寶石的故事。第 1 題的四個選項都是動詞，但是能夠與介系詞 with 連用的只有 share，表示「分享」，所以正確選擇為 (C)。第 2 題要選擇合適的代名詞。根據語法知識，通常用代名詞 so 來指代所做的事情，所以最符合題意的選項是 (A)。第 3 題考時態的用法。閱讀全文可知，本篇短文所用的時態是過去式，而本題說明的情況是假設的，還沒有發生，要用 would have，所以正確選項是 (C)。第 4 題空格處所填的動詞在句中引導伴隨副詞，要用現在分詞，即 hoping，所以選項 (B) 符合題意。第 5 題的四個選項都是介系詞片語，將其一一代入可知，in return 表示「作為回報」符合題意，所以選 (D)。

解答＆技巧｜ 01 (C)　 02 (A)　 03 (C)　 04 (B)　 05 (D)

適用 TIP 1　適用 TIP 2　適用 TIP 7　適用 TIP 9　適用 TIP 11

補充

generously ad 慷慨地；ask sb. to do sth. ph 要求某人做某事；give sth. to sb. ph 給某人某物；without hesitation ph 毫不遲疑；give back ph 歸還

7,000 單字

- wise [waɪz] a 2 聰明的
- woman [ˈwʊmən] n 1 女人
- precious [ˈprɛʃəs] a 3 珍貴的
- stone [ston] n 1 石頭
- hungry [ˈhʌŋɡrɪ] a 1 饑餓的
- bag [bæg] n 1 包
- rest [rɛst] n 1 休息
- day [de] n 1 天

- back [bæk] ad 1 還，往回
- valuable [ˈvæljuəbl] a 3 貴重的
- please [pliz] int 1 請
- heart [hɑrt] n 1 心
- generous [ˈdʒɛnərəs] a 2 慷慨的
- hope [hop] n 1 希望
- record [ˈrɛkɚd] n 2 記錄

DAY 6

Part 1
詞彙題
Day 6
完成 25%

Part 2
綜合測驗
Day 6
完成 50%

Part 3
文意選填
Day 6
完成 75%

Part 4
閱讀測驗
Day 6
完成 100%

According to the study, noise will pose an immediate __01__ to people's health. Whether it's day or night, at home or at work, noise can always produce physical and psychological stress to people, and no one could be __02__ to it. Though most people choose to ignore the noise in order to adjust to it, our ears actually never close, and our bodies still __03__ to it, sometimes even with extreme tension to some strange sounds at night.

When faced with noise, we may feel annoyance which is the most common symptom of the stress that noise does to our bodies. Of all the health __04__ of noise, hearing loss may be the most observable and measurable. Unfortunately, we usually pay less attention to the more serious health hazards __05__ with the stress caused by noise. Therefore, when we get annoyed or irritable by noise, we should consider it to be a warning that something dangerous to our health may be happening.

01 _____ (A) boss   (B) danger
         (C) employer   (D) constituent

02 _____ (A) spiritual   (B) neural
         (C) accustomed   (D) immune

03 _____ (A) respond   (B) reply
         (C) correspond   (D) answer

04 _____ (A) education   (B) system
         (C) hazards   (D) management

05 _____ (A) pertaining   (B) associated
         (C) belonged   (D) alluding

DAY 6

Part 1
詞彙題
Day 6
完成 25%

Part 2
綜合測驗
Day 6
完成 50%

Part 3
文意選填
Day 6
完成 75%

Part 4
閱讀測驗
Day 6
完成 100%

中譯 | 研究指出，噪音會對人們的健康造成直接危害。不管是白天還是夜晚，不管在家還是在上班，噪音總能對人們造成生理以及心理壓力，沒有人能夠不受這種壓力的影響。儘管大多數人選擇忽視噪音，為的是要適應它，但是我們的耳朵從來沒有關閉，我們的身體仍然會做出反應，有時甚至對夜裡的一些奇怪的聲音感到極度緊張。

當面對噪音時，我們可能會感到惱怒，這是噪音對我們的身體造成壓力的最常見的症狀。在噪音造成的所有健康危害中，聽力損耗可能是最顯著的，也是最可衡量的。但不幸的是，噪音導致與壓力有關的健康危害愈嚴重，我們對此的關注卻愈少。因此，當我們為噪音感到厭煩和煩躁時，應該將它當成是一種警告，提醒我們某些對健康有害的事情可能正在發生。

解說 | 本篇短文講述了噪音對人們的健康所造成的危害。第 1 題是四個選項都是名詞。依據題意，應該是對人們的健康造成危害，而 danger 表示「危害」，所以正確選擇為 (B)。第 2 題根據上下文的內容可知，應該用 be immune to 表示「對～有免疫力；不受～的影響」，最符合題意的選項是 (D)。第 3 題要選擇能夠與介系詞 to 搭配使用的動詞。依據題意，respond to 表示「反應，回應」，符合題意，即正確選項是 (A)。第 4 題考名詞片語的用法。依據題意，應該是「健康危害」，可以用 health hazards 來表達，所以選項 (C) 符合題意。第 5 題要選擇能夠與介系詞 with 連用的分詞。將其一一代入可知，只有 associated 能夠與 with 連用表示「與～有關，與～相聯繫」，符合題意，所以選 (B)。

解答＆技巧 | 01 **(B)**　02 **(D)**　03 **(A)**　04 **(C)**　05 **(B)**

適用 TIP 1　適用 TIP 2　適用 TIP 7　適用 TIP 11

補充

at home ph 在家；at work ph 在工作；annoyance n 惱怒；observable a 看得見的；annoyed a 惱怒的

7,000 單字

- pose [poz] v 2 造成
- night [naɪt] n 1 夜晚
- psychological [ˌsaɪkəˈlɑdʒɪk] a 4 心理的
- ignore [ɪgˈnor] v 2 忽視
- ear [ɪr] n 1 耳朵
- close [kloz] v 1 關閉
- tension [ˈtɛnʃən] n 4 緊張
- common [ˈkɑmən] a 1 普通的

- measurable [ˈmɛʒərəbl] a 2 可測量的
- hazard [ˈhæzəd] n 6 危險
- irritable [ˈɪrətəbl] a 6 急躁的
- employer [ɪmˈplɔɪə] n 3 雇主
- constituent [kənˈstɪtʃuənt] n 6 成分
- spiritual [ˈspɪrɪtʃuəl] a 4 精神的
- correspond [ˌkɔrɪˈspɑnd] v 4 符合

Some theorists consider children passive when they are receiving experience, __01__ others think them active in organizing and creating their own worlds. The scientists who consider children to be passive do not think that they are unresponsive because all the knowledge that the children __02__ is given by the environment. In addition, children are stimulated by the external environment and driven by internal needs because they have little control __03__ them. Thus these scientists are in favor of direct and structured teaching methods.

On the other hand, those scientists who think children are active assume that they can learn very well on the __04__ that they explore and select their own learning materials and tasks, for the reason that human beings have an inborn tendency to be curious; thus they could explore the environment and organize the experience themselves. Therefore, what the children learn depends mainly on their interest which comes from their levels of understanding, and the teaching materials and methods should __05__ to their interest, too.

01 _____   (A) what   (B) when
            (C) while   (D) where

02 _____   (A) absorb   (B) shed
            (C) topple   (D) utilize

03 _____   (A) with   (B) for
            (C) upon   (D) over

04 _____   (A) turmoil   (B) condition
            (C) warranty   (D) transition

05 _____   (A) uncover   (B) surpass
            (C) sprawl   (D) correspond

中譯｜一些理論家認為兒童在接受經驗時很被動，而其他理論家認為，他們在組織以及創造他們自己的世界時很主動。那些覺得兒童比較被動的科學家們認為，兒童並不是沒有反應，因為他們吸收的所有知識都是環境所給予的。此外，兒童受到外界環境的刺激，並受到內部需求的驅使，是因為他們無法對這些事物進行控制。於是這些科學家支持直接的、有組織的教學方法。

另一方面，那些覺得兒童比較主動的科學家們認為，兒童能夠學得很好，前提是他們探索以及選擇自己的學習材料和任務，因為人類天生就有好奇的傾向，這樣他們自己就能夠探索環境、組織經驗。因此，兒童所學習的知識主要取決於他們依理解程度而產生的興趣，並且教材和方法也應該與他們的興趣一致。

解說｜本篇短文講述了兒童對知識以及外界環境的認知和接受能力。第 1 題空格前後所說明的現象是相反情況，需要用表示轉折意義的連接詞來引導，四個選項中只有 while 是轉折連接詞，表示「然而」，所以正確選擇為 (C)。第 2 題的四個選項都是動詞。依據題意，「吸收知識」可以表示為 absorb knowledge，要用動詞 absorb，最符合題意的選項是 (A)。第 3 題要選擇合適的介系詞。根據所學是知識，「能控制～」可以表達為 have control over，要用介系詞 over，即正確選項是 (D)。第 4 題考介系詞片語的用法。將四個選項一一代入可知，只有 condition 可以構成 on the condition that 表示「在～條件／前提下」，所以只有選項 (B) 符合題意。第 5 題將四個選項代入空格可知，correspond to 表示「符合」符合題意，所以選 (D)。

解答&技巧｜ 01 (C)　02 (A)　03 (D)　04 (B)　05 (D)

適用 TIP 1　適用 TIP 2　適用 TIP 7　適用 TIP 8　適用 TIP 11

補充
theorist ⓝ 理論家；unresponsive ⓐ 沒有反應的；structured ⓐ 有組織的；
teaching method ⓟⓗ 教學方法；come from ⓟⓗ 來自

7,000 單字
- passive [`pæsɪv] ⓐ 4 消極的
- organize [`ɔrgə,naɪz] ⓥ 2 組織
- think [θɪŋk] ⓥ 1 想
- because [bɪ`kɔz] ⓒⓞⓝⓙ 1 因為
- external [ɪk`stɜnəl] ⓐ 5 外部的
- drive [draɪv] ⓥ 1 驅動
- control [kən`trol] ⓝ 2 控制
- favor [`fevɚ] ⓝ 2 支持

- assume [ə`sjum] ⓥ 4 假定，認為
- explore [ɪk`splor] ⓥ 4 探索
- tendency [`tɛndənsɪ] ⓝ 4 趨勢
- curious [`kjurɪəs] ⓐ 2 好奇的
- therefore [`ðɛr,for] ⓐⓓ 2 因此
- utilize [`jutḷ,aɪz] ⓥ 6 利用
- sprawl [sprɔl] ⓥ 6 蔓延

DAY 6

Part 1
詞
彙
題
Day 6
完成 25%

Part 2
綜
合
測
驗
Day 6
完成 50%

Part 3
文
意
選
填
Day 6
完成 75%

Part 4
閱
讀
測
驗
Day 6
完成 100%

8 ▶ 97 年指考英文

The fruits and vegetables we eat often come in distinctive colors. The rich colors, __01__, are not there only to attract attention. They perform another important function for the plants.

Research shows that the substances __02__ these colors actually protect plants from chemical damage. The colors come mainly from chemicals known as antioxidants. Plants make antioxidants to protect themselves from the Sun's ultraviolet (UV) light, __03__ may cause harmful elements to form within the plant cells.

When we eat colorful fruits and vegetables, the coloring chemicals protect us, too. Typically, an intensely colored plant has __04__ of these protective chemicals than a paler one does. Research on how chemicals in blueberries affect brain function even suggests that these chemicals may help our own brains work more __05__. In other words, eating richly colored fruits and vegetables makes us both healthier and smarter.

01 _____   (A) almost   (B) rarely
            (C) however   (D) relatively

02 _____   (A) capable of   (B) different from
            (C) inferior to   (D) responsible for

03 _____   (A) which   (B) so
            (C) what   (D) such

04 _____   (A) more   (B) less
            (C) most   (D) least

05 _____   (A) obviously   (B) diligently
            (C) efficiently   (D) superficially

DAY
6

Part 1
詞
彙
題
Day 6
完成 25%

Part 2
綜
合
測
驗
Day 6
完成 50%

Part 3
文
意
選
填
Day 6
完成 75%

Part 4
閱
讀
測
驗
Day 6
完成 100%

中譯│我們吃的水果和蔬菜通常都有著獨特的顏色。豐富的色彩不僅僅是為了引起注意，它們為植物發揮另一項重要的功能。

研究顯示，導致這些顏色產生的物質實際上是為了保護植物免受化學損傷。這些顏色主要源於抗氧化劑的化學物質。植物產生抗氧化劑來保護自己免受太陽紫外線的照射，而紫外線可能會導致植物細胞內部形成有害元素。

我們在吃顏色鮮豔的水果和蔬菜時，造色的化學物質也會保護我們。很典型地，顏色特別鮮豔的植物要比顏色較淺的植物含有更多的防護性化學物質。針對藍莓中的化學物質如何影響大腦功能的研究甚至顯示，這些化學物質可能會幫助我們自己的大腦更有效地運作。換句話說，吃顏色豐富的水果和蔬菜使我們更加健康，也更加聰明。

解說│本篇短文介紹了蔬菜和水果的顏色的作用。第 1 題依據題意可知，要選擇合適的連接詞來連接前後兩個句子，而四個選項中，只有 however 可以作連接詞，其他三個選項都是副詞，所以正確選擇為 (C)。第 2 題考形容詞片語的用法。將四個選項一一代入空格，只有 responsible for 表示「導致，是～的原因」符合題意，所以最佳選項是 (D)。第 3 題依據題意，要選擇合適的代名詞，來指代前一句中的 ultraviolet (UV) light，而根據語法知識，指物的名詞一般用 which 來指代，即正確選項是 (A)。第 4 題句中有表示比較的連接詞 than，所以空格處要用比較級。依據題意，要用 more 表示「更多」，只有選項 (A) 符合題意。第 5 題將四個副詞一一代入空格，只有 efficiently 表示「有效率地」符合題意，所以選 (C)。

解答＆技巧│ 01 (C)　 02 (D)　 03 (A)　 04 (A)　 05 (C)

適用 TIP 2　適用 TIP 7　適用 TIP 8　適用 TIP 9　適用 TIP 11

補充
UV light ph 紫外線；colored a 有色的；typically ad 典型地；blueberry n 藍莓；richly ad 豐富地

7,000 單字

- fruit [frut] n 1 水果
- vegetable [ˋvɛdʒətəbl] n 1 蔬菜
- distinctive [dɪˋstɪŋktɪv] a 5 有特色的
- color [ˋkʌlɚ] n 1 顏色
- perform [pɚˋfɔrm] v 3 執行
- function [ˋfʌŋkʃən] n 2 功能
- protect [prəˋtɛkt] v 2 保護
- harmful [ˋhɑrmfəl] a 3 有害的
- element [ˋɛləmənt] n 2 要素
- colorful [ˋkʌlɚfəl] a 2 彩色的
- protective [prəˋtɛktɪv] a 3 防護的
- own [on] a 1 自己的
- both [boθ] conj 1 兩者都
- inferior [ɪnˋfɪrɪɚ] a 3 下級的
- least [list] a 1 最少的

A company's public image can play a __01__ role in attracting the employees, customers, stockholders, suppliers, as well as government officials. Then what is public image? It involves to __02__ a firm is viewed by its customers, suppliers, and stockholders, and can influence the product, price, place, and even promotional methods.

If a company's public image is good, it should be treasured and protected because it is usually built up over a long time and __03__ relationship with its public. Thus it could be a valuable asset of a company. Moreover, a quality image could enable a company to charge higher prices and to attract the best employees and dealers, which could also help the company __04__ the market.

Some factors could affect the public image of a company, such as the quality of the employees, company facilities, product quality and price, customer service, advertising and other public relations. Therefore, a company should take all possible measures to __05__ the good public image.

01 _____ (A) vital   (B) stationary
           (C) rigorous   (D) punctual

02 _____ (A) what   (B) which
           (C) where   (D) how

03 _____ (A) satisfied   (B) satisfying
           (C) satisfy   (D) to satisfy

04 _____ (A) ransom   (B) propel
           (C) win   (D) oblige

05 _____ (A) maintain   (B) collide
           (C) commence   (D) assert

中譯│一個公司的公眾形象，能夠在吸引員工、顧客、股東、供應商以及政府機構方面，發揮至關重要的作用。那麼什麼是公眾形象呢？公眾形象涉及到客戶、供應商和股東如何看待一個公司，能夠影響到產品、價格、位置，甚至是促銷手段。如果一個公司有好的公眾形象，那麼應該重視並加以保護，因為它通常需要很長時間及令人滿意的公共關係來建立。因此，它就可能是公司的寶貴財產。此外，品質形象能夠確保公司收取更高的價格、吸引最優秀的員工和經銷商，這也可以幫助公司贏得市場。

一些因素能夠影響到公司的公眾形象，例如員工的素質、公司設施、產品品質和價格、客戶服務、廣告以及其他的公共關係。因此，公司應當採取所有可能的措施來維護良好的公眾形象。

解說│本篇短文的主旨是「公眾形象」，介紹了公眾形象對於一個公司或企業的重要性。第 1 題的四個選項都是形容詞，將其一一代入可知，只有 vital 表示「至關重要的」符合題意，所以正確選擇為 (A)。第 2 題依據題意可知，空格處要選擇表示方式的副詞，四個選擇中只有 how 符合題意，所以最佳選項是 (D)。第 3 題要選擇合適的形容詞來修飾名詞 relationship，而四個選項中，只有 satisfying 是形容詞，表示「令人滿意的」符合題意，即正確選項是 (B)。第 4 題考動詞的用法。將四個選項的動詞一一代入，只有 win the market 表示「贏得市場」符合題意，所以正確選擇為 (C)。第 5 題的四個選項中，只有 maintain 表示「維持」符合題意，所以選 (A)。

解答&技巧│ 01 (A)　02 (D)　03 (B)　04 (C)　05 (A)
適用 TIP 1　適用 TIP 2　適用 TIP 7　適用 TIP 11

補充
stockholder ⓝ 股東；supplier ⓝ 供應商；promotional ⓐ 促銷的；customer service ⓟⓗ 顧客服務；advertising ⓝ 廣告

7,000 單字
- public [ˋpʌblɪk] ⓐ ① ⓝ ① 社會的
- employee [ˌɛmplɔɪˋi] ⓝ ③ 員工
- refer [rɪˋfɝ] ⓥ ④ 涉及
- company [ˋkʌmpənɪ] ⓝ ② 公司
- asset [ˋæsɛt] ⓝ ⑤ 資產
- moreover [morˋovɚ] ⓐⓓ ④ 而且
- enable [ɪnˋebl] ⓥ ③ 使能夠
- dealer [ˋdilɚ] ⓝ ③ 零售商
- facility [fəˋsɪlətɪ] ⓝ ④ 設施
- relation [rɪˋleʃən] ⓝ ② 關係
- rigorous [ˋrɪgərəs] ⓐ ⑥ 嚴格的
- punctual [ˋpʌŋktʃʊəl] ⓐ ⑥ 準時的
- ransom [ˋrænsəm] ⓥ ⑥ 贖回
- propel [prəˋpɛl] ⓥ ⑥ 推進
- collide [kəˋlaɪd] ⓥ ⑥ 碰撞

Many people may have thought about the __01__ questions: if women become managers of a company, will they bring different styles and skills to the job? Will they behave better than men? Could they be more motivated and committed than __02__ managers?

A recent research shows that women may show different attitudes to the management job. They may bring different skills, such as greater cooperativeness and an emphasis on affiliation to the job, and also be willing to take emotional factors into __03__ when making decisions, which could expand the range of techniques so as to help the company __04__ its workforce effectively.

The research also discovers that the "interactive leadership" style used by some female managers is different from the command-and-control style which is usually used by male managers. It is said that female managers often use the "interactive leadership" __05__ to encourage participation, share power and information with employees and get them satisfied with their work, which could lead to a win-win situation at work.

01 _____ (A) follow   (B) followed
        (C) following   (D) to follow

02 _____ (A) male   (B) female
        (C) young   (D) old

03 _____ (A) contradiction   (B) conviction
        (C) credibility   (D) consideration

04 _____ (A) deem   (B) manage
        (C) devalue   (D) escalate

05 _____ (A) familiarity   (B) fragment
        (C) hunch   (D) approach

中譯｜很多人或許都思考過下列問題：如果女人成為了一家公司的管理者，她們會為工作帶來不同的風格以及技巧嗎？她們會比男人表現得更好嗎？她們能夠比男性管理者更積極、更堅定嗎？

最近的一項調查顯示，女人會在管理工作上展現出不同的態度。她們或許會在工作中引入不同的技巧，像是更多的合作關係和加強聯繫，也願意在做決定時考慮到情感因素，這可以擴大技巧範圍，以便幫助公司更有效地管理員工。

研究也發現，女性管理者通常使用的「互動式領導」風格與男性管理者通常使用的「命令控制式」風格有所不同。據說，女性管理者通常使用「互動式領導」這種方法來鼓勵參與、與員工共享權力與資訊，以及使他們對工作感到滿意，這會讓工作中出現一種雙贏的局勢。

解說｜本篇短文的主旨是「女性管理者」，講述了女性和男性作為管理者時，在工作中表現出的不同之處。第 1 題的四個選項中，只有 following 表示「下列的」可以修飾名詞 questions，所以正確選擇為 (C)。第 2 題依據題意可知，空格處是將女性與男性管理者進行比較，應該用 male 表示「男性」，最符合題意的選項是 (A)。第 3 題根據上下文的內容可知，「將～考慮在內」應該表達為 take... into consideration，即正確選項是 (D)。第 4 題的四個選項都是動詞，將其一一代入可知，manage 表示「管理」最符合題意，所以正確選擇為 (B)。第 5 題的四個選項都可以作為名詞，但 approach 表示「方法」最符合題意，所以選 (D)。

解答＆技巧｜ **01** (C)　**02** (A)　**03** (D)　**04** (B)　**05** (D)

適用 TIP 1　適用 TIP 2　適用 TIP 7　適用 TIP 11

> **補充**
> motivated ⓐ 有積極性的；committed ⓐ 盡忠職守的；cooperativeness ⓝ 協同性；affiliation ⓝ 聯繫；workforce ⓝ 勞動力

> **7,000 單字**
> - manager [ˋmænɪdʒɚ] ⓝ ③ 管理者
> - company [ˋkʌmpənɪ] ⓝ ② 公司
> - bring [brɪŋ] ⓥ ① 帶來
> - skill [skɪl] ⓝ ① 技術
> - emphasis [ˋɛmfəsɪs] ⓝ ④ 強調
> - factor [ˋfæktɚ] ⓝ ③ 因素
> - range [rendʒ] ⓝ ② 範圍
> - technique [tɛkˋnik] ⓝ ③ 技術
> - leadership [ˋlidɚˏʃɪp] ⓝ ② 領導能力
> - encourage [ɪnˋkɝɪdʒ] ⓥ ② 鼓勵
> - participation [pɑrˏtɪsəˋpeʃən] ⓝ ④ 參與
> - share [ʃɛr] ⓥ ② 分享
> - situation [ˏsɪtʃuˋeʃən] ⓝ ③ 形勢
> - conviction [kənˋvɪkʃən] ⓝ ⑥ 確信
> - escalate [ˋɛskəˏlet] ⓥ ⑥ 逐步增強

DAY 6

Part 1
詞 彙 題
Day 6
完成 25%

Part 2
綜合測驗
Day 6
完成 50%

Part 3
文意選填
Day 6
完成 75%

Part 4
閱讀測驗
Day 6
完成 100%

Part 3 文意選填｜Cloze Test

1 ▶

Most people in the Untied States speak English, but they may not use the same word for the same thing. For __01__ , there is a kind of round flat breakfast food __02__ with maple syrup. Usually the food is __03__ pancakes. Still, some people may say flapjacks or griddlecakes. And people living in the hills of Arkansas or Tennessee may say battercakes.

When talking about dragonflies, people in Florida will say mosquito hawks, while people in nearby Georgia may say snake doctors! Still, there is another __04__ for dragonflies—snake feeders.

Building a __05__ might not be very easy if you live in the Untied States. A language __06__ once found 169 different words for the wood used to build a fire, such as lightered knots, kindling wood, lightning wood, etc.

When in the fruit store, you may __07__ people say cling peaches, plum peaches, green peaches, or pickle peaches. You don't have to feel __08__ about that because all of these sayings just __09__ to the same thing.

If you buy some fruit, you can put it in a paper bag, a nack, or a poke. All of these words __10__ the same thing. Besides, you may use porch, veranda or gallery for the same place at home; use friend or buddy for the same close relationship; and use snack, chow or grub for the same food.

(A) instance　(B) hear　(C) called　(D) refer　(E) mean
(F) served　(G) expert　(H) fire　(I) confused　(J) saying

---

01 _____　02 _____　03 _____　04 _____　05 _____

06 _____　07 _____　08 _____　09 _____　10 _____

選項中譯｜例子；聽到；稱為；指代；意味著；上菜；專家；火；困惑的；說法

中譯｜在美國，大多數人們都說英語，不過，對於同一種事物，也許會有不同的說法。例如，有一種圓圓扁扁、塗有楓糖漿的早餐食物，通常稱為 pancakes。不過，也有人稱為 flapjacks 或是 griddlecakes，而住在阿肯色州或者田納西州山區的人們，則是稱之為 battercakes。

提及蜻蜓，佛羅里達州的人會說 mosquito hawks，而喬治亞州附近的人們也許會說 snake doctors。還有另一種說法，稱之為 snake feeders。

如果你住在美國，生火可能都不太容易。有位語言學家曾經發現，用來生火的木頭有一百六十九種不同的說法，例如 lightered knots、kindling wood 和 lighting wood 等。

在水果店的時候，你也許會聽到人們說 cling peaches、plum peaches、green peaches 或是 pickle peaches。不必為此感到困惑，因為這些說法所指的都是同一種東西。

如果你買了水果，可以放在 paper bag、nack 或者 poke 裡。這些說法所指的都是同一種東西——袋子。此外，你也可以用 porch、veranda 或是 gallery 來表示家裡的同一處地方——門廊，還可以用 friend 或是 buddy 來表示同樣的親密關係——朋友，也可以用 snack、chow 或是 grub 來表示同一種食物——點心。

解譯｜閱讀全文可知，這篇文章的主題是英語中事物名稱的不同表達。

縱觀各選項，選項 (A)、(G)、(H)、(J) 是名詞，選項 (B)、(C)、(D)、(E)、(F) 是動詞，選項 (I) 是形容詞。根據題意，第 1、4、5、6 題應選名詞，第 2、3、7、9、10 題應選動詞，第 8 題應選形容詞。然後根據文章，依次作答。

第 1 題是選擇名詞，有四個名詞可供選擇，即為選項 (A)、(G)、(H)、(J)，選項 (A) 意為「例子」，選項 (G) 意為「專家」，選項 (H) 意為「火」，選項 (J) 意為「說法」，for instance 可以視為固定搭配，意為「例如」，所以選 (A)。第 4 題所選名詞，根據句意，應當是「還有另一種說法」，所以選 (J)。第 5 題所選名詞，也可以視為固定搭配，build a fire 意為「生火」，所以選 (H)。第 6 題則是選 (G)，language expert 意為「語言學家」。

第 2 題是選擇動詞，有五個動詞可供選擇，即為選項 (B)、(C)、(D)、(E)、(F)。只有選項 (F) 符合要求，視為固定表達，serve food 意為「提供食物，將食物擺上桌」。第 3 題所選動詞，也可以視為固定搭配，be called... 意為「被稱為～」，所以選 (C)。第 7 題所選動詞，根據句意，應當是「聽到人們說～」，所以選 (B)。第 9 題所選動詞，是與介系詞 to 進行搭配，refer to 意為「指的是」，所以選 (D)。第 10 題則是選 (E)，意為「這些說法所指的都是同一種東西」。

第 8 題是選擇形容詞，有一個形容詞可供選擇，即為選項 (I)，feel confused about 意為「對～感到困惑」。

DAY **6**

Part 1
詞
彙
題
Day 6
完成 25%

Part 2
綜
合
測
驗
Day 6
完成 50%

Part 3
文
意
選
填
Day 6
完成 75%

Part 4
閱
讀
測
驗
Day 6
完成 100%

解答&技巧│ 01 **(A)**　02 **(F)**　03 **(C)**　04 **(J)**　05 **(H)**
06 **(G)**　07 **(B)**　08 **(I)**　09 **(D)**　10 **(E)**

適用 TIP 1　適用 TIP 2　適用 TIP 6　適用 TIP 7　適用 TIP 8
適用 TIP 9　適用 TIP 10　適用 TIP 11

補充
Arkansas ⃞n 阿肯色州；Tennessee ⃞n 田納西州；Florida ⃞n 佛羅里達州；Georgia ⃞n 喬治亞州；
buddy ⃞n 朋友

7,000 單字
- maple [ˈmepl] ⃞n ⃞5 楓樹
- syrup [ˈsɪrəp] ⃞n ⃞4 糖漿
- pancake [ˈpænˌkek] ⃞n ⃞3 薄煎餅，鬆餅
- dragonfly [ˈdrægənˌflaɪ] ⃞n ⃞2 蜻蜓
- mosquito [məˈskito] ⃞n ⃞2 蚊子
- hawk [hɔk] ⃞n ⃞3 鷹
- nearby [ˈnɪrˌbaɪ] ⃞a ⃞2 附近的
- knot [nɑt] ⃞n ⃞3 結

- lightning [ˈlaɪtnɪŋ] ⃞n ⃞2 閃電
- peach [pitʃ] ⃞n ⃞2 桃子
- pickle [ˈpɪkl] ⃞n ⃞3 醃菜，泡菜
- poke [pok] ⃞n ⃞5 戳
- porch [portʃ] ⃞n ⃞5 門廊
- gallery [ˈgælərɪ] ⃞n ⃞4 走廊
- snack [snæk] ⃞n ⃞2 點心

MEMO

2 ▶ 95 年指考英文

With one out of every two American marriages ending in divorce, custody of children has become an issue in the American society. Up until the late 1970s, it had been common practice in the United States to automatically __01__ custody to the mother when a divorce occurred.

However, since the 1970s, this practice has been __02__ . Most custody battles today are decided, in theory, on the basis of who is the more suitable parent for the child. The reality, nevertheless, is that most women still win custody of their children in a __03__ .

This legal change was the result of the social changes that __04__ in the United States during the 1960s and 1970s. These changes challenged many of the __05__ roles men and women were expected to play. As a __06__ , it is not uncommon nowadays to find women working outside their homes and being very __07__ about their careers and personal lives. It is also not __08__ to see men accepting roles that were once considered the exclusive domain of women, such as shopping for groceries, driving their children to and from school, or cleaning their homes.

Because of the __09__ in the divorce rate, the change in the roles that men and women are expected to play, and the changing attitude of the judicial system toward child custody, more men have started to __10__ for and win custody of their children when divorce occurs.

DAY
6

Part 1
詞
彙
題
Day 6
完成 25%

Part 2
綜
合
測
驗
Day 6
完成 50%

Part 3
文
意
選
填
Day 6
完成 75%

Part 4
閱
讀
測
驗
Day 6
完成 100%

(A) award   (B) challenged   (C) concerned   (D) consequence
(E) divorce   (F) fight   (G) increase   (H) took place   (I) traditional
(J) unusual

01 _____   02 _____   03 _____   04 _____   05 _____

06 _____   07 _____   08 _____   09 _____   10 _____

選項中譯│判給；質疑；使關心；結果；離婚；爭取；增長；發生；傳統的；罕見的

中譯│在美國，有一半的婚姻最終都是以離婚收場，孩子的監護權也隨之成為美國社會主要的問題。直到二十世紀七〇年代，離婚時自然地將監護權判給母親，在美國都是慣例。

然而，二十世紀七〇年代之後，這種慣例已經受到質疑。如今，有多數的監護權之爭，從理論上來說，是根據哪一方更適合撫養孩子來決定的。不過事實上，離婚時仍然是大多數的母親贏得孩子的監護權。

這樣的合法轉變，要歸結於二十世紀六〇年代到七〇年代之間發生在美國的社會變化。這些變化挑戰男性和女性被期望扮演的很多傳統角色，導致的結果就是，如今女性離開家出去工作並不罕見，她們也十分重視自己的事業和個人生活。男性接受那些曾經被認為是女性獨佔領域的角色，例如購買雜貨、開車接送孩子上下學，或是打掃房子，這也並不罕見。

由於離婚率的增長、男性和女性被期望扮演的角色轉變，以及有關孩子監護權的司法體系的態度轉變，離婚時，更多的男性開始爭取孩子的監護權，並且獲得勝利。

解譯│閱讀全文可知，這篇文章的主題是美國孩子監護權的轉變及其原因。

縱觀各選項，選項 (D)、(E)、(G) 是名詞，選項 (A)、(B)、(C)、(F) 是動詞，選項 (H) 是動詞片語，選項 (I)、(J) 是形容詞。根據題意，第 3、6、9 題應選名詞，第 1、2、4、7、10 題應選動詞，第 5、8 題應選形容詞。然後根據文章，依次作答。

第 1 題是選擇動詞，須與介系詞 to 進行搭配，有五個動詞選項可供選擇，即為選項 (A)、(B)、(C)、(F)、(H)。只有選項 (A) 符合要求，award... to 意為「把～判給某人」。第 2 題所選動詞，是被動語態，根據句意，應當是「這種慣例已經受到質疑」，所以選 (B)。第 4 題是選動詞片語 (H)，意為「發生」。第 7 題所選動詞，可以視為固定搭配，be concerned about 意為「關心，重視」，所以選 (C)。第 10 題則是選 (F)，可以視為固定搭配，fight for 意為「爭取」。

第 3 題是選擇名詞，有三個名詞可供選擇，即為選項 (D)、(E)、(G)，選項 (D) 意為「結果」，選項 (E) 意為「離婚」，選項 (G) 意為「增長」，根據句意，應當是「離婚時自發地將監護權判給母親」，所以選 (E)。第 6 題所選名詞，可以視為固定搭配，as a consequence 意為「因此，結果」，所以選 (D)。第 9 題則是選 (G)，increase in... 意為「～的增長」。

第 5 題是選擇形容詞，修飾名詞 roles，有兩個形容詞可供選擇，即為選項 (I)、(J)。選項 (I) 意為「傳統的」，選項 (J) 意為「罕見的」，根據句意可知，應當是「男性和女性被期望扮演的傳統角色」，所以選 (I)。第 8 題則是選 (J)，句意為「男性接受那些曾經被認為是女性獨佔領域的角色，並不罕見」。

解答 & 技巧 | 01 (A) 02 (B) 03 (E) 04 (H) 05 (I)
06 (D) 07 (C) 08 (J) 09 (G) 10 (F)

適用 TIP 1 適用 TIP 2 適用 TIP 6 適用 TIP 7 適用 TIP 8
適用 TIP 9 適用 TIP 10 適用 TIP 11

補充

end in ph 以～而告終；up until ph 直到～為止；common practice ph 慣例；in theory ph 理論上；
on the basis of ph 按照，基於

7,000 單字

- divorce [də`vors] n 4 離婚
- society [sə`saɪətɪ] n 2 社會
- practice [`præktɪs] n 1 慣例，常規
- occur [ə`kɝ] v 2 發生
- battle [`bæt] n 2 爭鬥，鬥爭
- theory [`θiərɪ] n 3 理論
- suitable [`sutəbl] a 3 合適的
- reality [ri`æləti] n 2 事實

- challenge [`tʃælɪndʒ] v 3 挑戰
- expect [ɪk`spɛkt] v 2 期望
- accept [ək`sɛpt] v 2 接受
- exclusive [ɪk`sklusɪv] a 6 獨有的
- grocery [`grosərɪ] n 3 雜貨店
- attitude [`ætətjud] n 3 態度
- system [`sɪstəm] n 3 體系

Part 1
詞
彙
題
Day 6
完成 25%

Part 2
綜
合
測
驗
Day 6
完成 50%

Part 3
文
意
選
填
Day 6
完成 75%

Part 4
閱
讀
測
驗
Day 6
完成 100%

MEMO

3 ▶

Seeing a tree with lights and colored balls as decoration on it, you may think of __01__ . Gifts are usually __02__ to each other at Christmas. The custom may __03__ back to the gifts brought by the Wise Men to the young child Jesus. People in different countries have different opinions of Christmas, as well as different Christmas customs.

In England and in the United States, children usually hang up stockings on Christmas __04__ . On the morning of Christmas Day, they will find the stockings filled with __05__ .

In France, children usually put __06__ by the door on Christmas Eve. It is said that the Christ Child will put presents in the shoes.

In Spain, twelve days after Christmas, children will put __07__ in their shoes. The straw is for the camels of the Wise Men. They believe that when the camels pass by, they will eat the straw and leave gifts.

In Mexico, children will have a piñata at Christmas time. A piñata is a decorated paper __08__ , which is filled with candy and toys and suspended from a height with a rope. Children should have their eyes blindfolded and try to hit the piñata with a stick. This custom also __09__ as a part of birthday celebration at children's parties.

In Norway, children stand around the Christmas __10__ on Christmas Eve. They hold hands, sing Christmas songs and walk slowly around the tree.

(A) acts (B) given (C) gifts (D) Christmas (E) tree
(F) date (G) straw (H) Eve (I) container (J) shoes

01 _____ 02 _____ 03 _____ 04 _____ 05 _____

06 _____ 07 _____ 08 _____ 09 _____ 10 _____

選項中譯｜扮演；送；禮物；耶誕節；樹；追溯；稻草；前夕；容器；鞋子

中譯｜看到一棵樹上掛滿燈飾和彩球作為裝飾，你也許會想起耶誕節。耶誕節期間，人們要互贈禮物。這個習俗源自智者給年幼的耶穌送禮物。對於耶誕節，不同國家的人們有不同的看法，也有不同的聖誕習俗。

在英國和美國，聖誕前夕，孩子們通常要將長襪掛起來。在耶誕節的早上，他們會發現長襪裡裝滿了禮物。

在法國，聖誕前夕，孩子們通常在把鞋子放在門邊。據說，上帝之子會把禮物放在鞋子裡。

在西班牙，耶誕節過後十二天，孩子們要把稻草放在鞋子裡。稻草是為智者的駱駝準備的。他們認為，駱駝經過時會吃掉稻草，並且留下禮物。

在墨西哥，耶誕節期間，孩子們會玩一個擊打「皮納塔」的遊戲。這皮納塔是一種裝飾過的紙容器，裡面塞滿了糖果和玩具，用繩子懸掛在高處。孩子們要被蒙上眼睛，試圖用一根棍子去擊打皮納塔。這個習俗也適用於孩子們的生日慶祝會。

在挪威，聖誕前夕，孩子們圍繞在聖誕樹前。他們手牽手，唱著聖誕歌，緩慢地繞著樹走。

解譯｜閱讀全文可知，這篇文章的主題是各地的耶誕節習俗。

縱觀各選項，選項 (C)、(D)、(E)、(G)、(H)、(I)、(J) 是名詞，選項 (A)、(B)、(F) 是動詞。根據題意，第 1、4、5、6、7、8、10 題應選名詞，第 2、3、9 題應選動詞。然後根據文章，依次作答。

第 1 題是選擇名詞，有七個名詞可供選擇，即為選項 (C)、(D)、(E)、(G)、(H)、(I)、(J)，選項 (C) 意為「禮物」，選項 (D) 意為「耶誕節」，選項 (E) 意為「樹」，選項 (G) 意為「稻草」，選項 (H) 意為「前夕」，選項 (I) 意為「容器」，選項 (J) 意為「鞋子」，根據句意，應當是「看到樹上掛滿燈飾和彩球作為裝飾，也許會想起耶誕節」，所以選 (D)。第 4 題所選名詞，可以視為固定搭配，on Christmas Eve 意為「在耶誕節前夕」，所以選 (H)。第 5 題所選名詞，根據句意，應當是「發現長襪裡裝滿了禮物」，所以選 (C)。第 6 題所選名詞，根據句意，應當是「聖誕前夕，孩子們通常在把鞋子放在門邊」，所以選 (J)。第 7 題所選名詞，根據句意，應當是「把稻草放在鞋子裡」，所以選 (G)。第 8 題所選名詞，根據句意，piñata 應當是「是一種裝飾過的容器」，所以選 (I)。第 10 題則是選 (E)，Christmas tree 意為「聖誕樹」。

第 2 題是選擇動詞，須與名詞 gifts 進行搭配，有三個動詞可供選擇，即為選項 (A)、(B)、(F)。只有選項 (B) 符合要求，意為「送禮物」。第 3 題所選動詞，可以視為固定搭配，date back to 意為「追溯到」，所以選 (F)。第 9 題則是選 (A)，act as a part of 意為「作為～的一部分」。

DAY
6

Part 1
詞
彙
題
Day 6
完成 25%

Part 2
綜合測驗
Day 6
完成 50%

Part 3
文意選填
Day 6
完成 75%

Part 4
閱讀測驗
Day 6
完成 100%

解答＆技巧｜ 01 (D)　 02 (B)　 03 (F)　 04 (H)　 05 (C)
06 (J)　 07 (G)　 08 (I)　 09 (A)　 10 (E)

適用 TIP 1　適用 TIP 2　適用 TIP 6　適用 TIP 7　適用 TIP 8
適用 TIP 9　適用 TIP 10　適用 TIP 11

補充

the Wise Men ph 智者；Christmas Eve ph 聖誕前夕；the Christ Child ph 上帝之子，聖嬰；
piñata n 皮納塔；Christmas tree ph 聖誕樹

7,000 單字

- light [laɪt] n 1 燈
- Christmas [ˈkrɪsməs] n 1 耶誕節
- country [ˈkʌntrɪ] n 1 國家
- stocking [ˈstɑkɪŋ] n 3 長筒襪
- eve [iv] n 4 前夕
- gift [ɡɪft] n 1 禮物
- shoe [ʃu] n 1 鞋子
- present [ˈprɛznt] n 2 禮物

- straw [strɔ] n 2 稻草
- camel [ˈkæml] n 1 駱駝
- pass [pæs] v 1 經過
- candy [ˈkændɪ] n 1 糖果
- rope [rop] n 1 繩子
- hit [hɪt] v 1 打，擊
- stand [stænd] v 1 站立

MEMO

4 ▶

DAY
6

Part 1
詞
彙
題
Day 6
完成 25%

Part 2
綜
合
測
驗
Day 6
完成 50%

Part 3
文
意
選
填
Day 6
完成 75%

Part 4
閱
讀
測
驗
Day 6
完成 100%

When you do something over and over, it may become a ___01___. A habit is something that is ___02___. When a certain group of people come into the same habit, it becomes a ___03___.

People in different parts of the world usually have different customs. Customs that may seem ___04___ to you are not strange to others. Parents teach their children customs, and children will teach their own children the same customs in the ___05___. Years and years going by, customs are ___06___ down from generation to generation.

People in many different countries have a special day to ___07___ God. A long time ago, when Puritans came to America, they had hard times. Then the Indians helped them grow ___08___ and make a living on the new land. When the Puritans harvested the crops, they were greatly thankful and asked the Indians to come to a big dinner.

People in England give thanks on Harvest Festival Day. They bring food to churches. The food is then taken away by children and shared with the poor people of the community.

People in the Untied States have their Thanksgiving Day in November, well, the fourth Thursday to be ___09___. The festival was originally ___10___ to give thanks to God for the harvest and for health. Most people eat special food called turkey for Thanksgiving dinner.

People in Canada have a day of Thanksgiving, too. It falls on the second Monday in October.

(A) passed (B) custom (C) exact (D) acquired (E) habit
(F) crops (G) intended (H) future (I) thank (J) strange

---

01 _____   02 _____   03 _____   04 _____   05 _____

06 _____   07 _____   08 _____   09 _____   10 _____

選項中譯 | 傳遞；習俗；確切的；獲得；習慣；作物；意圖；將來；感謝；奇怪的

中譯 | 重複地做某件事情，很可能就會變成一種習慣。習慣是後天習得的。一群人都形成了相同的習慣時，這種習慣也就變成了一種習俗。

生活在世界上不同地方的人們，有著不同的習俗。也許，有些習俗在你看起來很奇怪，對其他人來說卻是平常。父母把習俗教給孩子們，日後孩子們也會把這些習俗教給自己的孩子。歲月流逝，這些習俗卻是代代相傳。

在許多不同的國家，人們都有一個特殊的日子來感謝上帝。很久以前，清教徒來到美洲，他們曾經有過很艱難的歲月。後來，印第安人幫助他們種莊稼，在這片新土地上生存。莊稼獲得豐收時，清教徒們十分感激，並邀請印第安人參加豐盛的晚宴。

英國人在豐收節這天表達感謝。他們帶食物去教堂，這些食物會被孩子們帶走，分給社區的窮人。

美國人有他們自己的感恩節，是在十一月，嗯，確切地說，是在第四個禮拜四。這個節日最初是用來感謝上帝賜予他們豐收和健康。在感恩節的晚宴上，大多數人都吃一種稱為火雞的特殊食物。

加拿大人也有感恩節，是在十月的第二個禮拜一。

解譯 | 閱讀全文可知，這篇文章的主題是感恩節習俗。

縱觀各選項，選項 (B)、(E)、(F)、(H) 是名詞，選項 (A)、(D)、(G)、(I) 是動詞，選項 (C)、(J) 是形容詞。根據題意，第 1、3、5、8 題應選名詞，第 2、6、7、10 題應選動詞，第 4、9 題應選形容詞。然後根據文章，依次作答。

第 1 題是選擇名詞，有四個名詞可供選擇，即為選項 (B)、(E)、(F)、(H)，選項 (B) 意為「習俗」，選項 (E) 意為「習慣」，選項 (F) 意為「作物」，選項 (H) 意為「將來」，根據句意，應當是「重複地做某件事情，很可能會變成一種習慣」，所以選 (E)。第 3 題所選名詞，根據句意，應當是「一定數量的人們都形成了相同的習慣時，這種習慣也就變成了一種習俗」，所以選 (B)。第 5 題所選名詞，可以視為固定搭配，in the future 意為「將來」，所以選 (H)。第 8 題則是選 (F)，grow crops 意為「種莊稼」。

第 2 題是選擇動詞，有四個動詞可供選擇，即為選項 (A)、(D)、(G)、(I)，根據句意可知，應當是「習慣是後天習得的」，所以選 (D)。第 6 題所選動詞，可以視為固定搭配，pass down from generation to generation 意為「代代相傳」，所以選 (A)。第 7 題所選動詞，意為「有個特殊的日子來感謝上帝」，所以選 (I)。第 10 題則是選 (G)，intend to do sth. 意為「意圖做某事」。

第 4 題是選擇形容詞，有兩個形容詞可供選擇，即為選項 (C)、(J)。選項 (C) 意為「確切的」，選項 (J) 意為「奇怪的」，根據句意可知，應當是「有些習俗在你看起來很奇怪，對其他人來說，卻是平常」，所以選 (J)。第 9 題則是選 (C)，to be exact 意為「確切地說」。

解答 & 技巧 | **01 (E)** **02 (D)** **03 (B)** **04 (J)** **05 (H)**
06 (A) **07 (I)** **08 (F)** **09 (C)** **10 (G)**

適用 TIP 1　適用 TIP 2　適用 TIP 6　適用 TIP 7　適用 TIP 8
適用 TIP 9　適用 TIP 10　適用 TIP 11

DAY 6

補充
Thanksgiving n 感恩節；go by ph 時間流逝；Puritan n 清教徒；give thanks ph 感恩；
share with ph 分享

7,000 單字
- habit [ˋhæbɪt] n 2 習慣
- acquire [əˋkwaɪr] v 4 獲得
- group [grup] n 1 群，團體
- custom [ˋkʌstəm] n 2 習俗
- different [ˋdɪfərənt] a 1 不同的
- strange [strendʒ] a 1 奇怪的
- teach [titʃ] v 1 教
- thank [θæŋk] v 1 感謝

- crop [krɑp] n 2 莊稼
- thankful [ˋθæŋkfəl] a 3 感激的
- harvest [ˋhɑrvɪst] n 3 豐收
- festival [ˋfɛstəvl] n 2 節日
- church [tʃɝtʃ] n 1 教堂
- community [kəˋmjunətɪ] n 4 社區
- November [noˋvɛmbɚ] n 1 十一月

Part 1 詞彙題 Day 6 完成 25%

Part 2 綜合測驗 Day 6 完成 50%

Part 3 文意選填 Day 6 完成 75%

Part 4 閱讀測驗 Day 6 完成 100%

MEMO

♫359

Scientists usually define a place as a desert if it gets only 10 inches (25 centimeters) or less of rain in a year. The __01__ of rain leads to little moisture in a desert. Most places get much more rain in a year. For instance, Chicago, Illinois, gets 20 to 40 inches of rain a year, and New York City 40 to 60 inches.

Most deserts are hot because they are near the __02__. On the earth, places nearer the equator are hotter, while places further away are colder. The North and South __03__ are quite cold because they are as far away from the equator as it is possible to be.

Deserts may come into being when moisture is stopped from __04__ there. Moisture is usually carried by __05__, but mountains may stop the clouds from bringing moisture to the desert. Also, as the earth moves around, it tends to create low rainfall in areas of high __06__. The areas with the highest rainfall are along the Tropic of Cancer and the Tropic of Capricorn.

Moisture gets into a cloud when water __07__ from a lake or ocean. The __08__ blows the clouds toward the mountains to reach the desert on the other side, but the moisture in the clouds falls out as it gets cooler going up the mountain. Thus, by the time the clouds get to the other side of the mountain, there is __09__ moisture left. In __10__, there is always no cloud left at all.

(A) latitudes (B) lack (C) little (D) Poles (E) equator
(F) fact (G) clouds (H) evaporates (I) wind (J) reaching

01 _____ 02 _____ 03 _____ 04 _____ 05 _____

06 _____ 07 _____ 08 _____ 09 _____ 10 _____

選項中譯｜緯度；缺少；很少的；地極；赤道；事實；雲；蒸發；風；到達

中譯｜通常，科學家把降雨量只有或不到十吋（二十五公分）的地方定義為沙漠。缺乏雨水意味著沙漠中少有水分。大多數的地方，一年中的降雨量都更多一些。例如，伊利諾州的芝加哥，年降雨量約二十到四十吋，紐約市的年降雨量則約四十到六十吋。

大多數的沙漠位於赤道附近，因而都十分炎熱。地球上，離赤道愈近的地方就愈熱，而離赤道愈遠的地區則是愈冷。南極和北極十分寒冷，就是因為它們是離赤道最遠的地方。

當水分受阻而無法到達某個地方時，那裡很可能就會形成沙漠。水分是由雲層攜帶的，然而山脈也許會阻止雲層把水分帶進沙漠。同樣，隨著地球的轉動，高緯度地區的降雨量會減少。降雨量最多的地區，是南北回歸線沿線。

水分從湖泊或海洋蒸發之後，進入雲層。風會把雲層吹過高山，抵達另一邊的沙漠，但是，雲層中的水分在沿著高山上升的過程中冷卻而形成降雨。因此，當雲層到達山的另一側時，所剩的水分寥寥無幾。事實上，通常連雲層都沒有了。

解譯｜閱讀全文可知，這篇文章的主題是沙漠的成因。

縱觀各選項，選項 (A)、(B)、(D)、(E)、(F)、(G)、(I) 是名詞，選項 (H)、(J) 是動詞，選項 (C) 是形容詞。根據題意，第 1、2、3、5、6、8、10 題應選名詞，第 4、7 題應選動詞，第 9 題應選形容詞。然後根據文章，依次作答。

第 1 題是選擇名詞，用於 of 結構，有七個名詞可供選擇，即為選項 (A)、(B)、(D)、(E)、(F)、(G)、(I)，選項 (A) 意為「緯度」，選項 (B) 意為「缺少」，選項 (D) 意為「極地」，選項 (E) 意為「赤道」，選項 (F) 意為「事實」，選項 (G) 意為「雲」，選項 (I) 意為「風」，根據句意，應當是「雨水缺乏」，所以選 (B)。

第 2 題所選名詞，是表示地點，根據句意，應當是「大多數的沙漠位於赤道附近，因而都十分炎熱」，所以選 (E)。第 3 題所選名詞，可以視為固定表達，North and South Poles 意為「南北極」，所以選 (D)。第 5 題所選名詞，根據句意，應當是「水分是由雲層攜帶」，所以選 (G)。第 6 題所選名詞，也可以視為固定表達，areas of high latitudes 意為「高緯度地區」，所以選 (A)。第 8 題則是選 (I)，意為「風把雲層吹過高山」。

第 4 題是選擇動詞，須為動名詞，有兩個動詞可供選擇，即為選項 (H)、(J)。只有選項 (J) 符合要求，stop... from doing sth. 意為「阻止～做某事」。第 7 題則是選 (H)，意為「水分從湖泊或海洋蒸發」。

第 9 題是選擇形容詞，只有一個形容詞可供選擇，即為選項 (C)，意為「很少的，幾乎沒有的」。

DAY
6

Part 1
詞
彙
題
Day 6
完成 25%

Part 2
綜
合
測
驗
Day 6
完成 50%

Part 3
文
意
選
填
Day 6
完成 75%

Part 4
閱
讀
測
驗
Day 6
完成 100%

解答＆技巧 | **01** (B)　**02** (E)　**03** (D)　**04** (J)　**05** (G)
　　　　　 06 (A)　**07** (H)　**08** (I)　**09** (C)　**10** (F)

適用 TIP 1　適用 TIP 2　適用 TIP 6　適用 TIP 7　適用 TIP 8
適用 TIP 9　適用 TIP 10　適用 TIP 11

補充
Chicago [n] 芝加哥；Illlnois [n] 伊利諾州；the Tropic of Cancer [ph] 北回歸線；
the Tropic of Capricorn [ph] 南回歸線；evaporate [v] 蒸發

7,000 單字

- scientist [ˈsaɪəntɪst] [n] [2] 科學家
- desert [ˈdɛzɚt] [n] [2] 沙漠
- inch [ɪntʃ] [n] [1] 英寸
- centimeter [ˈsɛntə‚mitə] [n] [3] 公分，釐米
- lack [læk] [n] [1] 缺乏
- moisture [ˈmɔɪstʃɚ] [n] [3] 水分
- instance [ˈɪnstəns] [n] [2] 例子
- further [ˈfɝðɚ] [a] [2] 更遠的

- pole [pol] [n] [3] 極地
- possible [ˈpɑsəbl] [a] [1] 可能的
- reach [ritʃ] [v] [1] 到達
- cloud [klaud] [n] [1] 雲
- mountain [ˈmauntn] [n] [1] 山
- latitude [ˈlætə‚tjud] [n] [5] 緯度
- wind [wɪnd] [n] [1] 風

MEMO

MEMO

DAY
6

Part 1
詞
彙
題
Day 6
完成 **25**%

Part 2
綜
合
測
驗
Day 6
完成 **50**%

Part 3
文
意
選
填
Day 6
完成 **75**%

Part 4
閱
讀
測
驗
Day 6
完成 **100**%

▶ 95 年學測英文

　　Tea was the first brewed beverage. The Chinese emperor Shen Nung in 2737 B.C. introduced the drink. Chinese writer Lu Yu wrote in A.D. 780 that there were "tens of thousands" of teas. Chinese tea was introduced to Japan in A.D. 800. It was then introduced to Europe in the early 1600s, when trade began between Europe and the Far East. At that time, China was the main supplier of tea to the world. Then in 1834, tea cultivation began in India and spread to Sri Lanka, Thailand, Burma, and other areas of Southeast Asia. Today, Java, South Africa, South America, and areas of the Caucasus also produce tea.

　　There are three kinds of tea: black, green, and oolong. Most international tea trading is in black tea. Black tea preparation consists mainly of picking young leaves and leaf buds on a clear sunny day and letting the leaves dry for about an hour in the sun. Then, they are lightly rolled and left in a fermentation room to develop scent and a red color. Next, they are heated several more times. Finally, the leaves are dried in a basket over a charcoal fire. Green tea leaves are heated in steam, rolled, and dried. Oolong tea is prepared similarly to black tea, but without the fermentation time.

　　Three main varieties of tea—Chinese, Assamese, and Cambodian—have distinct characteristics. The Chinese variety, a strong plant that can grow to be 2.75 meters high, can live to be 100 years old and survives cold winters. The Assamese variety can grow 18 meters high and lives about 40 years. The Cambodian tea tree grows five meters tall.

　　Tea is enjoyed worldwide as a refreshing and stimulating drink. Because so many people continue to drink the many varieties of tea, it will probably continue as the world's most popular drink.

01 In the early 1600s, tea was introduced to Europe due to _____.

(A) revolution

(B) marriage

(C) business

(D) education

02 According to the passage, which of the following is the most popular tea around the world?

(A) Green tea.

(B) Black tea.

(C) Oolong tea.

(D) European tea.

03 According to the passage, which of the following is TRUE about tea preparation?

(A) Black tea leaves need to be picked on a cloudy day.

(B) Green tea leaves need to be heated over a charcoal fire.

(C) The preparation of oolong tea is similar to that of black tea.

(D) Oolong tea leaves need to be heated in steam before they are rolled.

04 Which of the following statements can be inferred from the passage?

(A) People drink tea to become rich and healthy.

(B) Java developed tea cultivation earlier than India.

(C) Tea plants can grow for only a short period of time.

(D) People drink tea because of its variety and refreshing effect.

DAY
6

Part 1
詞
彙
題
Day 6
完成 25%

Part 2
綜
合
測
驗
Day 6
完成 50%

Part 3
文
意
選
填
Day 6
完成 75%

Part 4
閱
讀
測
驗
Day 6
完成 100%

中譯 | 茶是最先調製的飲品。早在西元前二七三七年，中國的炎帝神農氏推廣了這種飲品。西元七八〇年，中國作家陸羽寫道有「數以萬計」種茶。西元八〇〇年，中國的茶傳入日本，在十七世紀早期，歐洲和遠東貿易開始之時，又傳入歐洲。那時候，中國是全世界的主要茶葉供應國。後來，在一八三四年，茶的種植開始在印度興起，也傳入了斯里蘭卡、泰國、緬甸，以及東南亞的其他地區。如今，爪哇、南非、南美，以及高加索地區，都出產茶葉。

茶有三種：紅茶、綠茶和烏龍茶。大多數的國際茶葉貿易都是紅茶。紅茶的製作，主要是在晴朗的日子裡採摘嫩葉和葉芽，然後在陽光下晾曬一個小時左右，待這些茶葉稍顯捲曲時，送入發酵室，以提煉香味，並加深紅色色澤。接下來，要進行數次加熱。最後把這些葉子放在籃子裡，置於炭火上進行乾燥。綠茶茶葉會被置於蒸汽中加熱，捲曲，乾燥。烏龍茶則是與紅茶的製作相似，卻省去了發酵時間。

茶的主要品種有三——中國、阿薩姆、柬埔寨——各有其特色。中國茶品種生命力強，植株可以高達二‧七五公尺，存活一百年，也可以度過寒冬。阿薩姆品種可以高達十八公尺，存活四十年。而柬埔寨茶樹則是五公尺高。

茶作為一種提神的刺激性飲品，受到世界各地人們的喜愛。這麼多人都在持續飲用許多種類的茶，有鑒於此，茶也許會持續成為世界上最受歡迎的飲品。

解譯 | 在閱讀文章之前，先要預覽題目，然後再帶著問題有針對性地閱讀文章。第 1、2、4 題是文意理解，第 3 題是判斷正誤。理解了題目要求之後，閱讀全文，依次作答。

第 1 題是文意理解，問的是十七世紀早期茶傳入歐洲的原因。根據第 1 段第 5 句內容「It was then introduced to Europe in the early 1600s, when trade began between Europe and the Far East.」可知，十七世紀早期，歐洲和遠東貿易開始之時，又傳入歐洲，與選項 (C) 相符。選項 (A) 意為「變革」，選項 (B) 意為「婚姻」，選項 (D) 意為「教育」，在文中找不到相關敘述，可以排除。所以選 (C)。

第 2 題也是文意理解，問的是根據短文內容，哪一種茶在世界上最為流行。根據第 2 段第 2 句內容「Most international tea trading is in black tea.」可知，大多數的國際茶葉貿易都是紅茶，即是紅茶最為流行，所以選 (B)。

第 3 題是判斷正誤，考的是細節，問的是關於茶葉的製作，哪一項敘述是正確的。根據第 2 段最後一句內容「Oolong tea is prepared similarly to black tea」可知，烏龍茶與紅茶的製作相似，與選項 (C) 相符。同樣，此題也可以用排除法來解答。根據第 2 段第 3 句內容可知，紅茶的製作主要是在晴朗的日子裡進行，而不是在多雲的日子，排除選項 (A)；根據第 2 段第 6 句內容可知，是紅茶茶葉被置於炭火上進行乾燥，而不是綠茶茶葉，排除選項 (B)；根據第 2 段第 7 句內容可知，是綠茶茶葉會被置於蒸汽中加熱，捲曲，而不是烏龍茶茶葉，排除選項 (D)。所以選 (C)。

第 4 題同樣是文意理解，問的是根據短文，可以得出什麼推論。選項 (A) 意為「人們喝茶以變得健康富裕」，選項 (B) 意為「爪哇的茶文化比印度更早開始」，在文中並沒有提及，可以排除；選項 (C) 意為「茶葉只可以生長很短的一段時間」，與第 3 段內容不符，也可以排除；選項 (D) 意為「茶葉因其多樣性和提神功效而被人們飲用」，與最後一段內容相符。所以選 (D)。

解答＆技巧 | 01 **(C)**　02 **(B)**　03 **(C)**　04 **(D)**

適用 TIP 1　適用 TIP 2　適用 TIP 3　適用 TIP 7　適用 TIP 10
適用 TIP 11　適用 TIP 12　適用 TIP 13　適用 TIP 15　適用 TIP 16

補充
Sri Lanka n 斯里蘭卡；Thailand n 泰國；Burma n 緬甸；Java n 爪哇；Assamese a 阿薩姆的；Cambodian a 柬埔寨的

7,000 單字

- brew [bru] v 6 調製
- beverage [ˋbɛvərɪdʒ] n 6 飲料
- emperor [ˋɛmpərə] n 3 皇帝
- introduce [͵ɪntrəˋdjus] v 2 介紹，引入
- writer [ˋraɪtə] n 1 作家
- east [ist] n 1 東方
- preparation [͵prɛpəˋreʃən] n 3 準備
- bud [bʌd] n 3 芽

- scent [sɛnt] n 5 香味
- charcoal [ˋtʃɑr͵kol] n 6 木炭
- meter [ˋmitə] n 2 公尺
- revolution [͵rɛvəˋluʃən] n 4 革命
- cloudy [ˋklaʊdɪ] a 2 多雲的
- infer [ɪnˋfɝ] v 6 推斷
- healthy [ˋhɛlθɪ] a 2 健康的

MEMO

DAY 6

Part 1
詞彙題
Day 6
完成 25%

Part 2
綜合測驗
Day 6
完成 50%

Part 3
文意選填
Day 6
完成 75%

Part 4
閱讀測驗
Day 6
完成 100%

If you become angry easily and always tend to give vent to your anger in some ineffective ways, please put the following strategies into practice.

Try to recognize and accept your anger. When you get angry, you should think about your reaction and ask yourself: What made you get so angry? How will you intend to express it? Will you snap at others and say hostile and cutting words to them? Will it do something to you physically, such as making you clench your jaw or giving you a headache?

Take responsibility for your anger. You should know that it's up to you to decide whether to become angry or not. Just be responsible for your feelings, thoughts and behavior. Then there is little possibility for you to vent your anger on others incorrectly.

Talk about your anger with your family or friends. It is a fact that verbal expression of your feelings is a good way to deal with your anger. With the support from personal relationships, you may feel more confident in yourself and properly conduct yourself.

Cool off with all your efforts. As time goes on, you may understand what actually set you off and wonder whether your actions are necessary. So try to cool off with these steps: take deep breaths over and over again; remove yourself to a quiet place, or go for a walk; imagine a serene setting or experience; meditate on the event that made you angry from another perspective.

Learn appropriate ways to express your anger. Perhaps an anger management program or a therapist can help you learn to defuse your rage. It is just our inability to resolve wounds carrying from the past that makes us unable to deal with anger. Therefore, discussing your feelings with a professional can be a good way for you to untangle these emotions.

01 Which one of the following statements is true?

(A) There is actually no way to control your emotions.

(B) If you get angry, you should try to ask yourself what actually has caused your anger.

(C) You can always vent your anger on others at your will.

(D) Surroundings don't affect your feelings.

02 Which of the following strategies is not mentioned in the passage?

(A) Try to keep your emotions secret from others.

(B) Be responsible for your anger.

(C) Try your best to cool off.

(D) Try to express your anger appropriately.

03 The word "verbal" in the fourth paragraph is closest in meaning to _____.

(A) formal

(B) written

(C) oral

(D) informal

04 What is the main idea of the passage?

(A) How to develop a sense of responsibility.

(B) How to express your emotions.

(C) How to view your anger.

(D) How to control your anger effectively.

DAY
6

Part 1
詞
彙
題
Day 6
完成 25%

Part 2
綜
合
測
驗
Day 6
完成 50%

Part 3
文
意
選
填
Day 6
完成 75%

Part 4
閱
讀
測
驗
Day 6
完成 100%

中譯｜如果你是個易怒的人，也總是習慣用一些無效的方法來發洩自己的怒氣，那麼請將下列策略付諸實踐。

試著認識並接受你的憤怒。生氣的時候，應該思考自己的反應，問問自己：是什麼讓你如此生氣？你打算如何發洩？你會罵其他人，或是對他們說些有敵意的、挖苦的話嗎？它會對你的身體產生什麼影響，例如，讓你咬牙切齒，或是讓你感到頭疼？

你要對你的憤怒負責。你應該知道，要不要生氣是取決於你自己的。對自己的感情、想法和行為負責，那麼，你就不大可能會錯誤地將怒氣發洩在其他人身上。和你的家人或是朋友談談你的憤怒。事實上，口頭表達出你的感受，是應對憤怒的好方法。有了來自親密之人的支持，你也許會更加自信，並且表現出得體的行為舉止。

盡力冷靜。隨著時間的流逝，你可能會明白是什麼使你開始這樣做，並且反思自己的行為是否有必要。所以，試著用這些方式冷靜下來：不斷地深呼吸；移動到安靜的環境中去，或是去散步；想像寧靜的景色或是平和的經歷；沉思，從另一個角度來看待令你生氣的事件。

學會用合適的方式來發洩憤怒。憤怒管理課程或是治療師，也許可以幫你學會化解怒氣。很多時候，正是因為我們無法解決過去的一些創傷，才無法應對憤怒。因此與專業人士探討你的感受，可能是你理清這些情緒的好方法。

解譯｜在閱讀文章之前，先要預覽題目，然後再帶著問題有針對性地閱讀文章。第 1 題是判斷正誤，第 2 題是文意理解，第 3 題是詞義辨析，第 4 題是概括主旨。理解了題目要求之後，閱讀全文，依次作答。

第 1 題是判斷正誤，考的是細節，問的是哪一項敘述是正確的。根據第 2 段第 2 句內容「When you get angry, you should think about your reaction and ask yourself: What made you get so angry?」可知，生氣的時候，應該思考自己的反應，問問自己是什麼讓你如此生氣。與選項 (B) 敘述相符。同樣，此題也可以用排除法來解答。根據第 1 段內容可知，有些策略可以幫助抑怒，而不是沒有抑怒方法，選項 (A) 敘述錯誤，排除；根據第 3 段最後一句內容可知，不應該錯誤地將怒氣發洩在其他人身上，排除選項 (C)；根據第 5 段第 3 句內容可知，環境的轉換可以幫助你冷靜下來，而不是對情緒全無影響，排除選項 (D)。所以選 (B)。

第 2 題是文意理解，問的是哪一項策略在文中沒有提及。第 3 段首句內容與選項 (B) 相符，第 5 段首句內容與選項 (C) 相符，第 4 段首句內容與選項 (D) 相符。只有選項 (A)，在文中找不到相關敘述。所以選 (A)。

第 3 題是考 verbal 的同義字。選項 (A) 意為「正式的」，選項 (B) 意為「書面的」，選項 (C) 意為「口頭的」，選項 (D) 意為「非正式的」。根據第 4 段第 2 句內容可知，形容詞 verbal 在文中意為「口頭的」，所以選 (C)。

第 4 題是概括主旨。本篇結構是先總述後分述，第 1 段可以視為主旨段，根據第 1 段內容可知，文章主旨是介紹應對怒氣的策略，與選項 (D) 敘述相符。所以選 (D)。

解答＆技巧 | 01 (B) 02 (A) 03 (C) 04 (D)

適用 TIP 1　適用 TIP 2　適用 TIP 3　適用 TIP 7　適用 TIP 10　適用 TIP 11
適用 TIP 12　適用 TIP 13　適用 TIP 14　適用 TIP 15　適用 TIP 16

DAY 6

Part 1 詞彙題
Day 6
完成 25%

Part 2 綜合測驗
Day 6
完成 50%

Part 3 文意選填
Day 6
完成 75%

Part 4 閱讀測驗
Day 6
完成 100%

補充
ineffective [a] 效果不佳的；physically [ad] 身體上地；headache [n] 頭痛；defuse [v] 緩和；untangle [v] 解開

7,000 單字
- strategy [ˈstrætədʒɪ] [n] 3 策略
- clench [klɛntʃ] [v] 6 緊閉
- jaw [dʒɔ] [n] 3 下顎
- whether [ˈhwɛðɚ] [conj] 1 是否
- thought [θɔt] [n] 1 想法
- confident [ˈkɑnfədənt] [a] 3 自信的
- breath [brɛθ] [n] 3 呼吸
- remove [rɪˈmuv] [v] 3 移動
- imagine [ɪˈmædʒɪn] [v] 2 想像
- serene [səˈrin] [a] 6 平靜的
- meditate [ˈmɛdə͵tet] [v] 6 沉思
- perspective [pɚˈspɛktɪv] [n] 6 看法，洞察力
- therapist [ˈθɛrəpɪst] [n] 6 治療專家
- rage [redʒ] [n] 4 盛怒
- resolve [rɪˈzɑlv] [v] 4 解決

MEMO

Earthquakes usually occur without warning. It's quite important to take some steps in order to survive an earthquake. We should reserve water, food, clothes, medicine, tools and other things. Once an earthquake occurs, we should know at least how to live through the most dangerous and also the most precious 72 hours.

Generally speaking, a normal person needs at least 3.8 liters of drinking water per day. To ensure enough water, we should take the following factors into account. First, children and ill people need more water. Second, a medical emergency may require more water. Last, hot weather may double the amount of water needed. You can buy bottled water and keep it in its original container. Don't open it before you need to use it. Besides, you should also pay attention to its expiration date.

As for food, you could keep a supply of non-perishable food on hand. Remember to stock food that requires no refrigeration, cooking or special preparation, and food for infants or other special dietary needs should also be included. Avoid those food that will make you thirsty. Salt-free crackers, whole grain cereals and canned goods should be OK. In addition, some cooking utensils, such as a manual can opener, should also be prepared.

If you live in a cold area, you should think about warmth because you may not be able to have heating after an earthquake. In this case, you should prepare proper clothing and bedding supplies and have at least one complete change of clothing and shoes. Besides, coats, long pants, hats, gloves and blankets should also be taken into consideration.

01 Which one of the following statements is true?

(A) Warmth need not be taken into consideration in case of an earthquake.

(B) We should stock up with food that requires refrigeration or special preparation.

(C) Chilren and ill people may need less water.

(D) In case of hot temperatures, more water should be needed.

02 All the following items should be prepared in order to survive an earthquake except _____.

(A) non-perishable food

(B) bottled water

(C) books

(D) necessary medicine

03 The word "utensils" in the third paragraph is closest in meaning to _____.

(A) machines

(B) implements

(C) vehicles

(D) phones

04 What is the main idea of the passage?

(A) Preparation you need in order to survive an earthquake.

(B) Warning of an earthquake.

(C) Food and drinks.

(D) Clothes and bedding supplies.

DAY
6

Part 1
詞
彙
題
Day 6
完成 25%

Part 2
綜
合
測
驗
Day 6
完成 50%

Part 3
文
意
選
填
Day 6
完成 75%

Part 4
閱
讀
測
驗
Day 6
完成 100%

中譯｜地震通常是沒有預兆的，因此為了在地震中倖存下來，採取措施是十分重要的。我們應該儲存水、食物、衣服、藥品、工具和其他物品。一旦地震發生，我們至少應該知道，如何度過最危險的也是最寶貴的七十二小時。

通常來說，正常人每天需要三‧八公升的飲用水。為了確保有足夠的水，我們應該考慮以下因素。首先，兒童和病人需要更多的水。其次，醫療緊急情況也許會需要更多的水。最後，高溫天氣也許需要雙倍的水。可以購買瓶裝水，並且保持原包裝。在飲用之前，不要打開，也要注意保存期限。

至於食物，你應該在手邊儲存一些的不易腐壞的食品。要記得，儲存不需要冷藏、烹飪或是特殊處理的食品，嬰兒食品和有特殊飲食之人需要的食品，也應該準備。要避免那些會讓你感到口渴的食物。無鹽餅乾、全麥麥片和罐裝食品，都是很好的選擇。此外，手動開罐器之類的廚房用具，也要準備。

如果你生活在寒冷地區，應該考慮保暖問題，因為地震過後，你可能會無法取暖。在這種情況下，你應該準備合適的衣服和睡覺用品，至少要有一套換洗的衣服和鞋子。此外，外套、長褲、帽子、手套和毛毯，也應該考慮在內。

解譯｜在閱讀文章之前，先要預覽題目，然後再帶著問題有針對性地閱讀文章。第 1 題是判斷正誤，第 2 題是文意理解，第 3 題是詞義辨析，第 4 題是概括主旨。理解了題目要求之後，閱讀全文，依次作答。

第 1 題是判斷正誤，考的是細節，問的是哪一項敘述是正確的。根據第 2 段第 5 句內容「hot weather may double the amount of water needed」可知，高溫天氣也許需要更多的水，與選項 (D) 相符。同樣，此題也可以用排除法來解答。根據第 4 段首句內容可知，在寒冷地區需要考慮保暖問題，選項 (A) 敘述錯誤，排除；根據第 3 段第 2 句內容可知，應該儲存不需要冷藏或是特殊處理的食品，排除選項 (B)；根據第 2 段第 3 句內容可知，兒童和病人需要更多的水，排除選項 (C)。所以選 (D)。

第 2 題是文意理解，問的是為了在地震中倖存下來，哪一項物品是不需要準備的。第 4 段首句內容與選項 (A) 相符，第 2 段倒數第 3 行內容與選項 (B) 相符，選項 (D) 在文中沒有直接敘述，卻可以根據第 1 段第 3 句內容「We should reserve water, food, clothes, medicine, tools and other things.」加以推斷，也是需要準備的。只有選項 (C)，在文中找不到相關敘述。所以選 (C)。

第 3 題是考名詞 utensil 的同義字。選項 (A) 意為「機器」，選項 (B) 意為「工具」，選項 (C) 意為「交通工具」，選項 (D) 意為「電話」。根據第 3 段最後一句內容可知，utensil 在文中意為「用具」，所以選 (B)。

第 4 題是概括主旨。文中有明確的主旨句，本篇結構是先總述後分述，第 1 段可以視為主旨段，根據第 1 段內容可知，文章主旨是預防地震發生而採取的準備措施，與選項 (A) 敘述相符。所以選 (A)。

解答＆技巧｜ **01 (D)**　**02 (C)**　**03 (B)**　**04 (A)**

適用 TIP 1　適用 TIP 2　適用 TIP 3　適用 TIP 7　適用 TIP 10
適用 TIP 11　適用 TIP 12　適用 TIP 13　適用 TIP 14　適用 TIP 15

DAY
6

Part 1
詞彙題
Day 6
完成 25%

Part 2
綜合測驗
Day 6
完成 50%

Part 3
文意選填
Day 6
完成 75%

Part 4
閱讀測驗
Day 6
完成 100%

補充

survive an earthquake ph 在地震中倖存；non-perishable a 不易腐壞的；refrigeration n 冷藏；salt-free a 無鹽的；opener n 開蓋工具

7,000 單字

- earthquake [ˈɝθ.kwek] n 2 地震
- reserve [rɪˈzɝv] v 3 保留
- liter [ˈlitɚ] n 6 公升
- account [əˈkaʊnt] n 3 敘述
- ill [ɪl] a 2 生病的
- emergency [ɪˈmɝdʒənsɪ] n 3 緊急事件
- container [kənˈtenɚ] n 4 容器
- expiration [ˌɛkspəˈreʃən] n 6 到期，期滿

- infant [ˈɪnfənt] n 4 嬰兒
- thirsty [ˈθɝstɪ] a 2 口渴的
- manual [ˈmænjʊəl] a 4 手控的
- can [kæn] n 1 罐頭
- pants [pænts] n 1 長褲
- glove [glʌv] n 2 手套
- blanket [ˈblæŋkɪt] n 3 毛毯

MEMO

♫375

After a few months of a relationship, your parents have heard so much about your girlfriend or boyfriend after they know their existence. Then meeting your significant other's parents for the first time must be exciting and terrifying. Although so many things are out of your control, you can freely choose what clothes to wear. Learning how to match clothes will be a required lesson for you.

Many people believe that a conservative suit should be a good choice, and too revealing clothes would do the opposite. You should remember that all clothes you wear should give you a comfortable feeling. In a casual setting, a pair of comfy jeans and a simple top that you love could attract people's attention, and a pair of black heels would perfect the ensemble. All in all, clothes in your size should be the best because it cannot only boost your confidence, but also rub off on others around you. Don't wear clothes that are unfit for you.

If your meeting is in an afternoon barbecue, then boys are good with jeans or khakis with a polo or crewneck tee, and girls can match a dress or sundress with a denim jacket or scarf, and a pair of sandals should also be needed. Petite girls can also try a silk garment, skinny jeans and a wedge heel. No matter what clothes you choose, you must make yourself look pretty and cohesive.

On the other hand, if the meeting happens to be at a holiday gathering, dressing with a little festivity could be appropriate. It's nice to wear colors like dark blue or red because these colors are always inviting and appropriate.

01 Which one of the following statements is true?

(A) Clothes with dark blue or red color should be inviting and appropriate.

(B) Clothes have nothing to do with your confidence.

(C) A pair of comfy jeans and a simple top should be okay for a holiday gathering.

(D) Boys with jeans or khakis should be all right for a dinner party.

02 We can learn from the second paragraph that _____ should always be the best.

(A) clothes with the proper size

(B) revealing clothes

(C) a conservative suit

(D) comfy jeans

03 The word "festivity" in the last paragraph is closest in meaning to _____.

(A) fear

(B) anxiety

(C) sorrow

(D) rejoicing

04 What is the main idea of the passage?

(A) What to wear on formal occasions.

(B) What to wear on informal occasions.

(C) What to wear when meeting your lover's parents for the first time.

(D) What to wear at a holiday gathering.

DAY
6

Part 1
詞
彙
題
Day 6
完成 25%

Part 2
綜
合
測
驗
Day 6
完成 50%

Part 3
文
意
選
填
Day 6
完成 75%

Part 4
閱
讀
測
驗
Day 6
完成 100%

中譯｜ 經過幾個月的相處，你的父母知道你有了男／女朋友，也已經聽説了他／她的很多事情。這時候，第一次見對方家長，必定是既讓人興奮又害怕。很多事情你都無法掌握，但是你可以自由選擇要穿的衣著。學會如何搭配衣物，將會成為你的一門必修課。

很多人認為，傳統的套裝應該是最好的選擇，而過於暴露的衣服，則會有相反的效果。你要記住，所穿的所有衣服，都要帶給你舒適的感覺。在隨意的場合中，一條寬鬆牛仔褲，外加一件喜歡的簡單上衣，會引起人們的注意，再搭配一雙黑色的高跟鞋，將會使整體效果達到完美。最重要的是，合身的衣服就是最好的衣服，因為它不僅會增強你的自信心，還能引人注目。不要穿不合身的衣服。

如果你們是在下午的庭院燒烤見面，那麼男孩穿牛仔褲或是卡其褲，外加 polo 衫或是圓領 T 恤都不錯，女孩可以用牛仔外套或圍巾，來搭配長裙或是背心裙，加上一雙涼鞋。身材嬌小的女孩，也可以試試緞面上衣、緊身牛仔和楔形高跟鞋。無論你選擇什麼樣的衣服，都必須讓自己看起來漂亮而和諧。

另一方面，如果碰巧是在假期聚會上會面，那麼帶有一點歡慶氣息的裝扮，就很合適。穿深藍色或是紅色的衣服就很好，因為這些顏色總是既好看又適宜的。

解譯｜ 在閱讀文章之前，先要預覽題目，然後再帶著問題有針對性地閱讀文章。第 1 題是判斷正誤，第 2 題是文意理解，第 3 題是詞義辨析，第 4 題是概括主旨。理解了題目要求之後，閱讀全文，依次作答。

第 1 題是判斷正誤，問的是哪一項敘述是正確的。根據第 4 段最後一句內容「It's nice to wear colors like dark blue or red because these colors are always inviting and appropriate.」可知，穿深藍色或是紅色的衣服既好看又適宜，與選項 (A) 相符。同樣，此題也可以用排除法來解答。根據第 2 段倒數第 2 行內容可知，合適的衣服可以增加自信，選項 (B) 卻説衣服與自信無關，敘述錯誤，排除；根據第 2 段第 3 句內容可知，寬鬆牛仔褲和簡單上衣，適合隨意的場合，而不是節日聚會；排除選項 (C)；根據第 3 段第 1 句內容可知，男孩穿牛仔褲或是卡其褲，適合於下午燒烤時的會面，而不是晚宴，排除選項 (D)。所以選 (A)。

第 2 題是文意理解，考的是細節，根據第 2 段，什麼樣的衣著才是最好的。第 2 段第 4 句內容「clothes in your size should be the best」可知，合身的衣服才是最好的，與選項 (A) 相符。所以選 (A)。

第 3 題是考名詞 festivity 的同義字。選項 (A) 意為「恐懼」，選項 (B) 意為「憂慮」，選項 (C) 意為「悲傷」，選項 (D) 意為「歡樂」。根據第 4 段首句內容可知，festivity 在文中意為「歡慶，歡樂」，所以選 (D)。

第 4 題是概括主旨。文中有明確的主旨句，本篇結構是先總述後分述，第 1 段可以視為主旨段，根據第 1 段內容可知，文章主旨是初次見戀人的家長時的穿著，與選項 (C) 敘述相符。所以選 (C)。

解答 & 技巧 ┃ 01 **(A)** 02 **(A)** 03 **(D)** 04 **(C)**

適用 TIP 1　適用 TIP 2　適用 TIP 3　適用 TIP 7　適用 TIP 10

適用 TIP 11　適用 TIP 12　適用 TIP 13　適用 TIP 14　適用 TIP 15

DAY 6

補充

girlfriend n 女朋友；boyfriend n 男朋友；terrifying a 可怕的；comfy a 舒服的；
ensemble n 整體效果

7,000 單字

- existence [ɪɡˋzɪstəns] n ③ 存在
- conservative [kənˋsɝvətɪv] a ④ 保守的
- casual [ˋkæʒʊəl] a ③ 隨意的
- heel [hil] n ③ 鞋跟
- boost [bust] v ⑥ 增強
- rub [rʌb] v ① 擦
- meeting [ˋmitɪŋ] n ② 見面
- barbecue [ˋbɑrbɪˏkju] n ② 燒烤

- crewneck [ˋkrunɛk] n ③ 圓領
- jacket [ˋdʒækɪt] n ② 夾克
- scarf [skɑrf] n ③ 圍巾
- sandal [ˋsændl] n ⑤ 涼鞋
- garment [ˋɡɑrmənt] n ⑤ 衣服
- skinny [ˋskɪnɪ] a ② 瘦的
- gathering [ˋɡæðərɪŋ] n ⑤ 聚會

Part 1
詞彙題
Day 6
完成 25%

Part 2
綜合測驗
Day 6
完成 50%

Part 3
文意選填
Day 6
完成 75%

Part 4
閱讀測驗
Day 6
完成 100%

MEMO

DAY 7

Don't give up on something just because you think you can't do it.
— *ChandaKochhar*

不要因為覺得自己做不到，就放棄一件事。
——昌達・科赫哈

▶ **Part 1** │ 詞 彙 題

▶ **Part 2** │ 綜合測驗

▶ **Part 3** │ 文意選填

▶ **Part 4** │ 閱讀測驗

Part 1 　詞彙題 | Vocabulary Questions

01 London, the _____ of the United Kingdom, is the biggest financial center in Europe.

(A) abbreviation   (B) aborigine

(C) accommodation   (D) capital

補充
financial center ph 金融中心

7,000 單字
- kingdom [ˈkɪŋdəm] n ② 王國
- abbreviation [əˌbrivɪˈeʃən] n ⑥ 縮寫
- aborigine [æbəˈrɪdʒəni] n ⑥ 原住民
- accommodation [əˌkɑməˈdeʃən] n ⑥ 住處
- capital [ˈkæpət!] n ③ 首都

中譯│英國的首都倫敦是歐洲最大的金融中心。

解說│四個選項皆為名詞。依據題意，應該是「英國的首都倫敦」，選項 (D) capital 表示「首都」，符合題意，其他三個選項都不符合題意。

解答&技巧│**(D)** 適用 TIP 1　適用 TIP 4

02 According to the _____ sales figures, the sales have increased by thirty percent this month.

(A) ceramic   (B) arch

(C) latest   (D) broke

補充
sales figure ph 銷售數字

7,000 單字
- thirty [ˈθɝtɪ] num ① 三十
- ceramic [səˈræmɪk] a ③ 陶瓷的
- arch [ɑrtʃ] a ④ 主要的
- latest [ˈletɪst] a ② 最新的
- broke [brok] a ④ 破產的

中譯│最新的銷售數字顯示，這個月的銷售量成長了百分之三十。

解說│四個選項皆為形容詞。依據題意，應該是「最新的銷售數字」，選項 (C) latest 表示「最新的」，符合題意，其他三個選項都不符合題意。

解答&技巧│**(C)** 適用 TIP 1　適用 TIP 4

03 After negotiation, the young man agreed to _____ with the police for investigation.

(A) clash   (B) conquer

(C) cooperate   (D) construct

補充
agree to ph 同意

7,000 單字
- negotiation [nɪˌgoʃɪˈeʃən] n ④ 協商
- clash [klæʃ] v ⑥ 衝突
- conquer [ˈkɑŋkə] v ④ 戰勝
- cooperate [koˈɑpəˌret] v ④ 合作
- construct [kənˈstrʌkt] v ④ 建造

中譯│經過協商，這個年輕人同意配合警方進行調查。

解說│四個選項皆為動詞。依據題意，應該是「年輕人同意配合警方進行調查」，選項 (C) cooperate 表示「配合」，符合題意，其他三個選項都不符合題意。

解答&技巧│**(C)** 適用 TIP 3　適用 TIP 4

DAY 7

Part 1
詞
彙
題
Day 7
完成 25%

Part 2
綜
合
測
驗
Day 7
完成 50%

Part 3
文
意
選
填
Day 7
完成 75%

Part 4
閱
讀
測
驗
Day 7
完成 100%

04 At the meeting the manager _____ that he would quit the office and left the company next month.

(A) crushed　　　　　(B) cursed

(C) declared　　　　 (D) devised

補充
quit the office ph 辭職

7,000 單字
- quit [kwɪt] v ② 離職
- crush [krʌʃ] v ④ 壓碎
- curse [kɝs] v ④ 詛咒
- declare [dɪˋklɛr] v ④ 宣佈
- devise [dɪˋvaɪz] v ④ 設計

中譯｜經理在會議上宣佈，他將在下個月辭職並離開公司。

解說｜四個選項皆為動詞。依據題意，應該是「經理在會議上宣佈」，選項 (C) declared 表示「宣佈」，符合題意，是正確選項。

解答＆技巧｜**(C)** 適用 TIP 1　適用 TIP 4

---

05 When people feel uncomfortable or nervous, they may _____ their arms across their chests as if to protect themselves. 【98年學測英文】

(A) toss　　　　　　(B) fold

(C) veil　　　　　　 (D) discourage

補充
protect oneself ph 自我保護

7,000 單字
- to [tu] prep ① 到
- toss [tɔs] v ③ 投擲
- fold [fold] v ③ 折疊
- veil [vel] v ⑤ 遮蔽
- discourage [dɪsˋkɝɪdʒ] v ④ 使氣餒

中譯｜當人們感到不安或緊張時，他們就會抱住手臂，交叉在胸前，似乎想保護自己。

解說｜四個選項皆為動詞。依據題意，應該是「抱住手臂」，選項 (B) fold 表示「折疊」，符合題意，其他三個選項都不符合題意。

解答＆技巧｜**(B)** 適用 TIP 3　適用 TIP 4

---

06 The waitresses in this restaurant always treat every customer in a _____ manner.

(A) courteous　　　　(B) distinguished

(C) dusty　　　　　　(D) earnest

補充
in a manner ph 用一種方式

7,000 單字
- waitress [ˋwetrɪs] n ② 女服務員
- courteous [ˋkɝtjəs] a ④ 有禮貌的
- distinguished [dɪˋstɪŋgwɪʃt] a ④ 著名的
- dusty [ˋdʌstɪ] a ④ 落滿灰塵的
- earnest [ˋɝnɪst] a ④ 認真的

中譯｜這家餐廳的女服務員總是有禮貌地招待每一位客人。

解說｜四個選項皆為形容詞。依據題意，應該是「服務員禮貌地招待客人」，選項 (A) courteous 表示「有禮貌的」，符合題意，其他三個選項都不符合題意。

解答＆技巧｜**(A)** 適用 TIP 1　適用 TIP 4

07 The doctor told me that people who lived in _____ areas easily suffered from rheumatism.

(A) elastic   (B) elegant

(C) elementary   (D) damp

補充
live in ph 住在～

7,000 單字
- rheumatism [ˈrumə͵tɪzəm] n 6 風濕病
- elastic [ɪˈlæstɪk] a 4 有彈性的
- elegant [ˈɛləgənt] a 4 高雅的
- elementary [ˌɛləˈmɛntərɪ] a 4 基礎的
- damp [dæmp] a 4 潮濕的

中譯｜醫生告訴我，住在潮濕地區的人容易患風濕病。

解說｜四個選項皆為形容詞。依據題意，應該是「住在潮濕地區的人容易患風濕病」，選項 (D) damp 表示「潮濕的」，符合題意，其他三個選項都不符合題意。

解答&技巧｜**(D)** 適用 TIP 3   適用 TIP 4

---

08 I am ill, and I cannot eat spicy food; please give me some _____ porridge.

(A) eventual   (B) delicate

(C) experimental   (D) explosive

補充
be ill ph 生病

7,000 單字
- spicy [ˈspaɪsɪ] a 4 辛辣的
- eventual [ɪˈvɛntʃʊəl] a 4 最終的
- delicate [ˈdɛləkət] a 4 清淡可口的
- experimental [ɪkˌspɛrəˈmɛntl] a 4 實驗的
- explosive [ɪkˈsplosɪv] a 4 爆炸的

中譯｜我生病了，不能吃辛辣的食物，請給我一些清淡可口的粥。

解說｜四個選項皆為形容詞。依據題意，應該是「給我一些清淡可口的粥」，選項 (B) delicate 表示「清淡可口的」，符合題意，是正確選項。

解答&技巧｜**(B)** 適用 TIP 3   適用 TIP 4

---

09 The president had an emergency meeting with the shareholders before his _____ to San Franscisco.

(A) departure   (B) fantasy

(C) ferry   (D) fireplace

補充
emergency meeting ph 緊急會議

7,000 單字
- shareholder [ˈʃɛr͵holdə] n 4 股東
- departure [dɪˈpartʃə] n 4 離開
- fantasy [ˈfæntəsɪ] n 4 幻想
- ferry [ˈfɛrɪ] n 4 渡船
- fireplace [ˈfaɪr͵ples] n 4 壁爐

中譯｜總裁在前往舊金山之前，與股東們一起召開了緊急會議。

解說｜四個選項皆為名詞。依據題意，應該是「前往舊金山」，選項 (A) departure 表示「離開」，而 departure to 表示「離開去某地」，符合題意。

解答&技巧｜**(A)** 適用 TIP 2   適用 TIP 4

10 With the quality of honesty and modesty, he is really a _____ companion for most of the girls.

(A) frantic (B) fatal

(C) dependable (D) gigantic

補充
most of ph 大多數

7,000 單字
- modesty [ˈmɑdɪstɪ] n 4 謙虛
- frantic [ˈfræntɪk] a 5 狂亂的
- fatal [ˈfetl] a 4 致命的
- dependable [dɪˈpɛndəbl] a 4 可靠的
- gigantic [dʒaɪˈgæntɪk] a 4 巨大的

中譯｜他為人誠實、謙虛，對於大多數女孩來說，他真是一位可靠的伴侶。

解說｜四個選項皆為形容詞。依據題意，應該是「可靠的伴侶」，選項 (C) dependable 表示「可靠的」，符合題意，其他三個選項都不符合題意。

解答＆技巧｜ **(C)** 適用 TIP 3 適用 TIP 4

---

11 The _____ murderer suddenly vanished, and the police could not find any information about him.

(A) glorious (B) gracious

(C) mysterious (D) grammatical

補充
information about ph 有關～的資訊

7,000 單字
- murderer [ˈmɝdərə] n 4 兇手
- glorious [ˈgloriəs] a 4 光榮的
- gracious [ˈgreʃəs] a 4 親切的
- mysterious [mɪsˈtɪrɪəs] a 4 神祕的
- grammatical [grəˈmætɪkl] a 4 文法的

中譯｜那位神祕的殺人兇手突然消失了，警方找不到有關他的任何資訊。

解說｜四個選項皆為形容詞。依據題意，應該是「神祕的殺人兇手消失了」，選項 (C) mysterious 表示「神祕的」，符合題意，是正確選項。

解答＆技巧｜ **(C)** 適用 TIP 1 適用 TIP 4

---

12 My grandson is so _____ that he has to get a new prescription for glasses.

(A) greasy (B) harsh

(C) healthful (D) nearsighted

補充
get a prescription for glasses ph 配眼鏡

7,000 單字
- grandson [ˈgrænd.sʌn] n 1 孫子
- greasy [ˈgrizɪ] a 4 油膩的
- harsh [hɑrʃ] a 4 嚴厲的
- healthful [ˈhɛlθfəl] a 4 健康的
- nearsighted [ˈnɪrˌsaɪtɪd] a 4 近視的

中譯｜我外孫的眼睛近視得厲害，以致於他不得不配一副新眼鏡。

解說｜四個選項皆為形容詞。依據題意，應該是「眼睛近視得厲害」，選項 (D) nearsighted 表示「近視的」，符合題意，是正確選項。

解答＆技巧｜ **(D)** 適用 TIP 1 適用 TIP 4

DAY 7

Part 1
詞彙題
Day 7
完成 25%

Part 2
綜合測驗
Day 7
完成 50%

Part 3
文意選填
Day 7
完成 75%

Part 4
閱讀測驗
Day 7
完成 100%

13 He had tried his best to fulfill the task, but he knew he was fated to _____ the manager.

(A) horrify
(B) infect
(C) disappoint
(D) hasten

補充
be fated to ph 註定

7,000 單字
- fated [ˈfetɪd] a 3 命中註定的
- horrify [ˈhɔrə͵faɪ] v 4 使恐懼
- infect [ɪnˈfɛkt] v 4 感染
- disappoint [͵dɪsəˈpɔɪnt] v 3 使失望
- hasten [ˈhesn̩] v 4 加速

中譯｜他已經盡全力來完成任務，但是他知道他註定會讓經理失望。

解說｜四個選項皆為動詞。依據題意，應該是「讓經理失望」，選項 (C) disappoint 表示「使失望」，符合題意，其他三個選項都不符合題意。

解答＆技巧｜**(C)** 適用 TIP 1　適用 TIP 4

14 This math class is very _____; I have to spend at least two hours every day doing the assignments. 【98年指考英文】

(A) confidential
(B) logical
(C) demanding
(D) resistant

補充
math class ph 數學課
at least ph 至少

7,000 單字
- math [mæθ] n 3 數學
- confidential [͵kɑnfəˈdɛnʃəl] a 6 機密的
- logical [ˈlɑdʒɪkl̩] a 4 合邏輯的
- demanding [dɪˈmændɪŋ] a 4 苛求的
- resistant [rɪˈzɪstənt] a 6 抵抗的

中譯｜這門數學課很吃重，我每天必須花費至少兩個小時來做作業。

解說｜四個選項皆為形容詞。依據題意，應該是「數學課很吃重」，選項 (C) demanding 表示「要求苛刻的」，符合題意。

解答＆技巧｜**(C)** 適用 TIP 3　適用 TIP 4

15 If we take _____ methods in the production process, a lot of money can be saved.

(A) intermediate
(B) junior
(C) lawful
(D) economical

補充
production process ph 生產過程

7,000 單字
- can [kæn] aux 1 能，可以
- intermediate [͵ɪntəˈmidɪət] a 4 中間的
- junior [ˈdʒunjə] a 4 較年少的
- lawful [ˈlɔfəl] a 4 合法的
- economical [͵ikəˈnɑmɪkl̩] a 4 節約的

中譯｜如果我們在生產過程中採用經濟手段，我們就可以節省很多資金。

解說｜四個選項皆為形容詞。依據題意，應該是「採用經濟手段」，選項 (D) economical 表示「經濟的」，符合題意，是正確選項。

解答＆技巧｜**(D)** 適用 TIP 3　適用 TIP 4

16 The future commodity market situation is difficult to _____, so we should take all situations into consideration.

(A) lighten   (B) mislead

(C) evaluate   (D) negotiate

中譯｜ 未來的商品市場形勢難以評估，所以我們要將各種情況考慮在內。

解說｜ 四個選項皆為動詞。依據題意，應該是「市場形勢難以評估」，選項 (C) evaluate 表示「評估」，符合題意，其他三個選項都不符合題意。

解答＆技巧｜ **(C)** 適用 TIP 3   適用 TIP 4

> 補充
> market situation ph 市場形勢
>
> 7,000 單字
> - commodity [kə`mɑdətɪ] n 5 商品
> - lighten [`laɪtn] v 4 減輕
> - mislead [mɪs`lid] v 4 誤導
> - evaluate [ɪ`væljʊˌet] v 4 評估
> - negotiate [nɪ`goʃɪˌet] v 4 談判

---

17 We can make some concessions on terms of payment, but we cannot _____ on the price.

(A) offend   (B) overthrow

(C) compromise   (D) portray

中譯｜ 我們可以對付款方式做出讓步，但是在價格上不會妥協。

解說｜ 四個選項皆為動詞。依據題意，應該是「在價格上不會妥協」，選項 (C) compromise 表示「妥協」，符合題意，其他三個選項都不符合題意。

解答＆技巧｜ **(C)** 適用 TIP 3   適用 TIP 4

> 補充
> terms of payment ph 付款方式
>
> 7,000 單字
> - concession [kən`sɛʃən] n 6 讓步
> - offend [ə`fɛnd] v 4 冒犯
> - overthrow [ˌovə`θro] v 4 推翻
> - compromise [`kɑmprəˌmaɪz] v 5 妥協
> - portray [por`tre] v 4 描繪

---

18 The transnational company agreed to apologize to the customers and _____ for their economic losses.

(A) proceed   (B) publish

(C) quake   (D) compensate

中譯｜ 這家跨國公司同意向顧客道歉，並賠償他們的經濟損失。

解說｜ 四個選項皆為動詞。依據題意，應該是「賠償經濟損失」，選項 (D) compensate 表示「賠償」，符合題意，是正確選項。

解答＆技巧｜ **(D)** 適用 TIP 1   適用 TIP 4

> 補充
> compensate for ph 賠償，補償
>
> 7,000 單字
> - transnational [træns`næʃənəl] a 4 跨國的
> - proceed [prə`sid] v 4 開始
> - publish [`pʌblɪʃ] v 4 出版
> - quake [kwek] v 4 震動
> - compensate [`kɑmpənˌset] v 6 賠償

DAY 7

Part 1
詞彙題
Day 7
完成 25%

Part 2
綜合測驗
Day 7
完成 50%

Part 3
文意選填
Day 7
完成 75%

Part 4
閱讀測驗
Day 7
完成 100%

19 He had to _____ and please those local officials in order to obtain the management right of the land.

(A) regulate   (B) flatter

(C) rescue   (D) restore

> 補充
> management right ph 經營權

> 7,000 單字
> • obtain [əb`ten] v ④ 獲得
> • regulate [`rɛgjə,let] v ④ 調節
> • flatter [`flætɚ] v ④ 奉承
> • rescue [`rɛskju] v ④ 營救
> • restore [rɪ`stor] v ④ 恢復

中譯｜為了得到這塊土地的經營權，他不得不奉承討好那些地方官員。

解說｜四個選項皆為動詞。依據題意，應該是「奉承討好那些地方官員」，選項(B) flatter 表示「奉承」，符合題意，其他三個選項都不符合題意。

解答&技巧｜**(B)** 適用 TIP 3 適用 TIP 4

---

20 _____ examination is mainly to examine the examinee's speaking ability, so it is more difficult than the written one.

(A) Respectful   (B) Respectable

(C) Oral   (D) Shortsighted

> 補充
> speaking ability ph 口語能力

> 7,000 單字
> • examinee [ɪg,zæmə`ni] n ④ 應試者
> • respectful [rɪ`spɛktfəl] a ④ 恭敬的
> • respectable [rɪ`spɛktəbl] a ④ 值得尊敬的
> • oral [`orəl] a ④ 口頭的
> • shortsighted [`ʃɔrt`saɪtɪd] a ④ 目光短淺的

中譯｜口試主要檢驗考生的口語能力，所以比筆試難。

解說｜四個選項皆為形容詞。依據題意，應該是「口試檢驗考生的口語能力」，選項(C) Oral 表示「口頭的」，符合題意，其他三個選項都不符合題意。

解答&技巧｜**(C)** 適用 TIP 1 適用 TIP 4

---

21 For the sake of public safety, the government _____ anyone to set off firecrackers in the residential areas.

(A) shrugs   (B) sneezes

(C) sparkles   (D) forbids

> 補充
> residential area ph 住宅區

> 7,000 單字
> • residential [,rɛzə`dɛnʃəl] a ⑥ 住宅的
> • shrug [ʃrʌg] v ④ 聳肩
> • sneeze [sniz] v ④ 打噴嚏
> • sparkle [`spark!] v ④ 使閃耀
> • forbid [fɚ`bɪd] v ④ 禁止

中譯｜為了大家的安全著想，政府禁止任何人在住宅區內燃放鞭炮。

解說｜四個選項皆為動詞。依據題意，應該是「禁止在住宅區內燃放鞭炮」，選項(D) forbids 表示「禁止」，符合題意，是正確選項。

解答&技巧｜**(D)** 適用 TIP 1 適用 TIP 4

22 Not all the companys _____ by the law, which results in the market disorder and inefficiency.

(A) strive   (B) abide

(C) summarize   (D) transfer

中譯｜並非所有企業都遵守法律，這才導致了市場秩序混亂以及效率低下。

解說｜四個選項皆為動詞。依據題意，應該是「遵守法律」，選項 (B) abide 表示「遵守」，而片語 abide by 表示「遵守」，符合題意。

解答＆技巧｜**(B)** 適用 TIP 2 適用 TIP 4

補充
abide by ph 遵守

7,000 單字
- disorder [dɪsˋɔrdɚ] n 4 混亂
- strive [straɪv] v 4 努力
- abide [əˋbaɪd] v 5 忍受
- summarize [ˋsʌməˏraɪz] v 4 總結
- transfer [trænsˋfɝ] v 4 轉移

---

23 Mary and Jane often fight over which radio station to listen to. Their _____ arises mainly from their different tastes in music. 【99年指考英文】

(A) venture   (B) translation

(C) dispute   (D) temptation

中譯｜瑪麗和珍經常為了收聽哪個廣播電臺而爭吵，她們發生爭論主要是因為她們在音樂方面有著不同的品味。

解說｜四個選項皆為名詞。依據題意，應該是「發生爭論」，選項 (C) dispute 表示「爭論」，符合題意，其他三個選項都不符合題意。

解答＆技巧｜**(C)** 適用 TIP 1 適用 TIP 4

補充
fight over ph 為～而爭吵

7,000 單字
- mainly [ˋmenlɪ] ad 2 主要地
- venture [ˋvɛntʃɚ] n 5 企業
- translation [trænsˋleʃən] n 4 翻譯
- dispute [dɪˋspjut] n 4 爭論
- temptation [tɛmpˋteʃən] n 5 引誘

---

24 Compared with the outdated machines, the _____ equipment could rapidly improve productivity.

(A) tremendous   (B) troublesome

(C) advanced   (D) vain

中譯｜相較於那些過時的機器，這些先進的設備能夠快速提高生產效率。

解說｜四個選項皆為形容詞。依據題意，應該是「先進的設備」，選項 (C) advanced 表示「先進的」，符合題意，其他三個選項都不符合題意。

解答＆技巧｜**(C)** 適用 TIP 3 適用 TIP 4

補充
compared with ph 與～相比較

7,000 單字
- productivity [ˏprodʌkˋtɪvətɪ] n 6 生產力
- tremendous [trɪˋmɛndəs] a 4 極大的
- troublesome [ˋtrʌblsəm] a 4 麻煩的
- advanced [ədˋvænst] a 3 先進的
- vain [ven] a 4 徒勞的

DAY 7

Part 1
詞
彙
題
Day 7
完成 25%

Part 2
綜
合
測
驗
Day 7
完成 50%

Part 3
文
意
選
填
Day 7
完成 75%

Part 4
閱
讀
測
驗
Day 7
完成 100%

Part 2 · 綜合測驗 | Comprehensive Questions

A computer is a device that can perform numerical calculations. However, nowadays, a computer usually refers to an electronic device that can perform a __01__ of tasks according to some precise instructions. In 1953 only about 100 computers were used in the __02__ world, but today millions of computers are being widely used by students, businessmen, government officers and people in nearly every field.

Modern computers are more powerful than the huge and expensive ones which were used in the 1960s and 1970s, and they are used not only for household management and personal __03__ , but also for the tasks in business. It is said that the fastest computers have been generally used for scientific and engineering __04__ , but their capabilities are still continually being improved in order to maximize their working speed. Of all the kinds of computers, supercomputers cost billions of dollars and are large enough to __05__ two basketball courts. Thus they are primarily used by government agencies and large research centers.

01 _____ (A) hail   (B) series
         (C) feedback   (D) disclosure

02 _____ (A) dispensable   (B) drastic
         (C) emphatic   (D) whole

03 _____ (A) entertainment   (B) eruption
         (C) fraud   (D) hostility

04 _____ (A) ordeals   (B) momentums
         (C) applications   (D) inclines

05 _____ (A) overturn   (B) cover
         (C) pierce   (D) prescribe

中譯｜電腦是一種能夠執行數值運算的設備。然而，如今，電腦通常指一種能夠根據一些精確的指令，來完成一連串任務的電子設備。在一九五三年，全世界僅約有一百台電腦投入使用，但是如今，學生、商人、政府官員以及幾乎每一個領域的人們都在廣泛使用數百萬台電腦。

現代電腦比二十世紀六、七〇年代時使用的大型、昂貴的電腦更加強大，不僅用於家務管理和個人娛樂，也用於商業事物。據說，最快速的電腦一般已用於科學和工程應用，但是它們的性能仍然持續地加以改進，以盡可能提高它們的工作速率。在所有種類的電腦當中，超級電腦價值數十億美元，大到足以覆蓋兩個籃球場，主要用於政府機構以及大型的研究中心。

解說｜本篇短文的主旨是「電腦」，介紹了電腦的使用以及發展過程。第 1 題的四個選項中，只有 series 能夠構成 a series of 表示「一系列，一連串」，符合題意，所以正確選擇為 (B)。第 2 題的四個選項都是形容詞，但是依據題意應該是「在全世界」，可以表示為 in the whole world，所以最符合題意的選項是 (D)。第 3 題將四個選項的名詞一一代入空格，只有 entertainment 表示「娛樂」符合題意，即正確選項是 (A)。第 4 題的四個選項都是名詞，但是只有 applications 能夠與 engineering 搭配，表示「工程應用」，所以只有選項 (C) 符合題意。第 5 題要選擇合適的動詞。依據題意，cover 表示「覆蓋」符合題意，所以選 (B)。

解答＆技巧｜ 01 **(B)**　02 **(D)**　03 **(A)**　04 **(C)**　05 **(B)**

適用 TIP 1　適用 TIP 2　適用 TIP 7　適用 TIP 11

補充

numerical ⓐ 數字的；businessman ⓝ 商人；supercomputer ⓝ 超級電腦；primarily ⓐⓓ 主要地；government agency ⓟⓗ 政府機關

7,000 單字

- device [dɪ'vaɪs] ⓝ 4 裝置
- calculation [ˌkælkjə'leʃən] ⓝ 4 計算
- precise [prɪ'saɪs] ⓐ 4 精確的
- about [ə'baʊt] prep 1 大約
- modern ['mɑdən] ⓐ 2 現代的
- huge [hjudʒ] ⓐ 1 巨大的
- expensive [ɪk'spɛnsɪv] ⓐ 2 昂貴的
- task [tæsk] ⓝ 2 任務

- business ['bɪznɪs] ⓝ 2 商業
- capability [ˌkepə'bɪlətɪ] ⓝ 6 性能
- enough [ə'nʌf] ⓐ 1 足夠的
- feedback ['fid.bæk] ⓝ 6 回饋
- fraud [frɔd] ⓝ 6 欺詐
- ordeal [ɔr'diəl] ⓝ 6 折磨
- overturn [.ovə'tɜn] ⓥ 6 推翻

Part 1
詞彙題
Day 7
完成 25%

Part 2
綜合測驗
Day 7
完成 50%

Part 3
文意選填
Day 7
完成 75%

Part 4
閱讀測驗
Day 7
完成 100%

2 ▶ 97 年指考英文

Recent studies have shown that alcohol is the leading gateway drug for teenagers. Gateway drugs are substances people take that __01__ them to take more drugs. Alcohol works directly on the central nervous system and alters one's moods and limits judgment. Since its way of altering moods (changing one's state of mind) is generally expected and socially acceptable, oftentimes it __02__ overdrinking. Habitual drinkers may find alcohol not stimulating enough __03__ and want to seek other more stimulating substances. __04__ a circumstance often preconditions teenagers to the possibility of taking other drugs such as marijuana, cocaine or heroin. Another reason why alcohol is the main gateway drug is that the __05__ of teenagers it can affect is very wide. It is easily accessible in most societies and common in popular events, such as sports gatherings and dinner parties.

01	_____	(A) lead	(B) leads
		(C) leading	(D) led

02	_____	(A) applies to	(B) arrives at
		(C) results in	(D) plans on

03	_____	(A) in advance	(B) after a while
		(C) in the least	(D) at most

04	_____	(A) Since	(B) As
		(C) All	(D) Such

05	_____	(A) population	(B) popularity
		(C) pollution	(D) possibility

中譯 ｜ 最近的研究顯示，酒精是青少年主要的入門毒品。服用入門毒品之後，會導致人吸食更多的毒品。酒精直接作用於中樞神經系統，能夠改變一個人的情緒，並且限制判斷力。由於酒精會改變情緒（改變一個人的思想狀態）是預料中的事，並為社會所接受，所以時常會導致飲酒過量。酗酒成性的人不久會發現酒精不夠刺激，想要尋求其他令人刺激的物質。這種情況通常可能會導致青少年吸食其他的毒品，例如大麻、古柯鹼或者海洛因。酒精作為主要入門毒品的另外一個原因是，它能夠影響到的青少年人口非常多。酒精在大多數社會中很容易取得，在運動聚會和晚宴這樣的熱門場合中也很普遍。

解說 ｜ 本篇短文講述了酒精能夠誘導青少年犯罪。第 1 題是一個由 that 引導的限定子句，that 指代主詞 Gateway drugs，表示複數，後面的動詞也要用複數形式 lead，所以正確選擇為 (A)。第 2 題將四個選項的動詞片語一一代入，只有 results in 表示「導致」符合上下文的意思，所以最符合題意的選項是 (C)。第 3 題要選擇合適的介系詞片語。將四個選項的介系詞片語一一代入，after a while 表示「不久」符合題意，即正確選項是 (B)。第 4 題中，將四個選項一一代入空格，只有 such 表示「這樣的」可以修飾 a circumstance，所以正確選擇為 (D)。第 5 題的四個選項都是名詞，將其一一代入，只有 population 符合題意，所以選 (A)。

解答＆技巧 ｜ 01 (A)　02 (C)　03 (B)　04 (D)　05 (A)

適用 TIP 1　適用 TIP 2　適用 TIP 7　適用 TIP 11

補充

gateway ⓝ 入口處，門戶；central nervous system ⓟⓗ 中樞神經系統；socially ⓐⓓ 社會上；oftentimes ⓐⓓ 常常；precondition ⓥ 使事先具備條件

7,000 單字

- drug [drʌg] ⓝ ② 毒品
- teenager [ˈtinˌedʒɚ] ⓝ ② 青少年
- alter [ˈɔltɚ] ⓥ ⑤ 改變
- mood [mud] ⓝ ③ 情緒
- limit [ˈlɪmɪt] ⓥ ② 限制
- habitual [həˈbɪtʃʊəl] ⓐ ④ 習慣的
- seek [sik] ⓥ ③ 尋找
- possibility [ˌpɑsəˈbɪlətɪ] ⓝ ② 可能性

- heroin [ˈhɛroˌɪn] ⓝ ⑥ 海洛因
- main [men] ⓐ ② 主要的
- wide [waɪd] ⓐ ① 寬廣的
- dinner [ˈdɪnɚ] ⓝ ① 晚餐
- party [ˈpɑrtɪ] ⓝ ① 聚會
- while [hwaɪl] ⓝ ① 一會兒
- popularity [ˌpɑpjəˈlærətɪ] ⓝ ④ 流行

DAY 7

Part 1
詞彙題
Day 7
完成 25%

Part 2
綜合測驗
Day 7
完成 50%

Part 3
文意選填
Day 7
完成 75%

Part 4
閱讀測驗
Day 7
完成 100%

Nowadays, people have paid a great deal of __01__ to the digital divide which is the division of the information world into rich and poor. As the Internet becomes __02__ commercialized, more and more people hope that the digital divide will narrow because it is in the interest of business to __03__ the use of Internet, and the more people are online, the more potential customers there will be. Many governments are afraid that their countries will be left behind, so they want to spread Internet access. Maybe __04__ the next decade or two, half of the people in the world could be able to use the Internet, and the Internet may also become the most powerful tool to combat world poverty.

Of course, the Internet is not the only tool to defeat poverty, but I think most of us should take good __05__ of this tool. For example, some countries may think foreign investment is an invasion of their sovereignty, but using the Internet for foreign investment would contribute to the development of the economy.

01 _____ (A) attention   (B) prestige
         (C) refreshment   (D) serenity

02 _____ (A) entirely   (B) actually
         (C) continuously   (D) highly

03 _____ (A) tighten   (B) universalize
         (C) suspect   (D) shave

04 _____ (A) by   (B) up
         (C) within   (D) on

05 _____ (A) care   (B) out
         (C) heart   (D) advantage

中譯 | 如今，人們大量關注數位落差，它讓資訊世界有了貧富劃分。隨著網路變得高度商業化，愈來愈多的人希望這種數位落差會變小，因為普遍使用網路是為了商業利益，而上網的人愈多，潛在客戶就會愈多。很多政府害怕他們的國家會落後，因此他們想要普及網路的使用。或許在今後的十年或二十年裡，世界上一半的人口能夠使用網路，網路也會成為戰勝世界貧窮最強大的工具。

當然，網路並不是打敗貧窮的唯一工具，但是我認為我們大多數人應該好好利用這種工具。例如，一些國家可能會認為外資是一種主權侵略，但是使用網路運用外資將會有助於經濟的發展。

解說 | 本篇短文由數位落差講到網路，突顯了網路的重要性。第 1 題的四個選項都是名詞。依據題意，「關注」可以表達為 pay attention to，所以正確選擇為 (A)。第 2 題要選擇合適的副詞。依據題意，四個選項中，只有 highly 表示「高度化地」修飾形容詞 commercialized 最符合題意，所以最佳選項是 (D)。第 3 題依據題意，為了商業利益，要使電腦的使用普遍化，要用 universalize 表示「使普遍化」，即正確選項是 (B)。第 4 題的四個選項都是介系詞，但只有介系詞 within 可以表示時間範圍，所以只有選項 (C) 符合題意。第 5 題考動詞片語的用法。依據題意，「利用」可以表達為 take advantage of，所以選 (D)。

解答＆技巧 | **01 (A)** **02 (D)** **03 (B)** **04 (C)** **05 (D)**
適用 TIP 1　適用 TIP 2　適用 TIP 7　適用 TIP 11

補充

digital divide ph 數位落差；commercialized a 商業化的；potential customer ph 潛在顧客；
within the next decade or two ph 在之後的十或二十年裡；development of the economy ph 經濟發展

7,000 單字

- deal [dil] n 1 數量
- digital [ˈdɪdʒɪtl] a 4 數位的
- division [dəˈvɪʒən] n 2 分割
- rich [rɪtʃ] a 1 富裕的
- Internet [ˈɪntɚˌnɛt] n 4 網路
- use [jus] n 1 使用
- afraid [əˈfred] a 1 害怕的
- behind [bɪˈhaɪnd] ad 1 在後面

- next [ˈnɛkst] a 1 下一個的
- combat [ˈkɑmbæt] v 5 對抗
- poverty [ˈpɑvɚtɪ] n 3 貧窮
- sovereignty [ˈsɑvrɪntɪ] n 6 主權
- refreshment [rɪˈfrɛʃmənt] n 6 點心
- serenity [səˈrɛnətɪ] n 6 平靜
- suspect [səˈspɛkt] v 3 懷疑

DAY
7

Part 1
詞
彙
題
Day 7
完成 25%

Part 2
綜
合
測
驗
Day 7
完成 50%

Part 3
文
意
選
填
Day 7
完成 75%

Part 4
閱
讀
測
驗
Day 7
完成 100%

According to a new study, kids living in the inner-city where there are more green spaces gain less weight than kids living with fewer trees. Many people have __01__ obesity to eating too much junk food and watching TV for a long time, but that cannot be everything. Most experts agree to the idea that the changes of our health are __02__ to something in the environment, and they think that greenery can provide us with better health.

It is true that there should be more green places for kids to play; thus they will spend more time in taking __03__ outdoors, which can consume their excessive body heat. In addition, green space is also good for their mind. Although green space is not always easy to __04__ , you should try your best to get your family some grass and plants. Your children will love it so much, and their bodies and minds will also be __04__ to you.

01 _____ (A) trusted   (B) attributed
          (C) admired   (D) approved

02 _____ (A) awarded   (B) braked
          (C) confused   (D) related

03 _____ (A) exercise   (B) place
          (C) office   (D) stock

04 _____ (A) crash   (B) creep
          (C) find   (D) dodge

05 _____ (A) domestic   (B) grateful
          (C) energetic   (D) frequent

中譯│一項新的研究指出，生活在綠地更多的市中心的孩子，比起生活在樹木較少的地方的孩子，體重增加的幅度較少。很多人將肥胖歸因於吃太多的垃圾食品和看太多電視，但是這並不是全部的原因。大多數專家都認同我們的健康變化與環境事物有關，認為綠色植物能夠為我們提供更好的健康。

確實，應該要有更多的綠地供孩子們玩耍，這樣他們就會花更多的時間在戶外運動，能夠消耗他們多餘的身體熱量。此外，綠地也對我們的心智有益。儘管綠地並不總是輕易能找到，但是你應當盡全力為你的家人種植綠草和植物。你的孩子一定會非常喜愛，他們的身心也會感激你。

解說│本篇短文講述了綠色環境與兒童體重的關係。第 1 題的四個選項中，只有 **attributed** 能夠與介系詞 to 搭配，表示「歸因於」，所以正確選擇為 (B)。第 2 題的四個選項中，只有 related 能夠構成片語 be related to 表示「與～有關」，所以最符合題意的選項是 (D)。第 3 題的四個選項都可以與動詞 take 搭配構成片語，但依據題意，**take exercise** 表示「做運動，鍛鍊」最符合題意，即正確選項是 (A)。第 4 題的四個選項都是動詞，將其一一代入，**find** 表示「發現」符合上下文的意思，所以最佳選項是 (C)。第 5 題的四個選項都是形容詞，只有 **grateful** 能夠構成 be grateful to 表示「感謝，感激」符合題意，所以選 (B)。

解答＆技巧│ 01 **(B)**　02 **(D)**　03 **(A)**　04 **(C)**　05 **(B)**
　　　　　　適用 TIP 2　適用 TIP 4　適用 TIP 7　適用 TIP 11

補充
inner-city a 市中心貧民區的；obesity n 肥胖；junk food ph 垃圾食品；watch TV ph 看電視；greenery n 綠葉，綠色植物

7,000 單字

- kid [kɪd] n 1 小孩
- green [grin] a 1 綠色的
- tree [tri] n 1 樹木
- much [mʌtʃ] a 1 很多的
- junk [dʒʌŋk] n 3 垃圾
- time [taɪm] n 1 時間
- spend [spɛnd] v 1 花費
- outdoors [ˋaʊtˋdorz] ad 3 在戶外

- consume [kənˋsjum] v 4 消耗
- heat [hit] n 1 熱量
- family [ˋfæməlɪ] n 1 家人
- grass [græs] n 1 草地
- creep [krip] v 3 爬行
- dodge [dɑdʒ] v 3 躲避
- energetic [ˌɛnɚˋdʒɛtɪk] a 3 精力充沛的

DAY 7

Part 1
詞彙題
Day 7
完成 25%

Part 2
綜合測驗
Day 7
完成 50%

Part 3
文意選填
Day 7
完成 75%

Part 4
閱讀測驗
Day 7
完成 100%

5 ▶ 97 年指考英文

A new year means a new beginning for most of us. On December 28th last year, the New York City sanitation department offered people a new way __01__ farewell to 2007. For one hour on that day, a huge paper-cutting machine was set up in Times Square so that people could __02__ their lingering bad memories. Everything from photos of ex-lovers to lousy report cards could be cut into small pieces, as the organizers had announced __03__ the event. Recycling cans were also provided for items such as __04__ CDs and regrettable fashion mistakes. Former schoolteacher Eileen Lawrence won the event's $250 award for the most creative memory destined for __05__. She had created a painting from a photo of her ex-boyfriend, who Lawrence was happy to say goodbye to.

01 _____ (A) bid   (B) to bid
         (C) bidding   (D) bidden

02 _____ (A) destroy   (B) maintain
         (C) dislike   (D) create

03 _____ (A) until   (B) prior to
         (C) above all   (D) beforehand

04 _____ (A) available   (B) amusing
         (C) annoying   (D) artificial

05 _____ (A) machine   (B) machines
         (C) a machine   (D) the machine

中譯 | 對我們大多數人來說，新的一年意味著新的開始。在去年的十二月二十八號，紐約市的環境衛生部門為人們提供一種新的方式來告別二〇〇七年。那天的某一個小時裡，時代廣場上放置了一台巨大的裁紙機，讓人們可以將揮之不去的糟糕記憶破壞掉。如承辦方在活動之前所告知的，包括舊情人的照片和討厭的成績單在內的任何東西都可以裁成碎片。惱人的唱片和後悔購買的服飾和配件，也可丟入承辦方提供的垃圾回收桶。前任教師愛琳‧勞倫斯在活動中贏得了二百五十美元，獎勵她為這台機器提供了最具創意的記憶。她裁掉的是她根據自己前男友的照片創作的一幅繪畫，並且她很高興和他分手。

解說 | 本篇短文講述了紐約市在二〇〇七年的新年發生的一件事情。第 1 題空格處的動詞表示目的，要用不定詞來表示目的，即用 to bid，所以正確選擇為 (B)。第 2 題的四個選項都是動詞，將其一一代入空格，destroy 表示「破壞」符合題意，所以最佳選項是 (A)。第 3 題根據上下文的內容可知，要選擇副詞來修飾動詞 announced。四個選項中，只有 prior to 表示「在～之前」且後面可以接名詞，即正確選項是 (B)。第 4 題依據題意可知，要選擇表示貶義的形容詞來修飾名詞 CDs。四個選項中，只有 annoying 表示「討厭的」，所以選項 (C) 符合題意。第 5 題依據題意，machine 在前文中已經提到，此處表示特指，要用定冠詞 the，所以選 (D)。

解答＆技巧 | 01 (B)　02 (A)　03 (B)　04 (C)　05 (D)
適用 TIP 1　適用 TIP 2　適用 TIP 4　適用 TIP 7　適用 TIP 11

補充

New York City ph 紐約市；paper-cutting machine ph 裁紙機；Times Square ph 時代廣場；ex-lover n 前戀人；schoolteacher n （中小學）教師

7,000 單字

- December [dɪˋsɛmbɚ] n 1 十二月
- sanitation [ˌsænəˋteʃən] n 6 環境衛生
- offer [ˋɔfɚ] v 2 提供
- farewell [ˋfɛrˋwɛl] n 4 告別
- square [skwɛr] n 2 廣場
- memory [ˋmɛmərɪ] n 2 記憶
- lousy [ˋlaʊzɪ] a 4 討厭的
- announce [əˋnaʊns] v 3 宣佈

- event [ɪˋvɛnt] n 2 事件
- item [ˋaɪtəm] n 2 品項
- former [ˋfɔrmɚ] a 2 前者的
- destine [ˋdɛstɪn] v 6 預定，註定
- painting [ˋpentɪŋ] n 2 繪畫
- beforehand [bɪˋforˌhænd] ad 5 事先
- artificial [ˌɑrtəˋfɪʃəl] a 4 人造的

DAY 7

Part 1
詞彙題
Day 7
完成 25%

Part 2
綜合測驗
Day 7
完成 50%

Part 3
文意選填
Day 7
完成 75%

Part 4
閱讀測驗
Day 7
完成 100%

As we all know, the food we eat will have profound __01__ on our health. Although some foods have been made fit to eat, many other foods are still unfit to eat. According to a recent survey, eighty percent of the human illnesses are related to __02__ , and forty percent of cancer is related to the diet as well. It is true that different cultures may cause different illnesses because the food can be different in all cultures. Forty years ago, the researchers realized that nitrates which were used to __03__ color in meats caused cancer. Some other food additives could also cause cancer. Though those carcinogenic additives are still __04__ in our food, we could not know which food is helpful or harmful just according to its packaging. Farmers usually feed cows and living animals with penicillin, hence, penicillin has been found in the milk. Also the farmers try to __05__ the animals in order to gain a higher price on the market, which is controlled by the government.

01 _____ (A) roles   (B) effects
          (C) scores   (D) processes

02 _____ (A) pub   (B) receipt
          (C) response   (D) diet

03 _____ (A) rid   (B) snap
          (C) preserve   (D) stare

04 _____ (A) contained   (B) supposed
          (C) teased   (D) varied

05 _____ (A) weave   (B) amuse
          (C) fatten   (D) arise

DAY
7

Part 1
詞
彙
題
Day 7
完成 25%

Part 2
綜
合
測
驗
Day 7
完成 50%

Part 3
文
意
選
填
Day 7
完成 75%

Part 4
閱
讀
測
驗
Day 7
完成 100%

中譯 | 眾所周知，我們吃的食物對我們的健康有著深遠影響。儘管一些食物適合人們吃，但是很多其他的食物仍然不適合吃。最近的一項調查指出，百分之八十的人類疾病與飲食有關，百分之四十的癌症也與飲食有關。確實，不同的文化可能會導致不同的疾病，因為文化不同，所吃的食物也不同。四十年前，研究人員意識到，用於保持肉類顏色的硝酸鹽會導致癌症。一些其他的食品添加劑也會導致癌症。儘管那些致癌的添加劑仍然包含在我們的食物中，但是我們無法僅根據包裝就知道哪種食物是有益的還是有害的。農民通常餵盤尼西林給牛和活體動物，因此牛奶中也發現有盤尼西林。農民也試圖養肥動物，以便在政府管制的市場上賣更高的價錢。

解說 | 本篇短文介紹了食物對人類健康的影響。第 1 題依據題意，「對～有影響」可以表達為 have effects on，可以用 effect 表示「影響」，所以正確選擇為 (B)。第 2 題涉及到本篇短文的主旨，即健康與飲食的關係，所以此處應該選擇 diet，表示很多疾病都與飲食有關，最符合題意的選項是 (D)。第 3 題的四個選項都是動詞，將其一一代入空格，只有 preserve 表示「保持」符合題意，即保持肉類的顏色，即正確選項是 (C)。第 4 題根據上下文的內容可知，應該是致癌的添加劑仍然包含在我們的食物中，可以用 contained 來表示「包含」，所以只有選項 (A) 符合題意。第 5 題依據題意，要想賣更高的價錢，只有把動物養胖，可以用 fatten 表示「養肥」，所以正確選擇為 (C)。

解答＆技巧 | `01` **(B)** `02` **(D)** `03` **(C)** `04` **(A)** `05` **(C)**
`適用 TIP 2` `適用 TIP 4` `適用 TIP 7` `適用 TIP 11`

`補充`
unfit a 不合適的；illnesses n 疾病；nitrate n 硝酸鹽；carcinogenic a 致癌的；penicillin n 盤尼西林

`7,000 單字`
- eat [it] v ① 吃
- profound [prə`faʊnd] v ⑥ 深厚的
- fit [fɪt] a ② 適合的
- percent [pɚ`sɛnt] n ④ 百分比
- diet [`daɪət] n ③ 飲食
- researcher [rɪ`sɝtʃɚ] n ④ 研究員
- meat [mit] n ① 肉
- feed [fid] v ① 餵養

- cow [bif] n ② 母牛
- hence [hɛns] ad ⑤ 因此
- milk [mɪlk] n ① 牛奶
- pub [pʌb] n ③ 酒館
- snap [snæp] v ③ 猛咬
- tease [tiz] v ③ 取笑
- arise [ə`raɪz] v ④ 出現

The scientists have found that two factors will   01   an individual's intelligence. The first factor is the brain which an individual is born   02 . Some people can be more capable than others because human beings differ considerably. However, no matter how good a brain an individual can have in the   03 , if he has no opportunities to learn, he will have a low order of intelligence and become retarded in the future.

Therefore, the second factor is the environment in which an individual lives. If a person is handicapped environmentally, his brain cannot develop, and he will never   04   high intelligence to make himself capable. It is true that different environment will influence people's growth. A person who lives in a family with a high-level educational background proves to be more clever and capable than the one who has little or no opportunities to learn.   05   equal learning opportunities, two different people can develop into the same level of intelligence.

01 _____ (A) arouse   (B) determine
         (C) breed   (D) cherish

02 _____ (A) for   (B) in
         (C) up   (D) with

03 _____ (A) beginning   (B) climax
         (C) concept   (D) contribution

04 _____ (A) cram   (B) depress
         (C) attain   (D) enlarge

05 _____ (A) Giving   (B) Given
         (C) Gave   (D) Give

中譯｜科學家發現，兩種因素會決定一個人的智力。第一種因素是一個人天生原本的大腦。有些人會比其他人更有能力，這是因為人類之間的差別很大。然而，不管起初一個人所擁有的大腦多麼優秀，如果他沒有學習的機會，他的智商就會降低，將來會變得發展遲緩。

因此，第二個因素就是一個人所生存的環境。如果一個人的成長環境非常惡劣，他的大腦就不會發展，他就不會獲得高智商，從而變得有能力。確實，不同的環境會影響人們的成長。一個生活在高學歷背景家庭中的人證明要比一個沒有學習機會的人更聰明，也更有能力。給予平等的學習機會，兩個不同的人能夠發展成為相同水準的智商。

解說｜本篇短文講述了影響人類智力的兩個因素，即大腦和環境。第 1 題的四個選項都是動詞，將其一一代入空格，只有 determine 表示「決定」符合題意，即兩種因素會決定一個人的智力，所以正確選擇為 (B)。第 2 題要選擇合適的介系詞。依據題意，表示「天生的」可以說 be born with，要用介系詞 with 與 born 搭配，所以最符合題意的選項是 (D)。第 3 題考介系詞片語的用法。將四個選項一一代入空格，只有 beginning 能夠與介系詞 in 搭配構成 in the beginning 表示「起初」，即正確選項是 (A)。第 4 題根據上下文的內容可知，應該是獲得高智商，可以用動詞 attain 表示「獲得」，所以只有選項 (C) 符合題意。第 5 題根據題意可知，應該用過去分詞表示被動，動詞 give 要用 given 的形式，所以選 (B)。

解答＆技巧｜ **01 (B)**　**02 (D)**　**03 (A)**　**04 (C)**　**05 (B)**

適用 TIP 1　適用 TIP 2　適用 TIP 7　適用 TIP 11

補充
considerably ad 相當地；retarded a 發展遲緩的；environmentally ad 環境地；high-level a 高級的；develop into ph 發展為

7,000 單字

- intelligence [ɪn'tɛlədʒəns] n 4 智力
- first [fɝst] a 1 第一的
- differ ['dɪfə] v 4 使不同
- opportunity [ˌɑpə'tjunətɪ] n 3 機遇
- handicap ['hændɪˌkæp] v 5 妨礙
- never ['nɛvə] ad 1 從未
- growth [groθ] n 2 成長
- background ['bæk‚graund] n 3 背景

- little ['lɪtl] n 1 少量
- equal ['ikwəl] a 1 平等的
- arouse [ə'rauz] v 4 激發
- cherish ['tʃɛrɪʃ] v 4 珍愛
- climax ['klaɪmæks] n 4 高潮
- cram [kræm] v 4 塞滿
- enlarge [ɪn'lɑrdʒ] v 4 擴大

DAY **7**

Part 1
詞彙題
Day 7
完成 25%

Part 2
綜合測驗
Day 7
完成 50%

Part 3
文意選填
Day 7
完成 75%

Part 4
閱讀測驗
Day 7
完成 100%

When walking __01__ the huge department store, Susan found that it was really difficult to choose a suitable Christmas present for her father. As far as she knew, her father was not as easy to __02__ as her mother because her mother would only be delighted with perfume. With such a hot day outside and so many people in the department store, shopping at this time of the year was really a(an) __03__ experience.

In order to have a rest, Susan came to a counter where some attractive ties were on __04__. Although the assistant assured that all the ties were real silk, Susan knew that a tie could not please her father. Quite by chance, she saw a small crowd of men gathering around at a counter and found some good quality pipes on sale, whose prices were also very __05__. She was so happy because she knew that her father liked smoking, and this present would please him very much. However, when she went home with the pipe in her bag, her mother told her with delight, "Your father has decided to quit smoking."

01 _____   (A) over   (B) out
             (C) around   (D) of

02 _____   (A) please   (B) explore
             (C) grieve   (D) imitate

03 _____   (A) influential   (B) doubtful
             (C) drowsy   (D) disagreeable

04 _____   (A) earth   (B) sale
             (C) purpose   (D) duty

05 _____   (A) eager   (B) enjoyable
             (C) reasonable   (D) fashionable

DAY
7

Part 1
詞
彙
題
Day 7
完成 25%

Part 2
綜
合
測
驗
Day 7
完成 50%

Part 3
文
意
選
填
Day 7
完成 75%

Part 4
閱
讀
測
驗
Day 7
完成 100%

中譯 | 在大型百貨公司閒逛時，蘇珊發現真的很難為父親挑選一件聖誕禮物。據她所知，她的父親並不像她的母親那樣容易討好，因為她的母親只喜歡香水。外面天氣這麼熱，而百貨公司裡又有這麼多人，在一年中的這個時候來購物真是令人不快的經驗。

為了休息一下，蘇珊來到一個櫃檯，這裡銷售一些吸引人的領帶。儘管專櫃人員確保所有這些領帶都是真絲的，但是蘇珊知道一條領帶無法取悅她的父親。意外地，她看到一小群男人聚集在一個櫃檯那裡，發現那邊在銷售一些品質好的菸斗，而且價格也很合理。她很高興，因為她知道她的父親喜歡抽菸，這件禮物將會令他很開心。然而，當她將菸斗放在包包裡回到家時，她的母親卻高興地對她說：「你的父親已經決定戒菸了。」

解說 | 本篇短文講述了主角蘇珊為父親挑選聖誕禮物的故事。第 1 題考跟動詞 walk 相關的片語的用法。將四個選項一一代入空格，只有 walk around 表示「四處走動」，符合題意，所以正確選擇為 (C)。第 2 題的四個選項都是動詞。根據上下文的內容可知，蘇珊為父親買聖誕禮物是為了討好他，要用 please 表示「討好」，所以最符合題意的選項是 (A)。第 3 題根據上下文的內容可知，天氣熱和人多令人不愉快，四個選項中只有 disagreeable 表示「不愉快的」，即正確選項是 (D)。第 4 題考介系詞片語的用法。依據題意，應該是領帶在銷售，可以用 on sale 表示「出售」，所以只有選項 (B) 符合題意。第 5 題的四個選項都是形容詞，但是只有 reasonable 能夠用於修飾 prices，所以選 (C)。

解答＆技巧 | 01 (C) 02 (A) 03 (D) 04 (B) 05 (C)

適用 TIP 1   適用 TIP 2   適用 TIP 7   適用 TIP 11

補充
department store ph 百貨公司；have a rest ph 休息；delighted a 高興的；
quite by chance ph 偶然；smoke v 吸菸

7,000 單字
- walk [wɔk] v 1 走路
- store [stor] n 1 商店
- father [ˈfɑðɚ] n 1 父親
- easy [ˈizɪ] a 1 容易的
- perfume [ˈpɝfjum] n 4 香水
- outside [ˈaʊtˈsaɪd] ad 1 在外面
- counter [ˈkaʊntɚ] n 4 櫃檯
- assure [əˈʃʊr] v 4 保證

- silk [sɪlk] n 2 絲綢
- crowd [kraʊd] n 2 群眾
- pipe [paɪp] n 2 菸斗
- grieve [griv] v 4 使悲傷
- influential [ˌɪnfluˈɛnʃəl] a 4 有影響的
- reasonable [ˈriznəbl] a 3 合理的
- fashionable [ˈfæʃənəbl] a 3 流行的

9 ▶ 98 年學測英文

The Paralympics are Olympic-style games for athletes with disabilities. They were organized for the first time in Rome in 1960. In Toronto in 1976, the idea of putting together different disability groups __01__ sports competitions was born. Today, the Paralympics are sports events for athletes from six different disability groups. They emphasize the participants' athletic achievements __02__ their physical disability. The games have grown in size gradually. The number of athletes __03__ in the Summer Paralympic Games has increased from 400 athletes from 23 countries in 1960 to 3,806 athletes from 136 countries in 2004.

The Paralympic Games have always been held in the same year as the Olympic Games. Since the Seoul 1988 Paralympic Games and the Albertville 1992 Winter Paralympic Games, they have also __04__ in the same city as the Olympics. On June 19, 2001, an agreement was signed between the International Olympic Committee and the International Paralympics Committee to keep this __05__ in the future. From the 2012 bid onwards, the city chosen to host the Olympic Games will also host the Paralympics.

01 _____ (A) for   (B) with
         (C) as   (D) on

02 _____ (A) in terms of   (B) instead of
         (C) at the risk of   (D) at the cost of

03 _____ (A) participate   (B) participated
         (C) participating   (D) to participate

04 _____ (A) taken turns   (B) taken place
         (C) taken off   (D) taken over

05 _____ (A) piece   (B) deadline
         (C) date   (D) practice

中譯｜帕運會是給身心障礙運動員參加的奧運會，於一九六〇年首次在羅馬舉辦了這項活動。一九七六年在多倫多，將不同身心障礙團體聚集起來進行運動競賽的想法誕生了。如今，帕運會是由來自六個不同障礙團體的運動員們所進行的體育賽事，強調的是參與者的運動成就，而非他們的身體缺陷。帕運會的規模已逐漸擴大。參加夏季帕運會的運動員人數已經從一九六〇年，來自二十三個國家的四百名，增加到二〇〇四年，來自一百三十六個國家的三千八百〇六名。

帕運會總是和奧運會同年舉行。從一九八八年的首爾帕運會以及一九九二年的阿爾貝維爾冬季帕運會開始，帕運會也總是和奧運會舉行在同一個城市。二〇〇一年的六月十九日，國際奧運會和國際帕運會簽訂了一份協議，在將來繼續保持這一做法。從二〇一二年的申辦開始，被選為舉辦奧運會的國家也會舉辦帕運會。

解說｜本篇短文的主旨是「帕運會」，介紹了帕運會的發展史。第 1 題的四個選項都是介系詞。依據題意，空格處要選擇表示目的的介系詞，即不同身心障礙團體聚集起來是為了進行運動競賽，而介系詞 for 可以表示目的，所以正確選擇為 (A)。第 2 題考介系詞片語的用法。依據題意，空格處的介系詞片語用於肯定前者而否定後者，instead of 可以表達此種含義，所以最符合題意的選項是 (B)。第 3 題依據題意，空格處的動詞在句中作後位修飾，要用現在分詞 participating，即正確選項是 (C)。第 4 題考與動詞 take 有關的片語用法。依據題意，take place 表示「發生」符合題意，所以正確選擇為 (B)。第 5 題的四個選項都是名詞。依據題意，空格處指代的是前文中提到的奧運會在同一個城市舉行的這種做法，practice 更加符合題意，所以選 (D)。

解答&技巧｜ 01 **(A)**　02 **(B)**　03 **(C)**　04 **(B)**　05 **(D)**

適用 TIP 1　適用 TIP 2　適用 TIP 7　適用 TIP 11

補充

Paralympics ⓝ 帕運會；Olympic ⓐ 奧運會的；Rome ⓝ 羅馬；Toronto ⓝ 多倫多；Seoul ⓝ 首爾

7,000 單字

- athlete [ˈæθlit] ⓝ ③ 運動員
- disability [ˌdɪsəˈbɪlətɪ] ⓝ ⑥ 身心障礙
- sports [spɔrts] ⓐ ① 運動的
- born [bɔrn] ⓐ ① 出生的
- emphasize [ˈɛmfəˌsaɪz] ⓥ ③ 強調
- athletic [æθˈlɛtɪk] ⓐ ④ 運動的
- size [saɪz] ⓝ ① 大小
- winter [ˈwɪntɚ] ⓝ ① 冬天

- June [dʒun] ⓝ ① 六月
- sign [saɪn] ⓥ ② 簽署
- committee [kəˈmɪtɪ] ⓝ ③ 委員會
- host [host] ⓥ ② 主辦
- participate [pɑrˈtɪsəˌpet] ⓥ ③ 參加
- piece [pis] ⓝ ① 件
- deadline [ˈdɛdˌlaɪn] ⓝ ④ 截止日期

DAY **7**

Part 1
詞彙題
Day 7
完成 25%

Part 2
綜合測驗
Day 7
完成 50%

Part 3
文意選填
Day 7
完成 75%

Part 4
閱讀測驗
Day 7
完成 100%

Many scientists have said that if the population of the earth goes on __01__ at the present rate, not enough resources will be left to __02__ life on the earth. By the middle of the 21st century, we are quite likely to have used __03__ all the oil. Thus no oil can be used to drive our cars. Although the scientists have developed many new ways to feed the human beings in order to solve the crowded __04__ on the earth, it is still necessary for us to look for open spaces in other planets. But so far, no other planets in our solar system have been found capable enough to support life.

One of the scientists have said that before the earth's resources are completely __05__ , we can try to change the atmosphere of Venus in order to create a new world as large as earth. But the biggest problem is that Venus is much hotter than the earth, and only a tiny amount of water is there.

01 _____ (A) fastening   (B) freezing
         (C) increasing   (D) interrupting

02 _____ (A) sustain   (B) knit
         (C) leap   (D) loosen

03 _____ (A) for   (B) to
         (C) down   (D) up

04 _____ (A) memberships (B) conditions
         (C) miracles   (D) necessities

05 _____ (A) paused   (B) persuaded
         (C) exhausted   (D) released

DAY
7

Part 1
詞
彙
題
Day 7
完成 25%

Part 2
綜
合
測
驗
Day 7
完成 50%

Part 3
文
意
選
填
Day 7
完成 75%

Part 4
閱
讀
測
驗
Day 7
完成 100%

中譯｜很多科學家說，如果地球上的人數以目前的速率持續成長的話，地球上將不會有足夠的資源來維持所有的生命。到二十一世紀中期，我們很有可能早已用完所有的石油，這樣我們就沒有石油來駕駛汽車。儘管科學家們已經開發出了很多新的方法來供養人類，但是為了解決地球上的擁擠狀況，我們仍然有必要在其他星球尋找開放空間。不過迄今為止，我們在太陽系中沒有找到足以維持生命的其他星球。

其中一位科學家說，在地球的資源完全耗盡之前，我們可以試圖改變金星的大氣層，來創造一個像地球那麼大的新世界。但是最大的問題在於金星比地球熱得多，而且那裡的含水量真的不多。

解說｜本篇短文講述了地球資源面臨耗盡的問題。第 1 題要選擇合適的動詞。依據題意，人口應該是繼續增長，要用 increase 來表示「成長」，而介系詞 on 之後要用動名詞 increasing，所以正確選擇為 (C)。第 2 題的四個選項都是動詞。根據上下文的內容可知，表示「維持生命」可以說 sustain life，最符合題意的選項是 (A)。第 3 題考與動詞 use 相關的片語用法。依據題意，動詞 use 通常與介系詞 up 連用，表示「用完，耗盡」，符合文中的意思，所以正確選項是 (D)。第 4 題的四個選項都是名詞，將其一一代入空格，conditions 可以與 crowded 連用表示「擁擠狀況」，符合題意，所以正確選擇為 (B)。第 5 題依據題意應該是，地球資源被耗盡，要用 exhausted 表示「耗盡」，所以選 (C)。

解答＆技巧｜ 01 (C)　02 (A)　03 (D)　04 (B)　05 (C)

適用 TIP 1　適用 TIP 2　適用 TIP 7　適用 TIP 11

補充
solar system ph 太陽系；on the earth ph 在地球上；human beings ph 人類；Venus n 金星；
as large as ph 和～一樣大

7,000 單字

- population [ˌpɑpjəˈleʃən] n 2 人口
- rate [ret] n 3 速率
- resource [rɪˈsors] n 3 資源
- middle [ˈmɪdl̩] n 1 中間
- likely [ˈlaɪklɪ] a 1 有可能的
- oil [ɔɪl] n 1 石油
- new [nju] a 1 新的
- solve [sɑlv] v 2 解決

- necessary [ˈnɛsəˌsɛrɪ] a 2 必要的
- open [ˈopən] a 1 開放的
- planet [ˈplænɪt] n 2 行星
- sustain [səˈsten] v 5 維持
- knit [nɪt] v 3 編織
- membership [ˈmɛmbəˌʃɪp] n 3 會員資格
- pause [pɔz] v 3 暫停

Part 3 文意選填 | Cloze Test

1 ▶

From the map or __01__ , we can see that most of the earth is covered with water. If the earth's __02__ were divided into four parts, nearly three-fourths of it would be water.

The largest bodies of water are the oceans. There are four major oceans. The largest one is the Pacific Ocean, __03__ North and South America from Asia and Australia. The __04__ largest ocean is the Atlantic Ocean, separating America from Europe and Africa. The __05__ ocean is the Arctic Ocean around the North Pole. The Indian Ocean is larger than the Arctic, lying completely in the Eastern Hemisphere, to the south of Asia and to the east of Africa around the equator.

The ocean has many smaller parts that __06__ to the land. These parts are called bays, gulfs or straits. Just take the Gulf of Mexico as an __07__ . It is a part of the Atlantic Ocean. Speaking of the Atlantic Ocean, the Mediterranean Sea between Africa and Europe must be mentioned. And the Strait of Gibraltar connects the Mediterranean Sea to the Atlantic Ocean.

Bays that are deep and could serve as a __08__ from ocean storms often develop into harbors. These are safe places for ocean ships to berth and unload cargo. Cities are often built __09__ to good harbors, which makes it easier to trade with other places in the world. __10__ American cities, such as San Francisco, New York, Baltimore and New Orleans, are all built next to harbors.

(A) shelter   (B) separating   (C) globe   (D) next   (E) second
(F) Famous   (G) connect   (H) smallest   (I) surface   (J) example

---

01 _____   02 _____   03 _____   04 _____   05 _____

06 _____   07 _____   08 _____   09 _____   10 _____

選項中譯｜遮蔽處；分離；地球儀；鄰近的；第二的；著名的；連接；最小的；表面；例子

中譯｜從地圖或是地球儀上可以看到，地球的大部分區域都被水覆蓋著。如果把地球表面分成四等分，幾乎四分之三都是水域。

最大的水域是海洋。有四個主要的海洋。最大的是太平洋，它把南北美洲與亞洲、澳洲分隔開。第二大洋是大西洋，它把美洲和歐洲、非洲分隔開。最小的海洋是北冰洋（又稱北極海），位於北極附近。印度洋比北冰洋大一些，它完全是在東半球，位於赤道附近的亞洲南部和非洲東部。

海洋有許多小部分是與大陸相連，這些部分被稱為港灣、海灣或海峽。就以墨西哥灣為例，它是大西洋的一部分。說到大西洋，必然要提起地中海，它位於非洲和歐洲之間。直布羅陀海峽則是將地中海和大西洋連接在一起。

那些能夠躲避海洋暴風雨的深水港灣，通常會發展為海港，為海洋船隻的停泊和貨物的卸載提供了安全之所。城市通常是建在優良的海港邊，這樣會方便與其他地區進行貿易。著名的美國城市——例如舊金山、紐約、巴爾的摩和紐奧良——都是建立在港口邊的。

解譯｜閱讀全文可知，這篇文章的主題是海洋。

縱觀各選項，選項 (A)、(C)、(I)、(J) 是名詞，選項 (B)、(G) 是動詞，選項 (D)、(E)、(F)、(H) 是形容詞。根據題意，第 1、2、7、8 應選名詞，第 3、6 題應選動詞，第 4、5、9、10 題應選形容詞。然後根據文章，依次作答。

第 1 題是選擇名詞，與單數名詞 map 並列，有四個名詞可供選擇，即為選項 (A)、(C)、(I)、(J)，選項 (A) 意為「遮蔽處」，選項 (C) 意為「地球儀」，選項 (I) 意為「表面」，選項 (J) 意為「例子」，根據句意，應當是「從地圖或是地球儀上可以看到～」，所以選 (C)。第 2 題所選名詞，根據句意，應當是「如果把地球表面分成四等分」，所以選 (I)。第 7 題所選名詞，可以視為固定搭配，take... as an example 意為「以～為例」，所以選 (J)。第 8 題則是選 (A)，shelter from 意為「躲避～的地方」。

第 3 題是選擇動詞，須為動名詞，表示伴隨狀況，有兩個動詞可供選擇，即為選項 (B)、(G)。只有選項 (B) 符合要求。第 6 題則是選 (G)，可以視為固定搭配，connect... to 意為「把～連接在一起」。

第 4 題是選擇形容詞，有四個形容詞可供選擇，即為選項 (D)、(E)、(F)、(H)。選項 (D) 意為「鄰近的」，選項 (E) 意為「第二的」，選項 (F) 意為「著名的」，選項 (H) 意為「最小的」，根據句意可知，應當是「第二大洋是大西洋」，所以選 (E)。第 5 題所選形容詞，意為「最小的海洋是北極海」，所以選 (H)。第 9 題所選形容詞，與介系詞 to 連用，意為「鄰近～」，所以選 (D)。第 10 題則是選 (F)，意為「著名的美國城市」。

DAY
7

Part 1
詞
彙
題
Day 7
完成 25%

Part 2
綜
合
測
驗
Day 7
完成 50%

Part 3
文
意
選
填
Day 7
完成 75%

Part 4
閱
讀
測
驗
Day 7
完成 100%

解答 & 技巧 | **01** (C)　　**02** (I)　　**03** (B)　　**04** (E)　　**05** (H)
　　　　　　06 (G)　　**07** (J)　　**08** (A)　　**09** (D)　　**10** (F)

適用 TIP 1　　適用 TIP 2　　適用 TIP 6　　適用 TIP 7　　適用 TIP 8

適用 TIP 9　　適用 TIP 10　　適用 TIP 11

補充

the North Pole ph 北極；the Gulf of Mexico ph 墨西哥灣；the Mediterranean Sea ph 地中海；
the Strait of Gibraltar ph 直布羅陀海峽；New Orleans ph 紐奧良

7,000 單字

- map [mæp] n 1 地圖
- globe [glob] n 4 地球儀
- surface [ˋsɝfɪs] n 2 表面
- divide [dəˋvaɪd] v 2 劃分
- ocean [ˋoʃən] n 1 海洋
- separate [ˋsɛpə͵ret] v 2 分離
- Arctic [ˋarktɪk] n 6 北極
- connect [kəˋnɛkt] v 3 連接

- land [lænd] n 1 陸地
- bay [be] n 3 海灣
- gulf [gʌlf] n 4 海灣
- strait [stret] n 5 海峽
- sea [si] n 1 海
- shelter [ˋʃɛltə] n 4 庇護
- harbor [ˋharbɚ] n 3 海港

MEMO

❷▶

Look at the stars __01__ in the night sky. The __02__ one we can see is Sirius. Sirius is also known as the Dog Star. If we wanted to travel to Sirius, we would have to fly at the __03__ of light for eight and a half years.

The number of stars we can see on a clear night is around 3,000 to 5,000. According to the __04__, there may be more than thirty billion stars in our galaxy.

The Star of the East is a special star. Long time ago, this special star __05__ the Wise Men at night from Jerusalem to the child Jesus.

Another sign that God placed in the __06__, mentioned in the *Bible*, is the North Star. It is always in the same place—nearly over the earth's North Pole. The North Star, or pole star, serves as a guide of __07__ to people in the Northern Hemisphere. It is easy to find the North Star. First, find the Big Dipper. Then follow the pointer stars of the bowl of the dipper to __08__ the North Star.

The location of stars usually __09__ with seasons. However, the stars do not really change. __10__ to the revolution of the earth, the location of stars seems to change. We can see groups of stars called constellations as well. Each constellation appears in a different season of the year.

(A) guided　(B) twinkling　(C) astronomers　(D) Due　(E) locate
(F) brightest　(G) direction　(H) heaven　(I) speed　(J) changes

01 _____　02 _____　03 _____　04 _____　05 _____

06 _____　07 _____　08 _____　09 _____　10 _____

DAY 7

Part 1
詞彙題
Day 7
完成 25%

Part 2
綜合測驗
Day 7
完成 50%

Part 3
文意選填
Day 7
完成 75%

Part 4
閱讀測驗
Day 7
完成 100%

選項中譯｜引領；閃爍；天文學家；由於；定位；最明亮的；方向；天空；速度；變化

中譯｜仰望夜空中閃爍的繁星，我們所能看到最亮的那顆星是天狼星，也稱為天狗星。
如果我們想飛到天狼星，即便是以光速計算，也需要八年半的時間。
在晴朗的夜晚，我們能夠看到的星星，數量大約是在三千到五千個左右。天文學
家認為，在銀河系中，也許有超過三百億顆星星。
東方之星是一顆特殊的星星。很久以前，這顆星星在夜晚指引著智者，從耶路撒
冷一路找到了孩童時期的耶穌。
《聖經》中提及的上帝在天空中所設的另一個記號，就是北極星。它總是在同一
個位置——幾乎是在北極的上空。北極星為北半球的人們指引方向。北極星很容
易找得到，首先找出北斗七星，然後根據北斗七星碗狀結構的指引，就可以找到
北極星。
星星的位置通常會隨著季節變化而改變。不過，這些星星其實並沒有改變。由於
地球的公轉，星星的位置似乎是在發生變化。我們也可以看到被稱為星座的成群
的星星。每個星座會在一年中的不同季節出現。

解譯｜閱讀全文可知，這篇文章的主題是星星。
縱觀各選項，選項 (C)、(G)、(H)、(I) 是名詞，選項 (A)、(B)、(E)、(J) 是動詞，
選項 (D)、(F) 是形容詞。根據題意，第 3、4、6、7 題應選名詞，第 1、5、8、
9 題應選動詞，第 2、10 題應選形容詞。然後根據文章，依次作答。
第 1 題是選擇動詞，須為現在分詞作修飾語，修飾名詞 stars，有四個動詞可供
選擇，即為選項 (A)、(B)、(E)、(J)。只有選項 (B) 符合要求，句意為「夜空中
閃爍的繁星」。第 5 題所選動詞，根據句意可知，應當是「指引著智者找到了耶
穌」，所以選 (A)。第 8 題所選動詞，根據句意可知，應當是「找到北極星」，
所以選 (E)。第 9 題則是選 (J)，意為「星星的位置通常會隨著季節變化而改變」。
第 2 題是選擇形容詞，有兩個形容詞可供選擇，即為選項 (D)、(F)。選項 (D) 意
為「由於」，選項 (F) 意為「最明亮的」，根據句意可知，應當是「我們所能看
到最亮的那顆星是天狼星」，所以選 (F)。第 10 題則是選 (D)，due to 意為「由
於」。
第 3 題是選擇名詞，用於 of 結構，有四個名詞可供選擇，即為選項 (C)、(G)、
(H)、(I)，選項 (C) 意為「天文學家」，選項 (G) 意為「方向」，選項 (H) 意為
「天空」，選項 (I) 意為「速度」，at the speed of 可以視為固定搭配，意為「以～
的速度」，所以選 (I)。第 4 題所選名詞，是與 according to 進行搭配，根據句
意，應當是「天文學家認為」，所以選 (C)。第 6 題所選名詞，也可以視為固定
搭配，in the heaven 意為「在天空中」，所以選 (H)。第 7 題則是選 (G)，guide
of direction 意為「指引方向」。

解答＆技巧 | 01 **(B)**　02 **(F)**　03 **(I)**　04 **(C)**　05 **(A)**
06 **(H)**　07 **(G)**　08 **(E)**　09 **(J)**　10 **(D)**

適用 TIP 1　適用 TIP 2　適用 TIP 6　適用 TIP 7　適用 TIP 8
適用 TIP 9　適用 TIP 10　適用 TIP 11

補充
Bible n 聖經；the North Star ph 北極星；the Northern Hemisphere ph 北半球；dipper n 長柄杓；
constellation n 星座

7,000 單字
- star [stɑr] n 1 星星
- twinkle [ˈtwɪŋkl] v 4 閃爍
- sky [skaɪ] n 1 天空
- speed [spid] n 2 速度
- astronomer [əˈstrɑnəmə] n 5 天文學家
- billion [ˈbɪljən] n 3 十億
- galaxy [ˈgæləksɪ] n 6 星系，銀河系
- guide [gaɪd] v 1 引導

- sign [saɪn] n 2 標記
- heaven [ˈhɛvən] n 3 天空
- mention [ˈmɛnʃən] v 3 提及
- north [nɔrθ] n 1 北方
- direction [dəˈrɛkʃən] n 2 方向
- bowl [bol] n 1 碗
- due [dju] a 3 由～引起

Part 1
詞
彙
題
Day 7
完成 25%

Part 2
綜
合
測
驗
Day 7
完成 50%

Part 3
文
意
選
填
Day 7
完成 75%

Part 4
閱
讀
測
驗
Day 7
完成 100%

MEMO

The word "photography" means "writing with light." "Photo" __01__ from the Greek word "photos," which means light, while "graphy" comes from the Greek word "graphic," which means writing.

Of course, cameras don't literally write pictures. Instead, they imprint an image onto a piece of film. Even the most __02__ camera is basically a box with a piece of light-sensitive film inside. The box has a hole at the __03__ end from the film. The light __04__ the box from the hole—the camera's lens—and shines on the surface of the film to create a picture. The picture created on the film is the __05__, toward which the camera's lens is pointed.

A lens is made of glass, thinner at the edges and thicker in the center. The outer edges of the lens collect light rays and draw them together at the center of the lens.

The __06__ helps control the amount of light that enters the lens. It is quite important, since too much or too little light will both __07__ in an unsuccessful picture. __08__ flash—built into the camera or attached to the top of it—provides light when needed.

Cameras with automatic electronic flashes will automatically provide additional light. Electronic flashes—also known as flashes—require __09__. If the automatic flash or flash attachment __10__ working, a dead battery is probably the cause.

(A) image   (B) batteries   (C) quits   (D) sophisticated   (E) enters
(F) comes   (G) result   (H) opposite   (I) Electronic   (J) shutter

---

01 _____   02 _____   03 _____   04 _____   05 _____

06 _____   07 _____   08 _____   09 _____   10 _____

選項中譯│圖像；電池；停止；精密的；進入；來；導致；另一側的；電子的；快門

DAY
7

Part 1
詞
彙
題
Day 7
完成 25%

Part 2
綜
合
測
驗
Day 7
完成 50%

Part 3
文
意
選
填
Day 7
完成 75%

Part 4
閱
讀
測
驗
Day 7
完成 100%

中譯│photography 這個字意為「用光書寫」，photo 一詞源自希臘字 photos，意為「光」，而 graphy 一詞源自希臘字 graphic，意為「書寫的」。

從字面意思來說，照相機自然是不可能寫出圖片的，然而，照相機卻可以在膠捲上印出圖像來。實際上，即便是最精密的照相機，也只是個裝有感光膠捲的盒子。在膠捲另一端的盒子上，有個小孔。光從小孔──也就是照相機的鏡頭──射進盒子，然後照在膠捲的表面，形成圖像。在膠捲上形成的圖像，就是照相機的鏡頭所對準的物體。

鏡頭是由中間厚、邊緣薄的玻璃製成的。鏡頭外緣接收光線，並將其聚焦在鏡頭中央。

快門是用來控制進入鏡頭的光束。這是十分重要的，因為太多或是太少的光都會導致圖像攝取失敗。電子閃光燈是在相機內部或是在相機頂端，會在需要時提供光亮。

有自動電子閃光燈的照相機，將會自動增加光亮。電子閃光燈也稱為閃光燈，需要安裝電池使用。如果電子閃光燈或是閃光裝置不能正常使用，可能就是電池沒電的緣故。

解譯│閱讀全文可知，這篇文章的主題是照相機構造及其工作原理。

縱觀各選項，選項 (A)、(B)、(J) 是名詞，選項 (C)、(E)、(F)、(G) 是動詞，選項 (D)、(H)、(I) 是形容詞。根據題意，第 5、6、9 題應選名詞，第 1、4、7、10 題應選動詞，第 2、3、8 題應選形容詞。然後根據文章，依次作答。

第 1 題是選擇動詞，須與介系詞 from 進行搭配，有四個動詞可供選擇，即為選項 (C)、(E)、(F)、(G)，come from 可以視為固定搭配，意為「來自於」，所以選 (F)。第 4 題所選動詞，是第三人稱單數形式，根據句意，應當是「光從小孔射進盒子」，所以選 (E)。第 7 題所選動詞，是與介系詞 in 進行搭配，result in 意為「導致，產生～結果」，所以選 (G)。第 10 題則是選 (C)，可以視為固定搭配，quit doing sth. 意為「停止做某事」。

第 2 題是選擇形容詞，有三個形容詞可供選擇，即為選項 (D)、(H)、(I)。選項 (D) 意為「精密的」，選項 (H) 意為「另一側的」，選項 (I) 意為「電子的」，根據句意可知，應當是「最精密的照相機」，所以選 (D)。第 3 題所選形容詞，可以視為固定搭配，at the opposite end 意為「在另一側」，所以選 (H)。第 8 題則是選 (I)，electronic flash 意為「電子閃光燈」。

第 5 題是選擇名詞，有三個名詞可供選擇，即為選項 (A)、(B)、(J)，選項 (A) 意為「圖像」，選項 (B) 意為「電池」，選項 (J) 意為「快門」，根據句意，應當是「在膠捲上形成的圖像」，所以選 (A)。第 6 題所選名詞，根據句意，應當是「快門用來控制進入鏡頭的光束」，所以選 (J)。第 9 題則是選 (B)，句意為「需要安裝電池」。

解答＆技巧｜ **01** (F)　**02** (D)　**03** (H)　**04** (E)　**05** (A)
06 (J)　**07** (G)　**08** (I)　**09** (B)　**10** (C)

適用 TIP 1　適用 TIP 2　適用 TIP 6　適用 TIP 7　適用 TIP 8
適用 TIP 9　適用 TIP 10　適用 TIP 11

補充

literally ad 照字面意義地；imprint v 壓印；sophisticated a 精密複雜的；
basically ph 基本上，主要地；automatically ad 自動地

7,000 單字

- photography [fəˋtɑgrəfɪ] n 4 拍照，攝影
- graphic [ˋgræfɪk] a 6 書寫的
- camera [ˋkæmərə] n 1 照相機，攝影機
- instead [ɪnˋstɛd] ad 3 代替
- sensitive [ˋsɛnsətɪv] a 3 靈敏的
- opposite [ˋɑpəzɪt] a 3 另一側的
- lens [lɛnz] n 3 透鏡，鏡片
- shine [ʃaɪn] v 1 發光

- shutter [ˋʃʌtɚ] n 5 快門
- electronic [ɪlɛkˋtrɑnɪk] a 3 電子的
- flash [flæʃ] n 2 閃光燈
- automatic [ͺɔtəˋmætɪk] a 3 自動的
- additional [əˋdɪʃənl] a 3 另外的
- battery [ˋbætərɪ] n 4 電池
- quit [kwɪt] v 4 停止

MEMO

4 ▶

DAY
7

Part 1
詞
彙
題
Day 7
完成 **25%**

Part 2
綜
合
測
驗
Day 7
完成 **50%**

Part 3
文
意
選
填
Day 7
完成 **75%**

Part 4
閱
讀
測
驗
Day 7
完成 **100%**

Birds have always been a problem for farmers. When farmers plants ___01___ in the fields, birds may come to eat seeds. Most of these birds are crows. Farmers made scarecrows, supposing to ___02___ away these unwanted visitors.

The first scarecrows were made hundreds of years ago. They were actually sticks struck in the ground with rags tied to the top. When the wind blew, the rags ___03___ and frightened the birds away.

As time went on, farmers began making ___04___ scarecrows. They nailed a second stick across the top of the one in the ground. Later the scarecrows had arms and could wear old shirts. And farmers ___05___ the shirts with straw, making scarecrows look like real people.

When farmers began using modern ___06___, they didn't need scarecrows anymore. The machines usually made a lot of noise while working, naturally scaring birds away.

In the 1960s, with more attention having been paid to ___07___ art, scarecrows became popular again. People ___08___ scarecrows in their yards and vegetable gardens. Some people in cities also placed scarecrows in porches.

Today some artists make scarecrows for ___09___. These new scarecrows are still made of natural materials such as sticks and straw, but they are often dressed up in ___10___ clothes. Some scarecrows wear sunglasses, belts, or scarves, while others may wear beads, flowers, and purses.

(A) flapped   (B) folk   (C) fancy   (D) scare   (E) sale
(F) machines   (G) seeds   (H) stuffed   (I) better   (J) placed

01 _____   02 _____   03 _____   04 _____   05 _____

06 _____   07 _____   08 _____   09 _____   10 _____

選項中譯 | 擺動；人們；漂亮的；恐嚇；出售；機器；種子；填充；更好的；放置

中譯 | 鳥兒一直是困擾農夫的難題。農夫在田地裡播種，鳥兒也許會來偷食種子。大多
數的鳥兒是烏鴉。農夫們製作稻草人，希望嚇走這些不速之客。

最初的稻草人出現在幾百年前，其實就是插進地面、頂端繫著碎布的木棍。風吹
過時，碎布會迎風飄動，把鳥兒嚇走。

隨著時間的推移，農夫們開始製作更好的稻草人。他們把一根木棍插進土裡，並
在這根木棍頂端交叉釘上另一根木棍。後來，稻草人有了手臂，可以穿舊襯衫。
農夫們用稻草來填充襯衫，使得稻草人看起來和真人相似。

農夫開始使用現代機器時，就不再需要稻草人了。這些機器運作時，通常會發出
很大的噪音，自然會把鳥兒嚇跑。

二十世紀六〇年代，人們更加關注民間藝術，稻草人也隨之變得再度流行起來。
人們在院子和菜園裡放置稻草人。有些市民也在門廊裡放置稻草人。

如今，一些藝術家們製作稻草人出售。這些新式稻草人依然是用棍子、稻草這類
天然材料來製作，卻也用漂亮的衣服來裝飾。有些稻草人戴著太陽鏡、腰帶或是
圍巾，也有的稻草人佩戴珠子、鮮花和錢包。

解譯 | 閱讀全文可知，這篇文章的主題是稻草人。

縱觀各選項，選項 (B)、(E)、(F)、(G) 是名詞，選項 (A)、(D)、(H)、(J) 是動詞，
選項 (C)、(I) 是形容詞。根據題意，第 1、6、7、9 題應選名詞，第 2、3、5、8
題應選動詞，第 4、10 題應選形容詞。然後根據文章，依次作答。

第 1 題是選擇名詞，有四個名詞可供選擇，即為選項 (B)、(E)、(F)、(G)，選項
(B) 意為「人們」，選項 (E) 意為「出售」，選項 (F) 意為「機器」，選項 (G)
意為「種子」，plant seeds 可以視為固定搭配，意為「播種」，所以選 (G)。第
6 題所選名詞，根據句意，應當是「農夫開始使用現代機器時，就不再需要稻草
人了」，所以選 (F)。第 7 題所選名詞，也可以視為表達，folk art 意為「民間藝
術」，所以選 (B)。第 9 題則是選 (E)，for sale 意為「出售」。

第 2 題是選擇動詞，須與副詞 away 進行搭配，有四個動詞可供選擇，即為選項
(A)、(D)、(H)、(J)。只有選項 (D) 符合要求，scare... away 意為「把～嚇走」。
第 3 題所選動詞，根據句意可知，應當是「碎布迎風飄動，把鳥兒嚇走」，所
以選 (A)。第 5 題所選動詞，可以視為固定搭配，stuff... with 意為「用～填
充～」，所以選 (H)。第 8 題則是選 (J)，意為「人們在院子和菜園裡放置稻草
人」。

第 4 題是選擇形容詞，有兩個形容詞可供選擇，即為選項 (C)、(I)。選項 (C) 意
為「漂亮的」，選項 (I) 意為「更好的」，根據句意可知，應當是「製作更好的
稻草人」，所以選 (I)。第 10 題則是選 (C)，句意為「用漂亮的衣服來裝飾」。

解答＆技巧 | 01 **(G)** 02 **(D)** 03 **(A)** 04 **(I)** 05 **(H)**

06 **(F)** 07 **(B)** 08 **(J)** 09 **(E)** 10 **(C)**

適用 TIP 1   適用 TIP 2   適用 TIP 6   適用 TIP 7   適用 TIP 8

適用 TIP 9   適用 TIP 10   適用 TIP 11

DAY 7

Part 1
詞彙題
Day 7
完成 25%

Part 2
綜合測驗
Day 7
完成 50%

Part 3
文意選填
Day 7
完成 75%

Part 4
閱讀測驗
Day 7
完成 100%

補充

as soon as ph 一～就～；anymore ad 不再；folk art ph 民間藝術；suddenly ad 突然；
vegetable garden ph 菜園

7,000 單字

- crow [kro] n 1 烏鴉
- visitor [ˋvɪzɪtɚ] n 2 到訪者
- scarecrow [ˋskɛr͵kro] n 3 稻草人
- scare [skɛr] v 1 恐嚇
- hundred [ˋhʌndrəd] n 1 百
- rag [ræg] n 3 碎布
- flap [flæp] v 5 搖動
- shirt [ʃɝt] n 1 襯衫

- stuff [stʌf] v 3 塞滿
- noise [nɔɪz] n 1 噪音
- yard [jɑrd] n 2 院子
- artist [ˋɑrtɪst] n 2 藝術家
- belt [bɛlt] n 2 腰帶
- bead [bid] n 2 珠子
- purse [pɝs] n 2 錢包

MEMO

The organ starting, the carousel horses slowly begin to move. __01__ on the carousel hold tightly as the colorful horses go up and down and around and around. The carousel is another saying for merry-go-round.

Carousels have a long __02__ . In the 1400s, soldiers in France liked to play a ball game on __03__ . They had to throw and catch balls while their horses were running. The French then found a way to help the soldiers __04__ the game. Thus the first carousel came into being, but the horses involved were __05__ horses, quite different from modern carousels. Years later, carousels were used for fun. In the 1800s, carousels with __06__ replaced real horses.

Most merry-go-rounds in the United States were made in New York and Pennsylvania. Workers carved and __07__ the carousel horses. Some horses had fine saddles and roses around their necks, while others may have a wild look in their shiny glass eyes.

Some of these merry-go-rounds are now __08__ as historic places. One of the oldest merry-go-rounds is in Massachusetts. This carousel, known as the Flying Horses, was built around 1880. Riders can have some extra fun here. As the merry-go-round spins, riders should try to __09__ rings from a post on the wall. The person who gets the most rings is the __10__ , and the reward is a free ride.

(A) painted   (B) Riders   (C) horseback   (D) motors   (E) winner
(F) practice   (G) history   (H) real   (I) grab   (J) treasured

---

01 _____   02 _____   03 _____   04 _____   05 _____

06 _____   07 _____   08 _____   09 _____   10 _____

選項中譯｜為〜上色；騎乘的人；馬背；馬達；勝利者；練習；歷史；真正的；抓取；珍視

中譯｜當風琴響起，旋轉木馬也慢慢轉動。五顏六色的馬兒上上下下地不停旋轉，騎在馬上的人們都抓得緊緊的。carousel 是旋轉木馬 merry-go-round 的另一種說法。旋轉木馬歷史悠久。十五世紀時，法國的士兵喜歡騎馬玩一種球類遊戲。策馬前行時，他們要投球、接球。後來，法國人找到了一種方法來幫助士兵們練習這種遊戲。最初的旋轉木馬由此誕生，然而那時候所用的是真馬，與現代的旋轉木馬大有不同。多年後，旋轉木馬用於娛樂。十九世紀時，裝了馬達的旋轉木馬，取代了真馬。

過去美國大多數的旋轉木馬是在紐約和賓州製造的。工人們雕刻出木馬，並為之上色。有些木馬配有上等的馬鞍，脖頸處還纏繞著玫瑰花，也有些木馬閃閃發亮的玻璃眼睛中透露出野性。

如今這些旋轉木馬，有的已被視為古跡。最久遠之一的旋轉木馬在麻塞諸塞州，名為「飛奔的駿馬」，修建於一八八○年前後。在這裡，人們可以獲得額外的樂趣。木馬旋轉時，騎在木馬上的人要盡力從牆上的柱子上抓取吊環，拿到最多吊環的人就是贏家，獲得的獎勵就是免費坐一次旋轉木馬。

解譯｜閱讀全文可知，這篇文章的主題是旋轉木馬的由來及其發展狀況。

縱觀各選項，選項 (B)、(C)、(D)、(E)、(G) 是名詞，選項 (A)、(F)、(I)、(J) 是動詞，選項 (H) 是形容詞。根據題意，第 1、2、3、6、10 題應選名詞，第 4、7、8、9 題應選動詞，第 5 題應選形容詞。然後根據文章，依次作答。

第 1 題是選擇名詞，有五個名詞可供選擇，即為選項 (B)、(C)、(D)、(E)、(G)，選項 (B) 意為「騎乘的人」，選項 (C) 意為「馬背」，選項 (D) 意為「馬達」，選項 (E) 意為「勝利者」，選項 (G) 意為「歷史」，根據句意，應當是「騎在馬上的人們都抓得緊緊的」，所以選 (B)。第 2 題所選名詞，可以視為固定搭配，have a long history 意為「歷史悠久」，所以選 (G)。第 3 題所選名詞，是與介系詞 on 連用，on horseback 意為「在馬背上」，所以選 (C)。第 6 題所選名詞，根據句意，應當是「裝置了馬達的旋轉木馬，取代了真馬」，所以選 (D)。第 10 題則是選 (E)，意為「拿到最多吊環的人就是贏家」。

第 4 題是選擇動詞，有四個動詞可供選擇，即為選項 (A)、(F)、(I)、(J)，根據句意，應當是「練習這種遊戲」，所以選 (F)。第 7 題所選動詞，根據句意，應當是「工人們雕刻出木馬，並為之上色」，所以選 (A)。第 8 題所選動詞，是被動語態，且與介系詞 as 進行搭配，所以選 (J)。第 9 題則是選 (I)，意為「從牆上的柱子上抓取吊環」。

第 5 題是選擇形容詞，只有一個形容詞可供選擇，即為選項 (H)，意為「真正的」。

DAY 7

Part 1
詞彙題
Day 7
完成 25%

Part 2
綜合測驗
Day 7
完成 50%

Part 3
文意選填
Day 7
完成 75%

Part 4
閱讀測驗
Day 7
完成 100%

解答&技巧 | 01 (B)　02 (G)　03 (C)　04 (F)　05 (H)
06 (D)　07 (A)　08 (J)　09 (I)　10 (E)

適用 TIP 1　適用 TIP 2　適用 TIP 6　適用 TIP 7　適用 TIP 8
適用 TIP 9　適用 TIP 10　適用 TIP 11

補充

carousel [n] 旋轉木馬；merry-go-round [n] 旋轉木馬；horseback [n] 馬背；
Pennsylvania [n] 賓夕法尼亞州；Massachusetts [n] 麻塞諸塞州

7,000 單字

- organ [ˈɔrgən] [n] 2 風琴
- horse [hɔrs] [n] 1 馬
- merry [ˈmɛrɪ] [a] 3 高興的
- throw [θro] [v] 1 扔
- motor [ˈmotɚ] [n] 3 馬達
- carve [kɑrv] [v] 4 雕刻
- paint [pent] [v] 1 塗顏料於
- saddle [ˈsædl] [n] 5 馬鞍

- wild [waɪld] [a] 2 未馴化的，野性的
- treasure [ˈtrɛʒɚ] [v] 2 珍惜
- historic [hɪsˈtɔrɪk] [a] 3 歷史上的
- extra [ˈɛkstrə] [a] 2 附加的
- spin [spɪn] [v] 3 旋轉
- winner [ˈwɪnɚ] [n] 2 勝利者
- reward [rɪˈwɔrd] [n] 4 獎勵

MEMO

DAY
7

Part 1
詞
彙
題
Day 7
完成 25%

Part 2
綜
合
測
驗
Day 7
完成 50%

Part 3
文
意
選
填
Day 7
完成 75%

Part 4
閱
讀
測
驗
Day 7
完成 100%

Part 4   閱讀測驗 | Reading Questions

1▶

It was just 7 o'clock in the morning. The doorbell was ringing, I was quite unwilling to pull on a bathrobe and murmured to my husband David, "Who could that be? Today is Sunday!" "It must be the painters," he answered, and then rushed downstairs to open the door. In a minute I heard him chatting with those painters on the front porch.

"The painters?" I incredulously repeated his words. Although David and I had been talking about painting our new house for several weeks, our plan was still controversial. We had seen the color charts and paint samples, but we needed to further narrow down the choices.

Therefore, when he came back to the bedroom, I felt furious and shouted to him, "Why are the painters here? We haven't decided the main color! We need more time to sketch it out!"

"We will get started soon, and everything will be figured out." David said to me, "It's time to start."

Consequently, I was mad all day long. I thought painting the house was important, and it needed a mutual decision. But when I returned home in the evening, I was amazed. The painting was still in progress. I found that everything seemed to be satisfactory. I tried to defend my previous words and deeds, however, my argument fell apart.

"Maybe you are right, my dear." I said to David and gave him a big bear hug. Maybe each of us needed to be a dictator in the marriage life.

01 Which one of the following statements is true?

(A) The story happened on Sunday.

(B) When the doorbell rang, the wife went to open the door.

(C) David made an apology to his wife finally.

(D) David and his wife did not refer to the color charts and painted samples.

02 Which of the following statements is not mentioned in the passage?

(A) David chatted with the painters on the front porch.

(B) The wife was unable to believe it when the painters came.

(C) There is still a controversy over the plan of painting the house.

(D) David and his wife discussed the plan with the painters on that day.

03 The word "furious" in the third paragraph is closest in meaning to _____.

(A) worried

(B) happy

(C) angry

(D) embarrassed

04 We can learn from the passage that _____.

(A) couples always quarrel with each other

(B) painters always have to work hard

(C) mutual understanding is quite important in marriage life

(D) painting a house is difficult

DAY
7

Part 1
詞
彙
題
Day 7
完成 25%

Part 2
綜
合
測
驗
Day 7
完成 50%

Part 3
文
意
選
填
Day 7
完成 75%

Part 4
閱
讀
測
驗
Day 7
完成 100%

中譯｜才早上七點，門鈴響起，我很不情願地穿上浴衣，對丈夫大衛呢喃道：「會是誰？今天是星期天啊！」「肯定是油漆工。」他回答說，然後衝下樓去開門。不一會兒，我就聽見他和那些油漆工們在前面的門廊處交談。

「油漆工？」我不敢相信地重複他說的話。關於新房的刷漆問題，我和大衛已經討論了幾個星期，但是，我們的計畫仍有爭議。我們看過了比色圖表和塗料樣品，但是還需要進一步縮小選擇範圍。

因此當他回到臥室時，我感到很氣憤，對他大喊道：「為什麼那些油漆工會在這裡？我們還沒有決定用什麼主色調！我們需要更多的時間來把草圖畫出來！」

「我們就要開工了，一切問題都會得到解決的。」大衛對我說，「是時候開工了。」

因此，一整天我都很生氣。我想著，粉刷房子非常重要，需要我們共同做決定。但是，當我晚上回到家時，卻很吃驚。粉刷工程仍在進行當中。我發現，一切似乎都令人滿意。我試著為早上的言行進行辯解，然而我的這番爭論卻站不住腳。「親愛的，也許你是對的。」我對大衛說，並緊緊地擁抱他。也許，在婚姻生活中，我們每個人都需要當個獨裁者。

解譯｜在閱讀文章之前，先要預覽題目，然後再帶著問題有針對性地閱讀文章。第 1 題是判斷正誤，第 2、4 題是文意理解，第 3 題是詞義辨析。理解了題目要求之後，閱讀全文，依次作答。

第 1 題是判斷正誤，考的是細節，問的是哪一項敘述是正確的。根據第 1 段第 2 句內容「Today is Sunday!」可知，故事是發生在一個周日，與選項 (A) 相符。同樣，此題也可以用排除法來解答。根據第 1 段第 4 句內容可知，是大衛去開門，而不是他的妻子，選項 (B) 敘述錯誤，排除；根據第 4 段和第 6 段的內容可知，大衛最後並沒有向他妻子道歉，排除選項 (C)；根據第 2 段最後一句內容可知，大衛和他的妻子已經看過了比色圖表和塗料樣品，選項 (D) 錯誤，排除。所以選 (B)。

第 2 題是文意理解，問的是哪一項敘述在文中沒有提及。第 1 段最後一句內容與選項 (A) 相符，第 2 段首句內容與選項 (B) 相符，第 2 段第 2 句內容與選項 (C) 相符，只有選項 (D)，在文中找不到相關敘述。所以選 (D)。

第 3 題是考形容詞 furious 的同義字。選項 (A) 意為「擔心的」，選項 (B) 意為「高興的」，選項 (C) 意為「生氣的」，選項 (D) 意為「尷尬的」。根據第 3 段首句內容可知，furious 在文中意為「憤怒的」，所以選 (C)。

第 4 題也是文意理解，問的是我們可以從文中得出什麼結論。作者是借油漆房子一事，敘述了她和丈夫之間的矛盾，及至爭端最後得到解決，她才理解了丈夫。由此可知，夫妻之間需要相互理解，選項 (C) 意為「在婚姻生活中，相互理解十分重要」，與此相符。選項 (A) 意為「夫妻之間總是會發生爭吵」，選項 (B) 意為「油漆工總是不得不努力工作」，選項 (D) 意為「油漆房子是困難的」，並不是文章所要表達的意義。

解答 & 技巧 | **01 (A)** **02 (D)** **03 (C)** **04 (C)**

適用 TIP 1　適用 TIP 2　適用 TIP 3　適用 TIP 7　適用 TIP 10

適用 TIP 11　適用 TIP 12　適用 TIP 13　適用 TIP 14　適用 TIP 15

DAY
7

Part 1
詞
彙
題
Day 7
完成 25%

Part 2
綜
合
測
驗
Day 7
完成 50%

Part 3
文
意
選
填
Day 7
完成 75%

Part 4
閱
讀
測
驗
Day 7
完成 100%

補充

doorbell n 門鈴；bathrobe n 浴衣；incredulously ad 不相信地；amazed a 驚訝的；
marriage life ph 婚姻生活

7,000 單字

- murmur [ˋmɝmɚ] v 4 低聲説
- Sunday [ˋsʌnde] n 1 周日
- painter [ˋpentɚ] n 2 油漆工
- downstairs [ˏdaunˋstɛrz] ad 1 在樓下
- chat [tʃæt] v 3 聊天
- front [frʌnt] a 1 前面的
- controversial [ˏkɑntrəˋvɝʃəl] a 6 有爭議的
- chart [tʃɑrt] n 1 圖表

- sample [ˋsæmpl] n 2 樣品
- sketch [skɛtʃ] v 4 草擬
- mutual [ˋmjutʃuəl] a 4 共同的
- defend [dɪˋfɛnd] v 4 辯護
- argument [ˋɑrgjəmənt] n 2 爭論
- hug [hʌg] n 3 擁抱
- dictator [ˋdɪkˏtetɚ] n 6 獨裁者

MEMO

It is said that the falling dollars have grabbed the attention of Japan and Germany and forced them to take into consideration adopting economic policies advocated by the United States. With the devaluation of the dollars, the U.S. government feels delighted because on this occasion U.S. goods will become cheaper. The product sales of U.S. companies at home and abroad will increase, and U.S. trade deficit will decline.

The decline in price makes dollars cheaper. Many foreign investors can spend less money in snapping up U.S. stocks, which leads to a phenomenon that U.S. companies eventually become more competitive than those of other countries. Although more and more investors are considering buying shares of U.S. companies in anticipation of better profits in the future, it is only a faddish notion right now. When the corporate earnings become disappointing, the stock market will certainly come to a halt.

Improvement of U.S. competitiveness signifies the decline of other countries' competitiveness at the same time. In fact, Japan and Germany are suffering from recession. Their export-oriented economies have many problems now, causing many worries about the damage to their trade. Many other countries are considering cutting down interest rates to boost their economy.

However, what people really want to know is whether the falling dollars will get out of hand or not. If the dollars fall too far, those investors may lose confidence in U.S. investments, particularly the government bond market. And the money used to finance the federal budget and trade deficits will be turned to elsewhere. Once foreign manufacturers decide to carry on price hikes, the U.S. companies may follow suit to increase their profit margins. Then the high interest rate may slow down the economic development.

01 The word "boost" in the third paragraph is closest in meaning to _____.

(A) promote

(B) employ

(C) create

(D) build

02 Japan and Germany are _____ the falling dollars.

(A) happy about

(B) worried about

(C) indifferent to

(D) tired of

03 What would not happen if the falling dollars get out of hand?

(A) Money used to finance the federal budget and trade deficits would migrate elsewhere.

(B) Foreign investors might lose confidence in U.S. investments.

(C) It would contribute to the development of economy.

(D) Foreign manufacturers might decide to carry on price hikes.

04 What is the main idea of the passage?

(A) The consequence of the U.S. falling dollars.

(B) The benefit of U.S. falling dollars.

(C) Economic policies advocated by the United States.

(D) Economy of Japan and Germany.

DAY
7

Part 1
詞
彙
題
Day 7
完成 25%

Part 2
綜
合
測
驗
Day 7
完成 50%

Part 3
文
意
選
填
Day 7
完成 75%

Part 4
閱
讀
測
驗
Day 7
完成 100%

中譯 | 據說，美元價格下跌已經引起了日本和德國的注意，迫使他們考慮採用美國所提倡的經濟政策。美國政府樂意見美元貶值，因為在這種情況下，美國的商品會變得更為廉價。美國公司的產品銷量在國內外都會增加，美國的貿易逆差也將會減少。

價格下跌使美元變得更為廉價，很多外國投資商可以花費更少的錢來搶購美國股票，這就導致了美國公司最終會變得比其他國家的公司更具競爭力的現象。愈來愈多的投資商在考慮購買美國公司的股票，期望在日後獲得更好的收益。但是，目前這只是一時熱中的觀念。如果公司收入狀況變得令人失望，股票市場必然會陷入停滯。

提高美國的競爭力，就意味著降低了其他國家的競爭力。事實上，日本和德國正處於經濟蕭條時期，其以出口為主的經濟體目前都面臨著很多問題，致使很多人都擔心貿易受損。很多其他的國家正在考慮下調利率，來促進經濟發展。

然而人們真正想知道的是，美元下跌是否會無法控制。如果美元過度下跌，那些投資商可能會對美國投資喪失信心，特別是政府債券市場。用於資助聯邦預算和貿易逆差的資金，也將會另作他用。一旦外國製造商決定調漲價格，美國公司也許會隨之提高利潤率。而高利率也許會減緩經濟發展。

解譯 | 在閱讀文章之前，先要預覽題目，然後再帶著問題有針對性地閱讀文章。第 1 題是詞義辨析，第 2、3 題是文意理解，第 4 題是概括主旨。理解了題目要求之後，閱讀全文，依次作答。

第 1 題是考 boost 的同義字。boost 可以作名詞，意為「增長；幫助；鼓勵」；也可以作動詞，意為「提高；促進；增加；鼓勵」。根據第 3 段最後一句內容可知，boost 在文中意為「促進」。選項 (A) 意為「促進」，選項 (B) 意為「雇用」，選項 (C) 意為「創造」，選項 (D) 意為「修建」。所以選 (A)。

第 2 題是文意理解，問的是對於美元貶值，日本和德國持什麼態度。第 1 段中說，美元貶值，使美國的經濟暫時受益；第 2 段中說，美國公司更具競爭力；第 3 段則是說，日本和德國因此被削弱了經濟競爭力，正處於經濟蕭條時期，它們以出口為主的經濟體目前都面臨著很多問題，很多人都擔心貿易受損。由此可以推斷，日本和德國對於美元貶值是十分擔心的，與選項 (B) 相符。所以選 (B)。

第 3 題同樣是文意理解，問的是如果美元過度下跌，將不會發生什麼。可以定位於第 4 段。第 3 句內容與選項 (A) 相符，第 2 句內容與選項 (B) 相符，第 4 句內容與選項 (D) 相符。只有選項 (C)，在文中找不到相關敘述。所以選 (C)。

第 4 題是概括主旨。文中並沒有明顯的主旨句，需要根據各段內容加以概括。第 1 段是由美元貶值而引出話題，第 2 段講述的是美國公司更具競爭力，第 3 段講述的是日本和德國經濟蕭條，第 4 段講述的是美元過度貶值的影響。由此可知，短文內容是簡述美元貶值的後果，與選項 (A) 敘述相符，所以選 (A)。

解答＆技巧 | `01` **(A)** `02` **(B)** `03` **(C)** `04` **(A)**

適用 TIP 1　適用 TIP 2　適用 TIP 7　適用 TIP 10　適用 TIP 11
適用 TIP 12　適用 TIP 13　適用 TIP 14　適用 TIP 15　適用 TIP 16

DAY 7

Part 1
詞彙題
Day 7
完成 25%

Part 2
綜合測驗
Day 7
完成 50%

Part 3
文意選填
Day 7
完成 75%

Part 4
閱讀測驗
Day 7
完成 100%

補充

deficit n 赤字；investor n 投資者；faddish a 一時流行的，心血來潮的；
competitiveness n 競爭力；investment n 投資

7,000 單字

- grab [græb] v 3 奪取，抓
- economic [ˌikə`nɑmɪk] a 4 經濟的
- policy [`pɑləsɪ] n 2 政策
- advocate [`ædvəˌket] v 6 號召
- sale [sel] n 1 銷售
- competitive [kəm`pɛtətɪv] a 4 有競爭力的
- anticipation [ænˌtɪsə`peʃən] n 6 期望
- halt [hɔlt] n 4 停頓，暫停

- signify [`sɪgnəˌfaɪ] v 6 意味著
- recession [rɪ`sɛʃən] n 6 衰退，不景氣
- export [`ɛksport] n 3 出口
- federal [`fɛdərəl] a 5 聯邦政府的
- elsewhere [`ɛlsˌhwɛr] ad 4 在別處
- hike [haɪk] n 3 增加，提高
- margin [`mɑrdʒɪn] n 4 盈利，利潤

MEMO

♫ 433

3 ▶

The concept of home may be various for different people at different times and places. It is a fact that all people need homes. Married couples work together to create a new family, and then children can think of their parents' place as home. For those boarders, the school where they study and live is their home. However, travelers may have no places to call home, especially when they stay outside for a few nights.

Some regular travelers often take their own belongings—such as bed sheets, pillowcases and family photos—with them, no matter where they are. Thus they may feel like staying at home. Some travelers may stay in a hotel for long periods and become very familiar with the services, attendants and companions there. Therefore, they will call the hotel their home. Some of them may even give the hotel a bit of decoration, such as buying flowers and hanging colorful curtains, to make it more homely. If driving a camping car for traveling, travelers can take it as a moveable home.

Then, how will those travelers keep in contact with others during their trips? Some travelers contact them via Internet, letters, postcards, or photos. Others may call and say hello to their families and friends just to say that they are very well. In addition, travelers can also make friends on their way and become less homesick.

Nowadays, fewer and fewer people work in their hometown. A sense of belonging has become more and more important. Wherever they are, they can create a home and manage to live well.

01 According to the first paragraph, which one of the following statements is false?

(A) As for the definition of home, different people may have different ideas.

(B) Travelers may take many places as home.

(C) Children may take their parents' house as home.

(D) Boarders may take their school as home.

02 The word "attendants" in the second paragraph is closest in meaning to _____.

(A) scientists

(B) engineers

(C) teachers

(D) waiters

03 Which of the following statements is not mentioned in the passage?

(A) Travelers may keep in contact with others via letters.

(B) Travelers may keep in contact with others via Internet.

(C) Travelers may keep in contact with others via phones.

(D) Travelers don't need home or friends actually.

04 What is the main idea of the passage?

(A) The concept of home.

(B) Hotels.

(C) Travelers' home.

(D) Travelers' lifestyle.

7

Part 1
詞
彙
題
Day 7
完成 25%

Part 2
綜
合
測
驗
Day 7
完成 50%

Part 3
文
意
選
填
Day 7
完成 75%

Part 4
閱
讀
測
驗
Day 7
完成 100%

中譯 | 在不同的時代和地點，不同的人對於家有著不同的概念。事實上，人人都需要一個家。已婚夫妻一起努力建立新的家庭，孩子就可以把父母的住所當做自己的家。對於那些寄宿生來說，他們學習和生活的學校，就是他們的家。然而，旅行者也許並沒有什麼地方可以稱為家，尤其是當他們外宿的那些夜晚。

有些經常出門的旅行者，無論身處何地，都會隨身攜帶例如床單、枕套和家庭照之類的行李。這樣做，他們會覺得像是還留在家中一樣。有些旅行者也許會長時間地停留在飯店裡，對那裡的服務和侍者都很熟悉。因此他們將飯店稱為家。有些人甚至會為飯店進行簡單的裝飾，例如買一些花、懸掛彩色的窗簾，使它更有家的感覺。如果是開著露營車旅行，旅行者就可以將露營車稱為可以移動的家。

那麼，在旅行期間，那些旅行者如何與其他人聯繫？有些旅行者透過網路、信件、明信片或是照片與人聯繫，有些會打電話給家人或朋友，告知他們自己過得很好。此外，旅行者也可以在旅途中交朋友，就不會特別想家。

如今，愈來愈少的人在自己的家鄉工作，歸屬感也就愈來愈重要。不論他們身在何處，都可以建造家園，並且努力地生活得很好。

解譯 | 在閱讀文章之前，先要預覽題目，然後再帶著問題有針對性地閱讀文章。第 1 題是判斷正誤，第 2 題是詞義辨析，第 3 題是文意理解，第 4 題是概括主旨。理解了題目要求之後，閱讀全文，依次作答。

第 1 題是判斷正誤，考的是細節，問的是哪一項敘述是錯誤的。定位於第 1 段。根據最後一句內容「travelers may have no places to call home」可知，旅行者也許並沒有什麼地方可以稱為家，而不是有很多地方可以稱為家，選項 (B) 敘述錯誤。同樣，此題也可以用排除法來解答。第 1 句內容與選項 (A) 相符，第 3 句內容與選項 (C) 相符，第 4 句內容與選項 (D) 相符，都是正確的。所以選 (B)。

第 2 題是考名詞 attendant 的同義字。attendant 意為「侍者，服務員；隨行者；出席者」，根據第 2 段第 2 句內容可知，在文中意為「服務員」。選項 (A) 意為「科學家」，選項 (B) 意為「工程師」，選項 (C) 意為「教師」，選項 (D) 意為「服務員」。所以選 (D)。

第 3 題是文意理解，問的是哪一項敘述在文中沒有提及。根據第 3 段第 2、3 句內容可知，有些旅行者透過網路、信件、明信片或是照片與人聯繫，也有些旅行者會打電話給家人或朋友，與選項 (A)、(B)、(C) 相符。只有選項 (D)，在文中找不到相關敘述。所以選 (D)。

第 4 題是概括主旨。文中並沒有明顯的主旨句，需要根據各段內容加以概括。第 1 段是由家的不同概念而引出話題，第 2 段講述的是旅行者的家，第 3 段講述的是旅行者與他人的聯繫方式，第 4 段講述的是歸屬感。由此可知，短文內容是簡述旅行者的家，所以選 (C)。

解答＆技巧 ┃ **01** (B)　**02** (D)　**03** (D)　**04** (C)

適用 TIP 1　適用 TIP 2　適用 TIP 3　適用 TIP 7　適用 TIP 10

適用 TIP 11　適用 TIP 12　適用 TIP 13　適用 TIP 14　適用 TIP 15

補充

boarder n 寄宿者；especially ad 尤其；pillowcase n 枕頭套；become familiar with ph 對～熟悉；
moveable a 可移動的

7,000 單字

- belongings [bəˋlɔŋɪŋz] n 5 所有物
- sheet [ʃit] n 1 床單
- hotel [hoˋtɛl] n 2 旅館
- companion [kəmˋpænjən] n 4 夥伴
- bit [bɪt] n 1 少量
- flower [ˋflauɚ] n 1 花
- hang [hæŋ] v 2 懸掛
- via [ˋvaɪə] prep 5 經由

- postcard [ˋpostˏkɑrd] n 2 明信片
- hello [hɛˋlo] n 1 問候
- addition [əˋdɪʃən] n 2 增加
- homesick [ˋhomˏsɪk] a 2 思鄉的
- hometown [ˋhomˋtaun] n 3 家鄉
- wherever [hwɛrˋɛvɚ] conj 2 無論在哪裡
- well [wɛl] ad 1 好地，滿意地

Part 1
詞彙題
Day 7
完成 25%

Part 2
綜合測驗
Day 7
完成 50%

Part 3
文意選填
Day 7
完成 75%

Part 4
閱讀測驗
Day 7
完成 100%

MEMO

4 ▶ 96 年學測英文

Most American kids love Halloween treats, but a bucket of Halloween candy can be a dentist's nightmare. Some parents try to get rid of half of the candy after their children go to bed, but dentists say parents also need to separate the good kinds of treats from the bad.

It is not exactly what a child eats that truly matters, but how much time it stays in his mouth. According to pediatric dentist Dr. Kaneta Lott, the most damaging stuff is something that is sticky or very hard and thus stays in the mouth for a long time. This is because we all have bacteria in our mouths. When we eat, the bacteria take our food as their food and produce an acid that destroys the surface of the teeth, causing cavities to form. The longer the food stays in the mouth, the more likely cavities will develop. Therefore, potato chips are worse than candy because they get stuck between teeth. For the same reason, raisins and crackers are not the best choice. Hard candies take a long time to consume and are also a bad choice for Halloween treats.

If children really love candy, dentists recommend that they eat chocolate instead. Unlike hard candies, chocolate dissolves quickly in the mouth. Besides, chocolate contains tannins, which help to kill some of the bacteria in the mouth. But no matter what a child eats, brushing after each meal is still the best way to fight cavities.

01 What is the main purpose of this passage?

(A) To discuss how cavities can be treated.

(B) To point out the problems with Halloween celebrations.

(C) To tell parents what sweets are less damaging to their children's teeth.

(D) To teach parents the meaning of Halloween candies for their children.

02 Why are hard candies especially bad for teeth?

(A) They may break the child's teeth.

(B) They contain too much sugar.

(C) They help bacteria to produce tannins.

(D) They stay in the mouth for a long time.

03 According to the passage, which of the following is a better choice for Halloween treats?

(A) Chocolate.

(B) Crackers.

(C) Raisins.

(D) Potato chips.

04 According to the passage, which of the following is correct of tannins?

(A) They are produced when the bacteria digest the food.

(B) They help to get rid of some bacteria in the mouth.

(C) They help chocolate to dissolve more quickly.

(D) They destroy the surface of the teeth.

DAY
7

Part 1
詞
彙
題
Day 7
完成 25%

Part 2
綜
合
測
驗
Day 7
完成 50%

Part 3
文
意
選
填
Day 7
完成 75%

Part 4
閱
讀
測
驗
Day 7
完成 100%

中譯｜多數美國孩子喜歡吃萬聖節的糖果，但是，一桶萬聖節糖果很可能是牙醫的噩夢。有些家長試圖在孩子們睡覺之後丟掉一半的糖果，不過牙醫說，家長們也需要將那些好的糖果和不好的區分開來。

孩子吃什麼其實並不重要，真正重要的是，所吃的東西在口中停留多長時間。兒科牙醫金多・洛特博士說，那些黏性或是硬性的物質，會在口中停留較長的時間，造成的損害最大。這是因為我們口中都有細菌，吃東西的時候，這些細菌也會從我們吃的食物中攝取它們的食物，然後產生一種酸，破壞牙齒表層，形成蛀牙。食物在口中停留的時間愈久，就愈有可能出現蛀牙。洋芋片比糖果更具損害性，因為它會黏在牙齒之間。同樣地，葡萄乾和薄脆餅乾也不是最好的選擇。硬糖需要很長時間來溶化，也不是萬聖節糖果的好選擇。

牙醫建議，如果孩子們真的喜歡吃糖果，可以吃巧克力代替。和硬糖不同的是，巧克力在口中溶解得很快。此外，巧克力中含有單寧酸，可以幫助消滅口中的細菌。但是，不論孩子吃什麼，飯後刷牙都是抵抗蛀牙的最佳方式。

解譯｜在閱讀文章之前，先要預覽題目，然後再帶著問題有針對性地閱讀文章。第 1 題是概括主旨，第 2、3 題是文意理解，第 4 題是判斷正誤。理解了題目要求之後，閱讀全文，依次作答。主旨題可以留在最後解答。

第 2 題是問，為什麼硬糖於牙齒有害。流覽全文可知，第 2 段最後一句內容與第 2 題相符。根據「Hard candies take a long time to consume and are also a bad choice for Halloween treats.」可知，硬糖需要很長時間來溶化，不是萬聖節糖果的好選擇，所以選 (D)。

第 3 題是問，哪一樣是萬聖節糖果的好選擇。根據第 3 段首句內容「If children really love candy, dentists recommend that they eat chocolate instead.」判斷，應該選 (A)。此外，也可以用排除法來解答。根據第 2 段倒數第 3 行內容「raisins and crackers are not the best choice」，可知葡萄乾和薄脆餅乾不是最好的選擇，排除選項 (B)、(C)。再根據第 2 段倒數第 4 行內容「potato chips are worse than candy」可知，洋芋片比糖果更具損害性，排除選項 (D)。所以選 (A)。

第 4 題是判斷正誤，考的是細節，問的是關於單寧酸的敘述，哪一項是正確的。很明顯，其關鍵字是 tannins，即單寧酸，因此定位於第 3 段。直接提到 tannins 的，是第 3 段的倒數第 2 句內容「Besides, chocolate contains tannins, which help to kill some of the bacteria in the mouth.」可知，單寧酸可以幫助消滅口中的細菌，所以選 (B)。同樣，此題也可以用排除法來解答。根據第 2 段內容「the bacteria take our food as their food and produce an acid that destroys the surface of the teeth」可知，損害牙齒表層的是細菌產生的一種酸，而不是單寧酸，排除選項 (A)、(D)；而選項 (C) 在文中並未提及，也可以排除。所以選 (B)。

第 1 題是概括主旨。文中並沒有明顯的主旨句，需要根據各段內容加以概括。第 1 段是由萬聖節的糖果而引出牙齒問題，第 2 段講述的是對牙齒有害的食品及其原因，第 3 段講述的是選擇巧克力的原因，並且簡述了刷牙的重要性。由此可知，短文內容是簡述哪些食品對牙齒危害性較小，所以選 (C)。

解答＆技巧 | 01 **(C)** 02 **(D)** 03 **(A)** 04 **(B)**

適用 TIP 3　適用 TIP 11　適用 TIP 12　適用 TIP 13　適用 TIP 14　適用 TIP 15

補充

get rid of ph 除去，擺脫；**go to bed** ph 去睡覺；**separate... from...** ph 把～和～區分開；
pediatric dentist ph 兒科牙醫；**tannin** n 單寧酸

7,000 單字

- dentist [ˋdɛntɪst] n 2 牙醫
- nightmare [ˋnaɪt͵mɛr] n 4 惡夢
- half [hæf] n 1 一半
- mouth [maʊθ] n 1 嘴
- acid [ˋæsɪd] n 4 酸
- tooth [tuθ] n 2 牙齒
- cavity [ˋkævətɪ] n 6 洞
- potato [pəˋteto] n 2 馬鈴薯

- candy [ˋkændɪ] n 1 糖果
- raisin [ˋrezn̩] n 3 葡萄乾
- cracker [ˋkrækɚ] n 5 薄脆餅乾
- bad [bæd] a 1 不好的
- dissolve [dɪˋzɑlv] v 6 溶解
- sweets [swits] n 1 糖果
- correct [kəˋrɛkt] a 1 正確的

DAY
7

Part 1
詞
彙
題

Day 7
完成 25%

Part 2
綜
合
測
驗

Day 7
完成 50%

Part 3
文
意
選
填

Day 7
完成 75%

Part 4
閱
讀
測
驗

Day 7
完成 100%

MEMO

DAY 8

Never reject an idea, dream or goal because it will be hard work.
Success rarely comes without it.
— *Bob Proctor*

絕不要因為怕辛苦，就拒絕一個想法、夢想或目標，成功很少沒有伴隨辛苦。
——包柏‧普克

▶ **Part 1**｜詞 彙 題

▶ **Part 2**｜綜合測驗

▶ **Part 3**｜文意選填

▶ **Part 4**｜閱讀測驗

Part 1 | 詞彙題 | Vocabulary Questions

01 We could _____ in local newspapers, which can attract more applicants for interviews.

(A) assault　　　　(B) advertise
(C) astonish　　　　(D) beware

補充
local newspaper ph 地方報紙

7,000 單字
• applicant [ˋæpləkənt] n 4 申請人
• assault [əˋsɔlt] v 5 攻擊
• advertise [ˋædvɚͺtaɪz] v 3 登廣告
• astonish [əˋstɑnɪʃ] v 5 使驚訝
• beware [bɪˋwɛr] v 5 注意

中譯｜我們可以在地方報紙上登廣告，這樣就會吸引更多的求職者前來面試。

解說｜四個選項皆為動詞。依據題意，應該是「在地方報紙上登廣告」，選項 (B) advertise 表示「登廣告」，符合題意，是正確選項。

解答&技巧｜**(B)**　適用 TIP 1　適用 TIP 4

02 I _____ your talent for music so much that I decide to recommend you for further study in the conservatory of music in the United States.

(A) widen　　　　(B) vend
(C) appreciate　　　(D) vomit

補充
further study ph 深造

7,000 單字
• conservatory [kənˋsɝvəͺtorɪ] n 4 音樂學校
• widen [ˋwaɪdn] v 2 放寬
• vend [vɛnd] v 6 出售
• appreciate [əˋpriʃɪͺet] v 3 欣賞
• vomit [ˋvɑmɪt] v 6 嘔吐

中譯｜我非常欣賞你的音樂才華，所以我決定推薦你去美國的音樂學院深造。

解說｜四個選項皆為動詞。依據題意，應該是「欣賞你的音樂才華」，選項 (C) appreciate 表示「欣賞」，符合題意，其他三個選項都不符合題意。

解答&技巧｜**(C)**　適用 TIP 1　適用 TIP 4

03 Moving is really hard work; if you need help, I can _____ you in moving the furniture.

(A) withstand　　　(B) woo
(C) wrench　　　　(D) assist

補充
hard work ph 繁重的工作

7,000 單字
• really [ˋrɪəlɪ] ad 1 真地，很
• withstand [wɪðˋstænd] v 6 抵擋
• woo [wu] v 6 追求
• wrench [rɛntʃ] v 6 扭傷
• assist [əˋsɪst] v 3 幫助

中譯｜搬家真是辛苦，如果你需要幫忙，我可以幫你搬傢具。

解說｜四個選項皆為動詞。依據題意，應該是「幫你搬傢具」，選項 (D) assist 表示「幫助」，符合題意，是正確選項。

解答&技巧｜**(D)**　適用 TIP 1　適用 TIP 4

04 I told him to _____ me at 7 a.m., but he forgot, and then I was late for work.

(A) undo

(B) undergo

(C) awaken

(D) underestimate

補充
be late for ph 遲到

7,000 單字
- a.m. [`e`ɛm] abbr 4 上午
- undo [ʌn`du] v 6 取消
- undergo [ˌʌndə`go] v 6 經歷
- awaken [ə`wekən] v 3 叫醒
- underestimate [ˌʌndə`ɛstəˌmet] v 6 低估

中譯｜我叫他在早上七點叫醒我，可是他卻忘了，結果我上班遲到了。

解說｜四個選項皆為動詞。依據題意，應該是「在早上七點叫醒我」，選項 (C) awaken 表示「叫醒」，符合題意，其他三個選項都不符合題意。

解答＆技巧｜**(C)** 適用 TIP 1　適用 TIP 4

---

05 He is a famous Hollywood actor and has been _____ lots of prizes over the past ten years.

(A) uncovered

(B) trespassed

(C) trekked

(D) awarded

補充
lots of ph 很多

7,000 單字
- ten num 1 十
- uncover v 6 發現
- trespass v 6 侵入
- trek v 6 艱苦跋涉
- award v 3 榮獲

中譯｜他是一位著名的好萊塢演員，在過去十年裡已經榮獲了很多獎項。

解說｜四個選項皆為動詞。依據題意，應該是「榮獲了很多獎項」，選項 (D) awarded 表示「榮獲，授予」，符合題意，其他三個選項都不符合題意。

解答＆技巧｜**(D)** 適用 TIP 1　適用 TIP 4

---

06 It was _____ that he suffered from serious gunshot wounds but could not find a doctor.

(A) trivial

(B) awful

(C) truant

(D) superstitious

補充
gunshot wound ph 槍傷

7,000 單字
- gunshot [`gʌnˌʃɑt] n 4 射出的子彈
- trivial [`trɪvɪəl] a 6 瑣碎的
- awful [`ɔful] a 3 可怕的
- truant [`truənt] a 6 曠課的
- superstitious [ˌsupə`stɪʃəs] a 6 迷信的

中譯｜他受了很重的槍傷，但是卻找不到醫生，真是糟糕透了。

解說｜四個選項皆為形容詞。依據題意，應該是「糟糕透了」，選項 (B) awful 表示「糟糕的」，符合題意，其他三個選項都不符合題意。

解答＆技巧｜**(B)** 適用 TIP 1　適用 TIP 4

DAY
8

Part 1
詞彙題
Day
完成 25%

Part 2
綜合測驗
Day
完成 50%

Part 3
文意選填
Day
完成 75%

Part 4
閱讀測驗
Day
完成 100%

07 If you want to negotiate a shaky suspension bridge, you'd better stretch your arms to keep _____.

(A) superiority　　(B) successor

(C) balance　　(D) subscription

中譯｜如果你想順利通過搖晃的吊橋，你最好伸展手臂以保持身體平衡。

解說｜四個選項皆為名詞。依據題意，應該是「保持身體平衡」，選項 (C) balance 表示「平衡」，而片語 keep balance 表示「身體平衡」，符合題意，是正確選項。

解答＆技巧｜**(C)** 適用 TIP 2　適用 TIP 4

---

08 Many tourists took off their shoes, playing and collecting seashells on the beach with _____ feet.

(A) successive　　(B) superb

(C) spectacular　　(D) bare

中譯｜很多遊客脫去了鞋子，光腳在沙灘上玩耍、撿貝殼。

解說｜四個選項皆為形容詞。依據題意，應該是「光腳在沙灘上」，選項 (D) bare 表示「赤裸的」，符合題意，其他三個選項都不符合題意。

解答＆技巧｜**(D)** 適用 TIP 1　適用 TIP 4

---

09 At twelve, Catherine has won several first prizes in international art competitions. Her talent and skills are _____ for her age. 【99年指考英文】

(A) comparable　　(B) exceptional

(C) sophisticated　　(D) unconvincing

中譯｜十二歲時，凱薩琳就已經贏得了幾項國際藝術比賽的一等獎，她的才能和技藝與年齡不相符。

解說｜四個選項皆為形容詞。依據題意，應該是「才能和技藝與年齡不相符」，選項 (B) exceptional 表示「非凡的，罕見的」，符合題意。

解答＆技巧｜**(B)** 適用 TIP 3　適用 TIP 4

DAY
8

Part 1
詞
彙
題
Day
完成 25%

Part 2
綜
合
測
驗
Day
完成 50%

Part 3
文
意
選
填
Day
完成 75%

Part 4
閱
讀
測
驗
Day
完成 100%

10 The little girl's head struck the railing and was _____ profusely, so we should send her to the hospital right away.

(A) soothing
(B) socializing
(C) bleeding
(D) slashing

補充
right away ph 立刻，馬上

7,000 單字
• railing [ˋrelɪŋ] n 6 欄杆
• soothe [suð] v 6 安慰
• socialize [ˋsoʃə‚laɪz] v 6 交際
• bleed [blid] v 3 流血
• slash [slæʃ] v 6 猛砍

中譯｜這個小女孩的頭撞到了欄杆，正在大量出血，我們應該馬上送她去醫院。

解說｜四個選項皆為動詞。依據題意，應該是「正在大量出血」，選項 (C) bleeding 表示「出血」，符合題意，其他三個選項都不符合題意。

解答＆技巧｜**(C)** 適用 TIP 1 適用 TIP 4

---

11 In order to relieve her parents' economic _____, this 13-year-old girl dropped out of school and worked in a factory.

(A) skim
(B) seminar
(C) burden
(D) revelation

補充
drop out of school ph 輟學

7,000 單字
• old [old] a 1 ~歲的
• skim [skɪm] n 6 表層物
• seminar [ˋsɛmə‚nɑr] n 6 討論會
• burden [ˋbɝdn] n 3 負擔
• revelation [‚rɛvlˋeʃən] n 6 啟示

中譯｜為了減輕父母的經濟負擔，這個年僅十三歲的女孩輟學到工廠裡工作。

解說｜本題是一個目的副詞子句。依據題意，應該是「減輕父母的經濟負擔」，選項 (C) burden 表示「負擔」，而片語 economic burden 表示「經濟負擔」，符合題意。

解答＆技巧｜**(C)** 適用 TIP 2 適用 TIP 4

---

12 All the executives and staff attended the banquet so as to _____ the company's tenth anniversary.

(A) repress
(B) reinforce
(C) celebrate
(D) rein

補充
so as to ph 為了

7,000 單字
• tenth [tɛnθ] num 1 第十
• repress [rɪˋprɛs] v 6 抑制
• reinforce [‚riɪnˋfors] v 6 加強
• celebrate [ˋsɛlə‚bret] v 3 慶祝
• rein [ren] v 6 控制

中譯｜所有主管和員工都參加了這個宴會，來慶祝公司成立十周年。

解說｜四個選項皆為動詞。依據題意，應該是「慶祝公司成立十周年」，選項 (C) celebrate 表示「慶祝」，符合題意，其他三個選項都不符合題意。

解答＆技巧｜**(C)** 適用 TIP 1 適用 TIP 4

13 He defeated players from around the world in the match and finally became the world _____.

(A) regime
(B) radiant
(C) champion
(D) quench

補充
around the world ph 世界各地
7,000 單字
• player [ˋpleɚ] n 1 運動員
• regime [rɪˋʒim] n 6 政權
• radiant [ˋredjənt] n 6 發光體
• champion [ˋtʃæmpɪən] n 3 冠軍
• quench [kwɛntʃ] n 6 熄滅

中譯│他在比賽中打敗了來自世界各地的選手，最終成為了世界冠軍。

解說│四個選項皆為名詞。依據題意，應該是「成為世界冠軍」，選項 (C) champion 表示「冠軍」，符合題意，是正確選項。

解答＆技巧│**(C)** 適用 TIP 1 適用 TIP 4

14 She put on a thick down jacket, a hat and gloves as a protection against the _____ north wind.

(A) quarrelsome
(B) radical
(C) recreational
(D) chilly

補充
down jacket ph 羽絨夾克
7,000 單字
• hat [hæt] n 1 帽子
• quarrelsome [ˋkwɔrəlsəm] a 6 喜歡吵架的
• radical [ˋrædɪkl] a 6 激進的
• recreational [ˏrɛkrɪˋeʃənl] a 6 娛樂的
• chilly [ˋtʃɪlɪ] a 3 寒冷的

中譯│她穿上厚厚的羽絨夾克，戴上帽子和手套，來抵禦寒冷的北風。

解說│四個選項皆為形容詞。依據題意，應該是「抵禦寒冷的北風」，選項 (D) chilly 表示「寒冷的」，符合題意，其他三個選項都不符合題意。

解答＆技巧│**(D)** 適用 TIP 1 適用 TIP 4

15 Many companies are fiercely _____ with each other in order to contend for markets and customers.

(A) reconciling
(B) refining
(C) competing
(D) rendering

補充
contend for ph 爭奪
7,000 單字
• contend [kənˋtɛnd] v 5 競爭
• reconcile [ˋrɛkənsaɪl] v 6 使一致
• refine [rɪˋfaɪn] v 6 精煉
• compete [kəmˋpit] v 3 競爭
• render [ˋrɛndɚ] v 6 致使

中譯│為了爭奪市場和顧客，很多公司之間都在進行著激烈的競爭。

解說│四個選項皆為動詞。依據題意，應該是「公司之間進行著激烈的競爭」，選項 (C) competing 表示「競爭」，符合題意，其他三個選項都不符合題意。

解答＆技巧│**(C)** 適用 TIP 1 適用 TIP 4

16 I have always been looking for a(an) _____ learning method, trying to improve my English within the shortest time.

(A) relevant   (B) efficient

(C) reflective   (D) rational

中譯｜我一直在尋找有效的學習方法，試圖在最短的時間內提升英文能力。

解說｜四個選項皆為形容詞。依據題意，應該是「尋找有效的學習方法」，選項 (B) efficient 表示「有效的」，符合題意，是正確選項。

解答＆技巧｜**(B)**　適用 TIP 1　適用 TIP 4

> 補充
> learning method ph 學習方法
>
> 7,000 單字
> • learning [ˈlɜnɪŋ] n 4 學習
> • relevant [ˈrɛləvənt] a 6 有關的
> • efficient [ɪˈfɪʃənt] a 3 有效率的
> • reflective [rɪˈflɛktɪv] a 6 反射的
> • rational [ˈræʃənl] a 6 合理的

---

17 It is said that these two stars spent one million dollars on their wedding, which could be a _____ wedding.

(A) provincial   (B) pious

(C) optional   (D) luxurious

中譯｜據說，這兩位明星花費了一百萬美元辦婚禮，可稱得上是奢華婚禮。

解說｜四個選項皆為形容詞。依據題意，應該是「奢華婚禮」，選項 (D) luxurious 表示「奢華的」，符合題意，其他三個選項都不符合題意。

解答＆技巧｜**(D)**　適用 TIP 1　適用 TIP 4

> 補充
> spend on ph 在～方面花費
>
> 7,000 單字
> • dollar [ˈdɑlə] n 1 美元
> • provincial [prəˈvɪnʃəl] a 6 省的
> • pious [ˈpaɪəs] a 6 虔誠的
> • optional [ˈɑpʃən!] a 6 可選擇的
> • luxurious [lʌgˈʒʊrɪəs] a 4 奢侈的

---

18 The original price of this necklace was 200 dollars, but I bought it at a _____, and it only cost me 120 dollars.

(A) discount   (B) option

(C) newscaster   (D) neon

中譯｜這條項鍊原價兩百美元，但我用折扣價買了它，只花費了一百二十美元。

解說｜四個選項皆為名詞。依據題意，應該是「用折扣價買了它」，選項 (A) discount 表示「折扣」，而片語 at a discount 表示「打折」，符合題意。

解答＆技巧｜**(A)**　適用 TIP 2　適用 TIP 4

> 補充
> at a discount ph 打折
>
> 7,000 單字
> • necklace [ˈnɛklɪs] n 2 項鍊
> • discount [ˈdɪskaʊnt] n 3 折扣
> • option [ˈɑpʃən] n 6 選項
> • newscaster [ˈnjuz͵kæstə] n 6 新聞播報員
> • neon [ˈniɑn] n 6 霓虹燈

19 The police thought his motivation was _____ because his testimony was inconsistent.

(A) melancholy   (B) liable

(C) doubtful   (D) inherent

中譯｜員警認為他的動機很可疑，因為他所說的證詞前後不一。

解說｜四個選項皆為形容詞。依據題意，應該是「動機很可疑」，選項 (C) doubtful 表示「可疑的」，符合題意，其他三個選項都不符合題意。

解答＆技巧｜**(C)** 適用 TIP 1　適用 TIP 4

> 補充
> the police ph 員警
>
> 7,000 單字
> • testimony [ˋtɛstə͵monɪ] n 6 證詞
> • melancholy [ˋmɛlən͵kɑlɪ] a 6 憂鬱的
> • liable [ˋlaɪəbl] a 6 有責任的
> • doubtful [ˋdautfəl] a 3 可疑的
> • inherent [ɪnˋhɪrənt] a 6 固有的

---

20 The children were so _____ to see the clown appear on stage that they laughed, screamed, and clapped their hands happily.　【100年學測英文】

(A) admirable   (B) fearful

(C) delighted   (D) incentive

中譯｜孩子們很高興看到舞臺上的小丑，快樂地歡笑、尖叫和拍手。

解說｜四個選項皆為形容詞。依據題意，應該是「高興看到舞臺上的小丑」，選項 (C) delighted 表示「高興的」，符合題意，是正確選項。

解答＆技巧｜**(C)** 適用 TIP 3　適用 TIP 4

> 補充
> on stage ph 在舞臺上
>
> 7,000 單字
> • clown [klaun] n 2 小丑
> • admirable [ˋædmərəbl] a 4 令人欽佩的
> • fearful [ˋfɪrfəl] a 2 害怕的
> • delighted [dɪˋlaɪtɪd] a 4 高興的
> • incentive [ɪnˋsɛntɪv] a 6 激勵的

---

21 I believe the picnic in the forest could be _____ because everyone who hears the news is excited.

(A) delightful   (B) implicit

(C) imperative   (D) hysterical

中譯｜我相信在森林裡野餐會令人愉快，因為每一個聽到這個消息的人都非常興奮。

解說｜四個選項皆為形容詞。依據題意，應該是「野餐會令人愉快」，選項 (A) delightful 表示「令人愉快的」，符合題意，其他三個選項都不符合題意。

解答＆技巧｜**(A)** 適用 TIP 1　適用 TIP 4

> 補充
> in the forest ph 在森林裡
>
> 7,000 單字
> • forest [ˋfɔrɪst] n 1 森林
> • delightful [dɪˋlaɪtfəl] a 4 可愛的
> • implicit [ɪmˋplɪsɪt] a 6 含蓄的
> • imperative [ɪmˋpɛrətɪv] a 6 必要的
> • hysterical [hɪsˋtɛrɪkl] a 6 歇斯底里的

22 More than 500 people have applied for the positions in this utility company, but only 10 people will be _____ in the end.

(A) humiliated (B) harassed
(C) hacked (D) employed

補充
utility company ph 公共事業公司

7,000 單字
- utility [juˋtɪlətɪ] n 6 公用事業
- humiliate [hjuˋmɪlɪˌet] v 6 羞辱
- harass [ˋhærəs] v 6 使困擾
- hack [hæk] v 6 砍
- employ [ɪmˋplɔɪ] v 3 雇用

中譯│超過五百人來這家公共事業公司應徵，但最後只有十個人會被雇用。

解說│四個選項皆為動詞。依據題意，應該是「只有十個人會被雇用」，選項 (D) employed 表示「雇用」，符合題意，是正確選項。

解答＆技巧│**(D)** 適用 TIP 1 適用 TIP 4

---

23 Your visa is _____ for one year; therefore, you should remember to renew it one year later.

(A) gloomy (B) fragile
(C) valid (D) finite

補充
be valid for ph 有效期為～

7,000 單字
- renew [rɪˋnju] v 3 更新
- gloomy [ˋglumɪ] a 6 陰鬱的
- fragile [ˋfrædʒəl] a 6 易碎的
- valid [ˋvælɪd] a 6 有效的
- finite [ˋfaɪnaɪt] a 6 有限的

中譯│你的簽證一年之內有效，所以一年之後，請記得續簽。

解說│四個選項皆為形容詞。依據題意，應該是「簽證一年之內有效」，選項 (C) valid 表示「有效的」，符合題意，其他三個選項都不符合題意。

解答＆技巧│**(C)** 適用 TIP 3 適用 TIP 4

---

24 This office worker _____ the manager's unlawful acts, and then everyone knew that the manager embezzled public funds.

(A) flickered (B) revealed
(C) flared (D) extracted

補充
unlawful act ph 違法行為

7,000 單字
- embezzle [ɪmˋbɛzl] v 6 挪用
- flicker [ˋflɪkɚ] v 6 閃爍
- reveal [rɪˋvil] v 3 顯示
- flare [flɛr] v 6 閃耀
- extract [ɪkˋstrækt] v 6 提取

中譯│這名職員揭露了經理的違法行為，於是所有人都知道了經理挪用公款。

解說│四個選項皆為動詞。依據題意，應該是「職員揭露了經理的違法行為」，選項 (B) revealed 表示「揭露」，符合題意，其他三個選項都不符合題意。

解答＆技巧│**(B)** 適用 TIP 1 適用 TIP 4

DAY 8

Part 1 詞彙題 Day 完成 25%
Part 2 綜合測驗 Day 完成 50%
Part 3 文意選填 Day 完成 75%
Part 4 閱讀測驗 Day 完成 100%

♫451

Part 2 | 綜合測驗 | Comprehensive Questions

1 ▶

> The psychologists have seriously studied the meaning of color preference, as well as the __01__ that colors may have on human beings. If a person likes yellow, orange or red, he must be an optimist and an active person who __02__ life. But if a person prefers grays and blues, then he is probably a pessimist, quiet and shy, much willing to follow __03__ to lead. We should know that we are born with our color preference, but not to choose it as we grow up.
>
> No __04__, colors would influence our moods. For example, a yellow room could make people feel more cheerful and relaxed than a dark green one, and a red dress could bring people warmth and cheer on a cold winter day. Black is __05__, which may lead some people to suicide. All in all, light and bright colors can make people more active and happier, but dark and heavy colors make people more passive and sorrowful.

01 _____ (A) replacement   (B) effect
          (C) response   (D) scholarship

02 _____ (A) seeks   (B) shaves
          (C) shaves   (D) enjoys

03 _____ (A) and   (B) as
          (C) not   (D) so

04 _____ (A) doubt   (B) entrance
          (C) parking   (D) strength

05 _____ (A) stubborn   (B) interesting
          (C) cheerful   (D) depressing

中譯 心理學家已經認真研究了顏色喜好的意義，以及顏色對人類造成的影響。如果一個人喜歡黃色、橘色或紅色，他一定是一個樂天派，一個享受生活、積極主動的人。但是如果一個人偏愛灰色和藍色，那麼他可能是一個悲觀主義者，安靜又害羞，非常樂意遵從，而不是領導。我們應該知道，我們天生就具有顏色喜好，而不是隨著成長才選擇的。

毋庸置疑，顏色會影響我們的情緒。例如，一個黃色的房間會比一個深綠色的房間使人們感到更加歡快、放鬆，而一件紅色的洋裝在寒冷的冬天會給人們帶來溫暖和快樂。黑色令人沮喪，可能會導致一些人自殺。總之，輕快、明亮的顏色能夠使人們更加積極主動、更加高興，但是陰暗、深沉的顏色使人們更加消極、悲傷。

解說 本篇短文的主旨是「顏色」，講述了不同顏色所代表的不同含義。第 1 題的四個選項都是名詞。根據上下文的內容可知，應該是顏色會對人類造成的影響，effect 意思是「影響」，所以正確選擇為 (B)。第 2 題依據題意，積極主動地人通常會享受生活，可以用 enjoys 表示「享受」，最符合題意的選項是 (D)。第 3 題根據上下文的內容可知，空格處所填的詞表示否定關係，即肯定前者而否定後者，所以要用 not 表示否定，即正確選項是 (C)。第 4 題將四個選項一一代入，no doubt 表示「毋庸置疑」符合題意，即說明顏色會影響我們的情緒是事實，所以正確選擇為 (A)。第 5 題根據上下文的內容可知，黑色代表消沉、令人沮喪，所以形容詞 depressing 符合題意，最佳選項是 (D)。

解答＆技巧 01 **(B)** 02 **(D)** 03 **(C)** 04 **(A)** 05 **(D)**
適用 TIP 1　適用 TIP 2　適用 TIP 7　適用 TIP 11

補充
color preference ph 顏色喜好；optimist n 樂觀主義者；probably ad 可能地；pessimist n 悲觀主義者；all in all ph 總的來說

7,000 單字
- preference [ˋprɛfərəns] n 5 偏愛
- like [laɪk] v 1 喜歡
- gray [gre] n 1 灰色
- lead [lid] v 1 領導
- grow [gro] v 1 使成長
- room [rum] n 1 房間
- feel [fil] v 1 感覺
- dark [dɑrk] a 1 黑暗的
- warmth [wɔrmθ] n 3 溫暖
- cheer [tʃɪr] n 3 高興
- suicide [ˋsuəˏsaɪd] v 3 自殺
- sorrowful [ˋsɑrəfəl] a 4 悲傷的
- scholarship [ˋskɑlɚˏʃɪp] n 3 獎學金
- shave [ʃev] v 3 剃
- stubborn [ˋstʌbən] a 3 頑固的

2 ▶ 98 年指考英文

Keele University in the United Kingdom has developed a "virtual patient," created by a computer, to help train the pharmacists of the future. Students in the university's School of **01** work with the "patient" to gain experience in effective communication and decision-making.

Students talk with the "patient" directly or by typing questions into a computer. The "patient" responds verbally or with gestures to indicate **02** such as pain, stress or anxiety. As a result, students are forced to communicate clearly **03** that the "patient" understands them completely. The Virtual Patient can also be used to explore various medical situations. For example, the "patient" can be programmed to be allergic to certain medicine and can **04** serious reactions if students are not aware of the situation. This kind of practice allows students to learn from mistakes in a safe environment that would not be **05** with textbooks alone. The unique system can both be used in a classroom setting or for distance learning.

01 _____   (A) Education   (B) Business
              (C) Pharmacy   (D) Humanities

02 _____   (A) expressions   (B) emotions
              (C) elements   (D) events

03 _____   (A) in order   (B) in return
              (C) in case   (D) in addition

04 _____   (A) adapt to   (B) break into
              (C) provide with   (D) suffer from

05 _____   (A) exciting   (B) necessary
              (C) possible   (D) important

中譯｜英國基爾大學開發的「虛擬病人」是由電腦創造而成的，用來幫助訓練未來的藥劑師。大學藥學系的學生們與「病人」一起工作，透過有效溝通和決策來獲得經驗。

學生們直接與「病人」交談或是將問題輸入電腦。「病人」口頭進行回應或是用手勢來表示情緒，如疼痛、緊張或是焦慮。於是，學生們被迫清楚地進行溝通，以便「病人」能夠完全明白他們的意思。「虛擬病人」也可以用於探索各式各樣的醫療情況。例如，可以對「病人」進行程式設定，讓其對某種藥物過敏，如果學生沒有注意到這種狀況，「病人」將會遭受嚴重的不良反應。這種實踐活動可以讓學生在安全的環境中從錯誤中學習，而這種錯誤不可能單從課本上就能學到。這種獨特的系統可用於課堂上，也可用於遠端教學。

解說｜本篇短文介紹了「虛擬病人」這種由電腦創造的事物。第 1 題依據題意可知，本篇短文講的是未來的藥劑師與「虛擬病人」之間的互動，所以應該是「藥學系」，可以表達為 School of Pharmacy，所以正確選擇為 (C)。第 2 題的四個選項都是名詞，將其一一代入空格，只有 emotions 符合題意，因為 pain, stress or anxiety 這些都是情緒反應，所以最符合題意的選項是 (B)。第 3 題空格處的選項表示目的，四個選項中，in order 能夠與 that 連用表示「為了」，即正確選項是 (A)。第 4 題考動詞片語的用法。依據題意可知，應該是遭受嚴重的不良反應，可以用 suffer from 表示「遭受」，所以只有選項 (D) 符合題意。第 5 題依據題意可知，這種錯誤不可能從書本上學到，possible 表示「可能」符合題意，所以選 (C)。

解答＆技巧｜ 01 (C)　 02 (B)　 03 (A)　 04 (D)　 05 (C)

適用 TIP 2　適用 TIP 4　適用 TIP 7　適用 TIP 11

補充

Keele University ph 英國基爾大學；the United Kingdom ph 英國；verbally ad 口頭地；setting n 環境；distance learning ph 遠端教學

7,000 單字

- virtual [ˋvɝtʃʊəl] a 6 虛擬的
- patient [ˋpeʃənt] n 2 病人
- pharmacist [ˋfɑrməsɪst] n 6 藥劑師
- talk [tɔk] v 1 說話
- respond [rɪˋspɑnd] v 3 回答
- gesture [ˋdʒɛstʃɚ] n 3 手勢
- pain [pen] n 2 疼痛
- anxiety [æŋˋzaɪətɪ] n 4 焦慮

- force [fors] v 4 強迫
- communicate [kəˋmjunə͵ket] v 3 溝通
- medical [ˋmɛdɪk!] a 3 醫學的
- medicine [ˋmɛdəsṇ] n 2 藥
- mistake [mɪˋstek] n 1 錯誤
- pharmacy [ˋfɑrməsɪ] n 6 藥房
- humanity [hjuˋmænətɪ] n 4 人類

DAY
8

Part 1
詞彙題
Day 8
完成 25%

Part 2
綜合測驗
Day 8
完成 50%

Part 3
文意選填
Day 8
完成 75%

Part 4
閱讀測驗
Day 8
完成 100%

Nowadays, many social customs and manners have changed, and things which were considered impolite before have also been __01__ now. A few years ago, if a man smoked on the street, he would be considered impolite, but now it is quite normal.

Customs differ __02__ country to country. In different countries, a man can walk on the left or the right of a woman, and people can use their two hands or just one when they are eating.

Several researches have shown that the Americans and the British share a large number of social customs. For example, Americans and Englishmen both __03__ hands with others when they meet for the first time. And when eating at a restaurant, they will also __04__ their seats to the women. Promptness is important both for Americans and Englishmen. If a dinner is __05__ to begin at 7 o'clock, then all the guests should arrive just on time or a little earlier. Those people who are late must explain the delay.

01 _____ (A) acceptable   (B) sufficient
           (C) temporary   (D) tricky

02 _____ (A) to   (B) on
           (C) within   (D) from

03 _____ (A) unite   (B) shake
           (C) weaken   (D) accuse

04 _____ (A) analyze   (B) beam
           (C) offer   (D) circulate

05 _____ (A) identical   (B) equal
           (C) able   (D) scheduled

中譯 現今，很多社會習俗和禮儀都已經發生了變化，以前被認為是不禮貌的事情，現在也被接受了。幾年前，如果一個男人在大街上抽菸，會被認為不禮貌，但是現在很正常。

國家不同，習俗也不同。在不同的國家，男人可以走在女人的左邊，也可以走在右邊，人們可以用兩隻手吃飯，也可以用一隻手。

一些研究顯示，美國人和英國人很多社會習俗都相同。例如，美國人和英國人在第一次見到對方時都會握手。在餐廳吃飯時，他們也都會將自己的座位讓給女士。準時對於美國人和英國人來說很重要。如果晚宴預計在七點鐘開始，那麼所有客人都應該準時到達，或是稍微提前到達。那些遲到的人必須做出解釋。

解說 本篇短文介紹了各國風俗習慣的不同。第 1 題的四個選項都是形容詞，將其一一代入空格，acceptable 最符合題意，即以前被認為是不禮貌的事情，現在也被接受了，所以正確選擇為 (A)。第 2 題要選擇合適的介系詞。from country to country 表示各個國家，所以最符合題意的選項是 (D)。第 3 題考動詞片語的用法。依據題意，「握手」可以表達為 shake hands，要用動詞 shake，即正確選項是 (B)。第 4 題的四個選項都是動詞，但是能夠與 to 連用的只有 offer。offer sth. to sb. 表示「提供某物給某人」，是一個固定搭配，所以選項 (C) 符合題意。第 5 題四個選項都能夠構成固定搭配，但根據上下文的內容可知，應該是晚宴預計在 7 點鐘開始，be scheduled to 表示「安排，預定」符合題意，所以選 (D)。

解答＆技巧 01 **(A)** 02 **(D)** 03 **(B)** 04 **(C)** 05 **(D)**

適用 TIP 1　適用 TIP 2　適用 TIP 7　適用 TIP 11

補充

impolite a 無禮的；on the left ph 在左邊；Englishman n 英國人；for the first time ph 第一次；promptness n 準時

7,000 單字

- manners [ˋmænɚz] n 3 禮儀
- thing [θɪŋ] n 1 事情
- smoke [smok] v 1 吸菸
- left [lɛft] n 1 左邊
- hand [hænd] n 1 手
- just [dʒʌst] ad 1 正好
- meet [mit] v 1 見面
- seat [sit] n 1 座位

- important [ɪmˋpɔrtn̩t] a 1 重要的
- o'clock [əˋklɑk] n 1 ～點鐘
- then [ðɛn] ad 1 那麼
- arrive [əˋraɪv] v 2 到達
- tricky [ˋtrɪkɪ] a 3 狡猾的
- weaken [ˋwikən] v 3 變弱
- circulate [ˋsɝkjə͵let] v 4 使流通

DAY 8

Part 1
詞
彙
題
Day 8
完成 25%

Part 2
綜
合
測
驗
Day 8
完成 50%

Part 3
文
意
選
填
Day 8
完成 75%

Part 4
閱
讀
測
驗
Day 8
完成 100%

On Thursday afternoon Ms. Lauper dressed __01__, took her handbag with money and key in it, locked the window, pulled the door and locked it, and then went to a club __02__. She always did so on Thursdays because it could be an interesting experience for this lonely woman.

She came home at six o'clock as __03__, but she smelt cigarette smoke in her house. How could it be? She checked all the doors and windows, but they were all locked. Then what happened on __04__? Therefore, she decided to stay at home the following Thursday.

When another Thursday came, Ms. Lauper dressed and went out as usual. She didn't go to the club but returned to her home through her back garden. She waited at home quietly and until it was four o'clock, she heard someone outside __05__ to open her lock. She was so afraid that she quickly shouted out. At once she heard the sound of running feet behind the door.

01 _____ (A) herself   (B) her

(C) it   (D) itself

02 _____ (A) overseas   (B) backwards

(C) downwards   (D) nearby

03 _____ (A) particular   (B) usual

(C) perfect   (D) royal

04 _____ (A) moon   (B) planet

(C) earth   (D) galaxy

05 _____ (A) tried   (B) to try

(C) and try   (D) trying

DAY 8

Part 1 詞彙題 Day 8 完成 25%

Part 2 綜合測驗 Day 8 完成 50%

Part 3 文意選填 Day 8 完成 75%

Part 4 閱讀測驗 Day 8 完成 100%

中譯｜周四下午，羅波女士打扮好自己，帶著裝有錢和鑰匙的手提包，鎖好窗戶，把門拉上鎖起來，然後去了附近的一家俱樂部。她總是在周四這樣做，因為對於她這個孤獨的女人來說，那應該是有趣的經驗。

像往常一樣，她在六點鐘回到家，但是她在屋子裡聞到了菸味。這怎麼可能？她查看了所有的門窗，但是它們都是鎖著的。那麼究竟發生了什麼事？因此，她決定下周四待在家裡。

當周四來臨時，羅波女士像往常一樣打扮並出門。她並沒有去俱樂部，而是經過自己的後花園返回家中。她靜靜地在家裡等著，直到四點鐘的時候，她聽到有人在外面正試圖打開她的鎖。她很害怕，迅速大叫起來。她立刻聽到門的後面傳來了跑步聲。

解說｜本篇短文講述了主角羅波女士親身經歷的一件事情。第 1 題考人稱的用法。根據所學的知識，dress oneself 表示「打扮」，是一個固定搭配，所以空格處要填寫反身代名詞 herself，正確選擇為 (A)。第 2 題的四個選項都是地方副詞。根據上下文的內容可知，應該是附近的俱樂部，要用 nearby 表示「附近」，最符合題意的選項是 (D)。第 3 題考介系詞片語的用法。四個選項中，只有 usual 能夠與介系詞 as 連用，表示「像平常一樣」，所以正確選項是 (B)。第 4 題考與介系詞 on 相關的片語的用法。將四個選項一一代入空格，on earth 表示「究竟」符合短文的意思，所以只有選項 (C) 符合題意。第 5 題考動詞 hear 的用法。「聽到某人正在做某事」要用 hear sb. doing sth. 來表達，所以動詞 try 要用動名詞 trying，正確選項為 (D)。

解答＆技巧｜01 **(A)** 02 **(D)** 03 **(B)** 04 **(C)** 05 **(D)**
適用 TIP 2　適用 TIP 4　適用 TIP 7　適用 TIP 11

補充
handbag n 手提包；go out ph 出去；return to ph 返回；quietly ad 安靜地；behind the door ph 門後

7,000 單字
- Thursday [ˋθɝzde] n 1 星期四
- afternoon [ˋæftɚˋnun] n 1 下午
- key [ki] n 1 鑰匙
- lock [lɑk] v 2 鎖
- window [ˋwɪndo] n 1 窗戶
- door [dor] n 1 門
- club [klʌb] n 2 俱樂部
- lonely [ˋlonlɪ] a 2 孤獨的
- check [tʃɛk] v 1 檢查
- stay [ste] v 1 停留
- following [ˋfɑləwɪŋ] a 2 下面的
- usual [ˋjuʒʊəl] a 2 平常的
- garden [ˋgɑrdn̩] n 1 花園
- shout [ʃaʊt] v 1 呼喊
- royal [ˋrɔɪəl] a 2 皇家的

Many people believe that the glare from snow will cause snow blindness, especially for the troops. Most soldiers find themselves suffering __01__ headaches and even snow blindness if they keep on __02__ to snow light for a long time.

According to the study, a person's eyes could frequently find nothing to __03__ on in a broad snow-covered terrain. Therefore, his eyes would continually shift and jump back and forth over the entire landscape searching for something to look at. After several hours, though finding nothing, the eyes never stop searching. Then the eyeballs become sore and the eye muscles ache. As a __04__ to this irritation, the eye will produce more and more fluid until it covers the whole eyeball. Because of this, the vision begins to blur and becomes obscure, which results in the snow blindness at last. In order to overcome this problem, a person can focus his attention on one object at a __05__ . Thus he will not become snow-blind or lost.

01 _____ (A) to (B) in
(C) from (D) with

02 _____ (A) exposing (B) rushing
(C) shooting (D) sliding

03 _____ (A) stick (B) swing
(C) wake (D) focus

04 _____ (A) width (B) response
(C) accident (D) balance

05 _____ (A) stroke (B) guess
(C) time (D) barrel

中譯｜很多人相信，雪反射出的刺眼強光會導致雪盲症，尤其是對部隊。大多數士兵發現，如果他們長時間暴露在雪光中，他們就會遭受頭痛之苦，甚至是雪盲。

研究指出，一個人的眼睛在積雪覆蓋的寬闊地帶，會常常找不到可以專注的物體。因此，他的眼睛會不斷地移動，反覆來回搜尋整片土地，以尋求能注視的事物。幾個小時後，儘管什麼都沒找到，眼睛卻沒有停止搜尋，於是眼球和眼部肌肉就會疼痛。為了對這種刺激做出回應，眼睛會產生出愈來愈多的液體，直到這些液體覆蓋整個眼球。因此，視覺開始變得模糊不清，最終導致雪盲。為了克服這種困難，可以讓眼睛每次專注於一個物體，這樣就不會變成雪盲或是迷路。

解說｜本篇短文的主旨是「雪盲症」，講述了雪盲症的原因以及克服方法。第 1 題考動詞 suffer 的用法。suffer 通常與介系詞 from 連用表示「遭受」，所以正確選擇為 (C)。第 2 題的四個選項都是動名詞，因為介系詞 on 後面要接動名詞。依據題意，exposing 表示「暴露」符合上下文的意思，所以最符合題意的選項是 (A)。第 3 題的四個選項中，只有 focus 能夠與介系詞 on 搭配，表示「專注於」，符合題意，即正確選項是 (D)。第 4 題的四個選項都是名詞。根據上下文的內容，後面所提到的情況是對 irritation 的反應，要用 response 表示「反應」，只有選項 (B) 符合題意。第 5 題考介系詞片語的用法。四個選項中，只有 time 能與介系詞 at 搭配表示「一次」，所以選 (C)。

解答 & 技巧｜ 01 (C)　 02 (A)　 03 (D)　 04 (B)　 05 (C)

適用 TIP 2　適用 TIP 4　適用 TIP 7　適用 TIP 11

補充

blindness n 失明；snow-covered a 積雪覆蓋的；terrain n 地帶；eyeball n 眼球；snow-blind a 雪盲的

7,000 單字

- glare [glɛr] n 5 耀眼的光
- snow [sno] n 1 雪
- troop [trup] n 3 軍隊
- soldier [ˈsoldʒɚ] n 2 士兵
- nothing [ˈnʌθɪŋ] pron 1 沒有東西
- broad [brɔd] a 2 寬闊的
- forth [forθ] ad 3 向前
- landscape [ˈlænd.skep] n 4 風景

- sore [sor] a 3 疼痛的
- ache [ek] v 3 疼痛
- irritation [ˌɪrəˈteʃən] n 6 刺激
- fluid [ˈfluɪd] n 6 液體
- blur [blɝ] v 5 使模糊不清
- shoot [ʃut] v 2 射擊
- width [wɪdθ] n 2 寬度

DAY
8

Part 1
詞
彙
題

Day 8
完成 25%

Part 2
綜
合
測
驗

Day 8
完成 50%

Part 3
文
意
選
填

Day 8
完成 75%

Part 4
閱
讀
測
驗

Day 8
完成 100%

6 ▶ 98 年指考英文

In spite of modernization and the increasing role of women from all walks of life, the practice of the dowry in India is still widespread. The dowry system, money or property brought by a bride to her husband at marriage, was started centuries ago with the intention of providing security for a girl __01__ difficulties and unexpected circumstances after marriage. For this purpose, the parents gave __02__ they could to their daughter, which consequently went to the groom's family. By the beginning of the 21st century, however, the custom had deteriorated to a point whereby the groom and his family had become very __03__. When demands for dowry are not met, the bride is __04__ torture and often even killed. The more educated a man is, the __05__ the expectation is for dowry at the time of marriage. Girls who are highly educated are required to have larger dowries because they usually marry more educated men.

01 _____ (A) due to   (B) apart from
         (C) in case of   (D) with reference to

02 _____ (A) whoever   (B) whenever
         (C) whatever   (D) whichever

03 _____ (A) greedy   (B) pleasant
         (C) regretful   (D) sympathetic

04 _____ (A) aware of   (B) required by
         (C) furious with   (D) subject to

05 _____ (A) lower   (B) higher
         (C) better   (D) worse

中譯│ 儘管已經現代化了，且女性在各行各業中所擔任的角色不斷增加，但是在印度，嫁妝的實施仍然很普遍。嫁妝體制，即結婚時由新娘帶給她的丈夫的金錢或財產，早在幾世紀之前就已經開始了，其目的是為女孩婚後的生活提供保障，以防發生生活困難以及意想不到的情況。為此，父母給予女兒他們能給的任何東西，結果這些東西就成了新郎家的財產。然而，到了二十一世紀初，這種習俗已經惡化到新郎以及他的家人變得十分貪婪。當嫁妝不能滿足需求時，新娘就會遭受折磨，甚至經常遭到殺害。一個男人愈有教養，結婚時對於嫁妝的期望就會愈高。高學歷的女孩被要求準備更多的嫁妝，因為他們通常會和學歷更高的男人結婚。

解說│ 本篇短文的主旨是「嫁妝」，介紹了印度國家嫁妝體制的發展變化過程。第 1 題根據上下文的內容可知，介系詞片語 in case of 表示「萬一，假設」，符合題意，所以正確選擇為 (C)。第 2 題要選擇合適的代名詞。根據所學的語法知識，指代物體時一般用 whatever 或 whichever，但依據題意，whatever 表示「無論什麼」，在文中符合上下文的意思，所以最符合題意的選項是 (C)。第 3 題的四個選項都是形容詞，將其一一代入，只有 greedy 表示「貪婪的」符合上下文的意思，即正確選項是 (A)。第 4 題考片語的用法。將四個一一代入空格，is subject to 表示「易遭受」符合上下文的意思，只有選項 (D) 符合題意。第 5 題運用了 the more... the more... 的句型結構，空格處應當選用比較級。依據題意，higher 表示「更高的」最適合用來修飾 expectation，所以選 (B)。

解答&技巧│ 01 (C)　02 (C)　03 (A)　04 (D)　05 (B)
適用 TIP 2　適用 TIP 7　適用 TIP 9　適用 TIP 11

補充
all walks of life ph 各行各業；dowry n 嫁妝；unexpected a 意料之外的；consequently ad 因此；educated a 受教育的，有教養的

7,000 單字
• modernization [ˌmɑdənəˈzeʃən] n 6 現代化
• widespread [ˈwaɪdˌsprɛd] a 5 普遍的
• husband [ˈhʌzbənd] n 1 丈夫
• start [stɑrt] v 1 開始
• intention [ɪnˈtɛnʃən] n 4 意圖
• girl [ɡɝl] n 1 女孩
• daughter [ˈdɔtɚ] n 1 女兒
• deteriorate [dɪˈtɪrɪəˌret] v 6 惡化

• groom [ɡrum] n 4 新郎
• torture [ˈtɔrtʃɚ] n 5 折磨
• kill [kɪl] v 1 殺害
• highly [ˈhaɪlɪ] ad 4 高度地
• reference [ˈrɛfərəns] n 4 參考
• greedy [ˈɡridɪ] a 2 貪婪的
• furious [ˈfjʊrɪəs] a 4 激烈的

DAY
8

Part 1
詞
彙
題
Day 8
完成 25%

Part 2
綜
合
測
驗
Day 8
完成 50%

Part 3
文
意
選
填
Day 8
完成 75%

Part 4
閱
讀
測
驗
Day 8
完成 100%

Water pollution problems will become more intense and complex in the future because the __01__ population on the earth will tremendously increase the urban wastes, such as sewage. Many industries that __02__ a large number of complex chemical processes are producing large volumes of liquid wastes, most of which contain noxious chemicals. In addition, in order to __03__ the rapidly expanding population, people will also have to intensify the agriculture. However, large quantities of agricultural chemicals are still a big problem, therefore, it is apparent that we should take __04__ steps to develop corrective measures for the pollution problem.

Two effective ways can be used to solve the pollution problem. The first one is to dispose the wastes in order to reuse them and __05__ their pollution hazard. The second method is to economically use the wastes. For example, effluents from the sewage disposal plants can be used in some areas for irrigation, or as a supplemental source of water.

01 _____ (A) decreasing   (B) increasing
              (C) everlasting   (D) charming

02 _____ (A) cast   (B) chill
              (C) confuse   (D) involve

03 _____ (A) feed   (B) creep
              (C) define   (D) exchange

04 _____ (A) evil   (B) harmful
              (C) immediate   (D) impressive

05 _____ (A) interrupt   (B) decrease
              (C) kneel   (D) loosen

DAY
8

Part 1
詞彙題
Day 8
完成 25%

Part 2
綜合測驗
Day 8
完成 50%

Part 3
文意選填
Day 8
完成 75%

Part 4
閱讀測驗
Day 8
完成 100%

中譯｜未來水污染問題會變得更加嚴重，也更加複雜，因為地球上逐漸增加的人口將會大量增加城市廢棄物，如污水。很多需要大量複雜化工過程的工業正在製造大量的液體廢棄物，大多數都含有有毒的化學物質。此外，為了養活迅速增長的人口，人們也會不得不加強農業發展。然而，大量的農藥仍然是個問題，因此，很明顯我們應該立即行動來開發補救措施，以解決污染問題。

解決污染問題有兩種有效的方法。第一種方法是處理廢棄物，以重新使用，並且減少它們的污染危害。第二種方法是節約地使用這些廢棄物。例如，汙水處理廠排放出來的廢水能夠在某些地區用於灌溉，或是作為一種補充性水資源。

解說｜本篇短文的主旨是「水污染問題」，講述了水污染問題的嚴重性以及有效的解決方法。第 1 題要選擇合適的形容詞來修飾名詞 population。依據題意，increasing 表示「逐漸增加的」符合題意，所以正確選擇為 (B)。第 2 題根據上下文的內容應該是需要大量複雜的化工過程的工業，四個選項中 involve 意思是「需要，包含」，所以最符合題意的選項是 (D)。第 3 題的四個選項都是動詞，依據題意，應該是養活迅速增長的人口，可以用 feed 表示「餵養，供給」，即正確選項是 (A)。第 4 題將四個選項一一代入，take immediate steps 表示「立即採取措施」符合題意，所以最佳選項是 (C)。第 5 題依據題意，應該是減少污染危害，decrease 表示「減少」，所以選 (B)。

解答＆技巧｜ **01** (B)　**02** (D)　**03** (A)　**04** (C)　**05** (B)

適用 TIP 2　適用 TIP 4　適用 TIP 7　適用 TIP 11

補充

tremendously ad 驚人地；sewage n 污水，汙穢物；noxious a 有毒的；corrective a 矯正的；economically ad 經濟地

7,000 單字

- pollution [pəˋluʃən] n 4 污染
- intense [ɪnˋtɛns] a 4 強烈的
- complex [ˋkɑmplɛks] a 3 複雜的
- urban [ˋɝbən] a 4 都市的
- waste [west] n 1 廢物
- process [ˋprɑsɛs] n 3 過程
- contain [kənˋten] v 2 包含，需要
- intensify [ɪnˋtɛnsə͵faɪ] v 4 使加強

- agriculture [ˋægrɪ͵kʌltʃɚ] n 3 農業
- agricultural [͵ægrɪˋkʌltʃərəl] a 5 農業的
- apparent [əˋpærənt] a 3 明顯的
- dispose [dɪˋspoz] v 5 處理
- disposal [dɪˋspozl] n 6 處理
- chill [tʃɪl] v 3 冷卻
- kneel [nil] v 3 跪下

One day, my mother and I went to a grocery store for the __01__ grocery shopping. When my mother was selecting some spices, I just went to the dairy section where a large number of eggs were on __02__ .

I saw nearly all the eggs packed in dozen or half-dozen cartons, which were stacked three or four __03__ high. When I was looking at those stacks, a woman came by pushing her grocery cart and knocked off the stacks of cartons, but left quickly and quietly. I had no idea what to do and just bent __04__ to pick up the cartons and put them back together.

Just then the manager came over, and I was on my knees to inspect whether some of the eggs in the cartons were broken. But to him it looked as __05__ I broke the cartons. He severely criticized me and wanted me to pay for all the broken eggs. Though I had explained, he still did not trust me. Finally my mother came and paid for all the loss.

01 _____ (A) weekly   (B) week
         (C) weeklong   (D) weekdays

02 _____ (A) mess   (B) mixture
         (C) sale   (D) patience

03 _____ (A) head   (B) feet
         (C) hand   (D) bone

04 _____ (A) in   (B) to
         (C) upper   (D) down

05 _____ (A) whether   (B) if
         (C) weather   (D) but

中譯│ 有一天，我和媽媽去雜貨店進行每週一次的生活用品採購。當媽媽在挑選一些調味料時，我來到了乳製品區，那裡有很多雞蛋在特價。

我看到幾乎所有的雞蛋都用一打或半打的紙盒包裝著，堆放在三四呎高的地方。我在看這些雞蛋時，一個女人推著她的購物車走了過來，撞倒了堆放著的紙盒，但是很快就悄悄地離開了。我不知道該怎麼辦，就彎下腰把紙盒撿起來放回去。就在那時，經理過來了，而我正跪在地上檢查紙盒裡的一些雞蛋是否打破了。但是在他看來，好像是我把紙盒弄倒的。他嚴厲地批評了我，並且要讓我賠償所有損壞的雞蛋。儘管我已經做了解釋，他仍然不相信我。最終媽媽過來了，賠償了所有的損失。

解說│ 本篇短文講述了主角「我」在購物時所發生的事情。第 1 題的四個選項都與「星期」有關，但 weekly 是形容詞表示「每週一次的」，可以用於修飾 grocery shopping，所以正確選擇為 (A)。第 2 題依據題意應該是有很多雞蛋在特價，片語 be on sale 表示「拍賣中」，是常用的購物用語，所以最符合題意的選項是 (C)。第 3 題根據上下文的內容，表達「高度」時可以用 feet 表示「呎」，文中的意思就是三四呎高，所以正確選項是 (B)。第 4 題考動詞 bend 的用法。bend 通常與副詞 down 搭配表示「彎腰，蹲下」，在文中符合題意，所以選項 (D) 符合題意。第 5 題依據題意應該是「看起來好像」，可以表達為 look as if，其中 as if 表示「好像」，所以選 (B)。

解答＆技巧│ 01 **(A)**　02 **(C)**　03 **(B)**　04 **(D)**　05 **(B)**

適用 TIP 1　適用 TIP 2　適用 TIP 7　適用 TIP 11

補充
grocery store ph 雜貨店；dairy section ph 乳製品區；knock off ph 撞倒；on one's knees ph 跪著；severely ad 嚴厲地

7,000 單字
- spice [spaɪs] n 3 調味料
- egg [ɛg] n 1 蛋
- pack [pæk] v 2 包裝
- dozen [ˋdʌzn̩] n 1 一打
- carton [ˋkɑrtn̩] n 5 紙盒，紙箱
- stack [stæk] v 5 堆疊
- cart [kɑrt] n 2 手推車
- bend [bɛnd] v 2 彎曲

- put [pʊt] v 1 放
- inspect [ɪnˋspɛkt] v 3 檢查
- criticize [ˋkrɪtɪ.saɪz] v 4 批評
- trust [trʌst] v 2 信任
- weekly [ˋwiklɪ] a 4 每週的
- weekday [ˋwik.de] n 2 工作日
- bone [bon] n 1 骨頭

DAY
8

Part 1
詞
彙
題
Day 8
完成 25%

Part 2
綜
合
測
驗
Day 8
完成 50%

Part 3
文
意
選
填
Day 8
完成 75%

Part 4
閱
讀
測
驗
Day 8
完成 100%

9 ▶

Many young people enjoy different ___01___ of physical activities, such as walking, cycling, swimming, or skating or skiing in winter. The physical activities can also be football, golf, tennis or even mountaineering.

People who have a ___02___ for climbing mountains are often considered as brave and adventurous. Mountaineering is a sport, not a game. It has no man-made rules and is full of freedom, which may be the reason why it is ___03___ to many young people. Therefore, people who climb mountains are usually free to use their own methods.

Compared with other familiar sports, people might think mountaineering is not a team sport, which has been ___04___ to be wrong. Though there are no matches between the climbers, when they encounter danger or risks, they must work together to overcome it. The mountain climbers should always know that they must become stronger and more powerful to fight ___05___ the forces of nature with their high mental and physical qualities.

| 01 | _____ | (A) portions | (B) amounts |
| | | (C) kinds | (D) shapes |

| 02 | _____ | (A) passion | (B) relief |
| | | (C) representative | (D) scream |

| 03 | _____ | (A) sensitive | (B) shiny |
| | | (C) tricky | (D) attractive |

| 04 | _____ | (A) united | (B) proved |
| | | (C) warned | (D) appointed |

| 05 | _____ | (A) to | (B) up |
| | | (C) within | (D) against |

中譯 | 很多年輕人喜歡不同形式的體育活動，如散步、騎自行車、游泳，或者在冬天進行溜冰或滑雪。體育活動也可以是踢足球、打高爾夫、打網球，甚至登山。

喜歡登山的人通常被認為是勇敢的、愛冒險的。登山是一項運動，而不是一種比賽。它沒有人為的規則，充滿了自由，這也許就是它能夠吸引很多年輕人的原因。因此，登山的人通常可以自由地用自己的方法爬山。

與其他常見的運動相比，人們可能認為登山不是一項團隊運動，但這種觀點被證明是錯誤的。儘管登山者之間並沒有進行比賽，但是當遇到危險或風險時，他們必須團結一致來克服困難。登山者應當永遠了解到，他們必須變得更加強壯、更加強大，用他們高度的思想和身體素質來對抗自然力量。

解說 | 本篇短文的主題是「體育活動」，重點介紹了登山這項體育活動的特點。第 1 題依據題意應該是不同形式的體育活動，文中 different kinds of 表示「各種，不同種類的」，可以修飾 physical activities，所以正確選擇為 (C)。第 2 題四個選項中，只有 passion 能夠構成片語 have a passion for 表示「鍾愛，對～有強烈的愛好」，符合題意，所以最佳選項是 (A)。第 3 題根據上下文的內容，登山對年輕人非常具有吸引力，四個選項中 attractive 表示「吸引人的」符合題意，即正確選項是 (D)。第 4 題根據上下文的內容，登山不是一項團隊運動的觀點證明是錯誤的，通常用 prove to be 來表示「結果是，證明是」，所以選項 (B) 符合題意。第 5 題考動詞 fight 的用法。依據題意，「與～對抗」通常表達為 fight against，用介系詞 against 表示「反對，反抗」，所以選 (D)。

解答＆技巧 | 01 **(C)** 02 **(A)** 03 **(D)** 04 **(B)** 05 **(D)**

適用 TIP 1　適用 TIP 2　適用 TIP 7　適用 TIP 11

補充
mountaineering n 登山；adventurous a 愛冒險的；man-made a 人造的；team sport ph 團隊運動；climber n 登山者

7,000 單字
- enjoy [ɪn`dʒɔɪ] v 2 喜愛
- brave [brev] a 1 勇敢的
- rule [rul] n 1 規則
- full [fʊl] a 1 滿的
- freedom [`fridəm] n 2 自由
- young [jʌŋ] a 1 年輕的
- free [fri] a 1 自由的
- family [`fæməlɪ] n 1 家庭
- match [mætʃ] n 1 比賽
- danger [`dendʒɚ] n 1 危險
- risk [rɪsk] n 3 風險
- overcome [ˌovɚ`kʌm] v 4 克服
- high [haɪ] a 1 高的
- relief [rɪ`lif] n 3 寬慰
- representative [ˌrɛprɪ`zɛntətɪv] n 3 代表

10 ▶ 99 年學測英文

Anita was shopping with her mother and enjoying it. Interestingly, both of them __01__ buying the same pair of jeans.

According to a recent marketing study, young adults influence 88% of household clothing purchases. More often than not, those in their early twenties are the more __02__ consumers. There isn't a brand or a trend that these young people are not aware of. That is why mothers who want to keep abreast of trends usually __03__ the experts—their daughters. This tells the retailers of the world that if you want to get into a mother's __04__ , you've got to win her daughter over first.

With a DJ playing various kinds of music rather than just rap, and a mix of clothing labels designed more for taste and fashion than for a precise age, department stores have managed to appeal to successful middle-aged women __05__ losing their younger customers. They have created a shopping environment where the needs of both mothers and daughters are satisfied.

01 _____ (A) gave up   (B) ended up
(C) took to   (D) used to

02 _____ (A) informed   (B) informative
(C) informal   (D) informational

03 _____ (A) deal with   (B) head for
(C) turn to   (D) look into

04 _____ (A) textbook   (B) notebook
(C) workbook   (D) pocketbook

05 _____ (A) in   (B) while
(C) after   (D) without

DAY 8

Part 1
詞彙題
Day 8
完成 25%

Part 2
綜合測驗
Day 8
完成 50%

Part 3
文意選填
Day 8
完成 75%

Part 4
閱讀測驗
Day 8
完成 100%

中譯｜安妮塔和她媽媽一起購物，並且樂在其中。有趣的是，最後他們兩個都購買了相同的牛仔褲。

最近的市場調查指出，年輕人在家庭服裝購買方面的影響力占百分之八十八。通常，那些二十歲出頭的人是見多識廣的消費者，不會有這些年輕人不知道的品牌或潮流。這也就是那些想跟上潮流的媽媽們總是向專家——他們的女兒求助的原因。這就告訴了世界上的零售商一個道理，如果你想讓媽媽掏出錢包買東西，就必須先贏得她女兒的喜愛。

DJ 播放多樣音樂，而不僅僅是饒舌樂，且服裝品牌依品味和時尚混合展現，而非只針對特定年齡層，使百貨公司可在沒有流失年輕顧客的情況下，也吸引了成功的中年女性。

解說｜本篇短文講述了年輕人在購物時佔據了主要地位，會影響到家庭其他成員的購物需求。第 1 題考動詞片語的用法。將四個片語一一代入空格，只有 ended up 表示「結果為，以～結束」符合題意，且 up 後面可以跟動名詞 buying，所以正確選擇為 (B)。第 2 題的四個選項都是形容詞。根據詞義辨析，informed 表示「見多識廣的」最符合題意，所以最佳選項是 (A)。第 3 題的四個選項都是動詞片語。依據題意，turn to 表示「求助於」符合上下文的意思，即正確選項是 (C)。第 4 題根據主旨可知，短文主要講的是購物，那麼就跟 pocketbook（錢包）有關，其他選項皆不符合題意，只有選項 (D) 符合題意。第 5 題考介系詞的用法。依據題意，without 表示「沒有」符合題意，也就是沒有失去年輕的消費者，所以選 (D)。

解答＆技巧｜ **01 (B)**　**02 (A)**　**03 (C)**　**04 (D)**　**05 (D)**

適用 TIP 2　適用 TIP 7　適用 TIP 11　適用 TIP 14

補充
interestingly ad 有趣地；marketing study ph 市場研究；keep abreast of ph 跟上；retailer n 零售商；DJ ph 流行音樂節目主持人

7,000 單字
- shop [ʃɑp] v 1 購物
- mother [ˋmʌðɚ] n 1 母親
- same [sem] a 1 相同的
- pair [pɛr] n 1 一雙
- jeans [dʒinz] n 2 牛仔褲
- according [əˋkɔrdɪŋ] ad 1 依照
- often [ˋɔfən] ad 1 經常
- early [ˋɝlɪ] a 1 早的
- trend [trɛnd] n 3 趨勢
- tell [tɛl] v 1 告訴
- label [ˋlebl] n 3 標籤
- taste [test] n 1 品味
- fashion [ˋfæʃən] n 3 時尚
- informative [ɪnˋfɔrmətɪv] a 4 教育性的
- textbook [ˋtɛkst͵bʊk] n 2 課本

Part 3 文意選填 | Cloze Test

1 ▶ 98 年學測英文

Familiar fables can be narrated differently or extended in interesting and humorous ways. The end of the famous fable of "*The Tortoise and the Hare*" is well known to all: the tortoise wins the race against the hare. The moral lesson is that slow and steady wins the race. We all have grown up with this popular version, but the __01__ fable can be extended with different twists. At the request of the hare, a second race is __02__, and this time the hare runs without taking a rest and wins. The moral lesson is that __03__ and consistent will always beat slow and steady. Then it is the tortoise that __04__ the hare to a third race along a different route in which there is a river just before the final destination. This time, the tortoise wins the race because the hare cannot swim. The moral lesson is "First __05__ your strengths, and then change the playing field to suit them."

But the story continues. Both __06__ know their own drawbacks and limitations very well; therefore, they jointly decide to have one last race— not to decide who the winner or loser is, but just for their own pleasure and satisfaction. The two __07__ as a team. Firstly, the hare carries the tortoise on its back to the river. Then, the tortoise carries the hare and swims to the __08__ bank of the river. Lastly, the hare carries the tortoise again on its back. Thus they reach the __09__ line together. Overall, many moral lessons from the last match are highlighted. The most obvious one is the importance of __10__. Another moral which also means a great deal is "competition against situations rather than against rivals."

(A) arranged   (B) challenges   (C) competitors   (D) cooperate   (E) fast
(F) finishing   (G) identify   (H) opposite   (I) same   (J) teamwork

01 _____   02 _____   03 _____   04 _____   05 _____

06 _____   07 _____   08 _____   09 _____   10 _____

DAY
8

Part 1
詞
彙
題
Day 8
完成 25%

Part 2
綜
合
測
驗
Day 8
完成 50%

Part 3
文
意
選
填
Day 8
完成 75%

Part 4
閱
讀
測
驗
Day 8
完成 100%

選項中譯｜安排；挑戰；參賽者；合作；迅速的；終點的；辨明；對面的；同樣的；合作

中譯｜那些耳熟能詳的寓言故事可以用不同的方式來講述，或是用有趣的、幽默的方式來進行延伸。所有人都知道著名的寓言《龜兔賽跑》的結局：在和兔子的比賽中，烏龜獲得了勝利。寓意是說，緩慢而堅定的前行最終會贏得勝利。我們都是讀著這樣的通俗版本長大的，不過，同樣的寓言也可以用不同的轉折來進行擴展。應兔子的請求，進行了第二次比賽，這一次，兔子一直在跑，並沒有停下來休息，牠贏得了勝利。寓意是說，迅捷而持之以恆的前行，必定會勝過緩慢而堅定的前行。然後是烏龜向兔子挑戰，進行第三次比賽，這次是不同的路線，通往最終目的地的路上有一條河。因為兔子不會游泳，所以烏龜贏得了比賽。寓言是說，首先要辨明自己的長處，然後轉到合適的領域來加以應用。

不過，故事還在繼續。兩個參賽者都十分了解自己的缺點和不足之處，因此雙方共同決定，進行最後一次比賽，並不是為了決定誰勝誰負，而是為了尋求樂趣和滿足感。牠們兩個協同合作，兔子先背著烏龜跑到河邊，然後烏龜背著兔子遊到河對岸，之後兔子再次背著烏龜前行。就這樣，牠們一起到達了終點。總的來說，最後的這次比賽突顯出很多的寓意。最明顯的寓意是團隊合作的重要性；另一個意義深遠的寓意是，要與環境競爭，而不是與對手競爭。

解譯｜閱讀全文可知，這篇文章的主題是《龜兔賽跑》這則寓言的不同延伸。

縱觀各選項，選項 (C)、(J) 是名詞，選項 (A)、(B)、(D)、(G) 是動詞，選項 (E)、(F)、(H)、(I) 是形容詞。根據題意，第 6、10 題應選名詞，第 2、4、5、7 題應選動詞，第 1、3、8、9 題應選形容詞。然後根據文章，依次作答。

第 1 題是選擇形容詞，有四個形容詞可供選擇，即為選項 (E)、(F)、(H)、(I)。選項 (E) 意為「迅速的」，選項 (F) 意為「終點的」，選項 (H) 意為「對面的」，選項 (I) 意為「同樣的」，根據句意可知，應當是「同樣的寓言可以用不同的轉折來進行延伸」，所以選 (I)。第 3 題所選形容詞，是與下文的 slow 意義相對，所以選 (E)。第 8 題則是選 (H)，opposite bank of the river 意為「河的對岸」。第 9 題所選形容詞，可以視為固定搭配，the finishing line 意為「終點線」，所以選 (F)。

第 2 題是選擇動詞，有四個動詞可供選擇，即為選項 (A)、(B)、(D)、(G)，根據句意，應當是「應兔子的請求，安排第二次比賽」，所以選 (A)。第 4 題所選動詞，可以視為固定搭配，challenge... to... 意為「就～向某人挑戰」，所以選 (B)。第 5 題所選動詞，根據句意，應當是「首先要辨明自己的長處」，所以選 (G)。第 7 題則是選 (D)，意為「協同合作」。

第 6 題是選擇名詞，有兩個名詞可供選擇，即為選項 (C)、(J)，選項 (C) 意為「參賽者」，選項 (J) 意為「團隊合作」，根據句意，應當是「兩個參賽者都十分了解自己的缺點和不足之處」，所以選 (C)。第 10 題則是選 (J)，句意為「團隊合作的重要性」。

解答&技巧 | **01** (I)　**02** (A)　**03** (E)　**04** (B)　**05** (G)
　　　　　　 06 (C)　**07** (D)　**08** (H)　**09** (F)　**10** (J)

適用 TIP 1　適用 TIP 2　適用 TIP 6　適用 TIP 7　適用 TIP 8
適用 TIP 9　適用 TIP 10　適用 TIP 11

補充

at the request of ph 應～的請求；win the race ph 贏得比賽；grow up ph 長大；
take a rest ph 休息；rather than ph 而不是

7,000 單字

- narrate [næˋret] v 6 敘述
- tortoise [ˋtɔrtəs] n 3 烏龜
- race [res] n 1 比賽
- moral [ˋmɔrəl] a 3 道德的
- version [ˋvɝʒən] n 6 版本
- request [rɪˋkwɛst] n 3 要求
- consistent [kənˋsɪstənt] a 4 前後一致的
- steady [ˋstɛdɪ] a 3 堅定的

- river [ˋrɪvə] n 1 河流
- drawback [ˋdrɔ͵bæk] n 6 缺點，弊端
- loser [ˋluzə] n 2 失敗者
- pleasure [ˋplɛʒə] n 2 快樂
- overall [ˋovə͵ɔl] ad 5 總的來説
- obvious [ˋɑbvɪəs] a 3 明顯的
- rival [ˋraɪvl] n 5 競爭對手

MEMO

2 ▶

DAY
8

Part 1
詞
彙
題
Day 8
完成 25%

Part 2
綜
合
測
驗
Day 8
完成 50%

Part 3
文
意
選
填
Day 8
完成 75%

Part 4
閱
讀
測
驗
Day 8
完成 100%

Some people may think that the most important personal goal of Alexander Graham Bell was to invent the __01__ . However, this was not the __02__ .

Bell, __03__ in 1847, called himself "a teacher of the deaf." His father was a well-known speech teacher. Bell also taught speech at a school for the deaf in England. Bell __04__ to Canada with his family in 1870. After two years, he opened a school for the deaf in Massachusetts.

The idea for the telephone came to Bell in 1874. When Bell __05__ with the telephone, he also worked on a kind of equipment to help the deaf. It was in 1876 that Bell __06__ the first sentence over the telephone to his assistant, "Mr. Watson, come here; I want you." Bell received a __07__ for the telephone in the same year. Later, hundreds of cases were filed against Bell in court, though. Many people __08__ that they had already thought of the telephone. But Bell did not lose his patent.

The telephone was not the only __09__ of Bell. He received eighteen patents by himself, and another twelve with partners. Fourteen of the patents were for the telephone and telegraph. Others were for the photophone, phonograph, and different types of airplanes.

In 1888, Bell helped found the National Geographic Society. In 1890, he established the Alexander Graham Bell Association for the Deaf. Bell __10__ away in August, 1922.

(A) experimented   (B) case   (C) invention   (D) uttered   (E) born
(F) passed   (G) telephone   (H) claimed   (I) patent   (J) moved

01 _____   02 _____   03 _____   04 _____   05 _____

06 _____   07 _____   08 _____   09 _____   10 _____

選項中譯｜實驗；事實；發明；說；出生；去世；電話；聲稱；專利；搬家

中譯｜有人也許會認為，亞歷山大‧格雷厄姆‧貝爾最重要的個人目標就是發明電話，
事實卻並非如此。

貝爾出生於一八四七年，他自稱為「聾人的老師」。他的父親是一位著名的語言
老師。貝爾也在英格蘭的一所聾人學校教授口語表達。一八七〇年，貝爾隨家人
移居加拿大。兩年後，他在麻塞諸塞州創辦了一所聾人學校。

一八七四年，貝爾有了發明電話的想法，他在進行電話實驗的同時，也致力於研
發一種能幫助聾人的設備。一八七六年，貝爾透過電話對助手說出第一句話：
「沃森先生，快來，我需要你。」同年，貝爾獲得電話專利。然而，在法庭上，
卻有數百案例聲討貝爾。許多人聲稱，他們已經有過這樣的想法。但是，貝爾並
沒有失去他的專利。

電話並非是貝爾的唯一發明。他獨立獲得十八項專利，又與同伴們合作獲得了另
外的十二項專利。其中，因電話和電報而獲得的專利有十四個，也有其他的發
明，例如：光音機、留聲機以及不同類型的飛機。

一八八八年，貝爾協助成立了國家地理學會。一八九〇年，他創立了亞歷山大格
雷厄姆貝爾聽障協會。一九二二年八月，貝爾去世。

解譯｜閱讀全文可知，這篇文章的主題是電話發明者貝爾的生平。

縱觀各選項，選項 (B)、(C)、(G)、(I) 是名詞，選項 (A)、(D)、(E)、(F)、(H)、
(J) 是動詞。根據題意，第 1、2、7、9 題應選名詞，第 3、4、5、6、8、10 題
應選動詞。然後根據文章，依次作答。

第 1 題是選擇名詞，有四個名詞可供選擇，即為選項 (B)、(C)、(G)、(I)，選項
(B) 意為「事實」，選項 (C) 意為「發明」，選項 (G) 意為「電話」，選項 (I) 意
為「專利」，根據句意，應當是「貝爾最重要的個人目標就是發明電話」，所以
選 (G)。第 2 題所選名詞，可以視為固定表達，the case 意為「實情」，所以選
(B)。第 7 題所選名詞，也可以視為固定表達，receive a patent「獲得專利」，
所以選 (I)。第 9 題則是選 (C)，意為「電話並非是貝爾的唯一發明」。

第 3 題是選擇動詞，有六個動詞可供選擇，即為選項 (A)、(D)、(E)、(F)、(H)、
(J)，根據句意可知，應當是「貝爾出生於一八四七年」，所以選 (E)。第 4 題
所選動詞，根據句意可知，應當是「隨家人移居加拿大」，所以選 (J)。第 5 題
所選動詞，根據句意可知，應當是「進行電話實驗」，所以選 (A)。第 6 題所選
動詞，根據句意可知，應當是「透過電話對助手說出第一句話」，所以選 (D)。
第 8 題所選動詞，根據句意可知，應當是「許多人聲稱，他們已經有過這樣的想
法」，所以選 (H)。第 10 題則是選 (F)，pass away 意為「逝世」。

解答＆技巧 | **01 (G)**　**02 (B)**　**03 (E)**　**04 (J)**　**05 (A)**
06 (D)　**07 (I)**　**08 (H)**　**09 (C)**　**10 (F)**

適用 TIP 1　適用 TIP 2　適用 TIP 6　適用 TIP 7　適用 TIP 8
適用 TIP 9　適用 TIP 10　適用 TIP 11

DAY 8

補充

well-known ⓐ 著名的；Canada ⓝ 加拿大；photophone ⓝ 光音機；phonograph ⓝ 留聲機；
pass away ⓟⓗ 逝世

7,000 單字

- personal [ˋpɝsn̩l] ⓐ② 個人的
- goal [gol] ⓝ② 目標
- telephone [ˋtɛləˌfon] ⓝ② 電話
- deaf [dɛf] ⓐ② 耳聾的
- speech [spitʃ] ⓝ① 言語
- experiment [ɪkˋspɛrəmənt] ⓥ⑤ 實驗
- equipment [ɪˋkwɪpmənt] ⓝ③ 設備
- utter [ˋʌtɚ] ⓥ⑤ 說

- assistant [əˋsɪstənt] ⓝ② 助手
- receive [rɪˋsiv] ⓥ① 接收
- patent [ˋpætn̩t] ⓝ⑤ 專利
- court [kort] ⓝ② 法院，法庭
- invention [ɪnˋvɛnʃən] ⓝ④ 發明
- airplane [ˋɛrˌplen] ⓝ① 飛機
- August [ˋɔgəst] ⓝ① 八月

Part 1
詞彙題
Day 8
完成 25%

Part 2
綜合測驗
Day 8
完成 50%

Part 3
文意選填
Day 8
完成 75%

Part 4
閱讀測驗
Day 8
完成 100%

MEMO

Starfish are usually yellow, orange or brown. Most starfish are shaped like stars, with five arms __01__ from their bodies. A starfish can be as small as a paper clip, as long as a yardstick.

Rows of tiny spines __02__ the top of a starfish's arms. Spines are very sharp and have __03__ in them. They will move quickly when touched. Enemies that __04__ against a starfish may get a surprise.

Underneath each arm of a starfish are rows of __05__ holes, from which tube feet extend. The tube feet can act as a sucker to help starfish __06__ or cling to something. Even storm waves will not tear a starfish from a rock.

A starfish's mouth is on its underside, in the middle of its body. Starfish __07__ small animals as food. Sometimes they also eat mollusks with hard __08__, such as clams and oysters. A starfish __09__ its tube feet to each side of the shell. Then it slowly pries the shell open and pushes its stomach out through its mouth into the open shell to digest the soft flesh.

Fishers sometimes try to kill starfish by cutting them into __10__. This does not kill them, though. Starfish can grow new arms, even a new body.

(A) cover   (B) grip   (C) shells   (D) pieces   (E) poison
(F) extending   (G) swallow   (H) tiny   (I) brush   (J) attaches

---

01 _____   02 _____   03 _____   04 _____   05 _____

06 _____   07 _____   08 _____   09 _____   10 _____

選項中譯 | 覆蓋;緊抓;殼;碎片;毒素;延伸;吞咽;極小的;碰觸;吸附

中譯 | 海星通常是黃色、橘色或是棕色。大多數的海星形似五角星,體側延伸出五條手臂。海星可以是如迴紋針般的大小,或是長如碼尺。

海星的手臂上,覆蓋著成排的細小刺針。這些刺針非常鋒利,且含有毒素。被觸及時,這些刺針會快速地移動。觸及海星的敵人也許會為此吃驚。

海星的手臂下有成排的細小的孔,海星的管狀足就是透過這些細孔延伸出體外的。這些管狀足可以用做吸盤,有助於海星抓緊某物或是緊緊附著在某物體之上。即便是風暴潮,也無法將海星沖離岩石。

海星的嘴在底部,身體的正中間部位。海星以小型動物為食。有時候,海星也吃些有著堅硬外殼的軟體動物,包括蚌、牡蠣等。海星先是把牠的管狀足吸附在外殼兩邊,再慢慢地撬開硬殼,張開嘴把胃伸進硬殼裡,去消化柔軟的肉質。

有時,漁夫們會試圖把海星切成碎片,想以此來消滅牠們。然而,這樣做並不能夠殺死海星。海星會長出新的手臂,甚至是生成新的身體。

解譯 | 閱讀全文可知,這篇文章的主題是海星。

縱觀各選項,選項 (C)、(D)、(E) 是名詞,選項 (A)、(B)、(F)、(G)、(I)、(J) 是動詞,選項 (H) 是形容詞。根據題意,第 3、8、10 題應選名詞,第 1、2、4、6、7、9 題應選動詞,第 5 題應選形容詞。然後根據文章,依次作答。

第 1 題是選擇動詞,須與介系詞 from 進行搭配,有六個動詞可供選擇,即為選項 (A)、(B)、(F)、(G)、(I)、(J),根據句意,應當是「體側延伸出手臂」,所以選 (F)。第 2 題所選動詞,根據句意可知,應當是「海星的手臂上,覆蓋著成排的細小刺針」,所以選 (A)。第 4 題所選動詞,是與名詞進行搭配,所以選 (I)。第 6 題所選動詞,根據句意可知,應當是「有助於海星抓緊某物或是緊附著在某物體之上」,所以選 (B)。第 7 題所選動詞,根據句意可知,應當是「海星也吃軟體動物」,所以選 (G)。第 9 題則是選 (J),根據句意,應當是「把牠的管狀足吸附在外殼兩邊」。

第 3 題是選擇名詞,有三個名詞可供選擇,即為選項 (C)、(D)、(E),選項 (C) 意為「殼」,選項 (D) 意為「碎片」,選項 (E) 意為「毒素」,根據句意,應當是「刺針非常鋒利,且含有毒素」,所以選 (E)。第 8 題所選名詞,根據句意,應當是「有著堅硬外殼的軟體動物」,所以選 (C)。第 10 題則是選 (D),cut... into pieces 意為「切成碎片」。

第 5 題是選擇形容詞,只有一個形容詞可供選擇,即為 (H) 意為「極小的」。

DAY 8

Part 1
詞彙題
Day 8
完成 25%

Part 2
綜合測驗
Day 8
完成 50%

Part 3
文意選填
Day 8
完成 75%

Part 4
閱讀測驗
Day 8
完成 100%

解答&技巧 | 01 **(F)**　　02 **(A)**　　03 **(E)**　　04 **(I)**　　05 **(H)**
　　　　　　06 **(B)**　　07 **(G)**　　08 **(C)**　　09 **(J)**　　10 **(D)**

適用 TIP 1　適用 TIP 2　適用 TIP 6　適用 TIP 7　適用 TIP 8
適用 TIP 9　適用 TIP 10　適用 TIP 11

補充

starfish ⓝ 海星；yardstick ⓝ 碼尺；sucker ⓝ 吸盤；underside ⓝ 下側，底部；mollusk ⓝ 軟體動物

7,000 單字

- brown [braʊn] ⓐ 1 棕色的
- clip [klɪp] ⓝ 3 夾子，別針
- row [ro] ⓝ 1 排
- spine [spaɪn] ⓝ 5 刺
- brush [brʌʃ] ⓥ 2 觸及
- surprise [sə`praɪz] ⓝ 1 意外
- poison [`pɔɪzn̩] ⓝ 2 毒
- underneath [ˌʌndə`niθ] prep 5 在～下面

- tube [tjub] ⓝ 2 管
- grip [grɪp] ⓥ 5 緊抓
- storm [stɔrm] ⓝ 2 風暴
- swallow [`swɑlo] ⓥ 2 吞嚥
- clam [klæm] ⓝ 5 蛤
- oyster [`ɔɪstə] ⓝ 5 牡蠣
- digest [daɪ`dʒɛst] ⓥ 4 消化

MEMO

DAY
8

Part 1
詞
彙
題
Day 8
完成 25%

Part 2
綜
合
測
驗
Day 8
完成 50%

Part 3
文
意
選
填
Day 8
完成 75%

Part 4
閱
讀
測
驗
Day 8
完成 100%

4 ▶

　　Ostriches should be the world's largest bird, but they can't fly. An ostrich can be more than eight feet tall, and weigh more than 330 pounds. Ostriches usually live in the __01__ of Africa. They can run quite fast, about forty miles __02__ hour.

　　The __03__ ostrich lays from six to twelve eggs in the nest. Ostrich eggs are very large and weigh about four pounds. Both the male and female sit in the nest and take __04__ keeping them warm. The female usually sits in the nest from nine o'clock in the morning to four o'clock in the afternoon. Then the male sits through the night from four o'clock in the afternoon to nine o'clock in the morning. In this way the eggs are cared for every minute, and the growing chicks in the eggs will feel __05__ too hot nor too cold.

　　After about six weeks, the eggs __06__ out. The little chicks grow rapidly. When they are a month old, they can run as fast as their parents.

　　It is said that the frightened ostrich will __07__ its head in the sand. This is not __08__, actually. When an ostrich is __09__, it usually lies flat on the ground, with its head and neck stretching out. The loose feathers on its body may look like bushes. From a __10__, it looks as though it has buried its head.

(A) per　　(B) hatch　　(C) turns　　(D) distance　　(E) true
(F) grasslands　　(G) neither　　(H) female　　(I) frightened　　(J) bury

---

01 _____　　02 _____　　03 _____　　04 _____　　05 _____

06 _____　　07 _____　　08 _____　　09 _____　　10 _____

選項中譯｜每一；孵化；順序；距離；真實的；草原；兩者都不；雌性的；受驚的；埋

中譯｜鴕鳥是世界上最大的的鳥，但牠們卻不會飛。一隻鴕鳥可能超過八英尺高、超過三百三十磅重。鴕鳥通常生活在非洲草原上，牠們跑得很快，大約是每小時四十英里。

雌鴕鳥在鳥巢中下六到十二個蛋。鴕鳥蛋很大，重約四磅。雄鴕鳥和雌鴕鳥都在鳥巢裡，輪流為鳥蛋們保暖。通常，從早上九點一直到下午四點，雌鴕鳥都在鳥巢裡。之後，從下午四點到第二天早上九點，雄鴕鳥接替雌鴕鳥守在鳥巢裡。這樣，鳥蛋時時刻刻都被保護照顧，在鳥蛋裡成長的雛鳥也不會感到太熱或是太冷。

大約六周後，雛鳥從鳥蛋裡孵出。小雛鳥長得很快，一個月大的時候就可以和父母們跑得一樣快。

據説，鴕鳥受到驚嚇時，會把頭埋在沙子裡。這並非實情。當鴕鳥受到驚嚇時，通常會平躺在地面上，把頭和頸都伸得長長的。身上蓬鬆的羽毛看起來也許就像是灌木叢。從遠處看來，牠似乎是把頭埋了起來。

解譯｜閱讀全文可知，這篇文章的主題是鴕鳥。

縱觀各選項，選項 (C)、(D)、(F) 是名詞，選項 (B)、(J) 是動詞，選項 (E)、(H)、(I) 是形容詞，選項 (A) 是介系詞，選項 (G) 是代名詞。根據題意，第 1、4、10 題應選名詞，第 6、7 題應選動詞，第 3、8、9 題應選形容詞，第 2 題應選介系詞，第 5 題應選代名詞。然後根據文章，依次作答。

第 1 題是選擇名詞，有三個名詞可供選擇，即為選項 (C)、(D)、(F)，選項 (C) 意為「順序」，選項 (D) 意為「距離」，選項 (F) 意為「草原」，根據句意，應當是「鴕鳥通常是生活在非洲草原上」，所以選 (F)。第 4 題所選名詞，可以視為固定搭配，take turns doing sth. / take turns to do sth. 意為「輪流做某事」，所以選 (C)。第 10 題則是選 (D)，from a distance 意為「從遠處」。

第 2 題是選擇介系詞，只有一個介系詞可供選擇，即為選項 (A)，意為「每一」。

第 3 題是選擇形容詞，有三個形容詞可供選擇，即為選項 (E)、(H)、(I)。選項 (E) 意為「真實的」，選項 (H) 意為「雌性的」，選項 (I) 意為「受驚的」，根據句意可知，應當是「雌鴕鳥在鳥巢中下六到十二個蛋」，所以選 (H)。第 8 題所選形容詞，根據句意可知，應當是「這並非實情」，所以選 (E)。第 9 題則是選 (I)，句意為「鴕鳥受到驚嚇」。

第 5 題是選擇代名詞，只有一個代名詞可供選擇，即為選項 (G)，意為「兩者都不」。

第 6 題是選擇動詞，須與副詞 out 進行搭配，有兩個動詞可供選擇，即為選項 (B)、(J)。只有選項 (B) 符合要求，hatch out 意為「孵出」。第 7 題則是選 (J)，句意為「把頭埋在沙子裡」。

解答＆技巧│ **01** (F)　**02** (A)　**03** (H)　**04** (C)　**05** (G)
06 (B)　**07** (J)　**08** (E)　**09** (I)　**10** (D)

適用 TIP 1　適用 TIP 2　適用 TIP 6　適用 TIP 7　適用 TIP 8
適用 TIP 9　適用 TIP 10　適用 TIP 11

補充

grassland n 草原，草地；from... to... ph 從〜直到〜；neither... nor... ph 既不〜也不〜；
rapidly ad 快速地；frightened a 受驚嚇的

7,000 單字

- ostrich [ˈɑstrɪtʃ] n **5** 鴕鳥
- per [pɚ] prep **2** 每
- female [ˈfimel] a **2** 雌性的
- nest [nɛst] n **2** 窩
- weigh [we] v **1** 重
- minute [ˈmɪnɪt] n **1** 分鐘
- chick [tʃɪk] n **1** 雛鳥
- neither [ˈniðɚ] conj **2** 兩者都不

- bury [ˈbɛrɪ] v **3** 埋
- sand [sænd] n **1** 沙
- flat [flæt] a **2** 平的
- ground [graʊnd] n **1** 地面
- feather [ˈfɛðɚ] n **3** 羽毛
- bush [bʊʃ] n **3** 灌木
- distance [ˈdɪstəns] n **2** 距離

Part 1
詞
彙
題
Day 8
完成 25%

Part 2
綜
合
測
驗
Day 8
完成 50%

Part 3
文
意
選
填
Day 8
完成 75%

Part 4
閱
讀
測
驗
Day 8
完成 100%

MEMO

5 ▶

The Great __01__ started in 1929 in the United States, and continued for about ten years. It was a time of high __02__ rate and great poverty. What's __03__, the depression became a worldwide phenomenon that affected millions of people.

In the late 1920s, the price of shares on the New York Stock Exchange __04__ rapidly. More and more people bought stocks, in the __05__ of selling them again when the price went up and making a large profit. However, when prices __06__ in October, 1929, people rushed to sell their stocks and shares. But the prices on the stock market fell sharply soon. This is known as the Wall Street Crash. Thousands of people were brought to total __07__, many businesses and banks shut down, and unemployment __08__.

The situation in the U.S. became worse with sever droughts in the 1930s in the Midwest states. Thousands of farm workers were forced to make the long and difficult journey to look for work. Many people died of disease and hunger later.

The economic collapse in the United States had a __09__ effect on countries around the world. Banks in the U.S. __10__ funds from overseas and demanded the repayment of loans, triggering the closure of many European banks. Many European countries tried to protect their own trade by raising taxes on imports, which induced a slump in international trade, though.

(A) Depression   (B) increased   (C) ruin   (D) unemployment
(E) withdrew   (F) drastic   (G) soared   (H) worse   (I) hope
(J) dropped

01 _____   02 _____   03 _____   04 _____   05 _____

06 _____   07 _____   08 _____   09 _____   10 _____

選項中譯｜經濟蕭條時期；增長；毀滅；失業；撤回；嚴重的；激增；更糟糕的；希望；下降

中譯｜一九二九年，經濟大蕭條在美國發生，持續了將近十年的時間。這是一段高失業率和極度貧困的時期。更糟糕的是，經濟蕭條很快成為全球化現象，數百萬人受到影響。

二十世紀二〇年代晚期，紐約證券交易所的股票價格飛漲。愈來愈多的人購買股票，希望在股票價格上升的時候再次拋售，以獲取巨額利潤。然而，一九二九年十月，當股票價格下跌時，人們都急於賣掉股票。但是，股市價格依然急劇下跌。這次事件稱為華爾街崩盤。成千上萬的人傾家蕩產，許多企業和銀行倒閉，失業率激增。

二十世紀三〇年代，美國的中西部地區發生嚴重乾旱，加劇了經濟蕭條狀況。成千上萬的農場工人被迫長途跋涉去尋找工作，隨後很多人死於疾病和饑餓。

美國經濟的崩潰給世界各國帶來了嚴重的影響。美國銀行從海外撤資，要求償還貸款，致使歐洲的許多銀行紛紛倒閉。許多歐洲國家試圖透過增加進口稅來保護自己的貿易，卻引發了國際貿易衰退。

解譯｜閱讀全文可知，這篇文章的主題是經濟大蕭條。

縱觀各選項，選項 (A)、(C)、(D)、(I) 是名詞，選項 (B)、(E)、(G)、(J) 是動詞，選項 (F)、(H) 是形容詞。根據題意，第 1、2、5、7 題應選名詞，第 4、6、8、10 題應選動詞，第 3、9 題應選形容詞。然後根據文章，依次作答。

第 1 題是選擇名詞，有四個名詞可供選擇，即為選項 (A)、(C)、(D)、(I)，選項 (A) 意為「經濟蕭條時期」，選項 (C) 意為「毀滅」，選項 (D) 意為「失業」，選項 (I) 意為「希望」，Great Depression 可以視為固定表達，意為「經濟大蕭條」，所以選 (A)。第 2 題所選名詞，也可以視為固定表達，high unemployment rate 意為「高失業率」，所以選 (D)。第 5 題所選名詞，也可以視為固定表達，in the hope of 意為「希望」，所以選 (I)。第 7 題則是選 (C)，be brought to total ruin 意為「傾家蕩產」。

第 3 題是選擇形容詞，有兩個形容詞可供選擇，即為選項 (F)、(H)。選項 (F) 意為「嚴重的」，選項 (H) 意為「更糟糕的」，what's worse 可以視為固定搭配，意為「更糟糕的是」，所以選 (H)。第 9 題則是選 (F)，句意為「美國經濟的崩潰給世界各國帶來了嚴重的影響」。

第 4 題是選擇動詞，有四個動詞可供選擇，即為選項 (B)、(E)、(G)、(J)，根據句意可知，應當是「股票價格飛漲」，所以選 (B)。第 6 題所選動詞，根據句意可知，應當是「股票價格下跌」，所以選 (J)。第 8 題所選動詞，根據句意可知，應當是「失業率激增」，所以選 (G)。第 10 題則是選 (E)，意為「美國銀行從海外撤資」。

DAY **8**

Part 1 詞彙題 Day 8 完成 25%

Part 2 綜合測驗 Day 8 完成 50%

Part 3 文意選填 Day 8 完成 75%

Part 4 閱讀測驗 Day 8 完成 100%

解答＆技巧 | **01** (A)　**02** (D)　**03** (H)　**04** (B)　**05** (I)
　　　　　06 (J)　**07** (C)　**08** (G)　**09** (F)　**10** (E)

適用 TIP 1　適用 TIP 2　適用 TIP 6　適用 TIP 7　適用 TIP 8
適用 TIP 9　適用 TIP 10　適用 TIP 11

補充

Great Depression ph 經濟大蕭條；New York Stock Exchange ph 紐約證券交易所；
Wall Street Crash ph 華爾街崩盤；European a 歐洲的；repayment n 償還

7,000 單字

- depression [dɪˋprɛʃən] n 4 經濟蕭條期
- unemployment [ˏʌnɪmˋplɔɪmənt] n 6 失業
- stock [stɑk] n 5 股票，股份
- October [ɑkˋtobɚ] n 1 十月
- crash [kræʃ] n 3 崩潰
- shut [ʃʌt] v 1 關閉
- soar [sor] v 6 飛漲
- journey [ˋdʒɝnɪ] n 3 路程

- hunger [ˋhʌŋgɚ] n 2 饑餓
- drastic [ˋdræstɪk] a 6 極嚴重的
- collapse [kəˋlæps] n 4 崩潰
- withdraw [wɪðˋdrɔ] v 4 撤回，提取
- overseas [ˋovɚˋsiz] ad 2 海外
- loan [lon] n 4 貸款
- trigger [ˋtrɪgɚ] v 6 引發

MEMO

♫ 486

MEMO

DAY
8

Part 1
詞
彙
題
Day 8
完成 25%

Part 2
綜
合
測
驗
Day 8
完成 50%

Part 3
文
意
選
填
Day 8
完成 75%

Part 4
閱
讀
測
驗
Day 8
完成 100%

Part 4 閱讀測驗 | Reading Questions

1▶

Although we may feel worried and depressed in life, there are still many things that can console us a great deal. It is of great significance to shift those negative thoughts to something positive. No matter what adversities we have to confront, just keep in mind the following tips.

Call someone you love and tell them you love them. I don't think you have to spend much time in choosing who to call because it can be anyone you love. Your families, your relatives, your friends, your neighbors, your teachers and colleagues, all of them could be the person you love.

Listen to a favorite song. The world, admittedly, will not have an earth-shaking change within a few minutes. However, after you immerse yourself in music, you may calm down slowly and expel all the vexation from your mind.

Think about people who have a positive influence in your life. Close your eyes and think about them. You may find they are like the brilliant sunshine, giving you warmth and allowing you to be filled with inspiration and vigor. They will always give you a hand when you get into trouble. And when life is plain sailing for you, they will just stay beside you and accompany you quietly. Cherish these people, and then you will feel happy.

Be full of gratitude. Think about what you are grateful for every day. When you are in low spirits, just think about these things, and you may become more positive and active.

01 Which one of the following statements is false?

(A) When confronted adversities, we should immerse ourselves in despair or frustration.

(B) A favorite song may help you calm down.

(C) Those who have a positive influence in your life would help you gain inspiration and vigor.

(D) You should feel grateful for many things.

02 The word "vexation" in the third paragraph is closest in meaning to _____.

(A) disease

(B) happiness

(C) annoyance

(D) pressure

03 Which of the following tips is not mentioned in the passage?

(A) To call someone you love and tell them you love them.

(B) To listen to one of your favorite songs.

(C) To be grateful.

(D) To cherish the sunshine.

04 What is the main idea of the passage?

(A) How to get rid of those negative thoughts.

(B) How to be brave.

(C) People of spirits.

(D) Negative thoughts and positive thoughts.

DAY
8

Part 1
詞
彙
題
Day 8
完成 25%

Part 2
綜
合
測
驗
Day 8
完成 50%

Part 3
文
意
選
填
Day 8
完成 75%

Part 4
閱
讀
測
驗
Day 8
完成 100%

中譯｜在生活中，我們也許會覺得憂愁、沮喪，然而，還是有許多事情能帶給我們極大的慰藉。將消極的想法轉換為積極的想法，這是十分重要的。不論我們不得不面對的逆境為何，都要牢記以下建議。

打電話給你所愛的人，告訴他們，你愛他們。我認為，你不必花費很多的時間考慮要打給誰，因為只要是你愛的人都可以。你的家人、你的親戚、你的朋友、你的鄰居，你的老師和同事，他們都可以是你愛的人。

聽一首自己最喜歡的歌曲。在短短的幾分鐘內，世界固然不會發生翻天覆地的變化。然而沈浸在音樂之中，你也許會慢慢地冷靜下來，消除心中的所有煩惱。

想想那些在你的生活中有積極影響的人。閉上眼睛，想想他們。你也許會發現，他們如同燦爛的陽光，給予你溫暖，讓你充滿靈感和活力。當你陷入困境時，他們總是會對你施以援手；當你的生活一帆風順，他們會在你身邊，靜靜地陪伴。珍愛這些人吧，你會感到幸福。

心懷感恩。想想令你心懷感恩的事情。情緒低落的時候，就想想這些事情，這樣，你會有更加積極主動的心態。

解譯｜在閱讀文章之前，先要預覽題目，然後再帶著問題有針對性地閱讀文章。第 1 題是判斷正誤，第 2 題是詞義辨析，第 3 題是文意理解，第 4 題是概括主旨。理解了題目要求之後，閱讀全文，依次作答。

第 1 題是判斷正誤，考的是細節，問的是哪一項敘述是錯誤的。根據第 1 段最後一句內容「No matter what adversities we have to confront, just keep in mind the following tips.」可知，面對逆境，要牢記以下提示，再根據上文可知，應該保持積極的心態。選項 (A) 中則是說，面臨逆境，應該放任自己沉浸在絕望或是挫敗中，與此不符。同樣，此題也可以用排除法來解答。第 3 段最後一句內容與選項 (B) 相符，第 4 段第 3 句內容與選項 (C) 相符，第 5 段內容與選項 (D) 相符，都是正確的敘述，可以排除。所以選 (A)。

第 2 題是考 vexation 的同義字。選項 (A) 意為「疾病」，選項 (B) 意為「幸福」，選項 (C) 意為「煩惱」，選項 (D) 意為「壓力」。根據第 3 段最後一句內容可知，在文中意為「煩惱」，所以選 (C)。

第 3 題是文意理解，問的是哪一項建議在文中沒有提及。第 2 段首句內容與選項 (A) 相符，第 3 段首句內容與選項 (B) 相符，第 5 段首句內容與選項 (C) 相符。只有選項 (D)，在文中找不到相關敘述。所以選 (D)。

第 4 題是概括主旨。文中有明確的主旨句，根據第 1 段內容可知，文章主旨為擺脫消極情緒的方法，與選項 (A) 敘述相符。所以選 (A)。

解答＆技巧｜ **01 (A)** **02 (C)** **03 (D)** **04 (A)**

適用 TIP 1　適用 TIP 2　適用 TIP 3　適用 TIP 7　適用 TIP 10　適用 TIP 11

適用 TIP 12　適用 TIP 13　適用 TIP 14　適用 TIP 15　適用 TIP 16

補充

adversity n 災難，逆境；immerse v 沉浸；vexation n 煩惱，惱火；sunshine n 陽光；
slowly ad 緩慢地

7,000 單字

- console [kənˋsol] v 5 安慰
- confront [kənˋfrʌnt] v 5 面對
- someone [ˋsʌm͵wʌn] pron 1 某人
- relative [ˋrɛlətɪv] n 4 親戚
- neighbor [ˋnebɚ] n 2 鄰居
- colleague [ˋkɑlig] n 5 同事
- calm [kɑm] v 2 鎮靜，平靜
- expel [ɪkˋspɛl] v 6 驅除

- brilliant [ˋbrɪljənt] a 3 明亮的
- inspiration [͵ɪnspəˋreʃən] n 4 靈感
- vigor [ˋvɪgɚ] n 5 活力
- beside [bɪˋsaɪd] prep 1 在～旁邊
- accompany [əˋkʌmpənɪ] v 4 陪伴
- gratitude [ˋgrætə͵tjud] n 4 感激
- grateful [ˋgretfəl] a 4 感激的

MEMO

Part 1
詞彙題
Day 8
完成 25%

Part 2
綜合測驗
Day 8
完成 50%

Part 3
文意選填
Day 8
完成 75%

Part 4
閱讀測驗
Day 8
完成 100%

The following habits could help keep your life in order.

Write things down. You may feel amazed that someone can remember everyone's birthday and send cards for every occasion. It's not magic at all. You can do this if you write down the things you have to memorize. Compared with our brain, pens and papers are much more reliable to keep everything in perfect order. Surely, we can also use a computer or a smart phone. We can take notes of almost everything, including shopping lists, holiday gifts, home decor, meetings and birthdays. If you try to keep all the things in your mind, it will only complicate your life. Therefore, when you enter into a new company and have to get familiar with so many colleagues soon, you could write down their names. I dare say you could remember more names than you have anticipated.

Make schedules. There is a famous saying—procrastination is the thief of time. As we all know, succssful people never waste time. Make schedules, for the day and week, and strictly stick to them. This is very important. Once you set goals, try your best to achieve them. In contrast, if you always fail to meet the deadlines or achieve your goals, you may live a cluttered life. Hence, make a list, write down the things you want to do, and then do them right now. The longer you wait, the more difficult it will be to accomplish it.

Work hard. Once you have made a schedule, you need to put in a lot of efforts, and have a clear idea of what you need to do and when you can do it.

01 Which one of the following statements is false?

(A) We can take notes of almost everything that we need to remember.

(B) Compared to pens and papers, our brain is much more reliable to remember everything.

(C) Procrastination is believed to be the thief of time.

(D) Without schedules and goals, you may live a chaotic life.

02 The word "memorize" in the second paragraph is closest in meaning to _____.

(A) despise

(B) respect

(C) forget

(D) remember

03 Which of the following habits is not mentioned in the passage?

(A) To take notes of things.

(B) To make schedules.

(C) To work hard.

(D) To be confident.

04 What is the main idea of the passage?

(A) How to deal with your personal affairs.

(B) How to achieve success.

(C) Good habits you should keep in order to live an ordered life.

(D) How to keep everything in mind.

DAY
8

Part 1
詞
彙
題
Day 8
完成 25%

Part 2
綜
合
測
驗
Day 8
完成 50%

Part 3
文
意
選
填
Day 8
完成 75%

Part 4
閱
讀
測
驗
Day 8
完成 100%

中譯│以下習慣可以幫助你把生活管理得井然有序。

把事情寫下來。你也或許會為此感到驚訝，有些人能夠記住所有人的生日，並且在每一個節日裡都送出賀卡。這並不是魔法。如果你把那些需要記憶的事情都記下來，你也可以做到。相較於我們的大腦，筆和紙更為可靠，幫助我們將一切事情都安排得秩序井然。當然，我們也可以用電腦或是智慧型手機。我們幾乎可以記下一切事務，包括購物清單、節日禮物、家居裝飾、會議和生日。如果你試圖在心裡記住所有的事情，也只會讓你的生活變得更為複雜。因此，如果你進入了一家新的公司，並且需要儘快熟悉諸多的同事，就可以將他們的名字都寫下來。我敢說，你會記住的名字將遠遠超出預期。

制定時間表。正如俗語所說，拖延是時間之賊。我們都知道，成功的人都不會浪費時間。制定一天或是一周的時間表，並且嚴格遵守。這是很重要的。一旦設定了目標，就要盡力去實現。相反，如果你總是超出最後期限，或是無法實現目標，那麼，你的生活也許會混亂不堪。因此，列一張清單，將你想做的事情寫下來，然後立刻行動。等待的時間愈長，就愈難實現這些目標。

努力工作。一旦你制定了計畫表，就需要付出很多努力，也要清楚地知道，你需要做什麼事及什麼時候做。

解譯│在閱讀文章之前，先要預覽題目，然後再帶著問題有針對性地閱讀文章。第 1 題是判斷正誤，第 2 題是詞義辨析，第 3 題是文意理解，第 4 題是概括主旨。理解了題目要求之後，閱讀全文，依次作答。

第 1 題是判斷正誤，考的是細節，問的是哪一項敘述是錯誤的。根據第 2 段第 5 句內容「Compared with our brain, pens and papers are much more reliable to keep everything in perfect order.」可知，相較於我們的大腦，筆和紙更為可靠，幫助我們將一切事情都安排得秩序井然。選項 (B) 則是說，相較於筆和紙張，我們的大腦更為可靠，與文意不符。同樣，此題也可以用排除法來解答。第 2 段第 7 句內容與選項 (A) 相符，第 3 段第 2 句內容與選項 (C) 相符，第 3 段第 6 句內容與選項 (D) 相符。這三個選項的敘述都是正確的，可以排除。所以選 (B)。

第 2 題是考動詞 memorize 的同義字。選項 (A) 意為「輕視」，選項 (B) 意為「尊敬」，選項 (C) 意為「忘記」，選項 (D) 意為「記憶」。根據第 2 段第 3 句內容可知，memorize 在文中意為「記憶」，所以選 (D)。

第 3 題是文意理解，問的是哪一項習慣在文中沒有提及。縱觀全文，第 2 段首句內容與選項 (A) 相符，第 3 段首句內容與選項 (B) 相符，第 4 段首句內容與選項 (C) 相符。只有選項 (D)，在文中找不到相關敘述。所以選 (D)。

第 4 題是概括主旨。文中有明確的主旨句，本篇結構是先總述後分述，第 1 段可以視為主旨段，根據第 1 段內容「The following habits could help keep your life in order.」可知，以下習慣可以幫助你把生活管理得井然有序。選項 (C) 意為「把生活管理得井然有序的好習慣」，與此相符。所以選 (C)。

解答＆技巧｜ **01 (B)**　**02 (D)**　**03 (D)**　**04 (C)**

適用 TIP 1　適用 TIP 2　適用 TIP 3　適用 TIP 7　適用 TIP 10

適用 TIP 11　適用 TIP 12　適用 TIP 13　適用 TIP 14　適用 TIP 15

DAY
8

> 補充
>
> birthday ⓝ 生日；decor ⓝ 裝飾品；enter into ⓟⓗ 進入；waste time ⓟⓗ 浪費時間；cluttered ⓐ 混亂的
>
> 7,000 單字
>
> - card [kɑrd] ⓝ ① 卡片
> - occasion [əˋkeʒən] ⓝ ③ 時刻，時節
> - magic [ˋmædʒɪk] ⓝ ② 魔法
> - pen [pɛn] ⓝ ① 鋼筆
> - smart [smɑrt] ⓐ ① 聰明的
> - phone [fon] ⓝ ② 電話
> - complicate [ˋkɑmpləˌket] ⓥ ④ 使複雜
> - anticipate [ænˋtɪsəˌpet] ⓥ ⑥ 期望
>
> - schedule [ˋskɛdʒʊl] ⓝ ③ 計畫，進度表
> - week [wik] ⓝ ① 周，星期
> - set [sɛt] ⓥ ① 設定
> - list [lɪst] ⓝ ① 清單
> - wait [wet] ⓥ ① 等待
> - accomplish [əˋkɑmplɪʃ] ⓥ ④ 完成
> - effort [ˋɛfɚt] ⓝ ② 努力

Part 1
詞
彙
題
Day 8
完成 25%

Part 2
綜
合
測
驗
Day 8
完成 50%

Part 3
文
意
選
填
Day 8
完成 75%

Part 4
閱
讀
測
驗
Day 8
完成 100%

MEMO

According to a study, a person's voice can have a strong influence on the impression he gives to others, and its importance has greatly exceeded what he says. Many people believe that a strong and smooth voice can enhance the chances of promotion, while a raspy tone or a strident voice may lead to distractibility.

The study also shows that rough, weak, strained or breathy voices will make the speakers sound as negative, weak, passive or tense; in contrast, people with normal voices are usually seen as successful, sociable and smart. Some people may have no comment on others' voice, even though they are intolerable. The president of a famous company says that every person has a right to judge people. And when you hear somebody speak, the first thing you do is to form an opinion about him or her. Therefore, pay attention to your voice and the way you speak. In addition, gender, ethnicity, age and cultural background can also play an important role in the way people talk.

Not everyone's voice is excellent. But people's voice can be strengthened or improved through therapy, coaching or feedback. For example, voice can be strengthened through improving breath or strengthening the laryngeal muscles.

Up to now, many companies have provided their employees with voice coaching because there are usually many voice problems when the employees speak to the customers. After using sound-level equipment and audio recordings, the employees' voices can leave a better impression on the clients.

01 The word "strident" in the first paragraph is closest in meaning to _____.

(A) shrill

(B) pleasant

(C) comfortable

(D) boring

02 Which one of the following statements is false?

(A) Rough, weak, strained or breathy voices may create an unfavorable impression.

(B) A person's voice can greatly affect the impression he leaves on others.

(C) People's voice cannot be improved or strengthened anyway.

(D) When we hear someone talk, we always form an opinion about the speaker.

03 All of the following factors may have an effect on the way people talk except _____.

(A) voice

(B) cultural background

(C) marital status

(D) ethnicity

04 What is the main idea of the passage?

(A) The importance of a person's voice may exceed what he says.

(B) Employers and employees.

(C) How to improve one's voice.

(D) Excellent voice.

DAY
8

Part 1
詞
彙
題
Day 8
完成 25%

Part 2
綜
合
測
驗
Day 8
完成 50%

Part 3
文
意
選
填
Day 8
完成 75%

Part 4
閱
讀
測
驗
Day 8
完成 100%

中譯 | 一項研究指出，人的嗓音會強烈影響到他給別人留下的印象，其重要性也已經遠遠超過了說話內容。很多人認為，洪亮而流暢的說話聲音，會增加晉升的機會，而刺耳的語調或是尖銳的聲音，也許會導致注意力分散。

這項研究也顯示，沙啞、微弱、緊張或是帶有呼吸氣息的聲音，會使說話人聽起來消極、虛弱、消沉或是緊張；相反，說話聲音正常的人，通常會給人留下成功、友善和聰慧的印象。有些人或許對其他人的聲音不予評價，即便這些聲音難以容忍。一家著名企業的總裁說，每個人都有權評價他人。當你聽別人說話時，所做的第一件事情，就是對他們形成某種看法。因此，要注意你的聲音和你的說話方式。此外，性別、種族、年齡和文化背景，對於人們的說話方式，也有著重要作用。

並不是每個人的聲音都極為出色。然而，透過治療、訓練或是回饋資訊，人們的聲音可以得到加強或是改善。例如，透過改善呼吸或是強化喉部肌肉，可以讓聲音得到加強。

到現在為止，很多企業都為其員工提供了聲音訓練，這是因為員工與客戶交談時，通常會有很多的聲音問題。使用聲音位準設備和錄音設備之後，員工的聲音會給客戶留下更好的印象。

解譯 | 在閱讀文章之前，先要預覽題目，然後再帶著問題有針對性地閱讀文章。第 1 題是詞義辨析，第 2 題是判斷正誤，第 3 題是文意理解，第 4 題是概括主旨。理解了題目要求之後，閱讀全文，依次作答。

第 1 題是考形容詞 strident 的同義字。選項 (A) 意為「尖銳的，刺耳的」，選項 (B) 意為「愉快的」，選項 (C) 意為「舒適的」，選項 (D) 意為「厭煩的」。根據第 1 段第 2 句內容可知，strident 在文中意為「尖銳的」，所以選 (A)。

第 2 題是判斷正誤，考的是細節，問的是哪一項敘述是錯誤的。根據第 3 段第 2 句內容「But people's voice can be strengthened or improved through therapy, coaching or feedback.」可知，透過治療、訓練或是回饋資訊，人們的聲音可以得到加強或是改善。選項 (C) 則是說，人們的聲音無法改善或是加強，與文意不符。同樣，此題也可以用排除法來解答。第 2 段首句內容與選項 (A) 相符，第 1 段首句內容與選項 (B) 相符，第 2 段第 4 句內容與選項 (D) 相符。這三個選項的敘述都是正確的，可以排除。所以選 (C)。

第 3 題是文意理解，問的是影響人們說話方式的因素。可以定位於第 2 段。根據最後兩句內容可知，聲音、性別、種族、年齡和文化背景，都會影響人們的說話方式。選項 (A) 意為「聲音」，選項 (B) 意為「文化背景」，選項 (D) 意為「種族」，與文意相符。選項 (C) 意為「婚姻狀況」，在文中找不到相關敘述。所以選 (C)。

第 4 題是概括主旨。文中有明確的主旨句，本篇結構是先總述後分述，第 1 段可以視為主旨段。根據第 1 段內容可知，文章主旨是，說話聲音重於內容，與選項 (A) 敘述相符。所以選 (A)。

解答 & 技巧 | **01 (A)**　**02 (C)**　**03 (C)**　**04 (A)**

適用 TIP 1　適用 TIP 2　適用 TIP 3　適用 TIP 7　適用 TIP 10
適用 TIP 11　適用 TIP 12　適用 TIP 13　適用 TIP 14　適用 TIP 15

DAY 8

> **補充**
>
> raspy ⓐ 粗嘎刺耳的；strident ⓐ 尖銳刺耳的；distractibility ⓝ 注意力分散；
> breathy ⓐ 微弱的，不清晰的；intolerable ⓐ 難以容忍的

> **7,000 單字**
>
> - voice [vɔɪs] ⓝ 1 聲音
> - exceed [ɪkˋsid] ⓥ 5 超過
> - enhance [ɪnˋhæns] ⓥ 6 提高
> - promotion [prəˋmoʃən] ⓝ 4 晉升
> - tone [ton] ⓝ 1 聲音，語調
> - speaker [ˋspikə] ⓝ 2 說話者
> - tense [tɛns] ⓐ 4 緊張的
> - sociable [ˋsoʃəbl] ⓐ 6 好交際的
> - president [ˋprɛzədənt] ⓝ 2 總裁
> - speak [spik] ⓥ 1 說
> - gender [ˋdʒɛndə] ⓝ 5 性別
> - strengthen [ˋstrɛŋθən] ⓥ 4 加強
> - therapy [ˋθɛrəpɪ] ⓝ 6 治療
> - coach [kotʃ] ⓥ 2 訓練
> - audio [ˋɔdɪo] ⓐ 4 聲音的

Part 1
詞彙題
Day 8
完成 25%

Part 2
綜合測驗
Day 8
完成 50%

Part 3
文意選填
Day 8
完成 75%

Part 4
閱讀測驗
Day 8
完成 100%

MEMO

Seeking the love of your life online may not be the most romantic way, but it may lead to a happier and longer marriage than getting together through more traditional ways. A study has shown that people who meet and fall in love through cyberspace are less likely to separate or divorce than those who begin through friends or colleagues. This is because the former may have put a higher motivation to find love.

The psychologists have studied 20,000 people who are married and asked them a series of questions about their happiness. The results show that over a third of people have met their spouses online and lived a happier marriage life. They often communicate with each other via chat rooms and social networking sites. In contrast, people who meet and get married through work, bars, clubs or dates are among the least satisfied, and they are more likely to end their relationship.

It seems that people who meet online for the first time are more likely to see each other again because they share more information about themselves online. There indeed exists much anonymity online, and some of the information may be mendacious. However, these lies are mainly white lies about weight and height.

Currently more and more people surf the Internet. Take the UK for example. More than 5.7 million people in the UK have logged on to the Internet to chat or date with others. There is a 22 percent increase than that of the same month last year. The Internet has been popular with people who are among the 25-to-34 age group, and is becoming increasingly attractive to the older generation.

01 The word "cyberspace" in the first paragraph is closest in meaning to _____.

(A) computer

(B) Internet

(C) keyboard

(D) mouse

02 We can learn from the third paragraph that _____.

(A) online daters may be likely to meet each other again after the first meeting

(B) the white lies are seldom about weight and height

(C) all the information online are mendacious

(D) there exists no anonymity online

03 Which one of the following statements is false?

(A) Meeting the love of your life may lead to a happy marriage.

(B) People who get married in traditional ways may be likely to end their relationship.

(C) Websites are quite popular among the 25-to-34 age group.

(D) The older generation is indifferent to the Internet.

04 What is the main idea of the passage?

(A) How to surf the Internet.

(B) Seeking happiness in marriage.

(C) Finding Mr. or Mrs. Right online.

(D) Advantages of the Internet.

DAY
8

Part 1
詞
彙
題
Day 8
完成 25%

Part 2
綜
合
測
驗
Day 8
完成 50%

Part 3
文
意
選
填
Day 8
完成 75%

Part 4
閱
讀
測
驗
Day 8
完成 100%

中譯 | 透過網路尋找生命中的愛人，也許不是最浪漫的方式，但是，與那些透過傳統方式尋找愛人的婚姻相比，這也許會促成更加幸福、長久的婚姻生活。研究顯示，相較於那些從朋友或是同事開始發展的戀人，透過網路空間結識並相愛的人，較不會分手或是離婚。這種是因為，前者尋找愛情積極度更高。

心理學家對兩萬名已婚人士進行了研究，並且就幸福感向他們提出了一系列問題。結果顯示，超過三分之一的人在網上結識了配偶，並且有著更為幸福的婚姻生活。他們經常透過聊天室和社交網站彼此交流。相反，透過工作、酒吧、俱樂部和約會結識並結婚的人，對婚姻極不滿意，也更有可能分手。

一些其他的研究顯示，初次在網路上結識的人，更有可能再次見面，這是因為他們在網路上分享更多有關自己的資訊。網路的確是匿名性富，有些資訊也可能是虛假的。但是，這些大多是涉及體重和身高的善意謊言。

目前有愈來愈多的人上網。就以英國為例，有五百七十多萬人透過登入網路，同其他人聊天或是約會，與比去年同期相比增長百分之二十二。網路在二十五歲到三十四歲這個年齡層中很流行，對年長之人的吸引力也是逐漸增長。

解譯 | 在閱讀文章之前，先要預覽題目，然後再帶著問題有針對性地閱讀文章。第 1 題是詞義辨析，第 2 題是文意理解，第 3 題是判斷正誤，第 4 題是概括主旨。理解了題目要求之後，閱讀全文，依次作答。

第 1 題是考名詞 cyberspace 的同義字。選項 (A) 意為「電腦」，選項 (B) 意為「網際網路」，選項 (C) 意為「鍵盤」，選項 (D) 意為「滑鼠」。根據第 1 段第 2 句內容可知，名詞 cyberspace 在文中意為「網路空間」，所以選 (B)。

第 2 題是文意理解，問的是根據第 3 段，可以得出什麼結論。根據第 1 句內容可知，初次在網路上結識的人，更有可能再次見面，與選項 (A) 相符。同樣，此題也可以用排除法來解答。根據最後一句內容可知，善意的謊言大多是涉及體重和身高，而不是甚少涉及，排除選項 (B)；根據第 2 句內容可知，網路上的確是有很多匿名者，而不是沒有匿名現象，排除選項 (C)；有些資訊可能是虛假的，而不是所有資訊都是虛假的，排除選項 (D)。所以選 (A)。

第 3 題是判斷正誤，考的是細節，問的是哪一項敘述是錯誤的。根據第 4 段最後一句內容「The Internet... is becoming increasingly attractive to the older generation.」可知，網路對年長之人的吸引力是逐漸增長的。選項 (D) 則是說，年長之人對於網路漠不關心，與文意不符。同樣，此題也可以用排除法來解答。第 1 段第 1 句內容與選項 (A) 相符，第 2 段最後一句內容與選項 (B) 相符，第 4 段最後一句內容與選項 (C) 相符。這三個選項的敘述都是正確的，可以排除。所以選 (D)。

第 4 題是概括主旨。文中並沒有明顯的主旨句，需要根據各段內容加以概括。第 1 段是由網路情緣而引出話題，第 2 段講述的是有關已婚人士幸福感的研究結果，第 3 段講述的是透過網路約會更有發展的可能，第 4 段講述的是網路日益流行。由此可知，短文內容是簡述網路情緣，所以選 (C)。

解答&技巧 | **01** (B)　**02** (A)　**03** (D)　**04** (C)

適用 TIP 1　適用 TIP 2　適用 TIP 3　適用 TIP 7　適用 TIP 10
適用 TIP 11　適用 TIP 12　適用 TIP 13　適用 TIP 14　適用 TIP 15

DAY
8

Part 1
詞
彙
題

Day 8
完成 25%

Part 2
綜
合
測
驗

Day 8
完成 50%

Part 3
文
意
選
填

Day 8
完成 75%

Part 4
閱
讀
測
驗

Day 8
完成 100%

補充

online ad 線上地；anonymity n 匿名；mendacious a 虛假的，撒謊的；mainly ad 主要地；increasingly ad 逐漸地，日益地

7,000 單字

- may [me] v 1 也許
- romantic [rə`mæntɪk] a 3 浪漫的
- traditional [trə`dɪʃən] a 2 傳統的
- those [ðoz] pron 1 那些
- motivation [͵motə`veʃən] n 4 動機
- get [gɛt] v 1 變得，達到
- marry [`mærɪ] v 1 結婚
- bar [bɑr] n 1 酒吧

- lie [laɪ] n 1 謊話
- white [hwaɪt] a 1 白色的，無害的
- more [mor] pron 1 更多
- surf [sɜf] v 4 瀏覽
- than [ðæn] prep 1 比
- log [lɔg] v 2 註冊，登記
- with [wɪð] prep 1 和，與

MEMO

DAY 9

The best way to gain self-confidence is to do what you are afraid to do.
— *William Jennings Bryan*

獲得自信的最好方法是做你不敢做的事。
——威廉・詹寧斯・布萊恩

▶ **Part 1** | 詞 彙 題

▶ **Part 2** | 綜合測驗

▶ **Part 3** | 文意選填

▶ **Part 4** | 閱讀測驗

Part 1 詞彙題 | Vocabulary Questions

01 The two hairdressers were _____ in each other's ears so that I could not listen clearly to them.

(A) enlightening　　(B) whispering
(C) enacting　　(D) dooming

中譯｜那兩個髮型師在低聲耳語，我無法聽清楚他們在說些什麼。

解說｜四個選項皆為動詞。依據題意，應該是「髮型師在低聲耳語」，選項 (B) whispering 表示「低聲」，符合題意，其他三個選項都不符合題意。

解答＆技巧｜**(B)** 適用 TIP 1　適用 TIP 4

02 The two people who are playing badminton are Carl and Abby. The former is my neighbor, and the _____ is his sister.

(A) latter　　(B) diverse
(C) disposable　　(D) cumulative

中譯｜那兩個在打羽毛球的人是卡爾和艾碧。前者是我的鄰居，而後者是他的妹妹。

解說｜四個選項皆為形容詞。依據題意，應該是「後者是他的妹妹」，選項 (A) latter 表示「後者的」，與 former 相對應，符合題意。

解答＆技巧｜**(A)** 適用 TIP 2　適用 TIP 4

03 As a _____ businessman, he usually donates money to children living in rural areas in order to help them build schools.

(A) deadly　　(B) diplomatic
(C) disciplinary　　(D) wealthy

中譯｜作為一個富有的商人，他經常捐錢給農村的孩子，來幫助他們建造學校。

解說｜四個選項皆為形容詞。依據題意，應該是「富有的商人」，選項 (D) wealthy 表示「富有的」，符合題意，其他三個選項都不符合題意。

解答＆技巧｜**(D)** 適用 TIP 1　適用 TIP 4

04 Professor Wang is well known for his contributions to the field of economics. He has been _____ to help the government with its financial reform programs.

【100年指考英文】

(A) recruited　　　　(B) contradicted

(C) mediated　　　　(D) discharged

中譯｜王教授因在經濟學領域做出的貢獻而出名，政府聘請他來幫忙處理金融改革方案。

解說｜四個選項皆為動詞。依據題意，應該是「政府聘請他來幫忙處理金融改革方案」，選項 (A) recruited 表示「雇用，聘請」，符合題意。

解答&技巧｜**(A)** 適用 TIP 1　適用 TIP 4

> **補充**
> help with ph 在某方面幫忙
> financial reform ph 金融改革
>
> **7,000 單字**
> • known [non] a 6 知名的
> • recruit [rɪ`krut] v 6 聘用
> • contradict [ˌkɑntrə`dɪkt] v 6 反駁
> • mediate [`midɪˌet] v 5 調解
> • discharge [dɪs`tʃɑrdʒ] v 6 解雇

---

05 Reading the Bible is a _____ thing for the young man, so he feels quite boring.

(A) dreary　　　　(B) disgraceful

(C) edible　　　　(D) eloquent

中譯｜對於這個年輕人來說，讀聖經是一件枯燥乏味的事情，所以他感到很無聊。

解說｜四個選項皆為形容詞。依據題意，應該是「枯燥乏味的事情」，選項 (A) dreary 表示「枯燥乏味的」，符合題意，其他三個選項都不符合題意。

解答&技巧｜**(A)** 適用 TIP 3　適用 TIP 4

> **補充**
> feel boring ph 感到無聊
>
> **7,000 單字**
> • Bible [`baɪbl] n 3 聖經
> • dreary [`drɪərɪ] a 6 沉悶的
> • disgraceful [dɪs`gresfəl] a 6 可恥的
> • edible [`ɛdəbl] a 6 可食用的
> • eloquent [`ɛləkwənt] a 6 雄辯的

---

06 Compared with the barren soil, the farm crops can flourish better in the _____ one.

(A) wicked　　　　(B) artistic

(C) dread　　　　(D) fertile

中譯｜相較於那些貧瘠的土壤，農作物在這些肥沃的土壤中能夠生長得更加茂盛。

解說｜四個選項皆為形容詞。依據題意，應該是「在這些肥沃的土壤中能夠生長得更加茂盛」，選項 (D) fertile 表示「肥沃的」，符合題意。

解答&技巧｜**(D)** 適用 TIP 1　適用 TIP 4

> **補充**
> farm crop ph 農作物
>
> **7,000 單字**
> • flourish [`flɜɪʃ] v 5 茂盛
> • wicked [`wɪkɪd] a 3 邪惡的
> • artistic [ar`tɪstɪk] a 4 藝術的
> • dread [drɛd] a 4 可怕的
> • fertile [`fɜtl] a 4 肥沃的

DAY 9

Part 1
詞彙題
Day 9
完成 25%

Part 2
綜合測驗
Day 9
完成 50%

Part 3
文意選填
Day 9
完成 75%

Part 4
閱讀測驗
Day 9
完成 100%

07 Mother prepared _____ breakfast for us, including yogurt, fried eggs, sandwiches and fruit.

(A) cold 　　(B) delicious

(C) dear 　　(D) glad

補充
fried egg ph 煎蛋

7,000 單字
• yogurt [ˈjogɚt] n 4 優酪乳
• cold [kold] a 1 冷的
• delicious [dɪˈlɪʃəs] a 5 美味的
• dear [dɪr] a 1 親愛的
• glad [glæd] a 1 高興的

中譯 | 媽媽為我們準備了美味的早餐，有優酪乳、煎蛋、三明治和水果。

解說 | 四個選項皆為形容詞。依據題意，應該是「準備了美味的早餐」，選項 (B) delicious 表示「美味的」，符合題意。

解答&技巧 | **(B)** 適用 TIP 3 適用 TIP 4

---

08 I have learned to make a cake, so I know the main _____ of a cake are flour, eggs, butter and sugar.

(A) ingredients 　　(B) ghosts

(C) geese 　　(D) haircuts

補充
make a cake ph 做蛋糕

7,000 單字
• flour [flaʊr] n 2 麵粉
• ingredient [ɪnˈgridɪənt] n 4 原料
• ghost [gost] n 1 鬼
• goose [gus] n 1 鵝
• haircut [ˈhɛrˌkʌt] n 1 理髮

中譯 | 我學過做蛋糕，所以知道蛋糕的原料主要有麵粉、雞蛋、奶油和糖。

解說 | 四個選項皆為名詞。依據題意，應該是「蛋糕的原料」，選項 (A) ingredients 表示「原料」，符合題意，是正確選項。

解答&技巧 | **(A)** 適用 TIP 3 適用 TIP 4

---

09 You are so _____ to give your money to the stranger because he is actually a deceiver.

(A) lazy 　　(B) lucky

(C) foolish 　　(D) near

補充
give to ph 給予

7,000 單字
• deceiver [dɪˈsivɚ] n 5 騙子
• lazy [ˈlezɪ] a 1 懶惰的
• lucky [ˈlʌkɪ] a 1 幸運的
• foolish [ˈfulɪʃ] a 2 愚蠢的
• near [nɪr] a 1 近的

中譯 | 你把錢給那個陌生人真是太愚蠢了，因為他實際上就是一個騙子。

解說 | 四個選項皆為形容詞。依據題意，應該是「把錢給那個陌生人太愚蠢」，選項 (C) foolish 表示「愚蠢的」，符合題意，其他三個選項都不符合題意。

解答&技巧 | **(C)** 適用 TIP 1 適用 TIP 4

10 After a fierce competition, he _____ in getting into the finals and won the third prize.

(A) noted　　　　　　　(B) succeeded

(C) rode　　　　　　　(D) sailed

DAY 9

Part 1
詞彙題
Day 9
完成 25%

Part 2
綜合測驗
Day 9
完成 50%

Part 3
文意選填
Day 9
完成 75%

Part 4
閱讀測驗
Day 9
完成 100%

補充
succeed in ph 在～方面成功

7,000 單字
- fierce [fɪrs] a 4 激烈的
- note [not] v 1 記錄
- succeed [sək`sid] v 2 成功
- ride [raɪd] v 1 騎
- sail [sel] v 1 航行

中譯 | 經過激烈的競爭，他成功地進入了決賽，並贏得了第三名。

解說 | 四個選項皆為動詞。依據題意，應該是「成功地進入了決賽」，選項 (B) succeeded 表示「成功」，而片語 succeed in doing sth. 表示「成功做某事」，符合題意。

解答＆技巧 | **(B)** 適用 TIP 2　適用 TIP 4

---

11 The old man sat in an armchair and _____ at the sky, as if he had been lost in thought.

(A) sold　　　　　　　(B) shot

(C) gazed　　　　　　(D) sang

補充
lost in thought ph 陷入沉思

7,000 單字
- armchair [`ɑrm.tʃɛr] n 2 扶手椅
- sell [sɛl] v 1 賣
- shoot [ʃut] v 2 射擊
- gaze [gez] v 4 凝視
- sing [sɪŋ] v 1 唱歌

中譯 | 這位老人坐在扶手椅上，凝視著天空，仿佛陷入了沉思。

解說 | 四個選項皆為動詞。依據題意，應該是「凝視著天空」，選項 (C) gazed 表示「凝視」，符合題意，其他三個選項都不符合題意。

解答＆技巧 | **(C)** 適用 TIP 1　適用 TIP 4

---

12 If the government does not _____ the slavery, the slaves will unite together to resist the government.

(A) state　　　　　　　(B) win

(C) worry　　　　　　(D) abolish

補充
unite together ph 團結起來

7,000 單字
- unite [ju`naɪt] v 3 聯合
- state [stet] v 1 陳述
- win [wɪn] v 1 贏得
- worry [`wɝɪ] v 1 擔心
- abolish [ə`bɑlɪʃ] v 5 廢除

中譯 | 如果政府不廢除奴隸制，奴隸們就會團結起來共同反抗政府。

解說 | 本題是表示假設的條件句。依據題意，應該是「廢除奴隸制」，選項 (D) abolish 表示「廢除」，符合題意，是正確選項。

解答＆技巧 | **(D)** 適用 TIP 3　適用 TIP 4

13 The drunkard said that he saw a spacecraft and aliens in the mountain last night, which was so _____.

(A) absurd (B) worst
(C) yucky (D) alive

補充
in the mountain ph 在山上

7,000 單字
• drunkard [ˋdrʌŋkəd] n 6 醉漢
• absurd [əbˋsɝd] a 5 荒謬的
• worst [wɝst] a 1 最壞的
• yucky [ˋjʌkɪ] a 1 噁心的
• alive [əˋlaɪv] a 2 活著的

中譯｜那個酒鬼說，昨天晚上他在山上看到了太空船和外星人，這真荒唐。

解說｜四個選項皆為形容詞。依據題意，應該是「荒唐」，選項 (A) absurd 表示「荒謬的」，符合題意，其他三個選項都不符合題意。

解答＆技巧｜**(A)** 適用 TIP 1 適用 TIP 4

14 After a continuous interrogation for seven days, the goal keeper finally _____ that he was the murderer.

(A) bored (B) bet
(C) acknowledged (D) bounded

補充
goal keeper ph 守門員

7,000 單字
• interrogation [ɪn͵tɛrəˋgeʃən] n 6 審問
• bore [bor] v 3 鑽孔
• bet [bɛt] v 2 打賭
• acknowledge [əkˋnɑlɪdʒ] v 5 承認
• bound [baʊnd] v 5 束縛

中譯｜經過七天的連續審問，那位守門員終於承認他就是殺人兇手。

解說｜四個選項皆為動詞。依據題意，應該是「守門員承認他是殺人兇手」，選項 (C) acknowledged 表示「承認」，符合題意，其他三個選項都不符合題意。

解答＆技巧｜**(C)** 適用 TIP 1 適用 TIP 4

15 As a(an) _____ boy, you are only fifteen years old and should never come into contact with drugs.

(A) blank (B) adolescent
(C) costly (D) dishonest

補充
come into contact with
ph 接觸，聯繫

7,000 單字
• fifteen [ˋfɪfˋtin] num 1 十五
• blank [blæŋk] a 2 空白的
• adolescent [͵ædlˋɛsnt] a 5 青春期的
• costly [ˋkɔstlɪ] a 2 昂貴的
• dishonest [dɪsˋɑnɪst] a 2 不誠實的

中譯｜身為一個青春期男孩，你只有十五歲，絕對不能接觸毒品。

解說｜四個選項皆為形容詞。依據題意，應該是「青春期男孩」，選項 (B) adolescent 表示「青春期的」，符合題意，其他三個選項都不符合題意。

解答＆技巧｜**(B)** 適用 TIP 1 適用 TIP 4

DAY
9

Part 1
詞
彙
題
Day 9
完成 25%

Part 2
綜
合
測
驗
Day 9
完成 50%

Part 3
文
意
選
填
Day 9
完成 75%

Part 4
閱
讀
測
驗
Day 9
完成 100%

16 According to the meeting _____, the executives are scheduled to discuss the reform of the company in tomorrow's meeting.

(A) dinosaur   (B) dictionary
(C) agenda   (D) ending

> 補充
> meeting agenda ph 會議議程
>
> 7,000 單字
> • executive [ɪgˋzɛkjutɪv] n 5 行政主管
> • dinosaur [ˋdaɪnəˌsɔr] n 2 恐龍
> • dictionary [ˋdɪkʃənˌɛrɪ] n 2 字典
> • agenda [əˋdʒɛndə] n 5 議程
> • ending [ˋɛndɪŋ] n 2 結局

中譯｜根據會議議程，行政主管們計畫在明天的會議上討論公司的改革問題。

解說｜四個選項皆為名詞。依據題意，應該是「根據會議議程」，選項 (C) agenda 表示「議程」，符合題意，是正確選項。

解答＆技巧｜**(C)** 適用 TIP 3 適用 TIP 4

---

17 He has suffered from a severe seafood _____; once he eats seafood, he will fall in a faint at once.

(A) allergy   (B) dragon
(C) downtown   (D) eraser

> 補充
> fall in a faint ph 暈倒
>
> 7,000 單字
> • seafood [ˋsiˌfud] n 2 海鮮
> • allergy [ˋælədʒɪ] n 5 過敏症
> • dragon [ˋdrægən] n 2 龍
> • downtown [ˌdaunˋtaun] n 2 市中心
> • eraser [ɪˋresɚ] n 2 橡皮擦

中譯｜他對海鮮嚴重過敏，一旦吃了海鮮，就會立即暈倒。

解說｜四個選項皆為名詞。依據題意，應該是「對海鮮嚴重過敏」，選項 (A) allergy 表示「過敏症」，符合題意，其他三個選項都不符合題意。

解答＆技巧｜**(A)** 適用 TIP 3 適用 TIP 4

---

18 The soil in this area is so _____ that most of the walnut trees are not able to grow.

(A) fool   (B) gentle
(C) golden   (D) barren

> 補充
> walnut tree ph 核桃樹
>
> 7,000 單字
> • walnut [ˋwɔlnət] n 4 核桃
> • fool [ful] a 2 愚蠢的
> • gentle [ˋdʒɛntl] a 2 溫柔的
> • golden [ˋgoldn] a 2 金色的
> • barren [ˋbærən] a 5 貧瘠的

中譯｜這個地區的土壤過於貧瘠，以致於大多數的核桃樹都無法生長。

解說｜四個選項皆為形容詞。依據題意，應該是「土壤過於貧瘠」，選項 (D) barren 表示「貧瘠的」，符合題意，其他三個選項都不符合題意。

解答＆技巧｜**(D)** 適用 TIP 3 適用 TIP 4

19 In order to _____ her bedroom, she hung purple curtains on the window and decorated them with colored ribbon.

(A) beautify   (B) hammer

(C) handle   (D) hurry

中譯｜為了美化自己的臥室，她在窗戶上懸掛了紫色的窗簾，並用一些彩帶來裝飾。

解說｜四個選項皆為動詞。依據題意，應該是「美化自己的臥室」，選項 (A) beautify 表示「美化」，符合題意，其他三個選項都不符合題意。

解答＆技巧｜**(A)** 適用 TIP 1　適用 TIP 4

> 補充
> colored ribbon ph 彩帶
>
> 7,000 單字
> • ribbon [ˈrɪbən] n 3 緞帶
> • beautify [ˈbjutəˌfaɪ] v 5 美化
> • hammer [ˈhæmɚ] v 2 敲打
> • handle [ˈhændl] v 2 處理
> • hurry [ˈhɝɪ] v 2 趕快

---

20 In order to _____ his horizon, he visited more than 20 countries in five years and enjoyed many places of interest.

(A) jog   (B) lap

(C) broaden   (D) lick

中譯｜為了拓寬自己的視野，他在五年內參觀了二十多個國家，並且欣賞了很多名勝古跡。

解說｜四個選項皆為動詞。依據題意，應該是「拓寬自己的視野」，選項 (C) broaden 表示「拓寬」，符合題意，是正確選項。

解答＆技巧｜**(C)** 適用 TIP 3　適用 TIP 4

> 補充
> places of interest ph 名勝古跡
>
> 7,000 單字
> • horizon [həˈraɪzn] n 4 視野
> • jog [dʒɑg] v 2 慢跑
> • lap [læp] v 2 輕拍
> • broaden [ˈbrɔdn] v 5 拓寬
> • lick [lɪk] v 2 舔

---

21 The helicopters _____ over the sea, looking for the divers who had been missing for more than 30 hours.　【101年指考英文】

(A) nodded   (B) rustled

(C) strolled   (D) hovered

中譯｜直升機在大海上空盤旋，尋找那些已經失蹤三十多個小時的潛水夫。

解說｜四個選項皆為動詞。依據題意，應該是「直升機在大海上空盤旋」，選項 (D) hovered 表示「盤旋」，符合題意，其他三個選項都不符合題意。

解答＆技巧｜**(D)** 適用 TIP 3　適用 TIP 4

> 補充
> hover over ph 在～盤旋
> look for ph 尋找
>
> 7,000 單字
> • helicopter [ˈhɛlɪkɑptɚ] n 4 直升機
> • nod [nɑd] v 2 點頭
> • rustle [ˈrʌsl] v 5 使沙沙作響
> • stroll [strol] v 5 漫步
> • hover [ˈhʌvɚ] v 5 盤旋

22 As an experienced _____, she has worked in the nursing home for four years to take care of those poor old men.

(A) napkin   (B) caretaker

(C) motorcycle   (D) farm

補充
nursing home ph 養老院

7,000 單字
- four [for] num 1 四
- napkin [ˋnæpkɪn] n 2 餐巾
- caretaker [ˋkɛr͵tekɚ] n 5 看護人員
- motorcycle [ˋmotɚ͵saɪkl] n 2 摩托車
- farm [fɑrm] n 1 農場

中譯│作為一名有經驗的看護人員，她已經在養老院裡工作了四年，來照顧那些可憐的老人。

解說│四個選項皆為名詞。依據題意，應該是「有經驗的看護人員」，選項 (B) caretaker 表示「看護人員」，符合題意，是正確選項。

解答＆技巧│**(B)** 適用 TIP 1   適用 TIP 4

---

23 You should be _____ when you make data reports because even a punctuation mark could result in heavy loss.

(A) cautious   (B) neat

(C) naughty   (D) national

補充
heavy loss ph 重大損失

7,000 單字
- punctuation [͵pʌŋktʃuˋeʃən] n 6 標點
- cautious [ˋkɔʃəs] a 5 謹慎的
- neat [nit] a 2 靈巧的
- naughty [ˋnɔtɪ] a 2 頑皮的
- national [ˋnæʃən!] a 2 國家的

中譯│你在製作資料報告時要十分謹慎，因為即使一個標點符號也會造成重大損失。

解說│四個選項皆為形容詞。依據題意，應該是「在製作資料報告時要十分謹慎」，選項 (A) cautious 表示「謹慎的」，符合題意，是正確選項。

解答＆技巧│**(A)** 適用 TIP 1   適用 TIP 4

---

24 He _____ to the belief that he is able to receive a doctor's degree and find a high-paying job after graduation.

(A) omits   (B) pardons

(C) prays   (D) clings

補充
cling to ph 堅持

7,000 單字
- graduation [͵grædʒuˋeʃən] n 4 畢業
- omit [oˋmɪt] v 2 省略
- pardon [ˋpɑrdn̩] v 2 原諒
- pray [pre] v 2 祈禱
- cling [klɪŋ] v 5 堅持

中譯│他堅信他能夠獲得博士學位，並且在畢業後找到一份高薪工作。

解說│四個選項皆為動詞。依據題意，應該是「他堅信他能夠獲得博士學位」，選項 (D) clings 表示「堅持」，符合題意，是正確答案。

解答＆技巧│**(D)** 適用 TIP 2   適用 TIP 4

DAY
9

Part 1
詞彙題
Day 9
完成 25%

Part 2
綜合測驗
Day 9
完成 50%

Part 3
文意選填
Day 9
完成 75%

Part 4
閱讀測驗
Day 9
完成 100%

Part 2 綜合測驗 | Comprehensive Questions

1▶

We could not exactly know how many people with disabilities there are in the world, but we should know that when we get older, most of us would become __01__ of hearing or vision-impaired, which is also a kind of disablement.

Disablement can appear __02__ many forms and occur at any time of life. Some people are born with disabilities, and some people may become disabled in accidents. Other people may become disabled as a result of physical or mental illness. And __03__ time goes by, all these kinds of illness can become worse.

People with disabilities may face many physical __04__ . For example, when they go shopping or visit friends, they are not able to get up steps, get on or off the bus, and take the things themselves. But what's the most important is their attitude __05__ the disablement. No matter how serious the illness or trouble may be, people with disabilities should be full of confidence in their life and use their ability to overcome all the barriers.

01 _____ (A) easy (B) thick
(C) used (D) hard

02 _____ (A) in (B) of
(C) for (D) on

03 _____ (A) when (B) where
(C) as (D) with

04 _____ (A) voters (B) barriers
(C) wounds (D) youths

05 _____ (A) over (B) upon
(C) into (D) towards

DAY
9

Part 1
詞
彙
題
Day 9
完成 25%

Part 2
綜
合
測
驗
Day 9
完成 50%

Part 3
文
意
選
填
Day 9
完成 75%

Part 4
閱
讀
測
驗
Day 9
完成 100%

中譯｜我們無法確切知道世界上有多少身心障礙者，但是我們應該知道當我們年老時，我們大多數人會變得重聽或視力受損，這也是一種障礙。

身心障礙能夠以很多形式出現，並發生在一生中的任何時候。一些人天生就有缺陷，而一些人是由於意外而導致損傷不全。其他人可能是由於身體或心理上的疾病所引起。隨著時間的流逝，所有這些疾病將會變得更加嚴重。

身心障礙者可能會面臨許多身體上的障礙。例如，當他們去購物或者拜訪朋友時，他們不能夠上樓梯、上下公車，以及自己拿東西。但是最重要的是他們對於身心障礙的態度。不管疾病或麻煩多麼嚴重，身心障礙者都應該在生活中充滿信心，運用他們的能力去克服所有的障礙。

解說｜本篇短文的主旨是講述身心障礙產生的原因以及身心障礙者遇到的不便或困難。第 1 題的四個選項都是形容詞。依據題意，一旦人年紀大了，聽覺和視覺將很難變得清楚，hard 表示「困難的」，符合題意，所以正確選擇為 (D)。第 2 題考介系詞的用法。「以～形式」通常表達為 in... form，要用介系詞 in，所以最符合題意的選項是 (A)。第 3 題考連接詞的用法。依據題意，空格處的選項在句中引導伴隨副詞，根據意思可知，as 表示「隨著，伴隨」符合題意，即正確選項是 (C)。第 4 題的四個選項都是名詞，將其一一代入空格，physical barriers 表示「身體障礙」符合文中的意思，所以選項 (B) 符合題意。第 5 題考介系詞的用法。attitude 通常與介系詞 towards 連用，表示「對～的態度」，所以選 (D)。

解答&技巧｜ 01 (D)　02 (A)　03 (C)　04 (B)　05 (D)

適用 TIP 2　適用 TIP 7　適用 TIP 8　適用 TIP 11

補充
disability ⓝ 身心障礙；clearly ⓐⓓ 清晰地；disablement ⓝ 失能；disabled ⓐ 身心障礙的；as a result of ⓟⓗ 由於

7,000 單字
- vision [ˋvɪʒən] ⓝ 3 視力
- appear [əˋpɪr] ⓥ 1 出現
- any [ˋɛnɪ] ⓐ 1 任何的
- mental [ˋmɛnt!] ⓐ 3 精神的
- worse [wɝs] ⓐ 1 更糟的
- bus [bʌs] ⓝ 1 公共汽車
- confidence [ˋkɑnfədəns] ⓝ 4 自信
- ability [əˋbɪlətɪ] ⓝ 2 能力
- all [ɔl] ⓐ 1 所有的
- barrier [ˋbærɪr] ⓝ 4 障礙
- thick [θɪk] ⓐ 2 厚的
- hard [hɑrd] ⓝ 1 困難的
- voter [ˋvotɚ] ⓝ 2 選舉人
- wound [waund] ⓝ 2 傷口
- youth [juθ] ⓝ 2 青年

When people suddenly go abroad, they are most likely to __01__ culture shock. Once it occurs, newcomers may become anxious because they are not familiar with the foreign languages and cultures and could not understand the foreigners' behavior in daily life. Later, they find that when people say "yes," it may not mean __02__ , and more and more things are out of __03__ . They even have no idea when to shake hands and when to start conversations, or how to approach a stranger. Their life is filled with bewilderment and disorientation, which makes them feel afraid and frustrated. And what's __04__ , they are even deprived of some common sense, including understanding a transportation system, knowing how to make friends and __05__ for the university classes. After staying abroad for a period of time, some people begin to doubt about their own cultures and values. They make an attempt to identify with the new culture in order to be accepted by the foreign people.

01 _____ (A) achieve   (B) experience
        (C) bait   (D) erase

02 _____ (A) election   (B) entry
        (C) condition   (D) agreement

03 _____ (A) control   (B) cradle
        (C) credit   (D) cycle

04 _____ (A) more   (B) less
        (C) worse   (D) heavier

05 _____ (A) define   (B) register
        (C) dine   (D) explode

中譯 | 當人們突然出國時，他們很可能經歷文化衝擊。一旦發生了文化衝擊，新來者就可能會變得焦慮擔憂，因為他們不熟悉外國語言和文化，無法了解外國人在日常生活中的行為舉止。之後，他們發現當人們說 yes 時，可能並不意味著同意，而愈來愈多的事情超出了他們的控制。他們甚至不知道何時握手、何時開始談話，或者如何接近一個陌生人。他們的生活充滿了慌亂和迷惑，這使他們感到害怕、挫敗。更糟糕的是，他們甚至缺乏常識，包括了解運輸系統，知道如何交朋友以及報名參加大學課程。在國外待了一段時間之後，一些人開始懷疑他們自己的文化和價值觀。他們試圖認同新文化以得到外國人的認同。

解說 | 本篇短文的主旨是「文化衝擊」，主要講述了身處國外的人所面臨的文化方面的問題。第 1 題的四個選項都是動詞。依據題意，應該是經歷文化衝擊，experience 作動詞可以表示「經歷」，所以正確選擇為 (B)。第 2 題考單字的意思。yes 的意思是「是」，表示同意，即 agreement，所以最符合題意的選項是 (D)。第 3 題考介系詞片語的用法。將四個選項一一代入，out of control 表示「失去控制」符合題意，即正確選項是 (A)。第 4 題根據上下文的內容，空格後面所講的內容是更糟糕的情況，固定表達 what's worse 表示「更糟糕的是」，所以選項 (C) 符合題意。第 5 題依據題意，應該是報名參加大學課程，register for 表示「註冊，報名參加」符合題意，所以選 (B)。

解答＆技巧 | 01 (B)　02 (D)　03 (A)　04 (C)　05 (B)

適用 TIP 1　適用 TIP 2　適用 TIP 7　適用 TIP 11

補充
go abroad ph 出國；newcomer n 新來者；bewilderment n 迷惑；disorientation n 迷失方向；frustrated a 挫敗的

7,000 單字
- shock [ʃɑk] n 2 震驚
- daily [ˈdelɪ] a 2 日常的
- yes [jɛs] n 1 是
- shake [ʃek] v 1 搖動
- stranger [ˈstrendʒɚ] n 2 陌生人
- sense [sɛns] n 1 道理
- bait [bet] v 3 引誘
- erase [ɪˈres] v 3 抹去
- election [ɪˈlɛkʃən] n 3 選舉
- entry [ˈɛntrɪ] n 3 進入
- cradle [ˈkredl] n 3 搖籃
- credit [ˈkrɛdɪt] n 3 信用
- register [ˈrɛdʒɪstɚ] v 4 登記
- dine [daɪn] v 3 用餐
- explode [ɪkˈsplod] v 3 使爆炸

DAY 9
Part 1
詞彙題
Day 9
完成 25%

Part 2
綜合測驗
Day 9
完成 50%

Part 3
文意選填
Day 9
完成 75%

Part 4
閱讀測驗
Day 9
完成 100%

Compared with the societies where people are similar in many ways, social change is more likely to __01__ in societies where different kinds of people are mixed together because there are more different ways __02__ looking at things present in them. The more ideas, disagreements in interest, and groups and organizations with different beliefs there are in a society, the more likely it will have social change. In addition, greater worldly interest and tolerance will also be contained in a mixed society. It is all these factors that promote social change in a society.

In __03__ , social change is less unlikely to occur in a society where people are quite similar in many ways. Everything seems to be the same; thus people will have little or no opportunity to change. Even if the conditions may not be __04__ , they still become customary and undisputed to them. Besides, social change is also likely to occur more frequently in the material __05__ of the culture.

01 _____ (A) fade   (B) faint
         (C) occur   (D) hesitate

02 _____ (A) of   (B) to
         (C) in   (D) on

03 _____ (A) hand   (B) detail
         (C) contrast   (D) time

04 _____ (A) handy   (B) satisfactory
         (C) inferior   (D) liberal

05 _____ (A) lens   (B) justices
         (C) minorities   (D) aspects

中譯│與那些有著相似人群的社會相比，社會變化更有可能發生在那些不同人群彙集的社會，因為會有更多看待事物的不同方式出現在這裡。一個社會裡的思想、志趣分歧、團體和組織的不同信仰愈多，這個社會就愈有可能發生社會變化。此外，更為廣泛的世俗興趣和寬容也會被包含在一個混合的社會中。所有這些因素促使社會發生社會變化。

相比之下，社會變化不太可能發生在一個有著相似人群的社會中。所有事物看起來都一樣，那麼人們就沒有什麼機會進行改變。即使狀況不令人滿意，他們也變得習慣、無可爭議。此外，社會變化也有可能頻繁地發生在物質文化方面。

解說│本篇短文的主旨是「社會變化」，講述了導致社會變化的因素以及環境。第 1 題的四個選項都是動詞，將其一一代入，應該是發生社會變化，動詞 occur 表示「發生」符合題意，所以正確選擇為 (C)。第 2 題考介系詞的用法。根據所學的知識，way of 表示「～的方式」，是固定搭配，所以最符合題意的選項是 (A)。第 3 題空格處前後兩段內容表達的是相反的含義，此處應該用表示相反意義的介系詞片語。將四個選項一一代入，in contrast 表示「與此相反」符合題意，即正確選項是 (C)。第 4 題的四個選項都是形容詞，就其一一代入，satisfactory 表示「令人滿意的」符合上下文的意思，所以選項 (B) 符合題意。第 5 題考名詞片語的固定用法。依據題意，「物質方面」可以表達為 material aspects，所以選 (D)。

解答&技巧│ 01 (C)　02 (A)　03 (C)　04 (B)　05 (D)

適用 TIP 1　適用 TIP 2　適用 TIP 7　適用 TIP 11

【補充】
social change ph 社會變化；worldly a 世俗的；mixed a 混合的；everything n 一切事物；undisputed a 無可置疑的

【7,000 單字】
- similar [ˈsɪmələ] a 2 相似的
- mix [mɪks] v 2 混合
- look [lʊk] v 1 看
- tolerance [ˈtɑlərəns] n 4 容忍
- seem [sim] v 1 似乎
- customary [ˈkʌstəˌmɛrɪ] a 6 習慣的
- besides [bɪˈsaɪdz] ad 2 此外
- fade [fed] v 3 使褪色
- hesitate [ˈhɛzəˌtet] v 3 猶豫
- detail [ˈditel] n 3 細節
- contrast [ˈkɑnˌtræst] n 4 對比
- handy [ˈhændɪ] a 3 便利的
- liberal [ˈlɪbərəl] a 3 開明的
- justice [ˈdʒʌstɪs] n 3 正義
- minority [maɪˈnɔrətɪ] n 3 少數

④▶ 99 年學測英文

Many people like to drink bottled water because they feel that tap water may not be safe, but is bottled water really any better?

Bottled water is mostly sold in plastic bottles, and that's why it is potentially health __01__ . Processing the plastic can lead to the release of harmful chemical substances into the water contained in the bottles. The chemicals can be absorbed into the body and __02__ physical discomfort, such as stomach cramps and diarrhea.

Health risks can also result from inappropriate storage of bottled water. Bacteria can multiply if the water is kept on the shelves for too long or if it is exposed to heat or direct sunlight. __03__ the information on storage and shipment is not always readily available to consumers, bottled water may not be a better alternative to tap water.

Besides these __04__ issues, bottled water has other disadvantages. It contributes to global warming. An estimated 2.5 million tons of carbon dioxide were generated in 2006 by the production of plastic for bottled water. In addition, bottled water produces an incredible amount of solid __05__ . According to one research, 90% of the bottles used are not recycled and lie for ages in landfills.

01 _____	(A) frightening	(B) threatening
	(C) appealing	(D) promoting
02 _____	(A) cause	(B) causing
	(C) caused	(D) to cause
03 _____	(A) Although	(B) Despite
	(C) Since	(D) So
04 _____	(A) display	(B) production
	(C) shipment	(D) safety
05 _____	(A) waste	(B) resource
	(C) ground	(D) profit

中譯｜ 許多人都喜歡喝瓶裝水，因為他們覺得自來水可能不太安全，但是瓶裝水真的比較好嗎？

瓶裝水大多裝在塑膠瓶裡賣，這就是它潛在健康威脅的原因。塑膠加工的過程會導致有害的化學物質釋放至瓶子裡的水。化學物質被人體所吸收，導致身體不適，如胃痙攣和腹瀉。

不恰當地存儲瓶裝水也可能會導致健康風險。如果水在架子上放置過久，或是曝曬在高溫中或經陽光直射，細菌會開始繁殖。既然消費者不一定能輕易獲得瓶裝水的存儲和裝運資訊，那麼相比於自來水，瓶裝水就不一定是更好的選擇。

除了這些安全問題，瓶裝水還有其他的缺點，就是加劇全球暖化。據估計，二〇〇六年在為瓶裝水而生產塑膠的過程中，就產生了兩百五十萬噸二氧化碳。此外，瓶裝水還產生了數量驚人的固體垃圾。一項調查顯示，百分之九十用過的瓶子都沒有回收利用，而是長久地躺在垃圾掩埋場裡。

解說｜ 本篇短文講述了瓶裝水所存在的安全隱患，呼籲消費者注意。第 1 題考固定片語的搭配。依據題意，應該是健康威脅，可以用動詞 threaten 表示「恐嚇，威脅」，所以正確選擇為 (B)。第 2 題考句子結構。根據所學的文法知識，並列結構的句子中，前後動詞的時態應該保持一致。依據題意，句中的 and 表示並列，動詞 cause 應該和 be 一樣都用動詞原形，因為它們並列位於助動詞 can 之後，所以最符合題意的選項是 (A)。第 3 題考連接詞的用法。依據題意，since 表示「既然」符合上下文的意思，即正確選項是 (C)。第 4 題根據主旨可知，前一部分都是在講瓶裝水的安全問題，所以 safety 符合題意，正確選擇為 (D)。第 5 題考名詞片語的用法。依據題意應該是固體垃圾，即 solid waste，所以選 (A)。

解答＆技巧｜ 01 (B)　02 (A)　03 (C)　04 (D)　05 (A)

適用 TIP 1　適用 TIP 2　適用 TIP 7　適用 TIP 8　適用 TIP 11

補充

bottled ⓐ 瓶裝的；mostly ⓐⓓ 多半地；potentially ⓐⓓ 潛在地；diarrhea ⓝ 腹瀉；
inappropriate ⓐ 不恰當的

7,000 單字

- drink [drɪŋk] ⓥ 1 喝
- tap [tæp] ⓥ 3 水龍頭
- safe [sef] ⓐ 1 安全的
- bottle [ˋbɑtl] ⓝ 2 瓶子
- absorb [əbˋsɔrb] ⓥ 4 吸收
- discomfort [dɪsˋkʌmfət] ⓝ 6 不適
- stomach [ˋstʌmək] ⓝ 2 胃
- cramp [kræmp] ⓝ 6 痙攣
- storage [ˋstorɪdʒ] ⓝ 6 儲存
- bacteria [bækˋtɪrɪə] ⓝ 3 細菌
- multiply [ˋmʌltəplaɪ] ⓥ 2 繁殖
- ton [tʌn] ⓝ 3 噸
- generate [ˋdʒɛnəˏret] ⓥ 6 產生
- frighten [ˋfraɪtn] ⓥ 2 使驚嚇
- threaten [ˋθrɛtn] ⓥ 3 威脅

DAY 9

Part 1
詞
彙
題
Day 9
完成 25%

Part 2
綜
合
測
驗
Day 9
完成 50%

Part 3
文
意
選
填
Day 9
完成 75%

Part 4
閱
讀
測
驗
Day 9
完成 100%

After a busy day of work, our body needs to rest. Sleep would be the best and necessary way for us to __01__ good health because our body needs to recover from the activities of the __02__ day, and then the rest we get from sleep enables our body to prepare well for the next day.

According to the research, four levels of sleep have been found, and each one is a little deeper than the one __03__ . When we fall asleep, our mind slows down, our muscles relax little by little, our heart beats more and more slowly, and we will dream from time to time. Our eyeballs begin to move more quickly though our eyelids are still __04__ .

We can breathe deeply if we have trouble __05__ asleep. Other people believe that drinking warm milk and counting sheeps could help us become drowsy. But we should know that we'd better not eat too much food before sleeping, and little water should be drunk.

01 _____ (A) prevent   (B) pursue
        (C) keep   (D) recognize

02 _____ (A) previous   (B) reliable
        (C) rotten   (D) sincere

03 _____ (A) after   (B) intermediately
        (C) astride   (D) before

04 _____ (A) open   (B) closed
        (C) slippery   (D) stale

05 _____ (A) fall   (B) fell
        (C) falling   (D) to fall

中譯｜經過繁忙工作的一天後，我們的身體需要休息。睡眠對我們來說是保持身體健康的最佳也是最有必要的方式，因為身體需要從前一天的活動中恢復過來，那麼我們透過睡眠得到的休息將會使身體為第二天做好準備。

研究指出，人們已經發現了四個層次的睡眠，每一個層次都要比前一個稍微深。當入睡時，我們的思想變得緩慢，肌肉慢慢放鬆，心臟跳動得愈來愈慢，會時不時地做夢。儘管眼皮仍然緊閉，但是眼球開始更加快速地轉動。

如果入睡困難，我們可以深呼吸。其他人認為喝熱牛奶和數羊能夠幫助我們產生睡意。但是我們應該知道，最好不要在睡前吃太多食物，水也應該少喝。

解說｜本篇短文的主旨是「睡眠」，介紹了睡眠的幾個層次。第 1 題依據題意，應該是睡眠有助於保持身體健康，可以用 keep 表示「保持」，所以正確選擇為 (C)。第 2 題根據上下文的內容，睡眠是為了恢復前一天所消耗的體力，四個選項中，previous 表示「以前的，先前的」，符合題意，所以最佳選項是 (A)。第 3 題依據題意，睡眠層次是逐漸加深的，後來的比前面的睡眠層次深，所以要用 before 表示「之前」，即正確選項是 (D)。第 4 題依據題意，睡眠時眼皮是緊閉的，四個選項中 closed 表示「關著的」，所以選項 (B) 符合題意。第 5 題考固定片語的用法。根據所學的知識，「有困難做～」可以表達為 have trouble doing sth.，要用動名詞，所以動詞 fall 要用動名詞 falling，正確選擇為 (C)。

解答＆技巧｜ **01** (C)　**02** (A)　**03** (D)　**04** (B)　**05** (C)

適用 TIP 1　適用 TIP 2　適用 TIP 7　適用 TIP 11

補充
fall asleep ph 入睡；slow down ph 減速；deeply ad 深深地；warm milk ph 熱牛奶
have trouble doing sth. ph 做某事有困難

7,000 單字
- after [ˋæftɚ] prep 1 在～之後
- busy [ˋbɪzɪ] a 1 繁忙的
- body [ˋbɑdɪ] n 1 身體
- sleep [slip] n 1 睡覺
- best [bɛst] a 1 最好的
- recover [rɪˋkʌvɚ] v 3 恢復
- fall [fɔl] v 1 降落
- relax [rɪˋlæks] v 3 放鬆

- beat [bit] v 1 跳動
- asleep [əˋslip] a 2 睡著的
- sheep [ʃip] n 1 綿羊
- drowsy [ˋdraʊzɪ] a 3 昏昏欲睡的
- pursue [pɚˋsu] v 3 追求
- rotten [ˋrɑtn̩] a 3 腐爛的
- stale [stel] a 3 不新鮮的

DAY
9

Part 1
詞
彙
題
Day 9
完成 25%

Part 2
綜
合
測
驗
Day 9
完成 50%

Part 3
文
意
選
填
Day 9
完成 75%

Part 4
閱
讀
測
驗
Day 9
完成 100%

6 ▶ 99 年指考英文

The Sun is an extraordinarily powerful source of energy. In fact, the Earth __01__ 20,000 times more energy from the Sun than we currently use. If we used more of this source of heat and light, it __02__ all the power needed throughout the world.

We can harness energy from the Sun, or solar energy, in many ways. For instance, many satellites in space are equipped with large panels whose solar cells transform sunlight directly __03__ electric power. These panels are covered with glass and are painted black inside to absorb as much heat as possible.

Solar energy has a lot to offer. To begin with, it is a clean fuel. In contrast, fossil fuels, such as oil or coal, release __04__ substances into the air when they are burned. __05__, fossil fuels will run out, but solar energy will continue to reach the Earth long after the last coal has been mined and the last oil well has run dry.

01 _____ (A) repeats   (B) receives
       (C) rejects   (D) reduces

02 _____ (A) supplies   (B) has supplied
       (C) was supplying   (D) could supply

03 _____ (A) into   (B) from
       (C) with   (D) off

04 _____ (A) diligent   (B) harmful
       (C) usable   (D) changeable

05 _____ (A) Otherwise   (B) Therefore
       (C) What's more   (D) In comparison

中譯│太陽是一種非常強大的能源。事實上，地球從太陽接收到的能量要比我們目前所使用的多兩萬倍。如果我們使用更多這種熱源和光源，它可以提供全世界所需要的全部能量。

我們可以用很多方法來利用來自太陽的能量，或是太陽能。例如，許多太空衛星都裝配有巨型面板，面板上的太陽能電池能夠直接將太陽光轉化成電力。這些面板表面被玻璃所覆蓋，裡面被漆成黑色，以盡可能地吸收熱量。

太陽能可以提供很多東西。首先，它是一種乾淨的燃料。相比之下，石油和煤炭這些化石燃料在燃燒時，會向空氣中釋放有害物質。更重要的是，化石燃料會消耗殆盡，但是直到最後一塊煤炭被開採，最後一口油井乾涸，太陽能也會源源不斷地傳向地球。

解說│本篇短文的主旨是「太陽能」，介紹了太陽能的來源以及使用太陽能的好處。第 1 題的四個選項都是動詞。依據題意，應該是接收太陽能，可以用 receive 表示「接收」，所以正確選擇為 (B)。第 2 題所在的句子使用了假設語氣，空格處應該用假設語氣 could supply，最符合題意的選項是 (D)。第 3 題考介系詞的用法。依據題意，「將～轉化成～」可以表達為 transform... into...，要用介系詞 into，即正確選項是 (A)。第 4 題根據常識性的知識，化石燃料在燃燒時會向空氣中釋放有害物質，四個選項中，harmful 表示「有害的」，所以選項 (B) 符合題意。第 5 題空格處後面所說的內容是前面內容的遞進情況，可以用 What's more 表示「更重要的是」，表示遞進含義，所以選 (C)。

解答＆技巧│ 01 (B) 02 (D) 03 (A) 04 (B) 05 (C)

適用 TIP 1 適用 TIP 2 適用 TIP 7 適用 TIP 11

補充

extraordinarily ad 格外地；currently ad 目前；solar cell ph 太陽能電池；electric power ph 電力；fossil fuel ph 化石燃料

7,000 單字

- power [ˈpaʊɚ] n 1 力量
- way [we] n 1 方法
- satellite [ˈsætl̩ˌaɪt] n 4 衛星
- equip [ɪˈkwɪp] v 4 裝備
- transform [trænsˈfɔrm] v 4 轉變
- electric [ɪˈlɛktrɪk] a 3 電的
- cover [ˈkʌvɚ] v 1 覆蓋
- fossil [ˈfɑsl̩] a 4 化石的

- fuel [ˈfjuəl] n 4 燃料
- coal [kol] n 2 煤
- release [rɪˈlis] v 3 釋放
- reject [rɪˈdʒɛkt] v 2 反對
- diligent [ˈdɪlədʒənt] a 3 勤勉的
- changeable [ˈtʃendʒəbl̩] a 3 可改變的
- comparison [kəmˈpærəsn̩] n 3 比較

DAY
9

Part 1
詞
彙
題
Day 9
完成 25%

Part 2
綜
合
測
驗
Day 9
完成 50%

Part 3
文
意
選
填
Day 9
完成 75%

Part 4
閱
讀
測
驗
Day 9
完成 100%

Currently, more and more people choose to buy a used car as a primary __01__ or as a second car because the price of a used car is only about half what a new car costs. You must make right __02__ when you buy a used car, or else the investment you make on it would turn to be a big loss.

When you have a chance to buy a used car, you should pay much attention to when and where to buy, how to __03__ the car and even how to bargain __04__ the price. For example, it is good advice to buy during the day because lighting will make cars gleam like jewels at night, and the car will look dull but realistic in daylight.

Sometimes the seller would __05__ a high price on a used car. You should make an attempt to bargain with him, and any reason can be used to help you get a lower price.

01 _____ (A) stitch (B) tag
(C) tune (D) vehicle

02 _____ (A) selection (B) victim
(C) wisdom (D) accent

03 _____ (A) apologize (B) attach
(C) examine (D) blush

04 _____ (A) for (B) over
(C) with (D) at

05 _____ (A) carve (B) consist
(C) digest (D) set

DAY
9

Part 1
詞
彙
題
Day 9
完成 25%

Part 2
綜
合
測
驗
Day 9
完成 50%

Part 3
文
意
選
填
Day 9
完成 75%

Part 4
閱
讀
測
驗
Day 9
完成 100%

中譯｜目前，愈來愈多的人選擇購買二手車來作為主要的交通工具，或是當作自己的第二輛車，因為一輛二手車的價格只有大約一輛新車價格的一半。當你購買二手車時，你必須做出正確的選擇，否則你對它的投資將會轉變成重大損失。

當你有機會購買二手車時，你應該多加注意購買的時間和地點，如何檢查車輛，以及如何討價還價。例如，在白天買車是個好建議，因為晚上的燈光會使車輛閃閃發光，如同寶石一般，而車輛在白天看起來不閃亮，但是會比較真實。

有時賣方會為二手車設定比較高的價格。你應該試著跟他討價還價，任何理由都可以用來幫助你得到更低的價格。

解說｜本篇短文的主旨是「二手車」，主要介紹了如何正確地挑選二手車。第 1 題的四個選項都是名詞。依據題意，car 主要是作為交通工具來使用，空格處應該用 vehicle 表示「交通工具」，所以正確選擇為 (D)。第 2 題根據主旨，本篇短文講的是在購買二手車時如何進行挑選，四個選項中，selection 表示「選擇，挑選」，最符合題意的選項是 (A)。第 3 題要選擇合適的動詞。將四個選項一一代入可知，examine 表示「檢查」符合題意，即正確選項是 (C)。第 4 題考介系詞的用法。根據所學的知識，bargain over the price，表示「討價還價」，所以選項 (B) 符合題意。第 5 題考動詞片語的用法。「制定價格」通常表達為 set price，要用動詞 set 表示「制定」，所以選 (D)。

解答＆技巧｜ `01` **(D)** `02` **(A)** `03` **(C)** `04` **(B)** `05` **(D)**

適用 TIP 2   適用 TIP 4   適用 TIP 7   適用 TIP 11

補充
lighting n 照明；seller n 賣方；at night ph 晚上；make an attempt to do sth. ph 嘗試做某事；
bargain with sb. ph 與某人講價

7,000 單字
- used [juzd] a 2 二手的
- turn [tɜn] v 1 轉變
- loss [lɔs] n 2 損失
- chance [tʃæns] n 1 機會
- bargain [ˋbɑrgɪn] v 4 討價還價
- advice [ədˋvaɪs] n 3 建議
- gleam [glim] v 5 閃爍
- jewel [ˋdʒuəl] n 3 寶石

- dull [dʌl] a 2 （顏色）不鮮明的
- realistic [rɪəˋlɪstɪk] a 4 真實的
- stitch [stɪtʃ] n 3 針腳
- selection [səˋlɛkʃən] n 2 選擇
- accent [ˋæksɛnt] n 4 口音
- blush [blʌʃ] v 4 臉紅
- consist [kənˋsɪst] v 4 組成

8 ▶ 100 年指考英文

Handling customer claims is a common task for most business firms. These claims include requests to exchange merchandise, requests for refunds, requests that work __01__, and other requests for adjustments. Most of these claims are approved because they are legitimate. However, some requests for adjustment must be __02__, and an adjustment refusal message must be sent. Adjustment refusals are negative messages for the customer. They are necessary when the customer is __03__ or when the vendor has done all that can reasonably or legally be expected.

An adjustment refusal message requires your best communication skills __04__ it is bad news to the receiver. You have to refuse the claim and retain the customer __05__. You may refuse the request for adjustment and even try to sell the customer more merchandise or service. All this is happening when the customer is probably angry, disappointed, or inconvenient.

01 _____ (A) is correct (B) to be correct
(C) is corrected (D) be corrected

02 _____ (A) retailed (B) denied
(C) appreciated (D) elaborated

03 _____ (A) at fault (B) on call
(C) in tears (D) off guard

04 _____ (A) till (B) unless
(C) because (D) therefore

05 _____ (A) by and large (B) over and over
(C) at the same time (D) for the same reason

DAY
9

Part 1
詞
彙
題
Day 9
完成 25%

Part 2
綜
合
測
驗
Day 9
完成 50%

Part 3
文
意
選
填
Day 9
完成 75%

Part 4
閱
讀
測
驗
Day 9
完成 100%

中譯 │ 對於大多數企業來說，處理顧客索賠是平常事務。這些索賠包括要求換貨、退款、修正作業以及其他的調整要求。大多數索賠都會獲准，因為它們是合理的。然而，一些調整要求必須遭到拒絕，並且必須要發送拒絕調整的訊息。調整拒絕是發送給顧客的否定訊息。當顧客有過失，或是賣主已經做了預期中合理合法的所有事情，調整拒絕就是必要的。

傳達拒絕調整的訊息需要具備最好的溝通技能，因為對於接收者來說這是壞消息。你必須拒絕索賠，同時還要留住顧客。你或許要能拒絕調整要求，甚至還要試圖向顧客推銷更多的商品或服務。而這些都是在顧客有可能感到生氣、失望或不便時，必須進行處理的。

解說 │ 本篇短文講述了如何處理顧客索賠。第 1 題考動詞 request 的用法。request 意思是「請求，要求」，其後接受詞子句時，受詞子句的動詞要用動詞原形。依據題意，題目中的句子是由 that 引導的受詞子句，其後的動詞要用 be corrected 的被動形式，所以正確選擇為 (D)。第 2 題根據上下文的內容，空格後面出現了 refusal，則空格處應該表達的意思是「拒絕」，即 denied，最符合題意的選項是 (B)。第 3 題的四個選項都是介系詞片語，將其一一代入，at fault 表示「出錯」符合題意，即正確選項是 (A)。第 4 題要選擇合適的連接詞。依據題意，空格後面的內容說的是之前行動的原因，可以用 because 來連接，所以選項 (C) 符合題意。第 5 題根據上下文的內容可知，and 前後所說的事情是同時發生的，可以用時間副詞 at the same time 來表示「同時」，所以選 (C)。

解答＆技巧 │ 01 **(D)**　02 **(B)**　03 **(A)**　04 **(C)**　05 **(C)**

適用 TIP 2　適用 TIP 7　適用 TIP 8　適用 TIP 11

補充

customer claims ph 顧客抱怨；legally ad 合法地；communication skills ph 溝通技能；
disappointed a 失望的；inconvenient a 不方便的

7,000 單字

- include [ɪn`klud] v 2 包含
- merchandise [`mɝtʃən͵daɪz] n 6 商品
- refund [rɪ`fʌnd] n 6 退款
- approve [ə`pruv] v 3 贊成
- legitimate [lɪ`dʒɪtəmɪt] a 6 合法的，合理的
- refusal [rɪ`fjuzl] n 4 拒絕
- message [`mɛsɪdʒ] n 2 訊息
- vendor [`vɛndɚ] n 6 賣主

- require [rɪ`kwaɪr] v 2 要求
- refuse [rɪ`fjuz] v 2 拒絕
- retain [rɪ`ten] v 4 保持
- try [traɪ] v 1 試圖
- retail [`ritel] v 6 零售
- guard [gɑrd] n 2 守衛
- reason [`rizn] n 1 原因

Many people like to spend money on entertainment. Some people often enjoy movies, concerts and shows which are enjoyable but __01__ probably because they think that they can have a good __02__ only with spending a lot of money, and this is the life they dream of. However, sometimes a little reading or thinking can give them a pleasant surprise.

However, people may be the most interesting show in a large city. Just think that when you __03__ through the busy street, you can see what everybody is doing. You can see people of different ages and shapes from all over the world. And you can also enjoy a free fashion __04__ with so many people wearing clothes of various kinds and colors in the street.

Try to find something interesting around you. Maybe it is an interesting speech or debate in the college auditorium, or an attractive commercial advertisement, or just a free cooking __05__ in a department store which won't cost you a penny.

01 _____ (A) elegant   (B) envious
                (C) fragrant   (D) expensive

02 _____ (A) frame   (B) time
                (C) generosity   (D) grammar

03 _____ (A) wander   (B) harden
                (C) hasten   (D) install

04 _____ (A) instructor   (B) intensity
                (C) show   (D) limitation

05 _____ (A) literature   (B) demonstration
                (C) misfortune   (D) monument

中譯｜很多人都喜歡花錢來娛樂。一些人經常喜歡看電影、聽音樂會、觀看表演，這些活動令人愉快，卻價格昂貴，因為他們認為只有花很多錢，才能玩得高興，而這就是他們夢想的生活。不過有時一丁點的閱讀或是思考就能給予他們開心的驚喜。

然而，在一座大城市中，人類或許是最有趣的表演。試想一下，當你漫步穿過繁華的街道，你可以看到每個人都在做什麼。你可以看到來自全世界有著不同年齡和身材的人們。街道上有這麼多人身穿各種樣式和顏色的服裝，你也就可以欣賞到一場免費的時裝秀。

試著發現身邊有趣的事物。它也許是大學禮堂裡一場有意思的演講或辯論，或者是一則引人注目的商業廣告，或者只是一家百貨公司舉辦的免費烹飪示範，這些不會花費你一分錢。

解說｜本篇短文講述了消費與娛樂之間的關係。第 1 題的四個選項都是形容詞。依據題意，電影、音樂會和表演這些娛樂項目通常都比較昂貴，expensive 表示「昂貴的」符合題意，所以正確選擇為 (D)。第 2 題考動詞片語的用法。依據題意，「玩得高興」的固定表達為 have a good time，所以最符合題意的選項是 (B)。第 3 題要選擇合適的動詞。將四個選項的動詞一一代入，只有 wander 能夠與介系詞 through 連用表示「漫遊，閒逛」，即正確選項是 (A)。第 4 題根據上下文的內容，fashion show 是一個固定片語，意思是「時裝秀，時裝表演會」，符合題意，所以選項 (C) 符合題意。第 5 題的四個選項都是名詞，將其一一代入可知，demonstration 意思是「示範」，而 cooking demonstration 表示「烹飪示範」符合題意，所以選 (B)。

解答＆技巧｜ 01 (D) 02 (B) 03 (A) 04 (C) 05 (B)

適用 TIP 1　適用 TIP 2　適用 TIP 7　適用 TIP 11

補充

pleasant surprise ph 驚喜；everybody pron 每個人；all over the world ph 全世界；in the street ph 在街上；cost sb. sth. ph 花費某人某物

7,000 單字

- concert [ˋkɑnsɚt] n 3 音樂會
- enjoyable [ɪnˋdʒɔɪəbl] a 3 有樂趣的
- dream [drim] v 1 夢想
- shape [ʃep] n 1 身材
- wear [wɛr] v 3 穿
- clothes [kloz] n 2 服裝
- debate [dɪˋbet] n 2 辯論
- attractive [əˋtræktɪv] a 3 吸引人的

- penny [ˋpɛnɪ] n 3 美分
- envious [ˋɛnvɪəs] a 4 羨慕的
- generosity [ˌdʒɛnəˋrɑsətɪ] n 4 慷慨
- install [ɪnˋstɔl] v 4 安裝
- instructor [ɪnˋstrʌktɚ] n 4 指導員
- limitation [ˌlɪməˋteʃən] n 4 限制
- demonstration [ˌdɛmənˋstreʃən] n 4 示範

The medical profession have realized that the quality of the environment in the hospitals may play a(an) __01__ role in helping the patients gain a quick recovery __02__ illness. Therefore, many artists in Britain have been __03__ in to transform the old hospitals and to soften the modern buildings. So far, more than 100 hospitals have been decorated with significant collections of contemporary art in corridors, waiting areas and treatment rooms, where usually a large number of people gather.

Facts prove that the effect is striking. All the visitors could experience an enjoyable view of fresh colors and images in the corridors and waiting rooms, and the quality of the environment in the hospitals has __04__ the patients' need for expensive drugs when they are recovering from illnesses. According to the study, patients who have a view onto a garden need __05__ strong painkillers compared with patients who only look at brick walls in the hospitals.

01 _____ (A) muddy   (B) objective
         (C) significant   (D) offensive

02 _____ (A) into   (B) from
         (C) on   (D) over

03 _____ (A) overtook   (B) predicted
         (C) called   (D) recited

04 _____ (A) reduced   (B) increased
         (C) kept   (D) resembled

05 _____ (A) more   (B) equal
         (C) fewer   (D) no

DAY
9

Part 1
詞
彙
題
Day 9
完成 25%

Part 2
綜
合
測
驗
Day 9
完成 50%

Part 3
文
意
選
填
Day 9
完成 75%

Part 4
閱
讀
測
驗
Day 9
完成 100%

中譯｜醫療同業已經意識到，醫院的環境品質可能對病人的快速康復發揮重大作用。因此，英國的很多藝術家被召集起來，改造舊醫院，並且使當代的建築變得柔和。迄今為止，一百多家醫院的走廊、候診區和醫療室已經裝飾了具有重大意義的現代藝術收藏，因為這裡經常會有很多人聚集。

事實證明效果很顯著。所有來客都可以在走廊和候診室裡體驗清新色彩和圖像的愉悅景觀，當病人在恢復健康時，醫院的環境品質已經降低了他們對於昂貴藥物的需求。研究指出，相比於那些只看到醫院磚牆的病人，那些觀賞到花園的病人需要較少的強效止痛藥。

解說｜本篇短文講述了醫院的環境對於病人健康恢復的影響。第 1 題的四個選項都是形容詞，將其一一代入，play a significant role 表示「發揮重大作用」，符合題意，所以正確選擇為 (C)。第 2 題考介系詞的用法。recovery 作名詞通常與介系詞 from 連用，表示「從～中恢復」，是一個固定搭配，所以最符合題意的選項是 (B)。第 3 題考能夠與介系詞 in 連用的動詞。四個選項中，call in 表示「召集，召來」，符合上下文的意思，所以正確選項是 (C)。第 4 題依據題意，醫院的環境品質會降低病人對於昂貴藥物的需求，reduce 表示「降低」，所以選項 (A) 符合題意。第 5 題句中的 compared with 表示比較，所以空格處應該用比較級。依據題意應該用 fewer 表示「較少的」，所以選 (C)。

解答＆技巧｜ **01 (C)** **02 (B)** **03 (C)** **04 (A)** **05 (C)**

適用 TIP 2　適用 TIP 4　適用 TIP 7　適用 TIP 11

補充

so far ph 到目前為止；a large number of ph 很多的；waiting room ph 候診室；recover from illnesses ph 從疾病中恢復；painkiller n 止痛藥

7,000 單字

- profession [prəˋfɛʃən] n 2 同業，專業
- role [rol] n 2 角色
- quick [kwɪk] a 1 快速的
- old [old] a 1 老的
- soften [ˋsɔfṇ] v 5 使變柔和
- decorate [ˋdɛkəˏret] v 2 裝飾
- significant [sɪgˋnɪfəkənt] a 3 重大的
- collection [kəˋlɛkʃən] n 3 聚集
- contemporary [kənˋtɛmpəˏrɛrɪ] a 5 當代的
- corridor [ˋkɔrɪdə] n 5 走廊
- onto [ˋɑntu] prep 3 面向
- brick [brɪk] n 2 磚
- muddy [ˋmʌdɪ] a 4 泥濘的
- recite [rɪˋsaɪt] v 4 背誦
- resemble [rɪˋzɛmb!] v 4 類似

♫ 533

Part 3 文意選填 | Cloze Test

1 ▶

Sundews are a kind of __01__ little plants, seeming to be harmless. Around the edges of their leaves are tiny hairs that glisten with a shiny __02__ liquid. Insects may __03__ this liquid for food. Once an insect is attracted to land on the leaf, it cannot escape. The sundew will __04__ its leaves around the insect and swallow it.

Sundews are just one kind of __05__ plants. These plants may __06__ insects in different ways. The pitcher plant, for example, has bright colors to attract insects. When an insect lands on the colorful __07__, it will fall and slide down into the slippery insides of the plant. At the bottom is a pool of liquid. Special __08__ in the liquid will turn the insect into food of the plant.

Bladderworts are another kind of meat-eating plants living in water. Bladderworts have trapdoors in their sides. When an insect comes near the tiny hairs on the bladderwort leaf, the trapdoor opens, and the insect falls inside. A scientist once put four of the plants on a fence around a garden. Within eight days, these four plants trapped 136 insects.

Some plants __09__ rainwater at their root. When insects come to drink water, they cannot escape. The plants are lined with a powder, making it __10__ for the insects to get away.

(A) take　(B) trap　(C) meat-eating　(D) beautiful　(E) chemicals
(F) impossible　(G) sticky　(H) petals　(I) wrap　(J) collect

---

01 _____　**02** _____　**03** _____　**04** _____　**05** _____

06 _____　**07** _____　**08** _____　**09** _____　**10** _____

選項中譯｜誤以為；捕捉；食肉的；漂亮的；化學物質；不可能的；黏性的；花瓣；
包裹；收集

中譯｜茅膏菜是一種漂亮的低矮植物，似乎是無害的，葉子邊緣佈滿細小的絨毛，沾著
閃閃發亮的有黏性的液體。昆蟲也許會誤以為這種液體是食物。一旦有昆蟲受到
吸引而落在葉片上，就無法逃脫。茅膏菜會用葉子把昆蟲包裹起來吞掉。

茅膏草只是食肉植物中的一種。這些食肉植物也許會用不同的方式捕捉昆蟲。例
如，豬籠草是用鮮亮的顏色來吸引昆蟲。當昆蟲落到色彩鮮麗的花瓣上時，就會
掉落下去，滑進光滑的植物底部。底部是一灘液體，液體含有特殊的化學物質，
能把昆蟲分解成植物所需的食物。

狸藻也是一種食肉植物，生長在水中。狸藻側面有可以活動的蓋子。當昆蟲靠
近狸藻葉子上的細小絨毛時，活蓋會打開，昆蟲就會掉進去。有位科學家曾經
在花園的柵欄邊放了四株這種植物。在八天的時間裡，這四株植物就捕捉了
一百三十六隻昆蟲。

有些植物在根部收集雨水。當昆蟲前來喝水時，就無法逃開。這種植物上佈滿粉
末，讓昆蟲無法逃離。

解譯｜閱讀全文可知，這篇文章的主題是食肉植物。

縱觀各選項，選項 (E)、(H) 是名詞，選項 (A)、(B)、(I)、(J) 是動詞，選項 (C)、
(D)、(F)、(G) 是形容詞。根據題意，第 7、8 題應選名詞，第 3、4、6、9 題應
選動詞，第 1、2、5、10 題應選形容詞。然後根據文章，依次作答。

第 1 題是選擇形容詞，有四個形容詞可供選擇，即為選項 (C)、(D)、(F)、(G)。
選項 (C) 意為「食肉的」，選項 (D) 意為「漂亮的」，選項 (F) 意為「不可能的」，
選項 (G) 意為「黏性的」，根據句意可知，應當是「茅膏菜是一種漂亮的低矮植
物」，所以選 (D)。第 2 題所選形容詞，根據句意可知，應當是「閃閃發亮的有
黏性的液體」，所以選 (G)。第 5 題所選形容詞，根據句意可知，應當是「茅膏
草只是食肉植物中的一種」，所以選 (C)。第 10 題則是選 (F)，句意為「昆蟲前
來喝水時，就無法逃開」。

第 3 題是選擇動詞，有四個動詞可供選擇，即為選項 (A)、(B)、(I)、(J)，可以視
為固定搭配，take... for 意為「把～誤以為～」，所以選 (A) 符合要求。第 4 題
所選動詞，根據句意，應當是「茅膏菜將會用葉子把昆蟲包裹起來吞掉」，所以
選 (I)。第 6 題所選動詞，根據句意，應當是「用不同的方式捕捉昆蟲」，所以
選 (B)。第 9 題則是選 (J)，意為「有些植物在根部收集雨水」。

第 7 題是選擇名詞，有兩個名詞可供選擇，即為選項 (E)、(H)，選項 (E) 意為「化
學物質」，選項 (H) 意為「花瓣」，根據句意，應當是「色彩鮮麗的花瓣」，所
以選 (H)。第 8 題則是選 (E)，意為「液體含有特殊的化學物質」。

DAY 9

Part 1
詞 彙 題
Day 9
完成 25%

Part 2
綜 合 測 驗
Day 9
完成 50%

Part 3
文 意 選 填
Day 9
完成 75%

Part 4
閱 讀 測 驗
Day 9
完成 100%

解答&技巧｜ 01 **(D)**　 02 **(G)**　 03 **(A)**　 04 **(I)**　 05 **(C)**
　　　　　 06 **(B)**　 07 **(H)**　 08 **(E)**　 09 **(J)**　 10 **(F)**

適用 TIP 1　適用 TIP 2　適用 TIP 6　適用 TIP 7　適用 TIP 8
適用 TIP 9　適用 TIP 10　適用 TIP 11

補充

sundew n 茅膏菜；harmless a 無害的；bladderwort n 狸藻；meat-eating a 食肉的；
impossible a 不可能的

7,000 單字

- beautiful [ˋbjutəfəl] a 1 漂亮的
- edge [ɛdʒ] n 1 邊緣
- glisten [ˋglɪsn̩] v 6 發亮，閃耀
- shiny [ˋʃaɪnɪ] a 3 發亮的
- sticky [ˋstɪkɪ] a 3 黏性的
- insect [ˋɪnsɛkt] n 2 昆蟲
- wrap [ræp] v 3 包，裹
- pitcher [ˋpɪtʃə] n 6 罐，壺

- petal [ˋpɛtl̩] n 4 花瓣
- slide [slaɪd] v 2 滑動
- slippery [ˋslɪpərɪ] a 3 滑的
- bottom [ˋbɑtəm] n 1 底部
- pool [pul] n 1 一灘
- fence [fɛns] n 2 柵欄
- powder [ˋpaʊdə] n 3 粉末

MEMO

2 ▶

DAY
9

Part 1
詞
彙
題
Day 9
完成 25%

Part 2
綜
合
測
驗
Day 9
完成 50%

Part 3
文
意
選
填
Day 9
完成 75%

Part 4
閱
讀
測
驗
Day 9
完成 100%

St. Valentine's Day is a festival of __01__ and affection. This holiday is another interesting __02__ of pagan and Christian influences. Some of the customs probably come from an ancient Roman holiday called Lupercalia, a celebration to honor the __03__ Juno. During the Middle Ages, church leaders renamed Valentine and shifted the date from February 15 to the feast day of St. Valentine, February 14, in order to relate this __04__ holiday to Christianity.

Shortly after February 14, card shops, bookstores, __05__ stores, and drugstores display a wide assortment of greeting cards called valentines. Most valentines are usually __06__ with the symbolic red heart, as well as a picture of Cupid with his bow and __07__. Some are very fancy, decorated with paper lace, scented satin, feathers, ribbons, or bows, and contain tender verses. The plainest ones may simply say, "Be my Valentine." Besides, there are also special valentines, in every __08__ style—sentimental, sophisticated, or humorous.

Valentines may cost anywhere from a penny to more than a dollar, __09__ on the size and degree of decoration. School children often buy packages of small inexpensive valentines to give to classmates and teachers, along with small gifts. Youth often give flowers or candy (in a red heart box) for a Valentine's Day gift.

Today, Americans probably send more valentines than people in all other countries put together. The __10__ sale of valentines is more than 550 million dollars!

(A) illustrated   (B) goddess   (C) annual   (D) popular   (E) romance
(F) blend   (G) imaginative   (H) depending   (I) department   (J) arrow

01 _____   02 _____   03 _____   04 _____   05 _____

06 _____   07 _____   08 _____   09 _____   10 _____

537

選項中譯｜插圖；女神；年度的；流行的；浪漫；混合；富於想像的；取決於；部門；箭

中譯｜情人節是浪漫的節日，也是表達愛慕的節日，它是異教徒和基督教影響力的另一種有趣結合。有些傳統習俗是源自牧神節，這是古羅馬的節日，用以紀念女神朱諾。在中世紀時，教會領導人為情人節重新命名，日期也從二月十五日改為聖瓦倫丁節日的二月十四日，以便將這個流行的節日與基督教精神聯繫起來。

二月十四日之後，賀卡店、書店、百貨公司和藥妝店發行了各式各樣的賀卡，稱為 valentines（情人節賀卡）。情人節賀卡大多是畫著標誌性的紅心圖案，還有背著弓箭的丘比特。有些賀卡是用紙花邊、芳香緞帶、羽毛、絲帶或是蝴蝶結精心裝飾的，還有溫馨的詩詞。最簡單的也許只是寫著：「做我的戀人吧。」此外，也有些特別的賀卡，感性的、高雅的或是風趣的，種種風格極盡想像。

情人節賀卡價格不一，從一美分到一美元多都有，主要是根據其尺寸和裝飾程度而定。在校的孩子們通常是買盒裝的平價小賀卡，送給同學和老師，也會送些小禮物。年輕人通常是送花或是糖果（用紅色的心形盒子盛放），以此作為情人節禮物。

如今，美國人所送的情人節賀卡，也許要比所有其他國家的人所送的還多。每年的情人節賀卡花費，可高達五·五億美元！

解譯｜閱讀全文可知，這篇文章的主題是情人節賀卡。

縱觀各選項，選項 (B)、(E)、(F)、(I)、(J) 是名詞，選項 (A)、(H) 是動詞，選項 (C)、(D)、(G) 是形容詞。根據題意，第 1、2、3、5、7 題應選名詞，第 6、9 題應選動詞，第 4、8、10 題應選形容詞。然後根據文章，依次作答。

第 1 題是選擇名詞，有五個名詞可供選擇，即為選項 (B)、(E)、(F)、(I)、(J)，選項 (B) 意為「女神」，選項 (E) 意為「浪漫」，選項 (F) 意為「混合」，選項 (I) 意為「部門」，選項 (J) 意為「箭」，根據句意，應當是「情人節是浪漫的節日」，所以選 (E)。第 2 題所選名詞，根據句意，應當是「是異教徒和基督教影響力的另一種有趣結合～」，所以選 (F)。第 3 題所選名詞，根據句意，應當是「女神朱諾」，所以選 (B)。第 5 題所選名詞，可以視為固定搭配，department store 意為「百貨公司」，所以選 (I)。第 7 題則是選 (J)，句意為「背著弓箭的的丘比特」。

第 4 題是選擇形容詞，有三個形容詞可供選擇，即為選項 (C)、(D)、(G)。選項 (C) 意為「年度的」，選項 (D) 意為「流行的」，選項 (G) 意為「富於想像的」，根據句意可知，應當是「流行的節日」，所以選 (D)。第 8 題所選形容詞，意為「風格極盡想像」，所以選 (G)。第 10 題則是選 (C)，句意為「每年的情人節賀卡花費」。

第 6 題是選擇動詞，有兩個動詞可供選擇，即為選項 (A)、(H)，句意為「情人節賀卡大多是畫著標誌性的紅心圖案」，所以選項 (A)。第 9 題則是選 (H)，可以視為固定搭配，depend on 意為「取決於」。

解答&技巧 | **01 (E)**　**02 (F)**　**03 (B)**　**04 (D)**　**05 (I)**
　　　　　06 (A)　**07 (J)**　**08 (G)**　**09 (H)**　**10 (C)**

適用 TIP 1　適用 TIP 2　適用 TIP 6　適用 TIP 7　適用 TIP 8
適用 TIP 9　適用 TIP 10　適用 TIP 11

DAY 9

Part 1 詞彙題
Day 9
完成 25%

Part 2 綜合測驗
Day 9
完成 50%

Part 3 文意選填
Day 9
完成 75%

Part 4 閱讀測驗
Day 9
完成 100%

補充
St. Valentine's Day [ph] 情人節；Christian [a] 基督教的；pagan [a] 異教徒的；Lupercalia [n] 牧神節；the Middle Ages [ph] 中世紀；Cupid [n] 丘比特

7,000 單字
- romance [roˋmæns] [n] 4 浪漫
- blend [blɛnd] [n] 4 結合
- goddess [ˋgɑdɪs] [n] 1 女神
- February [ˋfɛbruˏɛrɪ] [n] 1 二月
- feast [fist] [n] 4 盛宴
- popular [ˋpɑpjələ] [a] 3 流行的
- drugstore [ˋdrʌgˏstor] [n] 2 藥妝店
- symbolic [sɪmˋbɑlɪk] [a] 6 象徵的
- arrow [ˋæro] [n] 2 箭
- fancy [ˋfænsɪ] [a] 3 精緻的
- imaginative [ɪˋmædʒəˏnetɪv] [a] 4 富於想像的
- humorous [ˋhjumərəs] [a] 3 幽默的
- degree [dɪˋgri] [n] 2 等級，程度
- package [ˋpækɪdʒ] [n] 2 包裝
- annual [ˋænjuəl] [a] 4 年度的

MEMO

> It was after midnight. A Dutch farmer made one last trip through his greenhouse before going to bed. When walking past rows and rows of tulips, suddenly he __01__ . There was a rare flower __02__ in the early morning hours. It was a black tulip. In the morning the __03__ farmer took the tulip to a flower show, and in the evening the farmer and his plant appeared on television.
>
> Most tulips are red, yellow, white or pink. A black tulip takes years to __04__ . The farmer worked on his midnight tulip for seven years. He crossed two dark purple tulips and got a seed. The seed grew into a round __05__ , and then a black flower grew from the bulb.
>
> Tulips are a major __06__ for the Dutch. Tulip sales bring in millions of dollars every year.
>
> The Dutch first got tulips from the __07__ East in the early 1600s. The Dutch loved the beautiful flowers and tried to __08__ new kinds of tulips. The results were striped-tulips, double tulips, and lily tulips, but black tulips were still very __09__ . Someone grew a black tulip in 1891, and another black tulip bloomed in 1955, known as Queen of the Night. Now black tulips can grow in __10__ gardens.

(A) Far (B) bulb (C) excited (D) ordinary (E) stopped
(F) rare (G) blooming (H) industry (I) produce (J) develop

---

01 _____   02 _____   03 _____   04 _____   05 _____

06 _____   07 _____   08 _____   09 _____   10 _____

選項中譯｜遠的；球莖；激動的；尋常的；停下；罕見的；開花；產業；創造出；發展

中譯｜午夜之後，一位荷蘭農民睡覺之前，最後一次穿過花房。他走過成排的鬱金香花叢，突然停了下來。有一株罕見的花，在凌晨時分盛開。這是一株黑色鬱金香。早上，這位激動的農民把這株鬱金香帶到了一個花展，到了晚上，這位農民和他的鬱金香都上了電視。

大多數的鬱金香是紅色的、黃色的、白色的或是粉紅色的。一株黑色的鬱金香要經過數年時間的培育。這位農民為午夜鬱金香花費了七年時間。他將兩株暗紫色的鬱金香雜交，得到了一粒種子。種子生長出了圓形球莖，而後從球莖中開出了黑色的花。

對於荷蘭人來說，鬱金香是一個主要的產業。鬱金香的銷售每年都會帶來數百萬美元的利潤。

十七世紀早期，荷蘭人才從遠東地區引入了鬱金香。荷蘭人喜歡這些漂亮的花，也試圖培育鬱金香的新品種。結果培育出了帶條紋的鬱金香、雙株鬱金香和百合鬱金香。但是，黑色的鬱金香還是很少見。一八九一年，曾有人培育出一株黑色鬱金香，另一株黑色鬱金香在一九五五年開花，稱為「夜后」。如今，黑色的鬱金香可以在普通的花園裡生長。

解譯｜閱讀全文可知，這篇文章的主題是鬱金香。

縱觀各選項，選項 (B)、(H) 是名詞，選項 (E)、(G)、(I)、(J) 是動詞，選項 (A)、(C)、(D)、(F) 是形容詞。根據題意，第 5、6 題應選名詞，第 1、2、4、8 題應選動詞，第 3、7、9、10 題應選形容詞。然後根據文章，依次作答。

第 1 題是選擇動詞，有四個動詞可供選擇，即為選項 (E)、(G)、(I)、(J)。句意為「他走過成排的鬱金香花叢，突然停了下來」，所以選 (E)。第 2 題所選動詞，為現在分詞作伴隨狀況，意為「在凌晨時分盛開」，所以選 (G)。第 4 題所選動詞，根據句意可知，應當是「一株黑色的鬱金香要經過數年時間的培育」，所以選 (J)。第 8 題則是選 (I)，意為「試圖培育鬱金香的新品種」。

第 3 題是選擇形容詞，有四個形容詞可供選擇，即為選項 (A)、(C)、(D)、(F)。選項 (A) 意為「遠的」，選項 (C) 意為「激動的」，選項 (D) 意為「尋常的」，選項 (F) 意為「罕見的」，根據句意可知，應當是「激動的農民」，所以選 (C)。第 7 題所選形容詞，可以視為固定搭配，the Far East 意為「遠東」，所以選 (A)。第 9 題所選形容詞，意為「黑色的鬱金香還是很少見」，所以選 (F)。第 10 題則是選 (D)，句意為「可以在普通的花園裡生長」。

第 5 題是選擇名詞，有兩個名詞可供選擇，即為選項 (B)、(H)，選項 (B) 意為「球莖」，選項 (H) 意為「產業」，根據句意，應當是「種子生長出了圓形球莖」，所以選 (B)。第 6 題則是選 (H)，意為「對於荷蘭人來說，鬱金香是一個主要的產業」。

DAY
9

Part 1
詞彙題
Day 9
完成 25%

Part 2
綜合測驗
Day 9
完成 50%

Part 3
文意選填
Day 9
完成 75%

Part 4
閱讀測驗
Day 9
完成 100%

7,000 單字大數據

解答＆技巧 | **01** (E)　**02** (G)　**03** (C)　**04** (J)　**05** (B)
06 (H)　**07** (A)　**08** (I)　**09** (F)　**10** (D)

適用 TIP 1　適用 TIP 2　適用 TIP 6　適用 TIP 7　適用 TIP 8
適用 TIP 9　適用 TIP 10　適用 TIP 11

補充
midnight n 午夜；Dutch a 荷蘭的；flower show ph 花展；the Far East ph 遠東；
unusual a 不尋常的

7,000 單字
- farmer [ˋfɑrmɚ] n 1 農民
- greenhouse [ˋgrin͵haʊs] n 3 花房，溫室
- tulip [ˋtjuləp] n 3 鬱金香
- rare [rɛr] a 2 罕見的
- bloom [blum] v 4 開花
- pink [pɪŋk] a 2 粉紅色的
- develop [dɪˋvɛləp] v 2 培育
- purple [ˋpɝpl̩] a 1 紫色的

- bulb [bʌlb] n 3 球莖
- industry [ˋɪndəstrɪ] n 2 產業
- million [ˋmɪljən] n 2 百萬
- double [ˋdʌbl̩] a 2 雙的
- lily [ˋlɪlɪ] n 1 百合
- queen [ˋkwin] n 1 女王，王后
- ordinary [ˋɔrdn͵ɛrɪ] a 2 尋常的

MEMO

♫ 542

4 ▸

DAY
9

Part 1
詞
彙
題
Day 9
完成 25%

Part 2
綜
合
測
驗
Day 9
完成 50%

Part 3
文
意
選
填
Day 9
完成 75%

Part 4
閱
讀
測
驗
Day 9
完成 100%

As we all know, a magician depends actually on his ability to __01__ at great speed to perform his tricks, rather than on "magic." However, this does not stop us from enjoying watching a magician's __02__ . The greatest magician of all time was probably Harry Houdini, who died in 1926. Mastering the art of escaping, Houdini could __03__ himself from the tightest knots or the most complicated locks in seconds. No one really knows how he did this, but there is no __04__ that he had made a close study of every type of lock. He liked to carry a small steel needle-like tool, which could be used in __05__ of a key, strapped to his leg.

Houdini once asked the Chicago police to lock him in __06__ . They bound him in chains and locked him up, but he freed himself in an __07__ . He was supposed to have used a tool, and was locked up again. This time he wore no clothes and had nothing at all with him, but he again __08__ in a few minutes. Houdini had probably hidden his "needle" in a wax like substance and dropped it on the floor in the passage. As he went past, he __09__ on it, so it stuck to the bottom of his foot.

His most famous escape, altogether, was astonishing. He was once heavily chained up and enclosed in an empty wooden chest, the lid of which was __10__ down. The chest was dropped into the sea in New York harbor. In one minute Houdini swam to the surface. When the chest was brought up and opened, the chains were found inside.

(A) act   (B) escaped   (C) free   (D) place   (E) prison
(F) nailed   (G) stepped   (H) performance   (I) instant   (J) doubt

01 _____   02 _____   03 _____   04 _____   05 _____

06 _____   07 _____   08 _____   09 _____   10 _____

選項中譯│表演；逃脱；使自由；位置；監獄；用釘子釘；踩；表現；立即的；懷疑

中譯│眾所周知，魔術師的表演，事實上所靠的是動作快速的表演能力，而不是靠所謂的「魔術」。不過，這並不妨礙我們欣賞魔術師的表演。最偉大的魔術師，也許是於一九二六年逝世的哈利・胡迪尼。他精通脱逃術，可以在很短的時間裡，從最緊的繩結或是最複雜的鎖中脱逃。沒有人知道他是怎麼做到的，不過無疑的是，他對所有類型的鎖都做過詳細的研究。他喜歡帶著一種像鐵針一樣的工具，捆綁在腿上，可以作為開鎖的鑰匙。

有一次，胡迪尼要求芝加哥的警方把他關進監獄。員警用鎖鏈捆綁住他，把他關了起來。但是，他立即就脱逃了。警方認為他是用了什麼工具，就再次把他關起來。這一次，他沒有穿衣服，也完全沒有帶東西，但是幾分鐘後，他還是脱逃了。胡迪尼可能是把他的「針」藏在一種像蠟一樣的物質中，然後把它扔在走道的地板上。當他經過的時候，踩在上面，它就黏在他的腳上了。

總而言之，他最著名的脱逃術，是很令人驚訝的。有一次，他被重重鎖鏈捆綁著，裝進一個空木箱中，這木箱的蓋子是用釘子釘著的。在紐約港，木箱被抛進海中。胡迪尼立即就游到了海面上。木箱被打撈起來，打開的時候發現，鎖鏈還留在箱子裡。

解譯│閱讀全文可知，這篇文章的主題是胡迪尼的魔術簡介。

縱觀各選項，選項 (D)、(E)、(H)、(J) 是名詞，選項 (A)、(B)、(C)、(F)、(G) 是動詞，選項 (I) 是形容詞。根據題意，第 2、4、5、6 題應選名詞，第 1、3、8、9、10 題應選動詞，第 7 題應選形容詞。然後根據文章，依次作答。

第 1 題是選擇動詞，有五個動詞可供選擇，即為選項 (A)、(B)、(C)、(F)、(G)。句意為「以極快的速度行動」，所以選 (A)。第 3 題所選動詞，可以視為固定搭配，free oneself from 意為「掙脱，擺脱」，所以選 (C)。第 8 題所選動詞，根據句意可知，應當是「幾分鐘後，他還是脱逃了」，所以選 (B)。第 9 題所選動詞，是與介系詞 on 進行搭配，意為「踩，踏」，所以選 (G)。第 10 題則是選 (F)，意為「木箱的蓋子是用釘子釘著的」。

第 2 題是選擇名詞，有四個名詞可供選擇，即為選項 (D)、(E)、(H)、(J)，選項 (D) 意為「位置」，選項 (E) 意為「監獄」，選項 (H) 意為「表現」，選項 (J) 意為「懷疑」，根據句意，應當是「欣賞魔術師的表演」，所以選 (H)。第 4 題所選名詞，可以視為固定搭配，there is no doubt 意為「毫無疑問」，所以選 (J)。第 5 題所選名詞，也可以視為固定搭配，in place of 意為「代替」，所以選 (D)。第 6 題則是選 (E)，lock... in prison 意為「把～關進監獄」。

第 7 題是選擇形容詞，只有一個形容詞可供選擇，即為選項 (I)，意為「立即的」。

解答&技巧 │ **01** (A) **02** (H) **03** (C) **04** (J) **05** (D)
　　　　　　 06 (E) **07** (I) **08** (B) **09** (G) **10** (F)

適用 TIP 1　適用 TIP 2　適用 TIP 6　適用 TIP 7　適用 TIP 8
適用 TIP 9　適用 TIP 10　適用 TIP 11

Part 1
詞
彙
題
Day 9
完成 **25%**

Part 2
綜
合
測
驗
Day 9
完成 **50%**

Part 3
文
意
選
填
Day 9
完成 **75%**

Part 4
閱
讀
測
驗
Day 9
完成 **100%**

補充

stop sb. from doing sth. ph 阻止某人做某事；in seconds ph 在很短的時間裡；
free oneself from ph 擺脫，脫逃；there is no doubt that ph 無疑；in an instant ph 立即，立刻

7,000 單字

- magician [mə`dʒɪʃən] n 2 魔術師
- doubt [daʊt] n 2 懷疑
- steel [stil] n 2 鋼
- needle [`nidl] n 2 針
- strap [stræp] v 5 綁，捆
- prison [`prɪzn] n 2 監獄
- chain [tʃen] n 3 鏈條
- again [ə`gɛn] ad 1 再次

- wax [wæks] n 3 蠟
- floor [flor] n 1 地板
- passage [`pæsɪdʒ] n 3 通道
- enclose [ɪn`kloz] v 4 裝入
- chest [tʃɛst] n 3 木箱
- nail [nel] v 2 用釘子釘
- swim [swɪm] v 1 游泳

MEMO

5 ▶ 100 年指考英文

The history of the written word goes back to 6,000 years ago. Words express feelings, open doors into the __01__ , create pictures of worlds never seen, and allow adventures never dared. Therefore, the original __02__ of words, such as storytellers, poets, and singers, were respected in all cultures in the past. But now the romance is __03__ . Imagination is being surpassed by the instant picture. In a triumphant march, movies, TV, videos, and DVDs are __04__ storytellers and books. A visual culture is taking over the world—at the __05__ of the written word. Our literacy, and with it our verbal and communication skills, are in __06__ decline.

The only category of novel that is __07__ ground in our increasingly visual world is the graphic novel. A growing number of adults and young people worldwide are reading graphic novels, and educators are beginning to realize the power of this __08__ . The graphic novel looks like a comic book, but it is longer, more sophisticated, and may come in black and white or multiple __09__ and appear in many sizes. In fact, some of the most interesting, daring, and most heartbreaking art being created right now is being published in graphic novels. Graphic novels __10__ the opportunity to examine the increasingly visual world of communications today while exploring serious social and literary topics. The graphic novel can be used to develop a sense of visual literacy, in much the same way that students are introduced to art appreciation.

(A) expense   (B) fading   (C) colors   (D) research   (E) replacing
(F) offer   (G) users   (H) rapid   (I) gaining   (J) medium   (K) circular
(L) unknown

---

01 _____   02 _____   03 _____   04 _____   05 _____

06 _____   07 _____   08 _____   09 _____   10 _____

選項中譯｜代價；消退；顏色；研究；代替；提供；使用者；迅速的；得到；媒介；
迴圈的；未知的

中譯｜書寫文字的歷史可以追溯到六千年前。文字可以用來表達情感，打開通向未知世界的門，創作前所未見的世界，使得那些不敢實踐的探險成為可能。因此，文字的最初使用者，例如故事的講述者、詩人和歌手，在過去的所有文明中都是受到尊敬的。但是如今，這種傳奇色彩卻在消退。速成的影像正在取代想像力。在競爭中獲勝的電影、電視、錄影、和光碟，正在取代故事講述者和書籍。以犧牲文字世界為代價，視覺文化正在掌控我們的世界。我們的讀寫能力，伴隨著言語溝通技能，正在迅速減退。

在迅速發展的視覺世界中，唯一得以繼續存在的一類小説，是圖像小説。世界上，愈來愈多的成年人和年輕人開始閱讀圖像小説，教育工作者也開始意識到這種媒介的力量。圖像小説類似於漫畫書，不過篇幅更長，情節更精細，也許是黑白的，也許是彩色的，尺寸不一。事實上，如今所創作過最有趣、最大膽、最令人悲痛的藝術中，某些是以圖像小説出版的。在探究值得深思的社會話題與文學話題的同時，圖像小説提供了機會，來審視如今這個日益發展的視覺世界。圖像小説可以用來培養視覺素養，就像學生們被引導著學習藝術鑒賞一樣。

解譯｜閱讀全文可知，這篇文章的主題是書寫文字的沒落與視覺世界中圖像小説的發展。

縱觀各選項，選項 (A)、(C)、(D)、(G)、(J) 是名詞，選項 (B)、(E)、(F)、(I) 是動詞，選項 (H)、(K)、(L) 是形容詞。根據題意，第 2、5、8、9 題應選名詞，第 3、4、7、10 題應選動詞，第 1、6 題應選形容詞。然後根據文章，依次作答。

第 1 題是選擇形容詞，有三個形容詞可供選擇，即為選項 (H)、(K)、(L)。選項 (H) 意為「迅速的」，選項 (K) 意為「迴圈的」，選項 (L) 意為「未知的」，根據句意可知，應當是「打開通向未知世界的門」，所以選 (L)。第 6 題則是選 (H)，句意為「我們的讀寫能力迅速減退」。

第 2 題是選擇名詞，有五個名詞可供選擇，即為選項 (A)、(C)、(D)、(G)、(J)，選項 (A) 意為「代價」，選項 (C) 意為「顏色」，選項 (D) 意為「研究」，選項 (G) 意為「使用者」，選項 (J) 意為「媒介」，根據句意，應當是「文字的最初使用者」，所以選 (G)。第 5 題所選名詞，可以視為固定搭配，at the expense of 意為「以～的代價」，所以選 (A)。第 8 題所選名詞，根據句意，應當是「教育工作者也開始意識到這種媒介的力量」，所以選 (J)。第 9 題則是選 (C)。

第 3 題是選擇動詞，有四個動詞可供選擇，即為選項 (B)、(E)、(F)、(I)，句意為「這種傳奇色彩在消退」，所以選 (B)。第 4 題所選動詞，根據句意，應當是「電影、電視、錄影、光碟正在取代故事講述者和書籍」，所以選 (E)。第 7 題所選動詞，根據句意，應當是「唯一得以繼續存在的一類小説」，所以選 (I)。第 10 題則是選 (F)，offer the opportunity 意為「提供機會」。

DAY
9

Part 1
詞彙題
Day 9
完成 25%

Part 2
綜合測驗
Day 9
完成 50%

Part 3
文意選填
Day 9
完成 75%

Part 4
閱讀測驗
Day 9
完成 100%

解答＆技巧 | **01** (L)　**02** (G)　**03** (B)　**04** (E)　**05** (A)
　　　　　　06 (H)　**07** (I)　**08** (J)　**09** (C)　**10** (F)

適用 TIP 1　適用 TIP 2　適用 TIP 6　適用 TIP 7　適用 TIP 8
適用 TIP 9　適用 TIP 10　適用 TIP 11

補充

take over ph 接管，取代；at the expense of ph 以犧牲～為代價；graphic novel ph 圖像小說
black and white ph 黑白的；visual literacy ph 視覺素養，圖像識讀能力

7,000 單字

- express [ɪkˋsprɛs] v 2 表達
- dare [dɛr] v 3 敢於
- singer [ˋsɪŋɚ] n 1 歌手
- respect [rɪˋspɛkt] v 2 尊敬
- imagination [ɪ͵mædʒəˋneʃən] n 3 想像
- surpass [sɚˋpæs] v 6 超過
- instant [ˋɪnstənt] a 2 速成的，立即的
- triumphant [traɪˋʌmfənt] a 6 勝利的

- march [mɑrtʃ] n 3 前進
- video [ˋvɪdɪo] n 2 錄影
- literacy [ˋlɪtərəsɪ] n 6 讀寫能力
- verbal [ˋvɝbl] a 5 言語的
- decline [dɪˋklaɪn] n 6 下降
- novel [ˋnɑvl] n 2 小說
- multiple [ˋmʌltəpl] a 4 多種的

MEMO

MEMO

DAY
9

Part 1
詞
彙
題
Day 9
完成 25%

Part 2
綜
合
測
驗
Day 9
完成 50%

Part 3
文
意
選
填
Day 9
完成 75%

Part 4
閱
讀
測
驗
Day 9
完成 100%

Part 4 　閱讀測驗│Reading Questions

1.

　　Business English correspondence, as a tool of human communication, is written for a special purpose. Normally, business English correspondence performs three functions: to inform, to influence and to entertain. Correspondence is designed to convey vast amount of information needed to complete day-to-day operations of the business—to explain instructions to employees, to announce meetings, to give responses to request letters, to place orders, etc. Business English correspondence can also be used to influence readers' attitudes and actions.

　　The layout of formal business English correspondence can be in three styles.

　　In the indented style, the first line of each paragraph is indented five spaces. The indention is necessary because there is not black division line between paragraphs. And the indented letter-space should be the same in one letter. When using either attention line or subject line, they are generally indented to comply with the paragraph indentation.

　　The block style is the most popular style for letters. It is now increasingly adopted in Britain and becomes more popular in America. In this format, each line should begin at the left margin—no colon after the salutation, and no comma after the complimentary close. There are two line-spacing between paragraphs. Components of the letter begin at the left margin.

　　The modified style has blocked-like and indented-like characteristics. All the paragraphs of the body begin at the left margin in block. Double-spaces are used between paragraphs. The inside address, the salutation and other parts use blocked style. The heading is at the right-hand top, while the complimentary close and signature are in the right-hand corner at the bottom of the page.

01 The word "correspondence" in the first paragraph is closest in meaning to _____.

(A) agreement

(B) similarity

(C) letter

(D) file

02 Which of the following functions of business Engligh correspondence is not mentioned in the passage?

(A) To research.

(B) To inform.

(C) To entertain.

(D) To influence.

03 Which one of the following statements is false?

(A) The first line of each paragraph should be indented five spaces in the indented style.

(B) Each line of the block style should begin at the left margin.

(C) Double spaces are used between two paragraphs in the modified style.

(D) The modified style should be the most popular.

04 What is the main idea of the passage?

(A) The indented style.

(B) Three styles of formal business English correspondence.

(C) The modified style.

(D) The block style.

DAY 9

Part 1
詞
彙
題
Day 9
完成 25%

Part 2
綜
合
測
驗
Day 9
完成 50%

Part 3
文
意
選
填
Day 9
完成 75%

Part 4
閱
讀
測
驗
Day 9
完成 100%

中譯 | 作為人際溝通的一種工具，商務英語書信是為著特殊目的而書寫的。商務英語書信通常有三個功用：告知、發揮影響和娛樂。書信用於傳達大量所需的資訊，來完成日常的商務運作，一一向員工說明指示、下達會議通知、回覆申請函、下訂單等。商務英語書信也可以用來影響讀者的態度和行動。

正式的商務英語書信有三種格式。

縮排式書信，每段首行要空五格。段落之間沒有黑色的分格線，因此這種縮排是必要的。同一封書信中，縮排空的格數也應該保持一致。使用注意線和主旨線時，通常要依照段落縮排格式來進行縮排。

齊頭式是最為流行的書信格式。如今，這種格式正逐漸被英國人所採用，並且日益受到美國人的喜愛。這種格式的書信，每一行都要從左邊緣開始書寫，稱呼語之後沒有冒號，結尾敬語之後也沒有逗號。段落之間要用兩行的間距。書信內容從左邊緣開始書寫。

混合式兼有齊頭式和縮排式的特點。正文的所有段落，都從左邊開始書寫。段落之間要用雙倍行距。信內位址、稱呼語和其他的部分用齊頭式的格式。信頭寫在右上角，結尾敬語和署名，則是寫在頁面右下角位置。

解譯 | 在閱讀文章之前，先要預覽題目，然後再帶著問題有針對性地閱讀文章。第 1 題是詞義辨析，第 2 題是文意理解，第 3 題是判斷正誤，第 4 題是概括主旨。理解了題目要求之後，閱讀全文，依次作答。

第 1 題是考名詞 correspondence 的同義字。名詞 correspondence 意為「相似；一致；信函」，根據第 1 段第 1 句內容可知，correspondence 在文中意為「書信」。選項 (A) 意為「一致」，選項 (B) 意為「相似」，選項 (C) 意為「書信」，選項 (D) 意為「檔案」。所以選 (C)。

第 2 題是文意理解，問的是關於商務英語書信的功用，哪一項在文中沒有提及。根據第 1 段第 2 句內容「business English correspondence performs three functions: to inform, to influence and to entertain.」可知，商務英語書信的三個功用，分別是告知、發揮影響和娛樂，與選項 (B)、(C)、(D) 相符。只有選項 (A)，在文中找不到相關敘述。所以選 (A)。

第 3 題是判斷正誤，考的是細節，問的是哪一項敘述是錯誤的。根據第 4 段首句內容「The block style is the most popular style for letters.」可知，齊頭式是最為流行的書信格式。選項 (D) 則是說，混合式最為流行，與文意不符。同樣，此題也可以用排除法來解答。第 3 段第 1 句內容與選項 (A) 相符，第 4 段第 3 句內容與選項 (B) 相符，第 5 段第 3 句內容與選項 (C) 相符。這三個選項的敘述都是正確的，可以排除。所以選 (D)。

第 4 題是概括主旨。短文第 1 段是由商務英語書信的功用而引出話題，第 2 段講述的是商務英語書信的三種格式，第 3、4、5 段分別對這 3 種格式加以闡釋。第 2 段「The layout of formal business English correspondence can be in three styles.」可以視為主旨段，由此可知，文章主旨是商務英語書信的三種格式，與選項 (B) 敘述相符。所以選 (B)。

解答&技巧 | **01** (C) **02** (A) **03** (D) **04** (B)

適用 TIP 1 適用 TIP 2 適用 TIP 3 適用 TIP 7 適用 TIP 10
適用 TIP 11 適用 TIP 12 適用 TIP 13 適用 TIP 14 適用 TIP 15

補充

indent Ⓥ 縮排；comply Ⓥ 順從，依從；indentation Ⓝ 縮排；colon Ⓝ 冒號；salutation Ⓝ 稱呼語；complimentary Ⓐ 讚美的

7,000 單字

- correspondence [ˌkɔrəˋspɑndəns] Ⓝ **5** 信件
- as [æz] prep **1** 作為
- and [ænd] conj **1** 和，與
- entertain [ˌɛntɚˋten] Ⓥ **4** 娛樂
- convey [kənˋve] Ⓥ **4** 傳遞
- layout [ˋleˌaʊt] Ⓝ **6** 設計，規劃
- five [faɪv] num **1** 五
- black [blæk] Ⓐ **1** 黑色的

- block [blɑk] Ⓝ **1** 印板，木板
- format [ˋfɔrmæt] Ⓝ **5** 版式
- line [laɪn] Ⓝ **1** 行
- no [no] ad **1** 無，不
- comma [ˋkɑmə] Ⓝ **3** 逗號
- component [kəmˋponənt] Ⓝ **6** 組成部分
- inside [ˋɪnˋsaɪd] Ⓐ **1** 裡面的，內部的

Part 1
詞
彙
題
Day 9
完成 25%

Part 2
綜
合
測
驗
Day 9
完成 50%

Part 3
文
意
選
填
Day 9
完成 75%

Part 4
閱
讀
測
驗
Day 9
完成 100%

MEMO

People of different countries have different attitudes towards marriage. Take Chinese people for example. They always pay much attention to interdependent and interpersonal relations, quite different from Americans in choosing spouses. For Chinese people, marriage means not only a simple combination of two individuals, but also the combination of two families. In traditional Chinese society, marriage is one of the most important events for a family. Before a man and a woman get married, according to the etiquette, they must meet each other's parents and gain their permission. Grand wedding will be held to celebrate it then.

We can see from above that the purpose of Chinese marriage is mainly to carry out the family obligation, to give birth to and bring up a new generation, and to serve both parties' parents. It is a bounden duty.

However, with the development of society, more and more young people have gradually got rid of some traditional bondage. They will not simply think marriage as a means to carry on the responsibility and obligations. It is, to some extent, related to their own personal rights. Therefore, as a member of the society, they should also take responsibility for their future.

In addition, late marriage seems to have become a trend in China, especially in large cities. And mixed marriage with different races or religions has also become more popular.

01 The word "etiquette" in the first paragraph is closest in meaning to

_____.

(A) manners
(B) language
(C) appearance
(D) clothing

02 Which of the following purposes of Chinese marriage is not mentioned in the passage?

(A) To carry out the family obligation.
(B) To bring up the new generation.
(C) To be responsible for the society.
(D) To support parents.

03 Which one of the following statements is false?

(A) Chinese people strongly reject the mixed marriage.
(B) Different people may have different ideas about marriage.
(C) Late marriage has become a trend in large cities in China.
(D) Many young people have gradually got rid of some traditional bondage.

04 What is the main idea of the passage?

(A) Chinese marriage.
(B) Different opinions of marriage.
(C) Late marriage.
(D) Mixed marriage.

DAY 9

Part 1
詞彙題
Day 9
完成 25%

Part 2
綜合測驗
Day 9
完成 50%

Part 3
文意選填
Day 9
完成 75%

Part 4
閱讀測驗
Day 9
完成 100%

中譯 │ 對於婚姻，不同國家的人們有著不同的態度。以中國人為例，他們十分重視相互依賴的人際關係，這與美國人極不相同。對於中國人來說，婚姻不只是意味著兩個人之間的簡單結合，也是兩個家庭的結合。在傳統的中國社會中，對於一個家庭來說，婚姻是家族中最為重要的事件之一。根據禮節，男女雙方結婚之前，必須面見對方的家長，獲得他們的許可。屆時，將會舉辦盛大的婚禮來慶祝。

由此我們可以看出，中國式婚姻的目的，主要是為了履行家庭義務，生養下一代，並且贍養雙方的父母。這是分內的義務。

然而，隨著社會的發展，愈來愈多的年輕人逐漸擺脫了某些傳統的束縛。他們不再將婚姻視為履行職責和義務的一種手段。在某種程度上，婚姻與他們自己的個人權利相關。因此，作為一名社會成員，他們也應當對自己的未來負責。

此外在中國，特別是在大城市中，晚婚似乎也已經成為趨勢。而且，不同民族或是不同宗教之間的通婚，也變得更為流行。

解譯 │ 在閱讀文章之前，先要預覽題目，然後再帶著問題有針對性地閱讀文章。第 1 題是詞義辨析，第 2 題是文意理解，第 3 題是判斷正誤，第 4 題是概括主旨。理解了題目要求之後，閱讀全文，依次作答。

第 1 題是考名詞 etiquette 的同義字。選項 (A) 意為「禮節」，選項 (B) 意為「語言」，選項 (C) 意為「外貌」，選項 (D) 意為「衣著」。根據第 1 段最後一句內容可知，etiquette 在文中意為「禮儀」，所以選 (A)。

第 2 題是文意理解，問的是關於中國式婚姻的目的，哪一項在文中沒有提及。關鍵字是「purposes of Chinese marriage」，定位於第 2 段。根據「the purpose of Chinese marriage is mainly to carry out the family obligation, to give birth to and bring up new generation, and to serve both parties' parents.」可知，中國式婚姻的目的，是為了履行家庭義務，生養下一代，贍養父母。選項 (A)、(B)、(D) 與此相符。只有選項 (C)，在文中找不到相關敘述。所以選 (C)。

第 3 題是判斷正誤，考的是細節，問的是哪一項敘述是錯誤的。根據第 4 段最後一句內容「mixed marriage with different races or religions has also become more popular.」可知，通婚在中國變得更為流行。選項 (A) 則是說，中國人強烈反對通婚，與文意不符。同樣，此題也可以用排除法來解答。第 1 段首句內容與選項 (B) 相符，第 4 段首句內容與選項 (C) 相符，第 3 段首句內容與選項 (D) 相符。這三個選項的敘述都是正確的，可以排除。所以選 (A)。

第 4 題是概括主旨。文中並沒有明顯的主旨句，需要根據各段內容加以概括。第 1 段是由中國式婚姻的傳統習俗而引出話題，第 2 段講述的是中國式婚姻的目的，第 3 段講述的是年輕一代婚姻觀念的變遷，第 4 段講述的是晚婚和通婚。由此可知，短文內容是簡述中國式婚姻，所以選 (A)。

解答&技巧 | **01** (A)　**02** (C)　**03** (A)　**04** (A)

適用 TIP 1　適用 TIP 2　適用 TIP 3　適用 TIP 7　適用 TIP 10
適用 TIP 11　適用 TIP 12　適用 TIP 13　適用 TIP 14　適用 TIP 15

DAY
9

Part 1
詞
彙
題
Day 9
完成 25%

Part 2
綜
合
測
驗
Day 9
完成 50%

Part 3
文
意
選
填
Day 9
完成 75%

Part 4
閱
讀
測
驗
Day 9
完成 100%

補充

interdependent ⓐ 互相依賴的；interpersonal ⓐ 人際的；etiquette ⓝ 禮節；
bounden ⓐ 分內的，義務的；carry on ⓟⓗ 繼續

7,000 單字

- for [fɔr] prep 1 為，給
- not [nɑt] ad 1 不
- two [tu] num 1 二
- but [bʌt] conj 1 然而
- man [mæn] n 1 男人
- must [mʌst] v 1 必須
- permission [pɚˋmɪʃən] n 3 許可
- grand [grænd] ⓐ 1 盛大的

- wedding [ˋwɛdɪŋ] n 1 婚禮
- hold [hold] v 1 舉行
- from [frɑm] prep 1 從，自
- carry [ˋkærɪ] v 1 承擔
- up [ʌp] ad 1 趨於，靠近
- serve [sɝv] v 1 服務
- duty [ˋdjutɪ] n 2 義務，責任

MEMO

♫ 557

No budget for your vacation? Try home exchanges—swapping houses with strangers. Agree to use each other's cars, and you can save bucks on car rentals, too.

Home exchanges are not new. At least one group, Intervac, has been facilitating such an arrangement since 1953. But trading online is gaining popularity these days, with several sites in operation, including Home Exchanges. Founded in 1992, with some 28,000 listings, this company bills itself as the world's largest home exchange club, reporting that membership has increased by 30% this year.

The annual fee is usually less than US$100. Members can access thousands of listings for apartments, villas, suburban homes and farms around the world. Initial contact is made via e-mail, with subsequent communication usually by phone. Before a match is made, potential swappers tend to discuss a lot.

However, the concept may sound risky to some people. What about theft? Damage? These are reasonable causes for concern, but equally unlikely. As one swapper puts it, "Nobody is going to fly across the ocean or drive 600 miles to come to steal your TV. Besides, at the same time they're staying in your home, you are staying in their home."

Exchange sites recommend that swappers discuss such matters ahead of time. They may fill out an agreement spelling out who shoulders which responsibilities if a problem arises. It does not matter if the agreement would hold up in court, but it does give the exchangers a little satisfaction.

Generally, the biggest complaint among home exchangers has to do with different standards of cleanliness. Swappers are supposed to make sure their home is in order before they depart, but one person's idea of "clean" may be more forgiving than another's. Some owners say if they come back to a less-than-sparkling kitchen, it may be inconvenient but would not sour them on future exchanges.

01 What is the second paragraph mainly about?

    (A) How to exchange homes.

    (B) How home exchange is becoming popular.

    (C) The biggest home exchange agency.

    (D) A contrast between Intervac and Home Exchange.

02 Which of the following is closest in meaning to "bills" in the second paragraph?

    (A) Advertises.

    (B) Dedicates.

    (C) Replaces.

    (D) Participates.

03 How do home exchangers normally begin their communication?

    (A) By phone.

    (B) By e-mail.

    (C) Via a matchmaker.

    (D) Via a face-to-face meeting.

04 What is recommended in the passage to deal with theft and damage concerns?

    (A) One can file a lawsuit in court.

    (B) Both parties can trade online.

    (C) Both parties can sign an agreement beforehand.

    (D) One can damage the home of the other party in return.

DAY
9

Part 1
詞
彙
題
Day 9
完成 25%

Part 2
綜
合
測
驗
Day 9
完成 50%

Part 3
文
意
選
填
Day 9
完成 75%

Part 4
閱
讀
測
驗
Day 9
完成 100%

中譯｜沒有度假的預算嗎？那就試試房屋交換吧——與陌生人交換住處。同意使用彼此的汽車，這樣你也可以節省租車費用。

房屋交換並不新鮮。至少，有個名為 Intervac 的團體從一九五三起，就一直在從事房屋交換事宜。但是近些日子以來，線上交易正受到大眾的歡迎，包括 Home Exchanges 在內的幾家網站，都有這樣的交易。Home Exchanges 成立於一九九二年，有兩萬八千項列表，自詡為世界上最大的換房交易俱樂部，並聲稱今年的會員人數已經增長了三成。

Home Exchanges 的年費通常不超過一百美元。會員們可以選擇列表中分布在世界各地的數千處公寓、別墅、市郊房屋和農場。交易雙方透過電子郵件進行初步接觸，之後通常是電話交流。在達成協議之前，有意願的交易者們傾向談論諸多事宜。

然而，對於有些人來說，這種觀念也許是有風險的。發生盜竊、遭到損失怎麼辦？這些都是值得關注的合理事項，卻也同樣是不可能發生的。正如一個交換者所說的：「沒有人會飛越海洋，或是驅車六百英里，來偷你的電視機。此外，他們在你家的同時，你也在他們的家裡。」

交換網站建議，交換者要提前討論這些事項。他們也許會填寫一項協議，以此申明如果出現了問題，將由誰來承擔責任。這份協議會不會訴諸法庭，並不重要，但是它可以為交換者帶來些許的滿意。

通常，房屋交換者抱怨得最多的，與房屋清潔的不同標準有關。交換者離開之前，應該確保他們的住宅秩序井然，但是對於清潔的概念，一個人的尺度也許會比另一個人的尺度更為寬鬆。有些屋主說，如果他們回來時看到一個較為髒亂的廚房，也許會感到不便，卻也並不妨礙他們在進行日後的房屋交換。

解譯｜在閱讀文章之前，先要預覽題目，然後再帶著問題有針對性地閱讀文章。第 1 題是概括段落主旨，第 2 題是詞義辨析，第 3、4 題是文意理解。理解了題目要求之後，閱讀全文，依次作答。

第 1 題是概括第 2 段主旨。文中有明確的主旨句，根據第 2 段首句「Home exchanges are not new.」可知，房屋交換並不新鮮，之後的敘述，也證明了房屋交換的普遍性。由此可知，段落主旨為房屋交換變得愈來愈流行，即為選項 (B)。選項 (A) 意為「如何進行房屋交換」，選項 (C) 意為「最大的房屋交換機構」，選項 (D) 意為「Intervac and Home Exchange 之間的比較」，都不能表現段落主旨。

第 2 題是考 bill 的同義字。bill 可以作動詞，意為「送交帳單；宣佈；貼廣告」；也可以作名詞，意為「帳單；廣告；法案」。選項 (A) 意為「廣告」，選項 (B) 意為「奉獻」，選項 (C) 意為「替換」，選項 (D) 意為「參加」。根據第 2 段最後一句內容可知，在文中 bill 是用作動詞，意為「宣佈，廣告」，所以選 (A)。

第 3 題是文意理解，問的是房屋交易者如何開始溝通。根據第 3 段第 3 句內容「Initial contact is made via e-mail」可知，交易雙方是透過電子郵件進行初步接觸，與選項 (B) 相符。所以選 (B)。

第 4 題同樣是文意理解，問的是文中應對關於盜竊和損失的擔憂的建議。根據第 5 段第 2 句內容「They may fill out an agreement spelling out who shoulders which responsibilities if a problem arises.」可知，他們可以填寫一項協議，以此申明，如果出現了問題，將由誰來承擔責任，與選項 (C) 相符。所以選 (C)。

解答＆技巧 | 01 (B)　02 (A)　03 (B)　04 (C)

適用 TIP 1　適用 TIP 2　適用 TIP 7　適用 TIP 10　適用 TIP 11

適用 TIP 12　適用 TIP 13　適用 TIP 14　適用 TIP 15

補充

equally [ad] 同樣地，同等地；unlikely [a] 不可能的；swapper [n] 交易者，交換者；risky [a] 冒險的；cleanliness [n] 清潔，乾淨

7,000 單字

- vacation [veˋkeʃən] [n] ② 假日
- swap [swɑp] [v] ⑥ 交換，交易
- buck [bʌk] [n] ① 美元
- rental [ˋrɛntl̩] [n] ⑥ 租金
- facilitate [fəˋsɪləˏtet] [v] ⑥ 使容易，使便利
- bill [bɪl] [v] ② 宣傳
- fee [fi] [n] ② 費用
- villa [ˋvɪlə] [n] ⑥ 別墅

- suburban [səˋbɝbən] [a] ⑥ 郊區的，市郊的
- initial [ɪˋnɪʃəl] [a] ④ 開始的，最初的
- subsequent [ˋsʌbsɪˏkwɛnt] [a] ⑥ 後來的，隨後的
- theft [θɛft] [n] ⑥ 盜竊，偷竊
- steal [stil] [v] ② 偷，竊取
- spell [spɛl] [v] ① 拼寫
- depart [dɪˋpɑrt] [v] ④ 離開

MEMO

DAY 9

Part 1 詞彙題
Day 9 完成 25%

Part 2 綜合測驗
Day 9 完成 50%

Part 3 文意選填
Day 9 完成 75%

Part 4 閱讀測驗
Day 9 完成 100%

Etiquette for banquets in China is always of great significance.

Banquets are usually held in restaurants or hotels that have been reserved. Guests will be led to the banquet room by the waiters. By tradition, the head of the delegation, who should arrive later, will be honored by loud applause on his arrival.

As for seating arrangement, it seems to be much stricter in China than in the west. Generally the guests should wait to be guided to their seat by the host. Traditionally, seats on the right should be superior to seats on the left. Therefore, on formal occasions, the guests of honor are always seated on the right side.

At formal banquets, other guests should not begin to eat before the host serves the guest of honor. And on informal occasions, the host may just raise his chopsticks to announce the beginning of eating. Then guests could enjoy the food as they like. But they should be careful not to eat too fast. If a guest stops eating in the middle of the banquet, he will be regarded as rude and offensive.

Drinking a toast, undoubtedly, has always been playing an important role. Generally the host will stand up, hold his glass with both hands, and then say a few words as good wishes. Then guests should hold their glasses and drink. Politely filling other guests' glasses full symbolizes respect and friendship.

When the last dish is finished, a banquet is usually getting close to the end. And then they will bid farewell to each other before they leave.

01 Why are guests of honor seated on the right side on formal occasions?

(A) Because they like to sit on the right side.

(B) Because seats on the right are superior to seats on the left.

(C) Because the host asks them to sit on the right side.

(D) It's not clearly stated in the passage.

02 The word "offensive" in the fourth paragraph is closest in meaning to _____.

(A) insulting

(B) favorable

(C) harmless

(D) acceptable

03 Which one of the following statements is false?

(A) Guests of honor usually arrive late at a banquet.

(B) Toasting is quite important at a banquet.

(C) When the banquet comes to an end, guests will bid farewell to each other before leaving.

(D) At formal banquets, guests can begin eating at will.

04 What is the main idea of the passage?

(A) Drinking a toast.

(B) Seating arrangement.

(C) Etiquette for banquet in China.

(D) Bidding farewell.

DAY
9

Part 1
詞
彙
題
Day 9
完成 25%

Part 2
綜
合
測
驗
Day 9
完成 50%

Part 3
文
意
選
填
Day 9
完成 75%

Part 4
閱
讀
測
驗
Day 9
完成 100%

中譯 | 中國的宴會禮節通常是極為重要的。

宴會通常是在預訂好的餐廳或是飯店裡舉行。客人們將由侍者引領前往宴會包廂。根據傳統，來客中的領導者通常會來得晚一些，當他到來時，其他人會以熱烈的掌聲以示尊敬。

中國的座位安排要比西方來得嚴格。通常情況下，客人們應該等著主人來引領入座。按照傳統，相較於左邊的座位，右邊的座位更為尊貴。因此在正式場合中，貴賓總是坐在右邊。

在正式的宴會中，在主人為貴客夾菜之前，其他客人不可以開始進餐。在非正式的場合，主人也許就只是簡單地抬起筷子，示意大家開始。之後賓客就可以隨意享用食物。不過客人應當注意，進餐速度不要太快。如果客人在宴會進行過程中停止進餐，則會認為是粗魯、無禮的。

祝酒無疑地一直都是十分重要的。通常情況下，主人會站起身來，雙手舉杯，說一些話以示美好祝福。客人們也要舉杯飲酒。禮貌地為其他客人的杯子斟滿酒，也象徵著尊重和友情。

通常用完最後一道菜後，宴會也就接近尾聲。離開之前，客人們要相互道別。

解譯 | 在閱讀文章之前，先要預覽題目，然後再帶著問題有針對性地閱讀文章。第 1 題是文意理解，第 2 題是詞義辨析，第 3 題是判斷正誤，第 4 題是概括主旨。理解了題目要求之後，閱讀全文，依次作答。

第 1 題是文意理解，問的是在正式的場合，貴客為什麼要坐在右手邊。定位於第 3 段。根據第 3 句內容「Traditionally, seats on the right should be superior to seats on the left.」可知，按照傳統，相較於左邊的座位，右邊的座位更為尊貴，與選項 (B) 相符。所以選 (B)。

第 2 題是考形容詞 offensive 的同義字。選項 (A) 意為「無禮的，侮辱的」，選項 (B) 意為「有利的」，選項 (C) 意為「無害的」，選項 (D) 意為「可接受的」。根據第 4 段最後一句內容可知，offensive 在文中意為「冒犯的」，所以選 (A)。

第 3 題是判斷正誤，考的是細節，問的是哪一項敘述是錯誤的。根據第 4 段第 1 句內容「At formal banquets, other guests should not begin to eat before the host serves the guest of honor.」可知，在正式的宴會中，在主人為貴客夾菜之前，其他客人不可以開始進餐。選項 (D) 則是說，在正式的宴會中，客人可以隨意開始用餐，與文意不符。同樣，此題也可以用排除法來解答。第 2 段第 3 句內容與選項 (A) 相符，第 5 段第 1 句內容與選項 (B) 相符，第 6 段最後一句內容與選項 (C) 相符。這三個選項的敘述都是正確的，可以排除。所以選 (D)。

第 4 題是概括主旨。本篇結構是先總述後分述，第 1 段可以視為主旨段，文中有明確的主旨句，根據「Etiquette for banquets in China is always of great significance.」可知，文章主旨為中國式宴會禮儀，與選項 (C) 敘述相符。所以選 (C)。

解答＆技巧 ┃ 01 **(B)**　02 **(A)**　03 **(D)**　04 **(C)**

適用 TIP 1　適用 TIP 2　適用 TIP 3　適用 TIP 7　適用 TIP 10

適用 TIP 11　適用 TIP 12　適用 TIP 13　適用 TIP 14　適用 TIP 15

補充

usually ad 通常；generally ad 一般地，普遍地；beginning n 開始；in the middle of ph 在～中間；get close to the end ph 接近尾聲

7,000 單字

- banquet [ˈbæŋkwɪt] n 5 宴會
- waiter [ˈwetɚ] n 2 侍者
- delegation [ˌdɛləˈgeʃən] n 5 代表團
- loud [laʊd] a 1 響亮的
- applause [əˈplɔz] n 5 掌聲
- west [wɛst] n 1 西方
- chopstick [ˈtʃɑpˌstɪk] n 2 筷子
- careful [ˈkɛrfəl] a 1 小心的

- stop [stɑp] v 1 停止
- toast [tost] v 2 祝酒
- say [se] v 1 說
- glass [glæs] n 1 杯子
- symbolize [ˈsɪmblˌaɪz] v 6 象徵
- dish [dɪʃ] n 1 菜肴
- bid [bɪd] v 5 說，問候

MEMO

DAY 9

Part 1
詞
彙
題
Day 9
完成 25%

Part 2
綜
合
測
驗
Day 9
完成 50%

Part 3
文
意
選
填
Day 9
完成 75%

Part 4
閱
讀
測
驗
Day 9
完成 100%

DAY 10

10天掌握 7,000 單字和題型

Where there is a will, there is a way.

有志者，事竟成。

▶ **Part 1** ｜詞 彙 題

▶ **Part 2** ｜綜合測驗

▶ **Part 3** ｜文意選填

▶ **Part 4** ｜閱讀測驗

Part 1 | 詞彙題 | Vocabulary Questions

01 It is _____ for this talkative child to keep silent in the class for a whole day.

(A) skillful   (B) snowy

(C) southern   (D) abnormal

中譯｜這個愛說話的小孩一整天都在課堂上保持沉默，真是反常。

解說｜四個選項皆為形容詞。依據題意，應該是「反常的」，選項 (D) abnormal 表示「反常的」，符合題意，其他三個選項都不符合題意。

解答＆技巧｜**(D)** 適用 TIP 3   適用 TIP 4

> 補充
> a whole day ph 一整天
>
> 7,000 單字
> • talkative [ˈtɔkətɪv] a 2 多話的
> • skillful [ˈskɪlfəl] a 2 熟練的
> • snowy [snoɪ] a 2 下雪的
> • southern [ˈsʌðən] a 2 南方的
> • abnormal [æbˈnɔrml] a 6 反常的

---

02 He has been worrying about his grandma's illness, so he is _____ in the group discussion.

(A) straight   (B) sudden

(C) absentminded   (D) tasty

中譯｜他一直在擔心奶奶的病情，所以在小組討論中表現得有些心不在焉。

解說｜四個選項皆為形容詞。依據題意，應該是「在小組討論中表現得有些心不在焉」，選項 (C) absentminded 表示「心不在焉的」，符合題意，其他三個選項都不符合題意。

解答＆技巧｜**(C)** 適用 TIP 1   適用 TIP 4

> 補充
> group discussion ph 小組討論
>
> 7,000 單字
> • grandma [ˈɡrændmɑ] n 1 奶奶
> • straight [stret] a 2 直的
> • sudden [ˈsʌdn] a 2 突然的
> • absentminded [ˈæbsəntˈmaɪndɪd] a 6 心不在焉的
> • tasty [ˈtestɪ] a 2 美味的

---

03 In order to get home before dark, the drivers decided to _____ their taxis from 60 to 100 miles per hour.

(A) trade   (B) trap

(C) vote   (D) accelerate

中譯｜為了在天黑之前趕到家，那些計程車司機決定將車速從每小時六十英里加快到每小時一百英里。

解說｜四個選項皆為動詞。依據題意，應該是「加快車速」，選項 (D) accelerate 表示「加速」，符合題意，是正確選項。

解答＆技巧｜**(D)** 適用 TIP 1   適用 TIP 4

> 補充
> per hour ph 每小時
>
> 7,000 單字
> • taxi [ˈtæksɪ] n 1 計程車
> • trade [tred] v 2 交易
> • trap [træp] v 2 設陷阱
> • vote [vot] v 2 投票
> • accelerate [ækˈsɛləˌret] v 6 加速

DAY
10

Part 1
詞
彙
題
Day 10
完成 25%

Part 2
綜
合
測
驗
Day 10
完成 50%

Part 3
文
意
選
填
Day 10
完成 75%

Part 4
閱
讀
測
驗
Day 10
完成 100%

04 The cafeteria is so large that it can _____ 500 people for meals at the same time.

(A) accommodate   (B) wet

(C) admire   (D) bless

補充
at the same time ph 同時

7,000 單字
- cafeteria [ˌkæfə`tɪrɪə] n 2 自助餐廳
- accommodate [ə`kɑmə,det] v 6 容納
- wet [wɛt] v 2 弄濕
- admire [əd`maɪr] v 3 欽佩
- bless [blɛs] v 3 祝福

中譯│這家自助餐廳很大，能夠同時容納五百人用餐。

解說│四個選項皆為動詞。依據題意，應該是「同時容納五百人用餐」，選項 (A) accommodate 表示「容納」，符合題意，其他三個選項都不符合題意。

解答＆技巧│ **(A)** 適用 TIP 1 適用 TIP 4

---

05 The supervisor's conduct didn't _____ with his words, so we all didn't buy his story.

(A) prosper   (B) buzz

(C) accord   (D) cast

補充
accord with ph 與～一致

7,000 單字
- supervisor [ˌsupɚ`vaɪzɚ] n 5 管理人
- prosper [`prɑspɚ] v 4 使繁盛
- buzz [bʌz] v 3 使嗡嗡叫
- accord [ə`kɔrd] v 6 使一致
- cast [kæst] v 3 投擲

中譯│那個管理人的言行不一致，所以我們都不相信他的話。

解說│四個選項皆為動詞。依據題意，應該是「言行不一致」，選項 (C) accord 表示「一致」，而片語 accord with 表示「與～一致」，符合題意。

解答＆技巧│ **(C)** 適用 TIP 1 適用 TIP 4

---

06 You should learn to act in _____ with the rules in our company, or else you will be dismissed.

(A) carriage   (B) carpenter

(C) accordance   (D) buffet

補充
in accordance with ph 依照

7,000 單字
- dismiss [dɪs`mɪs] v 4 解雇
- carriage [`kærɪdʒ] n 3 運輸
- carpenter [`kɑrpəntɚ] n 3 木匠
- accordance [ə`kɔrdəns] n 6 一致
- buffet [bu`fe] n 3 自助餐

中譯│在我們公司你應該學會按照章程行事，否則你會被開除。

解說│四個選項皆為名詞。依據題意，應該是「學會按照章程行事」，選項 (C) accordance 表示「一致，符合」，而片語 in accordance with 表示「按照」，符合題意。

解答＆技巧│ **(C)** 適用 TIP 2 適用 TIP 4

07 It snowed for a whole day yesterday, and the snow had _____ to a depth of six feet this morning.

(A) chewed   (B) accumulated

(C) choked   (D) confused

補充
accumulate to ph 積累到

7,000 單字
- depth [dɛpθ] n 2 深度
- chew [tʃu] v 3 咀嚼
- accumulate [əˋkjumjə‚let] v 6 積累
- choke [tʃok] v 3 窒息
- confuse [kənˋfjuz] v 3 使混亂

中譯│昨天下了一天的雪,今天早晨雪已經積到六呎深了。

解說│四個選項皆為動詞。依據題意,應該是「雪已經積了六呎深」,選項 (B) accumulated 表示「累積」,符合題意,其他三個選項都不符合題意。

解答&技巧│ **(B)** 適用 TIP 3 適用 TIP 4

---

08 Your aunt will sleep in this room, so you need to clean away the _____ of dirt here today.

(A) cone   (B) accumulation

(C) rectangle   (D) restroom

補充
clean away ph 清除

7,000 單字
- aunt [ænt] n 1 姑姑
- cone [kon] n 3 圓錐體
- accumulation [ə‚kjumjəˋleʃən] n 6 積累
- rectangle [rɛkˋtæŋgl] n 2 矩形
- restroom [ˋrɛstrum] n 2 (公共場所的)洗手間

中譯│你姑姑會睡在這個房間,所以你今天要把這裡的積塵清理一下。

解說│四個選項皆為名詞。依據題意,應該是「把這裡的積塵清理一下」,選項 (B) accumulation 表示「累積」,符合題意,是正確選項。

解答&技巧│ **(B)** 適用 TIP 1 適用 TIP 4

---

09 He has spent much time on the _____ of foreign language, so he can speak at least six languages now.

(A) acquisition   (B) runner

(C) suit   (D) wing

補充
at least ph 至少

7,000 單字
- six [sɪks] num 1 六
- acquisition [‚ækwəˋzɪʃən] n 6 獲得
- runner [ˋrʌnɚ] n 2 跑步者
- suit [sut] n 2 西服
- wing [wɪŋ] n 2 翅膀

中譯│他花費了大量時間來學習外語,所以現在他至少會說六種語言。

解說│四個選項皆為名詞。依據題意,應該是「花費大量時間來學習外語」,選項 (A) acquisition 表示「學習」,符合題意,其他三個選項都不符合題意。

解答&技巧│ **(A)** 適用 TIP 3 適用 TIP 4

10 They said that it was completely in conformity with the principle of _____ to local conditions, and we could do likewise in the future.

(A) wool
(B) gamble
(C) adaptation
(D) acquaintance

中譯｜他們說這完全符合因地制宜的原則，今後我們可以這麼做。

解說｜四個選項皆為名詞。依據題意，應該是「符合因地制宜的原則」，選項 (C) adaptation 表示「適應」，符合題意，其他三個選項都不符合題意。

解答＆技巧｜(C) 適用 TIP 3 適用 TIP 4

DAY 10

補充
in conformity with ph 符合

7,000 單字
• conformity [kənˋfɔrməti] n 6 一致
• wool [wʊl] n 2 羊毛
• gamble [ˋgæmbl] n 3 賭博
• adaptation [ˌædæpˋteʃən] n 6 適應
• acquaintance [əˋkwentəns] n 4 熟人

Part 1
詞彙題
Day 10
完成 25%

11 Human rights are fundamental rights to which a person is _____ entitled, that is, rights that she or he is born with. 　【101年指考英文】

(A) inherently
(B) imperatively
(C) authentically
(D) alternatively

中譯｜人權是一個人固有的基本權利，也就是她或他與生俱來的權利。

解說｜四個選項皆為副詞。依據題意，應該是「固有的基本權利」，選項 (A) inherently 表示「固有地」，符合題意。

解答＆技巧｜(A) 適用 TIP 1 適用 TIP 4

Part 2
綜合測驗
Day 10
完成 50%

補充
human rights ph 人權
be entitled to ph 有～的權利

7,000 單字
• she [ʃi] pron 1 她
• inherently [ɪnˋhɪrəntlɪ] ad 6 固有地
• imperatively [ɪmˋpɛrətɪvlɪ] ad 6 命令式地
• authentically [ɔˋθɛntɪklɪ] ad 6 真正地
• alternatively [ɔlˋtɝnəˌtɪvlɪ] ad 6 二者選一地

Part 3
文意選填
Day 10
完成 75%

12 Many students are _____ to the online games and thus negelct their studies.

(A) constant
(B) countable
(C) dramatic
(D) addicted

中譯｜很多學生沉迷於網路遊戲，因而荒廢了學業。

解說｜四個選項皆為形容詞。依據題意，應該是「沉迷於網路遊戲」，選項 (D) addicted 表示「沉迷的」，而片語 be addicted to 表示「沉迷於」，符合題意。

解答＆技巧｜(D) 適用 TIP 2 適用 TIP 4

Part 4
閱讀測驗
Day 10
完成 100%

補充
be addicted to ph 沉迷於

7,000 單字
• online [ˋɑnˌlaɪn] a 3 線上
• constant [ˋkɑnstənt] a 3 不變的
• countable [ˋkaʊntəbl] a 3 可數的
• dramatic [drəˋmætɪk] a 3 引人注目的
• addicted [əˋdɪktɪd] a 6 沉溺的

13 My uncle's drug _____ is so severe that he cannot live for one day without drugs.

(A) campus　　　　(B) expression
(C) addiction　　　(D) edition

補充
live for ph 為～而生活
7,000 單字
• uncle [`ʌŋkl] n 1 叔叔
• campus [`kæmpəs] n 3 大學校園
• expression [ɪk`sprɛʃən] n 3 表達
• addiction [ə`dɪkʃən] n 6 上癮
• edition [ɪ`dɪʃən] n 3 版本

中譯｜我叔叔的毒癮太深了，一天不吸毒，他就活不下去。

解說｜四個選項皆為名詞。依據題意，應該是「毒癮太深」，選項 (C) addiction 表示「上癮」，符合題意，是正確選項。

解答&技巧｜**(C)** 適用 TIP 3　適用 TIP 4

14 There are 10 network _____ in the Internet café, whose main work is to ensure the computers are in normal use.

(A) fans　　　　　(B) governors
(C) grasshoppers　(D) administrators

補充
normal use ph 正常使用
7,000 單字
• whose [huz] pron 1 誰的
• fan [fæn] n 3 迷
• governor [`gʌvənə] n 3 州長
• grasshopper [`græs͵hɑpə] n 3 蚱蜢
• administrator [əd`mɪnə͵stretə] n 6 管理人

中譯｜這家網咖有十名網路管理員，他們的主要工作是確保電腦能夠正常使用。

解說｜四個選項皆為名詞。依據題意，應該是「網路管理員」，選項 (D) administrators 表示「管理員」，符合題意，其他三個選項都不符合題意。

解答&技巧｜**(D)** 適用 TIP 3　適用 TIP 4

15 I dare _____ that the eggs must be very expensive during the Moon Festival because a lot of eggs will be needed to make mooncakes.

(A) affirm　　　　(B) heap
(C) heal　　　　　(D) leap

補充
Moon Festival ph 中秋節
7,000 單字
• mooncake [`munkek] n 6 月餅
• affirm [ə`fɜm] v 6 斷言
• heap [hip] v 3 堆積
• heal [hil] v 3 治癒
• leap [lip] v 3 飛躍

中譯｜我敢肯定，中秋節期間雞蛋的價格會很貴，因為需要大量雞蛋來製作月餅。

解說｜四個選項皆為動詞。依據題意，應該是「我敢肯定」，選項 (A) affirm 表示「肯定」，符合題意，其他三個選項都不符合題意。

解答&技巧｜**(A)** 適用 TIP 3　適用 TIP 4

16 Drinking lots of white spirits is not good for your health, so you can try low wine such as fermented _____ beverages instead.

(A) lively　　　　　　(B) magical

(C) alcoholic　　　　(D) marble

補充
alcoholic beverage ph 酒精飲料

7,000 單字
- spirit [ˋspɪrɪt] n 2 烈酒
- lively [ˋlaɪvlɪ] a 3 活潑的
- magical [ˋmædʒɪkl] a 3 魔術的
- alcoholic [͵ælkəˋhɔlɪk] a 6 含酒精的
- marble [ˋmɑrbl] a 3 大理石的

中譯｜喝大量白酒不利於健康，所以你可以用釀造酒這樣的低度酒來代替。

解說｜四個選項皆為形容詞。依據題意，應該是「用釀造酒來代替」，選項 (C) alcoholic 表示「酒精的」，符合題意，其他三個選項都不符合題意。

解答＆技巧｜**(C)** 適用 TIP 1　適用 TIP 4

---

17 The girl began to gradually _____ herself from her fiancé after she found he had a secret lover.

(A) mend　　　　　　(B) alienate

(C) pave　　　　　　(D) peel

補充
alienate from ph 使疏遠

7,000 單字
- fiancé [͵fiɑnˋse] n 5 未婚夫
- mend [mɛnd] v 3 修理
- alienate [ˋeljən͵et] v 6 疏遠
- pave [pev] v 3 鋪設
- peel [pil] v 3 剝落

中譯｜那個女孩發現自己的未婚夫有一位祕密情人後，就開始漸漸地疏遠他。

解說｜四個選項皆為動詞。依據題意，應該是「漸漸地疏遠他」，選項 (B) alienate 表示「疏遠」，符合題意，是正確選項。

解答＆技巧｜**(B)** 適用 TIP 3　適用 TIP 4

---

18 The supplies are limited, so please try to averagely _____ them to every victim in the earthquake-stricken region.

(A) plug　　　　　　(B) poll

(C) allocate　　　　(D) pretend

補充
earthquake-stricken region ph 地震災區

7,000 單字
- victim [ˋvɪktɪm] n 3 受害人
- plug [plʌg] v 3 插入
- poll [pol] v 3 投票
- allocate [ˋælə͵ket] v 6 分配
- pretend [prɪˋtɛnd] v 3 假裝

中譯｜物資有限，所以請儘量平均分配給每一位地震災區的災民。

解說｜四個選項皆為動詞。依據題意，應該是「平均分配給每一位災民」，選項 (C) allocate 表示「分配」，符合題意，其他三個選項都不符合題意。

解答＆技巧｜**(C)** 適用 TIP 3　適用 TIP 4

DAY 10

Part 1
詞
彙
題
Day 10
完成 25%

Part 2
綜
合
測
驗
Day 10
完成 50%

Part 3
文
意
選
填
Day 10
完成 75%

Part 4
閱
讀
測
驗
Day 10
完成 100%

19 The principal of this company said that if the first project failed, they would use a(an) _____ plan.

(A) sensible   (B) alternative

(C) rusty   (D) scary

中譯│這間公司的負責人說，如果第一個計畫失敗了，他們會使用備選方案。

解說│四個選項皆為形容詞。依據題意，應該是「使用備選方案」，選項 (B) alternative 表示「可供選擇的」，符合題意，其他三個選項都不符合題意。

解答＆技巧│**(B)** 適用 TIP 3   適用 TIP 4

---

20 There is an _____ in this sentence in the essay, so we could understand it from two different aspects.

(A) separation   (B) shallow

(C) ambiguity   (D) shepherd

中譯│散文中的這個句子有歧義，所以我們可以從兩個不同的方面來理解。

解說│四個選項皆為名詞。依據題意，應該是「句子有歧義」，選項 (C) ambiguity 表示「歧義，模稜兩可」，符合題意，是正確選項。

解答＆技巧│**(C)** 適用 TIP 1   適用 TIP 4

---

21 When I asked about her nationality, she gave me such an _____ answer that I didn't know where she came from on earth.

(A) ambiguous   (B) practical

(C) shady   (D) sexy

中譯│我詢問她的國籍時，她給了我一個模稜兩可的回答，以致於我不知道她究竟來自哪裡。

解說│四個選項皆為形容詞。依據題意，應該是「模稜兩可的回答」，選項 (A) ambiguous 表示「模稜兩可的」，符合題意，其他三個選項都不符合題意。

解答＆技巧│**(A)** 適用 TIP 3   適用 TIP 4

DAY
10

Part 1
詞
彙
題
Day 10
完成 25%

Part 2
綜
合
測
驗
Day 10
完成 50%

Part 3
文
意
選
填
Day 10
完成 75%

Part 4
閱
讀
測
驗
Day 10
完成 100%

22 The child fell down the stairway; you get a(an) ＿＿＿ and send him to the nearest hospital at once.

(A) shrink　　　　　(B) similarity

(C) ambulance　　　(D) skyscraper

補充
fall down ph 摔下

7,000 單字
- stairway [ˋstɛr͵we] n 3 樓梯
- shrink [ʃrɪŋk] n 3 收縮
- similarity [͵sɪməˋlærətɪ] n 3 類似
- ambulance [ˋæmbjələns]
  n 6 救護車
- skyscraper [ˋskaɪ͵skrepɚ]
  n 3 摩天樓

中譯｜那個小孩從樓梯上摔了下來，你馬上找一輛救護車把他送到最近的醫院。

解說｜四個選項皆為名詞。依據題意，應該是「找一輛救護車把他送到醫院」，選項 (C) ambulance 表示「救護車」，符合題意。

解答＆技巧｜**(C)** 適用 TIP 1　適用 TIP 4

---

23 The loudspeaker is of poor quality, so you need to ＿＿＿ its sound and make sure everyone at present can listen clearly.

(A) spade　　　　　(B) spill

(C) amplify　　　　(D) splash

補充
of poor quality ph 品質差的

7,000 單字
- loudspeaker [ˋlaud͵spikɚ]
  n 3 揚聲器
- spade [sped] v 3 鏟
- spill [spɪl] v 3 溢出
- amplify [ˋæmplə͵faɪ] v 6 放大
- splash [splæʃ] v 3 飛濺

中譯｜擴音器的品質不好，所以你要將它的聲音放大，以確定在場的每個人都能聽清楚。

解說｜四個選項皆為動詞。依據題意，應該是「把擴音器的聲音放大」，選項 (C) amplify 表示「放大」，符合題意，是正確答案。

解答＆技巧｜**(C)** 適用 TIP 1　適用 TIP 4

---

24 The ice cream made in this shop is so ＿＿＿ that hundreds of people buy it every day.

(A) yummy　　　　(B) sexual

(C) steep　　　　　(D) stiff

補充
hundreds of ph 數以百計

7,000 單字
- cream [krim] n 2 奶油
- yummy [ˋjʌmɪ] a 1 好吃的
- sexual [ˋsɛkʃuəl] a 3 性的
- steep [stip] a 3 陡峭的
- stiff [stɪf] a 3 呆板的

中譯｜這家店做的冰淇淋非常好吃，以致於每天都有數百人前來購買。

解說｜四個選項皆為形容詞。依據題意，應該是「冰淇淋非常好吃」，選項 (A) yummy 表示「好吃的」，符合題意，其他三個選項都不符合題意。

解答＆技巧｜**(A)** 適用 TIP 3　適用 TIP 4

 **Part 2** 綜合測驗 | **Comprehensive Questions**

 1 ▶ 100 年指考英文

> People may express their feelings differently on different occasions. Cultures sometimes vary greatly in this regard. A group of researchers in Japan, __01__ , studied the facial reactions of students to a horror film. When the Japanese students watched the film __02__ the teacher present, their faces showed only the slightest hints of reaction. But when they thought they were alone (though they __03__ by a secret camera), their faces twisted into vivid mixes of anguished distress, fear, and disgust.
>
> The study also shows that there are several unspoken rules about how feelings should be __04__ shown on different occasions. One of the most common rules is minimizing the show of emotion. This is the Japanese norm for feelings of distress __05__ someone in authority, which explains why the students masked their upset with a poker face in the experiment.

01 _____ (A) as usual   (B) in some cases
               (C) to be frank   (D) for example

02 _____ (A) of   (B) as
               (C) from   (D) with

03 _____ (A) were being taped   (B) had taped
               (C) are taping   (D) have been taped

04 _____ (A) rarely   (B) similarly
               (C) properly   (D) critically

05 _____ (A) with the help of   (B) in the presence of
               (C) on top of   (D) in place of

中譯｜人們表達情緒的方式會隨著場合而有所不同。在這一點上，文化有時會出現很大的差異。例如，日本的一組研究人員研究了學生們在觀看恐怖電影時的面部反應。當日本學生在有老師在場的情況下觀看電影時，他們的臉上僅僅表現出略微的反應跡象。但是當他們認為自己是獨處時（儘管他們正被一台隱藏式攝影機所拍攝），他們的臉龐生動地扭曲著，混合著極度痛苦的憂慮、害怕以及厭惡。

這項研究也顯示了，如何在不同的場合下恰當地表達情感，存在著一些不言而喻的規則。其中最常見的一個規則是將情感表現最小化。這就是日本人在權威人士面前處理痛苦感的標準，也解釋了學生們在實驗中為何要用面無表情來掩飾內心的慌亂。

解說｜本篇短文介紹了情感表達的影響因素。第 1 題考介系詞片語的用法。依據題意，空格後面的內容是為了舉例說明，所以應該用 for example 充當句子的插入語，正確選擇為 (D)。第 2 題考介系詞的用法。根據所學的知識，with sb. present 是一個固定搭配，表示「有某人在場」，所以最符合題意的選項是 (D)。第 3 題考時態的用法。依據題意，句子的主詞為 they，介系詞 by 表被動，所以動詞要用被動形式。而句子所表達的時態為過去進行式，所以要用過去進行式的被動語態，即 were being taped，正確選項是 (A)。第 4 題要選擇合適的副詞。四個選項中，properly 表示「恰當地」符合題意，所以正確選擇為 (C)。第 5 題將四個介系詞片語一一代入，in the presence of 表示「有某人在場」符合題意，所以選 (B)。

解答&技巧｜ 01 **(D)** 02 **(D)** 03 **(A)** 04 **(C)** 05 **(B)**

適用 TIP 1　適用 TIP 2　適用 TIP 7　適用 TIP 11

補充

differently ad 不同地；greatly ad 極大地；Japan n 日本；anguished a 痛苦的；unspoken a 不言而喻的

7,000 單字

- vary [ˋvɛrɪ] v 3 改變
- regard [rɪˋgɑrd] n 6 注意
- facial [ˋfeʃəl] a 4 面部的
- reaction [rɪˋækʃən] n 3 反應
- horror [ˋhɔrɚ] n 3 恐怖
- film [fɪlm] n 2 電影
- watch [wɑtʃ] v 1 觀看
- twist [twɪst] v 3 扭曲

- distress [dɪˋstrɛs] n 5 悲痛
- disgust [dɪsˋgʌst] n 4 厭惡
- minimize [ˋmɪnəˏmaɪz] v 6 最小化
- emotion [ɪˋmoʃən] n 2 情緒
- norm [nɔrm] n 6 規範
- frank [fræŋk] a 2 坦白的
- presence [ˋprɛzns] n 2 存在

Over the last ten years, a revolution has taken place in office work. At first, large computers were only used by large and rich companies which could __01__ them. But with the advancement of technology, small computers have come to the market, and they are able to do all the same work that larger and more expensive computers have __02__ done. Thus even the smallest company can use the computer now.

The main development in small computers has been __03__ the field of word processors. According to a rough statistic, about 70% of the secretaries and managers are making use of the word processors. With the help of these word processors, the secretaries can be freed __04__ a lot of routine work, and they can use this time to do something more interesting. Thus much money will be saved, and the secretarial time will also be made better use of. But a problem is that if a person uses word processors for a long time, he could slowly suffer from __05__ of sight.

01 _____ (A) revenge (B) scratch
(C) terrify (D) afford

02 _____ (A) before (B) ever
(C) ago (D) after

03 _____ (A) to (B) on
(C) in (D) up

04 _____ (A) from (B) with
(C) downward (D) outward

05 _____ (A) tragedy (B) usage
(C) loss (D) affection

DAY
10

Part 1
詞
彙
題
Day 10
完成 25%

Part 2
綜
合
測
驗
Day 10
完成 50%

Part 3
文
意
選
填
Day 10
完成 75%

Part 4
閱
讀
測
驗
Day 10
完成 100%

中譯｜在過去十年間，辦公室工作已經歷了重大變革。起初，只有大型且富有的公司才能用得起大型電腦。但是隨著技術的提升，小型電腦已經進入市場，能夠完成以往較大型、較昂貴的電腦所做的工作。因此現在即使是最小型的公司也能夠使用電腦了。

小型電腦的主要發展在於文字處理器。根據一項粗略數據，約有百分之七十的祕書和管理者在使用文字處理器。在這些文字處理器的幫助下，祕書能夠免除很多日常工作，而且能夠利用這些時間來做一些更有意思的事情。於是更多資金被節省下來，更多處理祕書工作的時間得到更好的利用。但是有一個問題，如果一個人使用文字處理器的時間過長，他可能會慢慢喪失視力。

解說｜本篇短文主要介紹了小型電腦的使用。第 1 題考動詞的用法。四個選項中，afford 表示「買得起」符合題意，所以正確選擇為 (D)。第 2 題要選擇合適的副詞來修飾動詞 done。依據題意，ever 作副詞表示「曾經」，可以修飾 done，其他選項不符合題意，所以最佳選項是 (B)。第 3 題考介系詞的用法。根據所學的知識，in the field of 表示「在～方面，在～領域」，所以正確選項是 (C)。第 4 題也是考介系詞的用法。根據上下文的內容，be freed from 表示「免於，免受」，是常用的固定搭配，所以選項 (A) 符合題意。第 5 題考名詞片語的用法。依據題意，應該是「視力喪失」，可以表達為 loss of sight，要用名詞 loss 表示「失去」，所以選 (C)。

解答＆技巧｜ 01 **(D)** 02 **(B)** 03 **(C)** 04 **(A)** 05 **(C)**

適用 TIP 1 　 適用 TIP 2 　 適用 TIP 7 　 適用 TIP 11

補充

office work ph 辦公室工作；processor n 處理器；with the help of ph 在～的幫助下；secretarial a 祕書的；make use of ph 利用

7,000 單字

- over [ˋovɚ] prep ❶ 在～之上
- small [smɔl] a ❶ 小的
- rough [rʌf] a ❸ 粗略的
- secretary [ˋsɛkrə⸴tɛrɪ] n ❷ 祕書
- routine [ruˋtin] a ❸ 日常的
- save [sev] v ❶ 節省
- sight [saɪt] n ❶ 眼界
- revenge [rɪˋvɛndʒ] v ❹ 報復

- scratch [skrætʃ] v ❹ 抓
- terrify [ˋtɛrə⸴faɪ] v ❹ 恐嚇
- afford [əˋford] v ❸ 買得起
- downward [ˋdaunwəd] ad ❺ 向下
- outward [ˋautwəd] ad ❺ 向外
- tragedy [ˋtrædʒədɪ] n ❹ 悲劇
- affection [əˋfɛkʃən] n ❺ 喜愛

Many parents have been anxious about their children's __01__ on the roads. Thus a new scheme has been decided to start by the education authorities. This scheme is mainly to solve the problem of getting children to and from school, and could set the parents at __02__ .

The schools have provided bus __03__ for children living more than three miles from their schools or less than three miles if other reasons exist. But now the schools have made a decision that if a group of parents ask for organizing transport for their children, they would be prepared to do that, so long as the schools will not __04__ money, and the children will be willing to attend the nearest school.

The new scheme will be tried out this semester. The schools have consulted with the bus company for the purpose that they can provide the service at a low __05__ . And most of the bus companies have agreed on it and made an extra journey to pick up the children who live further away.

01 _____   (A) aisle   (B) arena
          (C) bazaar   (D) safety

02 _____   (A) boyhood   (B) ease
          (C) bulge   (D) coastline

03 _____   (A) master   (B) stop
          (C) service   (D) bar

04 _____   (A) lose   (B) push
          (C) conduct   (D) discard

05 _____   (A) doorstep   (B) dressing
          (C) cost   (D) gorge

中譯｜很多家長一直擔心孩子們在路上的安全，於是教育當局已經決定展開一項新的方案。這項方案主要用於解決孩子們上下學的問題，使家長們能夠放心。

學校已經為住在三英哩外，或者三英哩內但有其他原因的孩童提供了公車服務。但是現在學校做出了決定，如果一群家長要求為他們的孩子安排接送，那麼學校將會準備那樣做，只要學校不會賠錢，而孩子們也願意去最近的學校上學。

新的方案將於本學期試行。學校已經與公車公司進行協商，讓他們能以低成本提供服務。大多數的公車公司已經就此達成了一致意見，增加額外行駛路程來接送住得更遠的孩童。

解說｜本篇短文講述了有關學校為孩童提供公車服務的問題。第 1 題根據上下文的內容可知，家長主要擔心孩子的安全問題，四個選項中，safety 表示「安全」，所以正確選擇為 (D)。第 2 題考與介系詞 at 相關的片語用法。依據題意，應該是使家長放心，可以用 at ease 表示「舒適，安逸」，最符合題意的選項是 (B)。第 3 題依據題意，應該是提供公車服務，名詞 service 表示「服務」符合題意，即正確選項是 (C)。第 4 題根據上下文的內容，學校要保證這樣做不會賠錢，而 lose money 可以表示「損失金錢，賠錢」符合題意，所以正確選擇為 (A)。第 5 題考介系詞片語的用法。依據題意，應該讓他們能以低成本提供服務，at a low cost 表示「以低成本」，所以選 (C)。

解答＆技巧｜ 01 (D) 02 (B) 03 (C) 04 (A) 05 (C)

適用 TIP 2　適用 TIP 4　適用 TIP 7　適用 TIP 11

補充

solve the problem ph 解決問題；make a decision ph 做決定；so long as ph 只要；
attend school ph 去上學；agree on ph 同意

7,000 單字

- scheme [skim] n 5 計畫
- ask [æsk] v 1 要求
- semester [sə`mɛstə] n 2 學期
- consult [kən`sʌlt] v 4 商議
- low [lo] a 1 低的
- pick [pɪk] v 2 挑選
- further [`fɝðə] ad 2 更遠地
- aisle [aɪl] n 5 通道

- arena [ə`rinə] n 5 競技場
- bazaar [bə`zɑr] n 5 集市
- bulge [bʌldʒ] n 5 膨脹
- master [`mæstə] n 1 主人
- push [puʃ] v 1 推
- discard [dɪs`kɑrd] v 5 拋棄
- gorge [gɔrdʒ] n 5 峽谷

DAY
10

Part 1
詞彙題
Day 10
完成 25%

Part 2
綜合測驗
Day 10
完成 50%

Part 3
文意選填
Day 10
完成 75%

Part 4
閱讀測驗
Day 10
完成 100%

4 ▶ | 101 年學測英文 |

Kizhi is an island on Lake Onega in Karelia, Russia, with a beautiful collection of wooden churches and houses. It is one of the most popular tourist __01__ in Russia and a United Nations Educational, Scientific, and Cultural Organization (UNESCO) World Heritage Site.

The island is about 7 km long and 0.5 km wide. It is surrounded by about 5,000 other islands, some of __02__ are just rocks sticking out of the ground.

The entire island of Kizhi is, __03__ , an outdoor museum of wooden architecture created in 1966. It contains many historically significant and beautiful wooden structures, __04__ windmills, boathouses, chapels, fish houses, and homes. The jewel of the architecture is the 22-domed Transfiguration Church, built in the early 1700s. It is about 37 m tall, __05__ it one of the tallest log structures in the world. The church was built with pine trees brought from the mainland, which was quite common in the 18th century.

01 _____ (A) affairs   (B) fashions
              (C) industries   (D) attractions

02 _____ (A) them   (B) that
              (C) those   (D) which

03 _____ (A) in fact   (B) once again
              (C) as usual   (D) for instance

04 _____ (A) except   (B) besides
              (C) including   (D) regarding

05 _____ (A) make   (B) making
              (C) made   (D) to make

DAY 10

Part 1
詞
彙
題
Day 10
完成 25%

Part 2
綜
合
測
驗
Day 10
完成 50%

Part 3
文
意
選
填
Day 10
完成 75%

Part 4
閱
讀
測
驗
Day 10
完成 100%

中譯｜基日島是俄羅斯卡累利阿共和國的一個島嶼，位於奧涅加湖上，島上彙集著漂亮的木質教堂和房屋。它是俄羅斯最受歡迎的旅遊景點之一，聯合國教科文組織將其列入世界遺產地。

這個島嶼長約七千公尺，寬約五百公尺，周圍被大約五千個其他島嶼所環繞，其中一些島嶼只是突出地面的岩石。

事實上，整個基日島是一個在一九六六年創建的木質建築戶外博物館。它容納了許多在歷史上有重大意義的、漂亮的木質構造，包括風車、船庫、小教堂、魚屋和住家。基日島上建築的瑰寶是有著二十二座穹頂的顯聖容天主堂，於一七〇〇年代早期建造，大約有三十七公尺高，使得它成為世界上最高的原木建築物。這座教堂是用由大陸帶來的松樹建造而成，這在十八世紀很常見。

解說｜本篇短文介紹了基日島的概況。第 1 題考名詞片語的用法。依據題意，「旅遊景點」可以表達為 tourist attractions，是一個固定搭配，所以正確選擇為 (D)。第 2 題考代名詞的用法。根據上下文的內容，空格處的代名詞指代 5,000 other islands，通常用 which 來指代，最符合題意的選項是 (D)。第 3 題考介系詞片語的用法。將四個選項一一代入，in fact 表示「事實上，實際上」符合題意，即正確選項是 (A)。第 4 題要選擇合適的介系詞。依據題意，空格後面所列舉的事物包含在前面的事物之內，四個選項中，只有 including 表示「包含，包括」，所以選項 (C) 符合題意。第 5 題依據題意，動詞 make 在句中修飾前面的句子，所以 make 要用現在分詞 making，正確選擇為 (B)。

解答＆技巧｜ 01 (D)　02 (D)　03 (A)　04 (C)　05 (B)

適用 TIP 1　適用 TIP 2　適用 TIP 7　適用 TIP 11

> 補充
>
> Kizhi n 基日島；Lake Onega ph 奧涅加湖；Karelia n 卡累利阿共和國；Russia n 俄國；UNESCO ph 聯合國教科文組織
>
> 7,000 單字
>
> - lake [lek] n 1 湖
> - wooden [ˈwʊdn̩] a 2 木製的
> - tourist [ˈtʊrɪst] n 3 遊客
> - educational [ˌɛdʒuˈkeʃən̩] a 3 教育的
> - heritage [ˈhɛrətɪdʒ] n 6 遺產
> - site [saɪt] n 4 地點
> - rock [rɑk] n 1 岩石
> - entire [ɪnˈtaɪr] a 2 整個的
> - outdoor [ˈaʊtˌdor] a 3 戶外的
> - architecture [ˈɑrkəˌtɛktʃɚ] n 5 建築式樣
> - fish [fɪʃ] n 1 魚
> - pine [paɪn] n 3 松樹
> - mainland [ˈmenlənd] n 5 大陸
> - fact [fækt] n 1 事實
> - include [ɪnˈklud] v 2 包含

Shirley came to visit me nearly every day, which made me feel quite
__01__ . Although she was only a nineteen-year-old girl, she smoked
continually and never used an ashtray. She often fought __02__ my daughter,
but they would make peace after a while. Sometimes she even followed me
to the kitchen when I was making tea or preparing dinner.

I really could not tell why she chose my __03__ because she had
graduated from a famous drama school, and I thought that she would have
been paid much attention to. Though she had been arranged by the director
to play a leading part with some fairly distinguished and experienced actors,
they didn't like her very much and always took every __04__ to run her down.
Although I felt troubled by her, I didn't dislike her because she actually had
much charm, and I enjoyed the feeling with her __05__ . She was just like my
lovely little sister.

| 01 | _____ | (A) forgetful | (B) uneasy |
| | | (C) extinct | (D) elaborate |

| 02 | _____ | (A) on | (B) over |
| | | (C) in | (D) with |

| 03 | _____ | (A) destination | (B) customs |
| | | (C) company | (D) counsel |

| 04 | _____ | (A) opportunity | (B) consent |
| | | (C) comrade | (D) journal |

| 05 | _____ | (A) instead | (B) around |
| | | (C) indeed | (D) roughly |

DAY 10

Part 1
詞彙題
Day 10
完成 25%

Part 2
綜合測驗
Day 10
完成 50%

Part 3
文意選填
Day 10
完成 75%

Part 4
閱讀測驗
Day 10
完成 100%

中譯｜雪麗幾乎每天都來拜訪我，這讓我感到很不自在。儘管她只是一個十九歲的女孩，但是她不停地抽菸，而且從來不用菸灰缸。她經常和我的女兒吵架，但是她們不久就會和好。有時甚至於我在廚房沏茶或是準備晚餐時，她也會跟著我。

我真的不懂她為什麼選擇跟我做朋友，因為她畢業於一所著名的戲劇學校，而我以為她本應該獲得更多的關注。儘管導演安排她跟其他相當著名和有經驗的演員一起扮演主要角色，但是他們非常不喜歡她，總是一有機會就指責她。儘管她使我感到困擾，但是我並不討厭她，因為她實際上很有魅力，而我喜歡她在身邊的感覺。她就像我可愛的小妹妹一樣。

解說｜本篇短文講述了主角「我」與一個女孩雪麗之間發生的故事。第 1 題的四個選項都是形容詞。依據題意，應該是雪麗的舉動使我感到很不自在，uneasy 表示「不自在的」，符合題意，所以正確選擇為 (B)。第 2 題考動詞 fight 的用法。fight 可以與介系詞 with 搭配使用，表示「與～打／吵架」，最符合題意的選項是 (D)。第 3 題根據上下文的內容可知，第二段內容講的是與工作相關的事情，空格處應該選擇 company 表示「同伴，作伴」，即正確選項是 (C)。第 4 題考動詞片語的用法。依據題意，take opportunity to do sth. 表示「抓住機會做某事」，所以選項 (A) 符合題意。第 5 題考副詞的用法。依據題意，with sb. around 表示「有人在附近／身邊」，符合題意，所以選 (B)。

解答＆技巧｜ 01 (B) 02 (D) 03 (C) 04 (A) 05 (B)
適用 TIP 1　適用 TIP 2　適用 TIP 7　適用 TIP 11

補充
ashtray n 菸灰缸；make peace ph 和解；after a while ph 過一會兒；distinguished a 著名的；experienced a 有經驗的

7,000 單字
- although [ɔlˋðo] conj 2 儘管
- fight [faɪt] v 1 打架
- graduate [ˋgrædʒu͵et] v 3 畢業
- director [dəˋrɛktɚ] n 2 導演
- part [pɑrt] n 1 角色
- fairly [ˋfɛrlɪ] ad 3 相當地
- actor [ˋæktɚ] n 1 演員
- dislike [dɪsˋlaɪk] v 3 不喜歡
- charm [tʃɑrm] n 3 魅力
- lovely [ˋlʌvlɪ] a 2 可愛的
- sister [ˋsɪstɚ] n 1 妹妹
- forgetful [fɚˋgɛtfəl] a 5 健忘的
- extinct [ɪkˋstɪŋkt] a 5 滅絕的
- counsel [ˋkaʊnsl] n 5 法律顧問
- comrade [ˋkɑmræd] n 5 同志

A firm should pay great attention to the training of its staff because there may be many __01__ in its departments. Staff training should have a purpose which usually refers to the introduction of job descriptions and job specifications.

As we know, the job description should give all details of the performance that is __02__ for a particular job, but the job specification should give the employees information about the behavior, knowledge and skills that are __03__. In order to make the employees perform successfully in the job, the Training Department must use the best methods to do the training.

Different training methods can have different advantages and disadvantages. Successful training programs not only teach the employees to learn about skills, but also teach them how to use these skills in the job. Generally, when the training comes to an __04__, the company will have an evaluation of it and then decide which employees are __05__, which is very important for every employee.

01 _____   (A) salaries   (B) settlers
                   (C) problems   (D) triumphs

02 _____   (A) required   (B) transformed
                   (C) wrecked   (D) alternated

03 _____   (A) battered   (B) browsed
                   (C) commuted   (D) expected

04 _____   (A) consent   (B) end
                   (C) distress   (D) exile

05 _____   (A) frantic   (B) grim
                   (C) qualified   (D) hoarse

DAY
10

Part 1
詞
彙
題
Day 10
完成 25%

Part 2
綜
合
測
驗
Day 10
完成 50%

Part 3
文
意
選
填
Day 10
完成 75%

Part 4
閱
讀
測
驗
Day 10
完成 100%

中譯│ 一家公司應該密切關注員工的培訓，因為公司的部門可能存在很多問題。員工培訓應該有目的性，通常是職務説明及工作規範的介紹。

正如我們所知，職務説明應該具體介紹一份特定的工作所要求的表現，而工作規範則應該向員工説明公司所期望的行為舉止、知識和技能的資訊。為了使員工在工作中表現成功，培訓部門必須採用最好的方法來進行培訓。

不同的培訓方法會有不同的優點和缺點。成功的培訓方案不僅要教會員工學習技能，還要教會他們如何在工作中使用這些技能。通常當培訓結束時，公司會對其進行評估，決定哪些員工合格，這對每一位員工來説都很重要。

解説│ 本篇短文的主旨是「員工培訓」，介紹了員工培訓的方法以及重要性。第 1 題依據題意，對員工進行培訓，是因為部門內部可能存在很多問題，名詞 problem 表示「問題」符合題意，所以正確選擇為 (C)。第 2 題根據上下文的內容，這些表現是工作中所需要的，required 表示「需要」，最符合題意的選項是 (A)。第 3 題的四個選項都是動詞，將其一一代入，expected 表示「期待」符合題意，即正確選項是 (D)。第 4 題考動詞片語的用法。依據題意，「結束」可以表達為 come to an end，是一個固定搭配，所以選項 (B) 符合題意。第 5 題的四個選項都是形容詞。依據題意，應該是公司決定哪些員工是合格的，可以用 qualified 來表示「合格的」，所以選 (C)。

解答＆技巧│ **01 (C)** **02 (A)** **03 (D)** **04 (B)** **05 (C)**

適用 TIP 2　適用 TIP 4　適用 TIP 7　適用 TIP 11

補充
staff training ph 員工培訓；refer to ph 指的是；specification n 説明；
in order to do sth. ph 為了做某事；training department ph 培訓部門

7,000 單字
- introduction [ˌɪntrəˈdʌkʃən] n 3 介紹
- description [dɪˈskrɪpʃən] n 3 描述
- performance [pəˈfɔrməns] n 3 業績
- successfully [səkˈsɛsfəlɪ] ad 2 成功地
- advantage [ədˈvæntɪdʒ] n 3 優點
- disadvantage [ˌdɪsədˈvæntɪdʒ] n 4 缺點
- program [ˈprogræm] n 3 計畫
- evaluation [ɪˌvæljuˈeʃən] n 4 評價

- salary [ˈsælərɪ] n 3 薪水
- wreck [rɛk] v 4 破壞
- alternate [ˈɔltənɪt] v 5 交替
- batter [ˈbætə] v 5 猛擊
- exile [ˈɛksaɪl] n 5 流放
- frantic [ˈfræntɪk] a 5 狂亂的
- hoarse [hors] a 5 嘶啞的

7 ▶ 101 年學測英文

There was once a time when all human beings were gods. However, they often took their divinity for granted and __01__ abused it. Seeing this, Brahma, the chief god, decided to take their divinity away from them and hide it __02__ it could never be found.

Brahma called a council of the gods to help him decide on a place to hide the divinity. The gods suggested that they hide it __03__ in the earth or take it to the top of the highest mountain. But Brahma thought __04__ would do because he believed humans would dig into the earth and climb every mountain, and eventually find it. So, the gods gave up.

Brahma thought for a long time and finally decided to hide their divinity in the center of their own being, for humans would never think to __05__ it there. Since that time humans have been going up and down the earth, digging, climbing, and exploring—searching for something already within themselves.

01	_____	(A) yet	(B) even
		(C) never	(D) rather

02	_____	(A) though	(B) because
		(C) where	(D) when

03	_____	(A) close	(B) apart
		(C) deep	(D) hard

04	_____	(A) each	(B) more
		(C) any	(D) neither

05	_____	(A) look for	(B) get over
		(C) do without	(D) bump into

DAY
10

Part 1
詞
彙
題
Day 10
完成 25%

Part 2
綜
合
測
驗
Day 10
完成 50%

Part 3
文
意
選
填
Day 10
完成 75%

Part 4
閱
讀
測
驗
Day 10
完成 100%

中譯 | 曾經有一段時間，所有人都是神。然而，他們卻經常認為自己的神性是理所當然的，甚至濫用神性。看到這種情況，主神梵天決定將他們的神性拿走，並藏在一個永遠也找不到的地方。

梵天找來諸神召開會議，來幫他選定一個隱藏神性的地方。諸神建議將神性藏在地底深處，或是將它帶到最高的山峰。但是梵天認為兩者都不妥，因為他相信人類會挖掘土地，並且攀登每一座山，最後總會找到它。因此，諸神都放棄了。

梵天思索了很長時間，最終決定將他們的神性藏在他們自身當中，因為人類永遠也不會想到去那裡尋找神性。從那個時候起，人類就一直在地球上上下下忙個不停——挖掘、攀爬、探索，來尋找已經存在於他們身上的東西。

解說 | 本篇短文講述了一則神話故事。第 1 題根據上下文的內容可知，應該是甚至濫用神性，副詞 even 表示「甚至」，符合題意，所以正確選擇為 (B)。第 2 題空格處應當選用表「地方」的關係副詞來指代地點。四個選項中，只有 where 表示地方，最符合題意的選項是 (C)。第 3 題根據上下文的內容可知，deep in the earth 表示「地底深處」，與 the top of the highest mountain 形成對照，所以正確選項是 (C)。第 4 題依據題意可知，梵天認為這兩個地方都不妥，要用 neither 表示「兩者都不」，所以選項 (D) 符合題意。第 5 題考動詞片語的用法。依據題意應該是「尋找」，四個選項中，只有 look for 表示「尋找」，所以選 (A)。

解答＆技巧 | 01 (B)　02 (C)　03 (C)　04 (D)　05 (A)

適用 TIP 1　適用 TIP 2　適用 TIP 7　適用 TIP 11

補充
divinity n 神性；Brahma n 梵天；eventually ad 最終；gave up ph 放棄；
up and down ph 上上下下

7,000 單字
- once [wʌns] ad 1 曾經
- god [gɑd] n 1 神
- abuse [əˋbjuz] v 6 濫用
- hide [haɪd] v 2 隱藏
- call [kɔl] v 1 召集
- top [tɑp] n 1 頂部
- dig [dɪg] v 1 挖
- into [ˋɪntu] prep 1 到～裡

- search [sɝtʃ] v 2 搜尋
- already [ɔlˋrɛdɪ] ad 1 已經
- rather [ˋræðɚ] ad 2 相當
- apart [əˋpɑrt] a 3 分離的
- deep [dip] a 1 深的
- each [itʃ] a 1 每一的
- bump [bʌmp] v 3 碰撞

The concept of reading has changed substantially __01__ the last century, and increased attention has been paid to defining and describing the reading process. Some experts believe that language is primarily a code which uses symbols to __02__ sounds, therefore, reading is simply the decoding process of symbols into the sounds they stand __03__ . Other experts think that reading is related to thinking. If a child just pronounces the sounds without interpreting their meanings, he is not truly reading.

Although many people have the ability to read, they actually do not read a book in its __04__ and thus could not be classified as readers. It is true that the philosophy, objectives, methods and materials of reading depend on the definition people use. According to the most satisfactory definition, reading should be the ability to unlock the symbol code of the language and to interpret its meaning for various purposes. In __05__ , reading is to interpret the ideas using symbols which represent sounds and ideas.

01 _____ (A) to (B) for
(C) as (D) over

02 _____ (A) hurl (B) represent
(C) impose (D) jeer

03 _____ (A) for (B) with
(C) upon (D) into

04 _____ (A) jury (B) mansion
(C) entirety (D) mileage

05 _____ (A) molecule (B) short
(C) notion (D) opponent

中譯│在上個世紀期間，閱讀的概念已經發生了顯著的改變，定義和描述閱讀過程已經獲得更高的關注。一些專家認為，語言主要是一種代碼，用符號來代表聲音，因此簡單說閱讀，就是解碼的過程，將符號破解成其所代表的聲音。其他專家則認為閱讀與思考有關。如果一個兒童只是發出讀音而沒有解讀其含義，他就不是真正地閱讀。

儘管很多人有能力進行閱讀，但是他們實際上並沒有全面地讀一本書，因此無法被歸類為讀者。確實，閱讀的哲理、目標、方法和材料取決於人們所使用的定義。最符合要求的定義指出，閱讀應該是開啟語言的符號代碼，並為了各種目的而解讀其含義的能力。總之，閱讀是用代表聲音和觀念的符號來解讀觀念。

解說│本篇短文的主旨是「閱讀」，介紹了閱讀的定義以及方法。第 1 題考介系詞片語的用法。依據題意，時間副詞「在上個世紀期間」可以表達為 over the last century，要用介系詞 over 來引導，所以正確選擇為 (D)。第 2 題的四個選項都是動詞。依據題意，應該是用符號來替代聲音，動詞 represent 表示「代表」，所以最符合題意的選項是 (B)。第 3 題考動詞 stand 的用法。根據所學的知識，stand 通常與介系詞 for 搭配使用，表示「代表」，所以正確選項是 (A)。第 4 題考介系詞片語的用法。依據題意，「全面地，從整體上看」可以表達為 in its entirety，所以選項 (C) 符合題意。第 5 題依據題意可知，最後一個句子是全文的總結，其前應該用表示總結性的介系詞片語來引導。而四個選項中，只有 short 能夠與介系詞 in 搭配，表示「總之，簡言之」，所以選 (B)。

解答＆技巧│ 01 (D)　02 (B)　03 (A)　04 (C)　05 (B)
適用 TIP 1　適用 TIP 2　適用 TIP 7　適用 TIP 11

補充
substantially ad 很大程度地；increased a 增加的；be related to ph 與～有關；truly ad 真正地；be classified as ph 被歸為

7,000 單字
• concept [ˈkɑnsɛpt] n 4 概念
• define [dɪˈfaɪn] v 3 下定義
• describe [dɪˈskraɪb] v 2 描述
• code [kod] n 4 代碼
• pronounce [prəˈnaʊns] v 2 發音
• satisfactory [ˌsætɪsˈfæktərɪ] a 3 令人滿意的
• unlock [ʌnˈlɑk] v 6 解開
• represent [ˌrɛprɪˈzɛnt] v 3 代表

• hurl [hɝl] v 5 投擲
• impose [ɪmˈpoz] v 5 利用
• jeer [dʒɪr] v 5 嘲笑
• mansion [ˈmænʃən] n 5 大廈
• mileage [ˈmaɪlɪdʒ] n 5 英里數
• notion [ˈnoʃən] n 5 見解
• opponent [əˈponənt] n 5 對手

9 ▶ 101 年指考英文

In 1985, a riot at a Brussels soccer match occurred, in which many fans lost their lives. The __01__ began 45 minutes before the start of the European Cup final. The British team was scheduled to __02__ the Italian team in the game. Noisy British fans, after setting off some rockets and fireworks to cheer for __03__ team, broke through a thin wire fence and started to attack the Italian fans. The Italians, in panic, __04__ the main exit in their section when a six-foot concrete wall collapsed.

By the end of the night, 38 soccer fans had died, and 437 were injured. The majority of the deaths resulted from people __05__ trampled underfoot or crushed against barriers in the stadium. As a result of this 1985 soccer incident, security measures have since been tightened at major sports competitions to prevent similar events from happening.

01 _____ (A) circumstance   (B) sequence
(C) tragedy   (D) phenomenon

02 _____ (A) oppose to   (B) fight over
(C) battle for   (D) compete against

03 _____ (A) a   (B) that
(C) each   (D) their

04 _____ (A) headed for   (B) backed up
(C) called out   (D) passed on

05 _____ (A) be   (B) been
(C) being   (D) to be

中譯 │ 一九八五年在布魯塞爾的足球比賽中，發生了一場暴亂，許多球迷都喪失了生命。悲劇發生在歐洲盃決賽開始前的四十五分鐘，英國隊預定要在比賽中對抗義大利隊。吵鬧的英國球迷們再釋放煙火為他們的球隊加油喝彩，突破了細鐵絲柵欄，開始對義大利球迷們發動攻擊。義大利人非常驚慌，起身前往所在場區的主要出口，此時一面六英尺高的水泥牆倒塌了。

到夜晚結束的時候，三十八位球迷死亡，四百三十七位球迷受傷。大多數死者是由於在體育場上遭到踐踏或是被柵欄所壓倒。由於一九八五年的這起足球事件，自此主要運動競賽的安全措施得到了加強，以防止類似事件的發生。

解說 │ 本篇短文講述了發生在布魯塞爾足球比賽中的一場暴亂。第 1 題的四個選項都是名詞。依據題意，這場暴亂導致很多人死亡，應該是一場悲劇，而 tragedy 表示「悲劇」，所以正確選擇為 (C)。第 2 題根據上下文的內容可知，應該是兩支球隊之間進行比賽，四個選項中，動詞片語 compete against 表示「與～競爭」，所以最符合題意的選項是 (D)。第 3 題考代名詞的用法。依據題意，空格處的代名詞指代的是 British fans，是複數名詞，所以要用複數代名詞 their 來進行指代，即正確選項是 (D)。第 4 題的四個選項都是動詞片語，將其一一代入可知，headed for 表示「前往」符合題意，所以正確選擇為 (A)。第 5 題中，介系詞 from 後面的動詞 be 應當用動名詞 being，所以選 (C)。

解答＆技巧 │ 01 (C)　　02 (D)　　03 (D)　　04 (A)　　05 (C)
適用 TIP 2　適用 TIP 7　適用 TIP 9　適用 TIP 11

補充

Brussels n 布魯塞爾；European Cup ph 歐洲盃；in panic ph 恐慌地；underfoot ad 在腳下地；security measures ph 安全措施

7,000 單字

- riot [ˈraɪət] n 6 暴亂
- final [ˈfaɪnl] n 1 決賽
- noisy [ˈnɔɪzɪ] a 1 嘈雜的
- firework [ˈfaɪr͵wɝk] n 3 煙火
- wire [waɪr] n 2 電線
- exit [ˈɛksɪt] n 3 出口
- section [ˈsɛkʃən] n 2 地區
- concrete [ˈkɑnkrit] n 4 混凝土

- injured [ˈɪndʒɚd] a 3 受傷的
- stadium [ˈstedɪəm] n 3 體育場
- incident [ˈɪnsədnt] n 4 事故
- tighten [ˈtaɪtn] v 3 變緊
- sequence [ˈsikwəns] n 6 順序
- phenomenon [fəˈnɑmə͵nɑn] n 4 現象
- oppose [əˈpoz] v 4 反對

Part 1
詞彙題
Day 10
完成 25%

Part 2
綜合測驗
Day 10
完成 50%

Part 3
文意選填
Day 10
完成 75%

Part 4
閱讀測驗
Day 10
完成 100%

DAY 10

A good modern newspaper should be extraordinary and remarkable. It usually contains some comments, interviews and __01__ of books, arts, theater, and music from the editorial page to feature articles. Many people read a newspaper in different ways. They may never read it __02__ or straight through, but by jumping from here to there or glancing __03__ one piece. They may also read certain article all the time or read just a few paragraphs.

In order to attract many different readers, a good modern newspaper provides a variety which is due to its topicality and immediate __04__ to what is happening in the world around them. Every person would pay attention to the content he is interested in, therefore, no two people really read the same paper. When reading the newspaper, each person may have a selection and get what he wants without missing anything he needs and without wasting time. Hence, the __05__ of reading can be an important thing for a reader to think about.

01 _____   (A) organizer   (B) patriot
             (C) criticism   (D) pinch

02 _____   (A) recklessly   (B) completely
             (C) substantially   (D) abnormally

03 _____   (A) at   (B) in
             (C) to   (D) on

04 _____   (A) acceleration   (B) certainty
             (C) diagnosis   (D) relation

05 _____   (A) donation   (B) technique
             (C) excerpt   (D) glamour

DAY 10

Part 1
詞彙題
Day 10
完成 25%

Part 2
綜合測驗
Day 10
完成 50%

Part 3
文意選填
Day 10
完成 75%

Part 4
閱讀測驗
Day 10
完成 100%

中譯｜一份好的當代報紙應該是特別且引人注目的。從社論到專題文章，它通常包含一些評論、訪談、以及對書籍、藝術、戲劇和音樂的評論。很多人用不同的方式來讀報紙。他們可能永遠不會讀完整份報紙或是從頭讀到尾，而是從這個地方跳到那個地方，瀏覽某一則報導。他們也可能一直閱讀某篇文章，或是只閱讀幾個段落。

為了吸引很多不同的讀者，一份好的當代報紙提供了多樣性，因為它具有時事性，與周圍世界正在發生的事情有著直接關聯。每個人都會關注自己感興趣的內容，因此沒有兩個人真的讀的是同一份報紙。看報紙時，每個人都可能會做出選擇，在不錯過任何所需要的資訊，且不浪費時間的情況下，獲得自己想要的東西。因此，對於讀者來說，閱讀技巧是需要思考的重要事情。

解說｜本篇短文的主旨是「報紙」，介紹了閱讀報紙的不同方法。第 1 題的四個選項都是名詞，將其一一代入，criticism 表示「評論」最符合題意，所以正確選擇為 (C)。第 2 題要選擇合適的副詞來修飾動詞 read。依據題意，應該是完全地閱讀，可以用 completely 表示「完全地」，所以最符合題意的選項是 (B)。第 3 題考動詞 glance 的用法。根據所學的知識，動詞 glance 通常與介系詞 at 連用，表示「瀏覽，看一下」，即正確選項是 (A)。第 4 題的四個選項中，只有 relation 能夠與介系詞 to 搭配使用，表示「與～相關」，所以選項 (D) 符合題意。第 5 題根據主旨可知，整篇短文都是在講閱讀報紙的方法，所以最後一句表現了這篇短文的主旨，四個選項中，technique 表示「方法，技巧」符合題意，所以選 (B)。

解答＆技巧｜ **01 (C)** **02 (B)** **03 (A)** **04 (D)** **05 (B)**
適用 TIP 1　適用 TIP 2　適用 TIP 7　適用 TIP 11

補充
straight through ⓟ 徑直；all the time ⓟ 一直；be due to ⓟ 由於；topicality ⓝ 時事性；read the newspaper ⓟ 看報紙

7,000 單字
- remarkable [rɪˋmɑrkəbl] ⓐ 4 引人注目的
- interview [ˋɪntɚˌvju] ⓝ 2 採訪
- editorial [ˌɛdəˋtorɪəl] ⓐ 6 編輯的
- page [pedʒ] ⓝ 1 頁
- jump [dʒʌmp] ⓥ 1 跳
- variety [vəˋraɪətɪ] ⓝ 3 種類
- content [kənˋtɛnt] ⓝ 4 內容
- waste [west] ⓥ 1 浪費

- patriot [ˋpetrɪət] ⓝ 5 愛國者
- pinch [pɪntʃ] ⓝ 5 （一）撮，少量
- acceleration [ækˌsɛləˋreʃən] ⓝ 6 加速
- diagnosis [ˌdaɪəgˋnosɪs] ⓝ 6 診斷
- donation [doˋneʃən] ⓝ 6 捐贈
- excerpt [ˋɛksɝpt] ⓝ 6 摘錄
- glamour [ˋglæmɚ] ⓝ 6 魅力

Part 3 文意選填 | **Cloze Test**

1▶

Unlike most sports, which evolved over time from street games, basketball was designed by Dr. James Naismith to suit a __01__ purpose. His purpose was to invent a __02__ game that could be played indoors in winter.

In 1891, Naismith was an instructor at a training school. That year the school was trying to find a physical activity that men could enjoy between the football and baseball __03__. None of the __04__ indoor activities held their interest for long. Naismith was asked to solve the problem.

He first tried to __05__ some of the popular outdoor sports, but they were all too rough. Players may be getting __06__ from tackling each other and being hit with equipment. So, Naismith decided to invent a game that would incorporate the most common elements of outdoor __07__ sports without having the real physical contact. Most popular sports used a ball, so he chose a soccer ball because it was soft and large enough. The sport required no equipment, such as a bat or a racket to hit it. Next he decided on an elevated goal so that __08__ would depend on skill and accuracy rather than on strength only. His goals were two peach baskets, fixed to ten-foot-high balconies at each end of the gym. The basic idea of the game was to throw the ball into the basket. Naismith set original rules for the game, many of which, though with some small changes, are still in __09__ now.

Basketball was an __10__ success. The new sport quickly took on. Today, basketball has been one of the most popular games throughout the world.

(A) standard   (B) vigorous   (C) scores   (D) immediate   (E) particular
(F) bruised   (G) seasons   (H) adapt   (I) team   (J) effect

01 ____   02 ____   03 ____   04 ____   05 ____

06 ____   07 ____   08 ____   09 ____   10 ____

選項中譯 │ 一般的；有活力的；得分；立即的；特別的；受傷；賽季；改編；團隊；
效果

DAY
10

Part 1
詞
彙
題

Day 10
完成 25%

Part 2
綜
合
測
驗

Day 10
完成 50%

Part 3
文
意
選
填

Day 10
完成 75%

Part 4
閱
讀
測
驗

Day 10
完成 100%

中譯 │ 大多數的運動是隨時間過去，從街頭比賽發展而來，籃球運動卻與此不同，是由
詹姆斯・奈史密斯博士為實現某種特殊目的而開創的。他的目的是開發一種冬天
時可以在室內進行的有活力的運動。

一八九一年，奈史密斯是一所訓練學校的教員。那一年，這所學校正在試圖尋找
一種可以在足球賽季和棒球賽季之間進行的體育活動。一般的室內活動都無法長
時間地引起人們的興趣。奈史密斯受命來解決這個難題。

最初他試圖去改造一些流行的戶外運動，不過那些戶外運動都過於粗暴。運動員
們互相拉扯，或是被運動器具擊中時，很可能會受傷。所以奈史密斯決定，開創
一種包含戶外團體運動中最為常見的要素，卻沒有實際身體接觸的運動。大多數
的流行運動都會用到球，所以他選擇了一種夠軟也夠大的足球。這種運動不需要
球棒、球拍之類的器具來擊球。然後，他決定使用一種架高的球門，這樣的話，
得分所要憑藉的就是技巧和準確度，而不僅僅是力度了。他的球門是兩個放桃子
的籃子，固定在體育館兩端的十英尺高的陽臺上。這項運動最初的設想，是要將
球扔進籃子裡。奈史密斯設定了最初的比賽規則，儘管後來大多有了些小小的改
變，但到現在仍然在沿用。

籃球運動很快取得了成功。這種新的運動方式很快被人們接受。現在，籃球已經
成為世界上最為流行的運動之一。

解譯 │ 閱讀全文可知，這篇文章的主題是籃球運動的起源。

縱觀各選項，選項 (C)、(G)、(I)、(J) 是名詞，選項 (F)、(H) 是動詞，選項 (A)、
(B)、(D)、(E) 是形容詞。根據題意，第 3、7、8、9 題應選名詞，第 5、6 題應
選動詞，第 1、2、4、10 題應選形容詞。然後根據文章，依次作答。

第 1 題是選擇形容詞，有四個形容詞可供選擇，即為選項 (A)、(B)、(D)、(E)。
選項 (A) 意為「一般的」，選項 (B) 意為「有活力的」，選項 (D) 意為「立即的」，
選項 (E) 意為「特別的」，根據句意可知，應當是「實現某種特殊目的」，所
以選 (E)。第 2 題所選形容詞，句意為「在室內進行的有活力的運動」，所以選
(B)。第 4 題所選形容詞，句意為「一般的室內活動」，所以選 (A)。第 10 題則
是選 (D)，an immediate success 意為「很快取得成功」。

第 3 題是選擇名詞，有四個名詞可供選擇，即為選項 (C)、(G)、(I)、(J)，選項
(C) 意為「得分」，選項 (G) 意為「賽季」，選項 (I) 意為「團隊」，選項 (J) 意
為「效果」，根據句意，應當是「在足球賽季和棒球賽季之間」，所以選 (G)。
第 7 題所選名詞，根據句意，應當是「團體運動」，所以選 (I)。第 8 題所選名
詞，根據句意，應當是「得分所要憑藉的就是技巧和準確度」，所以選 (C)。第
9 題則是選 (J)，be in effect 意為「在實行中，有效」。

第 5 題是選擇動詞，有兩個動詞可供選擇，即為選項 (F)、(H)，句意為「他試圖
去改造一些流行的戶外運動」，所以選 (H)。第 6 題則是選 (F)，get bruised 意
為「受傷」。

解答 & 技巧 | **01** (E)　　**02** (B)　　**03** (G)　　**04** (A)　　**05** (H)
　　　　　 06 (F)　　**07** (I)　　**08** (C)　　**09** (J)　　**10** (D)

適用 TIP 1　適用 TIP 2　適用 TIP 6　適用 TIP 7　適用 TIP 8
適用 TIP 9　適用 TIP 10　適用 TIP 11

補充

evolve from ph 由～發展而來；over time ph 隨著時間的推移，久而久之；
training school ph 訓練所；baseball season ph 棒球賽季；throw... into... ph 把～扔進～中

7,000 單字

- evolve [ɪˋvɑlv] v 6 進化，逐漸形成
- basketball [ˋbæskɪt͵bɔl] n 1 籃球
- particular [pəˋtɪkjəlɚ] a 2 特別的
- purpose [ˋpɝpəs] n 1 目的
- vigorous [ˋvɪgərəs] a 5 有活力的
- indoors [ˋɪnˋdorz] ad 3 室內
- standard [ˋstændəd] a 2 一般的，普通的
- indoor [ˋɪn͵dor] a 3 室內的

- team [tim] n 2 團隊
- soccer [ˋsakɚ] n 2 足球
- score [skor] n 2 得分
- accuracy [ˋækjərəsɪ] n 4 準確
- basket [ˋbæskɪt] n 1 籃子
- balcony [ˋbælkənɪ] n 2 陽臺
- gym [dʒɪm] n 3 體育館

MEMO

2 ▶

On the tip of each finger is a **01** pattern of ridges, known as the fingerprint. No two people in the world have the same **02** . Even twins have different fingerprints. A person's fingerprints last a **03** , unless they are altered by disease or injury. Fingerprints are believed to be the best way to **04** a certain person.

Fingerprints were not used as **05** until about 100 years ago. The English government kept the prints of its workers and prisoners. Sir Francis Galton made the first large **06** of fingerprints. Based on Galton's work, fingerprints began to be used to **07** down criminals. Sir Edward R. Henry created a system to **08** criminals by their prints later. And in 1924, the United States set up a print file at the FBI, with prints of more than 173 million people.

The original way to get one's fingerprint is very easy. First, soak the finger pulp in ink. Then roll the finger on a card from side to side. This step can be **09** for different fingers and different people.

You can also create your own prints. **10** with a pencil on a piece of paper until you get a gray smudge. Rub your finger pulp in the smudge, and then press a piece of clear tape on your finger. Next, stick the tape to a card, and it's done!

DAY 10

Part 1
詞
彙
題
Day 10
完成 25%

Part 2
綜
合
測
驗
Day 10
完成 50%

Part 3
文
意
選
填
Day 10
完成 75%

Part 4
閱
讀
測
驗
Day 10
完成 100%

(A) records   (B) fingerprints   (C) identify   (D) distinct   (E) repeated
(F) Scribble   (G) lifetime   (H) recognize   (I) collection   (J) track

01 _____   02 _____   03 _____   04 _____   05 _____

06 _____   07 _____   08 _____   09 _____   10 _____

選項中譯│記錄；指紋；辨別；清晰的；重複；亂畫；畢生；識別；收藏；追蹤

中譯│每根手指前端都有一圈清晰的凹凸紋路，這就是指紋。世界上沒有兩個人具有相同的指紋。即便是雙胞胎，也有不同的指紋。若非傷病，指紋是終生不變的。人們認為，指紋是確定某人身份的最佳方式。

直到一百年前，指紋才被記錄下來。英國政府保存了工人們和囚犯們的指紋。法蘭西斯‧高爾頓爵士建立了第一個大型的指紋收藏庫。基於高爾頓爵士的工作，指紋開始被用於追蹤罪犯。後來，愛德華‧R‧亨利爵士創立了用指紋來識別罪犯的系統。一九二四年，美國聯邦調查局設立指紋檔案，保存了一億七千三百多萬人的指紋。

最初採指紋的方法十分簡單。首先，把指腹沾上墨汁，然後在卡片上從一側滾到另一側，不同手指的指紋、不同人的指紋，都可以用這種方式重複採集。

你也可以採自己的指紋。在一張紙上用鉛筆隨意亂畫，直到出現一個灰色的印跡。將指腹在這個汙跡上摩擦，然後把手指按在透明膠帶上，接下來，把膠帶黏到一張卡片上。這樣就可以了。

解譯│閱讀全文可知，這篇文章的主題是指紋。

縱觀各選項，選項 (A)、(B)、(G)、(I) 是名詞，選項 (C)、(E)、(F)、(H)、(J) 是動詞，選項 (D) 是形容詞。根據題意，第 2、3、5、6 題應選名詞，第 4、7、8、9、10 題應選動詞，第 1 題應選形容詞。然後根據文章，依次作答。

第 1 題是選擇形容詞，只有一個形容詞可供選擇，即為選項 (D)，意為「清晰的」。

第 2 題是選擇名詞，有四個名詞可供選擇，即為選項 (A)、(B)、(G)、(I)，選項 (A) 意為「記錄」，選項 (B) 意為「指紋」，選項 (G) 意為「畢生」，選項 (I) 意為「收藏」，根據句意，應當是「世界上沒有兩個人具有相同的指紋」，所以選 (B)。第 3 題所選名詞，可以視為固定搭配，last a lifetime 意為「持續終生」，所以選 (G)。第 5 題所選名詞，根據句意，應當是「直到一百年前，指紋才被記錄下來」，所以選 (A)。第 6 題則是選 (I)，意為「建立了第一個大型的指紋收藏庫」。

第 4 題是選擇動詞，有五個動詞可供選擇，即為選項 (C)、(E)、(F)、(H)、(J)，句意為「指紋是確定某人身份的最佳方式」，所以選項 (C)。第 7 題所選動詞，可以視為固定搭配，track down 意為「追蹤」，所以選 (J)。第 8 題所選動詞，根據句意可知，應當是「用指紋來識別罪犯」，所以選 (H)。第 9 題所選動詞，意為「可以用這種方式重複採集」，所以選 (E)。第 10 題則是選 (F)，意為「在一張紙上用鉛筆隨意亂畫」。

解答&技巧 | **01** (D)　**02** (B)　**03** (G)　**04** (C)　**05** (A)
06 (I)　**07** (J)　**08** (H)　**09** (E)　**10** (F)

適用 TIP 1　適用 TIP 2　適用 TIP 6　適用 TIP 7　適用 TIP 8
適用 TIP 9　適用 TIP 10　適用 TIP 11

DAY
10

Part 1
詞
彙
題
Day 10
完成 25%

Part 2
綜
合
測
驗
Day 10
完成 50%

Part 3
文
意
選
填
Day 10
完成 75%

Part 4
閱
讀
測
驗
Day 10
完成 100%

補充

fingerprint n 指紋；because of ph 由於；a piece of paper ph 一張紙；scribble v 草草書寫；
smudge n 汙跡

7,000 單字

- tip [tɪp] n 2 尖端
- finger [ˋfɪŋgɚ] n 1 手指
- distinct [dɪˋstɪŋkt] a 4 清晰的
- ridge [rɪdʒ] n 5 脊
- lifetime [ˋlaɪf͵taɪm] n 3 畢生
- injury [ˋɪndʒərɪ] n 3 傷害
- identify [aɪˋdɛntə͵faɪ] v 4 分辨
- prisoner [ˋprɪznɚ] n 2 囚犯

- track [træk] v 2 追蹤
- criminal [ˋkrɪmɪn̩] a 3 犯人
- recognize [ˋrɛkəg͵naɪz] v 3 識別
- file [faɪl] n 3 檔案
- ink [ɪŋk] n 2 墨水
- repeat [rɪˋpit] v 2 重複
- tape [tep] n 2 膠帶

MEMO

Plants around us are always changing. It is usually hard to see these changes __01__ with eyes.

The sunflower is a big yellow flower that grows __02__ the light. It is said that the sunflower gets its name because it often __03__ its head following the sun. Another plant that changes in the __04__ is known as "Joseph's Coat of Many Colors." When this plant is put in the sunlight, its leaves turn bright red. If not, the leaves should be green.

Some plants may change if they are __05__. When the leaves of some plants are touched, they __06__ and hide themselves. The gardenia is a beautiful white flower, which has a pleasant smell. If you touch the smooth white blossoms of gardenias, they will turn brown and __07__ soon.

In addition, plants may change because of some other reasons. Some plants sleep at night. The morning glory, for example, __08__ in the morning, and in the afternoon the flowers naturally close. And the Prayer Plant closes its leaves together at night, just like a person closes his hands in prayer.

In a word, plants may change for many __09__, such as the time of day, the season, the heat, the cold, the rain, etc. These changes are miracles. Human __10__ can make plants change as well. For instance, farmers save seeds from their best fruits like cherries, apples and plums, and keep planting the best seeds every year. In this way they may get fruits better and better.

(A) touched   (B) turns   (C) reasons   (D) directly   (E) roll
(F) effort   (G) wither   (H) sunlight   (I) blooms   (J) toward

01 _____   02 _____   03 _____   04 _____   05 _____

06 _____   07 _____   08 _____   09 _____   10 _____

選項中譯｜觸摸；轉動；原因；直接地；捲起；努力；枯萎；陽光；開花；朝

中譯｜我們週遭的植物總是在變化。這些變化通常很難用眼睛直接看見。

向日葵是一種朝陽光生長的大黃花。據說，向日葵就是因為經常隨著太陽轉動而得名。另一種在太陽光下會發生變化的植物，被稱為「約瑟夫的彩色外衣」。置於太陽下時，它的葉子會變成亮紅色。如若不然，葉子會是綠色的。

一些植物被觸碰時也許會發生變化。有些植物的葉子被觸碰時，葉子會捲起來以示躲避。梔子花是一種漂亮的白色的花，有著甜美的芳香。如果你觸碰到梔子花光滑的白色花朵，它們會很快變為褐色，並且枯萎。

此外，植物有可能會因為其他的原因而發生變化。有些植物會在夜晚睡覺。例如，牽牛花是在早上開花，到了下午，花朵就會自然閉合。而竹芋屬（祈禱植物）的葉子在夜裡會合攏起來，就像一個人合攏手掌在禱告一樣。

簡言之，植物變化也許是有許多的原因，例如一天中的時間、季節、熱量、寒冷和雨水等。這些變化是奇蹟。人力也可以使植物發生變化。例如，農民們從最好的果實中——如櫻桃、蘋果和李子——留下種子，每年都種下最好的種子。用這樣的方式，農民們收穫的果實也許就會愈來愈好。

解譯｜閱讀全文可知，這篇文章的主題是植物的變化。

縱觀各選項，選項 (C)、(F)、(H) 是名詞，選項 (A)、(B)、(E)、(G)、(I) 是動詞，選項 (D) 是副詞，選項 (J) 是介系詞。根據題意，第 1 題應選副詞，第 2 題應選介系詞，第 4、9、10 題應選名詞，第 3、5、6、7、8 題應選動詞。然後根據文章，依次作答。

第 1 題是選擇副詞，只有一個副詞可供選擇，即為選項 (D)，意為「直接地」。

第 2 題是選擇介系詞，只有一個介系詞可供選擇，即為選項 (J)，意為「朝」。

第 3 題是選擇動詞，有五個動詞可供選擇，即為選項 (A)、(B)、(E)、(G)、(I)，句意為「向日葵就是因為經常隨著太陽轉動而得名」，所以選 (B)。第 5 題所選動詞，根據句意，應當是「一些植物被觸碰時也許會發生變化」，所以選 (A)。第 6 題所選動詞，是與名詞進行搭配，所以選 (E)。第 7 題所選動詞，句意為「如果你觸碰到梔子花光滑的白色花朵，它們會很快變為褐色，並且枯萎」，所以選 (G)。第 8 題則是選 (I)，意為「牽牛花是在早上開花」。

第 4 題是選擇名詞，有三個名詞可供選擇，即為選項 (C)、(F)、(H)，選項 (C) 意為「原因」，選項 (F) 意為「努力」，選項 (H) 意為「陽光」，可以視為固定搭配，in the sunlight 意為「在陽光下」，所以選 (H)。第 9 題所選名詞，根據句意，應當是「植物變化也許是有許多的原因」，所以選 (C)。第 10 題則是選 (F)，意為「人力也可以使植物發生變化」。

DAY
10

Part 1
詞彙題
Day 10
完成 25%

Part 2
綜合測驗
Day 10
完成 50%

Part 3
文意選填
Day 10
完成 75%

Part 4
閱讀測驗
Day 10
完成 100%

解答&技巧 | 01 (D)　02 (J)　03 (B)　04 (H)　05 (A)
　　　　　 06 (E)　07 (G)　08 (I)　09 (C)　10 (F)

適用 TIP 1　適用 TIP 2　適用 TIP 6　適用 TIP 7　適用 TIP 8
適用 TIP 9　適用 TIP 10　適用 TIP 11

補充

sunflower n 向日葵；in the sunlight ph 在陽光下；if not ph 如果不，不然；gardenia n 梔子花；
morning glory ph 牽牛花

7,000 單字

- toward [tə`word] prep 1 朝，向
- name [nem] n 1 名字
- coat [kot] n 1 外衣
- bright [braɪt] a 1 明亮的
- smooth [smuð] a 3 光滑的
- blossom [`blɑsəm] n 4 花朵
- roll [rol] v 1 捲起
- glory [`glorɪ] n 3 榮譽

- prayer [prɛr] n 3 祈禱
- season [`sizn̩] n 1 季節
- rain [ren] n 1 雨
- miracle [`mɪrək!] n 3 奇蹟
- seed [sid] n 1 種子
- cherry [`tʃɛrɪ] n 3 櫻桃
- plum [plʌm] n 3 李子

MEMO

❹▶

DAY
10

Part 1
詞
彙
題
Day 10
完成 25%

Part 2
綜
合
測
驗
Day 10
完成 50%

Part 3
文
意
選
填
Day 10
完成 75%

Part 4
閱
讀
測
驗
Day 10
完成 100%

The western philosophers and critics, during the 18th century, devoted much attention to such matters as natural __01__ —a trend reflecting the central position they had given to the philosophy of nature. Since then, the philosophy of art has gradually become even more __02__ and begun to supplant the philosophy of nature. Various central issues related to the philosophy of art have had a marked __03__ on the orientation of 20th-century aesthetics.

Still another far-reaching question has much to do with the value of art. Two opposing __04__ positions have been taken on this issue. One holds that art and its __05__ are a means to some recognized moral good, whereas the other __06__ that art is intrinsically valuable and is an end in itself. Underlying this whole issue is the concept of taste, one of the basic concerns of aesthetics. In recent years there has also been an increasing preoccupation with art as the prime object of critical judgment. Corresponding to the trend in contemporary aesthetic thought, critics have followed either of two approaches. On one hand, criticism is __07__ to the analysis and interpretation of the work of art. On the other hand, it is devoted to articulating the response to the aesthetic object and to __08__ a particular way of perceiving it.

Over the years, aesthetics has developed into a __09__ field of knowledge and inquiry. The concerns of __10__ aesthetics include diverse problems, such as the nature of style and its aesthetic significance, the relation of aesthetic judgment to culture, the relevancy of Freudian psychology and other forms of psychological study to criticism, etc.

(A) impact   (B) justifying   (C) theoretical   (D) contemporary   (E) beauty
(F) maintains   (G) restricted   (H) appreciation   (I) broad   (J) prominent

---

01 _____   02 _____   03 _____   04 _____   05 _____

06 _____   07 _____   08 _____   09 _____   10 _____

選項中譯｜影響；辯護；理論的；當代的；美麗；堅持；受限制；鑑賞；廣的；顯著的

中譯｜十八世紀時，西方的哲學家和評論家們十分關注自然美之類的事宜，這樣的潮流反映出他們對自然哲學所給予的主流地位。此後，藝術哲學逐漸地變得更為顯著，也取代了自然哲學。與藝術哲學有關的各種焦點議題，對二十世紀的美學走向有著顯著的影響。

不過，與藝術價值有關的，還有另一個意義深遠的問題。對此，有兩種不同的理論觀點。一方認為，藝術及其鑑賞是用以推行某些公認的德行；另一方則認為，藝術本質上就具有價值，本身也就是創造的目的。這些議題從根本上來說，其實是鑑賞力的觀念問題，這也是美學所關注的基本問題之一。近年來，也有愈來愈多的人把藝術作為批判性評論的主要目標。與當代美學觀點的潮流相一致的是，評論家們各自選擇以下兩種觀點之一。一方面，只限於藝術品本身的分析和闡釋的評論；另一方面，關注於清晰陳述對於審美目標的反應，並說明辯護特定的賞析方式。

多年來，美學已經發展為具備了知識和探究的廣域學科。當代美學所關注的，包括各式各樣的問題，例如，風格的本質及其美學意義，審美鑑定與文化的關係，佛洛伊德心理學和其他形式心理學研究在評論上的關聯所在。

解譯｜閱讀全文可知，這篇文章的主題是哲學與評論學的發展及其對美學的影響。

縱觀各選項，選項 (A)、(E)、(H) 是名詞，選項 (B)、(F)、(G) 是動詞，選項 (C)、(D)、(I)、(J) 是形容詞。根據題意，第 1、3、5 題應選名詞，第 6、7、8 題應選動詞，第 2、4、9、10 題應選形容詞。然後根據文章，依次作答。

第 1 題是選擇名詞，有三個名詞可供選擇，即為選項 (A)、(E)、(H)，選項 (A) 意為「影響」，選項 (E) 意為「美麗」，選項 (H) 意為「鑑賞」，根據句意，應當是「自然美」，所以選 (E)。第 3 題所選名詞，可以視為固定搭配，**have an impact on** 意為「對～有影響」，所以選 (A)。第 5 題則是選 (H)，意為「一方認為，藝術及其鑑賞是用以推行某些公認的德行」。

第 2 題是選擇形容詞，有四個形容詞可供選擇，即為選項 (C)、(D)、(I)、(J)。選項 (C) 意為「理論的」，選項 (D) 意為「當代的」，選項 (I) 意為「廣的」，選項 (J) 意為「顯著的」，根據句意可知，應當是「藝術哲學逐漸地變得更為顯著」，所以選 (J)。第 4 題所選形容詞，句意為「有兩種不同的理論觀點」，所以選 (C)。第 9 題所選形容詞，意為「廣域學科」，所以選 (I)。第 10 題則是選 (D)，**contemporary aesthetics** 意為「當代美學」。

第 6 題是選擇動詞，有三個動詞可供選擇，即為選項 (B)、(F)、(G)，句意為「另一方則認為，藝術本身是寶貴的，也只限於藝術本身」，所以選 (F)。第 7 題所選動詞，可以視為固定搭配，**be restricted to** 意為「受限於」，所以選 (G)。第 8 題則是選 (B)，意為「說明辯護特定的賞析方式」。

解答＆技巧｜ **01** (E)　**02** (J)　**03** (A)　**04** (C)　**05** (H)
　　　　　 06 (F)　**07** (G)　**08** (B)　**09** (I)　**10** (D)

適用 TIP 1　適用 TIP 2　適用 TIP 6　適用 TIP 7　適用 TIP 8
適用 TIP 9　適用 TIP 10　適用 TIP 11

補充

corresponding to ph 與～一致的；be restricted to ph 受～限制；work of art ph 藝術品；
on the other hand ph 另一方面；Freudian a 佛洛伊德的

7,000 單字

- beauty [ˋbjutɪ] n **1** 美麗
- prominent [ˋprɑmənənt] a **4** 顯著的，突出的
- various [ˋvɛrɪəs] a **3** 各式各樣的
- issue [ˋɪʃju] n **5** 議題
- impact [ˋɪmpækt] n **4** 影響
- theoretical [θiəˋrɛtɪkl] a **6** 理論的
- appreciation [ə͵priʃɪˋeʃən] n **4** 鑒賞
- critical [ˋkrɪtɪkl] a **4** 批評的，批判性的

- criticism [ˋkrɪtə͵sɪzəm] n **4** 批評，評論
- restrict [rɪˋstrɪkt] v **3** 限制
- analysis [əˋnæləsɪs] n **4** 分析
- articulate [arˋtɪkjə͵let] v **6** 清楚明白地說
- justify [ˋdʒʌstə͵faɪ] v **5** 證明～有理
- perceive [pəˋsiv] v **5** 理解
- inquiry [ɪnˋkwaɪrɪ] n **6** 探究

MEMO

DAY
10

Part 1
詞
彙
題
Day 10
完成 25%

Part 2
綜
合
測
驗
Day 10
完成 50%

Part 3
文
意
選
填
Day 10
完成 75%

Part 4
閱
讀
測
驗
Day 10
完成 100%

5 ▶

It might be hard to explain women's __01__ with Brad Pitt's face and George Clooney's eyes. According to a new research, women seem to judge a potential mate by how __02__ their features are. Men with square jaws and well-defined brow ridges are recognized as good short-term partners, while those with more feminine __03__ such as a rounder face and fuller lips are perceived as better long-term mates.

In the study, 854 subjects viewed a series of male head shots that had been digitally changed to __04__ or minimize masculine traits. They were then asked questions about how they expected the men in the photos to behave.

Most __05__ said that those with more masculine features were likely to be risky, competitive, and more apt to fight, challenge bosses, cheat on spouses and put less effort into parenting. Those with more feminine bodies were seen as good parents and husbands, hard workers and __06__ mates. But, despite all the __07__ characteristics, women would choose the more masculine seeming men for a short-term relationship.

From an evolutionary __08__ , this study makes sense. The key is testosterone, the hormone responsible for the development of masculine facial features and other sexual characteristics. It has been found to affect the body's ability to __09__ disease: men with high levels of the hormone are typically normal and healthy. However, increased testosterone has also been linked to cheating and violence in relationships. So, these men might produce high quality offspring. But they don't always make great parents or __10__ mates.

Skepticism has been shown toward physiognomy, which links facial characteristics to certain behavioral traits. Anyway, the research is a valuable tool for understanding mating strategies.

(A) fascination   (B) perspective   (C) fight   (D) participants   (E) faithful
(F) exaggerate   (G) traits   (H) masculine   (I) supportive   (J) negative

---

01 ____   02 ____   03 ____   04 ____   05 ____

06 ____   07 ____   08 ____   09 ____   10 ____

選項中譯│迷戀；角度；對抗；參與者；忠實的；誇大；特點；男子氣概的；支持的；負面的

中譯│女性對布萊德・彼特的臉和喬治・克隆尼的眼睛十分著迷的原因，也許很難解釋。一項新研究指出，女性們評價可能的伴侶時，所依據的似乎是他們的容貌是否有男子氣概。有著方形下顎和明顯的眉骨輪廓的男性，被認為是很好的短期伴侶；而那些有著更多女性特徵的男性，例如有著較圓的臉和更飽滿的唇形的男性，則會被視為較好的長期伴侶。

在這項研究中，有八百五十四位受試者仔細觀察了一系列的男性臉部特寫照片，這些照片都經過數位化修改，將男性特徵誇大或是減小到最低限度。看過照片之後，受試者被問及認為照片中的男性會有怎樣的行為舉止。

大多數的參與者們說，那些具備更多男性化特徵的男性，可能會喜歡冒險，有競爭意識，也更易於鬥毆，挑戰老闆，對配偶不忠，為人父母也不甚盡責。而那些具備女性化特徵的男性，則被視為好父親、好丈夫、勤奮的工作者、會支持另一半。然而，雖然有諸多負面的特質，女性們卻願意選擇那些看起來較為陽剛的男性，作為短期的伴侶。

從進化學的角度來說，這項研究是有道理的。關鍵在於睪固酮，也就是一種荷爾蒙，與男性化的容貌特徵和其他的性別特徵的發展有關。研究已經發現，睪固酮影響男性抵抗病症的能力：這種荷爾蒙較多的男性，明顯地更為健康。然而，更多睪固酮也與外遇和暴力有關。所以，這些男性的子女也許很優秀，不過本身卻通常不會是好父親或是忠實的伴侶。

相面術將面部特徵與某些行為特徵聯繫起來，對此已經有人提出懷疑。不論如何，對於了解擇偶策略，這項研究是一種可貴的工具。

解譯│閱讀全文可知，這篇文章的主題是女性的擇偶依據。

縱觀各選項，選項 (A)、(B)、(D)、(G) 是名詞，選項 (C)、(F) 是動詞，選項 (E)、(H)、(I)、(J) 是形容詞。根據題意，第 1、3、5、8 題應選名詞，第 4、9 題應選動詞，第 2、6、7、10 題應選形容詞。然後根據文章，依次作答。

第 1 題是選擇名詞，有四個名詞可供選擇，即為選項 (A)、(B)、(D)、(G)，選項 (A) 意為「魅力」，選項 (B) 意為「角度」，選項 (D) 意為「參與者」，選項 (G) 意為「特點」，根據句意，應當是「女性對布萊德・彼特的臉和喬治・克隆尼的眼睛十分著迷」，所以選 (A)。第 3 題所選名詞，根據句意，應當是「女性特徵」，所以選 (G)。第 5 題所選名詞，根據句意，應當是「大多數的參與者們」，所以選 (D)。第 8 題則是選 (B)，from a... perspective 意為「從～角度」。

第 2 題是選擇形容詞，有四個形容詞可供選擇，即為選項 (E)、(H)、(I)、(J)。選項 (E) 意為「忠實的」，選項 (H) 意為「男子氣概的」，選項 (I) 意為「支持的」，選項 (J) 意為「負面的」，根據句意可知，應當是「他們的容貌是否有男子氣概」，所以選 (H)。第 6 題所選形容詞，意為「會支持另一半」，所以選 (I)。

DAY
10

Part 1
詞
彙
題

Day 10
完成 25%

Part 2
綜
合
測
驗

Day 10
完成 50%

Part 3
文
意
選
填

Day 10
完成 75%

Part 4
閱
讀
測
驗

Day 10
完成 100%

第 7 題所選形容詞，意為「負面的特質」，所以選 (J)。第 10 題則是選 (E)，意為「忠實的伴侶」。

第 4 題是選擇動詞，有兩個動詞可供選擇，即為選項 (C)、(F)，只有選項 (F) 符合要求，句意為「將男性特徵誇大或是減小到最低限度」。第 9 題則是選 (C)，fight disease 意為「抵抗疾病」。

解答＆技巧｜ 01 (A)　02 (H)　03 (G)　04 (F)　05 (D)
06 (I)　07 (J)　08 (B)　09 (C)　10 (E)

適用 TIP 1　適用 TIP 2　適用 TIP 6　適用 TIP 7　適用 TIP 8
適用 TIP 9　適用 TIP 10　適用 TIP 11

補充

according to ph 根據；judge... by... ph 根據～判斷～；be likely to do sth. ph 有可能做某事；be apt to do sth. ph 易於做某事；cheat on sb. ph 對～不忠

7,000 單字

- fascination [ˌfæsnˈeʃən] n 6 著迷，迷戀
- masculine [ˈmæskjəlɪn] a 5 男子氣概的
- feature [ˈfitʃɚ] n 3 面貌，容貌
- feminine [ˈfɛmənɪn] a 5 女性的
- trait [tret] n 6 特徵
- subject [ˈsʌbdʒɪkt] n 2 受試者
- male [mel] a 2 男子的
- exaggerate [ɪgˈzædʒɚˌret] v 4 誇張
- cheat [tʃit] v 2 欺騙
- spouse [spauz] n 6 配偶
- characteristic [ˌkærəktəˈrɪstɪk] a 4 特徵
- hormone [ˈhɔrmon] n 6 荷爾蒙
- disease [dɪˈziz] n 3 疾病
- violence [ˈvaɪələns] n 3 暴力
- faithful [ˈfeθfəl] a 4 忠實的

MEMO

MEMO

DAY
10

Part 1
詞
彙
題
Day 10
完成 25%

Part 2
綜
合
測
驗
Day 10
完成 50%

Part 3
文
意
選
填
Day 10
完成 75%

Part 4
閱
讀
測
驗
Day 10
完成 100%

閱讀測驗｜Reading Questions

When you make friends with Americans, remember not to overstep any cultural boundaries that may be taboo. Most Americans like to go to churches, restaurants, parks and sport clubs. Thus when you make an appointment with them, these places can be good choices for you.

When you stay with Americans, you'd better not wait for them to approach you. They may not know whether you can speak English or not. It is a good advice to start conversation with common topics. You can ask them where they come from, their hobbies, their work, etc. However, you should avoid any invasion of their privacy, such as age, salary, marital status, appearance, weight, and so on. Otherwise, they may feel offended or resentful. Besides, you can show an interest in their culture, their jobs and their countries. You can exchange your views on these things.

At the end of the conversation, you can invite them to join you for dinner, coffee or tea. Set a specific time for that if you have got permission. Americans sometimes make general invitations like "Let's get together sometime." In this case, you should know that this is just a way for them to show friendship. It is actually not a real or formal invitation.

When you come into contact with Americans for the first time, don't expect too much. They may just be friendly to anyone, but it takes some time before they decide whether they really want to be your friend or not. Americans cherish lifelong friendship. So if you have a chance to make friends with them, you are very lucky.

01 Which one of the following statements is false?

(A) When making an appointment with Americans, you can choose churches, restaurants, parks and sport clubs.

(B) You should wait for Americans to start a conversation with you.

(C) If you come into contact with Americans for the first time, you should not expect too much.

(D) You can talk about culture, jobs, etc. with Americans.

02 When talking with Americans, you should try to avoid these topics except _____.

(A) salary

(B) weight

(C) age

(D) hobbies

03 When Americans say "Let's get together sometime," it probably means _____.

(A) a formal invitation

(B) a real invitation

(C) a way to show friendship

(D) nothing

04 The word "cherish" in the last paragraph is closest in meaning to _____.

(A) conquer

(B) qualify

(C) disregard

(D) treasure

DAY 10

Part 1 詞彙題
Day 10 完成 25%

Part 2 綜合測驗
Day 10 完成 50%

Part 3 文意選填
Day 10 完成 75%

Part 4 閱讀測驗
Day 10 完成 100%

中譯│和美國人交朋友時，要記住，不要逾越任何可能是禁忌的文化界限。大多數的美國人都喜歡去教堂、餐廳、公園和運動俱樂部。所以和他們約時間見面時，這些地方都是很好的選擇。

和美國人在一起時，最好不要等他們來接近你。也許，他們並不知道你是否會講英語。以常見的話題來交流，是個好建議。你可以問他們來自哪裡，問他們的愛好、工作等。然而，要避免侵犯個人隱私，例如年齡、薪水、婚姻狀況、樣貌、體重等。不然，他們也許會覺得被冒犯或是反感。此外，你可以表示對他們的文化、工作和國家感興趣，也可以就這些話題交換意見。

結束交談之後，你可以邀請他們，和你一起吃飯或是喝咖啡、喝茶。如果他們接受邀請，就要說定具體的時間。有時候，美國人會提出一般性的邀請，例如「咱們找個時間聚聚吧」。在這種情況下，你要知道這只是他們表達友誼的一種方法，而不是真正的或是正式的邀請。

初次和美國人接觸時，不要有太多的期待。他們也許會對任何人都表示友善，但是，在他們決定要不要和你成為真正的朋友之前，需要一定的時間。美國人珍惜終身的友誼。因此，如果有機會和他們交朋友，是非常幸運的。

解譯│在閱讀文章之前，先要預覽題目，然後再帶著問題有針對性地閱讀文章。第 1 題是判斷正誤，第 2、3 題是文意理解，第 4 題是詞義辨析。理解了題目要求之後，閱讀全文，依次作答。

第 1 題是判斷正誤，考的是細節，問的是哪一項敘述是錯誤的。根據第 2 段首句內容「When you stay with Americans, you'd better not wait for them to approach you.」可知，和美國人在一起時，最好不要等著他們來接近你。選項 (B) 則是說，應該等美國人主動與你交談，與文意不符。同樣，此題也可以用排除法來解答。第 1 段第 2、3 句內容與選項 (A) 相符，第 4 段首句內容與選項 (C) 相符，第 2 段倒數第 2 行內容與選項 (D) 相符。這三個選項的敘述都是正確的，可以排除。所以選 (B)。

第 2 題是文意理解，問的是與美國人交談時，應該避免什麼話題。根據第 2 段第 5 句內容「you should avoid any invasion of their privacy, such as age, salary, marital status, appearance, weight」可知，要避免侵犯個人隱私的話題，例如年齡、薪水、婚姻狀況、樣貌、體重等，與選項 (A)、(B)、(C) 相符。而根據第 2 段第 4 句內容「You can ask them where they come from, their hobbies, their work, etc.」可知，選項 (D) 是可以討論的話題。所以選 (D)。

第 3 題同樣是文意理解，問的是，如果美國人說「Let's get together sometime」，可能是意味著什麼。關鍵字是「Let's get together sometime」，定位於第 3 段。根據第 4、5 句內容可知，這只是他們表達友誼的一種方法，而不是真正的或是正式的邀請，與選項 (C) 相符，所以選 (C)。

第 4 題是考動詞 cherish 的同義字。選項 (A) 意為「征服」，選項 (B) 意為「合格」，選項 (C) 意為「不重視」，選項 (D) 意為「珍惜」。根據第 4 段第 3 句內容可知，cherish 在文中意為「珍惜」，所以選 (D)。

解答＆技巧 | **01 (B)** **02 (D)** **03 (C)** **04 (D)**

適用 TIP 1　適用 TIP 2　適用 TIP 3　適用 TIP 7　適用 TIP 10
適用 TIP 11　適用 TIP 12　適用 TIP 13　適用 TIP 15

DAY
10

Part 1
詞
彙
題
Day 10
完成 25%

Part 2
綜
合
測
驗
Day 10
完成 50%

Part 3
文
意
選
填
Day 10
完成 75%

Part 4
閱
讀
測
驗
Day 10
完成 100%

補充

make an appointment with ph 預約；marital a 婚姻的；show an interest in ph 對～感興趣；come into contact with ph 接觸，打交道；too much ph 太多

7,000 單字

- cultural [ˋkʌltʃərəl] a 3 文化的
- boundary [ˋbaundrɪ] n 5 界限
- when [hwɛn] ad 1 什麼時候
- or [ɔr] conj 1 或者
- where [hwɛr] ad 1 哪裡
- so [so] ad 1 這樣，那樣
- these [ðiz] pron 1 這些
- invite [ɪnˋvaɪt] v 2 邀請

- join [dʒɔɪn] v 1 加入
- sometime [ˋsʌm͵taɪm] ad 3 在某個時候
- friendship [ˋfrɛndʃɪp] n 3 友誼
- invitation [͵ɪnvəˋteʃən] n 2 邀請
- friendly [ˋfrɛndlɪ] a 2 友好的
- lifelong [ˋlaɪf͵lɔŋ] a 5 一生的，終身的
- very [ˋvɛrɪ] ad 1 很，十分

MEMO

When Americans are invited to attend get-togethers or banquets, either formal or informal, they always try to make other people feel comfortable. On the whole, they usually behave informally. Men may not shake hands with others when they're introduced. If male friends and business associates haven't seen each other for a period of time, when they get together again, they would shake hands to say hello. However, when a woman is introduced to a man, she usually doesn't shake hands with the man. In addition, Americans rarely shake hands to say good-bye.

American women have always been used to being independent. They live alone, go to work, and make a living by themselves. They seldom ask men for help, if not necessary. They may actively start conversations with men, or ask men to dance in a ball. It is, therefore, not clear whether men should open doors or offer seats to women in public.

A lot of Americans don't smoke or drink, nor do they want other people to do these things in their house. So if you are with unfamiliar people, you'd better think twice about it before you light up a cigarette or bring wine to a dinner. In America, there are usually special sections for smokers, such as smoking sections in restaurants and hotels. And non-smokers can choose to stay in non-smoking sections.

Americans usually bring gifts when they come to visit someone. They will also ask the host or hostess if there's anything they can do to help in the kitchen. This is considered to be polite.

01 When a woman is introduced to a man, she _____.

(A) offers a seat to the man

(B) will start a conversation with the man

(C) will shake hands with the man

(D) usually prefers not to shake hands with the man

02 The word "associates" in the first paragraph is closest in meaning to _____.

(A) relatives

(B) enemies

(C) companions

(D) strangers

03 Which one of the following statements is false?

(A) American women prefer to be independent.

(B) Many Americans don't want others to smoke or drink at their house.

(C) Americans always shake hands to say good-bye.

(D) There are usually smoking sections in restaurants or hotels in America.

04 What is the main idea of the passage?

(A) Etiquette for get-togethers or banquets in America.

(B) Whether to shake hands or not.

(C) American women.

(D) How to behave when you go to visit Americans.

DAY 10

Part 1
詞
彙
題
Day 10
完成 25%

Part 2
綜
合
測
驗
Day 10
完成 50%

Part 3
文
意
選
填
Day 10
完成 75%

Part 4
閱
讀
測
驗
Day 10
完成 100%

中譯｜美國人受邀參加正式或非正式的聚會或是宴會時，總是盡力讓其他人感到舒適。總的來說，他們的舉止通常是隨意的。男性在被介紹給其他人時，也許不會與對方握手。如果男性朋友和生意夥伴有一段時間沒有見面，再次相聚時，會握手問好。然而，女性被介紹給男性之時，通常是不與對方握手的。美國人也很少握手告別。

美國的女性向來習慣獨立。她們獨自居住，自己去工作、謀生。若非必要，她們很少向男性求助。她們或許會主動和男性交談，或是在舞會上邀請男性跳舞。因此在公共場合，男人也不太清楚是否應該為女性開門，或是讓座給她們。

很多美國人不吸菸，也不喝酒，也不希望其他人在他們家中吸菸或是喝酒。因此，如果你是和不太熟識的人在一起，在你點菸或是帶酒去參加晚宴之前，最好慎重考慮。在美國，通常都有為吸菸者設置的特定區域，比如餐廳或飯店裡的吸菸區。而不吸菸的人則可以選擇無菸區。

前去拜訪別人的時候，美國人通常會攜帶禮物。他們也會詢問男主人或是女主人，是否需要到廚房幫忙。這樣做是被認為有禮貌的。

解譯｜在閱讀文章之前，先要預覽題目，然後再帶著問題有針對性地閱讀文章。第 1 題是文意理解，第 2 題是詞義辨析，第 3 題是判斷正誤，第 4 題是概括主旨。理解了題目要求之後，閱讀全文，依次作答。

第 1 題是文意理解，問的是女性被介紹給男性時，她會怎麼做。關鍵字「a woman is introduced to a man」，定位於第 1 段。根據第 5 句內容「when a woman is introduced to a man, she usually doesn't shake hands with the man.」可知，女性被介紹給男性時，通常不與對方握手，與選項 (D) 相符。所以選 (D)。

第 2 題是考 associate 的同義字。associate 可以作動詞，意為「聯繫；打交道」；可以作形容詞，意為「合夥的；准的」；也可以作名詞，意為「夥伴，合夥人」。根據第 1 段第 4 句內容可知，associate 在文中是用作名詞，意為「夥伴」。選項 (A) 意為「親戚」，選項 (B) 意為「敵人」，選項 (C) 意為「夥伴」，選項 (D) 意為「陌生人」。所以選 (C)。

第 3 題是判斷正誤，考的是細節，問的是哪一項敘述是錯誤的。根據第 1 段最後一句內容「Americans rarely shake hands to say good-bye.」可知，美國人很少握手告別。選項 (C) 則是說，美國人經常握手告別，與文意不符。同樣，此題也可以用排除法來解答。第 2 段首句內容與選項 (A) 相符，第 3 段首句內容與選項 (B) 相符，第 3 段第 3 句內容與選項 (D) 相符。這三個選項的敘述都是正確的，可以排除。所以選 (C)。

第 4 題是概括主旨。文中並沒有明顯的主旨句，需要根據各段內容加以概括。第 1 段講述的是握手禮儀，第 2 段講述的是對待女性的禮儀，第 3 段講述的是有關菸酒的禮儀，第 4 段講述的是做客拜訪的禮儀。由此可知，短文內容是簡述美國的聚會或是宴會禮儀，所以選 (A)。

解答＆技巧 ｜ **01** (D) **02** (C) **03** (C) **04** (A)

適用 TIP 1　適用 TIP 2　適用 TIP 3　適用 TIP 7　適用 TIP 10
適用 TIP 11　適用 TIP 12　適用 TIP 13　適用 TIP 14　適用 TIP 15

補充

get-together n 社交聚會；informal a 非正式的；on the whole ph 總的來說；
shake hands ph 握手；non-smoking section ph 無菸區

7,000 單字

- they [ðe] pron **1** 他們
- if [ɪf] conj **1** 如果
- good-bye [gʊdˋbaɪ] n **1** 再見
- used to [ˋjust ˏtu] ph **2** 過去常常
- independent [ˏɪndɪˋpɛndənt] a **2** 獨立的
- go [go] v **1** 去
- dance [dæns] v **1** 跳舞
- ball [bɔl] n **1** 舞會

- clear [klɪr] a **1** 無疑的，肯定的
- nor [nɔr] conj **1** 也不
- want [wɑnt] v **1** 想要
- wine [waɪn] n **1** 酒
- come [kʌm] v **1** 到來
- hostess [ˋhostɪs] n **2** 女主人
- polite [pəˋlaɪt] a **2** 禮貌的

Part 1
詞
彙
題
Day 10
完成 25%

Part 2
綜
合
測
驗
Day 10
完成 50%

Part 3
文
意
選
填
Day 10
完成 75%

Part 4
閱
讀
測
驗
Day 10
完成 100%

MEMO

In China, the Spring Festival should be the most important celebration. When the Spring Festival comes, Chinese people will wish each other health and good luck. The celebration usually lasts for fifteen days. People usually paste couplets, have the family reunion dinner, set off firecrackers, and give New Year's greetings.

When the Spring Festival is drawing near, all households will be busy cleaning their houses, sweeping the floor, and doing the laundry. And they will paste couplets on doors to welcome the coming new year.

On New Year's Eve, the whole family will get together and stay up late, waiting for the arrival of the new year. Also they will have a family banquet with all the family members getting together. In the south, people will eat "niangao," which means "higher and higher every year," while in the north, people eat dumplings.

Setting off firecrackers has always played an important part in the celebration of the Spring Festival. Once the clock strikes twelve at midnight on New Year's Eve, all households will set off firecrackers and fireworks. The glitter can be seen everywhere, and the sound can be deafening.

On the first day of the Spring Festival, everybody will wear new clothes, visit relatives and friends, and offer them congratulations. It may be the best time for children because they can receive lucky money as gifts from grandparents or elders in the family. The lucky money is usually put in red envelopes. Red is believed to be a lucky color. It is said that lucky money in red envelopes will bring good luck and ward off monsters.

01 Which of the following statements is not included in the celebration of the Spring Festival?

(A) Giving New Year's greetings.

(B) Pasting couplets.

(C) Eating mooncakes.

(D) Setting off firecrackers.

02 The word "households" in the fourth paragraph is closest in meaning to _____.

(A) families

(B) children

(C) societies

(D) institutions

03 Which one of the following statements is false?

(A) Children receive lucky money in red envelopes as gifts.

(B) Chinese people have the family reunion dinner on New Year's Eve.

(C) Peole visit relatives and friends on the first day of the Spring Festival.

(D) The celebration of the Spring Festival lasts for a week.

04 What is the main idea of the passage?

(A) New Year's Eve.

(B) The celebration of the Sping Festival.

(C) New Year's Day.

(D) The family reunion dinner.

DAY
10

Part 1
詞
彙
題
Day 10
完成 25%

Part 2
綜
合
測
驗
Day 10
完成 50%

Part 3
文
意
選
填
Day 10
完成 75%

Part 4
閱
讀
測
驗
Day 10
完成 100%

中譯｜在中國，春節是最重要的節日。春節來臨時，中國人會相互祝福，希望彼此身體健康、好運連連。慶祝活動通常會持續十五天。人們通常要貼對聯、吃年夜飯、燃放鞭炮、表達新年祝福。

春節將至之時，家家戶戶都忙著打掃房屋，清掃地板，清洗衣物。他們也要在門上貼春聯，來迎接即將到來的新年。

除夕夜，全家人將聚在一起，熬夜守歲，等待著新年的到來。全家人都要聚在一起，吃團圓飯。在南方，人們要吃「年糕」，意味著「步步高升」；而在北方，人們要吃餃子。

在春節的慶祝活動中，燃放鞭炮向來都是很重要的。在除夕夜，當午夜十二點鐘的鐘聲敲響時，家家戶戶都要燃放煙花爆竹，光輝處處，聲震欲聾。

春節的第一天，每個人都要穿上新衣服，探訪親友，恭賀新年。對孩子們來說，這或許是最令人高興的時刻，因為祖父母或是家族中的長輩要給他們發壓歲錢，作為禮物。壓歲錢通常是裝在紅包裡。中國人認為紅色是個幸運的顏色，據說，裝在紅包中的壓歲錢可以帶來好運，並且驅趕猛獸。

解譯｜在閱讀文章之前，先要預覽題目，然後再帶著問題有針對性地閱讀文章。第1題是文意理解，第2題是詞義辨析，第3題是判斷正誤，第4題是概括主旨。理解了題目要求之後，閱讀全文，依次作答。

第1題是文意理解，問的是哪一項敘述不屬於春節的慶祝活動。根據第1段第4句內容「People usually paste couplets, have the family reunion dinner, set off firecrackers, and give New Year's greetings.」可知，春節的慶祝活動，包括貼對聯、吃年夜飯、燃放鞭炮、表達新年祝福。選項 (A)、(B)、(D) 與此相符。只有選項 (C)，在文中找不到相關敘述。所以選 (C)。

第2題是考名詞 household 的同義字。選項 (A) 意為「家庭」，選項 (B) 意為「孩子們」，選項 (C) 意為「協會」，選項 (D) 意為「機構」。根據第4段第2句內容可知，在文中意為「家庭」，所以選 (A)。

第3題是判斷正誤，考的是細節，問的是哪一項敘述是錯誤的。根據第1段第3句內容「The celebration usually lasts for fifteen days.」可知，慶祝活動通常會持續十五天。選項 (D) 則是說，慶祝活動持續一周，與文意不符。同樣，此題也可以用排除法來解答。第5段第2、3句內容與選項 (A) 相符，第3段第2句內容與選項 (B) 相符，第5段第1句內容與選項 (C) 相符。這三個選項的敘述都是正確的，可以排除。所以選 (D)。

第4題是概括主旨。文中有明確的主旨句，本篇結構是先總述後分述，第1段可以視為主旨段，根據第1段內容可知，文章主旨是春節的慶祝活動，與選項 (B) 敘述相符。所以選 (B)。

解答&技巧 ┃ 01 (C)　02 (A)　03 (D)　04 (B)

適用 TIP 1　適用 TIP 2　適用 TIP 3　適用 TIP 7　適用 TIP 10

適用 TIP 11　適用 TIP 12　適用 TIP 13　適用 TIP 14　適用 TIP 15

補充

couplet [n] 對聯，對句；New Year's Eve [ph] 除夕；wait for [ph] 等待；set off [ph] 燃放；
grandparents [n] 祖父母

7,000 單字

- wish [wɪʃ] [v] 1 希望
- celebration [ˌsɛləˈbreʃən] [n] 4 慶祝
- firecracker [ˈfaɪrˌkrækə] [n] 4 鞭炮，爆竹
- greetings [ˈgritɪŋz] [n] 4 問候
- clean [klin] [v] 1 打掃
- sweep [swip] [v] 2 清掃
- paste [pest] [v] 2 張貼
- south [sauθ] [n] 1 南方

- dumpling [ˈdʌmplɪŋ] [n] 2 餃子
- glitter [ˈglɪtə] [n] 5 光輝
- deafen [ˈdɛfn] [v] 3 使人感到震耳欲聾
- congratulation [kənˌgrætʃəˈleʃən] [n] 2 祝賀
- red [rɛd] [a] 1 紅色的
- ward [wɔrd] [v] 5 擋開，避開
- monster [ˈmɑnstə] [n] 2 野獸

Part 1
詞
彙
題

Day 10
完成 25%

Part 2
綜
合
測
驗

Day 10
完成 50%

Part 3
文
意
選
填

Day 10
完成 75%

Part 4
閱
讀
測
驗

Day 10
完成 100%

MEMO

As a young country in the world, America is composed of vast areas and has numerous immigrants from other countries. Now a massive number of immigrants are still pouring into the United States every year. Under the diversified culture, Americans have a strong sense of competition, and always make conscious effort to insist on personal struggles. They believe such a life creed that every person is the architect of his own future.

As for marriage, Americans believe it means to combine two individuals together in a legal way. As long as a man and a woman reach the legal age and fall in love with each other, they can surely get married; nobody can interfere.

Once Americans decide to get married, they will find a marriage counselor. Americans' marriage is only for themselves. They find a permanent partner in their life and then get married for the sake of their physical, psychological or social demands. Americans usually choose a spouse who shares the same temperament and interest with them. For them, marriage should be a personal right, rather than an obligation. And it is just a way to seek happiness, rather than the bondage of responsibility. They can surely decide by themselves who they will marry and when and where to hold the wedding.

Most Americans accept premarital sex. According to statistics, about 20% of the women had already been pregnant before they got married. This phenomenon can be seen everywhere in America.

01 Which one of the following statements is false?

(A) With vast areas and numerous immigrants, America has a highly diversified culture.

(B) Americans regard marriage as the bondage of responsibility.

(C) A man and a woman can surely get married if they reach the legal age and fall in love with each other.

(D) Premarital sex is not unusual in America.

02 Which of the following reasons is not considered when Americans plan to get married?

(A) The obligation.

(B) The physical demand.

(C) The social demand.

(D) The psychological demand.

03 The word "bondage" in the third paragraph is closest in meaning to _____.

(A) requirement

(B) development

(C) encouragement

(D) constraint

04 What is the main idea of the passage?

(A) American culture.

(B) Immigrants in America.

(C) Americans' opinion about marriage.

(D) The introduction of America.

DAY
10

Part 1
詞
彙
題
Day 10
完成 25%

Part 2
綜
合
測
驗
Day 10
完成 50%

Part 3
文
意
選
填
Day 10
完成 75%

Part 4
閱
讀
測
驗
Day 10
完成 100%

中譯｜作為新興的國家，美國地域廣闊，也有來自其他國家的大量移民。現在，每年仍有大量移民湧進美國。受多元文化的影響，美國人有著很強的競爭觀念，也總是刻意要求自己，保持競爭意識。他們相信這樣的人生信念：每個人都是自己的未來的建築師。

至於婚姻，美國人認為這意味著兩個人的合法結合。只要男女雙方都達到法定年齡，而且彼此相愛，就可以結婚，沒有人可以干預。

一旦美國人決定要結婚，他們會尋找一名婚姻顧問。美國人只是為了他們自己而結婚。他們找到了生命中的固定伴侶，然後結婚，以滿足在生理、心理或是社會層面的需求。美國人通常會選擇那些有著相同性情和興趣的人作為配偶。對於他們來說，婚姻是個人權利，而不是義務；只是一種尋求幸福的方式，而不是責任的束縛。他們當然可以自己決定和誰結婚，在何時何地舉辦婚禮。

大多數的美國人接受婚前性行為。據統計，大約有百分之二十的女性，在結婚之前就已經懷孕。這種現象在美國十分常見。

解譯｜在閱讀文章之前，先要預覽題目，然後再帶著問題有針對性地閱讀文章。第 1 題是判斷正誤，第 2 題是文意理解，第 3 題是詞義辨析，第 4 題是概括主旨。理解了題目要求之後，閱讀全文，依次作答。

第 1 題是判斷正誤，考的是細節，問的是哪一項敘述是錯誤的。根據第 3 段第 6 句內容「And it is just a way to seek happiness, rather than the bondage of responsibility.」可知，對於美國人來說，婚姻只是一種尋求幸福的方式，而不是責任的束縛。選項 (B) 則是說，美國人將婚姻視為責任的束縛，與文意不符。同樣，此題也可以用排除法來解答。第 1 段第 1、3 句內容與選項 (A) 相符，第 2 段第 2 句內容與選項 (C) 相符，第 4 段內容與選項 (D) 相符。這三個選項的敘述都是正確的，可以排除。所以選 (B)。

第 2 題是文意理解，問的是美國人打算結婚的時候，哪一項原因不在他們的考慮範圍之內。定位於第 3 段。根據第 3 句內容「and then get married, for the sake of their physical, psychological or social demand.」可知，美國人結婚，是為了滿足他們在生理、心理或是社會層面的需求。選項 (B)、(C)、(D) 與此相符。只有選項 (A)，在文中找不到相關敘述。所以選 (A)。

第 3 題是考名詞 bondage 的同義字。選項 (A) 意為「要求」，選項 (B) 意為「發展」，選項 (C) 意為「鼓勵」，選項 (D) 意為「束縛」。根據第 3 段第 6 句內容可知，在文中意為「束縛」，所以選 (D)。

第 4 題是概括主旨。文中並沒有明顯的主旨句，需要根據各段內容加以概括。第 1 段是由美國的概況而引出話題，第 2、3 段講述的是美國人對於婚姻的看法，第 4 段講述的是婚前性行為。由此可知，短文內容是簡述美國人對於婚姻的看法，所以選 (C)。

解答&技巧 | 01 **(B)** 02 **(A)** 03 **(D)** 04 **(C)**

適用 TIP 1　適用 TIP 2　適用 TIP 3　適用 TIP 7　適用 TIP 10
適用 TIP 11　適用 TIP 12　適用 TIP 13　適用 TIP 14　適用 TIP 15

補充

creed n 信條；fall in love with ph 墜入愛河；hold the wedding ph 舉行婚禮；
premarital a 婚前的；everywhere ad 到處

7,000 單字

- immigrant [ˈɪməgrənt] n 4 移民
- now [naʊ] ad 1 現在
- massive [ˈmæsɪv] a 5 大量的
- under [ˈʌndə] prep 1 在～下
- diversify [daɪˈvɝsəˌfaɪ] v 6 使多樣化
- conscious [ˈkɑnʃəs] a 3 自覺的，刻意的
- architect [ˈɑrkəˌtɛkt] n 5 設計師

- combine [kəmˈbaɪn] v 3 聯合，結合
- interfere [ˌɪntəˈfɪr] v 4 干預，干涉
- partner [ˈpɑrtnə] n 2 夥伴
- sake [sek] n 3 緣故
- temperament [ˈtɛmprəmənt] n 6 性情
- sex [sɛks] n 3 性行為
- pregnant [ˈprɛgnənt] a 4 懷孕的

MEMO

DAY
10

Part 1
詞彙題
Day 10
完成 25%

Part 2
綜合測驗
Day 10
完成 50%

Part 3
文意選填
Day 10
完成 75%

Part 4
閱讀測驗
Day 10
完成 100%

a matter of course	理所當然的事
abide by	堅持
abide by	遵守
above all	尤其是
above all	最重要的
absent-minded	心不在焉
abundant in	富有
access to	進入
account for	說明
accuse... of...	指控～
act as	扮演
act for	代理
act on	奉行
adapt oneself to	使（人）適應於～
adapt... for	改編～
adhere to	粘附
adjust oneself to	使（人）適應於～
adjust to	適應
admit of	認錯
after all	畢竟
agree on sth.	同意（事）
agree to do sth.	同意做（事）
agree to sb.	建議
agree to	同意
agree to	贊成
agree up sth.	在某一點上取得一致意見
agree with	贊同
ahead of time	提前
ahead of	在～之前
all at once	突然
all but	幾乎
all in all	大體上說
allow for	考慮到
amount to	等於

answer for	對～負責
answer to	符合
anxious for	為～焦急不安
apologize to sb. for sth.	為～向～道歉
appeal to sb. for sth.	為某事向某人呼籲
appeal to sb.	對某人有吸引力
apply for	申請
apply to sb. for sth.	為～向～申請
apply to	與～有關，適用
apply to	適用
approve of	贊成
arise from	由～引起
arrange for	安排～做～
arrive at	到達某地（小地方）
arrive in	到達某地（大地方）
arrive on	到達～
as a consequence of	由於～的結果
as a matter of course	當然地，自然地
as a result	結果
as known to all	眾所周知
as the last thing	最後一點
as the representative of	以～名義
as well as	除～外
assure sb. of sth.	向～保證
at all costs	不惜任何代價
at any cost	無論如何
at any price	無論如何
at any rate	無論如何
at birth	在出生時
at one's back	支援
at one's convenience	在（人）方便的時間或地點
at one's ease	自在，不拘束

at one's own risk	自行負責	be concentrated on	專注於～
at one's wit's end	無法可想	be concerned with	與～有關
at the back of	在～後面	be confident of	有信心
at the conclusion of	當～結束時	be confronted with	面對
at the cost of	以～為代價	be conscious of	意識到
at the risk of	冒～險	be conscious of	覺察
at the very start	一開始	be consistent in	一貫的
attach to	附屬於	be consistent with	與～一致
attend on	侍候	be content to do sth.	願意做（事）
attend to	注意	be content with	滿足於
attitude toward...	對～的態度	be convenient to / for	對～方便
attribute... to...	把～歸因於～	be critical of	愛挑毛病的，批評的
be absent from...	缺席～	be dependent on	依靠
be absorbed in	全神貫注於～	be different from	與～截然不同
be accustomed to	習慣於～	be distinct from	與～截然不同
be acquainted with	習慣於	be due to	是由於
be all in	極累	be eager for	想得到，盼望
be anxious about	為～焦急不安	be entitled to	有權～，有資格～
be ashamed of	以～為羞恥	be equal to	等於
be at an end	結束了	be equipped with	裝備有
be aware of	知道	be faithful to	忠於
be aware of	意識到	be focused on	專注於～
be based on / upon	基於	be ill in bed	臥病不起
be brought face to face wit	面臨	be in a tight corner	陷入困境
be brought into effect	生效	be in agreement with	與～一致
be busy doing sth.	忙於做某事	be in agreement with	遵照
be busy with sth.	於某事	be in blossom	開花（狀態）
be capable of	～的可能	be in danger of	處於～危險中
be capable of	能夠	be in effect	有效
be caught in the rain	被雨淋	be in favor of	贊成
be caused by	由～引起	be in operation	有效
be cautious of	謹防	be in the habit of	習慣於～
be certain of	一定	be known for sth.	以～出名
be composed of	由～組成的	be liable for	對～負責

be on duty	值班	bring down	使倒下
be out of danger	脫離危險	bring force	使產生
be proud of	引以為豪	bring forward	提出建議
be rich in	富饒於	bring in	使得到某種收入
be satisfied with	滿足於	bring to an end	結束
be sure of	有把握	bring up sb.	撫養某人
be the result of...	認為～的結果	bring up sth.	提出
be used to	習慣於～	bring up	嘔吐
be well supplied with	富於	but for	要不是
beat... at	在～運動項目上打贏	by accident	偶然
because of	由於	by accident	意外
because of	由於	by birth	在出生上
become responsible for 負責管理（照顧）		by chance	偶然
before in time	預告	by chance	偶然地
begin with	以～開始	by comparison	比較起來
behind one's back	背著某人（說壞話）	by contrast	對比之下
believe in	相信	by oneself	依靠自己
benefit from	受益	call at	訪問
beyond dispute	不容爭議的，無可爭議	call for sb.	去接某人一起去做某事
blame sb. for sth.	因～責備某人	call for	需要
blame sb. for sth. 因為（事）指責（人）		call in	請進來
blame sth. on sb.	把～推在某人身上	call off	取消（計畫、比賽）
boast of	吹噓	call on sb.	拜訪，號召
break away from	脫離	call out	大聲地叫
break down	（物）壞掉	call up sb.	打電話
break in	闖入，插話	carry away	拿走，入迷，被～吸引
break off	休息	carry forward	推進，發揚（精神）
break out	（戰爭等）爆發	carry off	搶走，奪走／獲得獎品
break through	打破包圍	carry on	進行下去，堅持下去
break up	驅散	carry out	使～生效
bring about	實現	carry out	進行到底，貫徹執行
bring back to one's mind	使回想起	carry sb. through	使～渡過難關
		carry through	進行到底，完成計畫
		catch at	想抓住

catch on	勾住，絆倒
catch up with	趕上某人
catch up	趕上
center one's attention on	把某人的注意力集中在～上
charge sb. with	～控告某人犯有～
charge sb. with sth.	控告某人犯有～
charge... for...	因～索取（費用）
charge... with	控告
clear away	清除掉，去掉，消散
clear off	消除
clear up	整理收拾
cling to	堅持
close to	臨近的
come across	偶然發現，偶然遇到
come at	向～撲過來，向～襲擊
come down	倒下
come forward	湧現
come from	來自於
come from	起源於
come in	進來
come into blossom	開花
come into effect	生效
come off duty	下班
come out	出來
come to an end	結束
come to one's rescuers	明
come to	蘇醒
come true	實現
come up	～被提出
come up sb.	走進
comment on	評論
commit oneself to	使自己承擔～
commit sb. to prison	把某人送進監獄

compare... to...	把～比作～
compare... with...	把～與～比較
compensate for	補償
complain about	抱怨，訴苦，控告
complain about	抱怨～
complain about	抱怨某人或事情
complain to sb. about sth.	向某人抱怨
comply with	照～辦
comply with	遵守
comply with	遵守
comply with	遵守，依從
conceive of	想像
concentrate on	集中，專心
concern oneself with	關心
condemn sb.to	判決（人）
confess to	承認，供認
confide in	對～講真心話
confidence in sb. / sth.	對～的信賴
confine... to...	把～限制在某範圍內
confirm sb. in	～使某人更堅定
conform to	符合
conform to	適合
conform to	遵循
congratulate sb. on	祝賀
consent to	同意
consent to	贊成
consider good	贊成
consist in	主要在於
consist of	由～組成的
consist with	符合，與～一致
consult sb. on sth.	就～向～請教
contrary to	與～相反
contrast... with	對照

contribute to	有助於	do away with	除去
convince sb. of	使某人確信	do away with	廢除
cope with	應付	do out	打掃，收拾
correspond to	相當於	do up one's hair	盤起長髮
correspond with	符合，一致	do up sth.	包起來
correspond with	通信	do with	涉及到
counting everyone / everything		drop in	順便來訪
	總共，總計	emerge from	出現
cut away	切除	end in	以～為結束
cut down	砍倒	end up with	以～而結束
cut off	切斷，中止	engage in	從事
cut out	停止	enter into	開始
cut sth. in half	把～砍成兩半	enter upon	開始
cut through	走近路，刺穿	fall a sleep	去睡覺（= go to sleep）
date back to	可追溯到	fall across	遇見（偶然）
date from	從某時期開始	fall back	後退，後撤
deal with	處理	fall back	撤退
deal with	論及	fall behind	落後，跟不上
delight in	喜歡	fall ill	病了
demand sth. from sb.	向某人要求～	fall in	集合，陷入
demand sth. of sb.	向某人要求～	fall into	陷入＋名詞
deprive sb. of sth.	剝奪某人某物	fall off	減少，從～摔下來
derive from	起源於	fall on	看到，落在～上面
derive... from	從～取得	fall out of	放棄
despair of	絕望	fall short of	缺乏
deviate from	偏離	feel shame	以～為羞恥
die away	聲音變弱	first of all	首先
die down	慢慢地熄滅（風、火）	first of all	第一
die off	因年老，疾病而死亡	focus one's attention on	
die out	變弱，消失，滅絕（動物）		把（人）的注意力集中在～上
differ from... in	與～的區別在於～	for a change	換換環境
dispose of	處理掉	for all that	儘管
distinguish between	辨別	for certain of	肯定地
distinguish... from	把～與～區別開	for fear that	萬一

for sure	有把握地	give over	讓位於
for the benefit of	為了～的利益	give rise to	引起，導致
for the better	好轉	give up	放棄
get about	到處走，消息的傳開	give way to	被取代
get across	穿過	give... an account of	說明～
get along with sb.	相處	go about	隨便走，進行
get along with sth.	進展得	go after	追趕
get around	傳開	go all out to do sth.	全力以赴去做～
get away	逃掉，離開，擺脫	go around	分配
get down	從～下來	go at	從事於
get in a word	策劃	go back to	追溯到～
get in	進去	go bad	變壞
get into trouble	陷入	go beyond	超出
get off	離開，下車	go by	經過，過去
get on	上車	go down	下降
get out	拔出	go hungry	挨餓
get over	克服	go into effect	生效
get rid of	去掉	go into	進入
get rid of	處理掉	go off	消失，腐敗，壞的
get rid off	擺脫	go on duty	上班
get the better of	打敗	go out	過時了
get through	完成	go over	復習，檢查
get to	到達	go through	經歷了（痛苦、困難）
get together	聚會，聯歡	go too far	太過分了，走太遠了
give an explanation or reason for		go up	提高
	解釋	go well with	協調
give away to	被取代	go with	相配
give away	贈送	go wrong	身體垮了，終止談話
give birth to	出生	go wrong	出錯，發生故障
give effect to	實行	have an advantage over	勝過
give in	屈服	have an effect on	對～有影響
give off	放出（氣體、光）	have confidence in	對～有信心
give one's attention	注意	have faith	依賴
give out	人筋疲力盡	have sb.. at one's back	有～支援

have the advantage of		in comparison with	和～比起來
	由於～處於有利條件	in conclusion	最後一點
have the advantage of sb.		in confidence	推心置腹地
	知道某人所不知道的事	in connection with	關於
have ～ to do with	與～有關係	in consequence	結果
having consciousness	知道	in consequence of	由於～的結果
hold back	阻擋，保留，隱瞞	in consideration of	由於
hold down	控制	in contrast to	和～比起來
hold off	延誤	in contrast to / with	和～形成對比
hold on	堅持下去	in decline	下降
hold out	維持	in demand	有需求
hold to	堅持某個看法（路線）	in despair	絕望
hold up	主持	in detail	詳細地
hunt for	尋找	in difficulties	～有困難，處境困難
hunt out	找出來	in disorder	慌亂地，狼狽不堪
hunt throw	翻找	in dispute	在爭議中
in / out of condition	健康狀況好／不好	in doubt	對～表示疑惑
in a short cut	訣竅	in effect	實際上
in accord with	與～一致	in fact	實際上
in accordance with	根據	in good / bad condition	
in addition to	此外		處於良好／壞狀態
in addition	此外	in no case	在任何情況下都不
in advance	事先	in no case	無論如何也不
in agreement with	同意	in no case	絕不要～
in agreement with	依照	in one's turn	輪到某人做某事
in any case	無論如何	in opposition to	與～相反
in as few words as possible	簡言之	in return for	由於
in blossom	開花（指樹木）	in spite of	不管，儘管
in brief	簡言之	in that	因為
in bulk	成批地	in the air	不肯定
in case of	如果發生～萬一	in the back of	在～後部
in case	萬一	in the case of	至於～
in charge of	負責（某事）	in the charge of	～由～管
in common	（和～）有共同之處	in the corner of	在角落裡

in the course	在～過程中	lead to	導致
in the distance	在遠處	leave alone	不要管（人），不要碰（物）
in the end	最終		
in the event of	如果發生～萬一	leave behind	遺留，遺志
insist on	堅持	leave off	～停止
it is one's turn to do sth.		leave out	刪掉，漏掉
	輪到某人做某事	leave over	剩下的，暫時不去解決的
keep back	留在後面，阻止，忍住	leave room for	留有～的餘地
keep company with	和～要好	let alone	不要管
keep down	控制	let down	失望
keep off	避開，遠離，讓開	let off	放過～
keep out	使其等在外面，不讓進入	let out	洩露
keep sb. from doing	阻止某人做某事	look after	照料
keep sth. from sb.	把某事瞞著某人	look after	侍候
keep to	堅持某種習慣，靠（左右）	look around	到處看
keep up with	跟上	look at	看
keep up	保持，維持	look back	回顧
knock at	敲（門）	look down on sb.	輕視～
knock into sb.		look down upon sb.	輕視～
	撞到某人身上，偶然遇到	look forward	期待
knock off	下班	look in	順便來訪
knock sb. up	把某人叫醒	look into sth.	調查
knock sb. up	敲門把～叫醒，使～疲倦	look on as	把～看作～
knock sth. down	拆除	look out	小心
know about	了解	look over	審閱，翻閱
know of	聽說	look through	仔細地檢查
last but one	倒數第二	look to	負責，留意
lay aside	放在～一邊，積蓄	look up to sb.	尊敬某人
lay down one's life for	為～獻出生命	look up	仰視
lay down	放下	lose all hope of	絕望
lay emphasis on sth.	強調	make an attempt at doing sth.	
lay in	積蓄		試圖做～
lay off	解雇	make certain	弄清楚
lay out	設計	make coffee	沖咖啡

make for	有助於	on the average	平均
make off	逃跑	on the back of	在～後部
make out	辯認出	on the basis of	根據～
make phone of	嘲笑，和某人開玩笑	on the contrary	相反
make tea	泡茶	on the decline	在衰退中
make the best of	充分利用	on the increase	在增加
make the best of	利用	once and for all	只此一次
make up for	補償	open fire on sb.	向某人開火
make up of	由～組成	open into	門打開後通向
make up one's mind	決定，下決心	open out	打開
make up	構成	open to the public	向公眾開放
make use of	利用	open to	道路通向
most important of all	最重要的	open traffic	通車
next to	毗鄰的	open up	開墾
no end of	很多，大量	other than	除～外
not at all	一點也不	out of breath	喘不過氣來
now that	既然	out of control	無法控制
obtain... from	由～來的	out of date	過時的
of one's own accord	自願地	out of one's accord with	與～不一致
on a diet	吃某種特殊飲食，節食	pass away	消磨（時間）
on account of	因為	pass by	從某人身邊經過，過去
on account	賒賬	pass for	冒充，假扮
on average	平均	pass off	消失
on behalf of	以～名義	pass on	傳下去
on board	到船上火車或飛機	pass through	經歷
on business	出差辦事	persist in	堅持於～
on condition that	以～為條件，假如	pick out	挑選，認出（某人），領會
on credit	賒購	pick up	
on demand	受到要求時	撿起來，中途把某人裝上車，恢復健康	
on display	陳列	profit from	利用
on earth	究竟	pull down	拆掉
on no account	絕不要～	pull off a plan	實現計畫
on no consideration	無論如何也不	pull off	脫衣帽
on one's own account	為了某人的緣故	pull out	拔出，離開

「單字」和「情境」相結合，
自然反射記憶不用死背。

實境照片 + 必考單字 + 模擬試題 + 聽力練習
＝自學也能學好英文！

單字是死的，
但是死背無法記牢單字。

情境是活的，
靈活運用單字
才是學好英文的關鍵！

圖解真正會考的7,000單字：
用實境圖解的方式記英文單字
（1書＋1MP3）
定價／379元

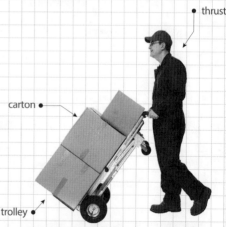

我識出版集團
I'm Publishing Group

我識客服：（02）2345-7222　http://www.17buy.com.tw
我識傳真：（02）2345-5758　iam.group@17buy.com.tw

〔全國各大書店熱烈搶購中！大量訂購，另有折扣〕
劃撥帳號◆19793190 戶名◆我識出版社

國家圖書館出版品預行編目（CIP）資料

題解一定會考的7,000單字 / 林芯著. -- 初版.
-- 臺北市：易富文化, 2018.09
　　面；　公分

ISBN 978-986-407-107-4（平裝附光碟片）

1.英語 2.詞彙

805.12　　　　　　　　　107011855

題解 in Topic
Vocabulary at a Glance!

一定會考的 7,000 單字

只要10天，掌握7,000單字和題型

書名 / 題解一定會考的7,000單字

作者 / 林芯

出版事業群總經理 / 廖晏婕

銷售暨流通事業群總經理 / 施宏

總編輯 / 劉俐伶

顧問 / 蔣敬祖

執行編輯 / 黃怡婷

校對 / 許祐瑄、陳書瑩、劉兆婷

視覺指導 / 姜孟傑、鍾維恩

排版 / 張靜怡

法律顧問 / 北辰著作權事務所蕭雄淋律師

印製 / 金濱印刷事業有限公司

初版 / 2016年9月

二版一刷 / 2018年9月

出版單位 / 我識出版集團—懶鬼子英日語

電話 / (02) 2345-7222

傳真 / (02) 2345-5758

地址 / 台北市忠孝東路五段372巷27弄78之1號1樓

郵政劃撥 / 19793190

戶名 / 我識出版社

網址 / www.17buy.com.tw

E-mail / iam.group@17buy.com.tw

facebook 網址 / www.facebook.com/ImPublishing

定價 / 新台幣379元 / 港幣126元

總經銷 / 我識出版社有限公司出版發行部

地址 / 新北市汐止區新台五路一段114號12樓

電話 / (02) 2696-1357 傳真 / (02) 2696-1359

地區經銷 / 易可數位行銷股份有限公司

地址 / 新北市新店區寶橋路235巷6弄3號5樓

港澳總經銷 / 和平圖書有限公司

地址 / 香港柴灣嘉業街12號百樂門大廈17樓

電話 / (852) 2804-6687 傳真 / (852) 2804-6409

2011 不求人文化

2009 懶鬼子英日語

I'm 我識出版集團
I'm Publishing Group
www.17buy.com.tw

2006 意識文化

2005 易富文化

2004 我識地球村

2001 我識出版社

2011 不求人文化

2009 懶鬼子英日語

www.17buy.com.tw

2006 意識文化

2005 易富文化

2004 我識地球村

2001 我識出版社